THE YEAR'S BEST

Fantasy

& Horror

2008

TWENTY-FIRST ANNUAL COLLECTION

THE YEAR'S BEST

Fantasy & Horror

2008

TWENTY-FIRST ANNUAL COLLECTION

Edited by

Ellen Datlow and

Kelly Link & Gavin J. Grant

St. Martin's Griffin  New York

THE YEAR'S BEST FANTASY AND HORROR. Copyright © 2008 by James Frenkel & Associates. All rights reserved. Printed in the United States of America. For information, address St. Martin's Press, 175 Fifth Avenue, New York, N.Y. 10010.

Summation 2007: Fantasy copyright © 2008 by Kelly Link and Gavin J. Grant
Summation 2007: Horror copyright © 2008 by Ellen Datlow
The Year in Media of the Fantastic: 2007 copyright © 2008 by Edward Bryant
Fantasy in Comics and Graphic Novels: 2007 copyright © 2008 by Jeff VanderMeer
Music of the Fantastic: 2007 copyright © 2008 by Charles de Lint

www.stmartins.com

ISBN-13: 978-0-312-38047-2 (hc)
ISBN-10: 0-312-38047-X
ISBN-13: 978-0-312-38048-9 (pbk)
ISBN-10: 0-312-38048-8

First Edition: October 2008

10 9 8 7 6 5 4 3 2 1

For Gwenda Bond and Christopher Rowe

Copyright Acknowledgments

Contents

Acknowledgments

Thanks to the editors, publishers, publicists, authors, artists, and readers who sent us review material and suggestions, but most especially thanks to Jim Frenkel, Ellen Datlow, Charles Brown, and the staff at *Locus*, *Rain Taxi*, and *Publishers Weekly*. We were grateful for the generous assistance of Jonathan Strahan, Jedediah Berry, and Michael DeLuca.

Please do contact us if you read something wonderful in an unexpected venue that you think we might otherwise overlook.

Any omissions or mistakes are always, of course, our own.

Because we can only select from what we see, please submit or recommend fantasy material to the address on this page: www.lcrw.net/yearsbest/

—G.J.G. & K.D.L.

Acknowledgments to Shane Jiraiya Cummings, Eugene Myers, and Stefan Dziemianowicz

Thanks to Jim Frenkel, our hardworking packager, and his assistant, Alan Rubsam and interns Emily Attwood, Emily Bradley, Jonathan Gelatt, Carla Hartwig, Leslie Matlin, Julie Olsson, Corinna Ranweiler, Joanna Reilly, Karissa Strand, Gretchen Treu, and Carl Weitkamp.

Also, a special thanks to Tom Canty for his unflagging visual imagination. Finally, thanks to my co-editors, Kelly Link and Gavin Grant.

I'd like to acknowledge the following magazines and catalogs for invaluable information and descriptions of material I was unable to obtain: *Locus*, *Publishers Weekly*, *Washington Post Book World*, *The New York Times Book Review*, *Prism* (the quarterly journal of fantasy given with membership to the British Fantasy Society), and *All Hallows*. I'd also like to thank all the magazine editors who made sure I saw their magazines during the year and the publishers who got me review copies in a timely manner.

—E.D.

My thanks to our very talented and hardworking editors, Ellen Datlow, Gavin Grant, and Kelly Link. And to my assistant, Alan Rubsam, and interns, all of whom Ellen has already mentioned above. The twenty-first collection was as much work as the first, though computers have helped us speed certain parts of the process. And thanks as well to our St. Martin's editor Marc Resnick and his assistant, Sarah Lumnah; their help is essential to the success of this enterprise. Also, thanks to the authors and agents who have granted permission to reprint the works in this volume, and to Tom Canty, who continues to produce fresh, effective design and imagery.

Lastly, my thanks to my wife, Joan D. Vinge, who for twenty-one years now has, with kindness and understanding, allowed the project to continue.

—J.F.

Summation 2007: Fantasy

Kelly Link and Gavin J. Grant

Welcome to the summation of the year in fantasy for the twenty-first annual edition of *The Year's Best Fantasy and Horror*.

This was another year in which many of our favorite short stories were published in original anthologies and online venues. Of the longer work that we read, much of the best work was published in young adult. The young adult (YA) fantasy field just keeps growing—do some browsing in your local bookstore, and you'll see that YA fantasy novels outnumber realistic YA novels—so perhaps it's not surprising that we found so many titles of interest there. And perhaps this isn't such a recent development, either, considering that so many of the ur-texts of fantasy were originally published for children and young adults (the Earthsea books, C.S. Lewis's Narnia books, and *The Hobbit*). We hope that readers of this anthology will follow our recommendations and explore what continues to be the heart of the genre.

Every year we attempt to reduce this summary by a few thousand words so that we can include more fiction. Readers who come away from this introduction wishing for more information about the state of publishing will want to check out the following resources.

Resources

We enthusiastically recommend *Locus* magazine and Mark R. Kelly's *Locus Online*—as well as the Locus Awards Database (www.locusmag.com)—for news, reviews, and links to readings, new books, and news in the field. We always recommend readers try their local independent bookshops for books as they may very likely offer a curated selection of the latest in the genre. Otherwise DreamHaven, Ziesing, Borderlands Books, and Powells.com offer excellent online catalogs and newsletters. We were very pleased to see short-fiction review zine *The Fix* brought back online (www.thefix-online.com). The Speculative Literature Foundation (www.speculativeliterature.org) continues to serve a diverse community of writers and publishers. *Rain Taxi Review of Books* unfailingly offers unusual and rewarding recommendations. *Prism*, the newsletter of the British Fantasy Society, keeps us up to date on the U.K. fantasy field. Other resources, most online but not all, include: *Ansible, Green Man Review, the Internet Review of Science Fiction, New York Review of Science Fiction, NewPages, Ralan,*

Revolution SF, *Rambles*, *SF Site*, *Speculations*, and *Tangent*. Bloggers like Gwenda Bond (bondgirl.blogspot.com), Rich Horton (ecbatan.livejournal.com), and Matt Cheney (mumpsimus.blogspot.com) provide lively, thoughtful commentary and reviews as well as covering industry related news.

Disclosure: We are the editors and publishers of Small Beer Press and the zine *Lady Churchill's Rosebud Wristlet*.

Favorite Books of 2007

Powers (Harcourt) is the third of Ursula K. Le Guin's young adult series, Annals of the Western Shore. Gavir, kidnapped as a child, grows up a slave who is both distinguished and put into danger by his eidetic memory and his ability to "remember" glimpses of the future. As with the first two books in this series, *Powers* is a coming-of-age story, and although it stands on its own, readers will recognize characters from *Voices* and *Gifts*. The Annals of the Western Shore novels are heart-of-genre work—a pre-industrial setting, a character-driven narrative in which the stakes are high—and yet the vividness and power of the prose gives these narrators and their stories immediacy and a feeling of contemporary relevance. Le Guin offers a nuanced examination of the consequences of slavery and war on one side, and on the other, the worth of storytelling and the act of bearing witness. This series is one of Gavin's recent favorites.

Ysabeau Wilce's debut young adult novel, *Flora Segunda: Being the Magickal Mishaps of a Girl of Spirit, Her Glass-Gazing Sidekick, Two Ominous Butlers (One Blue), a House with Eleven Thousand Rooms, and a Red Dog* (Harcourt) introduces a firecracker of a character, Flora Fyrdraaca, a "girl of Spirit" who lives in a sort of alternate, historical, and magical version of San Francisco at uneasy truce with the Aztec Empire. Wilce's prose style is energetic, eccentric, and wilfully baroque—a style which absolutely suits the setting (one that readers of *The Magazine of Fantasy & Science Fiction* will recognize), and the narrator who, all for the sake of a library book, takes a forbidden shortcut through her magick-saturated, booby-trapped house (11,000 rooms and only one potty). Flora's subsequent adventures and entanglements are improbable, delightful, and genuinely moving. This is an utterly engaging book, not least for offering one of the most original settings in recent fantasy.

Dreamquake (FSG, US; Fourth Estate, U.K.) is the second half of Elizabeth Knox's marvelous, young adult two-book Dreamhunter Duet. (The first book was published in the U.S. as *Dreamhunter*.) The setting is Antipodean, the system of magic is inventive, and Knox is a lyrical and gripping prose stylist. This is, perhaps, a story that would have been better served if it had been published in one volume and read straight through—a quibble, perhaps, since now readers can do exactly that. One of Kelly's favorite books of the year.

Daniel Abraham's Long Price Quartet goes from strength to strength in the second entry, *A Betrayal in Winter* (Tor). Royal succession, gender politics, and a huge amount of intrigue keep this one at a constant boil. Fans of George R. R. Martin waiting for the next installment of *A Song of Fire and Ice* would do well to seek out Abraham's series.

Guy Gavriel Kay's *Ysabel* (Roc) is a myth-infused fantasy that dips into the kind of territory that thrillers make use of so successfully. Ned, whose narration is endearingly adolescent in its mixture of naivety and cynicism, accompanies his photographer father to France for six weeks. While his father scouts with his team, Ned meets a fellow American traveler, Kate. The two teenagers, upon encountering a mysterious figure in a cathedral crypt, soon discover that the area around them is alive with history and danger. While this is Kay's first foray into contemporary fantasy, there are thematic echoes from the Fionavar trilogy that will reward his long-time fans.

The list of contributors to Gardner Dozois and Jack Dann's *Wizards: Magical Tales from the Masters of Modern Fantasy* (Berkley) reads like a Who's Who of contemporary fantasy, beginning with the first chapter of an as-yet-unpublished Neil Gaiman novel ("The Witch's Headstone") and closing with Orson Scott Card's novella "Stonefather." In the middle the reader will encounter work by Jane Yolen, Gene Wolfe, Patricia A. McKillip, and Tanith Lee. We reprint Elizabeth Hand's "Wizard's Wife" in this anthology. Garth Nix's "Holly and Iron" is also a standout in a year in which there was a wealth of good short fiction from this writer.

Naomi Novik's fourth Temeraire novel, *Empire of Ivory* (Del Rey), continues to expand the scope of her narrative as Captain William Laurence attempts to discover the cure for the deadly disease that has struck down the British dragon fleet. For the reader, there's the pleasure of seeing yet more of this alternate version of the world, and how the existence of dragons alters/thwarts the course of European colonial rule in China and now Africa. Novik's series of cliffhanger endings are deliciously frustrating. As soon as you finish the latest volume, you're instantly longing to have the next book in the series safely in hand.

We reprint in this anthology three stories from Ellen Datlow and Terri Windling's young adult anthology *The Coyote Road: Trickster Tales* (Viking). Like the first two anthologies in this series (*The Green Man* and *The Faery Reel*), there are illustrations by Charles Vess as well as a thoughtful introduction by Windling. Besides work by Holly Black, Delia Sherman, and Kij Johnson, we were particularly taken by Will Shetterly's "Black Rock Blues."

John Klima has edited for Tor Books and for the last few years has published the science-fiction-leaning zine *Electric Velocipede*. This year he edited his first anthology, *Logorrhea: Good Words Make Good Stories* (Bantam). Klima's brilliant idea was to ask contributors to write stories based on prizewinning spelling bee words. We reprinted Daniel Abraham's story, which was written for the word "cambist," in this anthology. Other highlights included stories by Marly Youmans ("smaragdine"), Theodora Goss ("dulcimer"), and Jeff VanderMeer ("appoggiatura").

The Adventures of Amir Hamza (Modern Library) by Ghalib Lakhnavi and Abdullah Bilgrami is the first complete translation (by Musharraf Ali Farooqi) of a classic epic saga based on the life of the uncle of the Prophet Mohammed. Like the *Odyssey* and *Beowulf*, the *Hamzanama* is a blend of history and religion and fantasy that comes out of the oral traditions of storytelling. We confess we aren't all the way through it yet—perhaps it should be read over one thousand and one nights?

Un Lun Dun (Del Rey) is China Miéville's first young adult novel. His considerable strengths are on display here: the urban landscape reinvented; the tropes and conventions of genre fiction turned inside out to excellent effect; a palpable sense of delight in wordplay transmitted from writer to reader. This is a future classic novel, the kind of book that young readers will rediscover as adult readers.

Terry Pratchett's *Making Money* (Harper) follows recurring trickster figure Moist van Lipwig (introduced in *Going Postal*) from his triumphant reformation of the postal system to the Government Mint. The latest novel from Pratchett offers his trademark blend of humor, keen insights, and more of the ongoing, fast-forward evolution/transformation of the pre-industrial city, Ankh-Morpork.

Beasts! A Pictorial Schedule of Traditional Hidden Creatures from the Interest of 90 Modern Artisans (Fantagraphics Books), "curated" by Jacob Covey, is a beautifully produced contemporary bestiary, featuring ninety illustrations of mythological creatures—vampires, the Erinyes, the Golem, and cliff ogres—by artists like Jordan Crane, Anders Nilsen, Seonna Hong, and Tom Gauld. Essential reading for crypto-zoologists as well as anyone interested in the work of contemporary comic-book artists.

Eclipse One: New Fantasy and Science Fiction (Night Shade Books) is the first of what will be an original annual anthology series edited by Jonathan Strahan. The excellent stories range from horror to comic fantasy, and we reprint here Eileen Gunn's "Up the Fire Road" and Jeffrey Ford's "The Drowned Life." If space had allowed, we would have included Ysabeau Wilce's "Quartermaster Returns" as well. Other standouts are Andy Duncan's "Unique Chicken Goes in Reverse" as well as work by Gwyneth Jones, Maureen McHugh, and Garth Nix. It's been a long time since genre readers had a yearly, original, mixed genre unthemed anthology to look forward to—our hats are off to Strahan and Night Shade.

Acclaimed writer David Anthony Durham has drawn on his strengths as an historical novelist to produce the first book of a promising fantasy series that promises to rival, in scope, George R. R. Martin's Song of Fire and Ice series. Durham's *Acacia: The War With the Mein* (Doubleday) is an epic doorstopper of a book: huge, detailed, and engrossing. There's an empire in decline here, as well as war, plague, heirs, and assassins.

In the Woods (Viking) by Tana French is an assured, page-turner of a debut thriller/police procedural/psychological portrait. There's a kernel of the fantastic at the core of one of the two mysteries here, and the narrative arc is all the more satisfying for the ways in which French leaves it open. Without ever making direct mention of fairy abductions or Pan narratives, French plays on these types of narratives and evokes a sense of the numinous and the awful in its original sense. This was one of Kelly's favorite books of the year.

Although, strictly speaking, there is no overt fantasy element in *The Brief Wondrous Life of Oscar Wao* (Riverhead) by Junot Diaz, his eponymous Dominican-American nerd-hero uses the language and conventions of genre fantasy—J.R.R. Tolkien, Dungeons & Dragons—to explain his own cultural heritage and baggage. At the heart of the book is a family curse that goes all the way back to 1492 and the arrival of Christopher Columbus in the New World. This is a wrenching, dazzling, epic, pyrotechnical masterpiece of a book.

Traditional Fantasy

Shadowbridge (Ballantine Del Rey) is the engaging first installment of Gregory Frost's long-awaited sequence about a world in which all communities and cities exist along the span of a single bridge. There are echoes here of Jack Vance, Fritz Leiber, and Roger Zelazny. Frost's characters—a shadow puppeteer and her chance-met companions—swap stories and secrets. There are gods, trickster figures, and tall tales. While the multi-stranded narrative will be completed in Frost's forthcoming *Lord Tophet*, the world of Shadowbridge is a large enough canvas for any number of novels.

Ink (Del Rey) concludes Hal Duncan's acclaimed, ambitious, brash, marvelous two-volume *The Book of All Hours*. It's a dazzlingly inventive, epic stew of science fiction elements like nanotechnology mixed in with various classic mythologies.

There are apocalypses and adventures, tricksters and gods aplenty in the overlapping arcs and worlds of Duncan's story.

Like Duncan, Catherynne M. Valente has braided together multiple strands of narrative in *In the Cities of Coin and Spice* (Bantam), the second of her Orphan's Tales series. (The first book, *In the Night Garden*, was co-winner of the James Tiptree, Jr. Award.) The reader will be reminded of the Arabian Nights, and of various incarnations of fairy tales, from the Brothers Grimm to Angela Carter's. The two books are copiously illustrated by Michael Kaluta, which adds to the lush, dream-like atmosphere of poet Valente's recursive, imagery-saturated prose.

Warren Rochelle's Celtic-inspired fantasy *Harvest of Changelings* (Golden Gryphon) is set in his native North Carolina and introduces Ben Tyson, a librarian, whose half-fey son is struggling with his interracial heritage.

U.S. readers get to catch up with a couple of notable Australian writers courtesy of Orbit and Eos. *Devices and Desires* (Eos) is the first of K.J. Parker's complex steampunk series in which an exiled weapon maker builds a tremendous machine to reunite his family. Fiona McIntosh begins the Percheron Saga in *Odalisque* (Eos). On a visit to Australia in 2007, it seemed to us there were hundreds (surely an exaggeration, but that's how it felt) of fantasy series that we hadn't yet seen over here. Readers are encouraged to check on the Web sites of Infinity Books, or Pulp Fiction, both independent Australian bookstores, to discover Australian writers whose work might not yet be available here.

Also noted: Charles Saunders's revised *Imaro 2: The Quest for Cush* (Night Shade Books) offers all the sword-and-sorcery adventure an H. Rider Haggard fan could ask for. Lois McMaster Bujold's second Sharing Knife novel, *Legacy* (Eos) is a character-driven fantasy that follows the conventions of a romance novel. Carole McDonnell's *Wind Follower* (Juno) builds into a story with mythic Christian resonances. The landscape and the characters draw, refreshingly, from African, Asian, Native American, and Latino cultures and histories. Drawing on Norse and German mythology, co-authors Elizabeth Bear and Sarah Monette rework the usual conventions of novels in which men and animals form telepathic bonds in *A Companion to Wolves* (Tor). This is an atypical historical fantasy: there's plenty of mud, blood, pack-psychology, and fairly graphic depictions of sex. David B. Coe begins a new series, Blood of the Southlands, with *The Sorcerers' Plague* (Tor) set across the ocean from his previous Winds of the Forelands. *Chronicles of the Black Company* (Night Shade Books) collects the first three novels of Glen Cook's popular series. Matthew Hughes continues his Henghis Hapthorn series in *The Spiral Labyrinth* (Night Shade Books). Readers will also want to look for Payseur and Schmidt's beautifully produced chapbook edition of Hughes's story *The Farouche Assemblage*. The first two books in Greg Park's Earthsoul Prophecies series are *Veil of Darkness* and *Cleansing Hunt* (Bladestar).

Small Beer Press published *Water Logic*, the third part of Laurie J. Marks's Elemental Logic series. Marks's epic fantasy has always been notable for its depth of characterization, wry humor, thoughtful portrayal of both natural world and the political landscape, and its hopefulness about the ability of individuals and cultures to reach compromise. Her Elemental Logic novels are also gripping reads.

Contemporary and Urban Fantasy

The heroine of Nalo Hopkinson's new novel, *The New Moon's Arms* (Warner) is the menopausal and enchantingly nicknamed Chastity Theresa Lambkin, who now goes by the more appropriate nickname Calamity. Calamity is an earthy, itchy (literally) narrator to whom strange things happen. Hopkinson deftly handles the mixture of magic realism, folklore, romance, and mystery, and the Caribbean setting is beautifully rendered.

Carol Emshwiller is one of our favorite authors and in the last few years it has been a pleasure to try to keep up with her body of work which has been both prolific and powerful. *The Secret City* (Tachyon) is an incandescent rendering of some of Emshwiller's classic themes: worries of disappearing within pop culture, aliens and alienation, and how to relate to the stranger beside you.

Blood Engines (Bantam) is the first of a series by Tim Pratt (published under the name T. A. Pratt). Marla Mason, the main series character, stands out among her peers in contemporary fantasy. She's sexually active, but utterly pragmatic and ruthless, and therefore all the more believable in how she handles her professional life (as a sorcerer) and her romantic life. Pratt's style is engaging, his take on magic is fresh, and the series begins, rather smartly, in the middle of things. Recommended to even those readers who have reservations about this corner of the genre.

The Gospel of the Knife (Tor) is a Vietnam-era sequel to Will Shetterly's wonderful *Dogland*, following the adventures of Chris Nix, whom we last saw in the titular dog-themed Florida tourist attraction. As in the first book, the engines driving Shetterly's coming-of-age fantasy are social. The underpinnings derive from Judeo-Christian mythology, but politics and racial tensions are equally central to the plot.

Ekaterina Sedia's short fiction has popped up in magazines such as *Analog* and *Baen's Universe* and she is, as well, the editor of several anthologies, including *Paper Cities* (Senses Five Press). Her recommended second novel, *The Secret History of Moscow* (Prime) is set in a murky mythic Russian underworld (as opposed to the criminal underworld more familiar from pop culture) in which myths and legends are juxtaposed with hard-nosed denizens of modern-day Moscow.

Cameron Rogers's *A Music of Razors* (Del Rey) made a splash several years ago, when published in Australia, a dark fantasy told in a braided narrative that jumps between the lives of a doctor practicing medicine in 1840 and a twentieth-century boy's attempt to banish a childhood monster. Rogers's prose is lush and atmospheric.

Caitlín R. Kiernan's dark fantasy *Daughter of the Hounds* (Roc) is set in the same world as *Low Red Moon* and is both lyrical and unsettling.

Whiskey and Water (Roc) is the second novel in Elizabeth Bear's series, The Promethean Age, in which the Faerie courts and the Promethean League remain on unsettled terms. There's plenty of personal and political intrigue here, as well as appearances by Christopher Marlowe, God, and Lucifer. Along with writers Emma Bull, Will Shetterly, and Sarah Monette, prolific author and blogger Bear has created an online site in 2007 where they have steadily published fanfiction for *Shadow Unit*, a paranormal investigations television show that doesn't actually exist.

Cherie Priest's *Neither Flesh Nor Feathers* (Tor) is the third dark fantasy featuring Eden Moore.

Steps Through the Mist: A Mosaic Novel (Aio Publishing, translated by Alice Copple-Tošić) is another strong collection from the prolific Zoran Živković.

Also noted: Overlook Press began to reprint John Crowley's revised version of his Ægypt series with *The Solitudes*, originally titled *Ægypt*. This will be followed by *Love & Sleep*, *Dæmonomania*, and *Endless Things*. This year Small Beer published *Endless Things*, the long-awaited conclusion of Crowley's series about itinerant historian Pierce Moffett, Giordano Bruno, John Dee, and multiple histories of the world.

Historical, Alternate History, and Arthurian Fantasy

Mary Gentle's *Ilario* (Eos) has been published in the U.S. in two parts, "The Lion's Eye" and "The Stone Golem." It's rooted in an alternate history—is it fantasy? science fiction? plain old fiction?—where the city of Carthage never fell but now exists in a permanent semi-darkened state named the Pestilence. Ilario, a hermaphroditic artist, flees there on discovering that his/her mother wants him/her killed to avoid embarrassment.

Since publishing her debut novel, the now-classic urban fantasy *War for the Oaks*, Emma Bull has written historical fantasy, techno-fantasy, and a wonderful epistolary novel (co-written with Steven Brust). Her latest is the excellent *Territory* (Tor) a Western featuring Doc Holliday, Wyatt Earp, witches, blood magic, and enough frontier detail to keep both history buffs and fantasy fans happy.

Mainspring, the first novel in a series for Tor by the prolific and versatile Jay Lake, is an old-fashioned big-idea science fantasy in which the world's titular spring has to be kept wound to keep the world going.

Justin Allen's debut *Slaves of Shinar* (Overlook) is set at the dawn of written history, as two men help fight the Niphilim—an early iron-using warrior culture.

The late David Gemmell's wife, Stella Gemmell, worked with the writer to complete the third of his novels retelling the Trojan story, *Troy: Fall of Kings* (Ballantine).

Pirates get the Gene Wolfe treatment in *Pirate Freedom* (Tor), a story involving time travel, the priesthood, and feats of derring-do. As usual with a Gene Wolfe novel, there is more here than meets the eye on a first read.

Also of note: In *Amberlight*, one of promising new fantasy imprint Juno Books' ventures into mass market paperback publishing, Sylvia Kelso explores gender and power dynamics in a matriarchal society. Kelso's style is rich and rewarding. *Dragon's Keep* (Harcourt) is a young adult Arthurian novel by Janet Lee Carey in which the banishment of Arthur's sister, Evaine, leads to an intricate series of intrigues between the royal family and dragons. In *Tracing the Shadow* (Bantam), Sarah Ash begins a new series, The Alchymist's Legacy, set in the same world as her previous Tears of Artamon trilogy, mixing elements of traditional fantasy with elements of steampunk. Diana Pharoah Francis begins what could be an intriguing new series, Crosspointe, with *The Cipher*, in which Lucy Trenton gets into trouble when she lets slip that she can detect magic. Nathalie Mallet's debut *The Princes of the Golden Cage* kicks off her Prince Amir series as well as a new line of mass-market paperbacks from small-press powerhouse Night Shade Books. Illustrator Mark J. Ferrari's debut novel *The Book of Joby* (Tor) combines elements of the Arthurian legend with the contemporary story of a boy, Joby, who becomes the subject of a bet between God and the Devil.

A few books crossed our desks that were of associational interest to fantasy readers: the latest in Diana Gabaldon's ongoing series, *Lord John and the Brotherhood of the Blade* (Delacorte); a young girl tells stories as she learns to support her family in Anita Amirrezvani's debut *The Blood of Flowers* (Little, Brown); Geoff Ryman, whose short stories appeared in this series, sets his novel, *The King's Last Song* (HarperCollins), in Cambodia, where an archaeologist uncovers an ancient king's book written on gold leaves.

Humorous Fantasy

Christopher Moore's *You Suck: A Love Story* (Morrow) offers his fans some cameo appearances from established characters, as well as newer and even more hapless protagonists. There are some nice comic set pieces, and as usual, Moore's laconic style and West Coast hipster setting offers an almost Maupin-like contemporary charm.

Eliot Fintushel's *Breakfast with the Ones You Love* (Bantam Spectra) is, as readers of his short fiction might be prepared for, a high energy, gonzo love story with some chance of the end of the world occurring.

Richard Kadrey's *Butcher Bird* (Night Shade Books) may belong in Ellen Datlow's horror half of the book but there's enough humor here for us to recommend it to readers who like their fantasy on the darker end of the spectrum.

Fantasy in the Mainstream

Helen Oyemi's excellent postcolonial novel, *The Opposite House* (Doubleday), is set, alternatively, in London and the "somewherehouse." Maja, a young Cuban immigrant, is pregnant in London, and her story intersects with the story of Aya, a Santerian goddess, who lives in a house where one door opens on London while the other door opens on Lagos. Oyemi moves between the worlds of realism and fantasy with assurance. This book is a delight.

The ghost in historian Rebecca Stott's debut *Ghostwalk* (Spiegel & Grau) is Isaac Newton, who may be haunting a Cambridge scholar. This is a secret history for fans of Neal Stephenson, Mary Gentle, and Tim Powers.

Serialized in the *New York Times*, and set in the mythical kingdom of Khazaria, Michael Chabon's *Gentlemen of the Road* (Del Rey) is a romp of an "adventure tale" in the style of writers like Fritz Leiber and Robert E. Howard. Best of all, the working title, Chabon notes, was "Jews with Swords." Readers of this anthology should also seek out—if they haven't, already—Chabon's excellent detective novel/alternate history *The Yiddish Policeman's Union*, which takes place against the backdrop of Sitka, Alaska, temporary home of Jewish refugees displaced after WWII.

Matthew Sharpe's *Jamestown* (Soft Skull) is a mashup of historical events and characters like Pocahontas and Captain John Smith, with sharp, contemporary political commentary and postmodern flourishes. Sharpe's prose is slangy, inventive, anachronistic, and wildly engaging.

Stephen Marche's *Shining at the Bottom of the Sea* (Riverhead) invents an island in the North Atlantic and maps its literary history in the style of a faux-academic anthology.

Blood is the New Black (Three Rivers) by Valerie Stivers is an interesting looking fashion industry/vampire novel crossover.

Also noted: *Samedi the Deafness* (Vintage) by poet Jesse Ball is a somewhat fractured novel of the surreal recommended to fans of Paul LaFarge and such like. *Place Names* by Jean Ricardou (Dalkey Archive, translated by Jordan Stump), written in 1969 in the *nouveau roman* experimental style, is a weightlessly odd novel sure to delight those who take the time to explore it. *Spring Tides* by Jacques Poulin (Archipelago, translated by Sheila Fischman), another French translation, is equally as odd; sillier, but also darker.

Brian Francis Slattery's *Spaceman Blues: A Love Song* (Tor) is an apocalyptic, anarchic novel concerning pop music, an alien invasion, and the origin of an unlikely superhero. Daniel Wallace's *Mr. Sebastian and the Negro Magician* (Doubleday) is a reworking of a fairly traditional genre, the deal with the devil story. Randall Silvis's *In a Town Called Mundomuerto* (Omnidawn) is a novella firmly grounded in the traditions of magic realism.

First Novels

Christopher Barzak's, *One for Sorrow* (Bantam) is a lyrical debut novel of Midwestern magic realism. Barzak handles the material of adolescent protagonist Adam McCormick's coming-of-age—sexuality, alienation, longing for community and genuine connection—with sensitivity, empathy, and originality. The ghosts here feel real and the secondary characters, particularly in the relationship between Adam's alcoholic mother and the drunk driver who leaves her paralyzed, are finely drawn.

Vintage: A Ghost Story (Lethe Press) by Steve Berman, originally published last year by Haworth, is a lovely, dark fantasy about a gay Goth teen growing up in Weird, NJ, who is haunted by—and attracted to—the ghost of a 1950s-era jock.

Patrick Rothfuss's bestselling debut, *The Name of the Wind* (DAW), the first novel in his Kingkiller Chronicle, has found a large and enthusiastic audience.

Alaya Dawn Johnson's *Racing the Dark* (Agate Bolden) is a the first of a series, a coming-of-age story set on a Polynesian island, where a young girl becomes apprentice to a witch.

Felix Gilman's debut *Thunderer* (Bantam) is a labyrinthine fantasy, first in a series set in the city of Ararat.

Kathleen Bryan begins The War of the Rose in *The Serpent and the Rose* (Tor), a romance-tinged epic fantasy set in the Kingdom of Lys.

English writer David Bilsborough's *The Wanderer's Tale* (Tor) is the first in what promises to be a doughty series set in an almost-medieval Europe. This debut is mostly set-up with the requisite plucky band of warriors gathering to fight the dark lords. Fans of Middle English will enjoy the proper nouns.

Alex Bledsoe's *The Sword-Edged Blonde* (Night Shade Books) is an enjoyable genre-muddler in which private eye Eddie LaCrosse has to do an old friend—who happens to be the King of Arentia—a favor and, in turn, face his own past.

Poetry

Last year we were happy to note the appearance of *Goblin Fruit*, an online zine devoted to fantastic poetry. This year it went from strength to strength—we had more honorable mentions than we could honorably mention. While the design of *Goblin Fruit* is not entirely browser friendly, its content is first class. *Farrago's Wainscot* is another new Web site that provides a wealth of excellent contemporary speculative poetry—including Catherynne M. Valente work which appears in this volume.

In print, *Dreams and Nightmares*, *Mythic Delirium*, *Star*Line*, and *The Magazine of Speculative Poetry* provide a range of speculative poetry while *Strange Horizons* and *Lone Star Stories* continue to regularly feature the same online. Many literary magazines, such as *Jubilat*, publish poetry that slips over into the fantastic genre.

We first encountered Laotian American poet Bryan Thao Worra's work when he was Special Guest at Diversicon 14 in Minneapolis. For that convention he had produced a PDF-only collection, *Monstro*. *On the Other Side of the Eye* (Sam's Dot) is his first long collection and well worth seeking out.

Simon Armitage's new translation of *Sir Gawain and the Green Knight* (Norton) runs on parallel pages to the original Middle English.

Sandra Kasturi's *The Animal Bridegroom* (Tightrope) is an eclectic collection that ranges from the disquieting to the whimsical. Kasturi's sense of language and play is remarkable: Kelly has been a fan of Kasturi's work for a long time, and was enormously pleased to see this new collection.

Claudia Carlson's *The Elephant House* (Marsh Hawk Press) included the excellent poem "Hell-in-the-Box."

Prolific poet JoSelle Vanderhooft and artist Erzebet YellowBoy collaborated on *Ossuary* (Sam's Dot).

Linda D. Addison's latest collection, *Being Full of Light, Insubstantial* (Space and Time), contains a large selection of mostly personal poetry with some flashes of the fantastic.

Lawrence Schimel's tiny *Fairy Tales for Writers* (A Midsummer Night's Press) is a lot of fun for anyone with a passion for fairy tales and an interest in writing.

The Science Fiction Poetry Association published *The 2007 Rhysling Anthology: The Best Science Fiction, Fantasy and Horror Poetry of 2006* (edited by Drew Morse) to encourage readers to participate in reading speculative fiction and poetry, join the association, and to vote for the award.

More from Elsewhere

Scott Lynch's *Red Seas Under Red Skies* (Bantam) is his second pirate adventure fantasy. If we're picky, this is really science fiction—the adventures of his engaging cast of orphans and thieves are, after all, set on another planet. But however you classify these books, they're lovely caper novels with all the satisfying trappings of epic fantasy, so perhaps one of us will push one into your hands (while the other cuts your purse strings).

Peter Straub is, of course, more usually to be found in our co-editor's territory. However, we'd at least like to mention *Sides* (Cemetery Dance), the first collection of Straub's essays, introductions, and afterwords, which is enlivened by his wide-ranging and informed enthusiasms for various kinds of fiction and creative work. The collection is rounded off by the essays of Straub's alter ego, the academic Putney Tyson Ridge.

Children's/Teen/Young Adult Fantasy

J. K. Rowling finished her best-selling seven-volume series with *Harry Potter and the Deathly Hallows* (Scholastic). *Deathly Hallows* is full of plot twists and set pieces, and Rowling's humor and gift for lively details are on display throughout. Among other revelations, we find out more about Snape's tragic past, and toward the end, readers will recognize echoes of C.S. Lewis and J.R.R. Tolkien.

Ironside: A Modern Faery's Tale (Simon & Schuster) is the third and final book in Holly Black's contemporary fantasy trilogy, following *Tithe* and *Valiant*, bringing back the characters of Roiben and changeling Kaye. All three books are gritty, smart, emotionally engaging, believable renderings not only of adolescence, but of Faery. Black's secondary characters are an added pleasure. Highly recommended to adult readers as well as teenagers.

Libba Bray's wonderful Gemma Doyle books have offered readers huge dollops of romance, tragedy, the boarding school genre, Victorian costume drama, and secondary-world fantasy. *The Sweet Far Thing* (Delacorte) is a bittersweet and powerful conclusion to Bray's trilogy.

M is for Magic includes uncollected stories by Neil Gaiman, as well as work that appeared previously in *Fragile Things* and *Smoke and Mirrors*. This is a mixed-genre collection, and highlights include "How to Talk to Girls at Parties" and "The Witch's Headstone," an excerpt from Gaiman's forthcoming young adult novel *The Graveyard Book*.

Cassandra Clare's *City of Bones* (McElderry), first in her Mortal Instruments series, is a fast-paced, immensely entertaining contemporary fantasy novel set in New York City. There are tattooed demon hunters, warring vampires and werewolves, and plenty of amusing, snarky repartee. Fans of *Buffy the Vampire Slayer* will enjoy both the wordplay and the swordplay.

Loosely following her previous Arthurian trilogy, Elizabeth Wein began a new series in the first Mark of Solomon novel, *The Lion Hunter* (Viking). Set in sixth-century Africa, this is a compelling, character-driven read, and one of the best young adult novels of the year.

Kathleen Duey's *Skin Hunger* (Atheneum) is the first volume in the trilogy *A Resurrection of Magic*. It's a truly dark fantasy that follows two alternating storylines, one involving a school for magic, the other following the founders of the academy. The price of magic is steep here—students who don't master magic begin to starve to death, and they are told that only one apprentice will graduate. The others will die. Readers beware: the ending is a cliffhanger.

One of our favorite authors, Peter Dickinson follows up his excellent secondary-world fantasy *The Ropemaker* with quest-novel *Angel Isle* (Wendy Lamb Books).

Stand-alone novella *The Game* (Firebird) displays Diana Wynne Jones's gifts for portraying complicated family dynamics, the cost of magic.

Robin McKinley has put a great deal of thought into what it might actually be like for a contemporary adolescent to become entangled with dragons. In *Dragonhaven* (Putnam), dragons are an endangered species: messy, complicated, and utterly believable.

Magic's Child (Razorbill) is the final book of Justine Larbalestier's compelling contemporary fantasy trilogy about teenager Reason Cansino, who must learn to cope with magic, madness, and her own pregnancy—not necessarily in that order.

Rafael Ábalos's *Grimpow: The Impossible Road* (Delacorte), translated by Noël Baca Castex, is an intricate historical fantasy that incorporates cryptography, the Knights Templar, and medieval lore.

Lloyd Alexander's posthumously published *The Golden Dream of Carlo Chuchio* (Holt) is a picaresque fantasy, similar in feel to *The Remarkable Journey of Prince Jen*.

Shannon Hale's *Book of a Thousand Days* (Bloomsbury) takes the form of a journal kept by the serving maid who, with her mistress, is walled up in a tower for the eponymous thousand days. Hale, whose *Goose Girl* novels we highly recommend, reworks a lesser-known Grimm's tale into an unexpected and affecting novel.

In *Iris, Messenger* (Harcourt) by Sarah Deming, Iris has to deal with the Greek gods and goddesses who, down on their luck, are scraping a living on the Jersey shore and surrounds. How Iris helps the pantheon makes for a great read—and don't miss the hilarious appendix.

Joanne Harris's first young adult novel, *Runemarks* (Knopf), is a comic, post-Ragnarok saga.

Marcus Sedgwick's *My Swordhand is Singing* (Wendy Lamb Books) is a dark fantasy about a village besieged by vampires.

Katherine Marsh, *The Night Tourist* (Hyperion), shifts the myth of Orpheus and Eurydice to contemporary New York City.

Lyn Gardner retells the tale of the Pied Piper in *Into the Woods* (David Fickling Books).

The Garden of Eve (Harcourt) by K.L. Going is an atmospheric ghost story that revolves around a decayed orchard and an apple tree whose fruit transports a grief-stricken girl named Evie to a mysterious garden.

A. A. Attanasio's *The Conjure Book* (Prime) features an environmentally conscious fox spirit, as well as teenaged witches.

The following new series intrigued us: Julia Golding's *Secrets of the Sirens* (Cavendish) successfully linked a contemporary awareness of environmental dangers with the survival of mythic creatures.

R.L. LaFevers's *Theodosia and the Serpents of Chaos* (Houghton, illustrated by Yoko Tanaka) has eleven-year-old Theodosia Throckmorton—who can tell when ancient artifacts carry a curse—at its heart. The resourceful heroine makes this one we recommend for reading aloud.

Sarah Beth Durst's debut *Into the Wild* (Razorbill) is a savvy, often funny mashup of fairy tales and the problem novel genre. Julie, Rapunzel's daughter, has a problem with the wildness under her bed (which isn't just the usual kid mess, it's Wildness itself). When it escapes she's not the only one in trouble.

J. & P. Voelkel's *Middleworld* (Smith and Sons) is the first book in their Jaguar Stones series. The five eponymous stones hold the power to change the world and it falls to twelve-year-old Max, whose archaeologist parents have disappeared, to keep the world safe.

Irish writer Michael Scott's *The Alchemyst: The Secrets of the Immortal Nicholas Flamel* (Delacorte) is a cinematic, fast-paced secret history.

In *Faeries of Dreamdark: Blackbringer* (Putnam) by Laini Taylor, faeries must try to rebottle the demons that humans have released. (Foolish humans!)

Twelve-year-old Stephanie inherits a houseload of trouble and finds herself protected by the titular hero of Derek Landy's swashbuckler *Skullduggery Pleasant* (HarperCollins).

And finally, Philip Reeve concluded his revelatory and energetic science fantasy Hungry City Chronicles with *A Darkling Plain* (Eos).

For younger readers: Holly Black and Tony DiTerlizzi manage the impossible by writing themselves into the first volume of a second series, Beyond the Spiderwick Chronicles, *The Nixie's Song*, in a cameo appearance. As with the first series, there's humor, realistically complicated characters, and family dynamics, but the setting is original: a new development in a Florida suburb.

Nancy Willard's *The Flying Bed* (Scholastic, illustrated by John Thomson), is a delightful fable set in Florence.

For those who enjoy Garth Nix's story in this volume, we recommend *One Beastly Beast* (Eos), which collects four stories aimed at a younger audience.

Dan Greenburg's Secret of the Dripping Fang series moved along three more notches with (and we love these titles) *Attack of the Giant Octopus*, *Please Don't Eat the Children*, and *When Bad Snakes Attack Good Children* (Harcourt).

Paul Stewart and Chris Riddell produced the eighth Edge Chronicle, *The Winter Knights* and the third Far Flung Adventure, *Hugo Pepper* (both David Fickling Books), the latter of which anyone with an interest in independent publishing will enjoy.

Also noted: Margaret Mahy's post-apocalyptic *Maddigan's Fantasia* (McElderry) involves a circus, time travel, and a quest to save the world. Gregory Maguire's *What-the-Dickens* (Candlewick) raises the specter of the Hurricane Katrina disaster and tells the story of an orphaned tooth fairy. Nnedi Okorafor-Mbachu's second young adult novel *The Shadow Speaker* (Jump at the Sun) is science fiction but uses some mythic elements that will interest our readers. Cornelia Funke's *Igraine the Brave* (translated by Anthea Bell) is a lighthearted quest by a spirited young girl. Mette Ivie Harrison's *The Princess and the Hound* (Eos) is an engrossing medieval fantasy in which magic is forbidden, and a prince must disguise his abilities, while also trying to solve the mystery of his potential bride and her close companion, a dog. Sid Fleischman's *The Entertainer and Dybbuk* (Greenwillow) is a strange and commanding short book of a post-WWII ventriloquist and a ghost who inhabits his puppet. Harcourt reprinted Joan Aiken's historical trilogy featuring Felix Brooke, a Spanish-English orphan, *Go Saddle the Sea*, *Bridle the Wind*, and *The Teeth of the Gale*.

Single-Author Story Collections

Readers waiting for the next installment of George R. R. Martin's Song of Ice and Fire series (as Kelly is), will be reminded of Martin's still prodigious gifts at the short-story length if they pick up Bantam's two-volume edition of *Dreamsongs*. As well as short fiction, Martin provides many pages of interstitial material about writing, working in Hollywood, and much more. These two volumes are essential reading.

Michael Swanwick's mixed-genre collection *The Dog Said Bow-Wow* (Tachyon) presents some of the excellent, twisty stories that make up 2008 Tor novel *The Dragons of Babel*, as well as the con-man tales of Darger and Surplus, and one original. In this outstanding collection Swanwick moves deftly from steampunk to science fiction to the fantastic landscape his readers first encountered in *The Iron Dragon's Daughter*.

In *The Secret Files of the Diogenes Club* (Monkey Brain Books), Kim Newman brings together half a dozen previously published stories and one original, all of which concern the eponymous club founded by Mycroft Holmes. Readers of this anthology will remember "The Gypsies in the Wood." Recommended especially to fans of Alan Moore et al.'s *League of Extraordinary Gentlemen*.

Editor and writer-to-watch Dean Francis Alfar is at the forefront of a recent and vigorous speculative fiction scene in the Philippines. His first collection, *The Kite of Stars and Other Stories* (Anvil) contains sixteen tales that draw on the traditions and tropes of magic realism.

Lucius Shepard is an acknowledged master of the novella, and *Dagger Key and Other Stories* (PS Publishing) contains nine longer works that range between fantasy and horror. Highlights include the tour-de-force "Dead Money," a story of zombies, poker, and doomed romance. It also includes Shepard's story notes and an introduction by China Miéville.

Tim Pratt's second collection, *Hart and Boot* (Night Shade Books), contains recent Hugo Award-winner "Impossible Dreams" as well as a dozen other well-crafted tales about superheroes, schmucks, wage-slaves, and problematic roommates. The title story alone, which appeared in *Best American Short Stories*, is worth the price of the collection.

Worshipping Small Gods (Prime) collects Richard Parks's stories about ghost hunter Eli Mothersbaugh, who can see and sometimes hear ghosts, as well as some quietly gorgeous work influenced by Japanese history and folklore. Includes three new stories.

Kelley Eskridge's *Dangerous Space: Short Fiction* (Aqueduct) is a long-awaited mixed-genre collection. Her often gender-ambiguous protagonists navigate subtle, beautifully written stories in which music and madness both feature prominently.

Readers who missed Ellen Klages's contemporary fable/fairytale "In the House of the Seven Librarians" in a previous volume of this anthology, should pick up a copy of her first collection *Portable Childhoods* (Tachyon). Many of Klages's charming stories revolve around the (literal) magic of childhood, but there are some excellent science-fiction stories here, too. Introduction by Neil Gaiman.

Turn and turn about: Ellen Klages provides the introduction to the prolific, multi-talented Jay Lake's latest collection, *The River Knows Its Own* (Wheatland Press). Although this is an unthemed collection, all twenty or so stories are set in Lake's home territory, the Pacific northwest.

The Girl Who Loved Animals and Other Stories (Golden Gryphon) collects seventeen of Bruce McAllister's stories—there are some subtle fantasies here, although the majority of the stories are science fiction.

Crimson Shadows: The Best of Robert E. Howard, Volume 1 is the latest in Del Rey's fine series The Fully Illustrated Robert E. Howard Library. The illustrations this time are by Jim and Ruth Keegan—collectors might wish these books were being published in hardcover editions, but readers who haven't read Howard's classic pulp stories will find these excellent value.

A fiftieth-anniversary edition of *Dandelion Wine* (PS Publishing) includes an introduction by Stephen King and the illustrations which accompanied the stories as they were originally published in magazines. The high-end edition is signed by both Bradbury and King and includes a companion volume, *Summer Night, Summer*, in which Donn Albright and Jon Eller have painstakingly collected most of Bradbury's Green Town stories. (A more affordable edition is forthcoming from Subterranean Press.)

Bradbury recently completed two novellas which Morrow has published as *Now and Forever: Somewhere a Band Is Playing & Leviathan '99*. The latter is *Moby Dick*-inspired science fiction while the former is one of Bradbury's small-town fantasias.

Sarah Monette's *The Bone Key* (Prime) collects her M. R. Jamesian antiquarian ghost stories about Kyle Murchison Booth. Strictly speaking, this is in Ellen Datlow's territory, but Kelly recommends it to fans of Robert Westall's collection *Antique Dust*.

Jeff VandeerMeer and Cat Rambo published a tiny, charming chapbook, *The Surgeon's Tale and Other Stories*, through their own Two Free Lancer Press.

Edward Gauvin, who has made it his mission to translate the works of French fabulist Georges-Olivier Châteaureynaud, produced a small enjoyable chapbook of Gauvin's stories, *Trois Contes* (One Horse Town).

Heather Shaw's first chapbook *When We Were Six* (Tropism Press) contains half-a-dozen stories including one of Kelly's favorites from last year, "Mountain, Man."

Night Shade Books published a couple of collections from stars in the field: both Elizabeth Moon's *Moon Flights* and S.M. Stirling's *Ice, Iron and Gold* have a few fantasy stories tucked in among the science fiction.

Susan Palwick moves with great dexterity between science fiction and fantasy in her debut collection *The Fate of Mice* (Tachyon). Standouts include the haunting werewolf story "Gestella" and "G.I. Jesus." Includes three original stories.

In *12 Collections & The Teashop* (PS Publishing, translated by Alice Copple-Tošić), Zoran Živković considers collectors. (Readers: know thyselves!)

Debut collection *Sparks and Shadows* (HW Press) from horror/dark fantasy writer Lucy Snyder collects most of her often-comic fiction and poetry, as well as some nonfiction. Also worth a look: *Installing Linux on a Dead Badger and Other Oddities* (Creative Guy Publishing).

Antediluvian Tales (Subterranean Press) by Poppy Z. Brite collects several stories set in pre-Hurricane Katrina New Orleans. Fans who have been lucky enough to read Brite's recent mystery novels (Kelly recommends them to anyone who likes food or love stories) will recognize some of the characters here.

Anthologies

Philippine Speculative Fiction III (Kestrel) edited by Dean Francis Alfar and Nikki Alfar was one of Gavin's favorite anthologies of the year, for stories like Joanna Paula L. Cailas's tall tale of familial monstrousness, "Hamog."

Steve Berman's *So Fey: Queer Fairy Fictions* (Haworth) was one of the stronger themed anthologies of the year. Favorite stories included Holly Black's heartbreaking "The Coat of Stars" and Eugie Foster's "Year of the Fox," as well as work by Craig Laurance Gidney and Laurie J. Marks.

Delia Sherman and Theodora Goss co-edited *Interfictions: An Anthology of Interstitial Writing* which was published by the Interstitial Arts Foundation (distributed by Small Beer Press). We reprint Veronica Schanoes's anti-fairytale "Rats" here, a story which is as representative of the anthology as any one story could be. That is, it isn't quite like anything we've ever read. There are a number of stories here by newer writers, as well as three translations. Michael DeLuca's, Vandana Singh's, and Jon Singer's stories were some of the standouts, and we would have reprinted Catherynne M. Valente's gloriously otherworldly "A Dirge for Prester John" if we'd had the space.

The James Tiptree Award Anthology series (Tachyon) edited by Jeffrey D. Smith, Karen Joy Fowler, Pat Murphy, and Debbie Notkin is one we recommend wholeheartedly. The third volume includes stories from Ted Chiang, Tiptree, Aimee Bender, as well as the first chapter of Geoff Ryman's Tiptree Award-winner *Air*.

Speculative Japan: Outstanding Tales of Japanese Science Fiction and Fantasy (Kurodahan Press), edited by Gene van Troyer and Grania Davis, has a high proportion of science fiction and horror tales (and some reprints from earlier translated anthologies). But this group of stories is very high quality; it shows work from the last thirty years and is certainly worth getting for those interested in speculative fiction in other traditions and languages.

Reliably good mixed-genre showcase of Canadian short fiction, *Tesseracts Eleven* (Edge) is edited this time around by Cory Doctorow and Holly Phillips.

Bandersnatch (Prime), edited by Paul Tremblay and Sean Wallace, is a pocket-sized hardcover without title or other text on the cover. It was wonderfully weird, and we found these stories particularly memorable: Nick Mamatas's "Summon Bind Banish," Vylar Kaftan's "Scar Stories," and Jack M. Haringa's "A Perfect and Unmappable Grace."

Jabberwocky 3 (Prime) edited by Sean Wallace, was a fine mix of poetry and fantasy, the best of which was perhaps Jennifer Rachel Baumer's "The Forgotten Taste of Chocolate and Joy."

Also of note: *Worlds Apart: An Anthology of Russian Science Fiction and Fantasy* (Overlook), edited by Alexander Levitsky, covers the 1700s to the 1950s in over seven hundred pages, and will be of interest especially to readers with an academic interest in genre fiction, although there is a wealth of stories here that will appeal to a more general audience as well.

This year there were two more *Daikaiju!* volumes from Agog! Press: *Revenge of the Giant Monsters* and *Giant Monsters vs The World,* both ably edited by Robert Hood and Robin Penn. If you have a soft spot for Gojiro and company, these anthologies are a ticket to giant-monster heaven.

Richard Peabody's latest pop-culture-themed anthology *Kiss the Sky: Fiction and Poetry Starring Jimi Hendrix* (Paycock Press) includes some fantasy-tinged work, both fiction and poetry.

Astounding Hero Tales: Thrilling Tales of Pulp Adventure (Hero Games), edited by James Lowder delivered on the promise of its title.

Other anthologies: *The Best of Jim Baen's Universe* (Baen), edited by Eric Flint; *The Solaris Book of New Fantasy* (Solaris), edited by George Mann, included a fun Hal Duncan pirate fantasy and a few other gems; *Shadow Plays*, edited by Elise Bunter and Ian McHugh was mostly darker fiction; *Text:UR: The New Book of Masks* (Raw Dog Screaming), edited by Forrest Aguirre, is for those whose taste runs more to the experimental end of the fantastic.

We edited *The Best of Lady Churchill's Rosebud* (Del Rey), a selection from the first ten years of our zine, including work by Nalo Hopkinson, Karen Joy Fowler, and David Schwartz. Introduction by Dan Chaon.

Magazines and Journals

This year we reprint two stories from *The Magazine of Fantasy & Science Fiction*, and after some whittling down of our list, we have eleven honorable mentions as well. Although *Asimov's* tends toward science fiction, we still found half-a-dozen honorable mentions, including Karen Joy Fowler's "Always," and we would have liked to reprint "Dead Money" by Lucius Shepard. UK genre bastion *Interzone* contains very little fantasy, but we recommend Paul Meloy's dark "Islington Crocodiles" (which will be the title of his forthcoming collection). There were two issues of the too-long-on-hiatus *Black Static* (previously *The Third Alternative*). The fiction here was mostly horror. *Realms of Fantasy* publishes perhaps the widest range of fantasy among the various magazines. In addition, they publish reviews by Gahan Wilson and scholarly articles by Terri Windling, and there are regular pieces on media, books, games, costuming, and so on. *RoF* published a number of Graham Edwards's dimension-hopping detective stories that Gavin and Kelly very much enjoyed, as well as effective stories from Elizabeth M. Glover, Von Car, and Jay Lake.

Fantasy Magazine published a couple of print issues before transitioning online. It's now published using the popular Word Press blog engine and continues to offer high-quality fiction as well as a range of columns and reviews. We reprint Lucy Kemnitzer's "The Boulder" in this anthology, and found much worth reading here.

Mixed-genre magazine *Postscripts* almost always contains stories worth noting, although very little of it ever seems to be written by women. We very much enjoyed stories by Paul Jessup, Joe Hill, and Graham Joyce.

Weird Tales has a new editor, Ann VanderMeer, and a gorgeous new design. In 2007 it was still too early to tell in what direction VanderMeer plans to move the magazine, but in the meantime there were enjoyable fantasy stories by Richard Parks and Patrice E. Sarath.

Black Gate: Adventures in Fantasy Literature managed two issues—which, with each issue running 224 large pages is akin to a regular quarterly schedule for almost any other magazine. Judith Berman's story "Awakening" made an appearance on the Nebula ballot, and there were also good stories from Martha Wells and James Enge.

Paradox: The Magazine of Historical and Speculative Fiction published one issue of fiction and poetry by writers including Sarah Monette and Darrell Schweitzer.

Subterranean Magazine moved online after its last print issue (guest edited by Ellen Datlow). The contents, which are put up over the course of each quarter, tends heavily toward first-class science fiction and darker fantasy. With stories by writers like Gene Wolfe, Elizabeth Bear, Joe Hill, Poppy Z. Brite, and Caitlín R. Kiernan available for free, let's hope that Bill Schafer continues this generous experiment.

We enjoyed a number of stories, including ones by Marie Brennan, Kevin Cockle, Jennifer Rachel Baumer, and Wesley Herbert, in Canada's lively and long-running *On Spec*.

Shimmer produced a splendid pirate-themed issue (guest edited by John Joseph Adams) which included Jeremiah Tolbert's escapade "Captain Blood's B00ty." There were two solid issues of *GUD: Greatest Uncommon Denominator* (pronounced "Good"), a dynamic new magazine experimenting with varied methods of delivery (print and/or PDF) and rates of payment (fixed plus possible bonuses on high sales). As reading patterns shift, this experiment will be one to watch.

Tales of the Unanticipated declared itself an anthology rather than a magazine. Whichever it is, it's a consistently broad-minded read. There were three strong issues of *Zahir*, two of *Talebones*, and one from zine *Sybil's Garage*: Steve Rasnic Tem and Ekaterina Sedia's stories particularly stood out.

Say: What's the Combination?, edited by Christopher Rowe and Gwenda Bond is a double-sized issue of their different-theme-each-time zine. Sarah Monette's "The Bone Key" (title story of her collection), as well as work by Melissa Moorer were two of a number of strong stories here.

Amy Beth Forbes's "The Gardener of Hell" was a standout in what continues to be one of our favorites of the small-press zines, Tim Pratt and Heather Shaw's twice-yearly *Flytrap*.

John Klima's zine *Electric Velocipede* is particularly strong on science fiction, but there is usually a sprinkling of fantasy poems and stories as well. *Kaleidotrope*, edited by Fred Coppersmith, is a new zine of similar ilk. Two issues came out in 2007 and we hope to see it going along the same steadily rising path of *EV*, *Flytrap*, etc.

Australian magazines continue to showcase interesting work and newer writers worth tracking down. *Aurealis* impressed with good stories from Adam Browne and Cat Sparks. It was nice to see a new issue of *Orb* (no.7) in which, again, Cat Sparks had a memorable story. *Andromeda Spaceways Inflight Magazine* reliably offers a couple of very good stories each year.

Long-running zine *Not One of Us* published its usual two issues as well as an annual themed one-off chapbook. *GrendelSong* zine, which had a promising start, seems to have disappeared.

Small Beer Press published the usual two issues of *Lady Churchill's Rosebud Wristlet*. Fiction by newer writers like Meghan McCarron and Alice Sola Kim were among the highlights, and we reprint in this anthology Karen Joy Fowler's "The Last Worders."

On the Internet, there are now whole constellations of new webzines to explore, including some, like *Subterranean* and *Fantasy* (both listed above, and both free) which have recently moved from print to Web site. Some of these zines offer free content; some are subscription based. Some pay their contributors while others don't. Below we have tried to note which webzines are subscription based.

Strange Horizons is a consistently rich source of work by new and slipstreamy writers, and one of our favorite magazines online or off. Although its content is free to readers, they pay their writers, depending on donations and yearly fund drives. As well as fiction, the site offers poetry, essays, and reliably provocative book reviews. We reprint Liz Williams's story "The Hide" in this anthology, and first-rate stories by Leah Bobet, Joy Comeau, Eliot Fintushel, and Theodora Goss are easy to find in their archives online. Seek them out!

Edited by Mike Resnick, *Jim Baen's Universe* is a mix of the new and old-school styles of genre fiction, and the columns published on their site by Barry Malzberg offer value to subscribers. We reprint Garth Nix's "Sir Hereward and Mister Fitz Go to War Again" in this anthology.

Orson Scott Card's Intergalactic Medicine Show is also subscription-based. Like *Jim Baen's Universe*, *Medicine Show* is an experiment in publishing that has collected a community of readers around it.

Clarkesworld Magazine has consistently published strong work as they put out their two stories a month. Some of the best work was by Caitlín R. Kiernan, Jeff VanderMeer, and Elizabeth Bear, and recently there has been interesting nonfiction as well. Chapbooks and an annual anthology mean that readers can choose to read this online magazine on paper instead.

We've reprinted Catherynne M. Valente's poem, "The Seven Devils of Central California" from *Farrago's Wainscot*, which, with its interstitial sibling *Behind the Wainscot*, tilt the balance toward poetry, but also include some excellent and weird short fiction. As with *Goblin Fruit*, the design ethos, although attractive, originally made for difficult reading and Gavin especially is pleased to see that changing. Online zines, often run by small coteries of determined, like-minded people, continue to expand our genre, it seems sometimes by sheer force of will. The establishment of Web sites that publish fantastic poetry are especially welcome.

Startup *Coyote Wild* published some good work including Emily Mah's "Coyote Discovers Mars."

Of the fantasy fiction published by Helix, we enjoyed Ann Leckie's "The Snake Wife" most.

We consistently find fiction of interest in *Ideomancer*, *Abyss and Apex*, *Aeon*, *Son and Foe*, *Susurrus*, *ChiZine*, *The Journal of Mythic Arts*, and *Lone Star Stories*. There are, of course, many other webzines. Finally, let us again point out that most print genre magazines, small-press zines, and even literary magazines usually have some sort of Web presence. Many have put up free content, ranging from teasers to entire stories. They may also offer message boards, columns, interviews. There's never before been such instant and direct communication with editors; among the most accessible are Gordon Van Gelder, John Klima, Andy Cox, and Ellen Datlow.

Among the literary journals this year, we would like to draw attention to *Mid-American Review*. Vol. 28, No. 1 featured a striking cover by Joey Remners, the poetry of Maggie Smith and Benjamin Russell, as well as work by Khaled Mattawa, reprinted herein. David Shumate's story "The Supernatural" is also of note.

Tin House's thirty-third issue was entitled "Fantastic Women." For the most part, the stories and poems came from the literary end of the spectrum. Highlights were Judy Budnitz's "Abroad" and Julia Elliott's "The Wilds" as well as work by Shelley Jackson, and an essay on Angela Carter by the issue's co-editor, Rick Moody. Kelly Link's story "Light" was published in this issue.

Alimentum: The Literature of Food was a surprise and delight, not only for including work that tipped over into the fantastic but for their overall theme and aesthetic sense. Susan Sampson's poem "Fishing Off Mount Olympus" was surreal and hilarious, while Dawn Tefft's somber "*El Día de los Muertos*" was also an introduction to a poet worth seeking out.

McSweeney's produced four eclectically designed issues. We reprint Alexander MacBride's debut story from the twenty-fifth issue.

Punk Planet included an enjoyable werewolf story, "Not Even the Zookeeper Can Keep Control" by Jonathan Messinger, before giving up the ghost to the difficulties of magazine distribution.

This year the always-excellent *Conjunctions* put out a terrific issue, "A Writers' Aviary." Included was a terrific story from Diane Ackerman. *The Paris Review* published work by Stephen King, a story titled "Ayana."

Literary journals and magazines that included a touch of the fantastic, and which, overall, we recommend checking out, included *One Story*, *A Public Space*, *Redivider*, *Virginia Quarterly Review*, *Ninth Letter*, *The Cincinnati Review*; *New England Review*; *Two Lines: World Writing in Translation*; *StoryQuarterly*; *The Southern Review*; *Southwest Review*; *The Georgia Review*; *The New Yorker*; *Alaska Quarterly Review*; *Massachusetts Review*; *Atlanta Review*; *Stand*; *Gargoyle*; *Kenyon Review*; *The Mississippi Review*; *Hobart*; *Fiddlehead*; *Salmagundi*; *Pindeldyboz*; *Diagram*; *Zoetrope: All-Story*; *The Paris Review*, and *Oxford American*.

The Fairy Tale Review's Violet issue came out at the start of 2008, and we will include it next year.

Art and Picture Books

We wrote up the best art book of the year, Shaun Tan's beautiful wordless tale of immigration, community, and the fantastic, *The Arrival* (Scholastic), in last year's volume. Since then, it's received many awards and, in perhaps an even great testimony to the power of Tan's book, the government of Mexico purchased 30,000 copies for distribution to schools. We're looking forward to Tan's next book, *Tales from Outer Suburbia*.

Spectrum 14: The Best in Contemporary Fantastic Art (Underwood Books), edited by Arnie Fenner and Cathy Fenner is, as always, both a resource and a browser's delight.

Emshwiller Infinity X Two: The Art & Life of Ed and Carol Emshwiller (Nonstop Press) by Luis Ortiz is a delight: informative, packed with illustrations and photos, and including an interview with Carol Emshwiller. Ortiz has reprinted many of Ed

"Emsh" Emshwiller's book and magazine covers, as well as photos of Carol Em-shwiller, who was often the model. Emsh was one of the most influential artists work-ing in the field, and longtime readers of *Fantasy & Science Fiction* will recognize his distinctive style.

Mervyn Peake: The Man and His Art (Peter Owen), compiled by Sebastian Peake and Alison Eldred and edited by G. Peter Winnington, is a book that readers inter-ested in Peake will want to seek out.

Rafal Olbinski's *Women: Motifs and Variations* (Hudson Hills) is a beautifully produced book featuring the work of this Polish-born surrealist.

Yoshitaka Amano's *Worlds of Amano* (DH Press) is a career-spanning book that ought to prove irresistible to anyone who has seen his work on the Final Fantasy videogames, manga, or on book covers. Amano is one of the most interesting artists currently working in the fantastic.

The Art of Bryan Talbot (NBM) showcases the diversity of Talbot's projects and interests: from Judge Dredd and Sandman to pen and ink illustrations for Lewis Carroll's "Jabberwocky," there's an embarrassment of riches here.

Origins: The Art of John Jude Palencar (Underwood) comprehensively covers the career of one of the most popular artists in the genre.

Brian Froud's *World of Faerie* (Imaginosis) comes in a hardcover and an ex-tremely expensive limited edition with all kinds of extras (unseen by us).

Two how-to books from Watson-Guptill crossed our desks: Christopher Hart's *Drawing Dragons and Those Who Hunt Them* and Bryan Baugh's *Swords & Sorcery: How to Draw Fantastic Fantasy Adventure Comics*. While both are filled with les-sons and illustrations, the former seems more suited to the beginner than the latter. Also worth a look: John Howe's *Fantasy Art Workshop* (Impact).

For younger readers: Lisbeth Zwerger, who is one of Kelly's favorite artists, provided marvelous, sly watercolors for *The Bremen Town Musicians* (Penguin/Minedition, translated by Anthea Bell).

The Luck of the Loch Ness Monster: A Tale of Picky Eating (Houghton, illus-trated by Scott Magoon) by A. W. Flaherty is a tall tale, explaining how the monster got to the Loch. (Answer: it involves a small girl on a sea voyage who throws her oat-meal overboard each morning.)

Beowulf: A Tale of Blood, Heat, and Ashes (Candlewick), is retold by Nicky Raven and illustrated by John Howe.

Mother Earth and Her Children: A Quilted Fairy Tale (Breckling, illustrated by Sieglinde Schoen-Smith) is translated by Jack Zipes.

New editions of old favorites included *Iron Hans* (Candlewick, illustrated by Matt Tavares), a Grimm tale retold by Stephen Mitchell, and Christopher Myers's illustrated *Jabberwocky* (Hyperion), a narrative-based version of Lewis Carroll's fa-mous nonsensical beast poem.

Of associational interest: *Didn't Didn't Do It* (Putnam) brings together Bradford Morrow (author, and editor of the journal *Conjunctions*) and Gahan Wilson in a picture book rich with wordplay.

General Nonfiction

Michael Swanwick's monograph, *What Can Be Saved from the Wreckage: James Branch Cabell in the Twenty-first Century* (Temporary Culture), is a welcome attempt to bring into the spotlight a writer whose books for the most part languish out of print. (Dover has an edition of *Jurgen*, and Wildside Press has some fifteen of his books available as print-on-demand trade paperbacks.) Even if you aren't familiar with Cabell, Swanwick's monograph is worth picking up for its own sake.

David Standish's *Hollow Earth: The Long and Curious History of Imagining Strange Lands, Fantastical Creatures, Advanced Civilizations and Marvelous Machines Below the Earth's Surface* (Da Capo) good-naturedly describes the theories of crackpots, scientists, as well as touching on the science-fiction narratives of Edgar Rice Burroughs, Edgar Allan Poe, and others.

Cartographia: Mapping Civilizations (Little, Brown) by Vincent Virga, with the aid of the Library of Congress, marries a history of maps and their historical, philosophical, and political purposes with a wealth of plates taken from the Library of Congress's collection. Should be of interest to readers of fantasy epics. Highly recommended to everyone else, too.

Collectors make note: small-press publishers Payseur & Schmidt have, in the last few years, put out a series of chapbooks and limited-edition items that are some of the most beautifully designed objects we've ever come across. This year they published *And Now We Are Going to Have a Party* by Nicola Griffith, a limited-edition biography in a boxed set that includes five volumes of Griffith's diary entries, ephemera, and juvenilia. There's also a CD of music by Griffith's '80s-era band, scratch-n-sniff cards, and a letterpressed preface by Dorothy Allison.

Frankenstein: A Cultural History (Norton) by Susan Tyler Hitchcock is an entertaining and sprawling history of Mary Shelley and her book, which touches on everything from Victorian musical theater to nineteenth-century publishing to contemporary bioethics.

Stephen Jones published his monograph, *H. P. Lovecraft in Britain* (British Fantasy Society), after researching Lovecraft's correspondence in Gollancz's files for *Necronomicon: The Best Weird Tales of H. P. Lovecraft.*

Hippocampus Press published the first book devoted to criticism of M.R. James's ghost stories, *Warnings to the Curious: A Sheaf of Criticism on M. R. James.*

Myth, Folklore, and Fairy Tales

One of our favorite aspects of this job is receiving various packages in the mail and then opening them to discover presses, writers, and projects that are new to us. Online, the Endicott Studio blog run by Midori Snyder, Terri Windling, and others provided the same experience on a weekly basis. We can't recommend highly enough that you take a look at their archives.

With regards to our own mailbox, one memorable packet this year came from Andrea Lawlor of Pocket Myths (pocketmyths.blogspot.com) who has produced three previous themed zines, *Persephone, Cupid & Psyche, Orpheus,* and, most recently, *The Odyssey,* which, besides the wide range of poetry and fiction, comes with a DVD.

Girl Meets Boy: The Myth of Iphis by Ali Smith, *Where Three Roads Meet* by Sally Vickers, and *Binu and the Great Wall: The Myth of Meng* by Su Tong are the latest in the ongoing Canongate Books series of contemporary retellings of ancient myths.

The Journal of Mythic Arts has closed. Any writer or reader short of inspiration or wishing to feast upon some new piece or form of art can still head to their archives.

Highlights included the weekly Sunday poem, features on artists working in various media, and reviews of work on the outskirts of the genre.

In Kate Bernheimer's *Brothers & Beasts: An Anthology of Men on Fairy Tales* (Wayne State University Press), a companion volume to her previous book *Mirror, Mirror on the Wall*, well-established and newer male writers, including Neil Gaiman, Robert Coover, Jeff VanderMeer, Gregory Maguire and David J. Schwartz write about their relationships to fairy tales.

Lancelot and the Lord of the Distant Isles: Or, the Book of Galehaut Retold (David R. Godine, illustrated by Judith Jaidinger) by Patricia Terry and Samuel N. Rosenberg is a beautiful and full retelling of the Arthurian tales.

Australian Juliet Marillier's *Wildwood Dancing* (Knopf) is a retelling of the Twelve Dancing Princesses set in Romania.

There was one online issue of *Cabinet des Fées* (edited by Helen Pilinovsky, Catherynne M. Valente, Erzebet YellowBoy, and JoSelle Vanderhooft) and one printed anthology (Prime).

New-Slain Knight (Thomas Dunne/SMP) is the fifth in Deborah Grabien's Haunted Ballad series in which the power of song and tradition is the only hope for a haunted child.

For younger readers: Fans of Shannon Hale's *Goose Girl* will enjoy Heather Tomlinson's debut, *The Swan Maiden* (Holt), where a girl who has been lied to about her ability to turn into a swan follows her heart and discovers the true cost of magic.

Awards

The 33rd annual World Fantasy Convention was held in Saratoga Springs, New York. Carol Emshwiller, Kim Newman, Robin Hobb, Lisa Tuttle, and Jean Giraud (Moebius) were the guests of honor. The following awards were given out: Life Achievement: Diana Wynne Jones and Betty Ballantine; Novel: *Soldier of Sidon*, Gene Wolfe (Tor); Novella: "Botch Town," Jeffrey Ford (*The Empire of Ice Cream*); Short Story: "Journey into the Kingdom," M. Rickert (*Fantasy & Science Fiction*, May); Anthology: *Salon Fantastique*, ed. Terri Windling and Ellen Datlow (Thunder's Mouth); Collection: *Map of Dreams*, M. Rickert (Golden Gryphon); Artist: Shaun Tan; Special Award, Professional: Ellen Asher (for work at the Science Fiction Book Club); Special Award, Non-Professional: Gary Wolfe (for reviews and criticism in Locus and elsewhere).

The James Tiptree, Jr. Memorial Award for genre fiction that expands or explores our understanding of gender was awarded to Shelley Jackson for *Half Life* (HarperCollins) and *The Orphan's Tales: In the Night Garden* by Catherynne M. Valente (Bantam/Spectra). The award was presented at WisCon in Madison, Wisconsin, and also at the World Science Fiction Convention in Yokohama, Japan.

The International Association for the Fantastic's William L. Crawford Fantasy Award went to *Map of Dreams* by M. Rickert (Golden Gryphon) and the IAFA Distinguished Scholarship Award was given to Jane Donawerth. The Mythopoeic Award winners were: Adult Literature: Patricia A. McKillip, *Solstice Wood* (Ace); Children's Literature: Catherine Fisher, *Corbenic* (Greenwillow); Scholarship Award in Inklings Studies: Wayne G. Hammond and Christina Scull, *The J.R.R. Tolkien Companion and Guide* (Houghton Mifflin); Scholarship Award in General

Myth and Fantasy Studies: G. Ronald Murphy, S.J., *Gemstone of Paradise: The Holy Grail in Wolfram's Parzival* (Oxford University Press).

As usual, there were more stories that we had pages for. Here is a list of a few more favorites which we encourage you to seek out:

Holly Black, "The Coat of Stars," *So Fey*.
Orson Scott Card, "Stonefather," *Wizards*.
Brian Evenson, "Alfons Kuylers," *Columbia* 45.
Eliot Fintushel, "How the Little Rabbi Grew," *Strange Horizons*, September 17.
Theodora Goss, "Singing of Mount Abora," *Logorrhea*.
Graham Joyce, "The Last Testament of Seamus Todd, Soldier of the Queen," *Postscripts* 10.
Lucius Shepard, "Dead Money," *Asimov's*, April/May.
Will Shetterly, "Black Rock Blues," *The Coyote Road: Trickster Tales*.
Sonya Taaffe, "The Windfalls" (poem), *Lone Star Stories*, April.
Catherynne M. Valente, "A Dirge for Prester John," *Interfictions*.
Ysabeau Wilce, "Quartermaster Returns," *Eclipse 1*.
Marly Youmans, "The Smaragdine Knot," *Logorrhea*.

We keep a small Web page for this book at www.lcrw.net/yearsbest and we encourage e-mail recommendations of works for consideration in next year's volume (please check this Summation and the Honorable Mention list to see the types of material we are already reading). As ever, thank you for reading. We hope you enjoy the following stories as much as we did.

Summation 2007: Horror

Ellen Datlow

The stories and poems chosen this year come from a variety of venues—nine are from magazines, ten stories are from anthologies, and one was first published online. Two of the three poems come from mainstream publications. Six of the contributors live in the U.K. (one born in the U.S.), one is Australian, and one (who I believe was born in the U.S.) has lived in Scandinavia most of his life.

Unlike last year, none of the works are from single author collections. If there were more room, I would have liked to have chosen Laird Barron's novella "Procession of the Black Sloth" from his excellent debut collection *The Imago Sequence*, or one of the two excellent novellas by Paul Finch in his collection *Stains*. Other novellas I very much enjoyed were "Vacancy" and "Dead Money" by Lucius Shepard, "Pen Umbra" by Gemma Files, "Cold Snap" by Kim Newman, "Dinckley Green" by Christopher Harman, and "The Magpies" by David Rix.

Awards

The Bram Stoker Awards for Achievement in Horror are given by the Horror Writers Association. The full membership may recommend in all categories but only active members can vote on the final ballot. The awards for material appearing during 2006 were presented at the organization's annual banquet held Saturday, March 31, 2007, at the World Horror Convention in Toronto, Ontario.

2006 Winners for Superior Achievement:

Novel: *Lisey's Story* by Stephen King (Scribner); First Novel: *Ghost Road Blues* by Jonathan Maberry (Pinnacle); Long Fiction: "Dark Harvest" by Norman Partridge (C.D. Publications); Short Fiction: "Tested" by Lisa Morton (*Cemetery Dance* magazine #55); Anthology: [Tie] *Retro Pulp Tales*, edited by Joe R. Lansdale (Subterranean) and *Mondo Zombie*, edited by John Skipp (C.D. Publications); Collection: *Destinations Unknown* by Gary A. Braunbeck (C.D. Publications); Nonfiction: [Tie] *Final Exits: The Illustrated Encyclopedia of How We Die* by Michael Largo (HarperCollins); and *Gospel of the Living Dead: George Romero's Visions of Hell on Earth* by Kim Paffenroth (Baylor University Press); Poetry: *Shades Fantastic* by Bruce Boston (Gromagon Press) Lifetime Achievement Award: Thomas Harris; Specialty Press Award: PS Publishing; Richard Laymon (President's) Award: Lisa Morton.

The International Horror Guild Awards were presented on November 1, 2007, at the Saratoga Hotel and Conference Center during the World Fantasy Convention in Saratoga Springs, New York. Nominations are derived from recommendations made by the public and the judges' knowledge of the field. Edward Bryant, Stefan R. Dziemianowicz, Ann Kennedy, and Hank Wagner adjudicated. Ramsey Campbell was honored as a Living Legend. Recognized for achievement in the field of horror/dark fantasy during 2006:

Novel: Conrad Williams. *The Unblemished* (Earthling); Long Fiction: Norman Partridge. "Dark Harvest" (C.D. Publications); Mid-length Fiction: Paul Finch. "The Old North Road" (*Alone on the Darkside*); Short Fiction: Stephen Gallagher. "The Box" (*Retro Pulp Tales*); Collection (Single Author) [Tie] Terry Dowling. *Basic Black* (C.D. Publications) and Glen Hirshberg. *American Morons* (Earthling); Anthology: William Sheehan and Bill Schafer, editors. *Lords of the Razor* (Subterranean Press); Periodical: *Subterranean*; Illustrated Narrative: Lewis Trondheim. A.L.I.E.E.E.N. (France: Editions Breal, 2004; US: Firstsecond Books, 2006); Nonfiction: S.T. Joshi, editor. *Icons of Horror and the Supernatural* (Greenwood Press); Art [Tie]: Aeron Alfrey. *Exhibits from the Imaginary Museum*, and John Picacio. *Cover Story: The Art of John Picacio* (MonkeyBrain).

The Winners of the 2007 British Fantasy Awards were announced during the award ceremony at the culmination of Fantasycon, September 23rd, in Nottingham, U.K. The winners: Sydney J. Bounds Best Newcomer Award (selected by a panel of judges including Ramsey Campbell, Marie O'Regan, David A. Sutton, Stephen Jones, Jo Fletcher and Philip Harbottle): Joe Hill; Best Non-Fiction: Mark Morris, for *Cinema Macabre* (PS Publishing); Best Artist: Vincent Chong; Best Collection: Neil Gaiman, for *Fragile Things* (Headline); Best Anthology: Gary Couzens, for *Extended Play: The Elastic Book of Music* (Elastic Press); Best Short Fiction: Mark Chadbourn, for "Whisper Lane (*The BFS: A Celebration*, British Fantasy Society); Best Novella: Paul Finch, for *Kid* (*Choices*, Pendragon Press); Best Small Press: Peter Crowther, PS Publishing; Karl Edward Wagner Award (BFS Committee Special Award): Ellen Datlow; August Derleth Award for Best Novel: Tim Lebbon for *Dusk* (Bantam Spectra).

Notable Novels of 2007

I rarely have time to read novels, so there are only a few about which I will say more than a few words. But if one judges the health of a field by the *number* of novels published, there seem to be no fewer horror novels published than in previous years. However, a good chunk of them are now published as mainstream fiction or as the newest "category"—paranormal romance and a type of urban fantasy in which the major players are often vampires or other supernatural creatures or hunters of those creatures.

Players by Paul McAuley (Simon and Schuster, UK) is a lively police procedural opening with the discovery of a dying naked teenage girl in a remote Oregon forest. A rookie detective hunts down a psychotic game designer so obsessed with his creation that he's had plastic surgery to model himself after one of his characters. Plenty of violence and some gore.

The Pilo Family Circus by Will Elliott (ABC Books, Australia) is a nightmarish story about an aimless young Australian who's warned by a bunch of wayward clowns that his audition is imminent—whoa! Who said he even *wanted* to be a clown? But it's down the rabbit hole for him, into a carnival existing in an alternate universe and run by a pair of sadistic brothers who answer to creatures even more monstrous than themselves . . . and no one—not even the customers—can leave the show intact.

Heart-Shaped Box by Joe Hill (William Morrow) is a solid first novel that, while not brilliant like his award-winning collection *Twentieth Century Ghosts,* is still very good. A jaded former rock star wins an eBay auction for a ghost that wants nothing less than total revenge. The book is smoothly written and expertly lays on the suspense as the protagonist and those he cares about are dragged into the influential sphere of a twisted and dangerous haunt.

In the Woods by Tana French (Viking) is another solid debut. In 1984, two children playing in a suburban British wood go missing, and the third child, found with blood in his sneakers and almost catatonic, has no memory of what happened to his two friends. Twenty years later, that survivor has become a homicide detective and is faced with a child murder in the same wood. This psychological suspense tale has enough of a hint of the supernatural to provide an extra creepiness.

Bangkok Haunts by John Burdett (Knopf) is the third in the remarkable series featuring the Thai Police detective Sonchai Jitpleecheep. The novel begins with the detective viewing what is apparently a snuff film showing the murder of a former lover with whom he was (and still is) obsessed. The story initially seems like a straightforward mystery, but as with the two previous novels, it achieves a richness and complexity that ultimately twists into a web of vengeance, mysticism, and magic.

The Somnambulist by Jonathan Barnes (Victor Gollancz) is an entertaining tale about a conspiracy afoot in Victorian England and the stage conjuror who is called upon to save London. The utterly unreliable narrator—the tall, silent titular character—and a cast of grotesques make for magical, bloody fun.

Generation Loss by Elizabeth Hand (Small Beer) is the author's first foray into the psychological suspense thriller and it's a doozy. Cass (Scary) Neary is a prickly, pill-popping protagonist best known for the photographs of dead people she took during the height of the punk scene. Now she's on an assignment/pilgrimage to backwoods Maine to interview the reclusive photographer who so strongly influenced her own work. What ensues is engrossing and horrifying.

Harry Potter and the Deathly Hallows by J.K. Rowling (Bloomsbury) is a satisfying conclusion to the Potter phenomenon. Despite some clunky writing and less than rounded characters, Rowling still manages to pull the reader into the adventures of "the boy who survived" and his friends. A few surprises, some nice touches, and a lot of death.

Spook Country by William Gibson (Putnam) is not horrific, but there's a dark undercurrent of paranoia threaded throughout this tense and satisfying, overtly political "caper" novel. The main characters are a former rocker, now a journalist on assignment for a magazine that doesn't yet exist, a pill-popping break-in wizard stuck with a paranoid secret ops loony, and a young Cuban involved in suspicious information transfers. And they're all converging on a huge shipping container with a mysterious *something* inside. Splendid entertainment.

Bottomfeeder by B.H. Fingerman (M Press) is a debut novel by a writer better known for his graphic novels. A normal guy from Queens, New York, is turned into a vampire at age twenty-seven by an unknown attacker, loses his wife, his home, and his job, and is forced to make it on his own in his strange new world. His only friend is a total loser he's known since high school who just won't let go. Funny, ironic, and ultimately moving as the guy meets other vampires and sees the possible lifestyles he could be "living."

Remainder by Tom McCarthy (Vintage) is a first novel about a man who received an 8.5 million pounds sterling settlement for an accident in which he almost died. The reader never finds out what actually happened but upon the guy's recovery, he becomes convinced that he has lost his connection to the world and that the only way he can recover is to recreate a specific living condition that he remembers. He does this by buying up property and peopling it with hirelings who will follow a specific script that he supplies—on call to his every whim. The pianist upstairs must practice a specific piece of music and when he makes mistakes, he has to practice over and over again. The concierge must stand by the door all day—in a mask—as the employer doesn't remember the face of the original concierge. Black cats must roam the red slate roof across the way. The end result is inevitable—monstrous, terrifying, and in a way, funny.

Deadstock by Jeffrey Thomas (Solaris) is an absorbing and well-told "Punktown" novel about a private eye hired by a rich man to find the missing, very expensive and unique doll that he has bioengineered for his daughter. In other parts of the city, an abandoned apartment building defends itself by bloodily slaughtering all intruders and a young girl has disappeared.

Stalin's Ghost by Martin Cruz Smith (Simon & Schuster) brings back Arkady Renko, the Moscow detective first introduced in *Gorky Park* and a recurring character in several other novels, including the terrific one about Chernobyl, *Wolves Eat Dogs*. In the new book, the ghost of Stalin appears to a subway car full of Muscovites, starting a chain of events that leads to political chicanery, death, revisiting past atrocities in Chechnya, and some great plot twists.

Fangland by John Marks (Penguin) is a surprisingly original vampire novel about a young associate producer sent to Transylvania to vet a mysterious crime lord for an interview on *The Hour* (modeled on *60 Minutes*, Marks's former employer). The crime lord, actually a vampiric creature who infects victims with the voices of humans killed in atrocities throughout history, uses the woman's connections to worm his way onto the twentieth floor of *The Hour*—dubbed "Fangland" by its denizens. Every time the reader thinks she knows where the story is going, it takes a neat half-turn away from the obvious.

Echo by Kate Morgenroth (Simon & Schuster Books for Young Readers) is a terrific young adult novel about a teenage boy whose brother was killed in a horrible accident. The surviving brother is not surviving very well, and a year later he begins to experience very strange things, as events spiral out of control. Only 135 pages, with a great cover.

The Terror by Dan Simmons (Little, Brown) is a brilliant, suspenseful novel about the doomed 1840s Franklin expedition to the Arctic that truly brings to life what it must have been like in that cold, cold place. Injected into this great adventure is a major supernatural element as "something" is ambushing and slaughtering men from the two ships. There are human monsters too, and heroes. Highly recommended.

The Witch's Trinity by Erika Mailman (Crown) is a marvelous novel that takes a common subject—witch trials during the 1500s—and makes it fresh. A tiny German village, like its neighbors, is afflicted by famine and so the Church sends a friar to investigate and root out the evil. The villagers realize too late that he believes someone in their midst is causing their bad luck, and the resulting hysteria rips apart the fabric of the close knit community.

Heartsick by Chelsea Cain (St. Martin's Press) is about a homicide detective obsessed with the beautiful serial killer who tortured him and then inexplicably saved his life and turned herself in. Dark and disturbing and graphic in its depiction of the killer's actions. This is definitely worth a read for those looking for "new" ideas in the serial killer sub-genre.

Softspoken by Lucius Shepard (Night Shade) is a short but powerful novel about a disaffected wife in a crumbling marriage who begins to hear and see ghosts in the antebellum mansion of her husband's boyhood. The interior life of the character is so troubled that the work is difficult to read, and while there's no real surprise to where the story's going, it's like a train wreck you can't help but stare at.

Also Noted

This is not meant to be all-inclusive but merely a sampling of dark fiction available during 2007.

Vampire fiction never dies. In addition to *Fangland* (reviewed above) there were a plethora of vampire novels by new and seasoned voices including *The Society of S* by Susan Hubbard (S&S), a coming of age story about a fledgling vampire searching for her missing mother, and *Let Me In* by John Ajvide Lindquist (Thomas Dunne Books/St. Martin's Press), a first novel by a Swedish former conjuror and stand-up comic about a murder and a twelve-year-old boy intrigued by the mysterious girl who moves in next door—and only comes out at night. Translated from the Swedish. Also, Jemiah Jefferson's *A Drop of Scarlet* (Leisure), the fourth book in her series about romantic bloodsuckers; *You Suck*, Christopher Moore's humorous novel about young vampires in love, (Morrow); Laurell K. Hamilton's fifteenth Anita Blake, vampire hunter novel, *The Harlequin* (Berkley); Chelsea Quin Yarbro's twentieth Saint-Germain novel, *Borne in Blood* (Tor); *The Forsaken* (St. Martin's), the seventh in L.A. Banks's vampire huntress series; and *Baltimore, or The Steadfast Tin Soldier and the Vampire* by Mike Mignola and Christopher Golden (Bantam), a dark fantasy illustrated by Mignola.

Dead Sea by Brian Keene (Leisure) is one of several zombie novels out in 2007. In addition, there were David Wellington's *Monster Planet*, third in a trilogy of zombie novels, originally published on the Web; *Dying to Live* (Permuted Press), a well-received first novel by Kim Paffenroth; and Sarah Langan's acclaimed second novel, *The Missing* (HarperCollins).

Ghosts and other hauntings were also popular in 2007, with novels such as *Taken* by Sarah Pinborough (Leisure); *The Everlasting* by Tim Lebbon (Necessary Evil Press/Leisure); *Angelica* by Arthur Philips (Random House); *The Servants* (Earthling), one of the two novels published by Smith in 2007; *Vintage*, a first novel written for young adults by Steve Berman (Haworth), nominated for both the Lambda and Andre Norton Awards. *One For Sorrow*, another first novel, this one by Christopher Barzak (Bantam Spectra), won the William Crawford Award for first book of fantasy; *Ghost* by Alan Lightman (Pantheon), about a man working in a mortuary who sees something that cannot be explained; and *Dead Man's Boots* by Mike Carey (Orbit), the third in his series about a ghost hunter. Michael Cisco's *The Traitor* (Prime) is a coming-of-age story about an itinerant spirit eater who meets his dark alter ego.

Demons are central to *Demon Eyes* by L.H. Maynard and M.P.N. Sims (Leisure), which features several mysterious deaths and a boss from Hell, *Butcher Bird* by Richard Kadrey (Night Shade Books), about a tattoo artist unaware that his partner was a demon; and *Mister B. Gone* by Clive Barker (HarperCollins), told by a medieval demon trapped in our world who alternately speaks directly to the reader and recounts his memoirs in a diary.

Ancient Eyes by David Niall Wilson (Bloodletting Press) is about old evil and modern men fighting it; Cherie Priest's *Dreadful Skin* (Subterranean), is a post-Civil War werewolf novel; Jonathan Maberry follows up his Stoker Award-winning novel *Ghost Road Blues* with *Dead Man's Song* (Pinnacle), taking place in the same town of Pine Deep. In Michael Marshall Smith's *The Intruders* (William Morrow), the wife of an ex-LAPD patrolman goes missing, and popular novelist John Farris's newest novel, *You Don't Scare Me* (Forge), is about a child abuser who, once dead, becomes something even worse. *The Castle in the Forest* by Norman Mailer (Random House), tells the story of Adolf Hitler from the point of view of a minion of Satan. Stephen King's *Duma Key* (Scribner) is about a man who suffers a life-changing accident that changes his personality, leading to the dissolution of his marriage and giving him a new, artistic talent. A second novel by King titled *Blaze*, under the Richard Bachman name (Scribner), is a trunk novel from 1973 about a man seeking revenge for the mistreatment he experienced as a boy. Laurell K. Hamilton's second 2007 novel, *A Lick of Frost* (Ballantine), is the sixth in her Meredith Gentry paranormal romance series. Kim Harrison's *For a Few Demons More* is book five in her Rachel Morgan series. *Mr. Hands* by Gary A. Braunbeck (Leisure) takes place in the fictional town of Cedar Hill and is about abuse, revenge, and redemption; *Morbid Curiosity* by Deborah LeBlanc (Leisure) is about magic out of control; *The Midnight Road* by Tom Piccirilli (Leisure) is a thriller about a man coming back from the dead, as is *Johnny Gruesome* by Gregory Lamberson (Bad Moon Books), with great looking fake-pulpy jacket art by Zach McCain; *Deeper* by Jeff Long (Atria) is a sequel to his 1999 novel *The Descent*; Edward Lee's *House Infernal* (Leisure), part three of the Infernal Saga, is about a nightmarish city.

The end of the world is well covered by John Shirley's *The Other End* (C.D. Publications), about Judgment Day, seen from the left, rather than the usual Fundamentalist point of view and Mark Morris's *The Deluge* (Leisure), taking place after a major flood destroys most of London; and *Twilight* by Brendan DuBois (Dunne /St. Martin's) is a post-apocalyptic novel about a UN peacekeeper's team investigating an atrocity in upstate New York after a devastating terrorist attack against the United States.

Some novels about returning and facing past experiences and mistakes: *The Dust of Wonderland* by Lee Thomas (Alyson Books) is about a man returning to face his demons in New Orleans, where he spent his youth. *A Good and Happy Child* by Justin Evans (Shaye Areheart) is about a New Yorker whose fear of holding his newborn son sends him into therapy and back to his troubled childhood in Virginia. *Winterwood* by Patrick McCabe (Bloomsbury) is about a newspaperman sent back to the town where he grew up to cover changing traditions in Ireland. His encounter with the local fiddler and teller of tall tales creates nasty cracks in his life. *Homeplace* by Beth Massie (Berkley), usually known as Elizabeth Massie, is about an artist who hopes to rediscover her muse in the Virginia of her childhood.

Last Rituals: An Icelandic Novel of Secret Symbols, Medieval Witchcraft, and Modern Murder by Yrsa Sigurdardóttir (William Morrow) is an Icelandic children's book author's first adult novel, and has been published all over the world. It introduces a female lawyer investigator who will appear in a subsequent novel in 2008. *Tokyo Year Zero* by David Peace (Knopf) is a noir novel taking place in post-WWII Japan described by one reviewer as a cross between Haruki Murakami and James

Ellroy. *The Darkest Evening* by Dean Koontz (Bantam) is about a woman who helps abused dogs, and the magical powers of a golden retriever. *After Dark* by Haruki Murakami (Knopf) is about two sisters and those they encounter in Tokyo between midnight and dawn. Another intriguing novel from Japan, *Grotesque* by Natsuo Kirino (Knopf) is about three Japanese women, two of them murdered prostitutes, the third, sister of one of the dead. *Death of a Murderer* by Rupert Thomson (Knopf) is about a policeman assigned to guard the body of a long imprisoned child murderer after she's died a natural death. *The Kingdom of Bones* (Shaye Areheart Books) is Stephen Gallagher's fourteenth novel, a dark historical with a former boxing champion as its protagonist. *Pig Island* by Mo Hayder (Atlantic Monthly Press) is about a journalist expert in exposing supernatural hoaxes and the havoc his presence wreaks when he visits a secretive religious community on a Scottish island. *The Big Girls* by Susanna Moore (Knopf) is the first foray into dark fiction since the author's excellent and perverse psychological crime novel, *In the Cut*. Set in an upstate New York women's prison, it examines the bond between an inmate and her psychiatrist. *The Grin of the Dark* by Ramsey Campbell (PS) is a novel about the search for the truth about a long-dead silent movie actor. *The Vanishing* by Bentley Little (Penguin/Signet) begins with a businessman slaughtering his family and leaving a cryptic message on the videotape he leaves behind. Brian Keene and J. F. Gonzalez follow up their first collaboration about a deadly alien invasion with *Clickers II: The Next Wave*, from Delirium Books. Keene had a third novel out called *Ghoul* (Leisure). *Echoes* by Joe R. Lansdale (Vintage) is a supernatural crime novel about a man who can see and hear violent events in the past. Jim Butcher's *White Knight* (Roc) is the ninth of this hardboiled supernatural crime series to feature Chicago wizard Harry Dresden. Michael Chabon's *The Yiddish Policeman's Union* (Harper-Collins) is a tour de force noir alternative history.

Two lost novels have been reprinted by Ash-Tree Press: *The Woman in Black* by M.Y. Halidom was originally published in 1906. The author's true identity only came to light in 2005 when his grandson revealed Halidom as Alexander Huth. Richard Dalby's introduction tells the story, in addition to examining the author's career. *Cold Harbour* by Francis Brett Young reprints a novel first published in 1924 by a regional novelist. Introduction by John Howard.

Anthologies

Travellers in Darkness, the Souvenir Book of the World Horror Convention 2007, edited by Stephen Jones, is a handsome limited edition hardcover book with tributes about the guests of the convention, and original stories, essays, reprints, and excerpts by them plus portfolios of work by World Horror Convention artist guest John Picacio and special Horror Writers Association artist guest Gahan Wilson.

The Mammoth Book of Monsters, edited by Stephen Jones (Robinson), is the most recent entry in Jones's consistently excellent Mammoth horror series, which reprints classics along with a handful of new stories. There were some very good originals among the twenty-two tales, including those by Scott Edelman, Tanith Lee, Jay Lake, and the late Sydney J. Bounds. The Tanith Lee is reprinted herein.

Summer Chills, edited by Stephen Jones (Carroll & Graf), has twenty horror stories about exotic vacations, six of them appearing for the first time. The originals are all good. The reprints include stories by Kim Newman, Nancy Holder, Elizabeth Massie, Glen Hirshberg, and Karl Edward Wagner.

Exotic Gothic: Forbidden Tales from Our Gothic World, edited by Danel Olson

(Ash-Tree Press), showcases twenty-three stories (eight original to the anthology) that take place around the world. The best of the originals are those by Terry Dowling and Barbara Roden.

Bare Bone, edited by Kevin L. Donihe and published by Raw Dog Screaming Press, changed from magazine to anthology format, although it's still numbered by issues. Number eleven had notable stories by Robert Dunbar, Paul Finch, and Jeremy C. Shipp.

666: The Number of the Beast, edited by Abby McAden (Point), is a lightweight horror anthology aimed at young teenagers. The most notable thing about it is that it has new stories by T.E.D. Klein, Joyce Carol Oates, P.D. Cacek, and Chet Williamson.

Phobic, edited by Andy Murray (Comma Press), is a very good anthology of fifteen wide-ranging horror stories by Ramsey Campbell, Nicholas Royle, Conrad Williams, Jeremy Dyson, Chaz Brenchley (from the 2006 anthology *Phantoms at the Phil II*, covered next), and Hanif Kureishi (reprint), and a host of other British writers with whom I'm not familiar.

Phantoms at the Phil: The Second Proceedings (Side Real/Northern Gothic, 2006) is the follow-up to the 2005 volume of three stories told for Christmas at the Literary & Philosophical Society of Newcastle-upon-Tyne. This edition has six original stories by Chaz Brenchley, Gail-Nina Anderson, Sean O'Brien, Simon Morden, Ann Cleeves, and Carol McGuigan plus an introduction by Christopher Fowler. Included in the limited edition are two CDs of the authors reading their stories. *Phantoms at the Phil: The Third Proceedings*, published late 2007, features two strong stories each by Chaz Brenchley, Gail-Nina Anderson, and Sean O'Brien. The Brenchley is reprinted herein.

The First Humdrumming Book of Horror Stories, edited by Ian Alexander Martin (Humdrumming), shows great promise as the debut showcase volume of horror stories by authors who have had books published by Humdrumming. My favorites of the twelve stories are by Garry Kilworth, James Cooper, John Travis, Gary Fry, and Gary McMahon, whose story is reprinted herein.

The Secret History of Vampires, edited by Darrell Schweitzer and Martin H. Greenberg (DAW), is a good batch of thirteen stories about historical figures who have dealings with (or who are) vampires. There are especially good stories by Tanith Lee, P. D. Cacek, Carrie Vaughn, Gregory Frost, and Harry Turtledove.

Dark Delicacies II: Fear, edited by Del Howison and Jeff Gelb (Carroll & Graf) follows up the duo's Stoker Award-winning first volume of non-theme "tales of terror and the macabre." The impressive line up includes strong stories by Caitlín R. Kiernan, Glen Hirshberg, Peter Atkins, Tananarive Due, John Farris, John Harrison, Joe R. Lansdale, James Sallis, and Steve Niles.

At Ease with the Dead: New Tales of the Supernatural and Macabre, edited by Barbara and Christopher Roden (Ash-Tree Press), is the fourth original anthology collaboration by the Rodens and it's full of excellent fiction. The strongest are by Reggie Oliver, Don Tumasonis, Barbara Roden, Steve Duffy, Helen Grant, John Whitbourn, and James Doig. The Tumasonis and Reggie Oliver stories are reprinted herein.

Strange Tales Volume II, edited by Rosalie Parker (Tartarus Press), is the worthy follow-up to the World Fantasy Award-winning volume of supernatural and psychological horror fiction. The wide-ranging original seventeen stories are all readable but the strongest are by Elizabeth Brown, Adam Golaski, Christopher Harman, Stephen Holman, Joel Knight, Don Tumasonis (under the pseudonym Hilbourne Carlone), A.G. Slatter, and a very strong novella by David Rix.

Inferno: New Tales of Terror and the Supernatural, edited by Ellen Datlow (Tor), is the first non-themed original horror anthology by the editor. Included are stories by Lucius Shepard, Glen Hirshberg, Lee Thomas, Pat Cadigan, P.D. Cacek, and others. Nathan Ballingrud's and Laird Barron's stories are reprinted herein.

The Restless Dead, edited by Deborah Noyes (Candlewick Press), is a follow-up to *Gothic!*, a young adult anthology of supernatural tales (2004). The new volume contains a good mix of ten stories, the strongest by Nancy Etchemendy, M. T. Anderson, Kelly Link, Annette Curtis Klaus, and Noyes herself.

High Seas Cthulhu, edited by William Jones (Elder Signs Press), is an anthology of twenty Lovecraftian tales set on the sea. All but one are original and although every story is readable, there isn't enough variety in tone, setting, or style. The more interesting stories are by Matthew Baugh, Tim Curran, John Shire, Stewart Sternberg, Charles P. Zaglanis, and Lee Clark Zumpe.

Read by Dawn II, edited by Adele Hartley (Bloody Books) is disappointing after last year's promising debut. However, there are notable stories by Patricia Russo, Suzanne Elvidge, Ken Goldman, Scott Stainton Miller, and Joshua Reynolds. For a book that positions itself as showcasing "international horror writing" it seems ironic not to provide biographies for any of the twenty-six contributors.

Classic Tales of Horror Volume 2, edited by Jonathan Wooding (Bloody Books) features fourteen stories, some overly familiar ("The Monkey's Paw" and "William Wilson") and some less so by writers including Joseph Sheridan LeFanu, Mary Shelley, E. Nesbit, and eleven others.

Legends of the Mountain State: Ghostly Tales from the State of West Virginia, edited by Michael Knost (Woodland Press), has thirteen original tales of phantom hitchhikers (a few too many), haunted coal mines, and oddities and haunts. The best is by Kealan Patrick Burke. Rick Hautala provides a Foreword.

In Bad Dreams, Volume One: Where Real Life Awaits, edited by Mark S. Deniz and Sharyn Lilley (Eneit Press), is the first in a proposed trilogy of original horror anthologies. It's curious that the contents *seem* to be thematically linked to crows as harbingers of death (and a painting of a crow is on the cover) but there's no introduction or other clarifying material. In any case, there are strong stories by Kaaron Warren, R.J. Barker, Robert Hood, and Stephanie Campisi.

Horrors Beyond 2: Stories of Strange Creations, edited by William Jones (Elder Signs Press) contains twenty-one original Lovecraftian tales of horror, with some science fiction. There's more variety and more panache than in most anthologies of this sort, with notable stories by Richard A. Lupoff, E. Sedia, Paul Melniczek, A. A. Attanasio, Tim Curran, Paul S. Kemp, Lucien Soulban, and Robert Weinberg.

Thrillers 2, edited by Robert Morrish (C.D. Publications), is the long-awaited follow-up to the original volume published in 1993. Following in the wake of the classic series *Night Visions*, each of four writers provide 20,000 words of fiction plus story notes. The contributors are Gemma Files, R. Patrick Gates, Tim Waggoner, and Caitlín R. Kiernan. Each has at least one very good story, and one, a long one by Kiernan, is terrific.

Five Strokes to Midnight, edited by Gary A. Braunbeck and Hank Schwaeble (Haunted Pelican Press), is the first book from a new press and it too is modeled slightly after the *Night Visions* series in that it showcases five writers with 20,000 words each, mixing better-known writers with a newcomer. Tom Piccirilli, Gary A. Braunbeck, Deborah LeBlanc, Hank Schwaeble, and Christopher Golden have each chosen a theme for their sections and the anthology ends up with thirteen stories and novellas. The good-looking jacket and interior art are by Ashley Laurence.

The Parasitorium: Parasitic Sands, edited by James Ossuary and Del Stone, Jr. (lulu), is the second volume of original stories published by a Yahoo writers group. The theme seems to revolve around beaches.

Gratia Placenti: For the Sake of Pleasing, edited by Jason Sizemore and Gill Ainsworth, is an all-original anthology of thirteen stories about the horrors that result from people getting what they want, consequences be damned. Only a few of the stories seem to fit the theme but there are notable stories by Mary Robinette Kowal and Neil Ayres.

Horror Library, Volume 2, edited by R. J. Cavender and Vincent Van Allen (Cutting Block Press), is a non-theme anthology with thirty stories, five of them reprints. The best of the originals are by Matt Hults, Marc Paoletti, Tom Pendergrass, Paul Walther, and Sunil Sadanand.

The Black Book of Horror (published by Mr. Black), edited by Charles Black (Mortbury Press), is the first title from this press and has eighteen non-theme horror stories, three reprints. The best of the originals are by Gary McMahon and Frank Nicholas. The publisher/editor includes one of his own stories.

A Dark and Deadly Valley, edited by Mike Heffernan (Silverthought), is an original anthology (but for the Graham Joyce) of horror about WWII. Darren Whalen's cover art—with skulls, Hitler, and sharp teeth—is striking, replicating the pulp covers of the 1950s, but doesn't accurately represent the stories inside—which are not pulpy at all. The stories are mostly very good, although a few are a little heavy-handed. My favorites are those by Brian Hodge, Lawrence Santoro, Brian Keene, Steve Vernon, and T.M. Wright.

Whispers in the Night: Dark Dreams III, edited by Brandon Massey (Dafina Books), is more consistent in quality than the previous book of this series of original dark fantasy, horror, and suspense by African American writers. There were notable stories by Tananarive Due, Anthony Beal, Christopher Chambers, Terence Taylor, and Wrath James White.

Midnight Premiere, edited by Tom Piccirilli (C.D. Publications), is the long-awaited horror/dark fantasy theme anthology about Hollywood and horror movies. It's got an entertaining mix, with strong entries by Thomas F. Monteleone, Richard Grove & Lisa Morton, Ray Garton, Tom Piccirilli, Brian Hodge, T.M. Wright, Gary A. Braunbeck, Mick Garris, Gerard Houarner, and Jack Ketchum.

Dark Passions: Hot Blood XIII, edited by Jeff Gelb and Michael Garrett (Kensington), has always been a mixed bag of erotic horror and this volume is no different. The best of the batch are by Graham Masterton, Steve Niles, and David J. Schow.

Classic Vampires Revisited: A Consuming Passion, edited by Tom English (Department of Dead Letters), is part of a chapbook series and has four stories important to the evolution of the vampire tale plus an essay about the stories by the editor. In this volume there are stories by Count Eric Stenbock, Augustus Hare, Mary E. Braddon, and Phil Robinson.

Tattered Souls, edited by Frank J. Hutton (Cutting Block Press), has six long stories that don't seem to be thematically connected. The best is a future noir piece by Matt Wallace.

Midnight Lullabies: The Harrow Anthology, edited by Kfir Luzzato, Dru Pagliassotti, Tyra Twomey, Jason Nolan, and Yuka Kajihara (The Harrow Press), is a good anthology of mostly original stories and poems focusing on childhood fears. There are notable dark stories by Rodney J. Smith and Alison J. Littlewood.

Frontier Cthulhu: Ancient Horrors in the New World, edited by William Jones

(Chaosium), is a pretty good mostly original-story anthology of fifteen Lovecraftian stories taking place in the American West. The best originals are those by Matthew Baugh, Lon Prater, and Jason Andrews.

Raw Meat, edited by Laurel Starling, Billie Jean Moran, and Tom Moran (Sideshow Press), bills itself as "bedtime stories for the sick and deranged." The stories are by members of an online writing group. The only notable one is by Liam Davies.

Book of the Dead, edited by Tina L. Jens and Eric M. Cherry (Twilight Tales), is an expanded edition of the original anthology from 1999. There are sixteen new tales, most brief. The best are by Alan Smale, Suzanne Church, Dan Waters, and John Weagly.

There's been a (largely unwelcome) proliferation of zombie anthologies in 2007. Unwelcome because most are filled with "flesh-eating zombies" which are dull after one or two of them. So original anthologies full of such junk become a real drag. *Flesh Feast: The Undead Volume Three*, edited by D.L. Snell and Travis Adkins (Permuted Press), is the third in a series of zombie anthologies. Despite the unwise decision to publish a novel excerpt by one of the editors, there are some notable contributions by Matthew Bey, Kevin Boon, Kriscinda Meadows, and Eric Turowski. The cover art is by James Ryman and the black and white interior illustrations are by a variety of artists. *Loving the Undead*, edited by Katherine Sanger (The Asylum Books and Press), has original stories about romantic liaisons between dead creatures. The best are by Doug Graves and E.C. Myers. *History is Dead*, edited by Kim Paffenroth (Permuted), initially confounded expectations because the cover art is evocative and attractive (with nice blood-spatters and a rotting head) and because of the excellence of the editor's nonfiction zombie book. And the first few stories seemed to foreshadow something different: historical zombie fiction with some nice touches and several atypical zombies. Alas, about halfway through, the flesh-eating zombies started coming fast and furious and overwhelm the more ambitious tales in the book. That said, there are imaginative, well-written stories by Carole Lanham, Christine Morgan, Joe McKinney, Douglas Hutcheson, and Jenny Ashford. And from Australia's Altair Books comes *Zombies*, edited by Robert N. Stephenson, which despite its cheesy cover art has fourteen pretty good stories by writers from Australia, Israel, the United States, the United Kingdom, and Canada. The best are by Martin R. Soderstrom, Hagy Averbuch, Gary Kemble, Jeff Harris, and Mike Brown.

Waiting for October (Dark Arts Books) has twelve stories, three each by Jeff Strand, Adam Pepper, Sarah Pinborough, and Jeffrey Thomas. Two from each contributor are original. With an introduction by Bill Breedlove.

The Sound of Horror, edited by David C. Montoya (Magus Press), has stories by John Edward Lawson, Joe McKinney, and six other writers.

Fried! Fast Food, Slow Deaths, edited by C. Morris and Joel A. Sutherland (Graveside Tales), has twenty-three pulpy stories written around the theme of fast food restaurants and wonderfully illustrated by artists such as Steve Lines, Steven Blondell, and others.

Nobody, edited by Kelly Gunter Atlas (DarkHart Press), celebrates the fourteenth anniversary of the Essex Writers and Artists' Guild, located in Massachusetts, by featuring eighteen stories by its members.

William Hope Hodgson's Night Lands volume II: Nightmares of the Fall, edited by Andy Robertson (Utter Tower), is a reprint volume of works by Gerard Houarner, John C. Wright, and others, originally published on the Web in tribute to Hodgson's creation.

American Supernatural Tales, edited by S. T. Joshi (Penguin Classics), has twenty-six stories by writers including Caitlín Kiernan, T.E.D. Klein, Thomas Ligotti, Stephen King, Shirley Jackson, Joyce Carol Oates, and others. With an introduction and reading list (bibliography).

Australian Gothic: An Anthology of Australian Supernatural Fiction, 1867–1939, edited by James Doig (Equilibrium), provides a rich sampling of work that has rarely been reprinted, by writers little known outside of Australia: Mary Fortune, Hume Nesbit, Frances Faucett, and many others. For anyone interested in older supernatural fiction far from the usual shores of the United States and the United Kingdom.

There were two other best of the year in horror anthologies in 2007, with *Australian Dark Fantasy & Horror: 2007 Edition*, edited by Angela Challis (Brimstone Press), covering Australian short fiction from 2006 and featuring eighteen stories, most from Australian venues. *The Mammoth Book of Best New Horror 18*, edited by Stephen Jones (Robinson), with—unlike most years—only one story overlapping with *The Year's Best Fantasy and Horror #20*. Jones provides an extensive overview of the year in horror, and he and Kim Newman collaborate on the necrology.

Mixed-genre Anthologies

Wizards, edited by Jack Dann and Gardner Dozois (Berkley), is an excellent theme anthology mixing fantasy and dark fantasy with excellent darker work by Elizabeth Hand, Jeffrey Ford, and Peter S. Beagle. The Elizabeth Hand is reprinted herein. *Love and Sacrifice*, edited by Robert Bratton (Zen Films), was published in conjunction with the British release of Zen Film's feature, *London Voodoo*. It has twelve original vignettes and tales that are a very mixed bag. For me, only the story by Jeremy C. Shipp stood out. *Fantasy*, edited by Paul G. Tremblay and Sean Wallace (Prime), is a sampler of the kind of fiction *Fantasy Magazine* is publishing. Unfortunately, the stories in the sampler don't provide as wide a range as the actual magazine does. Of the eleven stories only a few are dark, and the best of those are by Cat Rambo, Ekaterina Sedia, and Maura McHugh. *A Cross of Centuries: Twenty-Five Imaginative Tales About the Christ*, edited by Michael Bishop (Thunder's Mouth), contains a variety of stories including the sweet and the humorous. Five of the stories are original to the anthology. *Text: Ur, The New Book of Masks*, edited by Forrest Aguirre (Raw Dog Screaming) is a combination of the surreal, the experimental, and the just plain pretentious, all but two original. The best of the darker tales are by Sarah Totton and Tamar Yellin. *Logorrhea*, edited by John Klima (Bantam), is based on the intriguing idea of having writers choose a winning word from the Scripps National Spelling Bee and write a story using that word. For the most part, the stories are imaginative, although not all are engaging. The best of the darker ones are by Paolo Bacigalupi, Claire Dudman, Alex Irvine, Tim Pratt, David Prill, and Michelle Richmond. *Zencore!: Scriptus Innominatus*, edited by D.F. Lewis (Megazanthus Press), is the newest effort by Lewis, whose emphasis on at least short-term anonymity for the contributors to his Nemonymous series in order to confound expectations was admirable if not particularly useful. This anthology has the contributor names on the back cover but doesn't say who wrote which story—this information was revealed later by the publisher. Most of the stories are well-told and a few are excellent, including those by Reggie Oliver, Steven Pirie, Patricia Russo, E. Sedia, S.D. Tullis, and Mark Valentine, and the Tim Nickels, reprinted herein. *Speculative Japan*, edited by Gene van Troyer and Grania Davis (Kurodahan Press), showcases fifteen stories and vignettes by Japanese writers, some published for the first time in English, and although most are science fiction or fantasy, a couple are very dark, including the one by Kono Tensei. *The Solaris Book of New Science Fiction*, edited by George Mann (Solaris), has a handful of good, very dark sf stories by writers such as Simon Ings, Neal Asher, and Jeffrey Thomas. *Eclipse One*, edited by Jonathan Strahan (Night Shade Books), is the debut of a new non-theme series of science fiction and fantasy. There are some wonderful darker tales by Terry Dowling, Jeffrey Ford, and Margo Lanagan. The Dowling is reprinted herein. *Many Bloody Returns*, edited by Charlaine Harris and Toni L.P. Kelner (Ace), is a mixture of fantasy and dark fantasy about birthdays and vampires. The best are by Kelley Armstrong, Jim Butcher, and P.N. Elrod. *Tales from the Red Lion Inn*, edited by John Weagly and Andrea Dubnick (Twilight Tales), is an expansion of an anthology first published in 2000. There are eight new stories, some quite charming, but none are tonally dark enough to be considered horror, even the one with a serial killer. *The Best American Mystery Stories*, edited by Carl Hiaasen (Houghton Mifflin), includes some quite dark tales. *New Writings in the Fantastic*, edited by John Grant (Pendragon Press), is an all original non-theme mixed-genre anthology with forty stories, including some very good dark work by Paul L. Bates, Mark Justice, Stephen Kilpatrick, Paul Finch, Paul Pinn, Scott Emerson Bull, Gary McMahon, and Steve Redwood (and a brilliant darkish fantasy by Kate Riedel). *Daikaiju! 2: Revenge of the Giant Monsters* and *Daikaiju!: Giant Monsters vs the World* (Agog! Press) are both edited by Robert Hood and Robin Pen. Each has sixteen entertainingly pulpy but only occasionally scary stories by U.S., British, and Australian writers. There were strong darker stories by Leigh Blackmore and Steve Savile. *Astounding Hero Tales*, edited by James Lowder (Hero Games), has sixteen modern pulp tales, some of them dark. The best are by Hugh B. Cave, Richard Dansky, and William Messner-Loebs. *The Best of Lady Churchill's Rosebud Wristlet*, edited by Kelly Link and Gavin J. Grant (Del Rey), is an overview of the "boutique" zine's first ten years of publication, and includes stories light and dark, essays, poems, recipes, and other items. *Best New Paranormal Romance*, edited by Paula Guran (Juno), brings together stories by Elizabeth Hand, Delia Sherman, John Grant, Jane Yolen, and others. *Year's Best Fantasy 7*, edited by David G. Hartwell and Kathryn Cramer (Tachyon), covers fantasy of all stripes in self-identified genre publications, and includes some supernatural fiction, as evidenced by the stories by Lucius Shepard, Laird Barron, and M. Rickert, reprinted in this year's volume. In contrast, *Best American Fantasy*, guest edited by Ann and Jeff VanderMeer (series editor, Matthew Cheney) (Prime), appears to be aiming for the opposite of the Hartwell/Cramer anthology. In addition to only publishing American authors, the venues from which it draws the majority of its stories are mainstream publications that occasionally publish fantastic literature such as *The New Yorker, Tin House, The Georgia Review, Mississippi Review*, and *McSweeney's*. Even so, there is a bit of overlap with both *Year's Best Fantasy and Horror* and *The Mammoth Book of Best New Horror*. And surprisingly, there's even a story from *Analog*. *Perverted by Language: Fiction Inspired by The Fall*, edited by Peter Wild (Serpent's Tale), has some interesting dark stories, particularly by Stav Sherez, Michael Faber, Carlton Mellick III, Matthew David Scott, and Jeff VanderMeer. (I humbly admit to never having heard of the musical group, The Fall, before reading this book.) *Triangulation: End of Time*, edited by Pete Butler (Parsec Ink), has twenty very brief, mostly science fiction stories about the end of the world. There are a couple of horror stories included. *The Paramental Appreciation Society*, edited by P. Alan Beatts, is a chapbook with a variety of short-shorts written by the four members of a writing workshop meeting since October 2005 (Automatism

Press). *Brothers & Beasts: An Anthology of Men on Fairy Tales*, edited by Kate Bernheimer (Wayne State University Press), showcases poems, stories, and essays by men about their relationship to fairy tales. *The Best American Short Stories 2007*, edited by Stephen King (Houghton Mifflin), has twenty mixed-genre but mostly mainstream stories. Included are stories by T. Coraghessan Boyle, Karen Russell, and Bruce McAllister (with a story from *Fantasy & Science Fiction*). *Weird Tales: the 21st Century*, edited by Sean Wallace and Stephen H. Segal (Prime), is a sampling of mostly reprints of the revamped magazine, with one original. *Realms: The First Year of Clarkesworld Magazine*, edited by Nick Mamatas and Sean Wallace (Wyrm), has twenty-four stories, some of them dark, by Jeff VanderMeer, Catherynne M. Valente, Holly Phillips, Caitlín Kiernan, and others. *The Dedalus Book of Russian Decadence: Perversity, Despair and Collapse*, edited by Kirsten Lodge (Dedalus), has more than fifty stories, excerpts, and poems—some macabre—from the late nineteenth century. Translations by Grigory Dashevsky and Margo Shohl Rosen. *Rewired: The Post-Cyberpunk Anthology*, edited by James Patrick Kelly and John Kessel (Tachyon), unsurprisingly, contains a large dollop of dark SF by such writers as Jonathan Lethem and David Marusek. *Nebula Awards Showcase: 2008*, edited by Ben Bova (Roc), presents the 2006 award's short story winners and excerpts from the award-winning novel selected by the Science Fiction and Fantasy Writers of America©. Also included are essays, the Rhysling Award for poetry winners, an appreciation of Grandmaster James Gunn and a classic story by him, and a brief history of the Nebula awards and previous winners.

Collections

The Imago Sequence and Other Stories by Laird Barron (Night Shade) is probably the most eagerly anticipated debut horror collection of 2007 and it's one of the best of the year. Barron's a stylist who creates believable and flawed characters, and his short fiction (usually novellas or long novelettes) often delves into Lovecraftian depths and brings up new takes on very old monsters. The eight reprints and one original novella are completely engrossing. Three of the stories were reprinted in earlier volumes of our series and two others would have been if they'd been shorter. A special nod to the jacket artist and designer respectively: Eleni Tsami and Claudia Noble.

Stains by Paul Finch (Gray Friar) is the author's second collection. Finch's fiction is visceral and usually set in the contemporary U.K. His first collection, *Aftershocks*, won the British Fantasy Award and this new one will likely be on the award's short list. There are eight stories, three of them new novellas, and two of those very good. The attractive hardcover has jacket art by Zach McCain and an introduction by Simon Clark.

Old Devil Moon by Christopher Fowler (Serpent's Tail), the author's tenth collection, features twenty-one stories, most of them new, from this prolific writer of horror and mystery fiction. Although a few of the stories are a little thin, they're all entertaining, and there are a handful that are wonderfully creepy.

Omens by Richard Gavin (Mythos Books) is the second collection by this promising Canadian author of dark fiction. Of the twelve stories in the volume, seven are published for the first time. The evocative jacket art is by Harry O. Morris.

No Further Messages by Brett Alexander Savory (Delirium Books) is Book 9 in the Delirium Exclusive series, and demonstrates the maturation of a fine writer whose short fiction keeps getting better and better. Three of the twenty-one stories are original to the collection and one was reprinted in *The Year's Best Fantasy and Horror #20*. The good-looking jacket art is by Michael Gibbs.

Plots and Misadventures by Stephen Gallagher (Subterranean), the author's fine and varied second collection, contains ten reprints and one new novella. Two of the stories were in previous volumes of our series.

Masques of Satan by Reggie Oliver (Ash-Tree Press) is the author's third excellent collection, comprised of twelve supernatural stories and a novella, five previously published, all but one during 2007. Oliver's experience as an actor, producer, playwright, and theater director shows in several of the stories as he delves behind the bright lights and camaraderie of theatrical life. The jacket art and interior illustrations are all by the author. One of the stories, also appearing in the 2007 anthology *At Ease with the Dead*, is reprinted herein.

Passing of a God and Other Stories: The Collected Short Fiction of Henry S. Whitehead, Volume 1 (Ash-Tree), edited by Douglas A. Anderson and Stefan Dziemianowicz, is the first of a projected three-volume project reprinting all of Whitehead's short work. The extensive introduction by Dziemianowicz discusses Whitehead's history as a pulp writer. The excellent jacket art is by Jason Van Hollander.

Smothered Dolls by A.R. Morlan (Overlook Connection Press) is a major collection by an underappreciated writer who has been consistently writing sharply brilliant dark stories for two decades. The book contains two new pieces of fiction, and four of the stories were reprinted in earlier volumes of *The Year's Best Fantasy and Horror*. Critic Stefan Dziemianowicz provides an introduction.

Dirty Prayers by Gary McMahon (Gray Friar) has some effective stories among the twenty-five pieces of fiction, but it would have been a stronger collection if the interstitial "psalms" were deleted along with the vignettes, preserving only the cream of the crop. That said, there are some *very* good originals in the book.

The Attic Express and Other Macabre Stories by Alex Hamilton (Ash-Tree) brings together two earlier hard-to-find volumes of the author's short fiction, two stories from a third collection, and one original specially written for the new book. Hamilton started producing short, macabre stories for Herbert Van Thal's Pan paperback horror series in the sixties and many of the twenty-eight stories reprinted still pack a nice little wallop.

Strangers and Pilgrims, Tales by Walter de la Mare (Tartarus), is a selection of thirty-one of the author's uncanny supernatural and psychological stories. The introduction by Mark Valentine stresses that unlike much supernatural fiction, de le Mare's stories are about fear that comes from internal melancholy and that his characters are haunted "by loneliness, by lovelessness, by loss" rather than by external forces.

An Itinerant House and Other Ghost Stories by Emma Frances Dawson, edited by John Pinkney and Robert Eldridge (Thomas Loring), with an introduction by Robert Eldridge and illustrations by Ernest C. Peixotto. Dawson was born in Bangor and the original edition of *An Itinerant House* was published in 1898. This new edition includes her entire output of supernatural fiction: thirteen short stories, several of which were left out of the original volume because of space considerations. The illustrations are reproduced from the original. There is also an extensive introduction with a biography, and sections placing her stories in both an historical and critical context.

The God of the Razor by Joe R. Lansdale (Subterranean) celebrates the twentieth anniversary of the publication of *The Nightrunners*, reprinting the whole novel, along with six stories (one published for the first time) inspired by or drawn from the novel. The jacket art is by Tim Truman and the twenty black-and-white interior illustrations are by Glenn Chadbourne.

No-Man and Other Tales by Tony Richards (Pendragon) has four supernatural novellas, two of them new, two previously published in limited hardcover editions.

Five Stories by Peter Straub (Borderlands) contains the stories that the author has published between 2000 and 2004, including two picked up for a previous *Year's Best Fantasy and Horror*.

New Amsterdam by Elizabeth Bear (Subterranean) is a linked series of dark fantasy stories about a hard-boiled female sleuth, taking place in an alternative reality in which New Amsterdam is a Royal British colony ceded by the Dutch during the Napoleonic Wars.

Closing Time by Jack Ketchum (Gauntlet) has nineteen previously uncollected stories including one recent Bram Stoker Award winner and one being published for the first time. Each story has a brief afterword by the author.

The Spiraling Worm by David Conyers and John Sunseri (Chaosium) is a good collection of mostly new Lovecraftian adventures featuring secret service ops from the U.S., the U.K., and Australia. The original novella is impressive.

Secret Hours by Michael Cisco (Mythos Books) has fourteen eerie, chilling, and downright strange fragments, vignettes, and the occasional story wonderfully illustrated by Harry O. Morris, Jason C. Eckhardt, and Thomas Brown. If only there were a few more actual *stories* in the collection. With an introduction by Robert M. Price.

You Are the Fly by James Cooper (White Noise Press) is the first collection by the author and showcases sixteen stories, mostly psychological horror, seven original to the collection. There is an introduction by Greg F. Gifune and an afterword by Andrew Jury, an occasional collaborator with Cooper.

Lair of the Dreamer by Franklyn Searight (Hippocampus Press) features nine Lovecraftian stories by the author, an unpublished short mythos novel, and a posthumous collaboration with his father, Richard F. Searight.

When it Rains and Other Wreckage by Christopher Fulbright (Doorways Publications) has eighteen stories, two original to the collection.

Needles and Sins by John Everson (Necro Publications) is the author's third collection, with six of the nineteen stories appearing for the first time.

The Museum of Dr. Moses: Tales of Mystery and Suspense by Joyce Carol Oates (Harcourt) collects ten dark and often macabre stories by a master of the short form. Several of the stories were reprinted in earlier volumes of our series and another is reprinted herein.

Doomsdays by Jeffrey Thomas (Dark Regions Press) is filled with twenty-two brief apocalyptic visions. Four are new to the collection.

The Midnight Hour by Neil Davies (Screaming Dreams) features fourteen stories by this English author, five of them appearing for the first time.

In Fear and Dread by Derek M. Fox (Rainfall) is the author's third collection, and features twenty-one stories published between 1992 and 2007 (some repeats from earlier collections). One story is original.

Death Songs of Carcosa by John B. Ford and Steve Niles (Rainfall) is a chapbook featuring eight stories and poems, some of them collaborations.

World Wide Web by Gary Fry (Humdrumming) has a novella and six stories of Lovecraftian horror, four original to the collection. Some are serious, others pastiche and one is a very early previously unpublished story. There's an introduction by Mark Morris and afterword by the author. A second collection by Fry, *Sanity and Other Delusions: Tales of Psychological Horror* (PS), collects another six stories, two of them reprints. Stephen Volk provides the introduction.

Nightshadows by William F. Nolan (Darkwood Press) has twenty-three stories published between 2000 and 2007 with comments by the author on each one.

Voyeurs of Death by Shaun Jeffrey (Doorways) has eleven stories first published between 1993 and 2006 and four new stories. Of the originals, "Envy," about a special, new kind of dress, is the most interesting. The attractive cover and interior art is by Zach McCain.

Catalysts by Bill Gauthier (Dark Discoveries Publications) features thirteen stories written between 1998 and 2005. Three of the stories are previously unpublished. There's a foreword by Thomas F. Monteleone and story notes by the author.

Over the Darkening Fields by Scott Thomas (Dark Regions) is a good collection of twenty-six stories of varying lengths, more than half published for the first time. Thomas's work is always interesting and even the very brief stories are worth reading.

The Bone Key by Sarah Monette (Prime) features ten excellent dark stories, all published since 2004 in magazines such as *All Hallows* and *Tales of the Unanticipated*. One is original to the collection, and one was reprinted in an earlier volume of this series.

Scratching the Surface by Michael Kelly (Crowswing Books) is the first collection of a promising writer. Nine of the twenty-six stories appear for the first time and although a few are thin, others are quite good. John Pelan has provided a gracious introduction.

Triple Dare to Be Scared by Robert D. San Souci, illustrated by David Ouimet, (Cricket Books) is the third in this series of warmed-over spooky tales for kids. Most definitely not for the young adult or adult audience as they are too simplistic and derivative, but possibly a good introduction for very young readers.

God Laughs When You Die by Michael Boatman (Dybbuk Press) is a first collection with nine stories—two original—of brutal supernatural and psychological horror. Introduction by David J. Schow. There are black-and-white interior illustrations by John Perry, Amanda Rehagen, and Vanesa Littlecrow Wojtanowicz.

Dark Wisdom by Gary Myers (Mythos Books) has twelve entertaining but somewhat predictable Lovecraftian tales, more than half original to the collection. The interior illustrations are by the author. With an introduction by Robert M. Price.

13 Thorns by Gus Fink and Gina Ranalli (Afterbirth Books) is a collaboration between the outsider artist Fink and writer Ranalli.

Midnight in New England by Scott Thomas (Down East Books) is a collection of regional ghost tales. Some are mere vignettes, but others are solid, well-told stories.

The Taint and other novellas: Best Mythos Tales, Volume 1 by Brian Lumley (Subterranean) presents seven long Lovecraftian stories, the first of a two-volume set collecting all Lumley's fiction in this subgenre. With jacket art by Bob Eggleton.

Cthulhu Australis by David Conyers (A Rainfall Publication) features two reprints and one original Lovecraftian tale, taking place in Australia.

A Beckoning of Shadows by John Grover is the first collection by this author. More than half the seventeen brief stories appear for the first time. *Personal Headspace* by Nancy Jackson has four very short new stories by a new writer. *Tales From Darktowne* by Ran Cartwright has three short stories about the unlucky denizens of the bad part of town. *Zombies II* by Eric S. Brown features eight flesh-eating zombie tales, none more than a few pages long. All four titles were published by Naked Snake Press.

You Had Me at Arghhh! by Ken Goldman (Sam's Dot) belies the serious nature of the six stories, four of them published for the first time—none particularly humorous.

Installing Linux on a Dead Badger by Lucy A. Snyder (Creative Guy) consists of ten reprints and one original satirical horror story.

Match to Flame, The Fictional Paths to Fahrenheit-451 by Ray Bradbury (Gauntlet) is a collection of Bradbury stories that influenced the creation of his famous novel *Fahrenheit-451*. Until recently Bradbury believed that the book was mostly inspired by his story "The Pedestrian"—but came to realize that he's been interested in libraries and the destruction of libraries since he was eleven years old. Included in this volume are fragmentary notes, early stories, and anything else that might take the reader on the same journey Bradbury took in creating his masterwork. There's also a short preface by Richard Matheson, correspondence with Bradbury, an extensive introduction by William F. Touponce, and an essay about the text.

Hard Roads by Steve Vernon (Gray Friar) is made up of two very good stories by this Canadian writer. "Trolling Lores" is the mythic road trip of a dying man who has a running dialogue with the dead woman haunting the back seat of his car. "Hammurabi Road" is about three rednecks who plan to kill a fourth who they believe started a deadly hotel fire in town. But en route to their destination, things change when they encounter a bear.

Saint-Germain: Memoirs by Chelsea Quinn Yarbro (Elder Signs Press) has six stories about Yarbro's most famous creation, the popular gentleman vampire. Four are reprints, and two—a novelette and novella—are original to the collection.

City Pier: Above and Below by Paul G. Tremblay (Prime) is a dark novella comprised of four shorter pieces about a city above a pier and the lattice works below, both of which harbor criminals and outcasts who move between the two worlds. Originally published in 2005 by the webzine Lenox Avenue.

The Rising: Selected Scenes From the End of the World by Brian Keene (Delirium Books) has thirty-two brief stories and vignettes that fill out more of Keene's zombie world.

Indigo People: A Vampire Collection by Charlee Jacob (Wilder Publications) is made up of forty-five previously uncollected poems and stories.

Deadneck Hootenanny by Mark Justice (Novello) is a two-story chapbook of redneck horror humor, one a reprint, the other new.

Proverbs for Monsters by Michael A. Arnzen (Dark Regions) features thirty very short stories and thirty poems by the author, a few original to the collection.

The Mammoth Book of Modern Ghost Stories edited by Peter Haining (Carroll & Graf) spans one hundred years with forty stories by genre and non-genre names.

Phantasmapedia: An Alphabestiary of Little-Known Demons, Entities, Mutants, and Pseudo-Biological Aberrations by Mark McLaughlin (Dead Letter) is a cute series of definitions for imaginary critters with a cover illustration by the author.

Mixed-genre Collections

Living Shadows: Stories New and Preowned by John Shirley (Prime) is the author's seventh collection, with some of the twenty stories overlapping with those earlier books. Three stories are published for the first time (although two were also published in 2007 anthologies). Shirley has been writing dark science fiction, and supernatural and psychological horror for more than thirty years and this new collection reflects that versatility. *Worshipping Small Gods* by Richard Parks (Prime) is the author's second collection and has fourteen stories, three published for the first time. Most are fantasy stories originally published in *Realms of Fantasy*. A few are darker. *Defining Moments* by David Niall Wilson (Sarob Press) is the author's fourth collection, and has thirteen stories and novellas, three of them published for the first time. The author provides a preface. This is the final production of Robert Morgan's World Fantasy Award-winning press, begun ten years ago. He and his wife are shuttering the press and moving to France. *So Far, So Near* by Mat Coward (Elastic Press) has sixteen reprints with story notes by the author. *M is For Magic* by Neil Gaiman (HarperCollins) collects eleven of the author's stories and poems aimed at younger readers. The pieces are reprinted, mostly from anthologies, and range from charming and clever to clever and disturbing—all of them entertaining. The black-and-white interior illustrations are by Teddy Kristiansen. *Going Back* by Tony Richards (Elastic) is a very good collection featuring fourteen horror, mainstream, and mystery stories, one original to the collection. *Hebrew Punk* by Lavie Tidhar (Apex Publications) is a mini collection of four stories by this talented new writer. Three of the four stories were previously published (one by me) and all related to a mystical Judaic alternate history. With an introduction by Laura Anne Gilman. *The Involuntary Human* by David Gerrold (NESFA Press) showcases some of Gerrold's short fiction, an unproduced *Star Trek: The Next Generation* script, an excerpt from a yet unpublished book, and limericks. A few of the stories are dark ones. *Darker Loves: Tales of Mystery and Regret* by James Dorr (Dark Regions) presents fourteen fantasy and dark fantasy stories (two published for the first time) and ten poems. With an introduction by Brian A. Hopkins. *Twice Dead Things* by A. A. Attanasio (Elder Signs) is the author's first collection and brings together short fiction from 1975 through 2006, with a couple of original pieces. *The Space Between the Lines* by Peter Crowther (Subterranean) showcases twelve fantasy and dark fantasy stories by the award-winning author and editor, including one that appeared in this series a few years ago. The jacket art is by J.K. Potter. *Hart & Boot and Other Stories* by Tim Pratt (Night Shade) is the author's second collection, with thirteen elegant short stories (one original to the collection). *Just North of Nowhere* by Lawrence Santoro (Annihilation Press) is a collection of interconnected stories taking place in the town of Bluffton—some of the stories have been previously published. *When We Were Six* by Heather Shaw (Tropism Press) is a chapbook with six stories, one original, a few of them dark. *The Best of Robert E. Howard, volume 1, Crimson Shadows* (Del Rey) is the first of a two-volume collection of Howard's twenty-eight poems and stories, all restored to their original form. The pulp author, who created the hero Conan and wrote lots of sword and sorcery, also wrote horror. The book includes an extensive introduction and biography of Howard by Rusty Burke, and an essay by Charles Hoffman. With interior illustrations by Jim and Ruth Keegan. *Sparks and Shadows* by Lucy A. Snyder (HW Press) is a debut collection of seventeen SF, fantasy, satirical, and dark fantasy short stories, seven poems, and four essays. A few of the stories and poems appear for the first time. *The River Knows Its Own* by Jay Lake (Wheatland) presents twenty-two stories of fantasy and dark fantasy by this prolific writer—three of them are published for the first time. *Now and Forever* by Ray Bradbury (William Morrow) is a two-novella collection by one of fantastic literature's greatest practitioners. Both stories appear for the first time: one is science fiction and the other is a dark fantasy. *Secret Files of the Diogenes Club* by Kim Newman (MonkeyBrain Books) brings together another seven stories and novellas from the entertaining series about a secret club founded by Sherlock Holmes's brother that investigates supernatural doings in an alternate 1960s. Included is a new novella about a cold spot that appears in a remote part of England during a very long heat wave in the rest of the country. *The Fate of Mice* by Susan Palwick (Tachyon) is an excellent overview of Palwick's short fantasy and dark fantasy stories from the past twenty years. Three of the eleven stories appear for the first time. *The Girl Who Loved Animals and Other Stories* by Bruce McAllister (Golden Gryphon) has in it some of the most heartbreaking science fiction and fantasy (mostly darkish) that you'll ever read. In the mid to late '80s McAllister wrote two series of stories: about the Vietnam war and about a world in which the only animals left are in zoos. Then in 1994 he stopped writing fiction for about ten years and returned gloriously. The seventeen stories included show his remarkable range. One (from *Fantasy & Science Fiction*) was chosen for the *Best American Short Stories 2007*. *Dangerous Space* by Kelley Eskridge (Aqueduct Press) showcases the author's small but impressive output of seven stories and novelettes published between 1990 and 2007. There is one original, the title story. *Portable Childhoods* by Ellen Klages (Tachyon) is the debut collection by a bright star who began by dabbling in short fiction, with her first story published in 1998 but has in the past few years moved full steam ahead. The sixteen short stories collected here roam all over the genre firmament and are often thought-provoking, always entertaining. Three, including the title story, appear for the first time. *The Nail and the Oracle, Volume XI: The Complete Stories of Theodore Sturgeon* (North Atlantic Books) is comprised of twelve stories published between 1957 and 1970 and includes his controversial (at the time) "If All Men Were Brothers, Would You Let One Marry Your Sister." Harlan Ellison has written the foreword. *Balefires* by David Drake (Night Shade) brings together twenty-four fantasy, dark fantasy, and horror stories from early in the career of an author better known today for his military science fiction. *The Door to Saturn* by Clark Ashton Smith (Night Shade) is the second of the five-volume series collecting Smith's fantasy stories, edited by Scott Connor and Ron Hilger. The co-editors have tried to provide the definitive texts for each story and Tim Powers has written an introduction to the volume. *The Surgeon's Tale and Other Stories* by Cat Rambo and Jeff VanderMeer (Two Freelancer's Press) features six entertaining pieces of fantasy and dark fantasy, including one co-written by VanderMeer, M. F. Korn, and D. F. Lewis. *The Shadows, Kith and Kin* by Joe R. Lansdale (Subterranean) has nine entertaining stories—some original, some reprints—in a variety of genres from psychological and supernatural horror to a humorous tall tale. *The Winds of Marble Arch* by Connie Willis (Subterranean) is seven hundred pages chock full of twenty-three wonderful novellas and short stories, including several of her darkest visions. There is also some nonfiction. *Vanilla Bright Like Eminem* by Michel Faber (Harcourt) has sixteen stories, some of them with fantastic (light and dark) elements. Faber is the author of the historical novel *The Crimson Petal and the White* and the horror novel *Under the Skin*. *Dagger Key* by Lucius Shepard (PS) contains nine stories and novellas published between 2002 and 2007, and one, the title novella, is original to the collection. The hefty volume includes several dark pieces and story notes by the author. *The Collected Ed Gorman, Volume One: Out There in the Darkness* by Ed Gorman has nineteen stories, one reprinted in an earlier volume of this series, an introduction by Lawrence Block, and brief story notes by the author. *The Collected Gorman, Volume Two: The Moving Coffin* by Ed Gorman has an introduction by Max Allan Collins, twenty stories, and story notes. Both were brought out by PS Publishing. *The Last Mimzy* by Henry Kuttner (Del Rey) is a movie tie-in edition of the 1975 hardcover *The Best of Henry Kuttner*. In it are seventeen classics such as "Mimsy Were the Borogoves," the story from which the movie title is taken, and

"The Twonky." *Getting to Know You* by David Marusek (Subterranean) has ten science fiction stories by the author, some very dark. *Kite of Stars and Other Stories* by the Filipino writer Dean Francis Alfar (Anvil Publishing) features eighteen stories, most previously published in venues ranging from *Strange Horizons* and *Bewildering Stories* to the *Philippine Free Press*. Five of the stories were published in magazines and anthologies during 2007 and one is original to the collection. *The Complete Stories* by David Malouf (Pantheon) contains thirty-one stories and novellas by an award-winning Australian writer whose work often displays, dark elements.

The artists working in the small press toil hard and receive too little credit and money, and I feel it's important to recognize their good work. The following artists created art that I thought especially noteworthy during 2007: Anita Zofia Siuda, Tiffany Prothero, Eric Fortune, Brian Horton, Zach McCain, Paul Lowe, John Stewart, Alison Lovelock, Bryn Sparks, John Wyborn, Michele Guieu, Erica Leighton, Joe Kovach, Nicola Robinson, Erlend Mørk, Chris Green, Paul Bielaczyc, Michael Bielaczyc, Sandro Castelli, Keith Minnion, Lori Koefoed, John Stanton, Augie Wiedemann, Michael Gibbs, Kenn Brown, Bob Hobbs, Eric M. Turnmire, Richard Pellegrino, Rodger Gerberding, Suzanne Clarke, Kendall Anderson, Charlotte Thomson, Cameron Gray, H.E. Fassl, Ashley Laurence, Erzebet YellowBoy, Reggie Oliver, Christopher Nurse, Richard Marchand, James Owen, Dick Starr, and Steve Adams.

Magazines, Webzines, and Newsletters

There's an enormous annual turnover in small-press magazines that rarely last more than a year or two, so it's difficult to recommend buying a subscription to those that haven't proven their durability. But I urge readers to at least buy single issues of those that sound interesting. The following are, I think, the best in 2007.

Some of the most important magazines/webzines are those specializing in news of the field, market reports, and reviews. *The Gila Queen's Guide to Markets*, edited by Kathryn Ptacek, e-mailed to subscribers on a regular basis, is an excellent fount of information for markets in and outside the horror field. Ralan.com is *the* Web site for up-to-date market information. *Locus*, edited by Charles N. Brown, and *Locus Online*, edited by Mark Kelly, specialize in news about the science fiction and fantasy fields, but include a lot of horror coverage as well. The only major venues specializing in reviewing short genre fiction are *The Fix* (*http://thefix-online.com/*), *The Internet Review of Science Fiction* (*www.irosf.com/*), and *Locus*, but none of them specialize in horror.

After the demise in 1998 of *Necrofile*, an excellent critical journal, there were few other journals focusing on horror and the supernatural except for *Necropsy*, an online zine, which in winter 2008 posted its last issue. *Wormwood: Literature of the Fantastic, Supernatural and Decadent* edited by Mark Valentine and published by Tartarus Press was started in 2003 and has been an important source of criticism on the classics. Two issues were published in 2007 with articles by Joel Lane about the dark fiction of Theodore Sturgeon, an "Introduction to Degenerative Art" by Don LaCoss, focusing on an 1892 screed written by Max Nordau, "The Early Fantasies of David Lindsay" by Jeff Gardiner, a continuing series on the decadent worldview by Brian Stableford, and regular review columns by Douglas A. Anderson and Mark Valentine. *Dead Reckonings: A Review of Horror Literature* edited by S. T. Joshi and Jack M. Haringa and published by Hippocampus Press is a welcome second journal. This one focuses on contemporary work while also considering the classics. In its first year (two issues) the reviews were erudite and entertaining. Included were reviews of John Clute's lexicon of horror, *The Darkening Garden*, of novellas by Jack Ketchum, F. Paul Wilson and Norman Partridge, of two original anthologies inspired by Edgar Allan Poe from 2006, of two new novels by Michael Marshall Smith, Laird Barron's debut collection and T.E.D. Klein's first collection in many years, a novella and collection by Lucius Shepard, and a nonfiction title about Sheridan Le Fanu. The column "Ramsey Campbell, Probably" focused on M. R. James in the fall issue.

The Horror Fiction Review, edited by Nick C. Cato, is a quarterly fanzine with interviews and reviews of books, the occasional movie, and magazines. In 2007 there were interviews with Brian Hodge, John Little, and Mary SanGiovanni, an original piece of fiction per issue, and coverage of horror conventions.

Fangoria, edited by Anthony Timpone, is a monthly media magazine covering both big and small budget horror productions, the grislier the better. It features columns on film news, DVD releases, video games, and books. During 2007, there were interview/profiles of Clive Barker, actress Virginia Vincent who appeared in the original version of *The Hills Have Eyes*, and actor Robert Carlisle.

Rue Morgue, edited by Rod Gudino, is a quirky, entertaining monthly. While it does have some of the gore and mayhem of *Fangoria*, it manages to provide better and more articles about a variety of media. Although it focuses on movies and video, there are also regular columns on books, graphic novels, and audio. In 2007 the magazine featured profiles of authors Bentley Little and Jemiah Jefferson, artist Les Edwards, and Korean filmmaker Jooh-ho Bong (*The Host*). Other highlights were an overview of early silent horror movies such as *Der Golem* and Thomas Edison's *Frankenstein*, an article by Steve Niles about collaborating on a graphic novel with Bernie Wrightson, a twenty-five-year retrospective of John Carpenter's movie *The Thing*, and an article about the Burns Archive of Memorial (death) photography, dedicated to an art form that flourished in the early nineteenth century.

Video Watchdog, a bi-monthly edited by Tim Lucas, is one of the most exuberant film magazines around, and is one of my favorites, because I'm usually inspired to watch or re-watch at least one movie they review in every issue. The magazine is invaluable to the connoisseur of trashy, pulp, and horror movies and enjoyable for just about everyone. There was a wonderful guide to Greek fantastic cinema by Dimistris Koliodimos in the June issue.

The British Fantasy Society exists to promote and celebrate the genres of fantasy, science fiction, and horror in all its forms. It celebrated its thirtieth anniversary in 2001. Members receive a copy of every issue of *Prism*, the news magazine, with book and games reviews, an events column, and the occasional article. These are also all BFS special publications. *Dark Horizons*, edited by Peter Coleborn and Jan Edwards also comes free with membership to the BFS. The magazine celebrated its fiftieth issue with editorials from previous editors, articles on writers Karl Edward Wagner and Joyce Carol Oates, and the artist Anne Sudworth, an interview with John Connolly, and strong fiction by Sue Anderson, Ian Hunter, and Ewing Murray. There was a second issue out later in the year, with very good fiction by David Turnbull and Reggie Oliver, and an interview with me.

Cemetery Dance, edited by Robert Morrish, only published one issue as of July 2007, slipping from its schedule again. But # 57 was a very good one, with excellent stories by Stephen Graham Jones and A.R. Morlan and strong stories by David Prill and Charlee Jacob.

Weird Tales® published one last issue (#343) completely under the editorship of George H. Scithers, Darrell Schweitzer, and John Gregory Betancourt. That issue had cover art by Edward Miller. It was a Joe R. Lansdale special issue, with an interview with Lansdale, a classic reprint, and a new story. The magazine changed direction drastically with Issue 344, sporting a new logo, a paper upgrade, and more, under the creative direction of Stephen H. Segal, with assistance from a number of consulting editors. Officially, Ann VanderMeer then took over the reins with Issue 347 published late 2007. Only time will tell whether the magazine attracts new readers and keeps the old ones. There were notable darker stories by Patrice E. Sarath, Carrie Vaughn, Scott William Carter, Lisa Mantchev, Amanda Downum, Michael Shea, and a collaboration by M. Thomas and Paul G. Tremblay.

Postscripts #10, published for the 2007 World Horror Convention in Toronto and for Guest of Honor Michael Marshall Smith, was a 350-plus-page extravaganza edited by Peter Crowther and Nick Gevers and available in three hardcover editions. John Picacio did the striking cover art; the excellent interior illustrations were by Les Edwards, Wayne Blackhurst, Randy Broecker, James Hannah, and David Kendall. Four of the stories are reprints. The array of fiction is magnificent, with notable stories by Stephen Gallagher, Joe Hill, Graham Joyce, P.D. Cacek (more moving than horrific), Lucius Shepard, Lisa Tuttle (reprinted herein), Michael Marshall Smith (with a few originals, some reprints, a nonfiction article, and an excerpt from a forthcoming novel), Mark Morris, Stephen Volk, and Chaz Brenchley. Three more issues were published in 2007, but none had much horror. However, there were notable stories by Kealan Patrick Burke and Marly Youmans.

Supernatural Tales, edited by David Longhorn, is an excellent semi-annual (just having switched from annual) published in England. If you enjoy supernatural fiction you can't go wrong with this magazine and *All Hallows*, below. The best stories in 2007 were by Joel Lane, Mark Nicholls, Simon Strantzas, Mark Patrick Lynch, Duncan Barford, Gary Fry, Helen Grant, and D. Siddall. There were book reviews in the second issue of the year. The editor announced that with the next issue, the perfect-bound magazine was going back to a stapled booklet in order to save money. But that shouldn't matter as it's the content that counts.

All Hallows, edited by Barbara Roden and Christopher Roden, hails from Canada and is sent to members of the Ghost Story Society. It always contains quality fiction, an entertaining column by Ramsey Campbell, news updates, obituaries, reviews, and articles about noted ghost-story writers. The huge (324-page) Issue 42 was scheduled for October 2006 publication but wasn't actually published until well into 2007. It contained notable stories by Aaron Albrecht, Jameson Currier, David Dumitru, M. C. Grassly, Ian Harding, Edward Lodi, Tony Lovell, Gary McMahon, John Llewellyn Probert, Donald Pulker, Mark Silcox, and Simon Strantzas. Issue 43, with 304 pages, featured a goodly variety of notable stories, particularly those by Frances Hardinge, S.D. Tullis, John Alfred Taylor, Tom English, Helen Grant, Rhys Hughes, E. Michael Lewis, and Richard Tyndall. The utterly creepy cover illustration for #43 is by Paul Lowe.

Black Static, the magazine formerly known as *TTA*, published its first two issues in 2007. Much the same, but the magazine will focus on dark fiction even more than it previously did. There was notable dark stories by Joel Lane, Lynda E. Rucker, Mélanie Fazi, Tim Casson, Andrew Humphrey, Simon Avery, Jamie Barras, and a collaboration by Lisa Tuttle and Steven Utley. In addition to the fiction there were film and book reviews.

Not One of Us, edited by John Benson, has been around for a very long time now, and continues to publish unusual, often dark, fiction. There were two issues out in 2007 and an excellent special one-off called *Midrash*. The strongest stories and poems were by Chris Bell, Amanda Downum, Sonya Taaffe, Torger Vedeler, and Ian Rogers.

Dark Discoveries edited by James R. Beach brought out two issues in 2007, with good stories by Jay Lake and Tony Richard. There were also interviews with Jay Lake, Brian Hodge, T.M. Wright, John Maclay, Tim Waggoner, and John Everson, plus reviews.

Whispers of Wickedness, edited by Peter Tennant, Steve Pirie, Alison Littlewood, and Bob Lock, brought out two print issues in 2007 plus had original material on its Web site. There were notable stories in the print version by Dan McNeil, Charles A. Muir, R.J. Barker, and Jim Steel and an interesting story by Darren McCormick on the Web site.

Rainfall Books brought out a series of magazines in late 2006, including *Beyond the Borderland* Issue #2 (no editor credited), concentrating on Hodgsonian stories and poems. The best was a story by Gary McMahon. A second publication, *Lovecraft's Disciples*, edited by John B. Ford and Steve Lines, came out twice. Each issue contained three stories, one a parody by the always amusing Mark McLaughlin.

Doorways edited by Brian Yount, launched as a quarterly specializing in horror and the paranormal, includes interviews, book and movie reviews, and essays on the paranormal along with its fiction. The fiction was uneven but there was strong new work by Stephen Graham Jones, P.D. Cacek, Joel Arnold, Lee Thomas, and the collaborative team of M.P.N Sims and L.H. Maynard.

Jabberwocky, edited by Sean Wallace, is in its third year and it continues to showcase elegant and smart fantasy prose poems, poetry, and stories, some of them dark. For me, the strongest darker pieces were those by Sonya Taaffe, Catherine L. Hellisen, Shirl Sazynski, Erik Amundsen, Jennifer Rachel Baumer, Alison Campbell-Wise, Catherynne M. Valente, and a collaboration by Sonya Taaffe and John Benson.

Bandersnatch, edited by Paul G. Tremblay and Sean Wallace, is a new magazine companion to *Jabberwocky* and *Cabinet des Fées* from Prime. An adorable little hardback with wonderful cover art, there's a bit too much surrealism and not enough storytelling for my taste, although two of the darkest stories—those by Jack Haringa and Nick Mamatas—are quite good, and the Haringa is reprinted herein.

Mixed-genre Magazines and Webzines

Space and Time, edited by Gordon Linzner, reached its one hundredth issue in 2007, with strong horror stories by Lee Thomas, Jennifer Crow, and John Urbancik. The issue was the last to be edited by the magazine's long-time owner and publisher. Hildy Silverman takes the reins for future issues. *Sybil's Garage*, edited by Matthew Kressel, looks better visually with each issue and in 2007 had strong dark fiction and poetry by JoSelle Vanderhooft, Steve Rasnic Tem, and Ekaterina Sedia, plus interviews with Jeffrey Ford and the creative director of Wildside Press, Stephen H. Segal. *Subterranean*, edited by William Schafer, published an excellent issue #6 with some very good dark fiction by Joe R. Lansdale, William Browning Spencer (reprinted herein), Elizabeth Bear, Livia Llewellyn, and Cherie Priest. There was an interview with artist Edward Miller (a.k.a. Les Edwards) and book reviews by Dorman T. Shindler. Issue #7 was guest edited by myself and featured seven original short stories—the darkest were by Richard Bowes, Anna Tambour, Terry Bisson, M. Rickert (reprinted herein), a collaboration by Joel Lane and John Pelan, and a novella by Lucius Shepard. Subterranean started publishing fiction on its Web site in 2007, and by the end of 2007 went completely online.

On Spec, with fiction edited by Susan MacGregor, Steve Mohn, Diane L. Walton, and Peter Watts, is the only major Canadian science SF/F/H magazine. It's an attractive, perfect-bound quarterly that sometimes publishes dark fiction. In 2007 there were good dark stories and poems by Jerome Stueart, Cat Sparks, Catherine MacLeod, Kay Weathersby Garrett, A.M. Arruin, Trevor J. Morrison, Marie Brenner, Michael Vance, Nancy Chenier, Julia Campbell-Such, Claire Litton, and Paul Hosek. *Aurealis*, edited by Stephen Higgins and Stuart Mayne, is the premier mixed-genre magazine of Australia. Although #37 had a 2006 pub date, it only appeared in March 2007. Another issue was published late 2007. There were good dark stories by Kaaron Warren, Matthew Chrulew, and Lee Battersby and an intriguing non-horror story by Geoff Maloney.

Midnight Street, edited by Trevor Denyer, published two issues in 2007. There were interviews with Peter Straub, the writing team of Maynard and Sims, and book reviews. Also, there were good stories by Ken Goldman, Nick Jackson, Peter Tennant, John Paul Catton, and a collaboration by L.H. Maynard and M.P.N. Sims. *Apex Science Fiction and Horror*, edited by Jason Sizemore, is a quarterly with consistently readable fiction and regular interviews. The three issues published in 2007 had notable horror by Ian Creasey, Patrice Sarath, Cherie Priest, Stefani Nellen, Daniel G. Keohane, and Nancy Fulda. *New Genre*, edited by Adam Golaski, is a consistently literate annual, and issue 5 had an assortment of SF/F/H stories. The best of the dark fantasy and horror stories were by Joseph A. Ezzo and Jaime Corbacho and there's one very powerful tale by Paul Walther, which is reprinted herein. *Albedo One*, edited by John Kenny, Frank Ludlow, David Murphy and Bob Neilson, published two issues in 2007, neither with much horror, but there were strong dark stories by Michael Mathews, Andrew McKenna, and Nicola Caines. *Talebones*, edited by Patrick Swenson and Honna Swenson, is a well-produced perfect-bound quarterly that showcases science fiction and dark fantasy stories and poetry. Three issues came out in 2007 and there were strong dark stories by Hayden Trenholm, Andrew Tisbert, and Mark Ridney. Beginning with Issue 36, the magazine will be edited by Patrick Swenson solo. *Ellery Queen's Mystery Magazine*, edited by Janet Hutchings, doesn't usually have much horror but it often has good dark fiction. In 2007 the best were by William Scott Carter, Sheila Kohler, Laura Benedict, James Powell, Chris Simms, and a story by Joyce Carol Oates, which is reprinted herein. *Orson Scott Card's Intergalactic Medicine Show*, edited by Edmund Schubert, occasionally runs dark fiction and in 2007 there were very good stories by Peter S. Beagle, William Jon Watkins, Margit Elland Schmitt, and Michael Strahan. *The Magazine of Fantasy & Science Fiction*, edited by Gordon van Gelder, often publishes excellent horror and dark fantasy. In 2007 there were very good, dark stories by P.E. Cunningham, Ron Goulart, Donald Mead, M. Rickert, Daryl Gregory, Don Webb, and two very good novellas by Lucius Shepard and John Langan. The Donald Mead is reprinted herein. *Asimov's Science Fiction Magazine*, edited by Sheila Williams, published some very dark stories in 2007, including those by Kit Reed, Kim Zimring, James Van Pelt, Nancy Kress, Ted Kosmatka, Carol Emshwiller, Jim Grimsley, Tanith Lee, Bruce McAllister, and Liz Williams. *Cabinet des Fées*, edited by Helen Pilinovsky, Catherynne M. Valente, and Erzebet Barthold YellowBoy, is a gorgeous-looking double issue of this journal that focuses on fairy tales. There are four nonfiction pieces and ten stories, one a reprint. The darkest and my favorites are those by R. W. Day and Mike Allen (and the reprint, by Kimberly DeCina). The wonderful cover art is by Charles Vess and the black-and-white interior illustrations are by Daniel Trout. There is also an online version with original material on it. *Ideomancer*, published by Marsha Sisolak and edited by a team, is a quarterly online webzine that publishes science fiction, fantasy, and horror. There was a wonderfully imaginative collaborative project by Benjamin Rosenbaum, Christopher Barzak, Elad Haber, Greg van Eekhout, Kiini Ibura Salaam, Meghan McCarron, and Tim Pratt called "23 Small Disasters" which are hyperlinked through words in each piece of flash fiction. *GUD (Greatest Uncommon Denominator)*, edited by Kaolin Fire, debuted in the spring with an attractive perfect-bound magazine that looks like an anthology. It contains a mixed bag of fiction and poetry (and I think one journal entry about a trip to Taiwan—although it wasn't labeled as nonfiction). There was very little dark fiction but the best of it was by Steve J. Dines, Leslie Claire Walker, and a collaboration by Sarah Singleton and Chris Butler. *Tin House*, a literary quarterly edited by Will McCormick, has theme issues and in 2007 had very good dark fiction by Cate Marvin, Elizabeth Ziemska, and Nick Flynn (and a terrific, but not so dark story by Kelly Link). *Paradox*, edited by Christopher M. Cevasco, specializes in alternate histories and only occasionally publishes stories dark enough to be called horror. In 2007 there were good dark stories by Kenneth J. Sargeant, Tom Doyle, and Michael Livingston. *Andromeda Spaceways Inflight Magazine*, edited by an Australian cooperative, published more horror fiction and poetry than in previous years, with some very good work by Kaaron Warren, Jennifer Fallon, Kate Forsyth, Ian McHugh, Michael Merriam, and a story by Rick Kennett that I wanted for this volume but could just not fit in. *Realms of Fantasy*, edited by Shawna McCarthy, sometimes publishes dark fantasy and even horror. The best darker stories appearing during 2007 were by Christopher Barzak, Stephen Chambers, Noreen Doyle, Euan Harvey, Samantha Henderson, Trent Hergenrader, M.K. Hobson, Devon Monk, Richard Parks, and Josh Rountree. The magazine features a regular, always erudite column on "folkroots," plus book reviews, and a gallery of beautiful samples of fantastic art with text by Karen Haber.

The best webzines publishing horror in 2007 were: *ChiZine*, edited by Brett Alexander Savory, Sandra Kasturi, Gord Zajac, and Hannah Wolf Bowen, always has a good mix of fiction and poetry, and 2007 was no different. There was notable dark work by David De Beer, Barry Hollander, Bill Kte'pi, David Sakmyster, Marge Simon, Lavie Tidhar, and Paul G. Tremblay. *Lone Star Stories*, edited by Eric Marin, is a consistently interesting source of science fiction, fantasy, and dark fantasy prose and poetry and had good dark work by Mike Allen, Leah Bobet, Samantha Henderson, Jay Lake, Sarah Monette, Ben Peek, Sonya Taaffe (one poem reprinted herein), and Catherynne M. Valente. *Strange Horizons* is a Web site with fiction, reviews, and nonfiction columns and essays. The fiction is edited by Susan Marie Groppi, Jed Hartman, and Karen Meisner. 2007 was a very good year for dark fiction on the site, with excellent stories by Cat Rambo, Lori Selke, Stephanie Burgis, Theodora Goss, and Liz Williams. *Helix*, edited by William Sanders and Lawrence Watt-Evans, concentrates more on science fiction and fantasy but occasionally has excellent dark fiction and poetry. In 2007 there was a terrific story by Mike Allen, a very good one by Ann Leckie, and a very moving poem by Jane Yolen. *Clarkesworld*, edited by Nick Mamatas and Sean Wallace, publishes two new pieces of fiction a month, nonfiction articles, and interviews. The best of the dark stories in 2007 were by Jeff VanderMeer, Barth Anderson, Elizabeth Bear, David Charlton, Holly Phillips, Paul G. Tremblay, Cat Rambo, and Caitlín Kiernan.

The following magazines and webzines also had at least one very good horror/dark fantasy story in 2007: *Flytrap*, edited by Tim Pratt and Heather Shaw; *Zahir: A Journal of Speculative Fiction*, edited by Sheryl Tempchin; *Interzone*, edited by Andy Cox; *GrendelSong*, edited by Paul Jessup; *Out of the Gutter*, edited by Matthew Louis; *Outer Darkness*, edited by Dennis Kirk; *Mid-American Review*, edited by Karen Craigo and Michael Czyzniejewski; *Hub*, edited by Lee Harris; *The Harrow* online, edited by Michael R. Colangelo, Jason D. Nolan, Dru Pagliassotti, T.E. Twomey, and Kfir Luzzato; *Southern Gothic* online, edited by Jeff Crook; *Horror Literature Quarterly* online, edited by Paul Puglisi; *Orb*, edited by Sarah Endacott; *Sirenia Digest*, the e-mail journal of author Caitlín Kiernan, which often has original pieces of her dark fiction; *The Paris Review*, edited by Philip Gourevitch; *Esquire*, edited by David Granger; *Coyote Wild* online, edited by MacAllister Stone; *Say . . . what's the combination?*, edited by Christopher Rowe and Gwenda Bond; *The Cincinnati Review*, edited by Brock Clarke; *Ticonderoga* online, edited by Russell B. Farr, and Liz Grzyb; *Lady Churchill's Rosebud Wristlet*, edited by Kelly Link and Gavin J. Grant; *Ploughshares*, edited by Margot Livesey; *Hobart*, edited by Aaron Burch; *Withersin*, edited by Misty Gersley; *The New Yorker*, fiction editor Deborah Treisman; *Tales of the Unanticipated*, edited by Eric M. Heideman; *Conjunctions*, edited by Bradford Morrow; *Island*, edited by Gina Mercer; *Horrorworld* online, edited by Nanci Kalanta; *Dark Animus*, edited by James R. Cain; and *Electric Velocipede*, edited by John Klima.

Nonfiction Books

The Triumph of the Thriller: How Cops, Crooks, and Cannibals Captured Popular Fiction by Patrick Anderson (Random House) provides a survey of the field, first covering nineteenth-century pioneers such as Poe, Collins, and Conan Doyle and early twentieth-century writers such as Christie, Hammett, and Chandler. The balance of the book is about contemporary writers including Thomas Harris and George Pelecanos. *Vampires in Their Own Words: An Anthology of Vampire Voices* by Michelle Belanger (Llewellyn) contains almost two dozen essays by self-professed vampires. *When Man is Prey: True Stories of Animals Attacking Humans*, edited by Michael Tougias (St. Martin's). *The Dark-Hunter® Companion* by Sherrilyn Kenyon with Althea Kontis (St. Martin's). *The Dead Travel Fast: Stalking Vampires from Nosferatu to Count Chocula* by Eric Nuzum (St. Martin's) looks at vampires in pop culture. *The Devil of Great Island: Witchcraft & Conflict in Early New England* by Emerson W. Baker (St. Martin's) is about the witchcraft hysteria that took place in a small town ten years before the Salem witch trials and how that initial hysteria fueled copycat incidents elsewhere in New England. *Dinner with a Cannibal: The Complete History of Mankind's Oldest Taboo* by Carole A. Travis-Henikoff (Santa Monica Press) is a scholarly history of cannibalism from its early manifestations and its evolution into a taboo, analyzing the practice in anthropological and archaeological terms. *Hitchcock and Philosophy: Dial M for Metaphysics* edited by David Baggett and William A. Drumin (Open Court) has eighteen philosophers probe the auteur's movies in nineteen essays. *The Cramps: A Short History of Rock 'n' Roll Psychosis* by Dick Porter (Plexus) charts the history of the punk band that used EC comics imagery in their circus-like shows. *Television Fright Films of the 1970s* by David Deal

(McFarland) is a survey covering nearly one hundred fifty made-for-television fright movies, with credits, a plot synopsis, and critical commentary for each. *Bela Lugosi: Dreams and Nightmares* by Gary D. Rhodes and Richard Sheffield (Collectibles Press) is a scholarly study of Lugosi's life, focusing on the period between 1952 and 1956. It includes details of newly discovered stage, newsreel, radio and TV work, as well as a filmography. *Nightmare USA: The Untold Story of the Exploitation Independents* by Stephen Thrower (FAB Press) is a massive, 528-page encyclopedia of grindhouse cinema, covering the period between 1970 and 1985. *Stephen King: The Non-Fiction* by Rocky Wood and Justin Brooks (C.D. Publications) is a major reference work on King's nonfiction, covering his columns, book reviews, essays on writing, letters to the editor, and introductions. Extensive footnotes. *Horror Films of the 1980s* by John Kenneth Muir (McFarland) is a survey of three hundred movies; *J-Horror: The Definitive Guide to the Ring, the Grudge, and Beyond* by David Kalat (Vertical) guides the reader through the maze of the mostly Japanese horror movie franchises that took off in the late 1990s with Ringu and Ju-an. *Witchcraft Through the Ages: The Story of Häxan, the World's Strangest Film, and the Man Who Made It* by Jack Stevenson (FAB) is about an infamous silent, semi-documentary–style movie from 1922 and its Danish director Benjamin Christiansen, who cast himself as both Satan and Jesus. *Midnight Mavericks* by Gene Gregorits (FAB) has interviews with filmmakers John Waters, Abel Ferrara, and Larry Fessenden, writers Jack Ketchum, Joe R. Lansdale, artist J.K. Potter, and Lydia Lunch, among many others. *Mondo Lucha a Go-Go* by Dan Madigan (Rayo) is a look at the horror-influenced Mexican wrestling pop culture phenomenon. *I Was a TV Horror Host* by John Stanley (Atlas Books) is a memoir by the host of *Creature Features* from 1979 to 1984. *It Came from the Kitchen* by Geoff Isaac and Gordon Reid (BearManor Media) is a cookbook of favorite recipes by horror personalities. *Eija Tsuburaya: Master of Monsters* by August Ragone (Chronicle) is the first English-language biography of the Japanese master of monster special effects. *Hollywood Horror from the Director's Chair: Six Filmmakers in the Franchise of Fear* by Simon A. Wilkinson (McFarland) focuses on Wes Craven, Larry Cohen, Don Coscarelli, and three other directors. *Grimm Pictures: Fairy Tale Archetypes in Eight Horror and Suspense Films* by Walter Rankin (McFarland) compares elements in such fairy tales as "Little Red Cap" with those in *The Silence of the Lambs* and *Rosemary's Baby*, "Rapunzel" with *The Ring*, and "Cinderella" with Ripley in *Aliens*. *Dimensions Behind the Twilight Zone* by Stewart T. Stanyard (ECW) is a behind-the-scenes look at the show, with previously unseen photographs and the personal reminiscences of those who worked on it. *How to Survive a Horror Movie* by Seth Graham-Smith (Quirk) has humorous advice and illustrated instructions about avoiding ghosts, haunted cars, etc. *Encyclopedia Horrifica* by Joshua Gee (Scholastic) is a charming, attractive, and well-produced blend of fact and fiction aimed at a young adult readership. *Mario Bava: All the Colors of the Dark* by Tim Lucas (Video Watchdog) is the long-awaited tome about one of the masters of horror. With an introduction by Martin Scorsese, the book is almost 800,000 words and has over one thousand full-color illustrations. *The Portable Obituary: How the Famous, Rich, and Powerful Really Died* by Michael Largo (HarperCollins) is an entertaining, alphabetical compendium of exactly what the title says. *Horrifying Sex: Essays on Sexual Difference in Gothic Literature*, edited by Ruth Bienstock Anolik (McFarland), has sixteen essays about sex in gothic literature from Edgar Allan Poe to Clive Barker. *W. Paul Cook: The Wandering Life of a Yankee Printer*, edited by Sean Donnelly (Hippocampus), was a friend and publisher of H.P. Lovecraft and other authors of weird fiction. The book includes a thorough biography of Cook and memoirs about him by friends, plus a bibliography. The rest of the book features Cook's fiction, nonfiction, and poetry. *The Cryptopedia: A Dictionary of the Weird, Strange and Downright Bizarre* by Jonathan Maberry and David F. Kramer (Citadel) is divided into thirteen chapters, with a brief overview of the subject of the chapter and then definitions of terminology pertinent to that subject. A fun book to dip into. *What a Way to Go* by Geoffrey Abbott (St. Martin's Griffin) is a grim and disturbing little book about ways to kill someone, most of them torturously. *Collected Essays: Volume 5: Philosophy; Autobiography and Miscellany* by H.P. Lovecraft, edited by S.T. Joshi (Hippocampus), is the final volume of the series and features opinion pieces by Lovecraft on a wide range of political subjects. Also, his memorials for Henry S. Whitehead and Robert E. Howard, a "Confession of Unfaith," "Instructions in Case of Decease," and a variety of odds and ends that provide insights into the man. *H.P. Lovecraft in Britain*: A Monograph by Stephen Jones (BFS) is the first detailed history of the publication of Lovecraft's fiction in Britain, based on newly discovered files at the publisher, Victor Gollancz. *Warnings to the Curious: A Sheaf of Criticism on M. R. James* (Hippocampus), edited by S.T. Joshi and Rosemary Pardoe, is, according to the editors, the first volume on James to be devoted exclusively to his supernatural writing. Included in the book are memoirs by his friends, early criticism of his work, more recent criticism, and essays about individual stories. Not overly academic, the book is for anyone interested in James's work. *Sides* by Peter Straub (C.D. Publications) provides a mere peek at Straub's uncollected nonfiction work, including eleven introductions and afterwords (to books by Karl Edward Wagner, Rex Stout, Poppy Z. Brite, and to a contemporary edition of H.G. Wells's *The Island of Dr. Moreau*), and three longer essays, including one about his mother. The last section focuses on Putney Tyson Ridge, an imaginary former childhood friend and vicious critic of his (Straub's) work. *Vision and Vacancy: The Fictions of J. S. Le Fanu* by James Walton (University College Dublin Press) has been described by reviewers as being dense and authoritative yet readable. *Frankenstein: A Cultural History* by Susan Tyler Hitchcock (Norton) is entertaining throughout but most interesting in demonstrating how ubiquitous the use of the images and idea of "Frankenstein's monster" inundated western culture since the creature's creation by Mary Shelley in 1816. It's referred to by Dickens (in *Great Expectations*), used as a political bludgeon in the mid-nineteenth century, and has become a symbol of genetic modification today. *The Gothic*, edited by Gilda Williams (Whitechapel and MIT Press), is a survey of the influence of the "gothic in current art and visual culture." The word "gothic" in this context is applied to "works centering on death, deviance, the erotic macabre, psychologically charged sites, disembodied voices, and fragmented bodies." The liberal use of excerpts from novels and essays ranges from the mid-seventeenth century through 2006 but because the material is not given any context by the editor, the reader comes away with a patchwork of ideas and voices lacking cohesion. In contrast to Williams's book, *On Ugliness*, edited by Umberto Eco (Rizzoli), is a wonderful, profusely illustrated rumination on the dark, the monstrous, and the grotesque from ancient times to the present. In addition to the illustrations, Eco quotes from plays, religious tracts, fiction, poetry—and weaves his own analyses into the text.

Poetry Magazines and Web Sites

Goblin Fruit, edited by Amal El-Mohtar, Jessica P. Wick, and Oliver Hunter, is an attractive looking Web site with consistently good dark poetry, published quarterly. It debuted in spring 2006, but I only just discovered it. It's got excellent work by Karen

Romanko, Sonya Taaffe, Katharine Mills, Jaime Lee Moyer, Marlo Dianne, Jennifer Crow, Alex Dally MacFarlane, Catherynne M. Valente, and JoSelle Vanderhooft. *Mythic Delirium*, edited by Mike Allen, edging toward its tenth year, brought out two issues in 2007. In them, there was strong dark poetry by JoSelle Vanderhooft, Samantha Henderson, Jessica Paige Wick, Holly Cooley, Leah Bobet, and M. Frost. *Star*Line, the Journal of the Science Fiction Society*, edited by Marge Simon, is a bi-monthly magazine in its thirtieth year. There were good dark poems by Mary A. Turzillo and JoSelle Vanderhooft. *Poe Little Thing*, published by Naked Snake Press, brought out one issue in 2007, and then the press went on hiatus.

Poetry Chapbooks, Collections, and Anthologies

The Complete Poetry and Translations of Clark Ashton Smith Volume 3: The Flowers of Evil and Others, edited by S.T. Joshi and David E. Schultz (Hippocampus), in a remarkable achievement, presents all of Smith's translations of French and Spanish poets such as Baudelaire, Victor Hugo, Paul Verlaine, Amado Nervo, and others. He taught himself French in the 1920s and then Spanish in the 1940s in order to do this. All the texts are annotated by the co-editors.

Sam's Dot published *Sometimes While Dreaming* by Marcie Tentchoff, this relatively new poet's very promising first collection which includes forty-eight pieces of dark fantasy and horror, most of them original. The jacket and interior illustrations are by Marge Simon. Also, *Blood Verse* by Derek Clendening, a collection of ten poems about vampires, most of them appearing for the first time. And *On the Other Side of the Eye* by the Laotian American poet Bryan Thao Worra who writes fantasy and dark fantasy about his birthplace. Most of the poems are new to the collection. *Ossuary* by JoSelle Vanderhooft with art by Erzebet YellowBoy is an excellent, all-original poetry collection of mostly dark poetry, inspired by the art of Erzebet YellowBoy and focusing on the themes of decay and transformation. A second collection of eighteen poems (about half new) by Vanderhooft was published by Ash Phoenix and is titled *The Minotaur's Last Letter to His Mother*. It's illustrated by Marge Simon.

Tango in the Ninth Circle by Corinne De Winter (Dark Regions Press) has twenty-seven short, all original poems with an introduction by Denise Dumars and illustrations by Matt Taggart.

Vectors: A Week in the Death of a Planet by Charlee Jacob and Marge Simon (Dark Regions) is a chilling series of SF/horror poems about a plague rampaging over Earth, killing humans and animals alike. With cover art by Marge Simon.

Being Full of Light, Insubstantial by Linda D. Addison (Space & Time) is the third collection by this talented poet. The poems are a combination of fantasy and the personal, with some dark fantasy. The majority are original to the collection. The attractive jacket art and interiors are by Brian James Addison.

Your Cat & Other Space Aliens by Mary Turzillo (vanZeno Press) has, despite its title, much more than cute science fiction poetry. Among the over seventy new and reprinted works are some excellent dark fantasy poems.

Naked Snake Press published *chemICKals* by Karen L. Newman, which uses chemicals, compounds, and elements in a series of brief, nasty poems. Also, *Shades of Darkness, the Collected Works of Chad Hensley*, containing all of the poems from *What the Cacodaemon Whispered*, an earlier collection, and "Deep South Drifter," a section with fifteen new poems, some of them very effective.

Heresy by Charlee Jacob (Bedlam Press) is a strong all-original collection of twenty-five very dark poems. The nicely evocative cover art is by publisher David G. Barnett.

In Yaddath Time by Ann K. Schwader (Mythos Books) is a sonnet sequence inspired by Lovecraft's "Fungi from Yuggoth" but adding Schwader's sure and very modern touch. With cover art and interior illustrations by Steve Lines and an introduction by Richard L. Tierney.

Chapbooks and Other Small Press Items

Biting Dog Press published *The Resurrection and the Life* by Brian Keene, illustrated with woodblocks by George Walker. Also, *Midlisters* by Kealan Patrick Burke, a well-written tale about the author of several violent horror novels with a bad case of envy. The invitation to be a guest of honor at his first convention brings mixed blessings—his rival is another of the guests. With an introduction by Jack Ketchum and jacket and interior art by Keith Minnion.

The Session by Aaron Petrovich (Hotel St. George Press) is a humorous novella about two detectives who stumble upon a bizarre new religion while tracking a murder victim's stolen organs.

PS Publishing brought out *Illyria* by Elizabeth Hand, a marvelous novella about the lure of theater, a performance of Shakespeare's *Twelfth Night*, and the relationship between two cousins/soulmates growing up in a decaying mansion in north Yonkers. Not as dark as much of Hand's work, but riveting.

Magus Press published *Other Things Other Places* edited by David G. Montoya with three stories by John Dimes, David L. Tamarin, and Matt Staggs (not seen).

Burning Effigy Press published *General Slocum's Gold* by Nicholas Kaufmann, a well-told story about an ex-con, a treasure map, and a true-life historical tragedy in early twentieth-century New York City. Also, *The Distance Travelled: A Little Slice of Heaven* by Brett Alexander Savory and Gord Zajac, a sequel to Savory's 2006 novel. It's about what happens to a guy living in Limbo who will do anything to get out—even follow a weird quacking tomcat out into the dark. *Words Written Backwards* by Gemma Files is an effective story about a Native American shaman and a teenage girl he finds wandering in a blizzard on an island teeming with evil.

Naked Snake Press's products often have interesting cover art but inconsistent interior production values: Zombies zombies everywhere—caused by a mysterious wave of energy—that's what Eric S. Brown's chapbook, *The Wave*, is about. And the virtually unreadable (because of inferior reproduction) Scott A. Johnson story *The Journal of Edwin Grey* about a man who discovers his uncle's mysterious journal.

Lost in Translation by Gord Rollo from Nyx Books is a novella about a man plagued by voices in his head since being abducted by aliens as a child. Cover art is by Don Paresi.

Room 415 by Edward Lee (Necro Press) was originally in the limited edition of the publisher's 2004 *Damned: An Anthology of the Lost* anthology but with a different ending.

Black Tide by Del Stone, Jr. (Telos) is about a professor and his two students fighting to survive the results of an environmental disaster on a Florida island.

White Noise Press brought out several interesting chapbooks with new stories: *Brazen Bull*, by Elizabeth Massie, about an unemployed father with suspicions about the new family in town. *Smiling Faces Sometimes* by Gary A. Braunbeck is about a middle-aged man who, destroyed by bad luck in his life, returns to the town and tree house where almost forty years earlier, he and his friends used to be happy. The excellent covers and interior art for both chapbooks are by Keith Minnion. *All Your Gods Are Dead* by Gary McMahan is about a widower whose brother has been gruesomely murdered. The combination of body parts turning up, cryptic e-mail messages, and an act of self-mutilation he witnesses leads him to a cult that is preparing to take over. *The Last Stand of the Great Texas Packrat* by Steve Vernon is about a man obsessed with his books.

The Lazarus Condition by Paul Kane (Tasmaniac) is a short novel about a man mysteriously resurrected, who tries to go back to the life he lost when he died.

The Twilight Limited by Peter Atkins, Dennis Etchison, and Glen Hirshberg is an excellent three-story chapbook (the Etchison a reprint) compiled for the group's third west coast book tour. There is also a framing story/play.

From Bad Moon Books came: *You In?* by Kealan Patrick Burke, an effective, nasty little tale about an ex-gambler at the end of his rope who takes a job as night watchman at an abandoned inn; *Vampire Outlaw of the Milky Way* by Weston Ochse is something different by this author, a space opera. Cover art is by Chad Savage. *Wings of the Butterfly* by John Urbancik is a novella about a pack of shapeshifters led by a bullying wolf leader. The good-looking cover photo is by Laura Jack. *Restore from Backup* by J.F. Gonzales and Michael Oliveri is about a tech guy who takes a job at a mysterious company that won't tell him what it does.

The Fisherman by David A. Sutton (Gothic Press) is about a couple whose recent marriage is already troubled, vacationing on the coast of Wales, and their encounter with an old fisherman whose wife disappeared into the sea years before. The cover art and single interior illustration are by Marge Simon.

These four chapbooks came out from Rainfall: *The Mechanics of False Hilarity* by John B. Ford has two disturbing stories about clowns. The cover art is by Des Knight and the one interior illustration is by Steve Lines. *The Innsmouth Affair* by John Sunseri is a fast-moving tale about a gang of thieves who are pledged to protect humankind from various eldritch creatures with nefarious intentions. *A Little Job in Arkham* also by Sunseri is a two-story chapbook with the titular reprint and a second mythos tale. *Tales of the Phantom Moon* is a four-story chapbook of reprints by Andy McIlvain.

Double Act by L.H. Maynard and M.P.N. Sims (Pendragon Press) is a novella about a successful comedy act of 1950s England that's split up by the death of one of the two members (not seen).

This is Now by Michael Marshall Smith (Earthling) is a three-story chapbook published in honor of Smith's Guest of Honor appearance at the Toronto World Horror Convention in 2007. Two of the stories were previously published, the one original is a humorous SF story. The cover art is by Edward Miller. Most of the print run was given away in goodie bags at the convention. The rest (paperback and hardcover) were offered for sale to the public by the publisher.

Delirium Chapbooks 3 and 4: *Blood Wish* by Michael McBride is about a fatherless eight-year-old boy's encounter with a strange child in the woods outside his mother's hometown. *Pickman's Hotel* has two Lovecraftian-influenced humorous stories by Mark McLaughlin. The books in this series are adorable little hardcovers.

Ugly Heaven, Beautiful Hell by Jeffrey Thomas and Carlton Mellick III (Corrosion Press) presents two novellas, one by each author. *Beautiful Hell* is a kind of sequel to Thomas's earlier novel *Letters from Hades*.

Frayed by Tom Piccirilli (Creeping Hemlock Press) is an absorbing novella about two best friends who have competed in romance and literature for twenty years, all the while repressing a mutual anger and hatred that has been building from the time they were twelve. One, a "guest" in a weird mental hospital that seems more like a country club, has invited the other for a visit. The striking dust jacket and interior art is by publisher R. J. Sevin.

Bloodletting Books published some good-looking chapbooks such as *The Hollow Earth* by Steven Savile, a rousing tale about a theft from the British Museum that leads the members of London's Greyfriar's Club into a deadly fight with those who want to loose demons upon the world. Good cover and interior art by Daniele Serra. In *Tequila's Sunrise*, Brian Keene creates a charming dark fable for the modern world when a young Aztec meets temptation in the mountains just as the Spanish conquistadors are set to vanquish his people and destroy their way of life. The jacket art and interior illustrations are by Alex McVey and Keene supplies a brief afterword. The book's embossed green end papers and a brown ribbon bookmark make a very nice package. *Desecration* by Michael Laimo is about the desecration of a century-old church that is about to be demolished, and what it heralds for humanity. Jacket art by Mike Bohatch and again lovely endpapers, this time a quilted-looking orange.

Tattooing Violet by R.T. Mitchell (Scrybe Press) is about the power of tattoos on the bodies of two children abused by their stepfather. Cover art by Kirk Alberts.

Sam's Dot brought out *Living Stone*, a novella by Edward Cox about a series of brutal killings and the cop who tries to solve them. *Pretty* by Philip S. Meckley is about a young American visiting a friend's family estate in England and his attempt to stop a ghostly scenario played out over and over. *Darkness, Darkness* by Jane Gwaltney is a dark story about a troubled young woman who desperately wants her brand new relationship to work. *Widdershins* by Raymond Yeo is about two siblings in New Orleans, one of whom summons a demon.

Blood Coven by Christopher Fulbright and Angeline Hawkes (Dead Letter Press) begins very well with a "catcher" assigned by a secret agency to track down the spawn of a queen vampire in Victorian London, but ultimately disappoints. It has an effective cover illustration and design by Allen Koszowski. This is part of the "Literary Vampire Series" edited by Tom English.

Necessary Evil Press brought out *Placeholders* by John R. Little, an intriguing and fast-moving time-travel mystery about a man who repeatedly dies and is resurrected into different bodies. Introduction by Thomas F. Monteleone with cover art by Caniglia. *The Peabody-Ozymandias Traveling Circus and Oddity Emporium* by F. Paul Wilson is a revision and expansion of the original story that anchored the 1992 HWA Wilson-edited anthology *Freak Show*.

The Scalding Rooms by Conrad Williams (PS) takes place in a dystopian noir future in which sentient machines eat human spines, all manner of animals are processed for chopped meat, including pets, and death is everywhere. Powerful, gorgeously written and totally brutal. Gray Friar Press published a second novella by Williams, *Rain*, which is very different from *The Scalding Rooms*. *Rain* is a psychologically complex story about a domestic hell created by a couple whose relationship has been dying at least since the birth of their son four years earlier. After a break-in at their flat in the U.K., they move to rural France where things just get worse.

The Story of Noichi the Blind, edited by Alan Drew and Chet Williamson (CD), purports to be a lost manuscript by the great storyteller Lafcadio Hearn but is actually a clever homage about a woodcutter whose wife dies and his refusal to accept her death. Grisly, but also moving.

Art Books and Odds and Ends

Bookworm by Rosamond Purcell (Quantuck Lane Press) is by one of my favorite artist/photographers. *Finders, Keepers: Eight Collections* and *Special Cases: Natural Anomalies and Historical Monsters* were covered in earlier volumes of this series. *Bookwork* has introductions by Sven Birkerts and Purcell. To me, the most interesting photographs are those of naturally decrepit books partially destroyed by termites, water or fire damage, or just old age. I'm less interested in her more contrived collages but there's plenty of variety, with enough objects of decrepitude to please everyone.

Spectrum 14: The Best in Contemporary Fantastic Art, edited by Cathy Fenner and Arnie Fenner (Underwood Books), juried by major fantasy artists, continues to be *the* showcase for the best in genre art—the sheer variety of style and tone and media and subject matter is impressive. Futurist, *Blade Runner* designer and artist Syd Mead was celebrated as the 2006 Grand Master. Arnie Fenner covered the political and cultural year. There is also an appreciation of the late Stanley Meltzoff, whose art was on the Signet editions of Heinlein's *Tomorrow, the Stars* and *The Puppet Masters*. Plus, a necrology. The jury—all artists themselves—convene and decide on Gold and Silver awards in several categories. This is a book for anyone interested in art of the fantastic, dark or light.

Pet Noir: An Illustrated Anthology of Strange But True Pet Crime Stories, edited by Shannon O'Leary (Manic D Press), came out late 2006. It's divided into crimes by animals and crimes against animals and despite its initially breezy style (in comic art and text) it delves a bit deeper behind the headlines of infamous cases such as the mauling death of a San Francisco woman by a Presa Canario dog.

Eureka Production continues its series of Graphic Classics with a second edition of *H.P. Lovecraft Volume Four*, edited by Tom Pomplun. The 2002 first edition was not seen by me. The stories and excerpts are illustrated in a variety of styles by Matt Howarth, Pedro Lopez, Richard Corben, Mark A. Nelson, and other artists. Also, *Gothic Classics, Volume Fourteen* contains illustrated, retold tales of varying success by Jane Austin, Ann Radcliffe, J. Sheridan Le Fanu, Edgar Allan Poe, and Myla Jo Closser. And there was also a revised edition of *Graphic Classics: Bram Stoker, Volume Seven*, with forty-eight additional pages.

The Saga of the Bloody Benders written and illustrated by Rick Geary (NBM ComicsLit) is an entertaining graphic novel about a nineteenth-century couple, their adult son and his wife, who settle down in Lafayette County, Kansas, and build an inn and grocery at the nexus of travel across the prairie. Travelers disappear and just as the family is about to be accused of murder, they're gone. The house is dug up and the missing travelers are discovered butchered. Thereafter, sightings of the Benders are reported all over the west but it's not clear what happened to them.

ABC Spook Show by Ryan Heshka (Simply Read Books) is a charming little book that's perfect for introducing very young children to horror. Scary but not too scary. The colorful alphabet illustrates A-Z and includes three goofy-looking red-nosed ghosts gambling as "E for Ectoplasm," a bloated pig who ate too much "Yucky Candy," and of course Zombies running free for "Z as in Zombie."

Dog Trick or Cat Treat: Pets Dress up for Halloween by Archie Klondike (ECW Press) kind of says it all—photos sent in by the owners indexed in the back of the book. I hope their darlings can forgive them. A pit bull sports a rust-colored fur disguising it as a lion for a parade in Tompkins Square Park, New York City; a Dalmatian looks sheepish as a cowboy; Mabel the tabby looks self-satisfied in her Mexican sombrero and with her bottle of tequila; Ginger the dachshund wears a hot-dog bun and squiggles of mustard on top. And the pugs! Poor pugs.

Jan Švankmajer and Eva Švankmajer Exhibition: Alice or Pleasure Principle is the catalog from a terrific exhibit in Tokyo in 2007. Jan Švankmajer is a great Czech animator, who made the awe-inspiring movies *Alice, Faust, Conspirators of Pleasure,* and *Little Otik.* His work influenced the Brothers Quay (whose work I also love). The exhibit had props from some of the films as well as collages, drawings, and paintings by Jan and his wife Eva. The catalog is heavily illustrated but is in Japanese.

Dr. and Mr. Doris Haggis-on-Whey's World of Unbelievable Brilliance: Animals of the Ocean, in Particular the Giant Squid (McSweeney's) is a very silly, entertaining book that has a gold-foiled-embossed cover and is profusely illustrated—if there's *any* reliable information actually in here about the giant squid, they've fooled me. Sample pages: "Can I Keep Him? A Guide to Giant Squid Ownership," "Squid Trends and Fashions: west coast and dirty south," and "Seven Cautionary Tales about Octopuses and Otters."

The Legend of the Headless Horseman by Washington Irving (abridged) with illustrations by Gris Grimley (Atheneum) features two equally unpleasant characters (at least in this version): the gold-digging geeky schoolmaster Ichabod Crane and the uncouth and arrogant Brom Van Brunt—rivals for the hand of the village catch Katrina Van Tassel. Crane is scared off by a manifestation of the legendary headless horseman. Grimley's illustrations are scary but not too scary. For kids.

The Nightmare Factory based on the stories by Thomas Ligotti (Foxatomic) makes for an intriguing introduction to new readers and a good-looking addition for collectors of Ligotti's work. The book features adaptations of "The Last Feast of the Harlequin" by Stuart Moore and Colleen Doran, "Dream of a Mannikin" by Moore and Ben Templesmith, "Dr. Locrian's Asylum" by Joe Harris and Ted McKeever, and "Teatro Grottesco" by Harris and Michael Gaydos. The excellent cover art is by Ashley Wood. Ligotti has written a new introduction for each story.

Angel Skin by Christian Westerlund and Robert Nazeby Herzig (NBM/ComicsLit) is a nicely realized graphic novel about a young suicide who awakes in a dead city and embarks with an elderly companion on a search to find God. Enter grotesque yet beautiful fallen angels, a creature with his own reasons for finding God, and a population of depressives and you've got an atmospheric, mostly downbeat story with a bit of light at the end.

A Book of Unspeakable Things: Works inspired by H. P. Lovecraft's Commonplace Book, edited by Patrick J. Gyger was created for a French exposition commemorating the seventieth anniversary of Lovecraft's death. The introduction discusses Lovecraft as a "science fiction writer" and describes how his *Commonplace Book,* kept from 1919 and 1934, recorded ideas that the author planned to use in his later fiction. Twenty one-page pieces of text (in French and English) and one hundred pieces of art were commissioned. The book contains most of both. The first half showcases pieces by Lucius Shepard, Jeffrey Ford, James Morrow, Norman Spinrad, Ian Watson, Terry Bisson, Paul Di Filippo, Christopher Priest, and several French writers. The second half is filled with eighty-nine pieces of Lovecraft-inspired art by John Couthart, H. R. Giger, and other artists whose names are unfamiliar to me. All in all, a wonderful artifact that's available for purchase

The Bearskinner: A Tale of the Brothers Grimm retold by Amy Schlitz, illustrated by Max Grafe (Candlewick Press), is a dark tale about a poor soldier who makes a deal with the devil: unlimited riches as long as he wears a rotting bearskin for seven years without revealing the deal or praying to God. Otherwise, he loses his soul. The beautiful illustrations make wonderful use of various shades of brown and other dark colors, with brief, unexpected dashes of bright colors.

The Year in Media
of the Fantastic: 2007

Edward Bryant

2007 was a good year for the fantastic on screen. It might not have been a five-star, A-plus-plus year, but it was still pretty impressive. Here's an encapsulation of some of what happened. Essentially there was something for everyone.

Big Screen Horror

Probably the most impressive horror picture of the year was *The Orphanage*, from the expert Spanish director Antonio Bayona, and executive-produced by Guillermo del Toro. Laura (Belén Rueda) and her husband (Fernando Cayo) are the grieving parents of a young son who is HIV positive. Laura is a social worker whose ambition is to purchase the long-abandoned orphanage in which she grew up, and to refurbish it as a home for disabled children. Things go well until the supernatural phenomena begin to manifest. Spectral kids in burlap bag full-head masks are pretty spooky, along with the moody ocean waves constantly breaking in the background. Laura begins to discover that perhaps a child's life in the orphanage was not nearly so idyllic as she remembered. *The Orphanage* is a literate, understated, and disturbing work.

Sweeney Todd, adapted by Tim Burton from Stephen Sondheim's hit Broadway musical, opened late in the year, never quite becoming the mass audience's favorite Christmas movie. This retold urban myth about the wronged nineteenth-century London barber who returns from exile to take up a new identity but the same old straight razor, and to take revenge in grisly, graphic fashion, is played brilliantly by Johnny Depp. Helena Bonham Carter also takes a wonderful turn as the bake-shop lady who both falls for Sweeney and has the bright idea of serving up victims as cheap meat pies. The entire cast, including Alan Rickman and Sacha Baron Cohen, all do their own singing and do it well. *Sweeney Todd* is not a tonic for your spirits, but is the perfect antidote for sloppy, sentimental musicals. Perhaps the high point is a dream sequence in which Bonham Carter imagines what it would be like to have a conventional life with the demon barber.

Fido was already a year old and nearly invisible when Lionsgate released this alternate-world Canadian low-budget production in the United States. It's a brilliant lampoon of '50s American culture—with zombies. Director Andrew Currie's film begins with an expert vintage documentary explaining that after World War II, a Romero-esque radiation from space reanimated the dead. The Zombie Wars ensued, the living humans eventually getting the upper hand thanks to security corporation Zomco's domestication collars, gadgets akin to doggie shock devices that keep zombies docile. Those pacified undead are conscripted to do all the drudge jobs in an America of walled-off small towns. The great masses of free-range zombies still wander the countryside in between. In the cloistered town of Willard, young Timmy (a portentous name indeed) lives with his Leave-It-to-Beaver parents and a household zombie he names Fido. Carrie-Anne Moss is Mom, British comic Billy Connolly expertly tackles the nonverbal role of Fido. The family comic drama is rib-tickling, touching, horrifying, and utterly human. For a bonus, check out the big, shiny, custom '50s automobiles.

When it comes to coming-of-age fables, *Teeth* fills the bill. Written and directed by Mitchell Lichtenstein, this small independent dark fantasy tells the story of Dawn (Jess Weixler), a young woman who's grown up in a modest lower middle-class home right in the shadow of a nuclear plant. The clear suggestion is that radiation may have jiggered Dawn's genes and given her a unique quality. Dawn's already distinctive, as a sunny and devout young woman who conducts "purity assemblies" at her high school. As she reaches the threshold of womanhood, Dawn discovers she has a built-in defense mechanism that protects her from the depredations of date-rapists, incest-minded psycho stepbrothers, and gynecologists—that mythically fearsome quality of vagina dentata. *Teeth* is sincere and affecting, but not without its occasional moments of grisly amusement, real humor, and, of course, a few graphic bits. All in all, the film is quite a remarkable achievement.

If I'm interpreting the end credits of *George Romero's Diary of the Dead* correctly, this modestly budgeted latest entry in Romero's four-decade saga of the walking, lurching, masticating dead roaming the earth was supported through the clout (and cash) of a quintet of horror heavyweights. The conceit of this film is that it's a documentary of the zombie onslaught against humanity, filmed with hand-held cameras by a small group of Pittsburgh university students making their way cross-country to a prospective haven. The gimmick of homegrown video was used far less effectively in 2008's *Cloverfield*. In *Diary*, writer/director Romero knows how to impart the effect of unsteady-cam without triggering the audience's equilibrium-loss queasiness. With their cell-phone videos, hand-helds, and CCTV tapes, Romero's young cast are a diverse, empathic, and resourceful bunch of video and Net-aware people constantly dealing with the issue of whether the visual image is more real than what the human eye sees in real-time. It's a serious issue that the film treats thoughtfully, fairly and provocatively. At its heart, *Diary* is a straightforward horror movie that possesses both involving characters and is actually *about* something. Be sure to watch for the key moment in which a major character, bitten by a zombie and aware of his imminent fate, begs his colleagues, "Shoot me!"

Grindhouse, the complete double feature by Robert Rodriguez and Quentin Tarantino that pays homage to the exploitation movies of the '70s, comes with all the nostalgic bells and whistles, including print scratches, skipped frames, lost reels, and fake trailers such as one for a flick called *Machete* with the unforgettably rugged face of Danny Trejo front and center. Robert Rodriguez's feature, *Planet Terror*, is a survive-the-zombies melodrama featuring a cast including Bruce Willis, Freddy

Rodriguez, Rose McGowan, and two of the director's nieces playing a pair of kick-ass survivalist teens. Quentin Tarantino takes on a role as a zombified soldier and would-be rapist who comes to a truly disgusting and oozy punchline. The film is hyperkinetic and reasonably entertaining, but doesn't really add any new dimension to its predecessors of thirty years ago.

Tarantino's *Death Proof* is the second feature and the more successful part of the movie marathon program. Kurt Russell seems to be having an enormous amount of fun as the psychopathic stunt driver Mike, who picks up gorgeous women, then drives his car at speed into horrendous crashes. Russell's character has an effective crash cage; the passenger riding shotgun does not. All goes well with the driver's crazy hobby until he has the bad luck to meet up with a posse of four tough, resilient young women including Rosario Dawson, the omnipresent Rose McGowan and, playing herself, Zoe Bell, Uma Thurman's spectacular stunt double in *Kill Bill*. Murderous Mike is overmatched, to say the least. All in all, *Grindhouse* was critically undervalued when it was released. The double feature's three-plus hours of running time may seem like the Bataan death march to the patience-challenged. Both features have reached DVD as separate releases, so that may help. Still, I'd argue that *Grindhouse*, problematic enterprise or not, is still a major cinematic accomplishment. Hyperannuated, post-adolescent, nostalgic, exploitation appreciators have feelings, too.

The low-budget British film *Severance* builds off a terrific idea. A tour bus-load of U.K. defense contractor employees drive into deepest, darkest, Eastern Europe to spend a weekend of team-building exercises at a remote and creepy forest lodge. As you can doubtless imagine, things go horribly awry. The woods are full of nutso killers from the recent Balkan unpleasantness. There are priceless moments. Imagine something like *Friday the 13th* meets *The Office*. As high concepts go, it's not a bad risk.

Thomas Jane performed a far better acting turn in *The Mist* than he ever did in *The Punisher*. It wouldn't have taken much. Jane and Laurie Holden starred in Frank Darabont's nifty adaptation of Stephen King's novella. King's original story concerned a diverse group of townspeople trapped in a supermarket by a mysterious mist that harbors all manner of nasty alien creatures. There is the suggestion that all is due to a military experiment gone terribly wrong. Odd how cinematic military projects do that so frequently. The novella ended with both enormous vagueness and a modicum of hope. In his script, Darabont takes the story a bit further, ends the tale with some definition, but also uses a beautifully grim device borrowed wholecloth from the climax of the twice-filmed minor classic, *Only Five Came Back*.

The Host allows Korean director Bong Joon-ho to ring an effective change on the whole Godzilla notion. The film starts politically enough with a slipshod U.S. military installation in Korea screwing up, allowing toxic waste to be dumped, thereby triggering the rapid evolutionary mutation of what appears to be a highly steroidal lungfish with a nasty disposition. Before you can say "Gojira," the creature is clumping down the Seoul dock front, chomping passersby and raising all manner of other hell. *The Host* actually becomes a terrific family drama, as a local clan is separated by the creature, a daughter is thrown into jeopardy, and her relatives try to recover her safely. It's both effective and affecting, and the plot is leavened by a few terrific sight gags. Consider this one of the must-sees.

Like remakes of classics, movies based on video games don't get a lot of respect. I must say, though, that one of my guilty pleasures has been the Milla Jovovich vehicles based on *Resident Evil*. The first two features have been beautifully stylish exercises in cinematography with plenty of ultra-violence and a *noir*ish sensibility as soldiers and babes battle a multitude of urban zombies created by either the deliberate design or the sloppy behavior of the sinister Umbrella Corp., the corporate overlord of the doomed Raccoon City. Milla Jovovich plays the kick-ass agent of Umbrella Corp. who learns, to her sorrow, of her employer's duplicity. When the viewer joins the third and newest installment, *Resident Evil 3: Extinction*, we find Jovovich's character riding her motorcycle across America's interior desert. She runs afoul of a family using a small-town radio station to broadcast fake appeals for medical aid in order to attract victims to use as monster-chow for their pack of zombie dogs. After that adventure, our heroine continues her *Mad Max*-ish quest west. She finds allies, including Ali Larter, and they all meet up in a spectacularly ruined Las Vegas with more zombies, not to mention the (perhaps) final minions of the Umbrella Corp. End of the series? I doubt it. I hope not.

In *30 Days of Night*, based on the popular graphic novel, Josh Hartnett, Melissa George, and a handful of other hardy souls survive an onslaught of vampires who opportunistically attack Alaska's northernmost town during the winter when the sun doesn't rise for a whole month. The bloodsuckers, all looking and sounding like the most unsavory of Slavic illegal immigrants, sail their hijacked freighter to an icy and inhospitable coast, and come ashore to make the best of a dismal season. Meaner than a migratory pack of polar bears, the vampires do quite well for themselves. But you know humans—they always manage to find a way.

Remember Danny Boyle's *28 Days Later*, the terrific thriller about a nasty virus escaping in London and turning large numbers of citizens into hyperkinetic hordes of zombie-like killers? Now the sequel, *28 Weeks Later*, this time directed by Juan Carlos Fresnadillo, takes us a bit further into the future when the un-green zombies have overgrazed their territory and apparently died off. Unpopulated London is deemed by the government ready for resettlement. Optimistic fools, they. Bureaucrats and the military establish a secure Green Zone to start the ball rolling. Convoys of civilians head back into the city. Of course there are surviving zombies and they tend to view this plan as akin to hearing the chime of the dinner bell. Robert Carlyle plays one of the civil servants, a man carrying the guilty secret of having sacrificed his wife to save himself during the initial zombie attacks. What ensues is energetic and crisply filmed, but never quite captures the manic intensity of *28 Days Later*. This time the original's the best.

1408, adapted from the Stephen King short story, is a good old-fashioned ghost story about an intensely haunted hotel room in the Big Apple. John Cusack plays a guy who's been hunting ghosts—or any proof of post-death survival—for years, without any luck. Then he comes to room *1408* where there's evidence that scads of unlucky guests have come to terrible ends over the decades. Hotel manager Samuel L. Jackson isn't enthusiastic about letting Cusack spend the night in *1408*, but eventually relents. Cusack, a man with a secret agenda himself, then gets an object lesson in paranormal jeopardy. *1408* is a solid and classy lesson in spookiness.

As a rule of thumb, remakes of classics are generally a bad idea. John Carpenter's *Halloween* has held up extremely well for three decades. Structure, direction, and cinematography have endured, as has the splendid performance of the young Jamie Lee Curtis as the teen Midwestern protagonist who must learn extreme coping skills to survive the psychopathic murder rampage of the crazed Michael Myers. So when it came time to refurbish *Halloween*, the smart thing to do was bring to the table a sensibility both gifted and a little loony. Director and musician Rob Zombie was a good choice. Zombie has a love for edgy approaches to extreme graphic violence, and he adores the sleaziest of '70s horror movies. Thus the new *Halloween* becomes something both the same and very different. Possibly reflecting the interests of filmmaker Zombie, the new version pays an extreme amount of attention to Michael

Myers's back-story, to the detriment of treating the story of the Jamie Lee Curtis character. It all depends on who you believe is the protagonist of the piece. I'd vote for the heroine, but I'm probably too old-fashioned. At any rate, Jamie Lee's successor here is simply too forgettable. But Michael is not. Sic transit . . .

Director Eli Roth helms *Hostel: Part II* as he did the original *Hostel*, a film that cost me points with some of my friends when I lauded its wedding of astute and nasty political commentary to extreme horror movie violence. The sequel takes place directly after the events of its predecessor. Once again the post-Soviet collapse economy is in full capitalist bloom, and once again local military, police, and the business community are in the business of kidnapping locals, other Europeans, and, most prized of all, Americans, for sale to sadists from all over the globe as murder and torture victims. The money's big, the risks high, and the stakes major for impoverished pockets of Eastern European society. In short order the sole surviving protagonist of *Hostel* is dispatched and we meet a whole new cast of unwary innocents looking for fun and frolic (not to mention tourist bargains) in the spas and hostels of the east. This time, however, we're focusing on the women. You might think of *Hostel II* as the distaff version of the first feature. The young women are resourceful and tenacious, but they fare little better than the men. Final confirmation of that will have to wait for the inevitable *Hostel 3*.

How many *Saw* sequels do we need before the toolbox is full and we can move on to hammers, drill bits, and socket sets? *Saw IV* suggests it'll be a while before the audiences and producers will abandon serrated edges as a leitmotif. Even though actor Tobin Bell as the creepy antagonist, Jigsaw, died for good in the previous installment, he's back in *Saw IV* for a graphic autopsy and some occasional flashbacks. The novelty value of the post mortem, particularly the uncovering of Jigsaw's brain and the disclosure of his stomach contents is a perfect accompaniment for hot buttered popcorn. Seeing himself autopsied, with or without the presence of James Lipton, is probably good for any actor. The *Saw* premise has always been a self-proclaimed grasp at Old Testament morality. The perpetrators of atrocious deaths are presumably bad people who have one final opportunity to make a good decision under the pressure of knowing they'll end badly if they screw up. It is not uncommon for the people behind the picture to lose track of that rigorous ethic. Innocents do die. The other major reason to watch these movies is to see the jaggedly stylish cinematography of gloomy, grubby, monochromatic interiors; in short, Gray Line tours of urban hell. It perhaps appeals to a limited demographic, but box office receipts suggest otherwise.

In the tradition of *Lake Placid*, *Primeval* gives us yet another giant man- (and woman-) eating crocodile, this time in the wetlands of Burundi. Supposedly based on true events, the exploits of a mythic serial-killing reptile, named by the locals Gustave, draw a U.S. network news crew to film and capture the critter in time for sweeps after it devours a world-class forensic anthropologist investigating war crimes in the revolution-torn country. Yanks Dominic Purcell, Brooke Langton, and Orlando Jones draw the short straws when it comes to this dubious plum assignment. Jürgen Prochnow adds some substance as a local ace croc hunter. *Primeval* is a game, if uneven, attempt to fuse a political view of modern, chaotic Africa with the hunt for a primal killing force of nature. Gustave, of course, steals the show.

Best Monster of the Year

The most effective and memorable movie monster of the year was not an obvious supernatural manifestation or a masked guy with a machete. Spanish actor Javier

Bardem gets the nod for his turn as the calm and deliberate killer Anton Chigurh in the Coen brothers' adaptation of Cormac McCarthy's novel *No Country for Old Men*. Particularly favoring a compressed-air bolt gun ordinarily used for killing cattle in a slaughterhouse, Bardem's character is presented as a calm and collected, unstoppable killing machine, more force of nature than psychopath. One of Chigurh's few pleasures, it would seem, is determining a passerby's life or death with the call of a tossed coin. The film itself is a memorable suspense yarn of an '80s drug deal gone horribly wrong. Besides Bardem, the cast includes Josh Brolin, Tommy Lee Jones, Kelly Macdonald, and a host of others, all acquitting themselves magnificently. The role of Anton Chigurh is especially striking when measured against Javier Bardem's casting, the same year, as a tender, romantic, fragile poet in *Love in the Time of Cholera*. My runner-up for a monstrous film portrayal? Daniel Day Lewis's icily rapacious and fatally ambitious self-made oil tycoon in Paul Thomas Anderson's adaptation of Upton Sinclair's novel *Oil*, *There Will be Blood*. Lewis's character is someone you'd never want to run into in the dark. Or in a bowling alley.

Fantasy on the Big Screen

It was a good year for Neil Gaiman's work on screen. My favorite was a feature film adaptation by director Matthew Vaughn and Jane Goldman of his 1999 novel, *Stardust*. *Stardust* is a fable of romantic adventure, punctuated with sharp humor, and chockfull of wondrous incident. The time is the Victorian era in England; Tristan (Charlie Cox) is a smitten young man, pining for the attentions of the cold and distant beauty Victoria (Sienna Miller) in the village of Wall. The village is so named because of the nearby stone wall that separates a magical realm from our own. Tristan ventures across the wall in search of a fallen star to give Victoria as a token. He soon finds there are many beings in search of the fallen star—and even more amazingly, the fallen star is a young woman named Yvaine (Claire Danes). Tristan soon finds himself in competition with a gaggle of ambitious noblemen, both living and ghostly, who have outlived their king (Peter O'Toole), and with the supremely beautiful but evil witch-queen Lamia (Michelle Pfeiffer). Once Tristan teams with Yvaine and they desperately need rescue, the show is pretty much stolen by Robert De Niro as Captain Shakespeare of the sky-ship *Perdita*, an aerial vessel, the crew of which hunts and captures lightning in the clouds. While the captain is a bit player in the novel, he earns a lot more time in the film. De Niro doesn't just eat the scenery; he *becomes* the scenery when he has a tremendous reveal as a flaming crossdresser. Some observers have suggested the closest previous movie to *Stardust* is *The Princess Bride*. That's true in terms of tone and warmth. But *Stardust* is very much its own film, and it's a nonpareil fantasy for the year. For a bonus you get bit parts from the likes of Peter O'Toole, Ian McKellen, and Ricky Gervais.

Until I read certain reviews, I didn't realize *The Golden Compass* was supposed to be a virulent anti-Catholic screed. Well, perhaps so, but *my* viewing of the movie simply suggested that any alternate-world, magical steampunk culture could easily be ruled by a Magisterium, a sinister and tenaciously repressive bunch of status quo fans who just happened to all dress in black. Be that as it may, this adaptation, by writer/director Chris Weitz, of Philip Pullman's first volume in the *His Dark Materials* trilogy is a first-rate work of fantasy. In this alternate British history, each human is accompanied by a daemon, essentially a familiar in animal or bird form. If your daemon is a white tiger, that's pretty cool; if your daemon is a mere vole, well, you just have to live with it. The film introduces Dakota Blue Richards in a fine acting debut as Lyra Belacqua, the astute girl who gets tangled in the maneuverings of Lord Asriel (Daniel Craig) who believes he's found the means to access parallel worlds. The Magisterium counts this a heresy and tries to kill him. Soon the lord and the girl are on the way to the Arctic to prove the discovery, as well as to recover some kidnapped child friends of Lyra, with ace Magisterium agent Marisa Coulter (Nicole Kidman) in hot pursuit. We continue to meet intriguing characters such as the expatriate American aeronaut Lee Scoresby (Sam Elliot), accompanied by his daemon Hester (voiced by Kathy Bates). Our heroine is quickly taken under the wing (or paw) of the sentient, exiled, alcoholic polar bear Iorek (voiced by Ian McKellen). Perhaps the most striking fantasy film image of the year is the sequence of girl astride polar bear, loping across the starlit polar ice. As it turns out, the film ends a couple of chapters short of the novel's climax. This changes the whole tone of the work, but one can surmise why the adapter of the script did so. Presumably the final revelations of the book will be restored at the opening of the film sequel. But in spite of that little issue, *The Golden Compass* is an involving story, has first-rate performances, and is a sumptuous visual feast.

For a good long while now, the tradition of the magic shop (that store with genuine magical qualities—not a mere purveyor of stage magic paraphernalia) has been popular in fantasy fiction. So far it has resisted any urge to modernize itself with the notion of a magic mega-mall. Thus it was good to see *Mr. Magorium's Wonder Emporium* for the holidays in 2007. The store of the title is a truly wondrous toyshop in New York City, an apparently small but infinitely expansive place where one can obtain virtually any plaything, old or new, and the display toys possess amazing qualities of animation. The shopkeeper of the title is played by Dustin Hoffman as a gentleman a quarter-millennium in age, who knows he is reaching the end of his tenure. His assistant and cashier, played by Natalie Portman, has no idea of Mr. Magorium's actual nature or her own destiny. This fantasy is a genuine charmer.

Enchanted is as light as helium, but it does provide considerable charm and amusement, particularly for the Disney fan who doesn't hold St. Walt in completely reverential awe. Kevin Lima directed from a Bill Kelly script. The film begins with narration by Julie Andrews and an utterly over-the-top animation sequence in classic Disney fantasy style. But then the evil Queen Narissa (Susan Sarandon) shuffles the princess (Amy Adams) off to a terrible exile—into our world as a living flesh-and-blood human being. Pursued by the prince (James Marsden), the princess winds up smack in the middle of Manhattan where she is taken in by the good-hearted Philip family (headed by Patrick Dempsey) and does her best to adapt in this strange land. One set-piece scene is a complete hoot. I refer to when the princess stands in a sunny morning window and calls for her usual helpers to aid in cleaning up and working on new clothing. But instead of the customary trilling bluebirds and neatly scurrying mice, her new allies are hordes of pigeons, roaches, and rats. All comes to a good end, of course, with plenty of fun and the expenditure of nary a calorie.

The Water Horse: Legend of the Deep, from some of the makers of *Babe*, is a most pleasant and scenic kids' fable about a young boy named Angus (Alex Etel) who discovers a large and mysterious egg on the shore of a Scottish loch and takes it home. The egg hatches into an unusual-looking but playful creature, so Angus decides to raise it in his family's bathtub. Dad (Brian Cox) is dubious. If you can't plot out the rest of the story from the moment you know the body of water is Loch Ness, you should be ashamed.

Blackhawk gunships and dragons get to dogfight in L.A. airspace in writer/director Hyung-rae Shim's Korean-produced adaptation of the video game, *Dragon Wars* (aka

D-War). A good chunk of the movie is given over to a sequence interpreting a traditional Korean legend from the distant past. That set piece is a bookend for the present-day action in which characters have been reborn and are once again squaring off, using rather fearsome dragons as weapons, to control the world. The film is sincere enough, and it's good to see Robert Forster in action again, playing aged shopkeeper Jack who turns out to be an unexpected mentor for the young hero Ethan (Jason Behr).

And now for the other half of your Neil Gaiman double feature. In this version of *Beowulf*, the English-speaking world's oldest known monster fiction, the script is a collaboration between Gaiman and Roger Avary. The movie is filmed in a sophisticated form of rotoscopic animation much like the technique used for *Polar Express*. British actor Ray Winstone plays the titular hero wonderfully as an increasingly world-weary if ambitious man of action who is simply getting tired. Unlike many versions of the Anglo-Saxon myth, this film goes far beyond Beowulf's defeat of the monster mead-hall raider Grendel. Beowulf marries, succeeds the king (Anthony Hopkins), and assumes control of the kingdom, but eventually must deal with Grendel's scheming mother and the dragon. All in all, it's a dark and somber epic of courage and doomed heroism.

For a diverting historical fiction that probably never was, but should have been, try *Pathfinder*. Imagine that many centuries ago, a Viking raiding party meets disaster in the New World, and is survived only by a single small male child. The boy is discovered by a local Native American warrior, adopted by the tribe, and grows up never quite fully accepted by his fellows. As an adult untested warrior (Karl Urban), he wants to settle down with local girl Moon Bloodgood. But he meets quandary and crisis when a fierce new band of Viking raiders lands on the coast and starts raising havoc. Much fighting, chasing, overland treks across spectacular scenery, touches of folk magic, bad weather, and general mayhem ensue. Heroic melodrama, but fun.

It's often difficult to comment upon later entries in highly successful epic fantasy series. After all, what new can be said, other than perhaps pointing out that an entry has lost all its initial energy? So here goes. *Spider-Man 3* features the inarguably attractive Tobey Maguire and Kirsten Dunst as the Spider Guy and his love interest. Plenty of computer-generated effects keep us swooping through the urban canyons. But the film seems far too long, overstuffed even, as Spider-Man deals not only with the villainous Sandman, but with his dark alter ego, Venom, as well. It does go on.

Pirates of the Caribbean: At World's End features, as ever, Johnny Depp as the always-amusing Captain Jack Sparrow. Then there's the added attraction of Rolling Stone Keith Richards as Jack's grizzled dad. Unfortunately Richards's cameo is all too brief. Bill Nighy hangs in there as the tentacle-bearded ghost pirate, Davy Jones. There's plenty of swashbuckling, but not a whole lot that's notably new.

Harry Potter and the Order of the Phoenix, the fifth in the series about coming of age at the Hogwarts School of Wizardry, plays quite well. Some of the fun comes from the plot allowing the evil Lord Voldemort to return. But perhaps the most startling aspect of the film is the audience's realization that the young actors are aging not only as fast as their character roles, but perhaps a little bit faster. The personal dynamics among Harry, Ron, Hermione, Luna Lovegood, and the rest of the crew seem to be increasingly informed by hormones.

Slipstream Fantasy

When I saw Julie Taymor's truly visionary *Across the Universe* early in its run, I had a moment of pause immediately afterward. In the restrooms, audience members over, say, forty, were saying things like "Man, that brought it all back!" while younger viewers were saying, "Wow, I had no idea it was that cool!" Sorry, but *Across the Universe* is not literal history. It might more properly be called meta-history, as director Taymor reimagines the world of the late '60s by brilliantly mining the range of Beatles music not just for the tunes, but as well for the characters, mythology, and cultural resonances the Fab Four drew upon. That script is by Dick Clement and Ian La Frenais. Young Jude (Jim Sturgess) comes to America from Britain to see what's going on. He meets Lucy (Evan Rachel Wood) and we're off on a magical mystery tour through a phantasmagoric New York crammed with sex, mind-altering drugs, rock 'n' roll, social action, and war protests. It's a world that, if it really *wasn't* completely the way we remember it, should have been this way.

I'm *Not There*, directed by Todd Haynes from a script by Haynes and Oren Moverman, is a more modest but equally astute and freewheeling reimagining of recent history — in this case, the life and times of Bob Dylan. The most brash device is to place a different actor playing Dylan into each stage of the musician's life and career, beginning with depicting the very young Dylan as a black boy (Ben Whishaw) falling headlong into a lasting love affair with rhythm and blues. It's hard to divorce this section of the picture from treacherous memories of Steve Martin's role (in *The Jerk*) of a man raised as a young child by black sharecroppers. Christian Bale, Heath Ledger, Richard Gere, the others, all do well in their respective Dylan avatars. But the stunner is Cate Blanchett, portraying Dylan in his Brillo-haired turn at the Newport Festival when he shocked the crowd by going electric. Of all the versions of Dylan in *I'm Not There*, this is the one where the viewer loses any sense of watching an acting role. Blanchett *is* Dylan, and she indeed deserved an Oscar nod.

Are They Fantasy If They Seem to Empower Young People?

I didn't read just Robert Heinlein and Andre Norton juveniles when I was a boy. Nor Edgar Rice Burroughs. The Nancy Drew series? Loved it. The Hardy boys? Natch. I admit I stopped short at Cherry Ames, student nurse. I liked Tom Swift, along with the Zeppelin boys (yes, it was a real series). And I especially loved Howard Pease's seagoing adventures of Todd Moran, a young man who eventually became third mate of a rusty tramp steamer. They fueled the same fantasies as the later Andre Norton *Solar Queen* adventures. But I digress. One of the real sleepers of the film year was the engaging feature *Nancy Drew*, with Emma Roberts effectively cast as the ever-young detective. The film does a good balancing act, drawing back from making the girl detective as hip as, say, Veronica Mars, but not letting her fall into any kind of old-fashioned fuddy-duddy status either. Credit the crisp script by director Andrew Fleming and Tiffany Paulsen. Nancy is fun, resourceful, courageous, and above all, competent. The movie sets Nancy up to leave her childhood out there in the mythic Midwest and move with her father Carson (Tate Donovan) to L.A. where work now takes him.

So for the time being, *hasta luego* to Bess, Georgie, Ned, and the rest. The Drews are barely moved into the old house in Southern California when Nancy stumbles on clues that lure her into the long-cold case of the mysterious death of Dehlia Draycott, one-time movie queen. She proceeds to work with the mystery even as she scopes out the alien landscape of the west coast and makes friends with local kid Corky (Josh Flitter) who becomes her sometimes obnoxious assistant. The film has considerable charm. It's one of those rare family films that just about everyone can enjoy.

The world probably didn't need another reworking of Alfred Hitchcock's classic *Rear Window*, but *Disturbia* was made and released anyway This time instead of Raymond Burr playing the neighborhood's next-door killer, David Morse takes the role and makes it suitably creepy. Instead of Jimmy Stewart hobbled in a sick bed in the next house, Shia LaBeouf plays a mildly troubled teen who gets himself sentenced to home confinement with an electronic ankle bracelet. He's a bad boy, but not, of course, *that* bad. For a younger audience who wouldn't be caught dead watching a movie more than ten years old, it's an effective way to bring some of that old thriller sensibility to an appreciative new generation.

Science Fiction

Sunshine was one of the most impressive SF films of the year. It's also a terrible piece of science fiction. I suppose if one is going to create a terrific piece of film that will be both exuberantly loved and vehemently hated, the creator should be someone of immense talent and ambition. In this case, the culprit is Irish director Danny Boyle, responsible in the past for such sensational work as *Trainspotting* and *28 Days Later*. I suspect the script by Alex Garland was never intended to be scrupulously scientific. The time is the not-too-distant future, and Earth's second manned expedition is heading through space toward the sun on the good ship *Icarus*. The first ship met some mysterious but presumably disastrous fate. Here's the problem: our sun is dying. Humankind's only hope is to rekindle the solar furnace pretty much by dumping all the fissionable material left on Earth into the sputtering star. Say what? If you can get past the dubious scientific premise, you can pay attention to the spectacular cinematography and the quirky and diverse performances from the crew, an ensemble that includes the likes of Cillian Murphy, Cliff Curtis, Michelle Yeoh, Rose Byrne, and Hiroyuki Sanada. On the way, our protagonists intercept the lost ship and manage to up the odds of their mission's failure. Think of *Sunshine* ultimately as a savory blend of *2001: A Space Odyssey* and *Solaris* with a soupçon of *Alien* thrown in just for the hell of it. Don't be put off by the observation that much of the movie's real interest comes from the crew's serious speculations about life, the universe, and everything.

I didn't notice the observation in any of the reviews at the time, but the latest Billy Bob Thornton movie carries with it a very strong nostalgic fragrance of early Robert A. Heinlein. Yes, really. Remember *Rocketship Galileo*? Heinlein, a true Libertarian, felt that the pioneers of space flight ought to be brave, resourceful, entrepreneurial individuals rather than faceless governments or multinationals. Real spacemen should be guys who bring their brains and resources together in the middle of the New Mexico desert, cobble together an ingenious rocket ship, and blast off. As it happens, that's also much of the plot of *Astronaut Farmer*. The name of Billy Bob Thornton's character is Farmer, so the title *Astronaut Farmer* possesses multiple meanings. Farmer was, in fact, once a trainee astronaut but left the program when it became essential for someone to come home and take over the failing family farm. But he's never given up his dream of the stars. So with his extremely patient and long-suffering wife (Virginia Madsen) standing by, Farmer has spent years accumulating NASA junk and surplus, and welding and bolting a functional orbiter in the barn. It's no secret project. NASA and the rest of our government know that Thornton's going to attempt a blast-off, single orbit, and re-entry, and they hate the idea. So does the local law. The community is just bemused. No one wants to infringe on Farmer's rights, but no one wants to see him and his spaceship crash, explode, or burn down half the county. All in all, it's a wonderful character portrait of a true American individual, if also a trigger for memories of an era of technological optimism that really never was.

Southland Tales is pretty darned interesting, though it won't be everyone's cup of tea. It's the creation of Richard Kelly, the director of the cult sensation, *Donnie Darko*. It's also my nomination to be considered the best Philip K. Dick movie for 2007. Okay, so it's not actually a Dick film. But it *could* be. It walks, talks, acts like, sounds like, and feels like a Philip K. Dick project. Set in the near future, it's crammed with conspiracy, paranoia, amnesia, repressive corporations, political idealism and criticism, all suffusing a parched California southland teetering on the verge of social, economic, and political collapse. One might not expect it, but Dwayne "The Rock" Johnson does a marvelous job as the hero Boxer Santaros, a manipulated amnesiac action star. Sarah Michelle Gellar is also on hand to add to the paranoia. There are cameos from Wallace Shawn, Janeane Garofalo, Jon Lovitz, Seann William Scott, Mandy Moore, Amy Poehler, John Larroquette, Cheri Oteri, and even an alleged uncredited appearance by director Eli Roth as "man shot while sitting on toilet." Finally, if you need another reason to see this crazed fable of tomorrow's California, consider this: In what other movie will you see a glitzy corporate zeppelin shot down by an RPG fired from the tilted roof of an airborne ice cream truck? That touch alone should have received an awards nod.

2007 saw the third feature version of Richard Matheson's classic novel of vampirism and apocalyptic doom, *I Am Legend*. This time the filmmakers at least used Matheson's original title. (For completists, the previous film titles were *Last Man on Earth* and *The Omega Man*.) In this latest version, Will Smith stars as Dr. Robert Neville, the role previously played by, respectively, Vincent Price and Charlton Heston. We find Neville making do with his German shepherd, apparently the last survivors of the plague that doomed Manhattan. The bridges and tunnels have been bombed to ensure the quarantine, but there don't seem to be any survivors over in Brooklyn and New Jersey either. The first half of the film is absolutely terrific, with stunning vistas of an abandoned, decaying metropolis. We see great sequences where Neville and dog go hunting game for food, the prey coming from escaped Central Park Zoo deer. But there are also escaped predators from the zoo, and Neville tends to back off when large, hungry lions vie for the same prey. The second half starts to fall apart as we discover Neville's been trying to find a plague cure by experimenting on the other survivors—plague victims who have mutated into zomboid killers. Neville also gets some human companions when a small boat from Brazil carrying a woman and a young boy lands on Manhattan. It turns out Neville's been continuously broadcasting radio messages to the world. The story gets ever more melodramatic before finally crashing and burning. At that point, it definitely isn't Matheson.

The increasingly busy Shia LaBeouf starred, along with Tyrese Gibson, in the summer popcorn epic, *Transformers*, based on the toy, game, and animation franchise. LaBeouf plays a nerdy teen who unwittingly finds himself in possession of a key widget that could tip the balance of power in a centuries-old war between two rival groups of giant transformable robots. One group is, of course, benign, and the other simply wants to devastate everything. The special effects are superb. The CGI treatment of the cyber transformations is so detailed and rapid, the human eye can't truly see all the expertise that went into the process. True appreciation will probably only come to techies who watch the DVD in slo-mo. But everyone else can watch for the general noise, color, and hyperkinetic motion. This is no *Citizen Kane*, but it does the job of entertaining folks in the summer as it was designed to do. And I have to admit I got a kick out of the nice robot that transformed itself into a vintage Camaro in order to win the attention of LaBeouf's character.

Okay, so I miss Sigourney Weaver and Lance Henriksen. I even miss the Arnie of the first *Predator. Aliens vs. Predator: Requiem*, the second in this dubious jam-up of two successful SF monster franchises, sounds suspiciously like a whacked-out evening of lesser professional wrestling; something like, say *Monday Night WWF Raw*. This sequel takes up immediately after the events of the first *Alien vs. Predator*. The predators foolishly don't notice that a young alien has stowed away inside the body of the deceased leader they're taking back to the home world. The alien does its thing, the ship goes out of control, and then crashes into the mountains of Colorado where a small ski town becomes lunch for the creature. This film can be recommended only for those of you who desperately need your fix of Giger-esque creature designs.

2007's *I Am Legend* may have been the third version of Richard Matheson's novel, but *The Invasion* was the fourth version of Jack Finney's 1950s classic, *The Body Snatchers*. As you may recall, the basic plot of all the versions is that alien organisms from space are taking over the Earth by replacing each human being with a lookalike body that has all the memories and skills of the originals but boosts efficiency by possessing no emotions. Finney's original protagonist was Dr. Miles Bennell, the physician in the small town of Santa Mira, California. Now he has become a she—Carol Bennell, played by Nicole Kidman. It should be mentioned that Kidman also starred in the remake of *The Stepford Wives*. *The Invasion* is a step up. The location is changed to Washington, D.C. Kidman's husband is played by Daniel Craig, a CDC guy who's among the first on the scene when a chunk of crashed space shuttle starts infecting earthside humans with the alien organism. The essential plot of Jack Finney's novel is hard for filmmakers to screw up completely. It must be noted, though, that the bloodline tends to thin a bit with each new generational version. While it's definitely watchable, *The Invasion*'s blood is somewhat anemic compared to the best previous version.

Animation

Persepolis is, to my eye, the best animated feature of the year. It's not so much a film of the fantastic, but it's a terrifically effective work, adapted from her own graphic novel by Marjane Satrapi in collaboration with Vincent Paronnaud. This French-American production is an autobiographical coming-of-age story set during the chaotic days of the Iranian Islamic Revolution of the '80s. Chiara Mastroianni is terrific as the voice of the character Marji Satrapi. The film is richly human, poignant, and absolutely affecting.

Director Zack Snyder in collaboration with Kurt Johnstad adapted *300* from Frank Miller's graphic novel about the 300 Spartan warriors trying to hold off the Persian hordes at the narrow pass at Thermopylae in 480 B.C. The animation works well, turning Miller's paintings into realistic kinetic sculptures. Gerard Butler plays Leonidas, King of Sparta. Lena Headey is his Queen Gorgo. Everything's expectably macho, though Snyder does improve on Miller by giving female characters in the film something to do and say. As for the history, well, don't expect a History Channel documentary. Like so many films these days, *300* is visually stunning, but not terribly involving on a human level. If you want to see a funny take on this, check out a DVD of *Meet the Spartans* which includes a terrific parody of *300*, particularly a choreographed dance number with the Spartans in their brief leather outfits doing their best to morph into the Village People.

When the family leaves on holiday, the pet rat Roddy (voiced by Hugh Jackman) slips out of his cage and gets into big, big trouble when he encounters some wild rodent intruders. Then, as suggested by the title *Flushed Away*, he journeys down the plumbing into the literal London underworld. One might be so unkind as to suggest our hero reaches a *Neverwhere* destination for vermin, but the film is much kinder than that. This underground universe is full of sharp humor and clever invention, with the subterranean characters voiced by such as Kate Winslet, Ian McKellen, and Jean Reno as Le Frog.

Ratatouille, directed by Brad Bird and Jan Pinkava, is even cleverer. French country rat Remy (voiced by Patton Oswalt) isn't like the other rats. He has extraordinary senses of taste and smell, as well as a fantastic gift for the culinary arts. Through various circumstances he finds his destiny running a failing restaurant from behind the scenes, letting his front, an incompetent young French cook, have all the glory. That's all well and good until the humans fail him and Remy must call in his extended family for help. The sight of an entire kitchen being run by a gang of rats will feed the paranoia of any number of wary diners. The wit is sharp in *Ratatouille*, and the warmth is genuine.

Here's what Jerry Seinfeld's been doing in the four years since his TV series ended: making sure that *Bee Movie* got made. It's a decent film with all the bee jokes you ever imagined could be made. Young college graduate bee Barry B. Benson (voiced by Seinfeld) becomes disillusioned with his career choice (making honey) and heads off to the big city. He reaches New York City, gets in trouble, and is rescued by Manhattan florist Vanessa (voiced by Renée Zellweger). Barry discovers, to his horror, that people eat honey, so he decides to sue the human race. That's when things start to get weird.

If you like the TV series, you'll likely enjoy *The Simpsons Movie*. If the series annoys you, this feature film will probably not change your mind. All the familiar characters are on hand, along with a full measure of the customary skewed humor.

With *Shrek the Third*, that franchise about the large, green, lovable ogre continues, this time with Mike Myers's Scottish-brogued ogre going off to visit his in-laws. It's funny, but not nearly so fresh as it was in the first entry. Still, I'll go to see any Shrek movie, so long as it includes Antonio Banderas doing his turn as the suave hit-kitty, Puss in Boots.

How Fantastic Can the Small Screen Be?

So many shows; so little time. If you watched everything of a fantastical nature on cable and broadcast TV, you sadly would have no life at all. I have no life. Here's a quick gloss on just some of the offerings.

BBC America brought us *Torchwood*, spun off from *Dr. Who*. *Torchwood* is essentially a paranormal special ops group based in Cardiff, Wales, keeping track of the space-time rift beneath the city that's constantly allowing all manner of alien creatures and technology to filter through into our world. As Capt. Jack Harkness (John Barrowman), the Torchwood chief says, "The twenty-first century is when it all changes, and we've got to be ready." Think of *Torchwood* as a hybrid of *The X-Files* and *Buffy the Vampire Slayer*, but with a voice all its own. Adventure, horror, humor, pathos, it's all here. Enjoy. This one's a keeper.

Holly Hunter's new TNT series, *Saving Grace*, is also a keeper. This is an amazing seriocomic drama that comes as close as humanly possible to mainstreaming Christian programming. Hunter plays an unhappy Oklahoma cop, a dissatisfied woman who drinks, swears, and sleeps with men. Then, after a terrible accident, a redneck angel named Earl offers to save her butt. But there's a price. She has to agree to give faith a chance. She does, but grudgingly. Her struggles with her faith are a thread of dramatic tension that runs through the series. Hunter's good, and so is the supporting cast.

Pushing Daisies is the new fantasy series from the creators of the late, much lamented *Wonderfalls*. Our hero is a young man with a special power. With a single touch he can bring someone back from the dead. With a second touch he can make the resurrectees permanently dead again. He's already resurrected his childhood dog and the murdered love of his life, and he now has to learn to live without ever touching them. It sounds grim, but it's not. *Pushing Daisies* is a gentle, funny, whimsical, winning series. It's among the best fantasies of the season.

SciFi Channel adapted the graphic novel *Painkiller Jane* into a weekly series about a woman (Kristanna Loken) who can regenerate her body after any physical mishap. She's promptly recruited into an elite group of operatives whose job it is to ride herd on the neuros, people with paranormal powers and a healthy sense of evil. It's a simple, low-budget Canadian show that will give you your minimum weekly dose of melodrama.

SciFi Channel's *Flash Gordon* updated the old pulp scenario to the present, keeping the same characters, but giving them cell phones. It's passable entertainment, but perhaps a little too contemporary for the purists.

Sci-Fi Channel gave *The Dresden Files*, based on the Jim Butcher novels about Harry Dresden, a modern-day Chicago sorcerer detective for hire, a single season, then killed it. The show was succeeding in the marketplace, just not succeeding enough. It was a good adaptation and it'll be missed.

Lifetime's *Blood Ties* based on Tanya Huff's vampire novels, was a pleasant distraction. It had some horror and some romance as King Henry VIII's bastard vampire son teamed up with a female detective in contemporary Toronto. Solid entertainment.

Medium, with Patricia Arquette as a Phoenix housewife with psychic powers who helps out the local district attorney, continues to garner ratings after three years. The family relationships for Arquette, her kids, and her engineer husband continue to appeal.

Dr. Who, in whatever iteration, will no doubt live forever in the care of BBC and BBC America. David Tennant is the current avatar of the Doctor. The new series of the show are clearly higher-budgeted than the older seasons; the once bare-bones, cheesy sets now look like a much higher quality of cheese. Cybermen, Daleks, K-9—they go on forever. It can't be denied; *Dr. Who* is fun.

Battlestar Galactica is still the flagship drama of the Sci-Fi Channel, and it's still simply one of the best SF series ever made. 2007 saw its third and penultimate season, as the surviving men and women of the Colonies continued to attempt to elude their cybernetic adversaries, the Cylons, and find their way to the fabled but lost Earth. The appeal of the series is in its complexity. It's increasingly dark and gritty. The Cylons keep evolving their humanity; the humans continue to struggle with dysfunctional politics, economics, and general behavior. The show has become, Gods save us, startlingly like real drama.

Sci-Fi's *Stargate: SG-1* wound up its final season (the penalty of a show building its inventory to allow an appropriate syndication package), but the spin-off, *Stargate:*

Atlantis continues, allowing a weekly dose of tough U.S. soldiers and scientists gallivanting across the universe with their alien allies, kicking butt whenever they encounter forces of injustice.

So you're a young slacker and you discover your parents have sold your soul to the Devil. The Devil really doesn't care about your soul, but decides to employ you to work here on Earth as sort of a repo man, a guy whose job it is to track down escaped souls from Hell and return them. That's *Reaper*. It can be quite funny.

On the (Kansas) Beach

After CBS canceled *Jericho*, the post-apocalyptic drama of life in a small Kansas town after the mushroom clouds go up, a strident viewer protest brought the show new life. The new season came, the ratings didn't, and the show was again canceled. This time it looks like it'll be for good. Maybe the guy from *Pushing Daisies* could use his magic touch.

Showtime's *Dexter* adapted from Jeff Lindsey's novels about a reasonably moral and sympathetic serial killer, screened its second successful season.

Heroes, NBC's hit drama about ordinary people who develop extraordinary powers, is solidly in favored status at the network. Each new season brings new characters with new weird powers, and continued deepening of apparently interlocking conspiracies.

That's something of the same situation at *Lost* where the Oceanic Air crash survivors on the mysterious island have come a long way from the unexpected polar bears in the tropics and the invisible monster that bends trees and occasionally manifests itself as black smoke. The story arc and the plot revelations become ever more enigmatic. The producers swear that all will be revealed. We'll see.

Showtime's *Masters of Horror* lurched through its second and probably final season of twelve one-hour adaptations of known stories by known writers. It was an uneven anthology series. One episode was a Bentley Little story adapted by Richard Chizmar and Johnathon Schaech that dealt with a new family living in the Virginia suburbs, who discover that some of the founding fathers were members of a secret society that practiced cannibalism, a clandestine organization that still persists to the present day. The episode ended with one of the worst sight gags ever seen on television. On the other hand, there was a skillful and horrifyingly— but appropriately—bleak adaptation of James Tiptree, Jr.'s "The Screwfly Solution," in which aliens wishing to clean up the Earth employ a grimly efficient biological means to exterminate humankind. *Masters of Horror* was a brave attempt, but the tide seems to be inexorably opposed to anthology series. Bless producer/director Mick Garris for trying.

Masters of Science Fiction, the SF companion series to *Masters of Horror* never screened on its home channel, Showtime. Instead, a mere four dramas were broadcast at 9 P.M. Saturday nights on ABC. Adaptations for these one-hour dramas included stories by Robert A. Heinlein, John Kessel, Howard Fast, and Harlan Ellison. Nine at night on Saturday means death for any new show. Even so, ratings for series were rising throughout the month's episodes, climaxing with Ellison's "The Discarded."

Best Commercial of the Fantastic

Actually there are quite a few candidates from which to draw. Fantasy, SF, horror, they all furnish tropes that Madison Avenue seems only too happy to latch onto.

Finally I had to choose from the standpoint of both aesthetics and consumer considerations. And the winner is : . . the beer company's spot for Heineken's Draught Keg. This is the commercial featuring a serenely manic young woman who reveals additional cybernetic arms and discloses the keg hidden behind the shining steel panel in her abdomen. The cyborg animation, the music, and choreography all make for a sublime SF moment.

Playing with the Fantastic

Whether from Toys "R" Us or the fast food franchises, there was no lack for film tie-in toys in 2007. I finally had to choose the set of three toys from *The Golden Compass* made by Corgi. For a total of about $35, you can get the Magisterial sky ship, the steam taxi, and Lee Scoresby's aeronaut balloon, along with some character miniatures. The pieces are exquisitely detailed and are produced in full color. I wish the airships could fly, but one can't have everything.

Fantasy in Comics
and Graphic Novels: 2007

Jeff VanderMeer

For fantasy, the year 2007 was defined and made timeless by one graphic novel: Shaun Tan's *The Arrival* (Arthur A. Levine Books). Wordless yet containing worlds, *The Arrival* demonstrates the power of fantasy to show us our reality. It is also an example of the rare book that feels full and complete without conventional conflict and conflict resolution.

The story is simple: an immigrant arrives in a strange city and tries to make a life for himself so that one day he can send for his family. He encounters strange fantastical creatures that are as natural as breakfast, lunch, and dinner to the native inhabitants. He learns the stories of other immigrants who have come to the city. At the end, he is reunited with his family.

I'm giving nothing away by summarizing the plot because it is, as I've said, simple. The complexity and the richness of *The Arrival* come entirely from the painstaking and effortless execution of the central idea, using a myriad of panels that, mostly in warm sepia tones, convey not just movement but *the moment*.

One page is just small, square images of cloud formations. Another page is a panoramic bleed of an obelisk-and-symbol-strewn surreal city with vaguely birdlike iconography. But everywhere, in every type of panel, Tan has managed to convey a wealth of motion—the bustle and lively anarchy of urban life—while also conveying a profound and steadying silence and stillness. Tan's commitment to an art style that can accommodate these two extremes simultaneously explains the most odds-defying success of the book: that it seems static but is actually dynamic, that it is very personal and yet it has grandeur.

This dynamism wedded to depth seems to come from character. Even though the nameless immigrant appears in the panels rather than looking into them, I felt that the sturdy brilliance in Tan's style was a reflection of the strength of the character. True, we *see* the immigrant acting in a solid, honorable way as he tries to become comfortable with the strange, but it's also the warmth and texture of the images that conveys this about him.

. . . And yet, the city is truly *strange*, filled with odd metamorphosing creatures and bizarre buildings—even if, like all immigrants, the man eventually becomes so accustomed to them that they melt into the background, as familiar to him as an ATM machine, a cell phone, an automatic door is to us. Nothing in the warmth of the style can ever disguise the alienness of the grotesquely playful beast shown on the front cover of *The Arrival*. I only have to imagine what it would look like in real life to know that. Yes, this grotesquery works on a symbolic level, showing how foreign the city looks to a newcomer, but it is also highly effective as fantasy. You tend to believe in the world you are shown, and you believe, too, that it has hidden vistas and a purpose and causality.

I have not yet mentioned grace notes. This book is full of them, none quite so moving as the dozens of immigrant faces drawn on the inside boards and endpapers. These faces stare out at the reader with a luminous intensity and an undeniable wisdom of experience. They are often still visible in glimpses as you turn the pages. I've never been surer I was reading a classic than in experiencing *The Arrival*.

Major Books of the Year

Although everyone's idea of what constitutes a major publishing event will be different, I found six books that, in very different ways, define the contribution of fantasy to the comics field in 2007.

Alice in Sunderland by Bryan Talbot (Dark Horse Comics) is a truly stunning accomplishment. Talbot's heady collage of fantasy and reality is a modern classic of the graphic novel form. Relating the history of the city of Sunderland, Talbot meditates on history as it intersects with the personal and with myth. A plethora of drawing styles is nicely linked by the framing narrative, and the insertion of characters from *Alice in Wonderland* works extremely well. What I like best about this welter of ideas and images is the questing, searching aspect of it. Even when Talbot is relating historical fact, it's used not as a tool to lecture, but a way of opening up the reader's mind to an array of fascinating ideas. It's one of the few cases where the overwhelming complexity and cross-pollination of thought in a graphic novel context becomes, at times, almost wearying. That such a book now exists in the world suggests that comics have begun to realize their full intellectual potential.

Flight 4, edited by Kazu Kibuishi (Villard), might just be the best in the series to date. It opens with a tour de force by Michel Gagne, "The Saga of Rex," about a horned mammal critter that goes on an incredible adventure. The set pieces are muscular in both the visual and storytelling sense. The fluidity, sense of play, and imagination exhibited by Gagne get *Flight 4* off to a champagne-cork-popping start. The second comic, Amy Kim Ganter's "Food from the Sea," about a seaside community's predilection for one type of seafood over another, has a marvelously grotesque depiction of the seafood in question, and a story that generally holds together despite a couple of clunky bits.

From there, the anthology proceeds from strength to strength, reflecting a much greater diversity of art styles and storylines than volume 3. It's hard to know where to begin in praising this volume, or what to highlight, I enjoyed it all so much. Neil Babra's "The Blue Guitar," with its ragged, swooping panels and lyrical style, delighted me. "Igloo Head and Tree Head" by Scott Campbell has the kind of absurdist imagination behind it that exhibits an unholy originality, coupled to a deliberately "hand-made"-looking art style that provides just the right amount of whimsy. Even better is "The Story of Binny" by Lark Pien, in which a boy finds a strange talking animal that gradually manipulates him into worse and worse situations. The deconstruction of the usual cute mammal tale into something more sinister works marvelously well. Highly recommended for anyone who loves the kind of seamless sense of play that distinguishes the great from the merely good.

Out, out damn blot, but it won't come out—it just keeps growing. That's something of the premise behind *the blot* by Tom Neely (iwilldestroyyou.com), one of the most bizarre and original graphic novels I've ever read. In a crisp, clean, yet utterly surreal drawing style, Neely depicts the odd adventures of an Average Joe whose face is periodically ravaged by a giant ink blot. The man tries to escape the blot, control the blot, even meets a woman who helps him understand the blot. A giant black wolf attacks the man and woman. A suffocating froth of black blot comes out of the man's mouth. Throughout the narrative Neely uses, at most, five words. The story is all conveyed through the sometimes stark but always dynamic art. Black-and-white panels are supplemented with limited use of spot-color to accentuate an emotion. What starts out as semi-humorous and absurdist gains depth and poignancy. A luminous quality, a quality of something pulled whole out of the subconscious, permeates the latter portions of *the blot*. This quality is accentuated because the characters have been drawn in what I'd call a classic comics style, so when they are naked, when they are vulnerable, when the narrative opens up into a kind of surreal psychological portrait, it's that much more effective. It's as if Popeye suddenly had an existential crisis, and stood revealed as a three-dimensional person. Days after reading *the blot*, I was still thinking about it.

In *Essex County Volume I: Tales from the Farm* (Top Shelf Productions), a heartfelt and beautifully sparse tale of an orphaned ten-year-old named Lester, Jeff Lemire uses an illustration style that perfectly captures the wide open spaces of rural Ontario. After Lester's mother dies, he's sent to live on his uncle's farm. He hardly knows his uncle and his father has long since left the scene. Lester forms a friendship with a gas station attendant named Jimmy Lebeuf who used to be a professional hockey player until a bad hit knocked him out of the game. Together, the two comics fans build a rich fantasy life revolving around the possibility of an alien invasion. Another section, showing pages from Lester's own home-made comic book, is imaginative and funny. The book has four parts, corresponding to the four seasons, beginning with winter. If there wasn't a word spoken in this understated and genuinely moving tale, readers would still appreciate the strength and offhand precision of Lemire's landscapes. From fields to farm equipment to the simple shapes of a gas station, Lemire manages to find the essence of each object and somehow give it an emphasis that makes you see it with fresh eyes. *Tales from the Farm* often has the same effect as the best black-and-white photography: making you focus on what matters.

Regards from Serbia by Aleksandar Zograf (Top Shelf) recounts living through the horrors of Yugoslavia's disintegration and civil war. Throughout the book, you find yourself engaging in uncomfortable laughter, because Zograf fully grasps the awful absurdity of the human condition during wartime. Aiding this effort is his bold yet fluid line work and his willingness to include fantastical elements and portents that capture psychological truths about the situation. Zograf is also able to draw realistic scenes and yet include within them strangeness and exaggeration, all while remaining causal and consistent. Most important, perhaps, these vignettes, observations, and stories give a more complex and perhaps ultimately more horrific view of the conflict than a documentary. Perhaps this is simply because there are fewer constraints on a cartoonist. Perhaps it's because if we were to see video or actual photographs documenting Yugoslavia's disintegration we would have no distance from the horror. And by horror I mean not just the overarching horror of bloodshed and tor-ment, but the day-to-day stress and struggle of people caught in the crossfire who try to find some way of not only living but of having a normal life of sorts. Regardless, Zograf has done an excellent job of personalizing the experience, but, more impor-tant, making it universal—in a way that links the real world to the fantastical.

Finally, *Wormwood, Gentleman Corpse: Birds, Bees, Blood, and Beer* by Ben Tem-plesmith (IDW Publishing) luxuriates in its Lovecraft/Decadent origins. Temple-smith's witty and hallucinogenic Wormwood (indeed a gentleman corpse) hangs out with a ghost cop and battles tentacular horrors that tend to assail him fungally in bars and other shady places. Even the most horrific of supernatural scenes is leav-ened with humor, while the art and coloring are phantasmagorical in the best sense. Anyone who appreciates the cool appeal of squidly assailants and mushroom mon-strosities will appreciate this anti-Wonderland noir funhouse of a book. This first volume collects the initial four issues of the comic, as well as a number of amazing sketches and full-page paintings.

Other Worthy Comics

In 2007, high quality and diversity typified the many fantasy offerings.

Artesia 3: Afire by Mark S. Smylie (Archaia Studio Press) exemplifies the best of intelligent heroic fantasy, featuring a heroine who is brainy, fierce, and passionate. This latest collection offers an exceedingly high standard of storytelling, weaving to-gether battle sequences, court intrigue, and the supernatural. I have to admit when I started reading the Artesia books I didn't know what to expect, but I was quickly drawn in to this top-notch series.

The surreal *Bookhunter* by Jason Shiga (Sparkplug Comics), set in the 1970s, ap-plies the high-energy impact of a big budget Hollywood thriller to a story about the theft of a rare book from a library. This genius meshing of high-concept with low-key setting results in a funny romp, with Shiga taking the idea as far as it can go. A per-fect prologue, in which a book thief is tracked down by the Library Police and shot before he can put the hostage books to the torch, lets readers know they're not in Realityville anymore. What follows is a meticulous and exciting investigation of the disappearance of a rare book from the Oakland Public Library. It's quite an achieve-ment to make the examination of a card catalogue pulse-pounding. Shiga invests the details of book creation, collecting, and preservation with an urgency and fascina-tion that defies description. A bold, broad illustration style in sepia tones both evokes the 1970s and invests the action scenes with extra power.

The Boys (Volume One: The Name of the Game) by Garth Ennis and Darich Robertson (Dynamite Entertainment) might be a guilty pleasure, but it's actually a pretty highbrow one. Taking as their basic premise that some superheroes are too ar-rogant or predator-like to be allowed to conduct business unimpeded, Ennis and Robertson have postulated a CIA-backed team that counteracts thoughtless and pre-meditated abuse by the wearers of spandex. In this first story cycle, the team takes on a group of younger superheroes who are living a lifestyle close to that of Caligula. The level of violence, sex, and everything else is turned up to "11" in *The Boys*, but I say it's highbrow for one simple reason: Ennis and Robertson have really thought about the concept and fleshed it out to its maximum potential. The excesses here serve the plot and the context of the world they've created to house that plot. The bold, in-your-face art style helps accentuate those excesses. I don't know if I'm just odd for liking something like *the blot* (mentioned above) and something like *The*

Boys, but there it is, folks. Apparently I can hold two opposite and opposing thoughts in my mind at the same time without my skull exploding.

Moomin: Book 2 by Tove Jansson (Drawn & Quarterly Press) continues the valuable process of reissuing Tove Jansson's Moomin comic strips in graphic novel form. It's a beautiful oversized book featuring the antics of the hippo-like Moomin and his family. From dealing with obnoxious neighbors to doing ridiculous things for love, the Moomin family's adventures are funny, surreal, sometimes melancholy, and always richly whimsical. In less skilled hands, this would be fodder for sticking one's finger down one's throat in revulsion at the treacly whimsy of it all. However, Tove Jansson was a pragmatist and also, if her work is any indication, a wise person. Beneath the gentle surface of *Moomin* there is a sly, wicked wit and much trenchant commentary about the world and people's place in it. As Neil Gaiman says, "A lost treasure now rediscovered—one of the sweetest, strangest comics strips ever drawn or written. A surrealist masterpiece. Honest." This second volume is just as great as the first.

The Nightmare Factory: Based on the Stories of Thomas Ligotti, Various Creators (Fox Atomic Comics) acknowledges that Thomas Ligotti might be one of our best supernatural fiction writers. It's exciting to see some of his classic stories rendered in comics form by a host of amazing artists. Chief among these creators is Ben Templesmith, the marvelous artist behind *30 Days of Night* and *Wormwood: Gentleman Corpse*. This title seems to have fallen under most readers' radar, but is still available and highly recommended.

Set one hundred years after a worldwide catastrophe called The Big Wet, *Wasteland Book 1: Cities in Dust* by Antony Johnston and Christopher Mitten (Oni Press) follows the adventures of Michael, a desert scavenger. And strange adventures they are—action-packed but also at times contemplative, with all kinds of secrets for readers to discover. It's not just about surviving in a bleak landscape—there are multiple layers to this comic, and multiple mysteries. The drawing style is stark and evocative, with Johnston's writing bringing depth and excitement. Despite being set in the future, *Wastelands* is basically quest fantasy.

Mouse Guard: Fall 1152 by David Petersen (Archaia Studios Press) is a sumptuous hardcover collection of Petersen's lovingly illustrated Mouse Guard comics. For decades, the vaunted Mouse Guard has protected its citizens from external threats. But now they must deal with treachery, war, and even giant (to them) crabs. An extraordinary attention to detail defines the art, while the storyline is exciting and classic, with betrayal, intrigue, and several reversals of fortune. Readers will be left wanting even more Mouse Guard adventures.

Death by Chocolate: Redux by David Yurkovich (Top Shelf) is the story of an unlikely superhero, who, due to a freak accident, is made of chocolate, both sending up the superhero genre and paying tribute to it. Agent Swete, a member of the FBI's Food Crimes Division, is uniquely qualified to investigate bizarre, food-related mysteries. In this edition, readers get new material that tells the tale of how Agent Swete became the chocolate avenger. There is also an essay by the creator, and Yurkovich has re-mastered every page of this unique series.

Sardine in Outer Space, Vols. 3 and 4, by Emmanuel Gnibert and Joann Sfar, (First Second) is brawling, sprawling, silly, bursting with color, and highly imaginative, giving two French geniuses, Gnibert and Sfar, carte blanche to create a classic pirate adventure. Featuring Captain Yellow Shoulder, Little Louie, Doc Krok the Mad Scientist, Supermusclesman (chief executive dictator of the universe), and, of course, Sardine and her little black cat-creature, the series has given readers the shivery delights of flesh-eating tattoos, kidnapped suns, a space boxing championship, intergalactic yogurt thieves, and a space Santa Claus. The sense of play involved isn't as ironic or in-jokey as something like Futurama, and in many ways that's a relief. We're left to root for Sardine as she falls in and out of danger due mostly to the shenanigans of Doc Krok and the aforementioned Supermusclesman. In volume four, space leeches, cosmic squid, and talking clouds come into play, making for a grand finale indeed. Rest assured for those who prefer fantasy to SF, there's nothing particularly futuristic about Sardine. It's pure make-believe with a level of invention that kids and their parents alike can savor.

The Secret History, Book One: Genesis and Book Two: Castle of the Djinns by Jean-Pierre Pecau, Igor Kordey, and Carole Beau (Archaia Studios Press) extrapolate from what we know about the ancient world to create a riveting storyline based on rune stones—a magic possibly responsible for plague, division, and war. The series as a whole works off the idea that unseen forces have shaped the fate of Western civilization. Truly mind-blowing in scope, the Secret History will eventually cover Rome, Napoleon, and World War II. Fans of clandestine plots, alternate history, action-adventure, fantasy, and intricately detailed art will all enjoy this series.

Although not as complex as previous offerings in the series, Dungeon, Parade, Vol. 2: Day of the Toads by Joann Sfar, Lewis Trondheim, and Manu Larcenet (Nantier Beall Minoustchine) continues the English translation of the ultimate sword-and-sorcery adventure. Dungeon parodies heroic fantasy in hilarious fashion while also offering exciting battle scenes, deep and interesting characters, and fun plots.

Korgi: Book 1 by Christian Slade (Top Shelf) seems like another timeless classic in the making, with the feel of a kinder, gentler Maurice Sendak. It features a girl and her korgi (or "corgi" if you prefer that spelling) having a series of fantastical adventures, overcoming trolls and other beasties. The korgis in this book are also fantastical, with their own community in the trees. The illustration in this wordless tale is exceptional, with almost the quality of etchings. I'm not really that susceptible to the "cute" factor, but I have to say I fell for this book hook, line, and sinker. It's a great gift for kids or adults.

The Professor's Daughter by Joann Sfar and Emmanuel Gnibert (First Second) relates the adventures in London of a Victorian girl who discovers a mummy. Slapstick and follies ensue. Pleasant and deftly illustrated, light but satisfying fare.

In stark contrast, Micrographica by Renee French (Top Shelf), first published on the Internet, is subversive and disturbing fantasy about a mob of tiny rodents and the corpse they call continent. Darkly funny and original, this small book should not be read around dinner time.

Scarlet Traces: The Great Game by Ian Edginton and D'Israeli (Dark Horse Comics) is a superior example of "alternate-alternate history" fantasy that riffs off H.G. Wells's The War of the Worlds by supposing that Great Britain has adapted Martian technology in the wake of the aliens' defeat. In this installment, the Brits have been waging war on Mars for decades while hiding a terrible secret from their citizens. Intrepid photojournalist Charlotte Hemming travels to Mars, only to find that the British military are preparing a horrific solution to end the war. A dynamic, bright color scheme and eccentric approaches to portraying Martian technology nicely complement the exciting storyline.

B.P.R.D.: The Universal Machine by Mike Mignola, John Arcudi, and Guy Davis (Dark Horse) provides a sequel to last year's The Black Flame (in which whole cities were destroyed by a Lovecraftian monster). The Bureau for Paranormal Research and Defense is trying to find a cure for the "death" of their homunculus, Roger. That path leads Dr. Kate Corrigan to some rather shady parts of France, including the magically re-created castle of a long-dead marquis who isn't as inanimate as one would hope. Cabinets of curiosities and horrors play a large role in Dr. Corrigan's genuinely suspenseful adventures, all rendered in the blocky yet evocative style developed by Mignola.

Robotika by Alex Sheikman and Joel Jason O'Chun (Archaia Studios Press) uses sleek, ultra-violent color to create a fantasy set in the future. Imperfect cyborgs square off against imperfect humans in elaborate and hyper-real duels. A distinctly Asian aesthetic permeates the panels, and a generous use of space deliberately contradicts the usual clutter of action scenes in comics. The "future" cities are depicted as fancifully as anything in *Alice in Wonderland.* Anyone attempting to read *Robotika* as science fiction will be disappointed. Fantasy lovers, however, will glut themselves on the visuals.

Skyscrapers of the Midwest 4 by Joshua Cotter (AdHouse Books) continues the series' surreal trek into fantasy land with bizarre monsters, strange treks into deep forest, and creepy little cyborgs. Trying to describe this mixture of odd elements is almost as weird as experiencing it yourself.

Therefore Repent! by Jim Munroe and Salgood Sam (IDW Publishing) is the first foray into graphic novels by the indie innovator Jim Munroe, with able assistance from the illustrator. It features a war with angels, bird-headed men, and, after a Rapture-like catastrophe, the appearance of magic on Earth. The main characters, Raven and Mummy, must navigate this new world while also dealing with more personal issues. The art is extraordinarily fluid and the storyline ingenious and sharply intelligent.

Age of Bronze 3: Betrayal, Part One by Eric Shanower (Image Comics) continues one man's quest to detail all of Ancient History's greatest legends in comics form. *Age of Bronze: Betrayal* presents a complex, fascinating view of the Trojan War. You'll find all of your old favorites, like Achilles, Odysseus, and Helen, in Shanower's version, rendered in detailed, etching-like black-and-white illustrations. What strikes me as most impressive is that the story seems so effortless, despite its labyrinthine plot twists. The list of character names and descriptions, along with a copious bibliography of research materials, demonstrates how difficult it must have been to create such a seamless vision.

This is the first time I've read *Battle Royale* by Koushun Takami and Masayuki Taguchi, now in an Ultimate Edition hardcover from Tokyopop. Collecting the first three volumes, this stunning compilation is a blood-splattering kinetic adrenaline rush of a read—so much so that even as I was wincing at times from the extreme situations, I couldn't stop turning the pages.

As a latecomer to this series, I'm sure there's nothing much original that I can say about *Battle Royale,* except that it displays the same kind of consummate understanding of the storyteller's art as a movie series like *Saw.* (In fact, *Battle Royale* is a bit like a combination of *Saw, Survivor,* and *Lost,* with more bloodshed.) Yes, there is extreme violence, but there's also a skillful back-and-forth between past and present, a real brutality at the level of narrative that has to be admired, as the creators continually raise the stakes without compromising their stark vision. You have to respect that commitment to raising a B-movie premise to hyper-real brilliance through sheer bloody-minded power of will. Also, whether intentional or not, it's genius to wed the melodramatic situation to the melodrama that is being a teenager. In theory, this might have led to the whole series being one long shriek, but the two things tend to complement one another. I really enjoyed *Battle Royale*, and appreciated the chance to first experience it in this deluxe hardcover.

WarCraft: The Sunwell Trilogy (Ultimate Edition) by Richard A. Knaak and Jae-Hwan Kim (Tokyopop) will allow fans of the related game to revel in a sumptuous oversized book, which contains an eight-page, full-color prologue by the author, illustrated by Kim, a color art gallery, an artist's sketchbook, an afterword, a full-color unbound pin-up, and an Upper Deck World of WarCraft trading card. Oh, yes, and it also includes hundreds of pages of epic fantasy adventure with wonderful evocations of dragons.

I'm late in finding *Blurred Vision #1* and *#2* by various artists and Kevin Mutch and Alex Rader (Blurred Books) but I'm glad I found them, along with another offering from Blurred Books, *The Unbearable Cuteness of Being* by Ken Brown. Mix your Dada with your Surrealism and give it all a modern updating and you have an idea of all three of these titles. The Blurred Vision series combines all kinds of styles and approaches, often in a hallucinatory way. "Transgressive" is a word that also comes to mind. *The Unbearable Cuteness of Being* consists of odd color collages that come across as updated Max Ernst. For trippy and cool, you could do a lot worse than pick up any of these volumes.

Inexplicable yet worth noting since it comes to readers from the creator of the critically acclaimed *Box Office Poison*, *Lower Regions* by Alex Robinson takes place in a dungeon and features D&D-type creatures fighting one another.

Finally, brilliant French creator Michel Gagne released *Zed No. 8: Brotherhood of Metal* (available from www.ZEDcomic.com). If you don't know by now, Zed's a space alien who gets into trouble/has adventures that seem whimsical enough due to his cute nature, but some really strange things happen in these comics. In this case, there's an invasion by a space fleet, rendered in Gagne's lovely art style. Odd, beautiful, and fun.

Zed is also wordless, and thus we end as we began with *The Arrival*: with the purest form of comics, conveying emotion through image, conjuring fantasy out of colors and lines on a page. Thanks for letting me share some of my enthusiasms from 2007.

Thanks for information, opinions, and advice during the creation of this year's summation to: Andrew Wheeler who will be writing this summation starting next year (and will do a superb job); and creator Chris Reilly.

Music of the Fantastic: 2007

Charles de Lint

My album of the year is Calexico's *Tool Box* (self-released). Calexico is one of those savvy bands who usually tour with a self-produced album that's only available at their shows. If they have copies left over, they go up for sale on their Web site (check www.casadecalexico.com/index.php to see if it's still available).

Tool Box might seem an odd choice for my favorite given that it appears to be a collection of instrumental outtakes from their last studio album, but it has a surprising cohesiveness and I've yet to get tired of it after weekly plays throughout the year. It's like the soundtrack to a desert landscape with more Mariachi horn, pedal steel and nylon-string guitar flourishes than were on *Garden Ruin*, their last studio album. And Convertino's drumming really shines.

Mind you, I could be completely off-base and the music might be all new material recorded specifically for this album. It doesn't really matter. What matters is that it sounds terrific and I can't stop playing it.

And speaking of tour-only CDs, Howe Gelb, one-time cohort of the duo at the heart of Calexico, also has one: *Upside Down Home 2007: Return to San Pedro* (self-produced). It's a stripped-down affair, mostly just guitar and that world-weary voice, but it should still appeal to all you fans of Giant Sand, The Friends of Dean Martinez, The Band of Blacky Ranchette, and the like.

There have been a lot of young, fresh-faced female singer/songwriters coming out of the U.K. of late—Adele, Laura Marling, Duffy, Kate Walsh, Kate Nash—each creating a bit of a buzz, and some, like Duffy, topping the charts.

I didn't hear quite as much about Scotland's Amy MacDonald, but her debut *This Is the Life* (Mercury Records), is the one disc out of all of them that really did it for me: smart songs, gorgeous voice with that soft burr of an accent, terrific production. I love her original songs, but having been given the taste of her covering Dougie MacLean's "Caledonia" as the album's hidden track, I'd really like to hear her do an album of traditional Scots songs.

But whether she's doing her own material, or covering a Neil Diamond song as she did on a recent U.K. TV performance, what makes her performance such a stand-out is how completely she inhabits the song, then delivers it with complete conviction.

What do you get when you mash together traditional fiddler and singer Eliza Carthy, singer/songwriter/activist Billy Bragg, experimental folk acts like Tunng and Benjamin Zephaniah, Indian singer Sheila Chandra, DJ/beatboxers Transglobal Underground, village dance band Tiger Moth, and more? Not some lame world fusion experiment. Nor is this just some tired compilation album as the credits might make it seem.

No, you get The Imagined Village with their self-titled album (Real World), a mix of traditional and original songs and tunes, their English flavor spiced with twenty-first-century innovation. From the spoken word start to the raucous dance finale, there's not a moment out of place on the album. Don't stick this in your iPod and wait for a song to come up on the shuffle. This is an album that will reward you more when it's played through as a whole. It's one of the most defining traditional British albums since Fairport Convention's *Liege & Leaf* in 1969, with a fabulous reinvention of "Tam Lin" (a song that was a centerpiece of that seminal album).

And speaking of Billy Bragg, while working on his new album, he also found time to write a book, *The Progressive Patriot* (Bantam Press), that examines the symbolism of Britain and explores the idea of what it means to be British in a multicultural society. It's brilliant stuff, available in paperback from Black Swan. He also recorded a bit of a tribute to his old mates Joe Strummer and the Clash under the name Johnny Clash: a seven-inch vinyl single "Old Clash Fight Song"/"The Big Lie" for Jail Guitar Doors, an organization that's trying to provide musical instruments to help with the rehabilitation of U.K. prison inmates.

And speaking of Joe Strummer, his director and long-time friend Julien Temple has made one of the best documentaries I've seen in ages. *The Future Is Unwritten* tells Strummer's story, warts and all, and the brilliant soundtrack (with spoken word snippets from Strummer's old radio show) is available from Epic Records. The film's on DVD, but only in the U.K. as I write this.

Lastly, from the American side of the ocean, you really need to check out Eilen Jewell's *Letters from Sinners & Strangers* (Signature Sounds). For touchstones, think of a mix of Gillian Welch and Lucinda Williams, with a little Madeleine Peyroux and a bit of Hot Club to jazz it up. The album's a mix of originals and covers, sung in a dustbowl weary voice that still has a sparkle of hope in it. There's not a bad track on the album, but the standout for me was her reinvention of Eric Anderson's "Dusty Box Car Wall" that I was sure was some old traditional piece until I checked the credits.

I've been listening to a lot of older music this year: surf, hot rod & rockabilly, '60s girl groups, '30s and '40s hillbilly and country, and punk/garage music from the mid-seventies. This probably explains why I continue to be entranced with XFM's *Theme Time Radio Hour with Your Host Bob Dylan*, because where else can you hear all that and more on a weekly radio show?

·If you don't get XFM, the shows usually show up on the Internet and you can listen to them there.

Celtic/British folk

Kathryn Tickell obviously keeps busy since she gave us yet another new album this year. *Instrumental* (Park) is, as the title implies, a collection of traditional and original instrumental music with Tickell shining on her Northumbrian pipes and fiddle. I'm always delighted with how fresh she and her band sound. Though she's risen to great heights on previous albums, this might well be her best one yet.

There's nothing graceless about Kate Rusby's *Awkward Annie* (Pure Records). She might have had to make the album under difficult circumstances that included a breakup with her husband/producer, but it's hard to fault her first outing in the producer's chair. From a Kinks cover and a mix of traditional and original songs, the new album's as good as any she's made and solidifies her position as one of the best voices on the U.K. traditional scene, though June Tabor will always give her a run for her money. Tabor's mature and stately vocals on *Apples* (Topic) are a highlight of a career that spans over thirty years now.

And if women from the U.K. singing traditional music is your thing, you should also check out *Cuilidh* by Julie Fowlis (Spit & Polish), Rachel Unthank & the Winterset's *Bairns* (EMI), and *Fairest Floo'er* by Karine Polwart (Hegri/Proper).

Kevin Burke has been in more of the best duos and bands than I could possibly list here, but the one thing that always shines through is the tone of his fiddle. He plays with such easy grace that you don't quite realize the drive his music has until you try to play along. This year he teamed up with Cal Scott for *Across the Black River* (Loftus) and if you have to ask if it's any good, then you haven't been paying attention to Celtic music for the past twenty-five years or so. Pretty much any Irish sessions you go to anywhere in the world still play tune sets popularized by his old group, The Bothy Band.

Burke also shows up as a member of Patrick Street with a new album called *On the Fly* (Loftus).

Some other fine fiddle albums released this year (and highly recommended for the great playing and their avoidance of the same old/same old) include Nerea's *Footprints* (www.nereathefiddler.com) which earned her a Canadian Folk Music Award nomination for Young Performer of the Year, *A Letter Home* by Athena Tergis (Compass Records), Oliver Schroer's *Hymns and Hers* (www.oliverschroer.com), *In the Moment* by Alasdair Fraser and Natalie Haas (Culburnie Records), and Aly Bain and Ale Möller's *Beyond the Stacks* (Whirlie).

After breaking a silence of too many years, Loreena McKennitt put out a new album last year. This year she gives us the chance to revisit the tour she did for that disc with a new DVD/2 CD combo, *Nights from the Alhambra* (Verve/Quinlan Road) proving she's just as good live as she is in the studio.

And if you want more music along this vein, but with a bit of a different flavor, try *Verticordia* by Ariel (Ariel Rose Music — Google that with MySpace to get her page).

It's not all solo artists, of course. Some great band albums were also released such as Beoga's *A Lovely Madness* (Compass Records). Don't be put off by the fact the band is driven by two button accordion players; this is a killer album. Dàimh are sort of like a Scottish Lúnasa only with Gaelic vocals, but they too believe that acoustic instruments don't need to be amped up to deliver. Their CD is called *Crossing Point* (Greentrax).

Lastly a couple of stalwarts. Gráda moved away from traditional music with their new album *Cloudy Day Navigation* (Compass Records), proving they write as well as they play. The album comes with a bonus DVD featuring a live show in Dublin. And the venerable Battlefield Band are back with *Dookin'* (Temple Records), sounding just as fresh and lively as they did some twenty-five years or so ago.

Americana

Because Brock Zeman lives near me, I get to see him in concert a lot. His shows are invariably great, but what always surprises me is how many new songs he throws into the mix. He's always writing. Because of my familiarity with his music, I'm probably more critical of his songwriting than I'd be with someone I only see once a year when they're passing through town, but the thing is, the songs are always good. Not just good, they're great.

Think I'm exaggerating? Then check out his recent collaboration with Dan Walsh (one of the great accompanists, here on guitars and dobro), *The Bourbon Sessions* (Busted Flat Records), and see what I mean. It's a stripped down affair, mostly just the two of them with a little help from Walsh's wife LeeAnne Wesseling on vocals and Joel Williams. In a situation such as that, if the songs don't stand up, it shows. But there's not a bad track on the album.

Frankly, the more I hear Zeman, the more I realize that he's pretty much my favorite living songwriter. And if you're digging Walsh's accompaniments, he's all over David Essig and Romi Mayes's *Beverley Street* (Dollartone Records) which also features Winnipeg's The D. Rangers.

I don't know that Steve Earle will ever put out as good an album as 1997's *El Corazón*. It's not that he hasn't put out some great albums since then, it's just that one has a taste of everything I like best about his work, but as varied as the material is, it still seems to have a narrative flow. Having said that, his new love song to New York City and his wife Allison Moorer, *Washington Square Serenade* (New West Records), comes pretty damn close.

Ian Tamblyn's *Superior: Spirit and Light* (North Track Records) is the first in a series of albums that centers around various landscapes. First up is a look at Lake Superior, with songs dating back as far as Tamblyn's 1976 debut ("Northern Journey"). But the songs as presented here are all re-recorded, and in some cases reinvented, with the new arrangements giving the project a distinctive and consistent voice.

On paper it shouldn't work: hard rock bluesman Robert Plant collaborating with sweet-voiced bluegrass fiddler Alison Krauss on *Raising Sand* (Rounder). But maybe it shouldn't be so surprising that it does. Plant has a long history of working with indigenous musicians from other cultures, so why not a visit to Americana? And I remember reading somewhere that Krauss and her band listen to AC/DC, Led Zeppelin and the like in their tour bus. But the real proof is in the music, and this disc just shines with a roots groove that draws on both their strengths.

The Americana section of this essay is always the hardest to write, mostly because I have easy access to so much more of it through radio, friends, etc. than I do the music from other parts of the world. How do I break it down to just a few artists when so much of it isn't simply good, but excellent? Anyone who says there isn't any good music anymore just isn't paying attention. And do I really need to tell you about new releases by Bruce Springsteen, Lyle Lovett, and the like?

So I'm just going to name check a few lesser well-known artists and urge you to investigate further on your own, using the sources listed at the end of the essay as a jumping off point.

The Sky About to Rain is one of those bands that's actually just one person, in this case, Martyn Lee, based in the U.K., though after listening to *The Prison Notebooks* (www.cdbaby.com) you'd be forgiven for thinking he lived somewhere in the

Arizona desert. Ryan Bingham is from the American south (Texas, to be specific). His current release *Mescalito* (Lost Highway) is a raspy-voiced trip down some old highway, passing rundown truck stops with a slide guitar punctuating the throaty murmur of the car's engine.

Rising Appalachia's second album *Scale Down* (Unwound Records) takes us into the Appalachian Mountains with banjos, fiddles, and two-part harmonies riding an infectious and driving groove rhythm. Donna Hughes offers more traditional fare on her *Gaining Wisdom* (Rounder Records) with help from guests like Rhonda Vincent and Sam Bush, splitting the material between driving bluegrass rhythms and more introspective cuts.

Colleen Duffy performs under the name Devil Doll and calls herself a punk rock torch singer. You might want to add rockabilly to the description, but no matter what you call it, *The Return of Eve* (Lucky Bluebird Records) is a rocking follow-up to *Queen of Pain*.

While you're waiting for the next Fred Eaglesmith disc, you might want to check out Cliff Wagner & the Old No. 7's flavor of bluegrass on *My Native Land* (Wagco Records). Or if you want something that rocks just a little harder, slip a copy of The Steeldrivers's self-titled debut (Rounder) into the player and settle into its bluegrass meets Delta soul groove.

But sometimes, you don't want to hear about the good things in life. You'd rather commiserate with someone who knows the pain of living. For the real deal you can't do better than any of Mary Gauthier's albums. This year's release is called *Between Daylight and Dark* (Lost Highway).

Seriously, it was a great year for roots music with stellar new releases by the likes of Todd Snider, Sam Baker, The Sadies, Greg Brown, Basia Bulat, The Bible All-Stars, Southern Culture on the Skids, Nathan, Joe Henry . . .

But it's time to visit another part of the world.

Latin

Shakira's *Oral Fixation Tour* DVD (Epic) comes with a bonus CD that only features six songs from the concert, but the film itself is a delight from start to finish, showcasing the artist's Colombian and Lebanese heritage. The stage setting, Shakira's costume changes and dancing, and a top-notch band make for a terrific concert experience, even if it's just in your living room. The show also features duets with Alejandro Sanz and Wyclef Jean.

Jean had his own album this year, *Carnival Vol. II Memoirs of an Immigrant* (Sony), continuing the themes of immigration he addressed on his first release. It's hard to believe it's already been ten years since the first *Carnival* disc came out. Shakira returns the favor of Jean's producing her huge hit "Hips Don't Lie" by adding some vocals, but she's only one of a parade of fine guests that include everyone from Norah Jones and Paul Simon to Akon and Mary J. Blige.

Ojos de Brujo give value for the money with their DVD/CD combo, *Techarí Live* (Six Degrees Records), giving us the full show in both formats. I love this band and the way they combine hip-hop and flamenco with African and Asian flavors thrown into the mix. They're definitely a band to see live.

As are Ozomatli, the L.A.-based collective that throw a bit of everything into their music, but never lose their own distinctive flavor. Their latest is an iTunes exclusive EP, *Live from SoHo*. I should mention that it's a bit surprising how much of the music discussed here is available on iTunes and other on-line retailers. If you're looking for any of these releases and are having trouble getting them at your local music store (which you should be supporting first), try some of the on-line services. You don't get a booklet, but you do get to listen to the music right away.

Mala Rodríguez's *Malamarismo* (Machete Music) has a harder edge than her earlier releases—there's less flamenco and more of an urban feel—but it's no less successful for that.

If *In X-Ile* (Via Lactea) is anything to go by, London-based LaXuLa are a madcap fiesta of urban sounds, Spanish guitars, Gypsy fiddles, Arabic rhythms, and tango accordions, with Monte Palafox's vocals soaring over it all. It's both dark and colorful with a beat that doesn't stop.

Juanes is huge in the Latin market and for good reason. The Colombian singer/songwriter builds pop music out of traditional cumbias and boleros that ring with sincerity and activism. *La Vida Es Un Ratico* (Universal Latino) builds on the strengths of his previous albums, and when you listen to it, you'll understand why he's been called the Latin John Lennon.

They're both successful solo artists. James Keelaghan has made a career of bringing history to life with his heartfelt story songs, while Oscar Lopez is one of the big talents in the nouveau flamenco field. Put them together in Compadres with their new release *Buddy Where You Been* (Fusion) and you get what you're supposed to get with a good collaboration: something bigger than simply two artists combining their talents.

Seventeen years on, Café Tacuba are still one of Mexico's most innovative rock bands and *Si No* (Universal Latino) is a powerful reason why.

If you want to know why Gloria Estefan is so respected in the Latin community, you only have to listen to her new album *90 Millas* (Sony International). I always enjoy the combination of her voice taking on the compositions of her husband Emilio, but I especially like it when she sings in her native Spanish, and here the flavor is Havana from start to finish.

World

Better known as Sigur Rós's backup string section, the four women who make up Amiina add a mix of children's toys, harps, brass, and musical glasses to their strings to create their own version of a light Tom Waits soundscape for their debut album *Kurr* (Ever Records).

Mayra Andrade's *Navega* (Stern's) brings a light jazz flavor to traditional Cape Verdean music and offers hope in this young singer that we have someone to take up Cesaria Evora's mantle as Evora moves into her seventies.

It's been five years since Orchestra Baobab were reunited after a previous fifteen-year split, but the high spirit of their music remains unchanged. *Made in Dakar* (World Circuit) is a great introduction to their flavor of African rhythm and guitar, but really you can't go wrong with any of their albums.

Mano Negra's former singer Manu Chao doesn't break a lot of ground with his new album *La Radiolina* (Nacional Records), but he doesn't really need to. His Latin-tinged global rock—with touchstones to Bob Marley and Joe Strummer—continues to sell out concert halls across the world and the new album is a fine souvenir to bring home. Nothing like the live show, but recorded music never holds a candle to the live music experience anyway.

Yasmin Levy's *Mano Suave* (Harmonia Mundi) is an intoxicating blend of Arabic, Jewish, and Spanish influences, held together by Levy's fabulous voice.

Bob Marley and Jimmy Cliff are long gone, but their contemporary Toots Hibbert and his Maytals are still going strong, and still releasing terrific albums like this year's *Light Your Light* (Fantasy). I sometimes think of them as the Rolling Stones of reggae music for their longevity and tireless energy.

World music as a genre has a certain African/Latin bias, but there's a whole world of other music out there. For example, China gives us Sa Dingding with her major label debut *Alive* (Universal). Her voice is an ethereal delight, dancing above a wash of electrical guitars, keyboards, beatbox, and traditional Chinese instruments. And from India, Anoushka Shankar and Karsh Kale explore a mash-up of electronica and Indian music to great effect on *Breathing Underwater* (Manhattan Records). I've liked all of Shankar's solo discs, but this is easily her most adventurous and best to date.

If you're looking for more than an annual fix of the sorts of music discussed above, I'd like to recommend a few Web sites that carry timely reviews and news:

www.frootsmag.com
www.endicott-studio.com
www.pastemusic.com
www.globalrhythm.net
www.greenmanreview.com
www.rambles.net

If you'd like a monthly newsletter of Americana reviews, you should sign up for the Village Records newsletter at www.villagerecords.com. And for one more commercial site that provides excellent band/album information (and is probably the happiest shopping experience you'll have on the Web), point your browser to www.cdbaby.com.

Or if you prefer the written page, check out your local newsstand for copies of *fRoots* (two issues per year carry fabulous CD samplers), *Global Rhythm* (each issue includes a sampler CD), *Songlines* (also has a CD sampler), *Paste* (with CD sampler every issue; sometimes also a DVD sampler), *Sing Out!*, *Riddim* (with CD sampler), *Rock'n'Reel* (with CD Sampler), and *Dirty Linen*.

While I know there are lots of other great albums out there, I don't have the budget to try everything. But my ears are always open to new sounds. So, if you'd like to bring something to my attention for next year's essay, you can send it to me c/o P.O. Box 9480, Ottawa, ON, Canada K1G 3V2.

Remember to have fun with what you listen to. And try to keep an open mind. That style of music you think you hate just might become a favorite if you actually give it a try.

Special thanks, once again, to Cat Eldridge of *Green Man Review* and Ian and James Boyd and Megan Marshall of Compact Music, for helping to provide music in preparation of this essay.

Obituaries: 2007

James Frenkel

When we began this series of anthologies in 1987, nobody wanted to write about the deaths of those who had contributed to the culture of the fantastic arts, so as packager I started performing this necessary task. Necessary, because those who are gone should not be forgotten lest their works also be forgotten. Over the years it has become increasingly apparent that acknowledging those who have died is more than homage. It also gives readers a chance to learn, as we learn, of the contributions of some who may have been forgotten along the way, perhaps because their major contributions were decades ago.

So it is in the way of celebrating their contributions that we note the passing of people who gave us much to remember, whose work may yet inspire those who read these notes. And this year some very important creators were lost to us.

James O. Rigney, Jr., 58, who wrote as Robert Jordan, was best known for his Wheel of Time series. The series was comprised of eleven volumes, including *The Eye of the World*, *The Dragon Reborn*, *The Shadow Rising*, *Winter's Heart*, and *Knife of Dreams*. Known for its epic sweep, intricate plotting and large cast of complex characters, the Wheel of Time has been compared to the work of J.R.R. Tolkien in terms of its ability to exert a magnetic hold on readers. In a 1996 *New York Times Book Review* article, Edward Rothstein wrote, "Even a reader with literary pretensions can be swept up in Mr. Rigney's narrative of magic, prophecy, and battle." The series has been translated into more than twenty languages and has sold more than thirty million copies worldwide. Aside from this series, Rigney was also known for his help in continuing the Conan the Barbarian series, and he also wrote historical and adventure novels.

Lloyd Alexander, 83, was a much-honored, award-winning author of fantasy for young readers, loved by readers of all ages. The author of more than 40 books, Alexander was best known for the Prydain Chronicles, the last of which, *The High King* was awarded the Newbery Medal in 1969. He also won two National Book Awards, one for *The Marvelous Misadventures of Sebastion* and the other for *Westmark*, the first novel in a trilogy of that name. Alexander, whose work was deeply felt and beloved by readers for its universal themes, was also known for using fantasy settings to expose real world injustice.

Kurt Vonnegut, 84, was best known as the countercultural icon whose satirical, surreal novels such as *Slaughterhouse-Five, Cat's Cradle*, and *Breakfast of Champions* are recognized as American classics. Vonnegut also wrote plays, essays, and short fiction. His writing was informed by his harrowing experiences during the Second World War, in particular his survival in an underground bunker during the Allied forces' firebombing of Dresden, Germany, which destroyed the city. His dark, existential creations found a large, appreciative audience among college students in the 1960s. His reputation and popularity increased steadily over the next several decades as his oeuvre grew. By the end of his life he was considered one of the most important American writers of the second half of the twentieth century.

Jack Williamson, 98, was a seminal author of science fiction and fantasy. His best-known novels include *The Humanoids, The Legion of Space, Darker Than You Think, Terraforming Earth, The Silicon Dagger*, and his last novel *The Stonehenge Gate*. Williamson's work spanned more than eight decades, and he is often cited as a forefather of modern science fiction. His fiction was extremely diverse, ranging from the very darkest horror to flat-out adventure. He was also instrumental in the academic world, helping to legitimize the study of science fiction and fantasy as an academic discipline.

Fred Saberhagen, 77, was an author best known for his Berserker series of novels about intelligent machines out to destroy the human race. He wrote more than 60 novels and collections and edited three short story collections. In addition to his Berserker series he also wrote several books from Dracula's point of view as well as his Swords and Lost Swords series, and *Empire of the East*, a particular favorite.

Ira Levin, 78, was a playwright and novelist, known for his bestselling psychological thrillers, including *Rosemary's Baby, The Stepford Wives*, and *The Boys from Brazil*, all of which were adapted to the screen.

Fred Mustard Stewart, 74, was a novelist whose work ranged from horror to science fiction to adventure. Among his most popular novels were *The Mephisto Waltz*, which was also adapted for film, and *Century*. **Robert Anton Wilson**, 74, was an author, editor, and lecturer, best known for his Illuminatus! trilogy, cowritten with Robert Shea, published in 1975. Wilson also wrote more than 35 books on a wide range of subjects such as extrasensory perception, paranormal experiences, drugs, and conspiracy theories. The Illuminatus! trilogy has influenced many writers since, as evidenced by the ever-growing number of historical-conspiracy books and films.

Brant Parker, 86, was the co-creator of the long-running satiric medieval comic strip "The Wizard of Id." **Johnny Hart**, 76, was the creator of the award-winning comic strip "B.C." "B.C." was created in 1958 and since then has gone on to reach an audience of over 100 million readers. **Roy Kuhlman**, 83, was an improvisational painter whose works were featured on the covers of Samuel Beckett's *Krapp's Last Tape*, Hubert Selby, Jr.'s *Last Exit to Brooklyn*, and Jean Genet's *The Balcony*. **Marshall Rogers**, 57, was an illustrator whose work with writer Steve Englehart on Batman comics in 1977 and '78 helped redefine the hero, bringing him back to his roots as a dark vigilante and away from the camp element popularized by the 1960s television series. **Jay Kennedy**, 50, was editor-in-chief at King Features Syndicate and a scholar of comics, particularly 1960s-era underground comic strips. It was during his tenure at King that comics such as "Curtis," "Mutts," and "Zits" were introduced. **Joe Edwards**, 85, was an artist who worked on the very first issue of Archie Comics in 1942. Edwards was also the creator of the character Li'l Jinx. **Arnold Drake**, 83, was a comics writer who worked at Gold Key Comics, Marvel, and DC Comics. He was the creator of the Doom Patrol series and co-writer of *It Rhymes with Lust*—arguably America's first graphic novel.

Joseph Low, 99, was an illustrator who did absurdist covers for albums and *The New Yorker* and won Caldecott honors for his work on the children's book *Mice Twice*. **Martin J. Weber,** 102, worked in graphics, and invented several typographic and graphic techniques, most notably one that made two-dimensional photographs seems to spring off the page, popular in the 1960s with poster artists who used it to achieve a psychedelic look. **Iwao Takamoto,** 81, was the creator of the cartoon Scooby-Doo along with many other cartoons. He was originally hired by the Walt Disney Studios. He went on to work on animated films like *Lady and the Tramp, 101 Dalmatians*, and *Charlotte's Web*. **Jack Zander,** 99, was a pioneer of early television commercial animation. He is best known as the original animator of Jerry in "Tom and Jerry." He was honored by the Animated Film Society with the McCay award, for lifetime achievement.

Perry H. Knowlton, 80, was for many years the head of the Curtis Brown, Ltd. agency. Knowlton began his career at Charles Scribner's, where he worked in regional sales. He became an editor at Scribner's before joining Curtis Brown in 1959 to run the agency's book department. He represented such authors as Betty Friedan, John Knowles, C.S. Lewis and A.A. Milne. **Roger Elwood**, 64, was an editor of science fiction and fantasy. Elwood was responsible for the creation of the ill-fated Laser books science fiction imprint, now defunct. He is both blamed and credited for the plethora of anthologies in the 1970s. **Doug Hill**, 72, was an editor, poet, and writer. He was an editor for Aldus Books in Britain. Best remembered for his young adult fantasies, he was a master of combining violent action with strong condemnation of exploitation and corruption. His highly imaginative science fiction includes *World of the Stiks* and the Cade trilogy. **Sterling E. Lanier**, 79, was a writer and editor. His own works include *The War for the Lot, Hiero's Journey, Menace Under Marswood*, and his stories on the strange adventures of Brigadier Donald Fellowes. Lanier worked as an editor for the Winston Company, Chilton Books, and McRae-Smith. While at Chilton Books, he championed the publication of Frank Herbert's *Dune*, which became one of the best-selling science fiction novels of all time. **Robert Lantz,** 93, was a talent agent to such famous people as Bette Davis, Leonard Bernstein, Elizabeth Taylor, Milos Forman, and Yul Brynner. **Peter Haining**, 67, noted horror anthologist, was the editorial director at the New English Library and founded the NEL Young Writer of the Year Awards which was given to Philip Pullman in its first year. **Margaret Crawford**, 82, was an editor and publisher who worked with many authors, including L. Ron Hubbard, Robert E. Howard, and Olaf Stapledon. She was a publisher of *Spaceways* magazine and the magazine *Witchcraft and Sorcery*, which was originally titled *Coven 13*. **Emily Sunstein**, 82, was an independent scholar best known for her biographies of Mary Wollstonecraft and Mary Shelley.

Robert Goulet, 73, was a singer best known for his deep baritone voice. He got his big break as Lancelot in the original Broadway production of *Camelot*. His career included more than 60 albums and numerous roles both on Broadway, in television and on film. **Bobby Pickett**, 69, was known best for his hit novelty song "Monster Mash" which made it to the number one spot on the pop music charts in 1962, and returned to the charts in 1970 and 1973.

Michael Kidd, 92, was a dancer, and an award-winning stage and screen choreographer who worked on such works as *Finian's Rainbow, Guys and Dolls*, and *Seven Brides for Seven Brothers*. Mr. Kidd won five Tony awards and a special Academy Award "in recognition of his services to the art of dance in the art of the screen." **Henry LeTang**, 91, was a Tony award-winning choreographer best known for his work on such Broadways musicals as *Black and Blue* (1989), *Sophisticated Ladies*

(1981), and *Eubie!* (1978). He also choreographed films such as *The Cotton Club* (1981). **Ruthanna Boris**, 88, was a dancer and choreographer who starred in the Ballet Russes in the 1940s. She danced in such classics as *Swan Lake*, *The Nutcracker*, and *Les Sylphides* as well as *Frankie and Johnnie*.

    Tom Poston, 85, was an Emmy award-winning actor who worked on Broadway, on film, but most memorably on television. His most popular roles were on programs such as *Newhart*, *Mork & Mindy*, and on the original *Bob Newhart Show*. He was also a comic, and made a big impression on Steve Allen's weekly show in the early 1960s. **Gordon Scott**, 80, was best known for his repeated portrayal of Tarzan in the 1950s. **Jean-Pierre Cassel**, 74, was best known for his starring roles in 1960s French comedy films. His most successful roles were in the films of director Philippe de Broca. He was also known for his portrayal of Louis XIII in Richard Lester's memorable adaptations of Dumas' *Three Musketeers*. **Roscoe Lee Browne**, 81, was an actor best known for his work in films such as *The Liberation of L.B. Jones*, television shows such as the 1970s sitcom *Soap*, and the Broadway production *Two Trains Running*. Browne also performed a poetry anthology stage piece, *Behind the Broken Words*, and Anthony Zerbe Browne's poetry could be heard in these productions. **Yvonne De Carlo**, 84, was an actress who achieved her greatest level of success and popularity as Lily Munster on the sitcom *The Munsters*. She also appeared in nearly 100 films. **Richard Jeni**, 45, was a stand-up comedian and an actor featured in *The Mask*, among others films.

    Mala Powers, 75, was a film actress in the 1950s cinema. Her best-known role was that of Roxanne in *Cyrano de Bergerac*. Other film credits include *Edge of Doom*, *City Beneath the Sea*, and *City that Never Sleeps*. **Walker Edmiston**, 81, was an actor best known as the voice of Ernie the Keebler (Cookies) elf. He also had acting roles in various television shows. **Charles Lane**, 102, was a veteran character actor who appeared in hundreds of films from the 1930s to the '90s, including *It's a Wonderful Life* and *You Can't Take It With You*. In the 1950s Lane became a familiar presence on television and made guest appearances on series like *The Twilight Zone*. **Alice Ghostley**, 81, was a Tony Award-winning stage actress. She also acted on television, and was a regular on the show *Bewitched* from 1966-1972, playing Esmerelda, a shy, bumbling witch whose spells never worked. **George Grizzard**, 79, was a versatile actor best known for his roles in the plays of Edward Albee, such as *Who's Afraid of Virginia Woolf* and *A Delicate Balance*, and in many television roles. **Dick Wilson**, 91, a British actor, was best known for his role as Mr. Whipple in Charmin commercials. He also appeared in various television series, including *My Favorite Martian*, *Hogan's Heroes*, and *Bewitched*.

    László Kovács, 74, was an imaginative Hungarian cinematographer who worked on films such as *Easy Rider* and helped to create "the new Hollywood," or "the American new wave," pioneering improvisational techniques. His films include *Five Easy Pieces* and *Ghostbusters*, among many others. **Tom Moore**, 88, was the president of the ABC television network from 1962 to 1969 who helped revitalize a flagging ABC by aiming programming at younger viewers with shows such as *The Real McCoys*, *The Flintstones*, *The Untouchables*, *The Fugitive*, *The Addams Family*, and *Batman*. **Freddie Francis**, 89, was a British cinematographer and director known for his ability to use light and shadow to create an atmosphere of horror. He directed films such as *Tales from the Crypt* and *The Ghoul* and worked as director of photography on David Lynch's *The Elephant Man*. **Donfeld**, 72, was an Oscar-nominated Hollywood costume designer whose work can be seen in such films as *They Shoot Horses, Don't They?* and *Prizzi's Honor*. He also worked for television series, including *Wonder Woman,* which earned him an Emmy nomination. **Eustace Lycett,** 91, was a designer of special effects for Disney movies for 43 years. He worked on over 30 films including *Snow White and the Seven Dwarfs.* He received Oscars for his work on *Mary Poppins* and *Bedknobs and Broomsticks.* **Herman Stein,** 91, was a composer with nearly 200 film scores to his credit, including those for such science fiction and horror movies as *It Came from Outer Space, Creature from the Black Lagoon, This Island Earth,* and *The Incredible Shrinking Man.* **Steve Krantz,** 83, was a producer and author who produced *Fritz the Cat,* based on R. Crumb's sex-obsessed cat of the same name, the first full-length animated film to carry an X rating. **Curtis Harrington,** 80, was a film director best known for films like *Whoever Slew Auntie Roo?, What's the Matter With Helen?,* and *Killer Bees.* His films were noted for their inventive use of color and an overwhelming sense of the macabre. **Joel Siegel,** 63, was a movie critic known for his pithy commentary that became blurbs in his reviews on *Good Morning America.* **Willam J. Tuttle,** 95, was head of the makeup department for MGM and worked on over 300 films. He won an Oscar years before there was an official Academy Award for makeup, and received an honorary Oscar for *7 Faces of Dr. Lao.* **Charles Griffith,** 77, was the screenwriter behind the original *Little Shop of Horrors.* He wrote many films, including *The Wild Angels* and *Dr. Heckyl and Mr. Hype.*

Tillie Olsen, 94, was an author whose works voiced the struggles of women and working-class people. Her books included *Tell Me a Riddle* and *Silences.* Olsen was also an advisor to the Feminist Press, and at her suggestion the press began reprinting feminist classics. **Elizabeth Jolley,** 83, was an Australian novelist known for books termed "Australian Gothic." Her best-known novels include *Mr. Scobie's Ride, Miss Peabody's Inheritance, The Well,* and *The Sugar Mother.* **Madeleine L'Engle,** 88, was a Newbery Medal-winning author for her fantasy novel *A Wrinkle in Time.* Other novels in her Time series include *A Wind in the Door* and *A Swiftly Tilting Planet.* Her works included other children's books, poetry, and plays. **Alice Borchardt,** 67, was the author of the Silver Wolf series, the Tales of Guinevere series, and was the older sister of Anne Rice. **Leigh Eddings,** 69, was the wife of David Eddings and co-wrote every book published under his name.

That's a lot of talented people. Look for their works!

DANIEL ABRAHAM

The Cambist and Lord Iron:
A Fairy Tale of Economics

Daniel Abraham's "The Cambist and Lord Iron: A Fairy Tale of Economics"
was first published in the spelling bee anthology Logorrhea: Good Words
Make Good Stories, *edited by John Klima. Abraham is the author of the*
Long Winter Quartet of fantasy novels (an ongoing series wherein he again
manages to magically make trade and economics fascinating). He coau-
thored the science fiction novel Hunter's Run *with George R. R. Martin and*
Gardner Dozois, and, writing as M. L. N. Hanover, has begun a new series
of urban fantasy novels, the first book of which is Unclean Spirits. *Abraham*
lives in New Mexico with his family.

—K.L. & G.G.

For as many years as anyone in the city could remember, Olaf Neddelsohn had been the cambist of the Magdalen Gate postal authority. Every morning, he could be seen making the trek from his room in the boardinghouse on State Street, down past the street vendors with their apples and cheese, and into the bowels of the underground railway only to emerge at the station across the wide boulevard from Magdalen Gate. Some mornings he would pause at the tobacconist's or the newsstand before entering the hallowed hall of the postal authority, but seven o'clock found him without fail at the ticker tape checking for the most recent exchange rates. At half past, he was invariably updating the slate board with a bit of chalk. And with the last chime of eight o'clock, he would nod his respect to his small portrait of His Majesty, King Walther IV, pull open the shutters, and greet whatever traveler had need of him.

From that moment until the lunch hour and again from one o'clock until six, Olaf lived and breathed the exchange of foreign currencies. Under his practiced hands, dollars became pounds sterling; rubles became marks; pesos, kroner; yen, francs. Whatever exotic combination was called for, Olaf arranged with a smile, a kind word, and a question about the countries which minted the currencies he passed under the barred window. Over years, he had built nations in his mind; continents. Every country that existed, he could name, along with its particular flavor of money, its great sights and monuments, its national cuisine.

At the deep brass call of the closing gong, he pulled the shutters closed again.

From six until seven o'clock, he reconciled the books, filled out his reports, wiped his slate board clean with a wet rag, made certain he had chalk for the next day, paid his respects to the portrait of the king, and then went back to his boarding room. Some nights he made beans on the hotplate in his room. Others, he would join the other boarders for Mrs. Wells's somewhat dubious roasts. Afterward, he would take a short constitutional walk, read to himself from the men's adventure books that were his great vice, and put out the light. On Saturdays, he would visit the zoo or the fourth-rate gentleman's club that he could afford. On Sundays, he attended church.

He had a reputation as a man of few needs, tepid passions, and great kindness. The romantic fire that the exotic coins and bills awakened in him was something he would have been hard pressed to share, even had he anyone with whom to share it.

Which is to say there could not be another man in the whole of the city less like Lord Iron.

Born Edmund Scarasso, Lord Iron had taken his father's title and lands and ridden them first to war, then to power, and finally to notoriety. His family estate outside the city was reputed to rival the king's, but Lord Iron spent little time there. He had a house in the city with two hundred rooms arranged around a central courtyard garden in which trees bore fruits unfamiliar to the city and flowers bloomed with exotic and troubling scents. His servants were numberless as ants; his personal fortune greater than some smaller nations. And never, it was said, had such wealth, power, and influence been squandered on such a debased soul.

No night passed without some new tale of Lord Iron. Ten thousand larks had been killed, their tongues harvested, and their bodies thrown aside in order that Lord Iron might have a novel hors d'oeuvre. Lord Biethan had been forced to repay his family's debt by sending his three daughters to perform as Lord Iron's creatures for a week; they had returned to their father with disturbing, languorous smiles and a rosewood cask filled with silver as "recompense for his Lordship's overuse." A fruit seller had the bad fortune not to recognize Lord Iron one dim, fog-bound morning, and a flippant comment earned him a whipping that left him near dead.

There was no way for anyone besides Lord Iron himself to know which of the thousand stories and accusations that accreted around him were true. There was no doubt that Lord Iron was never seen wearing anything but the richest of velvets and silk. He was habitually in the company of beautiful women of negotiable virtue. He smoked the finest tobacco and other, more exotic weeds. Violence and sensuality and excess were the tissue of which his life was made. If his wealth and web of blackmail and extortion had not protected him, he would no doubt have been invited to the gallows dance years before. If he had been a hero in the war, so much the worse.

And so it was, perhaps, no surprise that when his lackey and drinking companion, Lord Caton, mentioned in passing an inconvenient curiosity of the code of exchange, Lord Iron's mind seized upon it. Among his many vices was a fondness for cruel pranks. And so it came to pass that Lord Iron and the handful of gaudy revelers who followed in his wake descended late one Tuesday morning upon the Magdalen Gate postal authority.

Olaf took the packet of bills, willing his hands not to tremble. Lord Iron's thin smile and river-stone eyes did nothing to calm him. The woman draping herself on Lord Iron's arm made a poor affectation of sincerity.

"Well," Olaf said, unfolding the papers. "Let me see."

These were unlike any currency he had ever seen; the sheets were just larger than a standard sheet of paper, the engraving a riot of colors—crimson, indigo, and a pale, delicate peach. The lordly face that stared out of the bill was Moorish. Ornate letters identified the bills as being valued at a thousand convertible guilders and issued by the Independent Protectorate of Analdi-Wat. Olaf wondered, as his fingers traced the lettering, how a protectorate could be independent.

"I'm very sorry, my lord," he said. "But this isn't a listed currency."

"And how is that *my* problem?" Lord Iron asked, stroking his beard. He had a rich voice, soft and masculine, that made Olaf blush.

"I only mean, my lord, that I couldn't give an exchange rate on these. I don't have them on my board, you see, and so I can't—"

"These are legal tender, issued by a sovereign state. I would like to change them into pounds sterling."

"I understand that, my lord, it's only that—"

"Are you familiar with the code of exchange?" Lord Iron asked. The dark-haired woman on his arm smiled at Olaf with all the pity a snake shows a rat.

"I . . . of course, my lord . . . that is . . ."

"Then you will recall the second provision of the Lord Chancellor's amendment of 1652?"

Olaf licked his lips. Confusion was like cotton ticking filling his head.

"The provision against speculation, my lord?"

"Very good," Lord Iron said. "It states that any cambist in the employ of the crown must complete a requested transfer between legal tenders issued by sovereign states within twenty-four hours or else face review of licensure."

"My . . . my lord, that isn't . . . I've been working here for years, sir . . ."

"And of course," Lord Iron went on, his gaze implacable and cool, "assigning arbitrary value to a currency also requires a review, doesn't it? And rest assured, my friend, that I am quite capable of determining the outcome of any such review."

Olaf swallowed to loosen the tightness in his throat. His smile felt sickly.

"If I have done something to offend your lordship . . ."

"No," Lord Iron said with something oddly like compassion in his eyes. "You were simply in the wrong place when I grew bored. Destroying you seemed diverting. I will be back at this time tomorrow. Good day, sir."

Lord Iron turned and walked away. His entourage followed. When the last of them had stepped out the street doors, the silence that remained behind was as profound as the grave. Olaf saw the eyes of the postal clerks on him and managed a wan smile. The great clock read twenty minutes past eleven. By noontime tomorrow, Olaf realized, it was quite possible he would no longer be a licensed cambist.

He closed his shutters early with a note tacked to the front that clients should knock on them if they were facing an emergency and otherwise return the next day. He pulled out the references of his trade—gazetteer, logs of fiscal reports, conversion tables. By midafternoon, he had discovered the location of the Independent Protectorate of Analdi-Wat, but nothing that would relate their system of convertible guilders to any known currency. Apparently the last known conversion had been into a system of cowrie shells, and the numbers involved were absent.

The day waned, the light pouring into the postal authority warming and then fading to shadows. Olaf sent increasingly desperate messages to his fellow cambists at other postal authorities, to the librarians at the city's central reference desk, to the office of the Lord Exchequer. It became clear as the bells tolled their increasing hours that no answer would come before morning. And indeed, no answer would come in time.

If Olaf delayed the exchange, his license could be suspended. If he invented some random value for the guilders, his license could be suspended. And there was no data from which to derive an appropriate equation.

Anger and despair warring in his belly, he closed his station, returned his books to their places, cleaned his slate, logged the few transactions he had made. His hand hovered for a moment over his strongbox.

Here were the funds from which he drew each day to meet the demands of his clientele. Pounds sterling, yen, rubles. He wondered, if he were to fill his pockets with the box's present contents, how far he would get before he was caught. The romance of flight bloomed in his mind and died all in the space of a breath. He withdrew only the bright, venomous bills of the Independent Protectorate of Analdi-Wat, replacing them with a receipt. He locked the box with a steady hand, shrugged on his coat, and left.

Lord Iron, he decided as he walked slowly down the marble steps to the street, was evil. But he was also powerful, rich, and well connected. There was little that a man like Olaf could do if a man of that stature took it as his whim to destroy him. If it had been the devil, he might at least have fallen back on prayer.

Olaf stopped at the newsstand, bought an evening paper and a tin of lemon mints, and trudged to the station across the street. Waiting on the platform, he listened to the underground trains hiss and squeal. He read his newspaper with the numb disinterest of a man to whom the worst has already happened. A missing child had been found alive in Stonemarket; the diary of a famous courtesan had sold at auction to an anonymous buyer and for a record price; the police had begun a policy of restricting access to the river quays in hopes of reducing accidental death by drowning. The cheap ink left more of a mark on his fingers than his mind.

At his boardinghouse, Olaf ate a perfunctory dinner at the common table, retired to his room, and tried in vain to lose himself in the pulp adventure tales. The presence of a killer among the members of the good Count Pendragon's safari proved less than captivating, even if the virtuous Hanna Gable was in danger. Near midnight, Olaf turned out his light, pulled his thin wool blanket up over his head, and wondered what he would do when his position at the postal authority was terminated.

Two hours later, he woke with a shout. Still in his night clothes, he rushed out to the common room, digging through the pile of small kindling and newspaper that Mrs. Wells used to start her fires. When he found the evening newspaper, he read the article detailing the sale of the courtesan's diary again. There was nothing in it that pertained directly to his situation, and yet his startling, triumphant yawp woke the house.

He arrived at work the next day later than usual, with bags as dark as bruises under his eyes but a spring in his step. He went through his morning ritual rather hurriedly to make up for the time he had lost, but was well prepared when the street doors opened at eleven o'clock and Lord Iron and his gang of rank nobility slouched in. Olaf held his spine straight and breathed deeply to ease the trip-hammer of his heart.

Lord Iron stepped up to the window like an executioner to the noose. The woman on his arm this morning was fair-haired, but otherwise might have been the previous day's twin. Olaf made a small, nervous bow to them both.

"Lord Iron," he said.

Lord Iron's expression was as distant as the moon. Olaf wondered if perhaps his lordship had been drinking already this morning.

"Explain to me why you've failed."

"Well, my lord, I don't think I can do that. I have your money here. It comes to something less than ten pounds, I'm afraid. But that was all the market would bear."

With trembling hand, Olaf slid an envelope across the desk. Lord Iron didn't look down at it. Fury lit his eyes.

"The *market*? And pray what *market* is that?"

"The glassblower's shop in Harrington Square, my lord. I have quotes from three other establishments nearby, and theirs was the best. I doubt you would find better anywhere."

"What do they have to do with this?"

"Well, they were the ones who bought the guilders," Olaf said, his voice higher and faster than he liked. He also ran on longer than he had strictly speaking intended. "I believe that they intend to use them as wrapping paper. For the more delicate pieces. As a novelty."

Lord Iron's face darkened.

"You sold my bills?" he growled.

Olaf had anticipated many possible reactions. Violence, anger, amusement. He had imagined a hundred objections that Lord Iron might bring to his actions. Base ignorance had not been one of them. Olaf's surprise leant a steadiness to his voice.

"My lord, *you* sold them. To me. That's what exchange is, sir. Currency is something bought and sold, just as plums or gas fixtures are. It's what we do here."

"I came to get pounds sterling for guilders, not sell wrapping paper!"

Olaf saw in that moment that Lord Iron genuinely didn't understand. He pulled himself up, straightening his vest.

"Sir," he said. "When a client comes to me with a hundred dollars and I turn him back with seventy pounds, I haven't said some Latin phrase over them. There aren't suddenly seventy more pounds in the world and a hundred fewer dollars. I *buy* the dollars. You came to sell your guilders to me. Very well. I have bought them."

"As wrapping paper!"

"What does that matter?" Olaf snapped, surprising both Lord Iron and himself. "If I invest them in negotiable bonds in Analdi-Wat or burn them for kindling, it's no business of yours. Someone was willing to buy them. From that, I can now quote you with authority what people are willing to pay. There is your exchange rate. And there is your money. Thank you for your business, and good day."

"You made up the price," Lord Iron said. "To place an arbitrary worth on—"

"Good God, man," Olaf said. "Did you not hear me before? There's nothing *arbitrary* about it. I went to several prospective buyers and took the best offered price. What can you possibly mean by 'worth' if not what you can purchase with it? Five shillings is worth a loaf of bread, or a cup of wine, or a cheaply bound book of poetry because that is what it will buy. Your tens of thousands of negotiable guilders will buy you nine pounds and seven shillings because that is what someone will pay. And there it is, in that envelope."

Never before in his life had Olaf seen nobility agape at him. The coterie of Lord Iron stared at him as if he had belched fire and farted brimstone. The fair-haired woman stepped back, freeing his lordship's sword arm.

I have gone too far, Olaf thought. He will kill me.

Lord Iron was silent for a long moment while the world seemed to rotate around him. Then he chuckled.

"The measure of a thing's worth is what you can purchase with it," he said as if tasting the words, then turned to the fair-haired woman. "I think he's talking about you, Marjorie."

The woman's cheeks flushed scarlet. Lord Iron leaned against the sill of Olaf's little, barred window and gestured Olaf closer. Against his best judgment, Olaf leaned in.

"You have a strange way of looking at things," Lord Iron said. There were fumes on his breath. Absinthe, Olaf guessed. "To hear you speak, the baker buys my five shillings with his bread."

"And how is that wrong, my lord?" the cambist asked.

"And then the wineseller buys the coins from him with a glass of wine. So why not buy the bread with the wine? If they're worth the same?"

"You could, my lord," Olaf said. "You can express anything in terms of anything else, my lord. How many lemon tarts is a horse worth? How many newspapers equate to a good dinner? It isn't harder to determine than some number of rubles for another number of yen, if you know the trick of it."

Lord Iron smiled again. The almost sleepy expression returned to his eyes. He nodded.

"Wrapping paper," he said. "You have amused me, little man, and I didn't think that could be done any longer. I accept your trade."

And with that, Lord Iron swept the envelope into his pocket, turned, and marched unsteadily out of the postal authority and into the noon light of Magdalen Gate. After the street doors were closed, there was a pause as long as three breaths together and then one of the postal clerks began to clap.

A moment later, the staff of the postal authority had filled the vaults of their chambers with applause. Olaf, knees suddenly weak, bowed carefully, closed the shutters of his window, and made his way back to the men's privacy room where he emptied his breakfast into the toilet and then sat on the cool tile floor laughing until tears streamed from his eyes.

He had faced down Lord Iron and escaped with his career intact. It was, no doubt, the greatest adventure of his life. Nothing he had done before could match it, and he could imagine nothing in the future that would surpass it.

And nothing did, as it turned out, for almost six and a half months.

If was a cold, clear February, and the stars had come out long before Olaf had left the Magdalen Gate authority. All during the ride on the underground train, Olaf dreamed of a warm pot of tea, a small fire, and the conclusion of the latest novel. Atherton Crane was on the verge of exposing the plot of the vicious Junwang Ko, but didn't yet know that Kelly O'Callahan was in the villain's clutches. It promised to be a pleasant evening.

He knew as soon as he stepped into the boardinghouse that something was wrong. The other boarders, sitting around the common table, went silent as he shrugged out of his coat and plucked off his hat. They pointedly did not look at him as Mrs. Wells, her wide, friendly face pale as uncooked dough, crossed the room to meet him.

"There's a message for you, Mr. Neddelsohn," she said. "A man came and left it for you. Very particular."

"Who was he?" Olaf asked, suspicion blooming in his heart more from her affect than from any guilt on his conscience.

"Don't know," Mrs. Wells said, wringing her hands in distress, "but he looked . . . well, here it is, Mr. Neddelsohn. This is the letter he left for you."

The envelope she thrust into his hand was the color of buttercream, smooth as linen, and thick. The coat of arms embossed upon it was Lord Iron's. Olaf started at the thing as if she'd handed him a viper.

Mrs. Wells simpered her apology as he broke the wax seal and drew out a single sheet of paper. It was written in an erratic but legible hand.

> Mr. Neddelsohn—
> *I find I have need of you to settle a wager. You will bring yourself to the Club Baphomet immediately upon receipt of this note. I will, of course, recompense you for your troubles.*

The note was not signed, but Olaf had no doubt of its authorship. Without a word, he pulled his jacket back on, returned his hat to his head, and stepped out to hail a carriage. From the street, he could see the faces of Mrs. Wells and his fellow boarders at the window.

The Club Baphomet squatted in the uncertain territory between the tenements and beer halls of Stonemarket and the mansions and ballrooms of Granite Hill. The glimmers behind its windows did little to illuminate the street, perhaps by design. From the tales Olaf had heard, there might well be members of the club who would prefer not to be seen entering or leaving its grounds. The service entrance was in a mud-paved alley stinking of piss and old food, but it opened quickly to his knock. He was bundled inside and escorted to a private sitting room where, it seemed, he was expected.

Of the five men who occupied the room, Olaf recognized only Lord Iron. The months had not been kind; Lord Iron had grown thinner, his eyes wilder, and a deep crimson cut was only half healed on his cheek. The other four were dressed in fashion similar to Lord Iron—well-razored hair, dark coats of the finest wool, watch chains of gold. The eldest of them seemed vaguely familiar.

Lord Iron rose and held his hand out toward Olaf, not as if to greet him but rather to display him like a carnival barker presenting a three-headed calf.

"Gentlemen," Lord Iron intoned. "This is the cambist I mentioned to you. I propose that he be my champion in this matter."

Olaf felt the rictus grin on his face, the idiot bobbing of his head as he made small bows to the four assembled gentlemen. He was humiliated, but could no more stop himself than a puppy could keep from showing its belly to beg the mercy of wolves.

One of the four—a younger man with gold hair and ice-blue eyes—stepped forward with a smile. Olaf nodded to him for what must have been the fifth time.

"I am Simon Cole," the gold-haired man said. "Lord Eichan, to my enemies."

At this, Lord Iron raised a hand, as if to identify himself as one such enemy. The other three men chuckled, and Lord Eichan smiled as well before continuing.

"Our mutual acquaintance, Lord Iron, has made a suggestion I find somewhat unlikely, and we have made a wager of it. He is of the opinion that the value of anything can be expressed in terms of any other valuable thing. I think his example was the cost of a horse in lemon mints."

"Yes, my lord," Olaf said.

"Ah, you agree then," Lord Eichan said. "That's good. I was afraid our little Edmund had come up with his thesis in a drug-soaked haze."

"We've made the agreement," Lord Iron said pleasantly. "Simon, Satan's catamite that he is, will set the two things to be compared. I, meaning of course *you*, will have a week to determine their relative worth. These three bastards will judge the answer."

"I see," Olaf said.

"Excellent," Lord Iron said, slapping him on the back and leading him to a chair upholstered in rich leather. It wasn't until Olaf had descended into the chair's depths that he realized he had just agreed to this mad scheme. Lord Eichan had taken a seat opposite him and was thoughtfully lighting a pipe.

"I think I should say," Olaf began, casting his mind about wildly for some way to remove himself from the room without offending either party. "That is, I don't wish that . . . ah . . ."

Lord Eichan nodded as if Olaf had made some cogent point, then shaking his match until the flame died, turned to face Olaf directly.

"I would like to know the value of a day in the life of His Majesty, King Walther," Lord Eichan said. "And I would like that value described in days of life of an inmate in the crown's prison."

"A day in the life of the king expressed in days of a prisoner's life?"

"Certainly you must agree that life is valuable," Lord Eichan said. "You wouldn't lightly part with your own."

"Well, certainly—"

"And you can't suggest that the king is the same as a bread thief."

"No, I wouldn't—"

"Well, then," Lord Eichan said. "It's settled."

"Come along, my boy," Lord Iron said, clapping Olaf on the shoulder. "I'll see you out."

"One week!" Lord Eichan said as Olaf and Lord Iron stepped from the room and into the corridor. Lord Iron was smiling; Olaf was not.

"My lord," Olaf said. "This is . . . I'm not sure I know how to go about something like this."

"That's why I got you a week to do it in," Lord Iron said. "The rat-licker wanted to limit it to three days."

"I don't know for a certainty that I can accommodate you, my lord," Olaf said.

"Do your best," Lord Iron said. "If we lose, Simon, Lord Eichan is going to kill me. Well, and you for that."

Olaf stopped dead. Lord Iron took another few steps before pausing and looking back.

"He's what?"

"Going to kill us," Lord Iron said. "And take five hundred pounds I've set aside in earnest as well. If we win, I'll kill him and bed his sister."

Olaf, unthinking, murmured an obscenity. Lord Iron grinned and pulled him along the dim corridor toward the back of the club.

"Well, you needn't bed his sister if you don't care to. Just do your best, boy. And be back here in a week."

With that, Lord Iron stepped Olaf out the door and into the cold, bleak alley. It wasn't until the door had closed behind him that Olaf realized Lord Iron hadn't recompensed him for the carriage ride.

In the morning, the whole affair had the air of a bad dream. Olaf made his way to Magdalen Gate as he always did, checked the ticker tape, updated his slate. What was the value of life, he wondered. And how was one life best to be measured against another.

And, behind it all, the growing certainty that Lord Eichan would indeed kill him if he couldn't find an acceptable answer.

Twice before noon, Olaf found he had made errors in his accounting. After bolting down the snowy street after a woman who had left with ten pounds fewer than she deserved, Olaf gave up. He wrote a note claiming illness, pinned it to his shuttered window, and left. He paused at the tobacconist to buy a pouch and papers.

In his room at the boardinghouse, Olaf sketched out every tack he could think of to address the issue. The most obvious was to determine how much money the state spent to keep his majesty and how much to run the prisons. But objections to that arose almost immediately; was that a measure of the worth of life or of operational expenses appropriate to each career? He considered the relative costs of physician's care for king and prisoner, but this again was not a concern precisely of life, but health. Twenty years coughing and twenty years free from illness were still twenty years.

For three days, he ate little and slept less. He ventured out to the library to search among the stacks of books and periodicals for inspiration. He found nothing on which he would have been willing to stake his life. Lord Iron had done that for him.

On the morning of the fourth day he rolled the last pinch of tobacco into the last paper, wet it, rolled it, and sat on his bed unable to bring himself to the effort of lighting the thing. Despair had descended upon him. He saw the next three days stretching before him in a long, slow sleep.

It was how he imagined the prisoners felt who had so occupied his thoughts. But he, at least, could go out for more tobacco. And beer. And good, bloody beefsteak. If he was to live like a prisoner, he might at least eat like a king. It wasn't as if he'd give himself gout in three days time, no matter how richly he ate or overmuch he drank.

Something stirred at the back of his mind, and he found himself grinning even before he knew why.

All that day and the two after it he spent in a whirl of activity, his despair forgotten. He visited physicians and the budget office, the office of the prison warden and the newspaperman who most reported on the activities of the king. The last day, he locked himself in his rooms with an abacus, a stub of pencil, and sheaves of paper.

When he came to the final accounting, his heart sank. He went through his figures again, certain that somewhere in the complexity of his argument, he had made an error. But the numbers tallied, and as little as he liked it, there was no more time. Putting on his best coat, he prepared the argument in his mind. Then, papers tucked under his arm, he went out past his silent fellow boarders and the stricken countenance of Mrs. Wells, down to the wintery street, and hailed a carriage to carry him back to Club Baphomet.

The furniture of the sitting room had been rearranged. A single table now dominated the space, with five chairs all along one side like an examiner's panel. The three judges sat in the middle with Simon, Lord Eichan on the left and Lord Iron on the right. Lord Eichan looked somewhat amused, but there was a nervousness in his movement with which Olaf identified. Lord Iron looked as relaxed as a man stepping out of a sauna; the wound on his face was visibly more healed. Glasses of wine sat before each man, and cigars rested in onyx ashtrays when the gentlemen of the club weren't making better use of them.

A straight-backed wooden chair faced them, a small student desk at its side. Olaf sat and arranged his papers. The eldest of the judges leaned forward and, with a smile more at home on the lips of a procurer, spoke.

"You may proceed, sir."

Olaf nodded his thanks.

"I will need to do just a bit of groundwork before I present my analysis," he said. "I hope you would all agree that a man who decries embezzlement and also diverts money into his private accounts is not actually opposed to the theft?"

The judges looked at one another in amusement.

"Or, similarly," Olaf went on, "A woman who claims to embody chastity and yet beds all comers is not, in point of fact, chaste?"

"I think even Lord Eichan will have to allow those to stand," the eldest judge said. "Your point?"

"My point, sirs, is that we judge people not by what they claim, but what they do. Public declarations of sentiment are not a fit judge of true character."

"You are preaching," the youngest of the judges drawled, "to the choir. There is no group in the nation more adept at saying one thing and doing another."

Olaf smiled awkwardly.

"Just so," he said. "I will move forward. I have come to the determination, after careful consideration, that a day in the life of his majesty the king equates to nineteen and three quarter hours of a prisoner of the crown."

There was a moment's silence. Simon, Lord Eichan blinked and an incredulous smile began to work its way onto his countenance. Lord Iron sat forward, his expression unreadable. One of the judges who had not yet spoken took a meditative puff on his cigar.

"I was never particularly good at sums," the man said in an unsettlingly feminine voice, "but it seems to me that you've just said a prisoner's life is *more* valuable than that of the king?"

"Yes," Olaf said, his belly heavy as if he'd drunk a tankard of lead. The eldest judge glanced at Lord Iron with a pitying expression.

"Let me also make some few observations," Olaf said, fighting to keep the desperation from his voice. "I have met with several physicians in the last few days. I am sorry to report that overindulging in strong liquor is thought by the medical establishment to reduce life expectancy by as much as five years. A habit of eating rich foods may reduce a man's span on the earth by another three to four years. A sedentary lifestyle by as much as eight. Indulging in chocolate and coffee can unbalance the blood, and remove as many as three years of life."

"You have now ceased to preach to the choir," said Lord Eichan. And indeed, the judges had grown more somber. Olaf raised a hand, begging their patience.

"I have used these medical data as well as the reports of the warden of Chappell Hill Prison and the last two years of his majesty's reported activities in the newspapers. I beg you to consider. A prisoner of the crown is kept on a simple diet and subjected to a mandatory exercise period each day. No spirits of any kind are permitted him. No luxuries such as coffee or chocolate. By comparison . . ."

Olaf fumbled with the sheaves of papers, searching for the form he had created. The eldest judge cleared his throat.

"By comparison," Olaf continued, "in the last two years, his majesty has taken vigorous exercise only one day in seven. Has eaten at banquet daily, including the richest of dishes. He regularly drinks both coffee and chocolate, often together in the French style."

"This is ridiculous," Lord Eichan said. "His majesty has the finest physicians in the world at his command. His life is better safeguarded than any man's in the realm."

"No, sir," Olaf said, his voice taking on a certainty that he was beginning to genuinely feel. "We *say* that it is, much as the embezzler claims honesty and the wanton claims virtue. I present to you the actions, as we agreed. And I would point out that his majesty's excesses are subject only to his personal whim. If he wished, he could drink himself insensible each morning, eat nothing but butterfat and lard, and never move from his seat. He could drink half a tun of coffee and play games with raw gunpowder. Unlike a prisoner, there is no enforcement of behavior that could rein him in. I have, if anything, taken a conservative measure in reaching my conclusions."

A glimmer of amusement shone in Lord Iron's eyes, but his face remained otherwise frozen. Simon, Lord Eichan was fidgeting with his cigar. The eldest judge sucked his teeth audibly and shook his head.

"And yet prisoners do not, I think, have a greater lifespan than monarchs," he said.

"It is impossible to say," Olaf said. "For many criminals and poor men, the time spent in the care of the crown can be when they are safest, best overseen, best clothed, best fed. I would, however, point out that his majesty's father left us at the age of sixty-seven, and the oldest man in the care of the crown is . . ."

Olaf paused, finding the name.

"The oldest man in the care of the crown is David Bennet, aged eighty. Incarcerated when he was sixteen for killing his brother."

He spread his hands.

"Your argument seems sound," the eldest judge said, "but your conclusion is ridiculous. I cannot believe that the king is of lesser value than a prisoner. I am afraid I remain unconvinced. What say you, gentlemen?"

But before the other two judges could answer Olaf rose to his feet.

"With all respect, sir, the question was not the value of the king or the prisoner, but of the days of their respective lives. I was not asked to judge their pleasures or their health insofar as their discomforts are less than mortal."

The effeminate judge lifted his chin. There was a livid scar across his neck where, Olaf imagined from his knowledge of men's adventure, a garrote might have cut. But it was Simon, Lord Eichan who spoke.

"How is it that a king can be more valuable than a prisoner, but his days be less? It makes no sense at all!"

"There are other things which his majesty has," Olaf said. He had warmed to his topic now, and the fact that his own life hung in the balance was all but forgotten. "A prisoner *must* take his exercise; a king has the power to refuse. A prisoner may wish dearly for a rich meal or a great glass of brandy, but since he cannot have them, he cannot exchange pleasure for . . . well, for some duration of life."

"This is a waste of—"

"Be quiet," the eldest judge said. "Let the man have his say."

"But—"

"Don't make me repeat myself, Simon."

Lord Eichan leaned back sneering and gripping his wine glass until his knuckles were white.

"It's a choice every man in this room has made," Olaf went on, raising his arm like a priest delivering a homily. "You might all live as ascetics and survive years longer. But like the king, you choose to make a rational exchange of some span of your life for the pleasure of living as you please. A prisoner is barred from that exchange, and so I submit a greater value is placed on his life precisely to the degree that strictures are placed on his pleasure and his exercise of power.

"Gentlemen, ask yourselves this; if I had two sons and saw that one of them kept from drink and gluttony while letting the other run riot, which of them would you say I valued? The prodigal might have more pleasure. Certainly the king has more pleasure than an inmate. But pleasure and power are not *life*."

"Amen," said Lord Iron. It was the first time he had spoken since Olaf had entered.

The silence that followed this declaration was broken only by the hissing of the fire in the grate and rush of blood in Olaf's ears.

"Your reports were accurate, Lord Iron," the drawling judge said. "Your pet cambist is *quite* amusing."

"Perhaps it would be best if you gave us a moment to discuss your points," the eldest judge said. "If you would be so kind as to step out to the antechamber? Yes. Thank you."

With the blackwood door closed behind him, Olaf's fear returned. He was in the Club Baphomet with his survival linked to Lord Iron's, and only an argument that seemed less and less tenable with each passing minute to protect him. But he had made his throw. His only other hope now was mad flight, and the door to the corridor was locked. He tried it.

What felt like hours passed, though the grandfather clock ticking away in the corner reported only a quarter hour. A pistol barked twice, and a moment later Lord Iron strode into the room. The door swung shut behind him before Olaf could make sense of the bloody scene. His gorge rose.

"Well done, boy," Lord Iron said, dropping something heavy into Olaf's lap. "I'll have you taken home in my personal carriage. I have Lord Eichan's sister to console this evening, and I won't be needing horses to do it. And I thought you should know; it wasn't unanimous. If his majesty hadn't taken your side, I think we might not have won the day."

"His majesty?"

Olaf's mind reeled. The face of the eldest judge resolved itself suddenly into the portrait he kept at his desk.

"You did well, boy," Lord Iron said. "Your country thanks you."

Without another word, Lord Iron unlocked the door, stepped out to the corridor, and was gone. Olaf looked down. A packet of bills squatted in his lap. Five hundred pounds at a guess, and blood smeared on the topmost bill.

He swore to himself in that moment that he would never answer another summons from Lord Iron, whatever the consequences. And, indeed, when the hour arrived, it was Lord Iron who came to him.

The weeks and months that followed were if anything richer in their tales of Lord Iron. While traveling in the Orient, he had forced a barkeep who had fallen into debt to choose between cutting off one of his infant daughter's toes or three of his own fingers in lieu of payment. He had seduced six nuns in Rome, leaving two of them with child. He had ridden an ostrich down the streets of Cairo naked at midnight. Of the untimely death of Lord Eichan there was no word, but apart from removing the portrait of the king from his desk, Olaf took no action. The less he personally figured into the debaucheries of Lord Iron, the better pleased he was.

Instead, Olaf plunged more deeply than ever into his work, his routine, and the harmless escapism of his men's adventure novels. But for the first time in memory, the perils of the heroines seemed contrived and weak; the masculine bravery of the heroes seemed overstated, like a boy who blusters and puffs out his chest when walking through the graveyard at dusk.

Clifford Knightly wrestled an alligator on the banks of the great Nile. Lord Morrow foiled the evil Chaplain Grut's plan to foul the waters of London. Emily Chastain fell gratefully into the mighty arms of the noble savage Maker-of-Justice. And Olaf found himself wondering what these great men would have done at Club Baphomet. Wrested the gun from Lord Iron? From Simon, Lord Eichan? Sternly spoken of God and truth and righteousness? Olaf doubted it would have had any great effect.

Winter passed into spring. Spring ripened to summer. Slowly, Olaf's discontent, like the nightmares from which he woke himself shouting, lessened. For weeks on end, he could forget what he had been part of. Many men who came to his window at the postal authority had traveled widely. Many had tales to tell of near misses: a runaway carriage that had come within a pace of running them down in the streets of Prague, a fever which had threatened to carry them away in Bombay, the hiss of an Afghan musket ball passing close to their head. Olaf had tales of his own now, if he ever chose to share them. That was all.

And still, when autumn with its golden leaves and fog and chill rain also brought Lord Iron back into his life, Olaf was not surprised.

It was a Tuesday night in September. Olaf had spent his customary hours at the Magdalen Gate postal authority, come back to his boardinghouse, and eaten alone in his room. The evening air was cool but not biting, and he had propped his window open before sitting down to read. When he woke, he thought for a long, bleary moment that the cold night breeze had woken him. Then the knock at his door repeated itself.

His blanket wrapped around his shoulder, Olaf answered the door. Lord Iron stood in the hall. He looked powerfully out of place. His fine jacket and cravat, the polished boots, the well-groomed beard and mustache all belonged in a palace or club. And yet rather than making the boardinghouse hall seem shabby and below him, the hallway made Lord Iron, monster of the city, seem as false as a boy playing dress-up. Olaf nodded as if he'd been expecting the man.

"I have need of you," Lord Iron said.

"Have I the option of refusal?"

Lord Iron smiled, and Olaf took it as the answer to his question. He stepped back and let the man come through. Lord Iron sat on the edge of the bed while Olaf closed his window, drew up his chair and sat. In the light from Olaf's reading lamp, Lord Iron's skin seemed waxen and pale. His voice, when he spoke, was distant as a man shouting from across a square.

"There is a question plaguing me," Lord Iron said. "You are the only man I can think of who might answer it."

"Is there a life at stake?" Olaf asked.

"No," Lord Iron said. "Nothing so petty as that."

When Olaf failed to respond, Lord Iron, born Edmund Scarasso, looked up at him. There was a terrible weariness in his eyes.

"I would know the fair price for a man's soul," he said.

"Forgive me?" Olaf said.

"You heard me," Lord Iron said. "What would be fit trade for a soul? I . . . I can't tell any longer. And it is a question whose answer has . . . some relevance to my situation."

In an instant, Olaf's mind conjured the sitting room at the Club Baphomet. Lord Iron sitting in one deep leather chair, and the Prince of Lies across from him with a snifter of brandy in his black, clawed hands.

"I don't think that would be a wise course to follow," Olaf said, though in truth his mind was spinning out ways to avoid being party to this diabolism. He did not wish to make a case before that infernal judge. Lord Iron smiled and shook his head.

"There is no one in this besides yourself and me," he said. "You are an expert in the exchange of exotic currencies. I can think of none more curious than this.

Come to my house on Mammon Street in a month's time. Tell me what conclusion you have reached."

"My lord—"

"I will make good on the investment of your time," Lord Iron said, then rose and walked out, leaving the door open behind him.

Olaf gaped at the empty room. He was a cambist. Of theology, he knew only what he had heard in church. He had read more of satanic contracts in his adventure novels than in the Bible. He was, in fact, not wholly certain that the Bible had an example of a completed exchange. Satan had tempted Jesus. Perhaps there was something to be taken from the Gospel of Matthew. . . .

Olaf spent the remainder of the night poring over his bible and considering what monetary value might be assigned to the ability to change stones to bread. But as the dawn broke and he turned to his morning ablutions, he found himself unsatisfied. The devil might have tempted Christ with all the kingdoms of the world, but it was obvious that such an offer wouldn't be open to everyone. He was approaching the problem from the wrong direction.

As he rode through the deep tunnels to Magdalen Gate, as he stopped at the newsstand for a morning paper, as he checked the ticker tape and updated his slate, his mind occupied itself by sifting through all the stories and folk wisdom he had ever heard. There had been a man who traded his soul to the devil for fame and wealth. Faust had done it for knowledge. Was there a way to represent the learning of Faust in terms of, say, semesters at the best universities of Europe? Then the rates of tuition might serve as a fingerhold.

It was nearly the day's end before the question occurred to him that put Lord Iron's commission in its proper light, and once that had happened, the answer was obvious. Olaf had to sit down, his mind afire with the answer and its implications. He didn't go home, but took himself to a small public house. Over a pint and a stale sandwich, he mentally tested his hypothesis. With the second pint, he celebrated. With the third, he steeled himself, then went out to the street and hailed a carriage to take him to the house of Lord Iron.

Revelers had infected the household like fleas on a dying rat. Masked men and women shrieked with laughter, not all of which bespoke mirth. No servant came to take his coat or ask his invitation, so Olaf made his own way through the great halls. He passed through the whole of the building before emerging from the back and finding Lord Iron himself sitting at a fountain in the gardens. His lordship's eyebrows rose to see Olaf, but he did not seem displeased.

"So soon, boy? It isn't a month," Lord Iron said as Olaf sat on the cool stone rail. The moon high above the city seemed also to dance in the water, lighting Lord Iron's face from below and above at once.

"There was no need," Olaf said. "I have your answer. But I will have to make something clear before I deliver it. If you will permit me?"

Lord Iron opened his hand in a motion of deference. Olaf cleared his throat.

"Wealth," he said, "is not a measure of money. It is a measure of well-being. Of happiness, if you will. Wealth is not traded, but rather is generated *by* trade. If you have a piece of art that I wish to own and I have money that you would prefer to the artwork, we trade. Each of us has something he prefers to the thing he gave away; otherwise, we would not have agreed on the trade. We are both better off. You see? Wealth is *generated*."

"I believe I can follow you so far," Lord Iron said. "Certainly I can agree that a fat wallet is no guarantor of contentment."

"Very well. I considered your problem for the better part of the day. I confess I came near to despairing; there is no good data from which to work. But then I found my error. I assumed that your soul, my lord, was valuable. Clearly it is not."

Lord Iron coughed out something akin to a laugh, shock in his expression. Olaf raised a hand, palm out, asking that he not interrupt.

"You are renowned for your practice of evil. This very evening, walking through your house, I have seen things for which I can imagine no proper penance. Why would Satan bother to buy your soul? He has rights to it already."

"He does," Lord Iron said, staring into the middle distance.

"And so I saw," Olaf said. "You aren't seeking to sell a soul. You are hoping to buy one."

Lord Iron sighed and looked at his hands. He seemed smaller now. Not a supernatural being, but a man driven by human fears and passions to acts that could only goad him on to worse and worse actions. A man like any other, but with the wealth to magnify his errors into the scale of legend.

"You are correct, boy," he said. "The angels wouldn't have my soul if I drenched it in honey. I have . . . treated it poorly. It's left me weary and sick. I am a waste of flesh. I know that. If there is no way to become a better man than this, I suspect the best path is to become a corpse."

"I understand, my lord. Here is the answer to your question: the price of a soul is a life of humility and service."

"Ah, is that all," Lord Iron said, as if the cambist had suggested that he pull down the stars with his fingers.

"And as it happens," Olaf went on, "I have one such with which I would be willing to part."

Lord Iron met his gaze, began to laugh, and then went silent.

"Here," Olaf said, "is what I propose. . . ."

Edmund, the new cambist of the Magdalen Gate postal authority, was by all accounts an adequate replacement for Olaf. Not as good, certainly. But his close-cropped hair and clean-shaven face lent him an eagerness that belonged on a younger man, and if he seemed sometimes more haughty than his position justified, it was a vice that lessened with every passing month. By Easter, he had even been asked to join in the Sunday picnic the girls in the accounting office sponsored. He seemed genuinely moved by the invitation.

The great scandal of the season was the disappearance of Lord Iron. The great beast of the city simply vanished one night. Rumor said that he had left his fortune and lands in trust. The identity of the trustee was a subject of tremendous speculation.

Olaf himself spent several months simply taking stock of his newfound position in the world. Once the financial situation was put in better order, he found himself with a substantial yearly allowance that still responsibly protected the initial capital.

He spent his monies traveling to India, Egypt, the sugar plantations of the Caribbean, the unworldly underground cities of Persia. He saw the sun set off the Gold Coast and rise from the waters east of Japan. He heard war songs in the jungles of the Congo and sang children's lullabies in a lonely tent made from yak skin in the dark of a Siberian winter.

And, when he paused to recover from the rigors and dangers of travel, he would retire to a cottage north of the city—the least of his holdings—and spend his time writing men's adventure novels set in the places he had been.

He named his protagonist Lord Iron.

KAREN RUSSELL

Vampires in the Lemon Grove

Karen Russell's "Vampires in the Lemon Grove" was published in the Winter *issue of* Zoetrope All-Story. *Russell's much acclaimed debut collection,* St. Lucy's Home for Girls Raised by Wolves, *was a finalist for the Young Lion's Award. Her short stories have appeared in* The New Yorker, Conjunctions, Granta, *and* The Oxford American. *She lives in New York City.*
—K.L. & G.G.
—E.D.

In October, the men and women of Sorrento harvest the *primofiore*, or "first fruit," the most succulent lemons; in March, the yellow *bianchetti* ripen, followed in June by the green *verdelli*. In every season you can find me sitting at my bench, watching them fall. Only one or two lemons tumble from the branches each hour, but I've been sitting here so long their falling seems contiguous, close as raindrops. My wife has no patience for this sort of meditation. "Jesus Christ, Clyde," she says. "You need a hobby."

Most people mistake me for a small, kindly Italian grandfather, a *nonno*. I have an old *nonno*'s coloring, the dark walnut stain peculiar to southern Italians, a tan that won't fade until I die (which I never will). I wear a neat periwinkle shirt, a canvas sunhat, black suspenders that sag at my chest. My loafers are battered but always polished. The few visitors to the lemon grove who notice me smile blankly into my raisin face and catch the whiff of some sort of tragedy; they whisper that I am a widower, or an old man who has survived his children. They never guess that I am a vampire.

Santa Francesca's Lemon Grove, where I spend my days and nights, was part of a Jesuit convent in the 1800s. Now it's privately owned by the Alberti family, the prices are excessive, and the locals know to buy their lemons elsewhere. In summers a teenage girl named Fila mans a wooden stall at the back of the grove. She's painfully thin, with heavy, black bangs. I can tell by the careful way she saves the best lemons for me, slyly kicking them under my bench, that she knows I am a monster. Sometimes she'll smile vacantly in my direction, but she never gives me any trouble. And because of her benevolent indifference to me, I feel a swell of love for the girl.

Fila makes the lemonade and monitors the hot dog machine, watching the meat rotate on wire spits. I'm fascinated by this machine. The Italian name for it translates as "carousel of beef." Who would have guessed at such a device two hundred years ago? Back then we were all preoccupied with visions of apocalypse; Santa Francesca, the foundress of this very grove, gouged out her eyes while dictating premonitions of fire. What a shame, I often think, that she foresaw only the end times, never hot dogs.

A sign posted just outside the grove reads:

CIGERETTE PIE
HEAT DOGS
GRANITE DRINKS
SANTA FRANCESCA'S LIMONATA—
THE MOST REFRESHING DRANK ON THE PLENET!!

Every day, tourists from Wales and Germany and America are ferried over from cruise ships to the base of these cliffs. They ride the funicular up here to visit the grove, to eat "heat dogs" with speckly brown mustard and sip lemon ices. They snap photographs of the Alberti brothers, Benny and Luciano, teenage twins who cling to the trees' wooden supports and make a grudging show of harvesting lemons, who spear each other with trowels and refer to the tourist women as "vaginas" in Italian slang. "*Buona sera*, vaginas!" they cry from the trees. I think the tourists are getting stupider. None of them speaks Italian anymore, and these new women seem deaf to aggression. Often I fantasize about flashing my fangs at the brothers, just to keep them in line.

As I said, the tourists usually ignore me; perhaps it's the dominoes. A few years back, I bought a battered red set from Benny, a prop piece, and this makes me invisible, sufficiently banal to be hidden in plain sight. I have no real interest in the game; I mostly stack the pieces into little houses and corrals.

At sunset, the tourists all around begin to shout. "Look! Up there!" It's time for the path of *I Pipistrelli Impazziti*—the descent of the bats.

They flow from cliffs that glow like pale chalk, expelled from caves in the seeming billions. Their drop is steep and vertical, a black hail. Sometimes a change in weather sucks a bat beyond the lemon trees and into the turquoise sea. It's three hundred feet to the lemon grove, six hundred feet to the churning foam of the Tyrrhenian. At the precipice, they soar upward and crash around the green tops of the trees.

"Oh!" the tourists shriek, delighted, ducking their heads.

Up close, the bats' spread wings are an alien membrane—fragile, like something internal flipped out. The waning sun washes their bodies a dusky red. They have wrinkled black faces, these bats, tiny, like gargoyles or angry grandfathers. They have teeth like mine.

Tonight, one of the tourists, a Texan lady with a big, strawberry red updo, has successfully captured a bat in her hair, simultaneously crying real tears and howling: "TAKE THE GODDAMN PICTURE, Sarah!"

I stare ahead at a fixed point above the trees and light a cigarette. My bent spine goes rigid. Mortal terror always trips some old wire that leaves me sad and irritable. It will be whole minutes now before everybody stops screaming.

The moon is a muted shade of orange. Twin discs of light burn in the sky and the sea. I scan the darker indents in the skyline, the cloudless spots that I know to be caves. I check my watch again. It's eight o'clock, and all the bats have disappeared into the interior branches. Where is Magreb? My fangs are throbbing, but I won't start without her.

I once pictured time as a black magnifying glass and myself as a microscopic, flightless insect trapped in that circle of night. But then Magreb came along, and eternity ceased to frighten me. Suddenly each moment followed its antecedent in a neat chain, moments we filled with each other.

I watch a single bat falling from the cliffs, dropping like a stone: headfirst, motionless, dizzying to witness.

Pull up.

I close my eyes. I press my palms flat against the picnic table and tense the muscles of my neck.

Pull UP. I tense until my temples pulse, until little black and red stars flutter behind my eyelids.

"You can look now."

Magreb is sitting on the bench, blinking her bright pumpkin eyes. "You weren't even *watching*. If you saw me coming down, you'd know you have nothing to worry about." I try to smile at her and find I can't. My own eyes feel like ice cubes.

"It's stupid to go so fast." I don't look at her. "That easterly could knock you over the rocks."

"Don't be ridiculous. I'm an excellent flier."

She's right. Magreb can shape-shift midair, much more smoothly than I ever could. Even back in the 1850s when I used to transmute into a bat two, three times a night, my metamorphosis was a shy, halting process.

"Look!" she says, triumphant, mocking, "you're still trembling!"

I look down at my hands, angry to realize it's true.

Magreb roots through the tall, black blades of grass. "It's late, Clyde; where's my lemon?"

I pluck a soft, round lemon from the grass, half a summer moon, and hand it to her. The *verdelli* I have chosen is perfect, flawless. She looks at it with distaste and makes a big show of brushing off a marching ribbon of ants.

"A toast!" I say.

"A toast," Magreb replies, with the rote enthusiasm of a Christian saying grace. We lift the lemons and swing them to our faces. We plunge our fangs, piercing the skin, and emit a long, united hiss: "*Aaah!*"

Over the years, Magreb and I have tried everything—fangs in apples, fangs in rubber balls. We have lived everywhere: Tunis, Laos, Cincinnati, Salamanca. We spent our honeymoon hopping continents, hunting liquid chimeras: mint tea in Fez, coconut slurries in Oahu, jet black coffee in Bogotá, jackal's milk in Dakar, cherry Coke floats in rural Alabama, a thousand beverages that purported to have magical quenching properties. We went thirsty in every region of the globe before finding our oasis here, in the blue boot of Italy, at this dead nun's lemonade stand. It's only these lemons that give us any relief.

When we first landed in Sorrento I was skeptical. The pitcher of lemonade we ordered looked cloudy and adulterated. Sugar clumped at the bottom. I took a gulp, and a whole small lemon lodged in my mouth; there is no word sufficiently lovely for the first taste, the first feeling of my fangs in that lemon. It was bracingly sour, with a delicate hint of ocean salt. After an initial prickling—a sort of chemical effervescence along my gums—a soothing blankness traveled from the tip of each fang to my fevered brain. These lemons are a vampire's analgesic. If you have been thirsty for a long time, if you have been suffering, then the absence of those two feelings—however brief—becomes a kind of heaven. I breathed deeply through my nostrils. My throbbing fangs were still.

By daybreak, the numbness had begun to wear off. The lemons relieve our thirst without ending it, like a drink we can hold in our mouths but never swallow. Eventually the original hunger returns. I have tried to be very good, very correct and conscientious about not confusing this original hunger with the thing I feel for Magreb.

I can't joke about my early years on the blood, can't even think about them without guilt and acidic embarrassment. Unlike Magreb, who has never had a sip of the stuff, I listened to the village gossips and believed every rumor, internalized every report of corrupted bodies and boiled blood. Vampires were the favorite undead of the Enlightenment, and as a young boy I aped the diction and mannerisms I read about in books: Vlad the Impaler, Count Heinrich the Despoiler, Goethe's bloodsucking bride of Corinth. I eavesdropped on the terrified prayers of an old woman in a cemetery, begging God to protect her from . . . me. I felt a dislocation then, a spreading numbness, as if I were invisible or already dead. After that, I did only what the stories suggested, beginning with that old woman's blood. I slept in coffins, in black cedar boxes, and woke every night with a fierce headache. I was famished, perennially dizzy. I had unspeakable dreams about the sun.

In practice I was no suave viscount, just a teenager in a red velvet cape, awkward and voracious. I wanted to touch the edges of my life. The same instinct, I think, that inspires young mortals to flip tractors and enlist in foreign wars. One night I skulked into a late Mass with some vague plan to defeat eternity. At the back of the nave, I tossed my mousy curls, rolled my eyes heavenward, and then plunged my entire arm into the bronze pail of holy water. Death would be painful, probably, but I didn't care about pain. I wanted to overturn my sentence. It was working; I could feel the burn beginning to spread. Actually, it was more like an itch, but I was sure the burning would start any second. I slid into a pew, snug in my misery, and waited for my body to turn to ash.

By sunrise, I'd developed a rash between my eyebrows, a little late-flowering acne, but was otherwise fine, and I understood I truly was immortal. At that moment I yielded all discrimination; I bit anyone kind or slow enough to let me get close: men, women, even some older boys and girls. The littlest children I left alone, very proud at the time of this one scruple. I'd read stories about Hungarian *vampirs* who drank the blood of orphan girls and mentioned this to Magreb early on, hoping to impress her with my decency. Not *children*! she wept. She wept for a day and a half.

Our first date was in Cementerio de Colón, if I can call a chance meeting between headstones a date. I had been stalking her, following her swishing hips as she took a shortcut through the cemetery grass. She wore her hair in a low, snaky braid that was coming unraveled. When I was near enough to touch her trailing ribbon she whipped around. "Are you following me?" she asked, annoyed, not scared. She regarded my face with the contempt of a woman confronting the town drunk. "Oh," she said, "your teeth . . ."

And then she grinned. Magreb was the first and only other vampire I'd ever met. We bared our fangs over a tombstone and recognized one another. There is a loneliness that must be particular to monsters, I think, the feeling that each is the only child of a species. And now that loneliness was over.

Our first date lasted all night. Magreb's talk seemed to lunge forward like a train without a conductor; I suspect even she didn't know what she was saying. I certainly wasn't paying attention, staring dopily at her fangs, and then I heard her ask: "So, when did you figure out that the blood does nothing?"

At the time of this conversation, I was edging on 130. I had never gone a day since early childhood without drinking several pints of blood. *The blood does nothing?* My forehead burned and burned.

"Didn't you think it suspicious that you had a heartbeat?" she asked me. "That you had a reflection in water?"

When I didn't answer, Magreb went on. "Every time I saw my own face in a mirror, I knew I wasn't any of those ridiculous things, a bloodsucker, a *sanguina*. You know?"

"Sure," I said, nodding. For me, mirrors had the opposite effect: I saw a mouth ringed in black blood. I saw the pale son of the villagers' fears.

Those early days with Magreb nearly undid me. At first my euphoria was sharp and blinding, all my thoughts spooling into a single blue thread of relief—*The blood does nothing! I don't have to drink the blood!*—but when that subsided, I found I had nothing left. If we didn't have to drink the blood, then what on earth were these fangs for?

Sometimes I think she preferred me then: I was like her own child, raw and amazed. We smashed my coffin with an ax and spent the night at a hotel. I lay there wide-eyed in the big bed, my heart thudding like a fish tail against the floor of a boat.

"You're really sure?" I whispered to her. "I don't have to sleep in a coffin? I don't have to sleep through the day?" She had already drifted off.

A few months later, she suggested a picnic.

"But the sun."

Magreb shook her head. "You poor thing, believing all that garbage."

By this time we'd found a dirt cellar in which to live in Western Australia, where the sun burned through the clouds like dining lace. That sun ate lakes, rising out of dead volcanoes at dawn, triple the size of a harvest moon and skull-white, a grass-scorcher. Go ahead, try to walk into that sun when you've been told your bones are tinder.

I stared at the warped planks of the trapdoor above us, the copper ladder that led rung by rung to the bright world beyond. Time fell away from me and I was a child again, afraid, afraid. Magreb rested her hand on the small of my back. "You can do it," she said, nudging me gently. I took a deep breath and hunched my shoulders, my scalp grazing the cellar door, my hair soaked through with sweat. I focused my thoughts to still the tremors, lest my fangs slice the inside of my mouth, and turned my face away from Magreb.

"Go on."

I pushed up and felt the wood give way. Light exploded through the cellar. My pupils shrank to dots.

Outside, the whole world was on fire. Mute explosions rocked the scrubby forest, motes of light burning like silent rockets. The sun fell through the eucalyptus and Australian pines in bright red bars. I pulled myself out onto my belly, balled up in the soil, and screamed for mercy until I'd exhausted myself. Then I opened one watery eye and took a long look around. The sun wasn't fatal! It was just uncomfortable, making my eyes itch and water and inducing a sneezing attack. (Magreb still has not let me forget this scene, and it happened two hundred years ago.)

After that, and for the whole of our next thirty years together, I watched the auroral colors and waited to feel anything but terror. Fingers of light spread across the gray sea toward me, and I couldn't see these colors as beautiful. The sky I lived under was a hideous, lethal mix of orange and pink, a physical deformity. By the 1950s we were living in a Cincinnati suburb; and as a day's first light hit the kitchen windows, I'd press my face against the linoleum and gibber my terror into the cracks.

"So-o," Magreb would say, "I can tell you're not a morning person." Then she'd sit on the porch swing and rock with me, patting my hand.

"What's wrong, Clyde?"

I shook my head. This was a new sadness, difficult to express. My bloodlust was undiminished but now the blood wouldn't fix it.

"It never fixed it," Magreb reminded me, and I wished she would please stop talking.

That cluster of years was a very confusing period. Mostly I felt grateful, above-ground feelings. I was in love. For a vampire, my life was very normal. Instead of stalking prostitutes, I went on long bicycle rides with Magreb. We visited botanical gardens and rowed in boats. In a short time, my face had gone from lithium white to the color of milky coffee. Yet sometimes, especially at high noon, I'd study Magreb's face with a hot, illogical hatred, each pore opening up to swallow me. *You've ruined my life*, I'd think. To correct for her power over my mind I tried to fantasize about mortal women, their wild eyes and bare swan necks; I couldn't do it, not anymore — an eternity of vague female smiles eclipsed by Magreb's tiny razor fangs. Two gray tabs against her lower lip.

But like I said, I was mostly happy. I was making a kind of progress.

One night, children wearing necklaces of garlic bulbs arrived giggling at our door. It was Halloween; they were vampire hunters. The smell of garlic blasted through the mail slot, along with their voices: "Trick or treat!" In the old days, I would have cowered from these children. I would have run downstairs to barricade myself in my coffin. But that night, I pulled on an undershirt and opened the door. I stood in a square of green light in my boxer shorts hefting a bag of Tootsie Roll Pops, a small victory over the old fear.

"Mister, you OK?"

I blinked down at a little blond child and then saw that my two hands were shaking violently, soundlessly, like old friends wishing not to burden me with their troubles. I dropped the candies into the children's bags, thinking: *You small mortals don't realize the power of your stories.*

We were downing strawberry velvet cocktails on the Seine when something inside me changed. Thirty years. Eleven thousand dawns. That's how long it took for me to believe the sun wouldn't kill me.

"Want to go see a museum or something? We're in Paris, after all."

"OK."

We walked over a busy pedestrian bridge in a flood of light, and my heart was in my throat. Without any discussion, I understood that Magreb was my wife.

Because I love her, my hunger pangs have gradually mellowed into a comfortable despair. Sometimes I think of us as two holes cleaved together, two twin hungers. Our bellies growl at one another like companionable dogs. I love the sound, assuring me we're equals in our thirst. We bump our fangs together and feel like we're coming up against the same hard truth.

Human marriages amuse me: the brevity of the commitment and all the ceremony that surrounds it, the calla lilies, the veiled mothers-in-law like lilac spiders, the tears and earnest toasts. Till death do us part! Easy. These mortal couples need only keep each other in sight for fifty, sixty years.

Often I wonder to what extent a mortal's love grows from the bedrock of his or her foreknowledge of death, love coiling like a green stem out of that blankness in a way I'll never quite understand. And lately I've been having a terrible thought: *Our love affair will end before the world does.*

One day, without any preamble, Magreb flew up to the caves. She called over her furry, muscled shoulder that she just wanted to sleep for a while.

"What? Wait! What's wrong?"

I'd caught her midshift, halfway between a wife and a bat.

"Don't be so sensitive, Clyde! I'm just tired of this century, so very tired, maybe it's the heat? I think I just need a little rest. . . ."

I assumed this was an experiment, like my cape, an old habit to which she was returning; and from the clumsy, ambivalent way she crashed around on the wind I understood I was supposed to follow her. Well, too bad. Magreb likes to say she freed me, disabused me of the old stories; but I gave up more than I intended: I can't shudder myself out of this old man's body. I can't fly anymore.

Fila and I are alone. I press my dry lips together and shove dominoes around the table; they buckle like the cars of a tiny train.

"More lemonade, *nonno?*" she smiles. She leans from her waist and boldly touches my right fang, a thin string of hanging drool. "Looks like you're thirsty."

"Please," I gesture at the bench. "Have a seat."

Fila is seventeen now and has known about me for some time. She's toying with the idea of telling her boss, weighing the sentence within her like a bullet in a gun: *There is a vampire in our grove.*

"You don't believe me, *signore* Alberti?" she'll say, before taking him by the wrist and leading him to this bench, and I'll choose that moment to rise up and bite him in his hog-thick neck. "Right through his stupid tie!" she says with a grin.

But this is just idle fantasy, she assures me. Fila is content to let me alone. "You remind me of my *nonno,*" she says approvingly, "you look very Italian."

In fact, she wants to help me hide here. It gives her a warm feeling to do so, like helping her own fierce *nonno* do up the small buttons of his trousers, now too intricate a maneuver for his palsied hands. She worries about me, too. And she should: lately I've gotten sloppy, incontinent about my secrets. I've stopped polishing my shoes; I let the tip of one fang hang over my pink lip. "You must be more careful," she reprimands. "There are tourists *everywhere.*"

I study her neck as she says this, her head rolling with the natural expressiveness of a girl. She checks to see if I am watching her collarbone, and I let her see that I am. I feel like a threat again.

Last night I went on a rampage. On my seventh lemon I found with a sort of drowsy despair that I couldn't stop. I crawled around on all fours looking for the last *bianchettis* in the dewy grass: soft with rot, mildewed, sun-shriveled, blackened. Lemon skin bulging with tiny cellophane-green worms. Dirt smells, rain smells, all swirled through with the tart sting of decay.

In the morning, Magreb steps around the wreckage and doesn't say a word.

"I came up with a new name," I say, hoping to distract her. "*Brandolino.* What do you think?"

Magreb and I have spent the last several years trying to choose Italian names, and every day that I remain Clyde feels like a defeat. Our names are relics of the places we've been. "Clyde" is a souvenir from the California Gold Rush. I was callow and blood-crazed back then, and I saw my echo in the freckly youths panning along the Sacramento River. I used the name as a kind of bait. It sounded innocuous, like someone a boy might get a malt beer with or follow into the woods.

Magreb chose her name in the Atlas Mountains for its etymology, the root word *ghuroob*, which means "to set" or "to be hidden." "That's what we're looking for," she tells me. "The setting place. Some final answer." She won't change her name until we find it.

She takes a lemon from her mouth, slides it down the length of her fangs, and places its shriveled core on the picnic table. When she finally speaks, her voice is so low the words are almost unintelligible.

"The lemons aren't working, Clyde."

But the lemons have never worked. At best, they give us eight hours of peace. We aren't talking about the lemons.

"How long?"

"Longer than I've let on. I'm sorry."

"Well, maybe it's this crop. Those Alberti boys haven't been fertilizing properly, maybe the *primofiore* will turn out better."

Magreb fixes me with one fish-bright eye. "Clyde, I think it's time for us to go."

Wind blows the leaves apart. Lemons wink like a firmament of yellow stars, slowly ripening, and I can see the other, truer night behind them.

"Go where?" Our marriage, as I conceive it, is a commitment to starve together.

"We've been resting here for decades. I think it's time . . . what is that thing?"

I have been preparing a present for Magreb, for our anniversary, a "cave" of scavenged materials—newspaper and bottle glass and wooden beams from the lemon tree supports—so that she can sleep down here with me. I've smashed dozens of bottles of fruity beer to make stalactites. Looking at it now, though, I see the cave is very small. It looks like an umbrella mauled by a dog.

"That thing?" I say. "That's nothing. I think it's part of the hot dog machine."

"Jesus. Did it catch on fire?"

"Yes. The girl threw it out yesterday."

"Clyde," Magreb shakes her head. "We never meant to stay here forever, did we? That was never the plan."

"I didn't know we had a plan," I snap. "What if we've outlived our food supply? What if there's nothing left for us to find?"

"You don't really believe that."

"Why can't you just be grateful? Why can't you be happy and admit defeat? Look at what we've found here!" I grab a lemon and wave it in her face.

"Goodnight, Clyde."

I watch my wife fly up into the watery dawn, and again I feel the awful tension. In the flats of my feet, in my knobbed spine. Love has infected me with a muscular superstition that one body can do the work of another.

I consider taking the funicular, the ultimate degradation—worse than the dominoes, worse than an eternity of sucking cut lemons. All day I watch the cars ascend, and I'm reminded of those American fools who accompany their wives to the beach but refuse to wear bathing suits. I've seen them by the harbor, sulking in their trousers, panting through menthol cigarettes and pacing the dock while the women sea-bathe. They pretend they don't mind when sweat darkens the armpits of their suits. When their wives swim out and leave them. When their wives are just a splash in the distance.

Tickets for the funicular are twenty lire. I sit at the bench and count as the cars go by.

That evening, I take Magreb on a date. I haven't left the lemon grove in upward of two years, and blood roars in my ears as I stand and clutch at her like an old man. We're going to the Thursday night show, an antique theater in a castle in the center of town. I want her to see that I'm happy to travel with her, so long as our destination is within walking distance.

A teenage usher in a vintage red jacket with puffed sleeves escorts us to our seats, his biceps manacled in clouds, threads loosening from the badge on his chest. I am jealous of the name there: GUGLIELMO.

The movie's title is already scrolling across the black screen: *Something Clandestine Is Happening in the Corn!*

Magreb snorts. "That's a pretty lousy name for a horror movie. It sounds like a student film."

"Here's your ticket," I say. "I didn't make the title up. If you wanted to see something else you should have said so."

It's a vampire movie set in the Dust Bowl. Magreb expects a comedy, but the Dracula actor fills me with the sadness of an old photo album. An Okie has unwittingly fallen in love with the monster, whom she's mistaken for a rich European creditor eager to pay off the mortgage on her family's farm.

"That Okie," says Magreb, "is an idiot."

I turn my head miserably and there's Fila, sitting two rows in front of us with a greasy young man, Benny Alberti. Her white neck is bent to the left, Benny's lips affixed to it as she impassively sips a soda.

"Poor thing," Magreb whispers, indicating the pigtailed actress. "She thinks he's going to save her."

Dracula shows his fangs, and the Okie flees through a cornfield. Corn stalks smack her face. "Help!" she screams to a sky full of crows. "He's not actually from Europe!"

There is no music, only the girl's breath and the *fwap-fwap-fwap* of the off-screen fan blades. Dracula's mouth hangs wide as a sewer grate. His cape is curiously still.

The movie picture is frozen. The *fwap*ing is emanating from the projection booth; it rises to a grinding *r-r-r*, followed by lyrical Italian cussing and silence and finally a tidal sigh. Magreb shifts in her seat.

"Let's wait," I say, seized with an empathy for these two still figures on the movie screen, mutely waiting for repair. "They'll fix it."

People begin to file out of the theater, first in twos and threes and then in droves.

"I'm tired, Clyde."

"Don't you want to know what happens?" My voice is more frantic than I intend it to be.

"I already know what happens."

"Don't you leave now, Magreb. I'm telling you, they're going to fix it. If you leave now, that's it for us, I'll never . . ."

Her voice is beautiful, like gravel underfoot: "I'm going to the caves."

I'm alone in the theater. When I turn to exit, the picture is still frozen, the Okie's blue dress floating over windless corn, Dracula's mouth a hole in his white greasepaint.

Outside I see Fila standing in a clot of her friends, lit by the marquee. These kids wear too much makeup, and clothes that move like colored oils. They all looked rained on. I scowl at them and they scowl back; and then Fila crosses to me.

"Hey, you," she grins, breathless, so very close to my face. "Are you stalking somebody?"

My throat tightens.

"Guys!" Her eyes gleam. "Guys, come over and meet the *vampire*."

But the kids are gone.

"Well! Some friends," she says, then winks. "Leaving me alone, defenseless . . ."

"You want the old vampire to bite you, eh?" I hiss. "You want a story for your friends?"

Fila laughs. Her horror is a round, genuine thing, bouncing in both her black eyes. She smells like hard water and glycerin. The hum of her young life all around me makes it difficult to think. A bat filters my thoughts, opens its trembling lampshade wings.

Magreb. She'll want to hear about this. How ridiculous, at my age, to find myself down this alley with a young girl: Fila powdering her neck, doing her hair up with little temptress pins, yanking me behind this Dumpster. "Can you imagine," Magreb will laugh, "a teenager goading you to attack her! You're still a menace, Clyde."

I stare vacantly at a pale mole above the girl's collarbone. *Magreb*, I think again, and I smile; and the smile feels like a muzzle. It seems my hand has tightened on the girl's wrist, and I realize with surprise, as if from a great distance, that she is twisting away.

"Hey, *nonno*, come on now, what are you—"

The girl's head lolls against my shoulder like that of a sleepy child, then swings forward in a rag-doll circle. The starlight is white mercury compared to her blotted-out eyes. There's a dark stain on my periwinkle shirt, and one suspender has snapped. I sit Fila's body against the alley wall, watch it dim and stiffen. Spidery graffiti weaves over the brick behind her, and I scan for some answer contained there: GIOVANNA & FABIANO. VAFFANCULO! VAI IN CULO.

A scabby-furred creature, our only witness, arches its orange back against the Dumpster. If not for the lock I would ease the girl inside. I would climb in with her and let the red stench fill my nostrils, let the flies crawl into the red corners of my eyes. I am a monster again.

I ransack Fila's pockets and find the key to the funicular office, careful not to look at her face. Then I'm walking, running for the lemon grove. I jimmy my way into the control room and turn the silver key, relieved to hear the engine roar to life. Locked, locked, every car is locked, but then I find one with thick tape in Xs over a busted door. I dash after it and pull myself onto the cushion, quickly, because the cars are already moving. The box jounces and trembles. The chain pulls me into the heavens link by link.

My lips are soon chapped; I stare through a crack in the glass window. The box swings wildly in the wind. The sky is a deep blue vacuum. I can still smell the girl in the folds of my clothes.

The cave system is vaster than I expected; and with their grandfather faces tucked away, the bats are anonymous as stones. I walk beneath a chandelier of furry bodies, heartbeats wrapped in wings the color of rose petals or corn silk. Breath ripples through each of them, a tiny life in its translucent envelope.

"Magreb?"
Is she up here?
Has she left me?
(I will never find another vampire.)

I double back to the moonlit entrance, the funicular cars. When I find Magreb, I'll beg her to tell me what she dreams up here. I'll tell her my waking dreams in the lemon grove: the mortal men and women floating serenely by in balloons freighted with the ballast of their deaths. Millions of balloons ride over a wide ocean, lives darkening the sky. Death is a dense powder cinched inside tiny sandbags, and in the dream I am given to understand that instead of a sandbag I have Magreb.

I make the bats' descent in a cable car with no wings to spread, knocked around by the wind with a force that feels personal. I struggle to hold the door shut and look for the green speck of our grove.

The box is plunging now, far too quickly. It swings wide, and the igneous surface of the mountain fills the left window. The tufa shines like water, like a black, heat-bubbled river. For a disorienting moment I expect the rock to seep through the glass.

Each swing takes me higher than the last, a grinding pendulum that approaches a full revolution around the cable. I'm on my hands and knees on the car floor, seasick in the high air, pressing my face against the floor grate. I can see stars or boats burning there, and also a ribbon of white, a widening fissure. Air gushes through the cracks in the glass box.

What does Magreb see, if she can see? Is she waking from a nightmare to watch the line snap, the glass box plummet? From her inverted vantage, dangling from the roof of the cave, does the car seem to be sucked upward, rushing not toward the sea but to another sort of sky? To a black mouth open and foaming with stars?

I like to picture my wife like this: Magreb shuts her thin eyelids tighter. She digs her claws into the rock. Little clouds of dust rise around her toes as she swings upside down. She feels something growing inside her, unstoppable as a dreadful suspicion. It is solid, this new thing, it is the opposite of hunger. She's emerging from a dream of distant thunder, rumbling and loose. Something has happened tonight that she thought impossible. In the morning, she will want to tell me about it.

M. RICKERT

Holiday

M. Rickert's short story collection, Map of Dreams, *won both the World Fantasy and William Crawford awards, and her story, "Journey into the Kingdom," won the World Fantasy Award for best short fiction. Her next collection,* Holiday, *will be published by Golden Gryphon Press in 2009. She lives in Cedarburg, Wisconsin.*

The story "Holiday" was first published in Subterranean *issue #7, which I had the honor to guest-edit.*

—E.D.

S he says her name is Holiday, but I know she's lying. I remember her face. It was all over the news for weeks, years even, but of course she doesn't know that. I briefly consider telling her, saying something like, "Hey, did you know you're a star?" But that would necessitate bringing up the subject of her death, and I'm not clear if she knows that she's a ghost, or that almost everyone thinks her parents killed her. That doesn't seem like the kind of thing any kid should have to hear, so instead I say, "Holiday? That's a pretty name."

Her body starts jerking in a strange way as she moves across my bedroom floor, her arms held out, her hands moving to some secret rhythm, and I think she's reenacting her death, the way some ghosts do, until I realize that she's tap dancing, her blonde curls bouncing, that little-Miss smile plastered across her face, bright red like she just finished eating a cherry Popsicle. I figured she came to tell me who offed her, but instead she came to dance and tell me lies.

"Why don't you come here," I pat beside me on the bed. Just like that she's gone. Like I'm a pervert or something. Poor dumb kid.

That's all there is until about a week later. This time I'm asleep on the couch and she wakes me up, singing a country western song. She's wearing a black cowboy hat with a big gold star on the front, a little black and red-fringed skirt, a denim shirt with silver buttons, and red tasseled cowboy boots that come about halfway up her calves. She looks pretty cute. She's singing in the dulcet tone of someone twice her age, and right away I understand the confusion people felt about her, the strange aura of sexuality that comes off her and shouldn't. When she sees me watching, she waves, her little fingers slightly bent, but she doesn't miss a beat, even when she winks.

This is so freaking weird I don't know what to do so I wait until she's finished and then I applaud.

She curtsies, holding out the skirt with the tips of her tiny fingers; her perfect blonde curls undisturbed by her dance and song.

"So," I say, "Holiday, right?"

She nods, her red lips smirked.

"You hungry?" I pick up the half-full bag of Doritos on the coffee table in front of the couch and extend it toward her. She shakes her head. "Wanna watch a movie?" I ask. She just stands there, staring at me, squinting slightly, looking like she just might start crying, as though I have awoken her from some dream about Barbie dolls and Christmas and a perfect life, into this reality of being murdered and stuck, for all eternity, at age six, tap dancing forever. I look through my DVD collection, *Kill Bill* (1 and 2), *Seven Samurai, The Shining, Howard Stern's Private Parts* (severely underrated and underappreciated, by the way), *City of Women, My Architect, Wild Weather Caught on Tape* (a gift from an old girlfriend) and *The Wet Women of California*, which, swear to God, I had forgotten all about. None of it exactly seems like the sort of thing to watch with a six-year-old murdered kid, so instead I turn on the TV and settle on the cooking channel, but I guess it wasn't the right choice because next thing I know, I'm sitting alone watching this chick with a giant smile, pouring liquid over hamburger meat. "Hey," I say to the air, "Come back, we don't have to watch this." But of course no one answers and no one appears. I pick up one of the DVDs, and put it in, just to get rid of the headache I feel coming on. In two seconds, I'm watching naked big-breasted women dive into the ocean, roll in the sand, and frolic with the waves and each other. I drink my warm beer and start to play with myself until I get the creepy feeling that maybe she's still in the room. I take my hand out of my pants, flick off the DVD, and turn over, my face pressed against the couch.

The next day I go to the library. There's a whole shelf devoted just to her. I page through the books and look at all the pictures. Yep, it's her all right. I don't check out the books, just in case she comes back. I don't want her to see them and get scared or anything. I don't know why she's coming to see me, but I want her to come back. When I read about how her father found her, wrapped in a blanket, as though someone was worried she would be cold, but with that rope around her neck, and all the rest, I feel like something inside me wakes up, and it's not a completely disturbing feeling. I spend the whole day at the library and when I leave I'm tired, and hungry, but before I do anything else, I go to Wal-Mart and buy the boxed collection of Shirley Temple DVDs. They were her favorite. Next time she comes, I'm going to be prepared. Sarah Vehler, who was in my brother's class in high school, is the checkout girl. She's gained about five hundred pounds since then and I barely recognize her, but she recognizes me just fine. "I didn't know you have kids," she says. What am I supposed to do, tell her I've got a ghost? Instead, I just shrug. Maybe that was a mistake. I don't know. This was all new territory for me. I tried to do what was right.

When Terry, my agent, calls to see how the book is coming along, I tell him it's just fine. "But hey," I say, "I'm thinking of going in another direction, sort of."

"Shoot," Terry says.

I stumble around a bit and even though he's thousands of miles away, I know he's chewing his Nicotine gum faster and faster until finally he says, "Listen, just give it to me in a sentence, all right?"

"I wanna write about—" and I say her name.

"Who?"

For a long time she was everyone's little girl. The whole country followed her story and wanted vengeance for what was done to her, but now, hardly anyone even remembers her name.

"Oh, wait, the little Miss America kid, right? What's she got to do with anything? Did your parents know her parents or something?"

"Well, not exactly, but—"

"Don't blow this, ok? Memoir writing isn't what it used to be, all right? Just stick to the facts, make sure it's all documented."

"But I—"

"Stick to your own story. You got enough there to keep you busy, right?"

"But Terry," I say, "When I think about her, I mean, don't you think what happened to her was a real travesty?"

"Travesty? Right. Of course it was. But what happened to you was a real travesty too, wasn't it? Your whole family torn apart by false accusations, your father dying in prison for something he didn't do. That's the travesty you know. That's the one you can write about."

"I just think—"

"Ok, I know what's happening here. Something in your mind, in your subconscious is trying to distract you from writing this, am I right? Huh?"

"I guess," I say, glancing at my computer.

"Tell you what, why don't you just take a couple of days? Give yourself a break. Watch movies. Take walks in the park. Get laid. Take some time off, is what I'm saying, not weeks or anything, but you know, take a few days, then you can come back to this all refreshed, OK?"

"OK," I say.

"Who cares if you're a few days late, right?"

"Right."

"Just forget about the kid," he says. "She's not your story."

We say good-bye and I walk over to the computer and click on the file. I stare at the blank screen, certain that if I could just come up with the title, I could probably sail through the whole thing. But the title is illusive. Instead I take Terry's advice and watch a movie, several in fact. Shirley Temple in black and white, highly, highly underrated. I don't even know when she appears. But suddenly we are sitting on the couch, laughing. It feels so good to laugh like that I decide not to say anything. I don't want to scare her off. I don't know when she left. I fell asleep and when I woke up, she was gone.

The next day I sit staring at the screen on my computer for two hours, I know it sounds like an exaggeration, but I timed it. I try several titles. *My Father's Rules. I Am Not His Son. Rising Above the Prison He Resides In. Last Chance.* You get the picture, right? Crap. I click off the computer and take Terry's advice. I go to the park.

They are so young. So perfect, with their perfect skin and little teeth and they are dirty, and bratty, and crying, and laughing and completely absorbed by the sand in the sandbox, or the need to traverse the bars, dangling above the dangerous ground, holding tight, and it's obvious it hurts, but they are determined, stubborn, wild, beautiful. I could watch them for hours, but instead I just watch for a little while, I know too well what the grownups will think about someone like me, a young man, all alone, watching children play. I turn away, hunched against the sudden cold, walking slowly, soon no longer able to hear the laughter and the sound of their voices, shouting names, or shouting nonsense.

God, how I envy them.

When I get home my brother is standing on my porch, hunched into his jacket, his hands in his pockets. "Hey," he says.

"Hey," I say. "What's up?"

He shrugs, glances at my door and then gives me that pretend smile of his.

"I don't have any," I say.

"What? Oh, that hurts, bro," he says. "I'm sincerely hurt. I just thought, you know, I'd stop by."

I nod, but I do it with a smirk so that he knows I know the truth even if we are going to play this game. I take the key out of my pocket and let us into the house.

"Christ," he says.

"What?"

"Don't you ever clean up after yourself? Mom would shit if she saw this."

"Well, she's not going to see it, all right? We both know that. What do you want?"

He shrugs, but he's casing the joint. I'm a writer. I notice these things. "Man, I'm just so hurt, bro," he says. "What, you think I only come when—"

"Yeah," I say. "Yeah, I do."

We stand there, staring at each other, then he shrugs and walks into my living room, sits on the couch, I'm only half paying attention, he picks up the remote control. "Wait," I say, but it's too late, Shirley Temple is dancing across the screen, all dimples and innocence.

I don't know what to do so I just stand there.

He's laughing so hard, he's bent over at the waist, and I start laughing too, and that's when he jumps up and grabs me by the collar and pushes me against the wall.

"I should fucking kill you," he says.

"It's not like that. I'm doing some research."

"Fucking pervert."

"I'm not the one," I say, only 'cause I'm desperate, only 'cause he's got this look in his eyes like he might really kill me.

He pushes me harder into the wall. He leans against me. "What did you say?"

"I'm not the one he liked most," I say and he lets go as if I'm on fire. For a moment we are just standing there, breathing heavy and staring at each other. I try to make it right. I reach over to touch his shoulder but he jerks away.

He wipes his hand through his hair, licks his lips, and then wipes them with the back of his hand, and his eyes stay cold.

"Come on," I try again.

He leans toward me, like he would kill me if he could stand to touch me. He speaks, real slow, breathing onion into my face, "But you're the one who's grown up to be just like him."

"It's fucking research," I shout. He nods, like: sure, he doesn't believe me. He walks out of my house, my fucking addict brother, thinking he's got it all together and that I'm the one falling apart. I lock the door behind him, and when I turn, she's there, tap dancing across the kitchen in the outfit that caused all the controversy, the one with the feathers, and the black net stockings. "Oh, hi," I say, "Did you catch any of that?"

She pirouettes in a furious twirl, a great flurry of tapping feet, and another twirl; I am sincerely amazed and clap until my hands feel raw. She smiles and smiles and then waves her arm, like a magician's assistant, and that's when I see the other little girl. She's taller, her skin is black, her hair in two ponytails high on her head, she's dressed just like a regular kid, a T-shirt, shorts, and flip-flops. "Hi," I say, "What's your name?"

She smiles, but it is a shy smile, her lips closed.

"Her name is Holiday, too."

I nod, puzzling this out.

"And today is her birthday."

I turn to the girl who looks up at me with her beautiful black eyes.

"Your birthday?"

Both girls nod solemnly.

"Well, I don't, let me see what I can find. I wasn't expecting . . ." I rummage through the kitchen drawers and cabinets, making excuses all the while. "I wish I had known, I'm just so unprepared. A birthday? If I had known, I would have, I mean, balloons and cake . . ." The girls look up at me, bright eyed, "But I'm sorry, I don't, this is the best I can, Happy Birthday," I say, and set a plate on the table. In the middle of the plate is a jelly sandwich, and in the center of the sandwich is the stub of a lit candle left over from when I was still trying to impress dates. The whole thing looks pretty lame but the girl claps all the same. She tries valiantly to blow the candle out, and then they both try, and after a while they just look up at me, and I do it for them.

I'm not sure what to do next so I ask them if they want to watch Shirley Temple movies, and we go into the living room and sit on the couch and I think they had a good time, though in the morning I discover the jelly sandwich untouched on the plate. It's stale but I eat it just the same, sitting in front of the computer, searching the Internet sites of missing and murdered children, looking for the birthday girl, but I never do find her.

Suddenly it's like I'm running some kind of day care center for dead kids. She keeps bringing them to me, I don't know why. We watch Shirley Temple movies, though she's the one who likes them best, and, I have to admit, she can be pretty bratty about it at times. Actually, they all can be pretty bratty. They're little kids, what can I say? They fight over which movie to watch, they run up and down the stairs, they jump off the kitchen table and the back of the couch. I recognize some of them. Without asking, I know some of their names. I mean, come on, some of these kids are famous. Others, like the little black girl, I never do figure out. When they're all around, I sometimes think I'm going to lose it, but when no one comes, when it's just me, all alone, staring at the computer again, still trying to find the perfect title, the perfect little phrase to describe what happened to my family, I miss their smelly mouths, their waxy ears, their noise, their demands, their little bodies twisted in odd positions of sleep and play, and I miss their laughter, the gorgeous sound of their laughter. Her dancing. I miss her dancing. And I miss her, most of all.

But she says it's getting boring at my house. She says it's too noisy. She says she might not come around any more and when I ask her to dance she just shakes her head, no; she doesn't feel like it. That's when I say, without thinking about it or anything, why don't we have a party, and she says, "You mean like a jelly sandwich with a candle stuck in it?" (I told you, she can be bratty.) But I say, no, I mean like a big party, with balloons and party hats and papier-mâché streamers, would you like that? "And a Christmas tree?" she asks. Well, I wasn't really thinking of that but I can tell she wants one so I say sure. She smiles, "And big red Valentine's hearts?" I say, all right, "And Easter baskets? And chocolate eggs?" And I say sure, of course, it'll be a holiday party, an every holiday party, and I don't say this part, but you know, for all the ones they've missed. She gives me a big hug then, her little arms tight around my neck and she kisses me right on the mouth.

I buy red, green, orange and black streamers, balloons that have "Happy Birthday" printed on them, a paper tablecloth with turkeys and pilgrims on it. I get a seventy-five percent discount on the scarecrow, the ceramic pumpkin, and a clown costume, but I have to pay a ridiculous price for the fake Christmas tree already decorated with lights and ornaments. I buy cupcakes, even though I'm not sure any of the dead kids eat, and I buy two kinds of paper plates, one with Barbie on them, and the other with dinosaurs. I get several different kid DVDs (I have to admit even I'm getting a little sick of Shirley Temple) and a CD of Christmas classics.

Sarah Vehler is working again, she is standing there, chewing on a hangnail, and not checking anyone out but I stand in line behind a woman with two little kids, a boy, and a girl. The boy is furiously sucking his thumb, and the girl is begging for candy. The woman, their mother, I assume, is ignoring them, paging through a *People* magazine. I smile at the little girl, and for just a second she stops asking for candy and stares at me. Her eyes remind me of beach glass. Sarah Vehler calls my name and when I look up, she waves me over. "Don't you have nothing better to do than stand in line all day?" she says. "Wow, looks like you're planning a full year of parties. How many kids you got anyway?" I shrug, and to change the subject tell her I like her earrings. I have long since learned that the real way to gain a woman's trust is to tell her you like her earrings but Sarah Vehler just looks at me like I said something crazy and of course that's when I realize she isn't wearing earrings. I laugh, "I mean last time," I say, "I remember the ones you had on last time, and I meant to tell you they were real nice." Then, things only get more ridiculous when she tells me she never wears earrings. "I'm sorry," I say, grabbing the bags and the box of cupcakes. "I thought it was you, but it must have been someone else." She just looks at me like she is thinking real hard, and then she says, "I saw your brother the other day and he says you don't have any kids at all."

I smile, to be polite, and then tilt my chin, like, you got another customer. She turns, and sees the guy who has a disturbingly blank expression on his face, but when she looks at me again, I shrug, as if to say, too bad we can't talk.

When I get home, I have to clean the place. I've let it go and my mother would shit if she saw it, but she never tries to visit, and doesn't even call. She's got her own life now, and doesn't like to be reminded of the old one, I guess, the one me and my brother are stuck in forever. I pick up beer cans and paper plates and realize this hasn't exactly been the best environment for children. I freaking hate to clean, but after a while I sort of get into it, I put one of the new DVDs in, I don't know what it was called but it was bright and noisy and cheerful, it kept me company. I even washed the windows. Then I hung up the streamers, twisting them from the ceiling in the kitchen and the living room, and I set up the tree, and the tablecloth, and the plates, and then I put the clown costume on, and I looked at myself in the mirror, I was wearing a bright red, yellow, blue, and green polka-dotted jumpsuit, giant red shoes that flopped six inches from my toes, a bright red wig, and a red nose. I looked at myself for a while, trying to figure out who I reminded myself of, and then I flashed back to a birthday party, was it for me or my brother, my father dressed up like a clown. I grab my phone and call. The answering machine picks up.

"The thing is," I say, "I mean, come on. Don't give up on me so fast, ok? It was just a movie. It's research, all right? Fuck. I mean really, fuck. Look, I didn't give up on you even with all the drugs and the stealing and shit, right? Right?" It seems like I should say something else, something perfect, but I can't think what that would be so I hang up and call Terry.

"The thing is," I say, "I haven't been completely honest."

There's a moment's pause. A long moment before he says, "Shoot."

"The thing is," I say, "what I want to write about isn't an innocent man." I wait, but he doesn't say anything. "The children . . ." She is standing there, in the middle of the living room, staring at the Christmas tree with the strangest expression on her face. She is dressed just like a regular little girl, in little girl pajamas and a bathrobe. I wave at her and point to the phone, signaling that I'll be winding the call up soon, but her expression doesn't change, she looks at me with confusion, and sorrow.

"What about the kids? What's your point? Can you just give it to me in a sentence?"

"The children were telling the truth, my father was not an innocent man."

Terry whistles, long and low. "Fuck," he says.

"You're the first person I ever told."

"Well, this puts us in the crapper without any shit, that's for sure."

"What?" She is reaching for the tree, touching it lightly with her fingertips, as though afraid it will disappear.

"Listen, if that's the case what we got is just another story about a fucking pedophile. Those are a dime a dozen. The market is saturated with them. It's not a special story anymore, it's just . . . now wait a second, that kid, you're not saying he had anything to do with that kid's murder are you, 'cause if you were saying that, well then we'd have a story."

"No." She is petting the tree, and this part really gets to me, she leans in to smell it, even though it is fake, she presses her face real close to the branches and then she realizes I am watching and she looks at me again, but in a new way, like she has something she wants to say, like she needs me. "I gotta go," I say.

"I mean even if you think he could have possibly had something to do with it, that we might be able to sell. It gets tricky, 'cause you know all of a sudden everyone's fact-checking the hell out of memoirs, but we might be able to work that angle, you know, not that you really believe he killed her, 'cause everyone knows her parents did it, right, but like you could tie her into your story and the idea that your father was someone like her father, you might have something there, ok? We might be able to sell that."

She has big eyes, and they are sad, and she wants to tell me something important, maybe she's going to tell me who did kill her, "Listen, I gotta go," I say. Terry keeps talking, he's getting excited now, just the way, all those years ago, everyone got excited about her murder. I click the phone off.

"What is it?" I say, "You can tell me."

"I wet myself," she says, in the softest little girl voice.

Sure enough, there's a wet stain down the front of her pajamas, and a puddle on the rug beneath the Christmas tree. "That's OK," I say, even as the dank odor reaches me, "sometimes that happens. Why don't you go in the bathroom and take off your clothes. Do you have a way, I mean, I don't know how this works, do you have some clean clothes with you?"

She shakes her head.

I nod, like, OK, no problem. The phone rings and she looks relieved when I don't make any move to answer it. Instead I search through the piles of clothes on my bedroom floor until I find a dingy white T-shirt and a brand new pair of boxer shorts, which of course will be huge on her, so I also give her a tie. She looks up at me with confusion when I hand her the stuff. "It'll be like a costume, for the party. Kind of different from the kind you usually wear, I know. Go in the bathroom, OK, and wash yourself off and take off your wet pajamas and put on the T-shirt, and these shorts, and tie these with this, see, like a belt."

"Will you wipe me?" she says.

I shouldn't be surprised by this; I've read all about how she still asked people to wipe her, even though she was dressed up like a movie star. "No. You have to do it yourself, OK?"

She shakes her head and starts to cry.

One thing I can't stand is a crying kid. "OK," I say, "OK, just don't cry, all right?"

We walk into the bathroom and I help her out of her pajamas, her skin is white, pure as fresh soap, and she is completely unembarrassed of her nakedness. She smiles when I wipe her, first with toilet paper, and then with a towel dampened with warm water and I just try not to think about anything, about how tiny she is, or how perfect. I help her put the clean T-shirt on and the boxer shorts, which I cinch around her little waist with the tie and by then she is laughing and I am too and we stand before the mirror to look at ourselves but all I see is me, in the ridiculous clown costume. Where does she keep disappearing to? I call her name, searching through all the rooms, thinking she's playing some kind of game, but I can't find her anywhere. The doorbell rings and I run to answer it, laughing because it's very funny the way she's hidden outside but when I open the door, my brother is standing there.

"Oh, fuck," he says.

"It's not the way it looks."

He looks behind me, at the streamers, the table set with Barbie and dinosaur plates, the cupcakes, the Christmas tree. "Fuck," he says.

"No, wait," I holler, and when he doesn't stop I follow him, flopping down the stairs, "Wait," I say, running after him, though it is difficult in the too-big red shoes, the red wig bouncing down my forehead, "it's not how it looks."

He turns, and I smile at him, knowing he'll understand, after all, we share the same childhood, but instead he looks at me with a horrified expression, as if I am a terrifying ghost, and then he turns his back on me and runs. I don't try to follow him; instead I walk back to my house. Someone in a passing car shouts something and throws a paper cup of soda at me, but misses. I am surprised by this, it seems to me clowns deserve a little respect; after all, they only exist to make people laugh.

When I get back inside, I shut the door and sit on the couch in front of the TV and watch the cartoon people, who are shaped like balloons. There are no dead children and there are no secrets in a world where everyone is brightly colored and devoid of the vulnerabilities of flesh. In balloon world all the problems explode or float away. Even though it's been cold and cloudy for weeks, the sun comes out and fills the room with an explosion of light until I can no longer see the picture on the TV screen. One of the streamers comes loose and dangles over my head, twirling, and I can't help but think that, in spite of what Terry said, there is plenty of shit for the crapper, but it doesn't matter, because in the distance, I hear the soft hum of a little girl singing. And just like that my mood improves, because I am waiting for the children, and just thinking about them makes me smile.

GARY McMAHON

Hum Drum

Gary McMahon lives, works, and writes in West Yorkshire, where he shares a home with an understanding wife and their weird and wonderful boy-child. McMahon's fiction has appeared in countless magazines and anthologies in both the U. K. and the U. S. He is the author of the British Fantasy Award–nominated novella "Rough Cut." Other books include All Your Gods Are Dead, *and* Dirty Prayers *(a collection of short fiction). A novel,* Rain Dogs, *is due out from U. K. publisher Humdrumming in mid-2008. Also forthcoming, from Screaming Dreams, is a double-novella collection called* Different Skins. *In 2009 Pendragon Press will publish* To Usher, the Dead, *a collection of further tales featuring Thomas Usher, the down-at-heel protagonist of "Hum Drum." McMahon can be found lurking online at www. garymcmahon.com.*

"Hum Drum" was originally published in The First Humdrumming Book of Horror Stories, *edited by Ian Alexander Martin.*

— E.D.

I was tired and half-drunk the night I first met William Probert, hence my memory of the occasion is rather hazy. I do recall that I'd spent a tough couple of days attending a faked exorcism in Bradford—a local Asian businessman had been convinced that his teenage daughter was inhabited by a djinn; upon closer inspection the whole situation had proved to be an elaborate blackmail plot perpetrated by the man's second cousin.

My head ached and my body was in desperate need of a massage, but being partial to the odd snifter, I'd decided to call in at a quiet city center bar called The Listening Post to ease my woes.

The quaint little pub had changed since my last visit to the city: now it wore the cheap lures and vulgar adornments of a venue desperate to attract the moneyed youth crowd rather than the serious drinkers of old. There was even a small stage at the back of the main room, where posters stated that "DJ & DANCERZ" were scheduled to perform every Friday night after ten. I shuddered to think what exactly that might entail.

It was getting late and I was relying on public transport to get me home, so I decided to make the next drink my last. I summoned the barman with raised hand and a friendly smile, and he sauntered over with an air of detached boredom. Before I could order, he poured me a double rum. Impressed that he'd taken the time to remember what I was drinking, I reached into my pocket to pay him—and leave a healthy gratuity.

"It's already paid for," said the lad, holding up a hand and backing away. "The gentleman over there said to make sure your next drink was on him."

I nodded, put away my wallet. Then I glanced over to where the barman had motioned with a tilted head to see who was standing me a round, and if I really wanted to accept it.

A well-dressed man with an expensive haircut smiled at me and raised his glass in a silent toast. I returned the gesture and took a swallow, hoping that the stranger would remain seated and not wander over to pester me.

I was out of luck.

I closed my eyes when I saw him stand, and when I felt his presence at my shoulder I felt like never opening them again. It's always like this: the needy seek me out, eager for my services. My reputation has spread through word of mouth, and sometimes it's all I can do not to scream at the people who approach me.

"I'm sorry to disturb you, but you are Thomas Usher, aren't you?"

I almost said that I wasn't, that he'd mistaken me for someone else. But I didn't. I never do. Instead I opened my eyes and turned to face him, once more accepting another's burden as my own.

"Please," I said, "take a seat."

The man smiled eagerly and pulled up a stool next to mine. He smelled of decent cologne and pricey whisky; this one would be willing to pay.

"I'm truly sorry to bother you, Mr. Usher, but I honestly have nowhere else to turn. I got your name from a mutual friend, Roger Deacon. The description he gave me was pretty much spot-on."

"Description? Please, do tell." I brushed lint from my trouser leg, trying my best to look disinterested. The ploy did not bear fruit.

"His words, exactly: a thin, cultured man of around forty dressed in a loose black suit and open-necked shirt, with close-cropped hair and eyes that wouldn't look out of place on a serial killer."

I laughed, which broke the ice, and the man visibly relaxed.

"How is Sir Roger? Last time I saw him he was running through the streets of West London clutching a bible and swearing off the booze."

"He's back on the booze, but has read that bible. He attends church twice a week, and swears to anyone who'll listen that you saved his life when a poltergeist tried to kill him.

"Anyway, I've been rude. Please allow me to introduce myself, however belatedly. My name is William Probert and I'm afraid that I need your help. Feel free to tell me to sod off, but at least allow me to explain myself first."

His eyes were wide and wet; if I refused to listen he was going to cry—I could see it in his face.

"Fire away, Mr. Probert. Any friend of Deacon's is a friend of mine."

I already knew who he was, of course. How could I not? At that time, William Probert was one of the hottest television directors in the country. He was tipped for stardom, and deservedly so; I'd seen most of the plays and dramas he'd done for the BBC, and been suitably impressed by their depth of vision. He was a considerable talent, and on the verge of making it big. I'd heard from people who knew about such things that his next project was to be a high profile murder mystery for a big-time American production company.

"It all started about a month ago, when I was browsing flea markets and antique shops in London. I was reaching the end of a weekend break, and was looking for something to buy my fourteen-year-old niece, Hazel. She's a very talented girl, and is interested in all things musical, so I was looking for a certain special something.

"I found it in a shop in Camden, a little place called Odds & Ends that specializes in the edgy and unusual. A drum, a handmade child's toy that perked my interest as soon as I saw it."

"Really?" I asked, growing more interested as he went on. "And why was that?"

"I'm not sure exactly, Mr. Usher. All I can say is that the thing seemed to call out to me. The drum was hanging on a nail from a shelf near the back of the shop, all dusty and forgotten. As soon as I saw it I fancied that I heard it make a sound—a whispery little percussion in my ear. Nonsense of course, but even then I knew it must be special."

I finished my drink and Probert bought me another. He'd barely touched his own, despite having to continually lick his lips in order to moisten them.

"Please," I said when the drink arrived. "Carry on."

"Thank you. Well, as I said, I had to have the drum. It was perfect for Hazel; I just knew she'd love it. The proprietor of the shop gave me some cock-and-bull story about it having belonged to a famous local criminal, no doubt anxious to add more to its value. In the end I paid over the odds, but I didn't care: I wanted that drum.

"I forgot about the thing during my journey home, and only remembered it when I was about to retire to bed the following evening. I got it out of my bag and studied it closely. It looked old and decrepit outside the shop, and there were scratches that looked like unintelligible words running around the casement of the drum. The skin was creased and torn, and I began to feel disappointed with my purchase.

"Then I was overtaken by the sudden urge to strike it. To make a sound against the thin hide that was stretched taut across the small bowl. There was a little timpani drumstick attached by a frayed length of twine, and I grasped it in my hand. I know this sounds silly, but I was suddenly afraid to make a noise, yet knew that I could not resist. I raised the stick and brought it down on the skin, making a few light taps that sounded nothing like music. I'm tone-deaf, and the sound I made was probably terrible, but all the same it seemed right. It *felt* like music of some kind or another."

He paused then, and gulped the rest of his drink. Then he wiped his brow with a hand that shook as if from tremors, and I realized that he was terrified.

"Since then . . . *odd* things have been happening. Muddy footprints on the path outside my window, wet marks on the floor by my bedroom door, and then last week I went into the bathroom one morning to find the sink filled with muddy water.

"I live alone, Mr. Usher, and I know damned well that I didn't fill that sink."

The barman brought more drinks without being asked; it was a quiet night in The Listening Post, and it was obvious from his demeanor that Probert needed more alcohol.

"And you think that I might be able to help you?"

"Yes, Mr. Usher. At least I hope so. I have nowhere else to go, no one to ask."

"I'll have to request a fee, Mr. Probert. I'm afraid that the last few jobs I've undertaken have been favors, and I find myself financially embarrassed."

"That isn't a problem. I'll pay anything you ask."

I sat for a moment and pondered Probert's case. It seemed quite obvious that there was something strange about the instrument he had bought, but formless doubts nagged at the back of my mind. Certain elements of his story sounded vaguely familiar. Perhaps I'd read of something similar, and just couldn't quite place the history.

"Do you understand what it is I do, Mr. Probert? I mean, did Deacon explain that I offer no guarantees? All I can do is attempt to aid whatever forces are at work in returning to wherever they belong. What I do is mainly of a passive nature; I have no power over these spirits, ghosts, phantoms—call them what you will—all I can do is try to communicate. I'm not much more than a bystander."

"Yes, I understand that completely. I realize that you are limited in what you can achieve. All I ask is that you try."

"Okay, Mr. Probert. I accept your offer. I'll accompany you home this evening and stay with you for a few days. Hopefully during that time another episode will occur, and we can take it from there."

The relief on his face was like a mask he'd suddenly put on. It altered his features to the point that he looked like a different man entirely. Someone more relaxed; someone who'd possibly found hope.

The drum was roughly the size of a soup bowl and looked older than sin. The material that formed it was cracked and torn, and the tough upper side that constituted the head was strained so much that it was discolored with age.

Running around the body of the drum was a series of words. As Probert poured us drinks I studied them, prying away loose dirt and dried flakes of leather with a fingernail.

Eventually I cleaned them up enough that I was able to read them.

"Bang a drum, who will come?"

"Pardon me?" said Probert, bringing over the drinks on a nice silver tray.

"That's what the words say: *'Bang a drum, who will come?'*"

"And what does that mean? Is it a warning? A child's verse? Considering what's happened since I did bang it, I'd suggest the former."

I said nothing, fascinated by the little instrument. It was a beautiful thing to behold; obviously handcrafted and with so much care poured into its construction. So much love.

The skin stretched across the drum's head had the look of smooth animal hide, and the hoop that held it in place was the color and texture of bone. The lugs that tightened the skin also reminded me of bone, and that tiny drumstick could have been made from a single human finger. The shell was surprisingly heavy for its diminutive size, and held the shape and approximate proportions of an undersized skull—perhaps one that had once belonged to a child or a midget.

I realized that this image was the product of my own overactive imagination, but the fancy was wonderfully chilling. Like something out of M. R. James.

"There's something else," said Probert abruptly. "Something I didn't tell you in case you thought I was mad."

"Come on, Mr. Probert. I've seen enough of the otherworldly to last a lifetime. I know the difference between the supernatural and the insane."

"Put your ear to the drum. Listen to it."

Puzzled yet intrigued, I did just that, lowering my right ear to the instrument. At first I failed to hear it, but after a little while the sound came through. A quiet humming noise, like the resonant twang of a tuning fork at the low end of its scale.

I glanced up at Probert. He looked stricken.

"It hasn't stopped humming since I struck it. That sound . . . that ghastly *reverberation*, has just kept on going. It's reached the stage now that I can hear it without trying. I even hear it in my sleep."

I listened again, and understood Probert's horror. The sound was unlike any other I'd ever heard; it was unearthly, a small-scale dirge, the faint soundtrack from a tuneless nightmare. I put down the drum and moved across to the other side of the room and pretended to look out of the window. I suddenly wanted to be as far away from that thing as possible. I could still hear the sound.

Before retiring to bed, Probert gave me the telephone number of Odds & Ends, and I resolved to contact the shop in the morning. I was hoping that the owner would know more than he had initially revealed about the drum.

Probert showed me to a nice room on the first floor of his converted farmhouse. It was a lovely old building, and the décor was effortlessly tasteful, retaining enough of the original features to create a homely air yet still boasting clean modern lines.

I was asleep before my head hit the pillow; when I dreamed it was of faceless entities pursuing me across a weird industrial landscape that echoed with the sound of beating drums. Morning arrived without incident, and I awoke to the smells of frying bacon and fresh coffee drifting up the staircase and into my nostrils. I was hungrier than I'd realized; the last time I'd eaten anything more substantial than a dry vegetable samosa had been two days ago.

I dressed without bathing, weighing up hunger against bodily hygiene and deciding on the call of the stomach. When I went downstairs to the kitchen, Probert was sitting at the breakfast bar and staring into his empty mug; he didn't even notice me as I entered the room.

"Ah, breakfast! I'm starving."

Probert twitched slightly, and looked up, remembering where he was and the identity of the stranger in his kitchen.

"Yes. It'll be ready soon."

"Are you okay? You look spooked."

He sighed, looked down at his silk-slippered feet. "Have you been in the upstairs bathroom?"

Feeling awkward, I shook my head.

"Take a look," he said. "Then come back down and tell me what you think."

Slowly climbing the stairs, I experienced the urge to flee. I would not be judged unfavorably if I left the house; I owed nobody anything; as far as my host was concerned, my slate was clean.

Gradually I pulled myself together, and padded along the landing, trying to remember which room Probert had identified as the bathroom the previous night. I did not have to look for long. The bathroom door had been left open and wet footprints led across the white tiles to the stand-alone, claw-footed tub. I followed them into the room and even before I reached the bathtub I knew what it would contain. It was filled to the brim with water: oily, black, murky water, like the sticky filth that coats a riverbed.

As I stared, a shape made itself known in the muck: the ragged outline of a human body. It was lying there in the bathtub, concealed by the dirty liquid, visible only to my eyes. I knew that Probert would have seen only the water; the rest was for me, exclusive to one who is allowed to see the seepage from another realm.

Not knowing what else to do, I stretched out an arm and held it inches above the surface of the water, if only to see what would happen. After a short while, I began to pull it away, sensing no movement beneath the surface. A hand shot out of the water, a scaly claw that was more bone than slick, syrupy flesh. Thin fingers enclosed my wrist, biting deep into the muscle. Then the hand let go and slipped back under the water. The revenant was not here for me; my presence was merely a distraction.

Bubbles escaped from the area located near where I assumed would be the nose; gaseous emissions from a thing long gone to rot.

I reached into the tub and groped for the plug, then watched as the water drained slowly away. It took quite some time; the stuff was thick as tar. When it was gone, no body was revealed. I washed up at the sink before leaving the room, trying to rid myself of the stink of something *other*.

After breakfast Probert went off to work—he had scenes to shoot for a short film he was making about a homeless man who slept in a metal bin outside a swanky restaurant in Leeds.

As soon as he left the house I picked up the phone, dialing the number for the shop where he'd bought the drum. It was answered on the first ring.

"Hello, Brooks here. How can I help?"

"My name is Usher. I'm calling on behalf of a customer of yours."

"We don't give refunds," said the loud, high voice. "Everything is bought and sold on good faith, and what you see is what you get."

"No, you misunderstand me, Mr. Brooks. I'm simply interested in the history of a piece bought by a friend of mine."

"Go on. . . ." The voice held a deep suspicion, but at least he hadn't hung up the phone.

"A drum. A small child's drum, bought there about a month ago."

"Ah, yes. The film director feller; I remember him well, the wife being a fan of his work. Nice chap, even signed me an autograph. For the wife, you understand."

"Of course: 'for the wife.' Can you tell me anything about the drum? It's a fascinating object."

Only then, under the duress of flattery, did he warm to the subject.

"That'll be the drum of Harvey Bellows," he said, sounding suddenly full of excitement at the chance of spinning a yarn. "He was a bad 'un; real rough trade. It was back in the days of old Queen Victoria—the early 1800s, I think. Bellows was a con man, a bloke who made his living by fleecing widows of their inheritance.

"He would mark out a suitable victim—a woman of means who had been left a fortune by a dead husband. He'd bide his time, befriending the woman's child; using that drum he made in the first instance to create a sort of rapport. After getting to know the young 'un, he would conspire to meet the mother. Then he'd simply work his wily ways and make her fall in love with him. He'd be in and out within three to six months, vanishing with a load of cash and leaving the poor widow and child destitute.

"Some time around 1819 or 1820, Bellows got his comeuppance. A mob tracked him down when he was recognized by one of his old victims. They chased him down to the river and threw him in to drown near the Embankment, under the old Waterloo Bridge—the original one, before someone decided to demolish it in 1936."

"And where did you come across his drum? Quite a find, if you don't mind me saying so. You must have a keen nose for such items."

Hubris loosened his tongue even more; I could almost feel the pride pouring from the other end of the line.

"It vanished off the face of the earth after Bellows's murder. They say one of the mob took it as a souvenir, but it didn't surface until 1958, when a man called Henry Stowell began to exhibit the drum in his amateur Murder Museum in Putney.

"I found it when I was involved in a house clearance on Stowell's estate. He had some good stuff, the old lad, and I copped for most of it. If there's anything particular you're interested in, I can always make some inquiries. . . ."

"No thank you, you've been a great help. If I'm ever in the area, I'll be sure to stop by and browse your stock."

"There's a curse, you know. On the drum."

This was it: the exact information I was fishing for.

"Really . . ."

"Oh, yes. They say that if it's drummed in a certain way, the ghost of Harvey Bellows will rise."

"And how is it stopped, this curse? It sounds fascinating."

"It can't be stopped. Once set in motion, the music must run its course. Per'aps old Harvey just wants his drum back, eh?"

I hung up the phone to the sound of his throaty laugher, and a chill caressed my spine, gently kissing the soft joints between each vertebra.

When Probert returned home early that afternoon, I told him of my intentions. He cooked a vegetable stir-fry and listened to my hastily cobbled plan as we ate, nodding and trying desperately to contain his gratitude. I even told him about my conversation with the talkative Mr. Brooks, and of the violent legend of Harvey Bellows.

Then he took me by surprise, voicing a theory I had not even considered.

"I have a thought," he said. "About the curse. Maybe it isn't *what* is banged upon the drum, but *he who bangs it*: the fatherless offspring of a wealthy widow?"

I stared at him quizzically.

"What I mean is, this Bellows character preyed on rich widows. His stock in trade was as a grifter, going for the long con. He used the drum to strike up friendships with the children of these women, and then moved in for the kill.

"My father died when I was still in the crib; he left my mother a fortune. This is what funded my education, and my mother is still a very rich lady. I banged the drum, and something answered the call."

He demanded that I use his Porsche; it was, he said, the quickest way to get there. I'd owned a fast car once, and a fast attitude to go with it. Neither had served me well, and it had all ended badly. My own ghosts are the only ones that I am afraid to see.

Sometimes grief is like a suit of clothing, a favorite outfit that we have held on to for far too long, worn too many times. We cannot bring ourselves to throw it away; it cost a lot to acquire and we have grown accustomed to its fit. Sometimes that grief is all we have at hand to wear, and the other clothes in our wardrobe are nothing more than a row of shoddy hanging corpses.

The roads were busy that time of the day, but still the journey was mercifully brief. I was in London by 4 P.M., and standing on the banks of the Thames as Big Ben struck the hour of five.

I held the drum in my hand, the jocular words of the shopkeeper running through my mind: *Per'aps old Harvey just wants his drum back.* It was the only hope I had of ending this; the alternative I had left in the capable hands of Probert, and I knew that he would not fail to make provisions.

I'd told him to wait until bedtime, and if by then I had not returned he was to put Plan B into action. Probert thought that he could pull together at least five thousand pounds in hard cash in less than three hours. Back in the Victorian era, that much would have been considered a vast amount of money; a fortune. If I was not back in Yorkshire before Probert retired for the night, he was to leave out the money for Bellows's restless spirit to collect. Hopefully, this would be enough to send him on his way, to pay off whatever debt Probert now owed.

Standing on the breezy embankment beneath the segmented concrete finger of Waterloo Bridge, I put the drum to my ear. That humming reverberation was still present, continuing like an endless echo, a subdued song of the dead. The sky reared above me like a huge airborne spirit threatening to swoop down and tear me to pieces; the voice of civilization was a quiet threat at my back—the distant thunder of traffic, the constant thrum of feet on concrete.

I took the drum from my ear and raised my hand to throw. In that instant, the sound ceased; the drum was silent. I hurled it into the lapping black waters, hoping that I was doing the right thing, that the hex would be broken.

The drum bobbed like a buoy for a while, and then dipped sharply down beneath the choppy surface as if pulled from below. As I watched, something appeared momentarily, a bulky oval shape rising from the water—a partially deflated football covered in river slime, or possibly a skull trailing muddy decomposed matter. The shape was gone before I could make out any details; I was never certain what it was that I saw there, floating atop the sharp gray waves.

Then I heard the noise again: a low, distant hum. The sound of the drum had not diminished; if anything it had increased in volume now that the instrument had been returned to its maker. Its hushed, solemn beat joined with the gentle swelling of the waves, and for an instant the whole world was filled with its monotonous rhythm. Stuck there beneath river and sky, I felt like an insect trapped between two sheets of glass, a specimen due for exhibit in a museum of extinct species.

The return journey north took far longer than I'd anticipated. Traffic was heavy and an accident had shut off one lane of the M1 motorway south of Birmingham. Try as I might, I could not summon a signal on my mobile phone. It was late by the time I reached Yorkshire, and long after midnight when I guided Probert's car onto his long graveled driveway.

The lights were on downstairs, but the upper story was in darkness. I wondered if Probert had fallen asleep in his armchair before setting out the money. Shadows stalked me as I approached the main door but I had nothing to fear from them. The thing I feared most was myself: the nagging ghost of my own futility.

I let myself in with the key he'd given me earlier, and hurried through into the lounge. I searched the entire ground floor and found no sign of the master of the house. Before going upstairs, I paused to listen for any sounds . . . like, perhaps, the quiet beating of a drum.

Then I climbed the stairs to the first floor.

Wet footprints marked the way, trailing up the stairs and along the passage to Probert's bedroom. The door was ajar, and a large carpetbag sat on the floor outside the room. The bag was open, and muddy footprints surrounded it; muddy smudges also decorated the clasps and the painted doorframe in which the bag sat. Most of the money was gone; only a few desultory five- and ten-pound notes remained, forgotten in the rush.

I followed the glistening footprints into the room and up to the side of Probert's huge four-poster bed.

He lay on his back on top of the covers, arms twisted up near his head, as if pinned there. His mouth was open. Gaping. Between his bloodless lips I could see clumps of black river mud wrapped around yet more used notes—*river* mud, cold and dank as the earth from an unhallowed grave. The stink was unbearable, like that of a thousand rotting corpses. The hideous stench of the bleak Thames invaded my senses: a sickening fetor created by the steady corruption of the many lives it had swallowed over the decades.

I reached out and respectfully closed Probert's eyes, no longer able to bear his accusatory stare. If I'd been a brighter man, more than just a bystander in this grim spectacle, perhaps I would have heeded those other words spoken by the sage old owner of that odd little shop in Camden.

Once set in motion, the music must run its course.

Early the following week I visited my usual tattooist to have William Probert's name inked alongside the others on my back; the neat little list that grows depressingly longer with each year that passes.

This list is my personal Wailing Wall of remembrance, a shrine to those I have failed. I bear their names upon me; it is a burden I must learn to carry with grace and dignity and patience, a load that I cannot shake off until I have fully earned the right to do so.

BILLY COLLINS

Scenes of Hell

Billy Collins's poem "Scenes of Hell" was published in the third issue of the literary journal A Public Space. *Collins, who was Poet Laureate from 2001 to 2003, has published a number of popular collections, including* The Trouble with Poetry and Other Poems, Nine Horses, *and* Picnic, Lightning. *He lives in Somers, New York.*

             —K.L. & G.G.

We did not have the benefit of a guide,
No crone to lead us off the common path,
No ancient to point the way with a staff,

But there were badlands to cross
Rivers of fire and blackened peaks,
And eventually we could look down and see

The jeweler running around a gold ring
The boss captured in an hourglass
The baker buried up to his eyes in flour

The banker plummeting on a coin
The teacher disappearing into a blackboard
And the grocer silent under a pyramid of vegetables.

We saw the pilot nose-diving
And the whore impaled on a bedpost
The pharmacist wandering in a stupor

And the child with toy wheels for legs
You pointed to the soldier
Who was dancing with his empty uniform

And I remarked on the blind tourist
But what truly caught our attention
Was the scene in the long mirror of ice:

You lighting the wick on your head,
Me blowing on the final spark,
And our children trying to crawl away from their eggshells

PAUL WALTHER

Splitfoot

Paul Walther has had stories published in numerous small press magazines, including New Genre *issue #1,* Space and Time, Night Terrors, *and* Horror Library Volume 2. *Several of his previous stories have received honorable mentions in* The Year's Best Fantasy and Horror. *He lives in Hopkins, Minnesota, with his wife and two teenage sons.*

"Splitfoot" was first published in New Genre *issue #5, edited by Adam Golaski.*

—*E.D.*

V iolet would never admit she was frightened. Certainly not to Royce and Trixie. But she wasn't going to be left alone. So she went out on the back stoop with them, even though she didn't smoke.

In truth, she couldn't bear to be in the house another moment without them. Yes. That was the truth. So she went out the back door with them, behind the house with Trixie and Royce, into the killing frigid cold of a snow-blasted prairie that came right up to the back step of the ugly little house like a pack of vicious wolves; always hungry, always vigilant, always waiting for the smallest sign of weakness so it could close in for the kill. It was a disheartening landscape, utterly dead and cold.

They had to smoke outside because the teenage daughter was asthmatic, and the smoke might trigger an episode. Another *kind* of episode, not the horror they'd lived through the night before.

So, the girl was troublesome in a couple of ways.

Trixie thought the little wench was lying. But then, it was in her favor to think so.

"She's afraid of change," Trixie said, her arms wrapped around her narrow torso. "Duh. It's a no-brainer."

Royce, with momentary possession of the cigarette they were sharing, shook his head. "I ain't taking no haunted house."

"It's not *haunted*," said Trixie, her slim fingers appearing briefly at the ends of her sweater sleeve to snatch the butt back from Royce, "I told you, she's making it up. She's *making* it happen."

"You would lie to your mother," said Royce, "you are *feral*."

If anything he appeared colder than Trixie, though he was better dressed for the weather and had sixty pounds on her. He winced at the sky. Violet knew Royce well enough to know what he was thinking. He was originally from Atlanta, so he didn't think the thirty-five degrees below zero was brutally cold, he thought it was *insane*.

"You are a superstitious southern cracker," said Trixie. The cigarette was down to the filter and she flicked it off her finger. It flew in a long, high arc against the motionless snow of the prairie, flipping cherry over filter like a tiny, smoking bomb, landing in a tiny black crater a few yards from the stoop among a dozen others just like it—Royce and Trixie's little downwind missile range.

It was a testament to the tenaciousness of the habit that the two of them would venture outside in such weather to beat one down in tandem, as fast as possible, like two runners passing the baton. It was also, possibly, a testament to the camaraderie of the habit that the two of them could share a single, saliva-tainted object like lovers, all the while arguing vehemently.

It had been this way all the way up north on the long, long car ride from the city on the previous afternoon. Violet, the fulcrum in the wide equilateral triangle of their relationship, sat in the back seat so they could better badger and aggravate each other.

Trixie drove, of course, steering her new black Mercedes with one hand, cigarette between her fingers, the other hand gripping her cell phone, coffee cup, mascara tube—anything other than the steering wheel, all the while talking, either on the phone, or to her passengers, or both. She had graceful, slim hands, Trixie did, and long blonde hair that she flipped out of her elfin face as she talked.

"She is nothing but a typical white bitch," Royce had said of her once, and Violet had taken offense. She and Royce were not lovers but they had been, once.

"Hey," she'd said. "I'm one too."

She did not point out that Trixie was twice as successful as him, at half his age, but it bothered her to hear him talk so poorly of her. *His* Mercedes, after all, was a decade old.

But he was looking at new ones.

Which had caused him to call in the loan to Violet, which she didn't have, of course, which had caused her to reluctantly call Trixie about . . . that old thing, which she didn't want to do but had to, because as nice as Royce was when you were on his good side, you did not want to test his patience on matters of money. She had once seen him break a pretty girl's nose, just because she didn't have what she owed him. As she'd fled, her smashed nose streaming blood, Royce had said, calmly, "She'll pay up next time, I suspect."

So she'd called Trixie about that little matter of the borrowed investment, which caused Trixie, predictably, to launch into her usual avalanche of hurt feelings and explanations and which, finally, when Violet, feeling Royce's hot breath on her neck, insisted, had caused this trip.

Because Trixie never had any cash. Not even enough to pick up a dinner check or a pack of cigarettes. What Trixie had was *things*, or rights to bits of things— automobiles and hocked jewelry and a part of an oil well in Texas and a quarter share in a private jet down in Columbia and . . . and . . . there was just no telling what all she had, and probably no inventory because it changed from day to day, as she traded parts of this for parts of that, or to cover some suddenly urgent debt.

Which is why they had driven all the way up to Pine Lake in the middle of winter, three hundred miles north of Minneapolis, to see a rental property on which Trixie held the deed and was willing to transfer to Royce via Violet, and Royce was buying all the gas and all the cigarettes, and he was buying the worst off-brands he could find in every gas station and convenience store, just to see the look on her face every time she put one of them in her mouth.

Which she did, in the freezing cold, every hour or so. The Mercedes, so sleek and strong on the highway, had become a block of expensive, inert metal in the lumpy gravel driveway within an hour of their arrival. There was no cell phone coverage— roaming or otherwise—within ten miles. Violet's phone was dead anyway, having been forgotten in the car long enough last night to kill its slim black battery thoroughly. Trixie and Royce still had functioning phones but no signal, and the cold had snapped the landlines to the little house more than a day before.

The renters—the Stoddards—mother, girl, boy, baby—didn't own any cell phones and had only an old pickup truck, also temporarily frozen to death. They lived in this tiny little place, this ugly little house on the edge of nothing, with little more than four beds, a few pots and pans, some ratty furniture, and a satellite television dish mounted on one corner of the low roof. *That* signal hadn't been killed by the cold.

So information was getting in to Violet's possible temporary new property, but none was getting out.

This much Violet knew: she had to have the place, if only for the few minutes it took for it to pass through her from Trixie to Royce. She'd already practiced saying it, to herself, just the way Trixie would: "Oh yes—I did have a piece of property up north, but I traded it in a business deal."

It would all be worth it, just to be able to drop that fact casually, in conversation, the way Trixie always did.

"I am freezing, again," said Royce, "and I tell you I ain't taking no haunted property."

"You are a superstitious fool," said Trixie, and she reached for the door.

It was warm inside, painfully warm, like hot water run over cold hands. Trixie's sunglasses frosted over immediately but she didn't take them off, giving her the appearance of a blonde, albino alien of some kind.

There wasn't much to see. The house, which the title indicated was over a hundred years old, consisted of a living room, with the television *always* going, a kitchen nook, and two bedrooms overlooking the back of nowhere to the north. The youngest girl was an infant, sharing a bedroom with her mother. The boy and girl, eight and twelve respectively, had been sharing the second bedroom. Now that Violet and company had been trapped, the entire sad-looking family was sleeping in the mother's bedroom, crashing on blankets and filthy comforters.

Violet looked at the ugly girl in question. She was a pudgy little thing with stringy blonde hair and fatty little breasts just starting under the thin fabric of her dirty tee shirt. Staring at the television, as usual, her slack little mouth was hanging open, her spattering of acne turned into craters of the moon by the flickering green light of the TV. She had no *reason* to obstruct this transfer of property, since it couldn't possibly make any difference to her whether Trixie owned the paper or Royce did (or Violet, for just a moment)—it was still just her mother's rent check, every month. Violet eyed her closely—this nasty little girl in ripped stretch pants. When it started up again— and it would start up again, as soon as the sun dipped under the horizon, Violet was sure of it—the awful thing that had prohibited sleep last night, and would certainly prohibit it again tonight, they would have a chance to catch the little schemer at it.

That first night, Violet, Royce and Trixie—stranded by the cold—had usurped the children's bedroom, but that arrangement had not lasted the night, because of the awful . . . *infestation*. Tonight, Violet was keeping an eye on the girl. She was not going to queer Violet's one and only real-estate deal. If that was, in fact, what was happening, Violet was not sure. She viewed every member of the family with suspicion, but her heart was not in it. She was afraid because, deep down, she believed it was real.

The evening news was on; the world was going on without them. Soon it would begin. Trixie was sitting at the kitchen table, her sunglasses still on. Royce squatted on a round footstool with stuffing leaking from the seams. There were candles everywhere, none of them lit, all of them bearing some image of the Virgin Mary or some anonymous, grimacing saint. Last night, at the height of the madness, Royce had gone through a trapdoor in the kitchen floor into the frigid crawlspace under the house with nothing but a cigarette lighter for light, looking for an explanation. He'd found none, and now he perched on his stool, looking grim.

The mother, Anna, sat at the table with Trixie. She was not talking. She was not making dinner, even though evening was approaching fast. She was just sitting there, looking old and tired and lumpy. Her head was in her hands.

"You never mentioned any of this," said Trixie, sitting at the table and addressing the gray top of the woman's head. "Four years of rent checks and you never mentioned it." She reached to her lips for an imaginary cigarette and, annoyed not to find one there, tapped her toe on the ragged linoleum floor.

"Didn't matter," said Anna, looking up and shrugging. "Did it?"

"Matters *now*, that you are screwing up my deal!"

"Shut up," Violet told Trixie. The baby was like a wax doll in a bassinet next to the table.

Royce was watching the girl on the couch. He could see through white women as if they were translucent on the surface. He knew what they were thinking before they thought it.

Violet was holding her breath.

The boy, though silent, was the only moving thing in the room. He was like a honeybee, buzzing everywhere, checking everyone out. His mother grounded him with a slap to the head.

"Sit down. These people are already nervous."

"Not nervous," said Royce from his footstool. "Just watching."

The woman laughed, an oddly phlegmy laugh for a woman who would not allow smoking in her home. Her face was flat from forehead to chin, as if somebody had already smashed her nose.

Outside, the sun kissed the flat white horizon of nothingness beyond the back door and the baby sighed, perhaps in anticipation. The winter wind howled around the side of the little house; a long, sustained moan that didn't help Violet's mood at all. Last night the wind had picked up this same way, surrounding the house like a continual, hostile force designed to trap the occupants. On the living room wall a cheap cuckoo clock whose little trapdoor never opened ticked loudly, its plastic gears whining as if there really was a bird trapped inside.

"No foolishness," said Royce, warning all of them. "None of that foolishness tonight."

Violet wished she could believe in his ability to threaten the whole thing away.

"Ain't nobody being foolish," said the woman quietly, "ain't nobody but—"

"No problems," said Trixie, laying a comforting hand on the woman's arm, "all he's saying is nobody wants any problems. I know you don't want any, either. It doesn't matter to you."

"No foolishness," said Royce, looking right at the girl.

"I ain't doing nothing," she said, picking at a scab on her cheek.

Outside the sun was disappearing on a cold horizon. The windows, covered over with a layer of insulating plastic filament, turned slowly into screens of greater and greater opacity until they became funhouse mirrors mocking the room's inhabitants.

An evil, incessant whisper came from the television. The cuckoo clock clicked and whined and rang a little muffled bell deep within its cheap plastic guts. Beside the malfunctioning clock hung a crucifix, suffering Christ on a skewed plastic cross, wearing a mantle of dust. Trixie fiddled with her cell phone, foolishly hoping for a signal. The boy, perched on the couch next to his sister, was chewing on his fingernails. Violet could see the TV screen reflected in the stretched plastic over the windows now, a flickering, multihued, electronic flame.

And it began.

The first pop came from behind the couch, directly behind where the girl was sitting. It was a sharp sound, just like last night, not particularly loud but clearly audible and not immediately identifiable. That was the whole problem, in a room so small.

"It's the walls again," Trixie said casually, "everything contracts in the cold."

"Ain't the cold," said the woman wearily.

"Shut up!"

Another pop. It was just a noise, but the quality of the noise was what made it so awful. It was right there in the room with them.

"Stop it now," said Royce.

The girl was motionless on the couch. The wind slapped the roof of the cottage like it intended to take the shingles off. Royce stood and snatched up the television's remote control, snapping the picture off. He stared at the girl. She put her hands up like a fugitive surrendering, but her eyes were hard.

"Okay," said Trixie, "You know what this is. You live here. Tell us what this is. Royce is just a businessman; that's all he is. He just wants to know what all this is."

"It's the devil," said Anna, "You don't have to believe in him, he believes in you."

"It's just going to be bad," said Trixie, "I am going to sell this property and it's going to be somebody else buying it. It doesn't matter to you—it's all the same. Just tell Royce what it is."

Pop! Pop! The noises came again, just like the night before. They were unnaturally loud. They were horrifying. They came from behind the couch, from behind the girl. Violet knew; this wasn't the pop of wood contracting; or stone settling. There was a wet, gristle tearing quality to these pops, like a great chicken bone being pulled loose. The television, not obeying the remote control in Royce's hand, turned itself back on again.

Trixie took the woman's hand again. "Tell her to stop. It's not funny—is it, Royce."

The woman shook her hand free. "She ain't doing it."

Violet couldn't take her eyes off the girl. "You better stop," she told her, "you are getting yourself into more trouble than you know."

The girl said nothing, and from behind Violet's head came a distinct, loud rap that made her flinch.

"Stop it," said Trixie.

"Ain't gonna stop," said Anna, "You—you girls come in here, you bring that . . . man—it ain't holy."

"We ain't gonna have another night like last," said Royce. He said it directly to the girl.

"Calm down," said Trixie, "Calm down, everyone."

Violet wasn't saying that, because she wasn't calming down herself. The house seemed to have gotten darker, and colder. She was afraid to look behind her chair, even though she knew there would be nothing there. The boy, who'd been silent, made a snuffling noise. Violet was surprised to see tears streaming down his cheeks.

He shuddered and clenched his fists, then suddenly leapt from his place on the couch.

"I hate you all!" he screamed, bolting for the bedroom.

The girl made a move as if to follow him.

Royce leaned forward. "You're gonna stay right where you are." .

Her mother, at the table, made no attempt to intervene. She was staring at the dark window. Outside, the wind increased the volume of its moaning. Violet could not stand the buffeting of the wind—it was getting under her skin.

"Listen," she said, "We shouldn't just sit here, letting this drive us crazy. Maybe we could play a game. Do you have any games?"

Over their heads, the roof let out a thunderous crack, as if the trusses were being torn from the walls.

"It's so cold," said Violet. "Do you see? It's doing funny things to the wood."

It was so cold. Around the kitchen window was a patina of frost. Violet had found a flashlight in one of the kitchen drawers the night before and now she turned it on, shining it through the window at the big plastic thermometer hung on a tree trunk in the yard. The big red hand pointed down, well below minus forty degrees. "You see?" she said, "It's—"

And then the popping started again, over by the girl on the couch. The lamp on the table next to her leaned precariously for what seemed an eternity, and then fell, smashing on the floor with a crash that left the room darker than before.

"You just did that," Royce told the girl.

"She did *not*!" shouted Violet. "I was standing right here and she did not!"

Trixie pulled on Anna's doughy arm. "Tell her to stop, for God's sake!"

A porcelain figurine that had recently occupied the windowsill flew through the air and shattered on the wall, just missing Royce's big head.

"No," said Violet, but Royce was already up, moving toward the flabby girl on the couch.

"No!" shouted Trixie, rising. All at once all the lights went out, and the television picture compressed to a tiny, white-hot dot before disappearing altogether.

It was all confusion, after that. There was a scream, and another scream, maybe the mother's, though it was so low and feral it was hard to believe it could be her. Something hit the house with the power of a locomotive, shaking it on the foundation, and when Violet turned the flashlight beam into the room it danced across the scene in a crazy jitterbug of fleeting images.

Each moment was captured like a flash photograph by the moving beam. There was Trixie, close by, her face turned into an albino caricature of itself, her mouth open in a pink, silent scream. There was Anna, her eyes and chin heavily shadowed, her mouth appearing to be curled in a demonic sneer. Out in the living room Royce was caught like a convict in the prison searchlight, and the girl was a dead body curled on the couch below him.

"Royce!" screamed Violet, but her voice was lost in a rending crash that seemed as if it must be the house coming down on them, and as her flashlight beam quivered the girl moved and Royce turned, but there was something else, too, something large and dark. Violet's flashlight beam only just caught it, a huge thing like a giant, whipping tail that snapped across the wall, tearing down pictures and sending a shelf full of figurines shattering across the floor. The flashlight was knocked from Violet's hand by something heavy and leathery. It fell and bounced on the floor to lie canted, its unattended beam throwing up monstrous shadows across the chaos that engulfed the room.

Royce was standing, and then he wasn't. It was as if he'd been knocked off his feet by a dark tidal wave. The girl was crawling across the floor toward Violet, her face smeared with a grotesque dark stain, her dark mouth hanging open.

Violet thought . . . she had believed it was real from the first moment. She had thought it was real from the first occurrences the night before, and she absolutely, with all her heart, believed the tired-looking woman at the table who thought it was all being caused by Satan. Or if not actually Satan, then some unidentified evil thing that had survived the awful cold and crept under cover of darkness to manifest itself in this tiny, run-down house. As far as she knew, all that now stood between them and its awful wrath was the feeble beam of her flashlight.

With perfect timing, her flashlight went dead and the room went black. She screamed, just from the shock of it.

Trixie hissed, "Damn it, Vi, what are you doing?"

Violet couldn't speak. Something was moving in the room, and she could sense it more than see it. It was stalking through the room, with feet like hooves, clicking on the uneven wood floor.

"Violet," said Royce dangerously, "turn that light back on."

As if she could—as if she had . . . "I didn't—I can't . . ."

"Violet, damn it!"

"I'm trying!" She scrambled on the floor, terrified, crawling as fast she could toward the last spot she'd seen the light. "I'm trying!"

"Violet!" screamed furious Trixie.

"I'm trying! I'm trying!"

Everyone was stumbling around in the dark. Someone stepped on Violet's hand— she screamed and they got off her, and she scrambled further. A few more feet and she had her hand around the barrel of the flashlight, rapping it on the floor, managing to get it lit again. She rolled onto her side, shining the light into the room.

It was chaos. Trixie was half out of her chair, leaning across the table. Across from her sat Anna, turned into a ghoul in the unflattering light, with dark pits under her eyes and chin. Royce had regained his feet and was in the center of the room, standing over the girl, and he was grabbing her by the arm, pulling her from the couch.

"Royce?" called Violet, trying to steady her beam.

"Royce!" Trixie echoed her, as if she was threatening a dog, "Royce, no!"

They were both drowned out by great slamming impacts to the house, again as if something was trying to knock it off its foundation. Violet screamed, just because it felt better than staying silent.

Royce roared like a wounded bear. Violet, watching, cringed. But he didn't swing—instead, to Violet's horror, a different figure appeared, coming out of the shadows behind Royce. It was an unimaginable thing, a creature with a grotesque head and hairy haunches, grabbing the girl by her throat, lifting her from the couch.

"No," begged Violet from the floor. The thing, with flashing hooves and twitching tail, lifted the girl.

"No!"

It was as if no one heard her, or cared. In the faltering beam of her flashlight the girl was suspended, her feet dangling. The grinning demon smacked her twice on the face.

"Stop it!" screamed Violet, her horror overcoming her terror that the monster would turn on her next. "Somebody stop it!"

Her flashlight died again. This time for good, she was sure. As she struggled with it, still trying to get light, the thing strode past her in the dark, smelling of stale sweat and something sickly sweet. Somewhere in the room someone was weeping; some-one else cursed softly under their breath. Violet was holding her breath, afraid to move. She wanted to stay low, out of the way, hidden, forever.

Trixie was suddenly talking, so suddenly that Violet, missing the first part of it, became cognizant that she was saying "Enough; enough, enough, enough," chant-ing it like a mantra in her reed-thin voice, as if that would do any good, as if . . . and then, about the sixth time she said it, the lights flickered and came back on. The television warmed back to life, starting with a spark and progressing through the stages of sentience until its sound and picture again dominated the room.

The girl lay at Royce's feet. Her upturned face was disfigured by a dark smear.

"You son of a bitch," said Trixie.

"No," said Violet, getting up off the floor. "He didn't do it. Didn't you see?"

"Shut up," said Royce, but she couldn't tell if he was talking to her, Trixie, or the girl moaning at his feet.

Violet was looking around the room, wildly hoping for some sign of the intruder, and she caught sight of it, moving in the dark doorway to the hall.

"There!" Violet stood and pointed. "Trixie, do you see it?" She shined her flash-light into the dark corner and caught the movement; a thick, dark red tail, mottled and tipped by a forked end, catching it in the beam as it slid quickly out of sight around the door frame. "Trixie!"

Anna had finally moved to hunch over her daughter. Royce was still standing in the middle of the room, looking down at them, and Trixie sat at the kitchen table, looking furious.

"Trixie," said Violet, "did you? Did you just see it? In the doorway? It hit the girl and then it went over there!"

"Sure," said Trixie, finally. "Sure, Violet. Just calm down."

"I'm not—did you not see it? You were looking right at it!"

"Goddamn hillbillies," said Royce. He nudged the women at his feet with a shiny loafer the way he would a pair of dogs copulating on the lawn. "Get yourselves up, now."

Trixie stood. "This doesn't change anything."

Violet, confused, finally understood the statement was directed at Royce.

"Don't have to change anything," he said, nudging Anna with his foot again. "You go on and get your girl cleaned up." Then he looked at Trixie and inclined his head toward the back door.

"I'm coming," said Violet. She could not bear to be in the house another mo-ment without them.

They stood on the back stoop and Royce kept one heel against the back door be-cause he suspected, probably fairly, that Anna might try to lock them out. The black sky was spattered with a million tiny, cold stars, and the wind had died down.

"Does it seem warmer?" asked Violet hopefully. She looked to the big thermome-ter, and the temperature had indeed gone up a good twenty degrees.

"Should try the car again," said Royce, handing Trixie one of his cheap cigarettes.

"You're a bastard," she said, looking at the thing.

"Bitch."

"You're going to take this place now."

Violet was lost. "Did you not see that thing? Trixie, I *know* you did."

Royce blew a great cloud of white smoke into the sky. "I reckon we've done *exor-cised* the place now. You say the property goes all the way back to that tree?"

"That's right. And to that row of pines over there."

"Guys," said Violet, "guys . . ."

Royce flicked the cigarette into the yard. "Violet, will you shut the hell up? And you—I'd go try to start that car now."

Trixie, nodding, trotted around the side of the house. Violet and Royce went back inside, into the warmth. Anna was washing her daughter's face at the sink. The girl, seeing them, made a little sound in her throat. The boy was crouched in a corner of the living room like a chubby gargoyle, watching the television.

"Is she okay?" asked Violet.

No one answered her.

Out in front of the house Trixie was grinding away at the starter, which was at least turning over. The car, miracle of German engineering that it was, coughed twice and then started with a triumphant roar. Royce grinned widely, his gold tooth glinting.

Trixie came in the front door, stamping her tiny feet to warm them. "I did it!"

And that was it. In less than ten minutes they were packed into the warming car, crunching over the frozen driveway, pointed toward the highway with the headlight beams throwing long, humanoid shadows behind every dark pine tree.

Trixie and Royce were in front, arguing over details of price. In the back seat Violet hugged her knees to her chest, finally getting warm. Her hand hurt, but she didn't care. There was a livid bruise there already, two sharply defined, anvil shaped marks. She paid no more attention to it than she did the two arguing in the front seat. She was sitting in the back seat, practicing it under her breath, over and over: "Well, yes, I did have some property up north, but I traded it in a business deal. . . ."

CHAZ BRENCHLEY

The House of Mechanical Pain

Chaz Brenchley has been making a living as a writer since he was eighteen. He is the author of nine thrillers, most recently Shelter, *and two major fantasy series:* The Books of Outremer, *based on the world of the Crusades, and* Selling Water by the River, *set in an alternate Ottoman Istanbul. He's currently working on a Chinese sequence of novels. A winner of the British Fantasy Award, he has also published three books for children and more than 500 short stories in various genres. His time as Crimewriter-in-Residence at the St. Peter's Riverside Sculpture Project in Sunderland resulted in the collection* Blood Waters. *2007 saw his debut as a professional playwright. He is a prizewinning ex-poet, and has been writer in residence at the University of Northumbria. He was Northern Writer of the Year 2000, and lives in Newcastle upon Tyne with two squabbling cats and a famous teddy bear.*

"The House of Mechanical Pain" was originally published in Phantoms at the Phil III.

—E.D.

Tasha's one of those people who live life on the razor's edge, who find the world too difficult to deal with, almost too difficult to bear.

She tries to be sweet about it, for our sake: greets every crisis with a glass of champagne, swallows down the fear and sees how far a smile and an endearing helplessness will get her this time. Seldom far enough, but when troubles reach their ragged ends she has an endless ability to suffer quietly, with an intolerable patience.

It's one of the reasons I adore her. Also one of the reasons why, when she asks for help, I'm just there. If she has to ask, then she really, really means it.

Also, she's not apologetic about it. This particular Friday, I was just settling down for the afternoon—Margaret Lockwood on the TV, paperwork all over the carpet, see which could hold my attention—when there's a hammer-hammer-hammer on the front door, familiar in every sense. Only one person I know deals so desperately with obstructions, kicking and flailing at them to get through to what she needs.

So I all but run to the door, and there she is, tight as a wire and twice as sharp; but bless her, she still takes the time for one of her trademark kisses, long and lingering and ironic. I think they're ironic.

Then, "Jonny. Thanks . . ."

"I haven't done anything yet."

"For being here, I meant."

"Always, for you. Why didn't you phone, if you wanted me?" I've never told her, but she's the reason I bought a mobile, the reason I always remember to carry it.

She shrugged and said, "I didn't think," which was classic Tash: she wanted me, so she came to get me. If I hadn't been in, that would have been one more complication to the crisis, one more struggle not to break down in the street. That's how she deals with the world. How badly she deals.

"So." I rubbed her long spine, feeling how the many tensions tangled through her body. "How are you doing, Tash?"

"Oh, not so great, really. You know."

"Yeah, I know. What do you need?"

"You. Come to Brookshurst with me?"

That was new. Usually it was an evening in the pub or holding her hand at a concert, being a warm body, reminding her that she was loved. Her family was one of those things she didn't talk about, but I did know that Brookshurst was her parents' place, and I knew how far away it was. This was a weekend trip she was talking about, that long at least; and I'd had my own plans for the weekend, and,

"Yes, of course," I said. "You sit here and watch the movie for me, while I pack."

"Thanks, sweetie. Bring your cameras, yeah?"

In the car going down—which meant in her car, because actually driving's one of the things she does really well, and you don't take that away from Tash; anything she's good at, you celebrate—I said, "Why do I need the cameras?"

"Because my stupid, hateful father wants to sell off the best of my childhood, and I'd like some pictures to remember it by."

"Seriously, Tash?"

"I am being serious. He's decided that we're all one step shy of the workhouse, and he needs to realize his assets. Which of course means our assets, the things that matter most to us, because those are the things that matter least to him. Not land, not shares, not the stuff that we could lose and never notice it was gone; no, it has to be what he calls clutter, what I call the soul of the house."

"I thought your family was rich?"

"We *are* bloody rich!"—and she proved it, stamping on the accelerator and breaking the speed limit, breaking the law by quite some distance as she showed me just how fast a TR7 can go, when it's impelled by a girl hiding her anxiety behind her temper.

She'd never really made a secret of her family's wealth; well, she couldn't. She depended on it. It wasn't only the car and the flat; trust-fund status was all she had to support the lifestyle. Champagne and troubles don't come cheap.

When she'd calmed down, when she'd slowed down, she said, "It's just in his head, that's all. He's always been like this. It's a bad mixture, meanness and blindness together. Technically, you're coming down to take pictures for him, for the sale catalog, because he likes to exploit our friends to get things done for nothing. Really, though, it's for me. Is this okay, Jonny? Really?"

It was a bit late to say no, but really it was okay, so I said so. "Really truly, hon. I'm fascinated." And it meant I got to spend the time with her, which was worth any amount of angst, only she'd never see that. Probably just as well.

Motorway, motorway, country lanes. And then we passed between high stone gateposts and under the overhanging branches of a long lime avenue, and so came to the ancestral mansion—

—which it was, rather, and for a moment I just wanted her to turn the car around and drive me all the way home again.

"Jesus, Tash . . ."

"Courage, mon brave," she murmured. "It's not so scary on the inside."

Maybe not, but I'd have been better convinced if she weren't so pale and thin-lipped as she said it. Tash has a face she puts on to meet the vicissitudes of the world, a kind of cheerful anticipation of calamity; here she was trying, I thought, for my sake, but she couldn't come near it.

On the outside, the house sported all the worst of Victorian Gothic: high pointed arches, gargoyles and gloom. And ivy, and narrow leaded windows. Turrets. Like that.

She drove us round to the back, to the stableyard; and I didn't need to ask if there were actually any horses in the stable, the muckheap assured me that there were, even before I saw their curious heads poking out to watch us.

I was intimidated already, before we even stepped out of the car, so I went camera-in-hand, which is my standard way of dealing. Tasha lacks the props; it took her another minute to move, which gave me time to shoot off a dozen frames, get my nerves settled, start reaching for a little perspective. It wasn't exactly a stately home, just a country house with ambitions; you could see clearly from the back how little was original, how much was dressing-up. Judging by the lines left visible, it was a plain Georgian cake with elaborate Victorian icing.

Even so, it was a three-story pile with all the attributes: a Land Rover in the yard and dogs barking joyously behind a door. Their noise rather underlined what we were missing, a figure in the doorway, a calling voice, any kind of family welcome for the prodigal daughter returned.

No great surprise, from what little she'd said. I should have screwed more out of her during the drive, at least a quick run-down of who I was likely to meet, but it's hard to ask Tash questions. She flinches, and puts on a bright helpful voice, and you know that for her this is third degree.

All unready, then, I followed her through that unlocked door into a room full of old sofas and Wellington boots and dogs who raised a fusillade to greet us, despite her best efforts to shush them; and on from there—the dog-room, she called it, un-surprisingly; I adjusted my mental landscape, to incorporate people who have whole rooms given over to their pets—into a chill stony corridor lined with stillrooms and storerooms, sculleries and larders.

This brought us into the kind of kitchen you only ever dream about: a long deal table and a great iron range; a Welsh dresser that must have been built in situ, it occupied an alcove so exactly; an Ulster sink and a wooden drainer that looked as old as the house. Tiles and mats underfoot, beams above.

Still no human bodies. It was starting to look pointed. I said, "Nobody home?" and she shrugged. "Oh, they'll be around, I expect. They'll find us if they want us. Are you hungry?"

Yes, of course I was hungry; but it was pushing six already, and I'd been nicely brought up. I said, "What time's dinner?"

"It's not that kind of house. We don't do sit-down dinners, people eat when they need to. Sorry. None of us can cook, see. . . ." And indeed she looked magnificently vague and helpless, turning a slow circle in the center of the kitchen, wafting her hands at the baffling intricacies of oven, freezer, fridge. "If you want food, you might as well do something about it now, save us coming back down later. . . ."

A quick search turned up ham, bread, eggs. Omelettes for two, then, and I made her eat; and then made coffee after, and still no one had come through to find us. This was more than pointed, it was the stuff of paranoia. I was convinced by now that she was wrong, that the house was empty.

And was just about to say so when there was a thunder of feet on uncarpeted wooden stairs, just beyond the wall. Tash stiffened visibly, then gave me an unquiet smile, pushed ineffectually at her hanging curtain of hair and just had time to say, "My brother," before he erupted into the room.

Late teenage, and not expecting to find us there; he did a more exaggerated version of Tash's little freeze, all gawky adolescent startlement, and then an even less accomplished version of her recovery.

"Nat. Hullo. I thought you'd gone upstairs. . . ."

Meaning, demonstrably, that he hoped she had, that he'd waited until he thought the coast was clear. She shrugged a negative and said, "Rufus, this is Jonny."

"The photographer, right?" And then he saw my camera on the table and slapped his forehead and said, "Duh. Sorry. I specialize in stating the obvious. Nat told us last week, she'd be bringing you down."

And had only told me this afternoon, but that was classic; she'd have spent all week hanging over the phone, quite incapable of asking. I was more interested to learn that she'd left a family name behind her, when she moved away. And that her brother had that swift public-school charm about him, albeit an abrupt and prickly version, and not available for use with his sister. Talking to her, he was all spikes.

He said, "I only came down for some grub; I'll just knock up a sandwich and get out of your way."

"Don't worry," Tash said, edging round the opposite side of the table, no easy touching here, "we were just going up. Mum and Dad in the library?"

"They are," and that was all too obviously family code for *let's not go there, then.*

If they had a code in common—and the same impetus, to avoid their parents—they couldn't dislike each other too badly. I wanted to sit them both down and make them talk, see what I could learn; but Tash was out of there already, with my bags. Hastening after, I realized that she'd come here with nothing, no bag of her own. Daughter of the house, of course she'd have a room, presumably with everything she needed, toothbrush and clean undies. Even so, to have nothing that she wanted to bring, that spoke volumes.

She led me up what must have been servants' stairs, narrow and steep. At the top was a short corridor: "Family rooms," Tasha said. "Rufus, my sister Alex. Our cousin Monty, when he's here." Which was what she meant by family, clearly, her own generation, close and difficult. Her parents were elsewhere: another wing of the house, another aspect of her life. I was catching on.

"This one's mine," she said, nudging at a door. "In case, you know, you need me in the night. . . ."

"Always, sweetheart."

That won me a smile, and, "Well, a girl can dream," but actually I thought she meant it the other way around; in case she needed me in the night, I'd know where to come. If I knew the need.

After that, a grand hall; we stood on the landing that overlooked it, with a divided staircase sweeping down from both ends, meeting halfway like a wishbone.

"The parents' rooms are along there," she said, wafting a hand at another corridor. "I'll show you upstairs later. You're in here."

Right at the heart of things, between one generation and another. No tucking the unprepared guest away in a corner, where he could be private if he needed to, where he could find an escape from other people's family tensions. This was Tasha; this was why I was here, to stand as a bulwark against oppression. To be leaned on, as and when needed. It wasn't really about the photographs.

Big square room, big squeaky bed that would announce to the house if anyone came sneaking in to join me. Just as well that wasn't in the game plan.

Surprisingly, I wouldn't need to traipse corridors in my dishabille; this room came with an en suite. That's en suite Victorian style, which meant another room equally large, equally square: this one tiled in black and white, and hosting an ancient cast-iron clawfoot bathtub, a decorated toilet bowl with a most unreliable-looking flushing mechanism above, and another contraption of pipes and chains that it took me a while to understand as a shower.

"Does that, um, *work?*"

"Scaldingly," she said. "Don't try to use it without help. I could show you, but it'd be better if you asked Ru—"

"I'll take baths," I said. "Now, why don't you introduce me to your parents?"

"Oh. Jonny . . ."

"Seriously, Tash. I can't stay here all weekend and not meet my hosts. And I don't want to be tiptoeing around, hoping not to bump into them in corridors, like some illicit boyfriend you've smuggled in behind their backs. Come on, let's just get it over with. Can't be that bad, surely?"

"You've no idea," she said. Darkly.

But she took me out, and down that long sweep of a staircase into the hall below; and then across a parquet floor to high double doors, where I almost thought she was going to knock before going in; and then she laid the flat of her hand against the oak, and hesitated, and I almost thought she was going to turn and walk away and leave me to go in alone; and then she pushed the door open and in we went.

For a library, it was a little short on books. But it had window-bays that looked out over the gardens, and ancient leather sofas, and ingrained aromas of tobacco and whisky and dust. Also a waiting generation, Tasha's father and mother: him sprawled on a sofa, glass in hand, her posed by the window gazing into the gloom outside, or else at her own reflection, or else at the reflection of the room behind her.

She didn't look round at her daughter's entrance; perhaps her eyes shifted slightly in the glass.

Tasha's father did at least stir, he did take notice. He gazed up at us and grunted, "Who's this, eh? Who's this?"

"My friend Jonny, Dad, I told you. He's come to take pictures."

"Unh. So you did. Photographer, are you, lad?"

"That's right, sir."

"Weddings and so forth, is it? Village fêtes?"

"Not those so much, perhaps. . . ."

"Well, so long as you can point a camera and not shake it, you'll be doing better than anyone here. While you're up there, you can look through the old stuff too, see if it's worth anything. Boxes and boxes of what-d'you-call-'ems, photographic plates, and all the gear that goes with 'em."

"Um, I don't really know very much about that."

"Do you not?" He frowned at me sharply above his glass. "Don't know the value of your own equipment, don't do weddings—what use are you, then?"

Well, I look after your daughter, when she'll let me—but I didn't say that, of course. I didn't say anything. Which was a mistake, perhaps, because it let Tash come blundering in on my behalf, trying to look after me. "He's an artist, Dad, he works for galleries and, and commissions, and . . ."

And it all meant nothing, less than nothing to her father, a grunt and a shrug; and her mother still hadn't spoken, still hadn't moved; and when Tasha grabbed my arm and pulled me none too gently toward the door, I was glad enough to go. Out in the hall again, she said, "I could take you up now, and show you the museum?"

I didn't know what that meant, except that it was presumably what she wanted me to photograph, what her father wanted to sell. I said, "Let's pick up Rufus on the way, get him to explain the shower to me."

She flinched. "You said you'd bathe . . . ?"

"I do like a shower in the mornings." And then, more honestly, as she turned reluctantly away from the stairs, "You shouldn't all be lurking in your own hidden corners of the house. Families are supposed to get on, you know?"

"It's not compulsory, Jonny. Sometimes they just don't. The Kilvallans have been dysfunctional, oh, for generations. Our grandparents couldn't stand each other—or, no, it's not that. They just couldn't *talk* to each other. And from what Grandma said, her own parents were worse. I think it's this house, it twists everything out of true. Unless it's just that all kids learn by example, and we've all had rotten examples to learn from. Ru and I are okay, actually. We just don't have much to, you know, say to each other. . . ."

I thought she and her brother were far from okay, even on the brief evidence I had; I also thought it was a bit much to blame the house. I liked the house, and I have limited sympathy for poor little rich kids. Just boundless, immeasurable sympathy for Tasha.

Rufus was still in the kitchen, chewing his way through half a loaf. He was startled to see us back, startled again to be asked to join us. He came, though, willingly enough, with a sandwich in his hand and his eyes full of a boy's curiosity.

Up to my room, then, and a slightly damp, steamy exploration of valves and levers, that left me thinking perhaps I would bathe after all; but once we'd done a little male bonding over the domestic engineering, it seemed only natural for Rufus to tag along as Tash took me further up into the house, into her family's history.

Every house should have a museum, I think, something to speak to its former occupants, its former occupations. Perhaps every house does have a museum, just that they're not all labeled so. Some houses are a museum in themselves, a record set in bricks and mortar. Perhaps Brookshurst is one of those and was trying to hide it, with the crudest possible misdirection: a locked door in an attic corridor, a wooden plaque professionally lettered, "Joshua Kilvallan: His Museum."

"Joshua was the younger son," Tash said, "back in the eighteen-sixties, eighteen-seventies. I think he was bored, he had nothing to do, so he got into collecting. Scientific instruments, mostly. I always loved this room. . . ."

Indeed, she had the key on her own key-ring, though it was presumably a copy; her father wouldn't let her keep him out.

She opened the door and turned on the lights inside, and I fell in love at first sight. Photographers like mechanisms. However fancy our cameras have become, they are still devices for capturing light; and I might not know much about their history, but I do know what I like.

I liked this room, and the mind that had created it. I understood Joshua, I thought, just from that swift and early glance. An intelligent and inquiring mind, trapped in the stultifying social conformity of his age and class. Bored rigid no doubt by rural ways of life, field sports and house parties, but kept at home by convention because he never would have thrived in the army and he must have spurned the church, he'd turned eyes and mind upward and outward: first to the horizons, then to the stars.

There were astrolabes and compasses, sextants and quadrants, devices for knowing where you stood upon the earth. There were cameras, original plate cameras on tripods, and never mind what I'd said to Tasha's father, those did surely have to be valuable; but they mattered more here, as devices for expressing where you stood, for seizing the moment.

There were telescopes for looking further, for reaching beyond mortal grasp; and, blessedly, under a great lead-lighted glass dome in the middle of the room stood an orrery.

The dome was covered with grime—well, everything in that room was covered with grime—but even so I could see enough to know what I was looking at: the little models of the planets, all in their proper orbits around a central stud to represent the sun. I stepped forward in a daze; I think I was making little crooning noises of desire. I know I heard Tasha laughing at me, though it didn't register at the time.

My sleeve made a swift duster, to clean the glass off and let me see properly. There were the inner planets, and out as far as Saturn, with five of its moons around it. I sighed, and stroked the glass, and said, "Eighteenth century, right?"

"That's right," Rufus confirmed, while Tash was still giggling. "How did you know?"

"They hadn't discovered Uranus, so it can't be later than 1780; but it's got all the early moons, which puts it later than, what, 1685. . . ."

"Jonny," Tash said behind me, "you're a geek."

"Am not. I just like this stuff. And I'm good at numbers."

"Geek," she asserted again. And, "You're supposed to be taking photographs, not drooling."

"If you clean the room up, I'll take your pictures. You don't want it coming out all dirty, do you?"

"Yes, I do," she asserted, "it's always been dirty; that's how I remember it."

"Well, your dad doesn't want it dirty."

"He can bloody clean it up, then. . . ." But her voice broke, she couldn't sustain the anger; I cursed myself silently, turned and hugged her. At first she was stiff and unresponsive, but my fingers walked up and down her spine, pressing deep into those tight tendons, and after a minute she was squirming, muttering protests she didn't mean.

"I've got your number, girl," I whispered. "Back-rub tomorrow. If you're good. If we get this room cleaned up tonight."

She scowled, angry with me now for knowing her weak spot, angry with herself for giving way so easily; she pushed hair back out of her eyes and said, "Ru can help."

"Oh, we'll all help. Promise."

She sniffed, and went off in search of cleaning-stuffs; I was pulled magnetically back to the orrery. The base plate was pierced, giving intimate views of the cogs and gears beneath; which led to the inevitable question, "Does it, you know, *work* . . . ?"

"It does, yeah. We're not supposed to, but, well . . ."

He went to the wall, where an old iron mechanism reached up the wall to the mean little dormer that gave the room its only natural light.

There was a crank leaning against the wall there, but it looked oddly too long to be anything to do with that mechanism, as well as too refined, too well made, totally wrong. . . .

"Old Joshua didn't believe in waste. One crank could perfectly well do two jobs at once, if the window's gearing was built to fit, but it belongs to the orrery. Just slots in at the bottom there. . . ."

It did, through a brassbound hole in the mahogany case. He slid it in, stepped back, gestured; I gripped the smooth handle of the crank and turned it slowly clockwise. Slowly, slowly the planets moved in their orbits, the moons turned around their planets, all the workings of God were laid bare. . . .

Well, no, but as a working model of the solar system, it was unbeatable. I wanted it, very badly. It should have been a museum piece, but if it had to be in private hands—if it could belong to Mr. Kilvallen, for crying out loud!—then why not to me?

Because he's a very rich man, Jonny, and you're not. My inner voice speaks a lot of sense sometimes, but I was still deeply covetous. I could understand something of Tasha's distress, even without the deep background of childhood possessiveness; how could anyone own this beautiful machine, and want to sell it . . . ?

Because it works, and he doesn't understand it. Nothing works in his life, and so he wants it out. That was my inner voice again, leaping to unjustified conclusions.

The orrery wasn't actually clockwork, you couldn't wind it up. You had to keep turning the crank, to keep the planets turning. So we did that, and so Tash came back to find us still playing; so we generously let her give the orrery a more thorough clean than I had, while we took J cloths off to the more boring corners of the museum.

Me, I headed straight for the cameras, naturally. I was in the mood to be intrigued; caught first by their awkward intricacies, the makeshift engineering of early bright ideas, my attention was snared soon by a photograph hung on the wall behind. That was just as early, it must have been taken with one of these cameras; and—once I'd rubbed the dust off—it turned out to be a family portrait, a small group of grim Victorians posed on the front steps outside this house.

"I guess no one had invented saying cheese," I said. "Or else it predates the smile. Do we know who these people are?"

They came to peer, and fingers pointed over my shoulder. Actually they didn't know names, but they thought this was Joshua's elder brother, his wife, their children; and that old man in the bathchair must be the paterfamilias. . . .

"Pity there's no Joshua," I said, "but he'll be taking the picture, of course. I wonder who she is?"—a girl standing off to one side of the group, head down, long loose hair falling like wings about her face.

"Poor relation?" Rufus hazarded, all heedless young heir. "Not Joshua's, he never married. She must be family or she wouldn't be let in the photo, but she really doesn't look like she belongs."

"Don't be cocky, Ru. If they ever took a family photo of us, none of us would look like we belonged."

And that, in an unexpected sentence, was why I love Tasha: that ruthless honesty, the unflinching glare into the spotlight of her own intelligence. She knows; oh, she does know. And she's not afraid of the knowledge. It's the world beyond that she can't deal with, anything outside her skin. Which is, first and foremost, her family, before she even gets to all the strangers.

We cleaned, or at least we shifted a lot of dust about; and then we needed ten minutes out in the air, on the roof, wheezing extravagantly and sharing a four-pack of lager. It should have been a classic, three young people intoxicated by height and night, stars and alcohol; but it wasn't, because there was no miracle going on here. Tash and Rufus were perennially edgy and uncomfortable with each other, almost silent under the weight of a lifetime's legacy of discord.

When we went back down, indeed, Rufus disappeared. I was sorry, but I couldn't blame him; it's not so interesting, watching a man take photos of a room. For me it was a constant fascination, as I kept getting closer to objects, seeing more. The or- rery was still the focus, but there was more and more at the fringes, around the walls, that I wanted to get deeper and deeper into. Deeper far than a photograph can take you; once I'd got enough shots to satisfy even Tasha, I put the cameras away and did some exploring with my hands, among the crumbling cardboard boxes in the cup- boards below the display cases.

It had been warm enough to stand out on the roof in shirtsleeves, a couple of hours earlier. Now suddenly I felt the night's chill coming at me. We'd opened the skylight earlier, to help clear the dust; I used that long crank to wind it closed again, and went back to rummaging. Tasha had gone off too, headed bedward; she'd left me with her key, though, and a bottle of her father's whiskey, and I had no plans to sleep yetawhile.

Just as well, because I'd just found the glass plates her father had told me about, stacks of them, interleaved with prints. Happy man: this family was starting to absorb me, and there's no such thing as too much information. I sat on the floor, whiskey close by, and looked at one image after another. And became more and more fasci- nated, because not all but most of them did have that stray girl, that footnote to the family, holding herself apart but still irredeemably there, inescapable; and that's where you start to wonder, is she there because she wants to be, or because the others want her to be, or because the photographer wants her to be? It's easy to forget that third factor, the eye behind the lens, when you're looking at family dynamics.

In this instance, I thought the question was easy to answer. The way she stood, the way she held herself, her body language was entirely saying no, she really didn't want to be there. And the others in every picture, the kids her age—and she was young, no more than twelve, not even a teenager yet—and the adults who really should have known better, they were doing the same thing, turning away from her, letting their bodies speak for them.

As everyone in this family still did, I thought, remembering Tasha and Rufus to- gether, remembering their parents. All turned away.

So that left Joshua. His hand composing these pictures, his voice commanding them, his eye deciding. Who on earth was she, that he should be insisting on her presence in his pictures?

I found the answer, part of the answer, in scribbled pencil on the back of one print. At last, someone had noted down names for future generations. Here were Victoria, Harold, Lucy and Georgina; here cousin Thomas and cousin Ned.

Which meant, logically and assuredly, that—if the boys were so explicitly picked out as cousins, separate from us—then the three girls must all be sisters together.

Which meant that my stray, my castaway Georgina was absolutely one of the tribe, not a poor relation at all; so why on earth was she so held apart, so disdained, so huddled in on herself?

She reminded me of Tasha, to be honest—especially now I'd seen her among her family, and seen how they all treated each other. The family in the photos looked healthier, in fact, because they only excluded one of themselves; as Tash had said, her own brood were all strangers to each other.

It was a mystery I didn't expect to solve, but I went on looking, because that's what I do. Give me pictures and a puzzle, and I am a dog with a bone, I am growling.

And there was a bottle of whiskey to be drunk, and the same applies. I'm very bad at putting the stopper in.

So I went on looking, one box of plates and then another; and then suddenly I was into another world. I'd have thought I'd found another photographer, if Joshua hadn't left his stylistic fingerprints all over these too, along with his obsession for Georgina.

I'd seen pix like these before, of course. Famously, Lewis Carroll made them. So did a host of other Victorians, and so have others since. Little girls naked, it's a theme. It's only our own generation that questions it; art has always invested nudity with purity, and youth the same. Take both together, youth and nudity, and nobody's been uncomfortable but us.

Sitting there, looking at these photographs from a hundred years ago and then some, I was very uncomfortable indeed. They were all Georgina, posed naked in various artificial settings; and here she couldn't hide behind the broken wings of her hair, but her face was truly saying how she felt, how she so very much did not want to be there and doing this.

They made me go back and look at the earlier pix again, how she'd always had her hair down to hide behind, how it wasn't actually her sisters or her parents she was flinching away from, so much as the camera itself. Or the man behind it.

But I was bringing my twenty-first century sensibilities to bear on a nineteenth-century story, and that's as corrupt as anything else. And it would probably be rude to drink all of Mr. Kilvallen's whiskey, on my first night under his roof. I put the cork in the bottle, locked the door behind me and went to bed.

Alien pipes make strange music. I slept badly, never more than drowsing and waking often, startling myself awake; much of the night I lay sleeplessly staring into the dark, listening to the noises in my bathroom, slight knocks and whisperings as though someone were shuffling around in there, trying to be quiet, not to disturb.

In the morning, Tash came in search of me: the usual thump on the door and she barged straight through, unworried by whatever state I might be in. As it happened, I'd risked the shower, just to wake myself up a bit; she found me still toweling my hair dry.

"Steamy," she said, wafting imagined clouds of vapor aside.

"Yeah, sorry, I didn't think to open a window. . . ."

"Joke, Jonny. It's fine."

She perched on the bed to watch me dress; I said, "How come there's a private bathroom here, anyway? The rest of you don't have an en suite."

"No, just this. It used to be the schoolroom; I know Joshua taught his brother's children here. The unmarried intellectual younger brother, of course he had to play at schoolmaster. The way I heard it, he had water and gas plumbed in to that room for his experiments, to make it a kind of science lab, I suppose. But the next generation was sent away to school, so they didn't need it here; and someone had the bright idea of converting the lab into a bathroom. Lucky you."

Oh, lucky me indeed. I was thinking more about Georgina. This was her uncle's space, to do with as he chose; one room opening privately off another with water plumbed in, doubtless that was his darkroom through there, and very possibly his studio also. At a guess, I'd just figured out where those photographs were taken.

I hadn't yet figured out what to do, who to tell, Tasha or her father. She'd be upset; he'd want to know if they were valuable. Tough call.

We went downstairs together, but she hadn't really needed my escort; the kitchen was empty when we got there, no awkward family to face. Toast and coffee for breakfast, then, and while we crunched I said, "You don't know what happened to the kids Joshua taught, do you? Only I found names for some of them on the back of a photo, and that just makes them more real somehow. Harold and Victoria, Lucy, Georgina . . . ?"

"I recognize the names," she said dubiously. "I'm sorry, I don't know anything about them. Ru might. Or there might be some kind of family record in the library somewhere, but . . ."

But she didn't want to go poking about in there, it was her parents' territory. Even at this time of day, nowhere to go trespassing. Indeed, she was swallowing toast in a hurry, glancing at her watch, saying, "I thought I'd go for a ride this morning, see if Lady Grey can remember any of her manners. There's an old hack of my father's, he'd be up to your weight, if you fancied . . . ?"

"Not me," I said. "Horses and me don't mix. You go do your thing, I'll do mine."

"Will you be all right? By yourself?" It was inconceivable to her, being left alone in a strange house, someone else's.

"Tash, I'll be fine. Go. Don't ride under any low branches."

I made another pot of coffee and waited, and ten minutes later there were brisk steps in the corridor. One of the family at least kept strict time, and Tasha knew it.

It turned out to be her mother. We did the polite smiling thing, I poured her a coffee, she refused toast; when it looked like she was heading for the window to do her silent staring out thing again, I intercepted her by asking what she knew about her family history.

"Not my family," she said sharply. "My husband's."

Which told me quite a lot right there, just not enough; so I asked her if she'd seen the photographs up in the museum.

"Some of them, yes," she said. "My husband wouldn't care about such things, but I—I disliked them, so I put them away. I'd have locked that cupboard, but the key is lost; keys do get lost, in this house. Lord only knows what else is up there, that's been locked away before. Frankly, I prefer not to know."

She was hugging her elbows in the same way her daughter did, confronted by a world too terrible to face. I could pity Tasha, born into this house and this life; it was harder to feel sorry for her mother, who had chosen to marry into it and chosen to stay.

I asked about surviving documents, in the library or elsewhere. She said she didn't know, but there was a family tree hanging in the hall. We went to see that, and she traced Joshua's line for me. There he was, as reported: no wife, no kids. And there was his brother, and the long line of his children: Harold the heir, and the three daughters. Harold had done his family duty, produced heirs of his own, a direct line down to Rufus and Tasha; Victoria and Lucy had married too, had children too; Georgina—

No. Georgina had barely made it out of childhood. Dead at fourteen, just a couple of years after those photos were taken. The chart didn't say why or how. And of course Victorian children did die, in numbers, there were all manner of diseases and accidents to carry them off; and even so it felt sinister to me that it should have been this girl, the outsider in her own home, who didn't survive. Not surprising, mind, I think I was looking for exactly that; she didn't have the look of a survivor.

I was still standing there, I suppose you'd call it thinking, when Mrs. Kilvallen said a sharp, "What's that?"

She was staring upward, at the gallery where my room stood. I'd left the door ajar, and white smoke was oozing out of the gap.

I took that long curving stair at a gallop, but she wasn't far behind me. When we reached the gallery, there was a hissing noise to be heard, then a great eruptive gurgle; I slowed and waited for her, relieved and baffled both at once.

"Not smoke," I said, before we'd even reached the door. "Steam. That's the shower running."

She frowned. "Natasha, then, I suppose?"

Of course she would think that, but I had to disabuse her. "No, she's gone riding. Rufus, maybe . . . ?"

But here came Rufus, along the corridor from his own room, come to see the fuss.

"Well," I said defensively, "I didn't leave it running. . . ."

"Well," she said sardonically, "I suggest you get in there to see."

We both went, Rufus and I. The bedroom was full of steam, the bathroom worse, a wall of white; plunging in, I could just make out a figure through the fog. She wasn't in the shower, only standing by the bath: naked, vulnerable, small. Too small for Tash, too small for anyone in this house, that I'd seen. . . .

Behind me, I heard swearing; that was Rufus, burning his hand on the pipes as he reached blindly through gushing scorching water for the lever that would turn it off. Only for a moment, he distracted me; when I turned my eyes back to find her again, she wasn't there.

The steam cleared, slowly. She wasn't anywhere in that room, or next door.

Rufus said, "Don't worry, Jonny, it's happened before. The whole system's haywire; I think water pressure builds up to the point where it can knock itself on, just from how hard the pipe shakes. No harm done, except a bit of water on the floor. I'll tell Mum."

No need; she was there in the bedroom, listening. Looking at me, seeing how fey I was, staring into corners. I don't think she believed that the shower turned itself on, any more than I did.

She said, "This was the master bedroom when the house came down to us. My husband wanted us to take it, but I couldn't sleep in here, I never could. I never liked the feel of, of that bathroom," a nod toward the dripping walls, the gathered pools of water on the floor. "I used to think I could hear someone moving about in there at night, while he was sleeping. . . ."

I went up to the museum, alone, with Tasha's key. I wasn't really going to talk to Georgina, but I think I did, as I sifted through the plates again: telling her how sorry

I was she'd been unhappy, hoping that she was easy now. I didn't believe it for a moment, but sometimes you just have to say these things.

The crank was back in the orrery. I was sure—no, I *knew* that I hadn't left it like that. Still, I went and turned it for a little, and watched how all the planets moved about each other on their wheels and cogs, all preordained and helpless. *Everybody hurts*, I thought; and, *everybody hurts each other.*

It didn't feel like an excuse.

There was another cupboard I hadn't got into last night, because it was locked against me. *Keys do get lost*, Tasha's mother had said, but old skills don't. I like devices, contraptions, mechanisms, and there's nothing more contraptual than a lock; I'd spent hours and hours in my teenage years, learning how to pick them.

This one was easy. In the cupboard, I wasn't at all surprised to find another stack of photographic plates. These didn't come with paper prints, but it didn't take long in that room to rig up a stand with a light source, so that I could project their images onto a white wall.

Even with black and white reversed, it was clear what I was looking at. These were the pictures that no Victorian, no man would ever want seen by other eyes: no artful posing of a naked child, these were pornography by any definition, abusive and exploitative, destructive. And all, all of Georgina.

I was appalled, sickened, but again not at all surprised. I think I'd been looking for them.

I wondered who else had seen them—Tasha's father? Very possibly. Her mother? Perhaps—and lost the key deliberately, perhaps. It would be impossible to ask.

Hard enough to tell them, though I had to find a way. Georgina had been locked up far too long in this limbo of secrecy and shame.

Even so, I left her so, me too: locking Joshua's museum behind me before I went downstairs.

Down and out, into the stable yard, for a breath of air perhaps. I found Tasha there, unsaddling her horse.

"Hi," I said. "You busy?"

"For a while. I just need to curry her. . . ."

"That's an idea," I said. "Fancy curry for lunch, after? Somewhere that isn't here?"

"God, yes," she said, explosively. "Gets to you, doesn't it?"

Oh, it does, I thought. *It does get to you. Yes, indeed. . . .*

If I'd been more generous to him, less kind to her, I'd have suggested taking Rufus too; but mostly I just wanted out of there, the two of us together. I could only look after one of the Kilvallens: one at a time, at least.

I kept her out all afternoon, so that we were driving into our own long shadow as we finally came back to the house, that last slow mile up the drive. It felt significant, somehow.

In, then, and straight up to the top floor, with me just shaking my head at all her questions. I unlocked the museum and we walked in to a waft of heat, the way an attic room can be after a day under the sun's hammer.

Tasha grunted, and went straight to open the skylight—but the crank wasn't there, although I'd left it there quite deliberately. It was back in the orrery again. Tasha reached for it, and,

"Jonny, it's stuck. I can't get it free. . . ."

No more could I, though I tugged and jerked with a will. Nor could I turn it, back or forth.

"Jonny, look. . . ."

Tash was staring, taking a step back from the orrery. I looked where her hand was pointing, and saw that one of the dome's panes was broken. Inside there was a scatter of glass between the planets, and more fallen down into the gearing; but more than that, worse than that, something was tangled between all the planets and their moons, long threads like fine black wires. . . .

I reached in gingerly and tried to pick one off, but it was all wound up too tightly. Tash scrabbled in her bag and found some nail-scissors; I snipped out a section and lifted it out, laid it on my palm and showed her.

"What is it?" I think she knew, but didn't want to say. No more did I; but,

"Hair," I said. "It's human hair, I think."

Long and dark, like a girl's hair: a girl who had hair like broken wings, that she could hide behind but never fly away.

"Who has, who could do . . . ?" She didn't finish her questions, she didn't need to; she knew the answers already, which were just as incomplete. Nobody here had hair like that, and nobody could come in where her key had locked them out. I'd been wrong before, there weren't any duplicates; keys could be misappropriated, as well as lost.

"It's getting dark," I said. "Let's grab a bottle of wine, and go out on the roof. I've got a story to tell you."

That kind of story, told in the gloaming to a girl you find it hard to look at, they're mostly grim. I had her house beneath my feet, her history in a box, her family in my head; she was in my heart, and I didn't dare take her hand.

I said, "Listen, then. There was a girl, lived here: not like you, she was probably happy once. When she was little. The house didn't breed pain then, it hadn't sharpened up its gears. But she had an uncle, who had nothing to do but play; and to her horror, to her shame, he was allowed to play with her.

"Why her and not her sisters, I can't say. She was youngest, she was spare, she was affordable. Or else there was something about her, maybe she was vulnerable already, maybe that drew him. Maybe he was that kind of predator, he could smell out the weakest. Whatever drove him, he made her his special target: cut her out of the herd, feasted on her.

"No," I said, "forget the metaphors. That's just another way to hide from what he did, and she's been hidden long enough. First he stripped her, then he took pictures of her naked, then he raped her. Over and over again. And took more pictures after, but that's not the worst of it. Her family's the worst of it. Her parents, her brother, her sisters. They let it happen, and go on happening. She couldn't bear that, I think it's what broke her in the end.

"I don't know if she killed herself, or just lost any reason to live. How it happened, I don't know that. She let death take her, but it wouldn't, it couldn't take her away. She's still here, still hurting." A figure in the roiling steam, where he'd hurt her most; a hand, a power, a motive force in that damned museum, where she was trapped, where her pain just went on happening. Wheels turned, cogs gripped, teeth locked together. Mechanical, eternal, inbuilt. Until someone smashed the machine.

"And all she can do," I said, "is pass it on. It's her gift to you, to all the generations of you." The flaw in the machine, the twisted gear that forced everything out of true: that ground one cog against another, broke teeth, buckled the framework. Did more and more damage, so long as someone kept on turning the crank.

"Here," I said, "you're good at breaking things. Break this."

I passed her one of those photographic plates, out of the box.

She held it for a moment, didn't try to look at it in the darkness. She looked at me. "Dad wants to sell these."

"Fuck him," I said, deliberately crude, violent almost. I could be violent tonight, if I needed to. If she needed me to. "If he knows what they are, if he's seen them, he has no right. I think your mother knows. These don't belong to your family, to any of you. They're Georgina's." That was the first time I'd said her name tonight, and I felt a breath of something stir my skin, chill and sorrowful. I wondered if she used to come up here, looking for escape. If she did, I didn't think she'd found it in far horizons and a solitary view. Nor in a swift plunge to earth, though I could feel the draw of that. I thought Tasha felt that too, maybe all her life.

She held the sheet of glass lightly between her fingers, then smashed it on the parapet.

I passed her another, and said, "You have to let him sell Joshua's things. Not these, but the rest of it. Sell them, scatter them, break up the collection. Dissipate him. Burn his notebooks, splinter that nameplate on the door. Expunge him, make him forgotten." Not just for Georgina: for herself, for all the generations. It might be too late for her, I wasn't sure; but for her children, for her brother's, for the future. They needed Joshua gone from here. He haunted the house as much as his victim did; they were all his victims now.

I'd made a start already, deleting all the photos that I'd taken. I wasn't going to let Tash carry him with her, wherever she went from here. She had baggage enough already.

She went on breaking Joshua's plates as I passed them to her, one by one. In the end, I thought, rain and wind together would finish the work; they'd wash Georgina free if we couldn't do it ourselves, leave nothing but clear glass and no memories, nothing to work with.

We did what we could, and then I took Tasha's hand and led her down through the house and out of the door and away from there. If there was a shadow in her driving mirror as we left, she didn't glance at it, not once. I know; I was watching.

KAREN JOY FOWLER

The Last Worders

Karen Joy Fowler's novels include the bestseller (and basis for the film of the same name) The Jane Austen Book Club *as well as* Sarah Canary, The Sweetheart Season, *and* Wit's End. *With the writer Pat Murphy, she created the James Tiptree, Jr. Award. Fowler lives in Santa Cruz, California. In 2007, Fowler published two excellent short stories: "Always," which appeared in* Asimov's, *and "The Last Worders," which we published in* Lady Churchill's Rosebud Wristlet *and which remains one of our favorite stories of the year.*

—K.L. & G.G.

Charlotta was asleep in the dining car when the train arrived in San Margais. It was tempting to just leave her behind, and I tried to tell myself this wasn't a mean thought, but came to me because I, myself, might want to be left like that, just for the adventure of it. I might want to wake up hours later and miles away, bewildered and alone. I am always on the lookout for those parts of my life that could be the first scene in a movie. Of course, you could start a movie anywhere, but you wouldn't; that's my point. And so this impulse had nothing to do with the way Charlotta had begun to get on my last nerve. That's my other point. If I thought being ditched would be sort of exciting, then so did Charlotta. We felt the same about everything.

"Charlotta," I said. "Charlotta. We're here." I was on my feet, grabbing my backpack, when the train actually stopped. This threw me into the arms of a boy of about fourteen, wearing a T-shirt from the Three Mountains Soccer Camp. It was nice of him to catch me. I probably wouldn't have done that when I was fourteen. What's one tourist more or less? I tried to say some of this to Charlotta when we were on the platform and the train was already puffing fainter and fainter in the distance, winding its way like a great worm up into the Rambles Mountains. The boy hadn't gotten off with us.

It was raining and we tented our heads with our jackets. "He was probably picking your pocket," Charlotta said. "Do you still have your wallet?" Which made me feel I'd been a fool, but when I put my hand in to check I found, instead of taking something out, he'd put something in. I pulled out an orange piece of paper folded like a fan. When opened, flattened, it was a flier in four languages—German, Japanese, French, and English. *Open mike,* the English part said. And then, *Come to the Last Word Cafe. 100 Ruta de los Esclavos by the river. First drink free. Poetry Slam. To the death.*

The rain erased the words even as we read them.

"No city listed," Charlotta noted. She had taken the paper from me to look more closely. Now it was blank and limp. She refolded it, carefully so it wouldn't tear, put it in the back pocket of her pants. "Anyway, can't be here."

The town of San Margais hangs on the edge of a deep chasm. There'd been a river once. We had a geological witness. We had the historical records. But there was no river now.

"And no date for the slam," Charlotta added. "And we don't think fast on our feet. And death. That's not very appealing."

If she'd made only one objection, then she'd no interest. Ditto if she'd made two. But three was defensive; four was obsessive. Four meant that if Charlotta could ever find the Last Word Cafe, she was definitely going. Just because I'd been invited and she hadn't. Try to keep her out! I know this is what she felt because it's what I would have felt.

We took a room in a private house on the edge of the gorge. We had planned to lodge in the city center, more convenient to everything, but we were tired and wanted to get in out of the rain. The guidebook said this place was cheap and clean.

It was ten-thirty in the morning and the proprietress was still in her nightgown. She was a woman of about fifty and the loss of her two front teeth had left a small dip in her upper lip. Her nightgown was imprinted with angels wearing choir robes and haloes on sticks like balloons. She spoke little English; there was a lot of pointing, most of it upwards. Then we had to follow her angel butt up three flights of ladders, hauling our heavy packs. The room was large and had its own sink. There were glass doors opening onto a balcony, rain sheeting down. If you looked out there was nothing to see. Steep nothing. Gray nothing. The dizzying null of the gorge. "You can have the bed by the doors," Charlotta offered. She was already moved in, toweling her hair.

"You," I said. I was nobody's fool.

Charlotta sang. "It is scary, in my aerie."

"Poetry?" the proprietress asked. Her dimpled lip curled slightly. She didn't have to speak the language to know bad poetry when she heard it, that lip said.

"Yes," Charlotta said. "Yes. The Last Word Cafe? Is where?"

"No," she answered. Maybe she'd misunderstood us. Maybe we'd misunderstood her.

A few facts about the gorge: The gorge is very deep and very narrow. A thousand years ago a staircase was cut into the interior of the cliff. According to our guidebook there are 839 stone steps, all worn smooth by traffic. Back when the stairs were made, there was still a river. Slaves carried water from the river up the stairs to the town. They did this all day long, down with an empty clay pitcher, up with a full one, and then different slaves carried water all during the night. The slave owners were noted for their poetry and their cleanliness. They wrote formal erotic poems about how dirty their slaves were.

One day there was an uprising. The slaves on the stairs knew nothing about it. They had their pitchers. They had the long way down and the longer way up. Slaves from the town, ex-slaves now, stood at the top and told each one as he (or she) arrived, that he (or she) was free. Some of the slaves poured their water out onto the stone steps to prove this to themselves. Some emptied their pitchers into the cistern as usual, thinking to have a nice bath later. Later all the pitchers were given to the former slave owners who now were slaves and had to carry water up from the river all day or all night.

Still later there was resentment between the town slaves, who had taken all the risks and made all the plans, and the stair slaves who were handed their freedom. The least grateful of the latter were sent back to the stairs.

Two or three hundred years after the uprising, there was no more water. Over many generations the slaves had finally emptied the river. To honor their long labors, in memory of a job well done, slavery was abolished in San Margais. There is a holiday to commemorate this every year on May 21. May 21 is also our birthday, mine and Charlotta's. Let's not make too much of that.

Among the many factions in San Margais was one that felt there was nothing to celebrate in having once had a river and now not having one. Many bitter poems have been written on this subject, all entitled "May 21."

The shower in our pensione was excellent, the water hot and hard. Charlotta reported this to me. Since I got my choice of bed, she got the first shower. We'd been making these sorts of calculations all our lives; it kept us in balance. As long as everyone played. We were not in San Margais for the poetry.

Five years before, while we were still in high school, Charlotta and I had fallen in love with the same boy. His name was Raphael Kaplinsky. He had an accent, South African, and a motorcycle, American. "I saw him first," Charlotta said, which was true—he was in her second period World Lit class. I hadn't seen him until fifth period Chemistry. I spoke to him first, though. "Is it supposed to be this color?" I'd asked when we were testing for acids.

"He spoke to me first," Charlotta said, which was also true since he'd answered my acid question with a shrug. And then, several days later, said "Nice boots!" to Charlotta when she came to school in calf-high red Steve Maddens.

My red Steve Maddens.

We quarreled about Raphael for weeks without settling anything. We didn't speak to each other for days at a time. All the while Raphael dated other girls. Loose and easy Deirdre. Bookish Kathy. Spiritual, ethereal Nina. Junco, the Japanese foreign exchange student.

Eventually Charlotta and I agreed that we would both give Raphael up. Charlotta made the offer, but I'd been planning the same; I matched it instantly. There was simply no other way. We met in the yard to formalize the agreement with a ceremony. Each of us wrote the words Ms. Raphael Weldon-Kaplinsky onto a piece of paper. Then we simultaneously tore our papers into twelve little bits. We threw the bits into the fishpond and watched the carp eat them.

I knew that Charlotta would honor our agreement. I knew this because I intended to do so.

When we were little, when we were just learning to talk, Mother says Charlotta and I had a secret language. She could watch us, towheaded two-year-olds, talking to each other and she could tell that we knew what we were saying, even if she didn't. Sometimes after telling each other a long story, we would cry. One of us would start and the other would sit struggling for a moment, lip trembling, and eventually we would both be in tears. There was a graduate student in psychology interested in studying this, but we learned English and stopped speaking our secret language before he could get his grant money together.

Mother favors Charlotta. I'm not the only one to think so; Charlotta sees it, too. Mother has learned that it's simply not possible to treat two people with equal love. She would argue that she favors us both—sometimes Charlotta, sometimes me. She would say it all equals out in the end. Maybe she's right. It isn't equal yet, but it probably hasn't ended.

Some facts from our guidebook about the San Margais Civil War. 1932–37: The underlying issues were aesthetic and economic. The trigger was an assassination.

In the middle ages, San Margais was a city-state ruled by a hereditary clergy. Even after annexation, the clergy played the dominant political role. Fra Nando came to power in the 1920s during an important poetic revival known as the Margais Movement. Its premiere voice was the great epistemological poet, Gigo. Fra Nando believed in the lessons of history. Gigo believed in the natural cadence of the street, the impenetrable nature of truth. From Day One these two were headed for a showdown.

Still, for a few years, all was politeness. Gigo received many grants and honors from the Nando regime. She was given a commission to write a poem celebrating Fra Nando's seventieth birthday. "Yes, I remember," Gigo's poem begins (in translation), "the great cloud of dragonflies grazing the lake . . ." If Fra Nando's name appeared only in the dedication, at least this was accessible stuff. Nostalgic even, elegiac.

Gigo was never nostalgic. Gigo was never elegiac. To be so now expressed only her deep contempt for Fra Nando, but it was all so very rhythmical; he was completely taken in. Fra Nando set the first two lines in stone over the entrance to the city-state library and invited Gigo to be his special guest at the unveiling.

"The nature of the word is not the nature of the stone," Gigo said at the ceremony when it was her turn to speak. This was also accessible. Fra Nando went red in the face as if he'd been slapped, one hand to each cheek.

A cartel of businessmen, angry over the graduated tariff system Nando had instituted, saw the opportunity to assassinate him and have the poets blamed. Gigo was killed at a reading the same night Fra Nando was laid in state in the Catedral Nacionales. Her last words were "blind hill, grave glass," which is all anyone could have hoped. Unless she said "grave grass," and one of her acolytes changed her words in the reporting as her detractors have alleged. Anyone could think up grave grass, especially if they were dying at the time.

All that remains for certain of Gigo's work are the contemptuous two lines in stone. The Margais Movement was outlawed, its poems systematically searched out and destroyed. Attempts were made to memorize the greatest of Gigo's verses, but these had been written so as to defy memorization. A phrase here and there, much contested, survives. Nothing that suggests genius. All the books by or about the Margais Movement were burned. All the poets were imprisoned and tortured until they couldn't remember their own names much less their own words.

There is a narrow bridge across the gorge that Charlotta can see from the doors by her bed. During the civil war, people were thrown from the bridge. There is still a handful of old men and old women here who will tell you they remember seeing that.

Raphael Kaplinsky went to our high school for only one year. We told ourselves it was good we hadn't destroyed our relationship for so short a reward. We dated other boys, boys neither of us liked. The flaws in our reasoning began to come clear.

1) Raphael Kaplinsky was ardent and oracular. You didn't meet a boy like Raphael Kaplinsky in every World Lit, every Chemistry class you took. He was the very first person to use the word later to end a conversation. Using the word later in this particular way was a promise. It was nothing less than messianic.

2) What if we did, someday, meet a boy we liked as much as Raphael? We were both bound to like him exactly the same. We hadn't solved our problem so much as delayed it. We were doomed to a lifetime of each-otherness unless we came up with a different plan.

We hired an Internet detective to find Raphael and he uncovered a recent credit card trail. We had followed this trail all the way to last Sunday in San Margais. We had come to San Margais to make him choose between us.

It was raining too hard to go out, plus we'd spent the night sitting up on the train. We hadn't been able to sit together, and had had a drunk on one side (Charlotta's) and a shoebox of mice on the other (mine). The mice were headed to the Snake Pit at the State Zoo. There was no way to sleep while their little paws scrabbled desperately, fruitlessly against the cardboard. I had an impulse to set them free, but it seemed unfair to the snakes. How often in this world we are unwillingly forced to take sides! Team Mouse or Team Snake? Team Fly or Team Spider?

Charlotta and I napped during the afternoon while the glass rattled in the doorframes and the rain fell. I woke up when I was too hungry to sleep. "I have got to have something to eat," Charlotta said.

The cuisine of San Margais is nothing to write home about. Charlotta and I each bought an umbrella from a street peddler and ate in a small, dark pizzeria. It was not only wet outside, but cold. The pizzeria had a large oven, which made the room pleasant to linger in, even though there was a group of Italian tourists smoking across the way.

Charlotta and I had a policy never to order the same thing off a menu. This was hard, because the same thing always sounded good to both of us, but it doubled our chances of making the right choice. Charlotta ordered a pizza called El Diablo, which was all theater and annoyed me, as we don't like hot foods. El Diablo brought tears to her eyes and she only ate one piece, picking the olives off the rest and then helping herself to several slices of mine.

She wiped her face with a napkin, which left a rakish streak of pizza sauce on her cheek. I was irritated enough to say nothing about this. One of the Italians made his way to our table. "So," he said with no preliminaries. "American, yes? I can kiss you?"

We were nothing if not patriots. Charlotta stood at once, moved into his arms, and I saw his tongue go into her mouth. They kissed for several seconds, then Charlotta pushed him away and now the pizza sauce was on him.

"So," she said. "Now. We need directions to the closest Internet cafe."

The Italian drew a map on her place mat. He drew well; his map had depth and perspective. The Internet cafe appeared to be around many corners and up many flights of stairs. The Italian decorated his map with hopeful little hearts. Charlotta took it away from him or there surely would have been more of these.

The San Margais miracle, an anecdotal account: About ten years ago, a little boy named Bastien Brunelle was crossing the central plaza when he noticed something strange on the face of the statue of Fra Nando. He looked more closely. Fra Nando was crying large milky tears. Bastien ran home to tell his parents.

The night before, Bastien's father had had a dream. In his dream he was old and crippled, twisted up like a licorice stick. In his dream he had a dream that told him to go and bathe in the river. He woke from the dream and made his slow, painful way down the 839 steps. At the bottom of the gorge he waited. He heard a noise in the distance, cars on a freeway. The river arrived like a train and stopped to let him in. Bastien's father woke up and was thirty-two again, which was his proper age.

When he heard about the statue, Bastien's father remembered the dream. He followed Bastien out to the square where a crowd was gathering, growing. "Fra Nando is crying for the river," Bastien's father told the crowd. "It's a sign to us. We have to put the river back."

Bastien's father had never been a community leader. He ran a small civil war museum for tourists, filled with faked Gigo poems, and rarely bought a round for the house when he went out drinking. But now he had all the conviction of the man who sees clearly amidst the men who are confused. He organized a brigade to carry water down the steps to the bottom of the gorge and his purpose was so absolute, so inspired were his words, that people volunteered their spare hours, their children's spare hours. They signed up for slots in his schedule and carried water down the stairs for almost a week before they all lost interest and remembered Bastien's father was not the mouth of God, but a tight-assed cheat.

By this time news of the crying statue had gone out on the Internet. Scientists had performed examinations. "Fakery cannot be ruled out," one said, which transformed into the headline, "No Sign of Fakery." Pilgrims began to arrive from wealthy European countries, mostly college kids with buckets, thermoses, used Starbucks cups. They would stay two or three days, two or three weeks, hauling water down, having visions on the stairs and sex.

And then that ended, too. Every time has its task. Ours is to digitize the world's libraries. This is a big job that will take generations to complete, like the pyramids. No time for filling gorges with water. "Live lightly on the earth," the pilgrims remembered. "Leave no footprint behind." And they all went home again, or at least they left San Margais.

On odd days of the week our people-finder detective e-mailed Charlotta and copied me. On even, the opposite. Two days earlier Raphael had bought a hat and four postcards. He had dinner at a pricey restaurant and got a fifty-dollar cash advance. That was Charlotta's e-mail. Mine said that this very night, he was buying fifteen beers at the Last Word Cafe, San Margais.

We googled that name to a single entry. *100 Ruta de los Esclavos by the river,* it said. *Open mike. Underground music and poetry nightly.* There were other Americans using the computers. I walked through, asking if any of them knew how to get to the Last Word Cafe. To Ruta de los Esclavos? They were paying by the minute. Most of them didn't look up. Those that did shook their heads.

Charlotta and I opened our umbrellas and went back out into the rain. We asked directions from everyone we saw, but very few people were on the street. They didn't know English or they disliked being accosted by tourists or they didn't like the look of our face. They hurried by without speaking. Only a single woman stopped. She took my chin in her hand to make sure she had my full attention. Her eyes were tinged in yellow and she smelled like Irish Spring soap. "No," she said firmly. "*Me entiendes?* No for you."

We walked along the gorge, because this was the closest thing San Margais had to a river. On one side of us, the town. The big yellow I of Tourist Information (closed indefinitely), shops of ceramics and cheeses, postcards, law offices, podiatrists, pubs, our own pensione. On the other cliff-face, the air. We crossed the narrow bridge and when we came to the 839 steps we started down them just because they were mostly inside the cliff and therefore covered and therefore dry. I was the one to point these things out to Charlotta. I was the one to say we should go down.

The steps were smooth and slippery. Each one had a dip in the center in just that place where a slave was most likely to put his (or her) foot. Water dripped from the walls around us, but we were able to close our umbrellas, leave them at the top to be picked up later. For the first stretch there were lights overhead. Then we were in darkness, except for an occasional turn, which brought an occasional opening to the outside. A little light could carry us a long way.

We descended maybe 300 steps and then, by one of the openings, we met an American coming up. In age she was somewhere in that long unidentifiable stretch from twenty-two to thirty-five. She was carrying an empty bucket, plastic, the sort a child takes to the seashore. She was breathless from the climb.

She stopped beside us and we waited until she was able to speak. "What the fuck," she said finally, "is the point of going down empty-handed? What the fuck is the point of you?"

Charlotta had been asking sort of the same thing. What was the point of going all the way down the stairs? Why had she let me talk her into it? She talked me into going back. We turned and followed the angry American up and out into the rain. It was only 300 steps, but when we'd done them we were winded and exhausted. We went to our room, crawled up our three ladders, and landed in a deep, dispirited sleep.

It was still raining the next morning. We went to the city center and breakfasted in a little bakery. Just as we were finishing, our Italian walked in. "We kiss more, yes?" he asked me. He'd mistaken me for Charlotta. I stood up. I was always having to do her chores. His tongue ranged through my mouth as if he were looking for scraps. I tasted cigarettes, gum, things left in ashtrays.

"So," I said, pushing him away. "Now. We need directions to the Last Word Cafe."

And it turned out we'd almost gotten there last night, after all. The Last Word was the last stop along the 839 steps. It seemed as if I'd known this.

Our Italian said he'd been the night before. No one named Raphael had taken the mic; he was sure of this, but he thought there might have been a South African at the bar. Possibly this South African had bought him a drink. It was a very crowded room. No one had died. That was just—how is it we Americans say? Poem license?

"Raphael probably wanted to get the feel of the place before he spoke," Charlotta said. "That's what I'd do."

And me. That's what I'd do, too.

There was no point in going back before dark. We checked our e-mail, but he was apparently still living on the cash advance; nothing had been added since the Last Word last night. We decided to spend the day as tourists, thinking Raphael might do the same. Because of the rain we had the outdoor sights mostly to ourselves. We saw the ruins of the old baths, long and narrow as lap pools, now with nets of morning glories twisted across them. Here and there the rain had filled them.

There was a Roman arch, a Moorish garden. When we were wetter than we could bear to be we paid the eight euros entrance to the civil war museum. English translation was extra, but we were on a budget; there are no bargains on last-minute tickets to San Margais. We told ourselves it was more in keeping with the spirit of Gigo if we didn't understand a thing.

The museum was small, two rooms only and dimly lit. We stood awhile beside the wall radiator, drying out and warming up. Even from that spot we could see most of the room we were in. There were three life-size dioramas—mannequins dressed as Gigo might have dressed, meeting with people Gigo might have met. We recognized the mannequin Fra Nando from the statue we'd seen in the city center, although this version was less friendly. His hand was on Gigo's shoulder, his expression enigmatic. She was looking past him up at something tall and transcendent. There was clothing laid out, male and female, in glass cases along with playbills, baptismal certificates, baby pictures. Stapled to the wall were a series of book illustrations—a bandito seizing a woman on a balcony. The woman shaking free, leaping to her death. A story Gigo had written? A family legend? A scene from the civil war? All of the above? The man who sold us our tickets, Señor Brunelle, was conducting a tour for an elderly British couple, but since we hadn't paid it would be wrong to stand where we could hear. We were careful not to do so.

We spoke to Señor Brunelle after. We made polite noises about the museum, so interesting, we said. So unexpected. And then Charlotta asked him what he knew about the Last Word Cafe.

"For tourists," he said. "Myself, my family, we don't go down the steps anymore." He was clearly sad about this. "All tourists now."

"What does it mean," Charlotta asked first. "Poetry to the death?"

"Which word needs definition? Poetry? Or Death?"

"I know the words."

"Then I am no more help," Señor Brunelle told her.

"Why does it say it's by the river when there's no river?" Charlotta asked second.

"Always a river. In San Margais, always a river. Sometimes in your mind. Sometimes in the gorge. Either way, a river."

"Is there any reason we shouldn't go?" Charlotta asked third.

"Go. You go. You won't get in," Señor Brunelle said. He said this to Charlotta. He didn't say it to me.

The Last Worders:

On the night Raphael took the open mic at the Last Word Cafe, he did three poems. He spoke ten minutes. He stood on the stage and he didn't try to move; he didn't try to make it sing; he made no effort to sell his words. The light fell in a small circle on his face so that, most of the time, his eyes were closed. He was beautiful. The people listening also closed their eyes and that made him more beautiful still. The women, the men who'd wanted him when he started to talk no longer did so. He was beyond that, unfuckable. For the rest of their lives, they'd be undone by the mere sound of his name. The ones who spoke English tried to write down some part of what he'd said on their napkins, in their travel journals. They made lists of words—

childhood, ice, yes. Gleaming, yes, yesterday.

These are the facts. Anyone can figure out this much.

For the rest, you had to be there. What was heard, the things people suddenly knew, the things people suddenly felt—none of that could be said in any way that could be passed along. By the time Raphael had finished, everyone listening, everyone there for those few minutes on that night at the Last Word Cafe, had been set free.

These people climbed the steps afterwards in absolute silence. They did not go back, not a single one of them, to their marriages, their families, their jobs, their lives. They walked to the city center and they sat in the square on the edge of the fountain at the feet of the friendly Fra Nando and they knew where they were in a way they had never known it before. They tried to talk about what to do next. Words came back to them slowly. Between them, they spoke a dozen different languages, all useless now.

You could have started the movie of any one of them there, at the feet of the stone statue. It didn't matter what they could and couldn't say; they all knew the situation. Whatever they did next would be done together. They could not imagine, ever again, being with anyone who had not been there, in the Last Word Cafe, on the night Raphael Kaplinsky spoke.

There were details to be ironed out. How to get the money to eat. Where to live, where to sleep. How to survive now, in a suddenly clueless world.

But there was time to make these decisions. Those who had cars fetched them. Those who did not climbed in, fastened their seat belts. On the night Raphael Kaplinsky spoke at the Last Word Cafe, the patrons caravanned out of town without a last word to anyone. The rest of us would not hear of the Last Worders again until one of them went on *Larry King Live* and filled a two-hour show with a two-hour silence.

Or else they all died.

Charlotta and I had dinner by ourselves in the converted basement of an old hotel. The candles flickered our shadows about so we were, on all sides, surrounded by us. Charlotta had the trout. It had been cooked dry, and was filled with small bones. Every time she put a bite in her mouth, she pulled the tiny bones out. I had the mussels. The sauce was stiff and gluey. Most of the shells hadn't opened. The food in San Margais is nothing to write home about.

We finished the meal with old apples and young wine. We were both nervous, now that it came down to it, about seeing Raphael again. Each of us secretly wondered, could we live with Raphael's choice? However it went? Could I be happy for Charlotta, if it came to that? I asked myself. Could I bear watching her forced to be happy for me? I sipped my wine and ran through every moment of my relationship with Raphael for reassurance. That stuff about the acid experiment. How much he liked my boots. "Let's go," Charlotta said and we were a bit unsteady from the wine, which, in retrospect, with an evening of 839 steps ahead of us, was not smart.

We crossed the bridge in a high wind. The rain came in sideways; the wind turned our umbrellas inside out. Charlotta was thrown against the rope rails and grabbed on to me. If she'd fallen, she would have taken me with her. If I saved her, I saved us both. Our umbrellas went together into the gorge.

We reached the steps and began to descend, sometimes with light, sometimes feeling our way in the darkness. About one hundred steps up from the bottom, a room had been carved out of the rock. Once slave owners had sat at their leisure there, washing and rewashing their hands and feet, overseeing the slaves on the stairs. Later the room had been closed off with the addition of a heavy metal door. A posting had been set on a sawhorse outside. THE LAST WORD CAFE, the English part of it said. NOT FOR EVERYONE.

The door was latched. Charlotta pounded on it with her fist until it opened. A man in a tuxedo with a wide orange cummerbund stepped out. He shook his head. "American?" he asked. "And empty-handed? That's no way to make a river."

"We're here for the poetry," Charlotta told him and he shook his head again.

"Invitation only."

And Charlotta reached into the back pocket of her pants. Charlotta pulled out the orange paper given to me by the boy on the train. The man took it. He threw it into a small basket with many other such papers. He stood aside and let Charlotta enter.

He stepped back to block me. "Invitation only."

"That was my invitation," I told him. "Charlotta!" She looked back at me, over her shoulder without really turning around. "Tell him. Tell him that invitation was for me. Tell him how Señor Brunelle told you you wouldn't get in."

"So?" said Charlotta. "That woman on the street told you you wouldn't get in."

But I had figured that part out. "She mistook me for you," I said. Beyond the door I could see Raphael climbing onto the dais. I could hear the room growing silent. I could see Charlotta's back sliding into a crowd of people like a knife into water. The door swung toward my face. The latch fell.

I stayed a long time by that door, but no sounds came through. Finally I walked down the last hundred steps. I was alone at the bottom of the gorge where the rain fell and fell and there was no river. I would never have done to Charlotta what she had done to me.

It took me more than an hour to climb back up. I had to stop many, many times to rest, airless, heart throbbing, legs aching, light-headed in the dark. No one met me at the top.

NATHAN BALLINGRUD

The Monsters of Heaven

Nathan Ballingrud was born in Massachusetts but grew up in the American
South. He's worked as a cook on offshore oil rigs, a bartender in New Or-
leans, and a housepainter. Currently he lives just outside of Asheville, North
Carolina, with his daughter.

Ballingrud's short fiction has been published in SCI FICTION, The
Third Alternative, The Magazine of Fantasy & Science Fiction, and The
Year's Best Fantasy & Horror, Seventeenth Annual Collection.

"The Monsters of Heaven" was originally published in Inferno: New Tales
of Terror and the Supernatural, edited by Ellen Datlow.

—E.D.

> "Who invented the human heart, I wonder? Tell me,
> then show me the place where he was hanged."
>
> —Lawrence Durrell, *Justine*

For a long time, Brian imagined reunions with his son. In the early days, these
fantasies were defined by spectacular violence. He would find the man who
stole him and open his head with a claw hammer. The more blood he spilled,
the further removed he became from his own guilt. The location would often
change: a roach-haunted tenement building; an abandoned warehouse along the
Tchoupitoulas wharf; a prefab bungalow with an American flag out front and a two-
door hatchback parked in the driveway.

Sometimes the man lived alone, sometimes he had his own family. On these latter occasions Brian would cast himself as a moral executioner, spraying the walls
with the kidnapper's blood but sparing his wife and child—freeing them, he imagined, from his tyranny. No matter the scenario, Toby was always there, always intact;
Brian would feel his face pressed into his shoulders as he carried him away, feel the
heat of his tears bleed into his shirt. You're safe now, he would say. Daddy's got you.
Daddy's here.

After some months passed, he deferred the heroics to the police. This marked
his first concession to reality. He spent his time beached in the living room, drinking more, working less, until the owner of the auto shop told him to take time off,
a lot of time off, as much as he needed. Brian barely noticed. He waited for the red
and blue disco lights of a police cruiser to illuminate the darkness outside, to give
some shape and measure to the night. He waited for the phone to ring with a glad

summons to the station. He played out scenarios, tried on different outcomes, guessed at his own reactions. He gained weight and lost time.

Sometimes he would get out of bed in the middle of the night, careful not to wake his wife, and get into the car. He would drive at dangerous speeds through the city, staring into the empty sockets of unlighted windows. He would get out of the car and stand in front of some of these houses, looking and listening for signs. Often, the police were called. When the officers realized who he was, they were usually as courteous as they were adamant. He'd wonder if it had been the kidnapper who called the police. He would imagine returning to those houses with a gun.

This was in the early days of what became known as the Lamentation. At this stage, most people did not know anything unusual was happening. What they heard, if they heard anything, was larded with rumor and embellishment. Fogs of gossip in the barrooms and churches. This was before the bloodshed. Before their pleas to Christ clotted in their throats.

Amy never told Brian that she blamed him. She elected, rather, to avoid the topic of the actual abduction, and any question of her husband's negligence. Once the police abandoned them as suspects, the matter of their own involvement ceased to be a subject of discussion. Brian was unconsciously grateful, because it allowed him to focus instead on the maintenance of grief. Silence spread between them like a glacier. In a few months, entire days passed with nothing said between them.

It was on such a night that Amy rolled up against him and kissed the back of his neck. It froze Brian, filling him with a blast of terror and bewilderment; he felt the guilt move inside of him, huge but seemingly distant, like a whale passing beneath a boat. Her lips felt hot against his skin, sending warm waves rolling from his neck and shoulders all the way down to his legs, as though she had injected something lovely into him. She grew more ardent, nipping him with her teeth, breaking through his reservations. He turned and kissed her. He experienced a leaping arc of energy, a terrifying, violent impulse; he threw his weight onto her and crushed his mouth into hers, scraping his teeth against hers. But there immediately followed a cascade of unwelcome thought: Toby whimpering somewhere in the dark, waiting for his father to save him; Amy, dressed in her bedclothes in the middle of the day, staring like a corpse into the sunlight coming through the windows; the playground, and the receding line of kindergarteners. When she reached under the sheets she found him limp and unready. He opened his mouth to apologize but she shoved her tongue into it, her hand working at him with a rough urgency, as though more depended on this than he knew. Later he would learn that it did. Her teeth sliced his lip and blood eeled into his mouth. She was pulling at him too hard, and it was starting to hurt. He wrenched himself away.

"Jesus," he said, wiping his lip. The blood felt like an oil slick in the back of his throat.

She turned her back to him and put her face into the pillow. For a moment he thought she was crying. But only for a moment.

"Honey," he said. "Hey." He put his fingers on her shoulder; she rolled it away from him.

"Go to sleep," she said.

He stared at the landscape of her naked back, pale in the streetlight leaking through the blinds, feeling furious and ruined.

The next morning, when he came into the kitchen, Amy was already up. Coffee was made, filling the room with a fine toasted smell, and she was leaning against the counter with a cup in her hand, wearing her pink terry cloth robe. Her dark hair was still wet from the shower. She smiled and said, "Good morning."

"Hey," he said, feeling for a sense of her mood.

Dodger, Toby's dog, cast him a devastated glance from his customary place beneath the kitchen table. Amy had wanted to get rid of him—she couldn't bear the sight of him anymore, she'd said—but Brian wouldn't allow it. When Toby comes back, he reasoned, he'll wonder why we did it. What awful thing guided us. So Dodger remained, and his slumping, sorrowful presence tore into them both like a hungry animal.

"Hey boy," Brian said, and rubbed his neck with his toe.

"I'm going out today," Amy said.

"Okay. Where to?"

She shrugged. "I don't know. The hardware store. Maybe a nursery. I want to find myself a project."

Brian looked at her. The sunlight made a corona around her body. This new resolve, coupled with her overture of the night before, struck him as a positive sign. "Okay," he said.

He seated himself at the table. The newspaper had been placed there for him, still bound by a rubber band. He snapped it off and unfurled the front page. Already he felt the gravitational pull of the Jack Daniels in the cabinet, but when Amy leaned over his shoulder and placed a coffee cup in front of him, he managed to resist the whiskey's call with an ease that surprised and gratified him. He ran his hand up her forearm, pushing back the soft pink sleeve, and he kissed the inside of her wrist. He felt a wild and incomprehensible hope. He breathed in the clean, scented smell of her. She stayed there for a moment, and then gently pulled away.

They remained that way in silence for some time—maybe fifteen minutes or more—until Brian found something in the paper he wanted to share with her. Something being described as "angelic"—"apparently not quite a human man," as the writer put it—had been found down by the Gulf Coast, in Morgan City; it had been shedding a faint light from under two feet of water; whatever it was had died shortly after being taken into custody, under confusing circumstances. He turned in his chair to speak, a word already gathering on his tongue, and he caught her staring at him. She wore a cadaverous, empty look, as though she had seen the worst thing in the world and died in the act. It occurred to him that she had been looking at him that way for whole minutes. He turned back to the table, his insides sliding, and stared at the suddenly indecipherable glyphs of the newspaper. After a moment he felt her hand on the back of his neck, rubbing him gently. She left the kitchen without a word.

This is how it happened:

They were taking Dodger for a walk. Toby liked to hold the leash—he was four years old, and gravely occupied with establishing his independence—and more often than not Brian would sort of half-trot behind them, one hand held indecisively aloft should Dodger suddenly decide to break into a run, dragging his boy behind him like a string of tin cans. He probably bit off more profanities during those walks than he ever did changing a tire. He carried, as was their custom on Mondays, a blanket and a picnic lunch. He would lie back in the sun while Toby and the dog played, and enjoy not being hunched over an engine block. At some point they would have lunch. Brian believed these afternoons of easy camaraderie would be remembered by them both for years to come. They'd done it a hundred times.

A hundred times.

On that day a kindergarten class arrived shortly after they did. Toby ran up to his father and wrapped his arms around his neck, frightened by the sudden bright surge of humanity; the kids were a loud, brawling tumult, crashing over the swings and monkey bars in a gabbling surf. Brian pried Toby's arms free and pointed at them.

"Look, screwball, they're just kids. See? They're just like you. Go on and play. Have some fun."

Dodger galloped out to greet them and was received as a hero, with joyful cries and grasping fingers. Toby observed this gambit for his dog's affections and at last decided to intervene. He ran toward them, shouting, "That's my dog! That's my dog!" Brian watched him go, made eye contact with the teacher and nodded hello. She smiled at him—he remembered thinking she was kind of cute, wondering how old she was—and she returned her attention to her kids, gamboling like lunatics all over the park. Brian reclined on the blanket and watched the clouds skim the atmosphere, listened to the sound of children. It was a hot, windless day.

He didn't realize he had dozed until the kindergarteners had been rounded up and were halfway down the block, taking their noise with them. The silence stirred him.

He sat up abruptly and looked around. The playground was empty. "Toby? Hey, Toby?"

Dodger stood out in the middle of the road, his leash spooled at his feet. He watched Brian eagerly, offered a tentative wag.

"Where's Toby?" he asked the dog, and climbed to his feet. He felt a sudden sickening lurch in his gut. He turned in a quick circle, a half-smile on his face, utterly sure that this was an impossible situation, that children didn't disappear in broad daylight while their parents were *right fucking there*. So he was still here. Of course he was still here. Dodger trotted up to him and sat down at his feet, waiting for him to produce the boy, as though he were a hidden tennis ball.

"Toby?"

The park was empty. He jogged after the receding line of kids. "Hey. *Hey!* Is my son with you? *Where's my son?*"

One morning, about a week after the experience in the kitchen, Brian was awakened by the phone. Every time this happened he felt a thrill of hope, though by now it had become muted, even dreadful in its predictability. He hauled himself up from the couch, nearly overturning a bottle of Jack Daniels stationed on the floor. He crossed the living room and picked up the phone.

"Yes?" he said.

"Let me talk to Amy." It was not a voice he recognized. A male voice, with a thick rural accent. It was the kind of voice that inspired immediate prejudice: the voice of an idiot; of a man without any right to make demands of him.

"Who is this?"

"Just let me talk to Amy."

"How about you go fuck yourself."

There was a pause as the man on the phone seemed to assess the obstacle. Then he said, with a trace of amusement in his voice, "Are you Brian?"

"That's right."

"Look, dude. Go get your wife. Put her on the phone. Do it now, and I won't have to come down there and break your fucking face."

Brian slammed down the receiver. Feeling suddenly light-headed, he put his hand on the wall to steady himself, to reassure himself that it was still solid, and that he was still real. From somewhere outside, through an open window, came the distant sound of children shouting.

It was obvious that Amy was sleeping with another man. When confronted with the call, she did not admit to anything, but made no special effort to explain it away, either. His name was Tommy, she said. She'd met him once when she was out. He sounded rough, but he wasn't a bad guy. She chose not to elaborate, and Brian, to his amazement, found a kind of forlorn comfort in his wife's affair. He'd lost his son; why not lose it all?

On television the news was filling with the creatures, more of which were being discovered all the time. The press had taken to calling them angels. Some were being found alive, though all of them appeared to have suffered from some violent experience. At least one family had become notorious by refusing to let anyone see the angel they'd found, or even let it out of their home. They boarded their windows and warned away visitors with a shotgun.

Brian was stationed on the couch, staring at the television with the sound turned down to barely a murmur. He listened to the familiar muted clatter from the medicine cabinet as Amy applied her makeup in the bathroom. A news program was on, and a handheld camera followed a street reporter into someone's house. The JD bottle was empty at his feet, and the knowledge that he had no more in the house smoldered in him.

Amy emerged from the kitchen with her purse slung over her arm and made her way to the door. "I'm going out," she said.

"Where?"

She paused, one hand on the doorknob. She wavered there, in her careful makeup and her push-up bra. He tried to remember the last time he'd seen her look like this and failed dismally. Something inside her seemed to collapse—a force of will, perhaps, or a habit of deception. Maybe she was just too tired to invent another lie.

"I'm going to see Tommy," she said.

"The redneck."

"Sure. The redneck, if that's how you want it."

"Does it matter how I want it?"

She paused. "No," she said. "I guess not."

"Well well. The truth. Look out."

She left the door, walked into the living room. Brian felt a sudden trepidation; this is not what he imagined would happen. He wanted to get a few weak barbs in before she walked out, that was all. He did not actually want to talk.

She sat on the rocking chair across from the couch. Beside her, on the television, the camera focused on an obese man wearing overalls smiling triumphantly and holding aloft an angel's severed head.

Amy shut it off.

"Do you want to know about him?" she said.

"Let's see. He's stupid and violent. He called my home and threatened me. He's sleeping with my wife. What else is there to know?"

She appraised him for a moment, weighing consequences. "There's a little more to know," she said. "For example, he's very kind to me. He thinks I'm beautiful." He must have made some sort of sound then, because she said, "I know it must be very hard for you to believe, but some men still find me attractive. And that's important to me, Brian. Can you understand that?"

He turned away from her, shielding his eyes with a hand, although without the TV on there was very little light in the room. Each breath was laced with pain.

"When I go to see him, he talks to me. Actually talks. I know he might not be very smart, according to your standards, but you'd be surprised how much he and I have to talk about. You'd be surprised how much more there is to life—to my life—than your car magazines, and your TV, and your bottles of booze."

"Stop it," I said.

"He's also a very considerate lover. He paces himself. For my sake. For me. Did you *ever* do that, Brian? In all the times we made love?"

He felt tears crawling down his face. Christ. When did that start?

"I can forget things when I sleep with him. I can forget about . . . I can forget about everything. He lets me do that."

"You cold bitch," he rasped.

"You passive little shit," she bit back, with a venom that surprised him. "You let it happen, do you know that? You let it all happen. Every awful thing."

She stood abruptly and walked out the door, slamming it behind her. The force of it rattled the windows. After a while—he had no idea how long—he picked up the remote and turned the TV back on. A girl pointed to moving clouds on a map.

Eventually Dodger came by and curled up at his feet. Brian slid off the couch and lay down beside him, hugging him close. Dodger smelled the way dogs do, musky and of the earth, and he sighed with the abiding patience of his kind.

Violence filled his dreams. In them he rent bodies, spilled blood, painted the walls using severed limbs as gruesome brushes. In them he went back to the park and ate the children while the teacher looked on. Once he awoke after these dreams with blood filling his mouth; he realized he had chewed his tongue during the night. It was raw and painful for days afterward. A rage was building inside him and he could not find an outlet for it. One night Amy told him she thought she was falling in love with Tommy. He only nodded stupidly and watched her walk out the door again. That same night he kicked Dodger out of the house. He just opened the door to the night and told him to go. When he wouldn't—trying instead to slink around his legs and go back inside—he planted his foot on the dog's chest and physically pushed him back outside, sliding him backwards on his butt. "*Go find him!*" he yelled. "*Go find him! Go and find him!*" He shut the door and listened to Dodger whimper and scratch at it for nearly an hour. At some point he gave up and Brian fell asleep. When he awoke it was raining. He opened the door and called for him. The rain swallowed his voice.

"Oh no," he said quietly, his voice a whimper. "Come back! I'm sorry! Please, I'm so sorry!"

When Dodger did eventually return, wet and miserable, Brian hugged him tight, buried his face in his fur, and wept for joy.

Brian liked to do his drinking alone. When he drank in public, especially at his old bar, people tried to talk to him. They saw his presence as an invitation to share sympathy, or a request for a friendly ear. It got to be too much. But tonight he made his way back there, endured the stares and the weird silence, took the beers sent his way, although he wanted none of it. What he wanted tonight was Fire Engine, and she didn't disappoint.

Everybody knew Fire Engine, of course; if she thought you didn't know her, she'd introduce herself to you posthaste. One hand on your shoulder, the other on your thigh. Where her hands went after that depended on a quick negotiation. She was a redhead with an easy personality, and was popular with the regular clientele, including the ones that would never buy her services. She claimed to be twenty-eight but looked closer to forty. At some unfortunate juncture in her life she had contrived to lose most of her front teeth, either to decay or to someone's balled fist; either way common wisdom held she gave the best blowjob in downtown New Orleans.

Brian used to be amused by that kind of talk. Although he'd never had an interest in her he'd certainly enjoyed listening to her sales pitch; she'd become a sort of bar pet, and the unselfconscious way she went about her life was both endearing and appalling. Her lack of teeth was too perfect, and too ridiculous. Now, however, the information had acquired a new kind of value to him. He pressed his gaze onto her until she finally felt it and looked back. She smiled coquettishly, with gruesome effect. He told the bartender to send her a drink.

"You sure? She ain't gonna leave you alone all night."

"Fuck yeah, I'm sure."

All night didn't concern him. What concerned him were the next ten minutes, which was what he figured ten dollars would buy him. After the necessary negotiations and bullshit they left the bar together, trailing catcalls; she took his hand and led him around back, into the alley.

The smell of rotting garbage came at him like an attack, like a pillowcase thrown over his head. She steered him into the alley's dark mouth, with its grime-smeared pavement and furtive skittering sounds, and its dumpster so stuffed with straining garbage bags that it looked like some fearsome monster choking on its dinner. "Now you know I'm a lady," she said, "but sometimes you just got to make do with what's available."

That she could laugh at herself this way touched Brian, and he felt a wash of sympathy for her. He considered what it would be like to run away with her, to rescue her from the wet pull of her life; to save her.

She unzipped his pants and pulled his dick out. "There we go, honey, that's what I'm talking about. Ain't you something."

After a couple of minutes she released him and stood up. He tucked himself back in and zipped his pants, afraid to make eye contact with her.

"Maybe you just had too much to drink," she said.

"Yeah."

"It ain't nothing."

"I know it isn't," he said harshly.

When she made no move to leave, he said, "Will you just get the fuck away from me? Please?"

Her voice lost its sympathy. "Honey, I still got to get paid."

He opened his wallet and fished out a ten dollar bill. She plucked it from his fingers and walked out of the alley, back toward the bar. "Don't get all bent out of shape about it," she called. "Shit happens, you know?"

He slid down the wall until his ass hit the ground. He brought his hand to his mouth and choked out a sob, his eyes squeezed shut. He banged his head once against the brick wall behind him and then thought better of it. Down here the stench was a steaming blanket, almost soothing in its awfulness. He felt like he deserved to be there, that it was right that he should sleep in shit and grime. He listened to the gentle ticking of the roaches in the dark. He wondered if Toby was in a place like this.

Something glinted further down the alley.

He strained to see it. It was too bright to be merely a reflection.

It moved.

"Son of a," he said, and pushed himself to his feet.

It lay mostly hidden; it had pulled some stray garbage bags atop itself in an effort to remain concealed, but its dim luminescence worked against it. Brian loped over to it, wrenched the bags away; its clawed hands clutched at them and tore them open, spilling a clatter of beer and liquor bottles all over the ground. They caromed with hollow music through the alley, coming at last to silent rest, until all Brian could hear was the thin, high-pitched noise the creature made through the tiny O-shaped orifice he supposed passed for a mouth. Its eyes were black little stones. The creature—angel, he thought, *they're calling these things angels*—was tall and thin, abundantly male, and it shed a thin light that illuminated exactly nothing around it. *If you put some clothes on it*, Brian thought, *hide its face, gave it some gloves, it might pass for a human.*

Exposed, it held up a long-fingered hand, as if to ward him off. It had clearly been hurt: its legs looked badly broken, and it breathed in short, shallow gasps. A dark bruise spread like a mold over the right side of its chest.

"Look at you, huh? You're all messed up." He felt a strange glee as he said this; he could not justify the feeling and quickly buried it. "Yeah, yeah, somebody worked you over pretty good."

It managed to roll onto its belly and it scrabbled along the pavement in a pathetic attempt at escape. It loosed that thin, reedy cry. Calling for help? Begging for its life?

The sight of it trying to flee from him catalyzed some deep predatory impulse, and he pressed his foot onto the angel's ankle, holding it easily in place. "No you don't." He hooked the thing beneath its shoulders and lifted it from the ground; it was astonishingly light. It mewled weakly at him. "Shut up, I'm trying to help you." He adjusted it in his arms so that he held it like a lover, or a fainted woman. He carried it back to his car, listening for the sound of the barroom door opening behind him, of laughter or a challenge chasing him down the sidewalk. But the door stayed shut. He walked in silence.

Amy was awake when he got home, silhouetted in the doorway. Brian pulled the angel from the passenger seat, cradled it against his chest. He watched her face alter subtly, watched as some dark hope crawled across it like an insect, and he squashed it before it could do any real harm.

"It's not him," he said. "It's something else."

She stood away from the door and let him come in.

Dodger, who had been dozing in the hallway, lurched to his feet with a sliding and skittering of claws and growled fiercely at it, his lips curled away from his teeth.

"Get away, you," Brian said. He eased past him, bearing his load down the hall.

He laid it in Toby's bed. Together he and Amy stood over it, watching as it stared back at them with dark flat eyes, its body twisting away from them as if it could fold itself into another place altogether. Its fingers plucked at the train-spangled bedsheets, wrapping them around its nakedness. Amy leaned over and helped to tuck the sheets around it.

"He's hurt," she said.

"I know. I guess a lot of them are found that way."

"Should we call somebody?"

"You want camera crews in here? Fuck no."

"Well. He's really hurt. We need to do something."

"Yeah. I don't know. We can at least clean him up I guess."

Amy sat on the mattress beside it; it stared at her with its expressionless face. Brian couldn't tell if there were thoughts passing behind those eyes, or just a series of brute reflex arcs. After a moment it reached out with one long dark fingernail and brushed her arm. She jumped as though shocked.

"Jesus! Be careful," said Brian.

"What if it's him?"

"What?" It took him a moment to understand her. "Oh my god. Amy. It's not him, okay? It's *not him.*"

"But what if it is?"

"It's *not.* We've seen them on the news, okay? It's a, it's a *thing.*"

"You shouldn't call it an 'it.'"

"*How do I know what the fuck to call it?*"

She touched her fingers to its cheek. It pressed its face into them, making some small sound.

"Why did you leave me?" she said. "You were everything I had."

Brian swooned beneath a tide of vertigo. Something was moving inside him, something too large to stay where it was. "It's an angel," he said. "Nothing more. Just an angel. It's probably going to die on us, since that's what they seem to do." He put his hand against the wall until the dizziness passed. It was replaced by a low, percolating anger. "Instead of thinking of it as Toby, why don't you ask it where Toby *is*. Why don't you make it explain to us why it happened."

She looked at him. "It happened because you let it," she said.

Dodger asked to be let outside. Brian opened the door for him to let him run around the front yard. There was a leash law here, but Dodger was well known by the neighbors and generally tolerated. He walked out of the house with considerably less than his usual enthusiasm. He lifted his leg desultorily against a shrub, then walked down to the road and followed the sidewalk further into the neighborhood. He did not come back.

Over the next few days it put its hooks into them, and drew them in tight. They found it difficult to leave it alone. Its flesh seemed to pump out some kind of soporific, like an invisible spoor, and it was better than the booze—better than anything they'd previously known. Its pull seemed to grow stronger as the days passed. For Amy, especially. She stopped going out, and for all practical purposes moved into Toby's room with it. When Brian joined her in there, she seemed to barely tolerate his presence. If he sat beside it she watched him with naked trepidation, as though she feared he might damage it somehow.

It was not, he realized, an unfounded fear. Something inside him became turbulent in its presence, something he couldn't identify but which sparked flashes of violent thought, of the kind he had not had since just after Toby vanished. This feeling came in sharp relief to the easy lethargy the angel normally inspired, and he was reminded of a time when he was younger, sniffing heroin laced with cocaine. So he did not object to Amy's efforts at excluding him.

Finally, though, her vigilance slipped. He went into the bathroom and found her sleeping on the toilet, her robe hiked up around her waist, her head resting against the sink. He left her there and crept into the angel's room.

It was awake, and its eyes tracked him as he crossed the room and sat beside it on the bed. Its breath wheezed lightly as it drew air through its puckered mouth. Its body was still bruised and bent, though it did seem to be improving.

Brian touched its chest where the bruise seemed to be diminishing. *Why does it bruise?* he wondered. *Why does it bleed the same way I do? Shouldn't it be made of something better?* Also, it didn't have wings. Not even vestigial ones. Why were they called angels? Because of how they made people feel? It looked more like an alien than a divine being. *It has a cock, for Christ's sake. What's that all about? Do angels fuck?*

He leaned over it, so his face was inches away, almost touching its nose. He stared into its black, irisless eyes, searching for some sign of intelligence, some evidence of intent or emotion. From this distance he could smell its breath; he drew it into his own lungs, and it warmed him like a shot of whiskey. The angel lifted its head and pressed its face into his. Brian jerked back and felt something brush his elbow. He looked behind him and discovered the angel had an erection.

He lurched out of bed, tripping over himself as he rushed to the door, dashed through it and slammed it shut. His blood sang. It rose in him like the sea and filled him with tumultuous music. He dropped to his knees and vomited all over the carpet.

Later, he stepped into its doorway, watching Amy trace her hands down its face. Through the window he could see that night was gathering in little pockets outside, lifting itself toward the sky. At the sight of the angel his heart jumped in his chest as though it had come unmoored. "Amy, I have to talk to you," he said. He had some difficulty making his voice sound calm.

She didn't look at him. "I know it's not really him," she said. "Not really."

"No."

"But don't you think he is, kind of? In a way?"

"No."

She laid her head on the pillow beside it, staring into its face. Brian was left looking at the back of her head, the unwashed hair, tangled and brittle. He remembered cupping the back of her head in his hand, its weight and its warmth. He remembered her body.

"Amy. Where does he live?"

"Who."

"Tommy. Where does he live?"

She turned and looked at him, a little crease of worry on her brow. "Why do you want to know?"

"Just tell me. Please."

"Brian, don't."

He slammed his fist into the wall, startling himself. He screamed at her. *"Tell me where he lives! God damn it!"*

Tommy opened the door of his shotgun house, clad only in boxer shorts, and Brian greeted him with a blow to the face. Tommy staggered back into his house, due more to surprise than the force of the punch; his foot slipped on a throw rug and he crashed to the floor. The small house reverberated with the impact. Brian had a moment to take in Tommy's hard physique and imagine his wife's hands moving over it. He stepped forward and kicked him in the groin.

Tommy grunted and seemed to absorb it. He rolled over and pushed himself quickly to his feet. Tommy's fist swung at him and he had time to experience a quick flaring terror before his head exploded with pain. He found himself on his knees, staring at the dust collecting in the crevices of the hardwood floor. Somewhere in the background a television chattered urgently.

A kick to the ribs sent Brian down again. Tommy straddled him, grabbed a fistful of hair, and slammed Brian's face into the floor several times. Brian felt something in his face break and blood poured onto the floor. He wanted to cry but it was impossible, he couldn't get enough air. *I'm going to die,* he thought. He felt himself hauled up and thrown against a wall. Darkness crowded his vision; he began to lose his purchase on events.

Someone was yelling at him. There was a face in front of him, skin peeled back from its teeth in a smile or a grimace of rage. It looked like something from hell.

He awoke to the feel of cold grass, cold night air. The right side of his face burned like a signal flare; his left eye refused to open. It hurt to breathe. He pushed himself to his elbows and spit blood from his mouth; it immediately filled again. Something wrong in there. He rolled onto his back and laid there for a while, waiting for the pain to subside to a tolerable level. The night was high and dark. At one point he felt sure that he was rising from the ground, that something up there was pulling him into its empty hollows.

Somehow he managed the drive home. He remembered nothing of it except occasional stabs of pain as opposing headlights washed across his windshield; he would later consider his safe arrival a kind of miracle. He pulled into the driveway and honked the horn a few times until Amy came out and found him there. She looked at him with horror, and with something else.

"Oh, baby. What did you do. What did you do."

She steered him toward the angel's room. He stopped himself in the doorway, his heart pounding again, and he tried to catch his breath. It occurred to him, on a dim level, that his nose was broken. She tugged at his hand, but he resisted. Her face was limned by moonlight, streaming through the window like some mystical tide, and by the faint luminescence of the angel tucked into their son's bed. She'd grown heavy over the years, and the past year had taken a harsh toll: the flesh on her face sagged, and was scored by grief. And yet he was stunned by her beauty.

Had she always looked like this?

"Come on," she said. "Please."

The left side of his face pulsed with hard beats of pain; it sang like a war drum. His working eye settled on the thing in the bed: its flat black eyes, its wickedly curved talons. Amy sat beside it and put her hand on its chest. It arched its back, seeming to coil beneath her.

"Come lay down," she said. "He's here for us. He's come home for us."

Brian took a step into Toby's room, and then another. He knew she was wrong; that the angel was not home, that it had wandered here from somewhere far away.

Is heaven a dark place?

The angel extended a hand, its talons flexing. The sheets over its belly stirred as Brian drew closer. Amy took her husband's hands, easing him onto the bed. He gripped her shoulders, squeezing them too tightly. "I'm sorry," he said suddenly, surprising himself. "I'm sorry! I'm sorry!" Once he began he couldn't stop. He said it over and over again, so many times it just became a sound, a sobbing plaint, and Amy pressed her hand against his mouth, entwined her fingers into his hair, saying, "Shhhh, shhhhh," and finally she silenced him with a kiss. As they embraced each other the angel played its hands over their faces and their shoulders, its strange reedy breath and its narcotic musk drawing them down to it. They caressed each other, and they caressed the angel, and when they touched their lips to its skin the taste of it shot spikes of joy through their bodies. Brian felt her teeth on his neck and he bit into the angel, the sudden dark spurt of blood filling his mouth, the soft pale flesh tearing easily, sliding down his throat. He kissed his wife furiously and when she tasted the blood she nearly tore his tongue out; he pushed her face toward the angel's body, and watched the blood blossom from beneath her. The angel's eyes were frozen, staring at the ceiling; it extended a shaking hand toward a wall decorated with a Spider-Man poster, its fingers twisted and bent.

They ate until they were full.

That night, heavy with the sludge of bliss, Brian and Amy made love again for the first time in nearly a year. It was wordless and slow, a synchronicity of pressures and tender familiarities. They were like rare creatures of a dying species, amazed by the sight of each other.

Brian drifts in and out of sleep. He has what will be the last dream about his son. It is morning in this dream, by the side of a small country road. It must have rained during the night, because the world shines with a wet glow. Droplets of water cling, dazzling, to the muzzle of a dog as it rests beside the road, unmenaced by traffic, languorous and dull-witted in the rising heat. It might even be Dodger. His snout is heavy with blood. Some distance away from him Toby rests on the street, a small pile of bones and torn flesh, glittering with dew, catching and throwing sunlight like a scattered pile of rubies and diamonds.

By the time he wakes, he has already forgotten it.

DELIA SHERMAN

The Fiddler of Bayou Teche

Delia Sherman's trickster tale "The Fiddler of Bayou Teche" comes from Ellen Datlow and Terri Windling's anthology The Coyote Road. *Sherman's name will be familiar to longtime readers of this series as this is her (lucky!) thirteenth appearance. Her short stories have also appeared in* The Armless Maiden; Ruby Slippers, Golden Tears; A Wolf at the Door; The Green Man; *and* The Magazine of Fantasy & Science Fiction. *She is a founding member of the Interstitial Arts Foundation and, with Theodora Goss, recently edited the anthology* Interfictions: An Anthology of Interstitial Writing. *She is at work on a second young adult novel set in New York (after* Changeling*), where she lives with her partner and sometime coauthor Ellen Kushner.*

—K.L. & G.G.

Come here, *cher*, and I tell you a story.

One time there is a girl lives out in the swamp. Her skin and hair are white like the feathers of a white egret and her eyes are pink like a possum's nose. When she is a baby, the loup-garous find her floating on the bayou in an old pirogue and take her to Tante Eulalie.

Tante Eulalie does not howl and grow hair on her body when the moon is full like the loup-garous. But she hides in the swamp same as they do, and they are all friends together. She takes *piquons* out of the loup-garous' feet and bullets out of their hairy shoulders, and doses their rheumatism and their mange. In return, the loup-garous build her a cabin out of cypress and palmetto leaves and bring her rice and indigo dye from town. On moonlit nights, she plays her fiddle at the loup-garous' ball. The loup-garous love Tante Eulalie, but the girl loves her most of all.

Yes, the girl is me. Who else around here has white skin and hair and pink eyes, eh? Hush now, and listen.

Tante Eulalie was like my mother. She named me Cadence and told me stories—all the stories I tell you, *cher*. When we sit spinning or weaving, she tell me about when she was a young girl, living with her pap and her good maman and her six brothers and three sisters near the little town of Pierreville. She tell me about her cousin Belda Guidry, the prettiest girl in the parish.

Now, when Belda is fifteen, there are twenty young men all crazy to marry her. She can't make up her mind, her, so her old pap make a test for the young men, to see which will make the best son-in-law. He make them plow the swamp and sow it with dried chilies and bring them to harvest. And when they done that, they have to catch the oldest, meanest gator in Bayou Teche and make a gumbo out of him.

I thought Tante Eulalie was making it all up out of her head, but she swore it was true. It was Ganelon Fuselier who won Belda, and Tante Eulalie was godmother to their second child, Denise.

Ganie cheated, of course. Nobody can pass a test like that without cheating some. Seemed to me like cheating was a way of life in Pierreville. The wonder was how the folks that were getting cheated never learned to be less trustful. I thought if I ever went to Pierreville, and Ganie Fuselier or Old Savoie tell me the sky is blue, I'd go outside and check. And if Murderes Petitpas came knocking at my door, I'd slip out the back.

Tante Eulalie's best stories were about Young Murderes Petitpas, who was like the grasshopper because he'd always rather fiddle than work, though 'Dres was too smart to get caught out in the cold. How smart was he? Well, I tell you the story of 'Dres and the Fiddle, and you can judge for yourself.

Once there's this old man, see, called Old Boudreaux. He has a fiddle, and this fiddle is the sweetest fiddle anybody ever hear. His old pap make it himself, back in eighteen-something, and when Old Boudreaux play, the dead get up and dance. Now, Young 'Dres thinks it's a shame that the best fiddler in St. Mary's parish—that is, Young 'Dres himself—shouldn't have the best fiddle—that is, Old Boudreaux's Pap's fiddle. So Young 'Dres goes to Old Boudreaux and he says, "Old Boudreaux, I'm afraid for your soul."

Old Boudreaux says: "What you talking about, boy?"

Young 'Dres says: "Last night when you were playing 'Jolie Blonde,' I see a little red devil creep out of the f-holes and commence to dancing on your fingerboard. The faster he dance, the faster you play, and he laugh like mad and wave his forked tail so I was scared half to death."

"Go to bed, 'Dres Petitpas," says Old Boudreaux. "I don't believe that for a minute."

"It's as true as I'm standing here," says Young 'Dres. "I got the second sight, me, so I see things other people don't."

"Hmpf," says Old Boudreaux, and starts back in the house.

"Wait," says Young 'Dres. "You bring your fiddle here, and I go prove it to you."

Of course, Old Boudreaux say no. But Young 'Dres got a way with him, and everybody know Old Boudreaux ain't got no more sense than a possum. So Old Boudreaux fetches his fiddle and goes to hand it to Young 'Dres. But Young 'Dres is wringing his bandana and moaning. "Mother Mary preserve me!" he says. "Can't you see its red eyes twinkling in the f-holes? Can't you smell the sulfur? You got to exercise that devil, Old Boudreaux, or you go fiddle yourself right down to hell."

Old Boudreaux nearly drop his fiddle, he so scared. He don't dare look in the f-holes, but he don't have to, because as soon as Young 'Dres name that devil, there's a terrible stink of sulfur everywhere.

"Holy Mother save me!" Old Boudreaux cry. "My fiddle is possessed! What am I going to do, 'Dres Petitpas? I don't want to fiddle myself down to hell."

"Well, I go tell you, Old Boudreaux, but you ain't going to like it."

"I'll like it, I promise. Just tell me what to do!"

"You give the fiddle to me, and I exercise that devil for you."

Old Boudreaux so scared, he hand his pap's fiddle right over to Young 'Dres. What's more, he tell him to keep it, because Old Boudreaux never go touch it again without thinking he smell sulfur. And that's how 'Dres Petitpas get the sweetest fiddle in the parish for nothing more than the cost of the bandana he crush the rotten egg in that make Old Boudreaux believe his fiddle is haunted.

Yes, that Young 'Dres made me laugh, him. But Tante Eulalie shook her head and said, "You go ahead and laugh, 'tit chou. Just remember that people like 'Dres Petit-pas are better to hear about than have dealings with, eh? You ever meet a bon rien like that—all smiling and full of big talk—you run as fast and as far as you can go."

That was Tante Eulalie. Always looking out for me, teaching me what I need to know to live in the world. By the time I could walk, I knew to keep out of the sun and stay away from traps and logs with eyes. When I got older, Tante Eulalie taught me to spin cotton and weave cloth and dye it blue with indigo. She taught me how to make medicine from peppergrass and elderberry bark and prickly pear leaves, and some little magic gris-gris for dirty wounds and warts and aching joints. Best of all, she taught me how to dance.

Tante Eulalie loved to play the fiddle, and she played most nights after supper was cleared away. The music she played was bouncing music, swaying music, twirl around until you fall music, and when I was very little, that's what I did. Then Tante Eulalie took me to the loup-garous' ball, where I learned the two-step and the waltz.

I took to dancing like a mallard to open water. Once I learned the steps, I danced all the time. I danced with the loup-garous and I danced by myself. I danced when I swept and I danced when I cooked. I danced to Tante Eulalie's fiddling and I danced to the fiddling of the crickets. Tante Eulalie laughed at me—said I'd wear myself out. But I didn't.

Then came a winter when the leaves were blasted with cold and ice skimmed the surface of the bayou. Long about Advent-time, Tante Eulalie caught a cough. I made her prickly pear leaf syrup and willow bark tea for the fever, and hung a gris-gris for strength around her neck. But it didn't do no good. At the dark of the year, she asked me to bring her the cypress wood box from under her bed. I opened it for her, and she pulled out three pieces of lace and a gold ring and put them in my hand.

"These are all I have to leave you," she said. "These, and my fiddle. I hope you find good use for them someday."

Not long after, the Bon Dieu called her and she went to Him. Her friends the loup-garous buried her under the big live oak behind the cabin and howled her funeral mass. I was sixteen years old now, more or less, and that was the end of my girlhood.

That was the end of my dancing, too, for a time. When I saw Tante Eulalie's fiddle lying silent across her cane-bottomed chair, I fell into sadness like a deep river. I lay in a nest of nutria skins next the fire and I watched the flames burn low and thought how nobody would know or notice if I lived or died.

Some time passes, I don't know how much, and then somebody knocks at the door. I don't answer, but he comes in anyway. It is Ulysse, the youngest of the loup-garous. I like Ulysse. He is quiet and skinny and he brings me peanut butter and white bread in a printed paper wrapper, and when we dance at the loup-garous' ball, everybody stops and watches us. Still, I wish he would go away.

Ulysse sniffs around a little, then digs me out of my nest and gives me a shake. "You in a bad way, chère," he says. "If Tante Eulalie see how you carry on, she pass you one big slap, for sure."

"Good," I say. "I like that fine. At least she be here to slap me."

Not much Ulysse can say to that, I think, and maybe he will go away now and let me be sad by myself. But he has another idea, him. He sniffs around again and starts to clucking like an old hen. "This place worse than a hog pen," he says. "Tante Eulalie see the state her cabin is in, she die all over again." He picks her fiddle and bow up off her chair. "Where she keep these at?"

To see Ulysse holding Tante Eulalie's fiddle gives me the first real feeling I have since it seems like forever. I get mad, me, so mad I go right up to Ulysse, who is bigger than me by a head, who has wild, dark hair and long teeth and sharp nails even when the moon is dark, and I hit him in the stomach.

"*Tiens, chère!* What is this? Why you hit your friend Ulysse?"

"Why? Because you touch Tante Eulalie's fiddle. Put it down, you, or I make you."

"Put it up, then," he says, "instead of curling up like a crawfish in winter."

I take the fiddle like it was an egg, and hang it on its hook over Tante Eulalie's bed. And then I start to cry, with Ulysse holding my shoulders and licking my hair like a wolf licks her cub till I am calm again.

After that, I clean the cabin and make myself a gumbo. I string Tante Eulalie's big loom with thread she spun and dyed, and I weave a length of pale blue cloth. The water rises to the edge of the porch and the nights get shorter. I set lines to catch fish, and make my garden with the seeds Tante Eulalie saved. The loup-garous still knock on my door, and I treat them for mange and rheumatism and broken bones, as Tante Eulalie always did. But I don't dance at their balls. I take my pirogue out at sunset and paddle between the big cypress trees and listen to the frogs sing of love and the roaring of the gators as they fight for their mates.

One night, paddling far from home, I see lights that are not the pale *feu follets* that dance in the swamp at night. They are yellow lights, lantern lights, and they tell me I have come to a farm. I am a little afraid, for Tante Eulalie used to warn me about letting people see me.

"You know how ducks carry on when a strange bird land in their water?" she says. "The good people of Pierreville, they see that white hair and those pink eyes, and they peck at you till there's nothing left but two-three white feathers."

I do not want to be pecked, me, so I start to paddle away.

And then I hear the music.

I turn back with a sweep of my paddle and drift clear. I see a wharf and a cabin and an outhouse and a hog pen, and a big barn built on high ground away from the water. The barn doors are open, and they spill yellow light out over a pack of buggies and horses and even cars—only cars I've seen outside the magazines Ulysse sometimes brings. I don't care about the cars, though, for I am caught by the fiddle music that spills out brighter than the lantern light, brighter than anything in the world since Tante Eulalie left it.

I paddle toward the music like a moth to a lit candle, not caring that fire burns and ducks peck and the people of Pierreville don't like strangers. But I am not stupid like Old Boudreaux. I am careful to hide my pirogue behind a buttonbush and I don't come out in the open. I stalk the music like a bobcat, softly, softly, and I find a place behind the barn where I think nobody will come. And then I dance. I dance the two-step with my brown striped shawl, tears wet on my face because Tante Eulalie is dead, because I am dancing alone in the dark, because the fiddle is crying and I cannot help but cry, too.

The moon rises, the crickets go to bed. The fiddler plays and I dance as if the dawn will never come. I guess I keep dancing when the music stops, because next thing I know, there's a shout behind me. When I open my eyes, the sky is pale and gray and there's a knot of men behind the barn with their mouths gaping like black holes in their faces.

One of them steps forward. He is tall, broad shouldered, and thick, and he wears a wide-brimmed hat pulled down low over his eyes, glittering in its shadow like the eyes of a snake in a hole. I throw my shawl around my shoulders and turn to run.

As soon as I move, all the men gasp and step back. I think that a little fear makes ducks mean, but a lot of fear makes them run. I give a hoot like a swamp owl, hold my shawl out like wings, and scoot low and fast into the cypress grove.

Behind me, there is shouting and lights bobbing here and there like lightning bugs. I creep to my pirogue and paddle away quiet as a water snake, keeping to the shadows. I am very pleased with myself, me. I think the men of Pierreville are as stupid as Old Boudreaux to be frightened by a small girl in a striped shawl. Maybe soon I will go and hear the music again.

Next night, Ulysse comes knocking at my door. He sits down at the table and I give him coffee and then I go to my wheel and set it spinning.

"I hear tell of a thing," says Ulysse over the whirr of the wheel. "It make me think."

I smile a little. "Think?" I say. "That *is* a piece of news. You tell your friends? Old Placide, he be surprised."

Ulysse shakes his head. "This is serious, Cadence. Up and down the bayou, everybody is talking about the haunt that bust up the Doucet *fais-do-do*."

I look down at the pale brown thread running though my fingers, fine and even as Tante Eulalie's. "There weren't no haunts at the Doucet *fais-do-do*, Ulysse."

"I know that. The Doucets say different. They say they see a girl turn into a swamp owl and fly away. What you say to that, *hein*?"

"I say they drink too much beer, them."

He brings his heavy black eyebrows together. "Why you go forget everything Tante Eulalie tell you, Cadence, and make a nine days' wonder with your foolishness?"

"Don't scold, Ulysse. The people of Pierreville for sure got more important things to talk about than me."

"Maybe so, maybe not," Ulysse says darkly. "What you doing at the Doucets'?"

"Dancing," I say, still teasing. "Who is the fiddler, Ulysse? He play mighty fine."

Ulysse is still not smiling. "He is a *bon rien*, Cadence, a bad man. Shake hands with Murderes Petitpas, you go count your fingers after."

I almost let the wheel stop, I'm so surprised. "You go to bed, Ulysse. Tante Eulalie make 'Dres Petitpas up out of her head."

"He's real, all right. Everybody say he sell his soul to the devil so he can play better than any human man. Then he fiddle the devil out of hell and keep him dancing all day and night until his hoofs split in two and the devil give 'Dres his soul back so he can stop dancing. 'Dres Petitpas is the big bull on the hill, and mean, mean. You stay away from him, you."

I maybe like Ulysse, but I don't like him telling me what to do—Ulysse, who eats rabbits raw and howls at the moon when it's full. I pinch the thread too tight and it breaks in two.

"Eh, Cadence," he says, "you going to hit me again? Ain't going to change what I say, but go ahead if it make you feel better."

I don't hit him, but I am maybe not very kind to him, and he leaves looking like a beaten dog. I hear howling, later, that I think is Ulysse, and I am a little sorry, but not too much.

Still, I do not go out again to dance. Not because Ulysse tell me, but because I am not a *couyon* like Old Boudreaux.

Two, maybe three nights after, I hear a thump against my porch and the sounds of somebody tying up a pirogue and climbing out. Not Ulysse—somebody heavier. Old Placide, maybe. I am already up and looking for my jar of fly blister for his rheumatism when there's a knock on the door.

I open it. I do not see Old Placide. I see a big man with a belly like a barrel, a big-brimmed hat, and a heavy black mustache. I try to shut the door, but 'Dres Petitpas shoves it back easy, and walks past me like he was at home. Then he sits down at my table with his hat pulled down to his snake-bright eyes and his hands spread on his thighs.

"Hey there, *chère*," he says, and smiles real friendly. His teeth are yellow and flat.

I stand by the door, thinking whether I will run away or not. Running away is maybe safer, but then 'Dres Petitpas is alone in my cabin, and I don't want that.

He eyes me like he knows just what I'm thinking. "I go tell you a story. You stand by the door if you want, but I think you be more comfortable sitting down."

I hate to do anything he say, but I hate worse looking foolish. I close the door and sit by the fire with my hands on my lap. I do not give him coffee.

"Well," he says, "this is the way it is. I am a good fiddler, me, maybe the best fiddler on the bayous. Maybe the best fiddler in the world. Ain't nobody in St. Mary's parish dance or court or marry or christen a baby without me. But St. Mary's parish is a small place, eh? I am too big for St. Mary's. I have an idea to go to New Orleans, fiddle on the radio, make my fortune, buy a white house with columns on the front."

He lifts his hands, his fingers square at the tips, his nails trimmed short and black with dirt, and he laughs. It is not a good laugh.

"You maybe don't know, little swamp owl girl, these hands are like gold. I fiddle the devil out of hell once and I fiddle him down again. I will make those *couyons* in New Orleans lie down and lick my bare feets."

He glances at me for a reaction, but I just sit there. Tante Eulalie is right. Close to, 'Dres Petitpas is not funny at all. He wants what he wants, and he doesn't care what he has to do to get it. He can't trick me, because I know what he is. What he go do, I wonder, when he finds that out?

As if he hears my thoughts, 'Dres Petitpas frowns. He looks around the cabin, and his eyes light on Tante Eulalie's fiddle I've hung on the wall. He gets up and goes to it, takes it down from its hook, and runs his thumb over the strings. They twang dully. "Good thing you loosen the strings," he says. "Keep the neck from warping, eh? Nice little fiddle. You play?"

I don't remember getting up, but I am standing with my hands twisted in my skirts. "No," I say as lightly as I can. "Stupid old thing. I don't know why I don't throw it into the bayou."

"You won't mind if I tune her, then." He brings the fiddle to the table and starts to tighten the strings. I sit down again. "One day," he says, picking up the story. "One day, my five sons Clopha and Aristile and 'Tit Paul and Louis and Télémaque come to me. Clopha is in love, him, and he wants my blessing to marry Marie Ey-mard.

"Now, I got nothing against marriage. My wife Octavie and me been married together twenty-two years, still in love like two doves. My sons are good boys, smart boys. Clopha can read anything you put in front of him—writing, printing, it don't matter. And young Louis adds up numbers fast as I can play my fiddle. But they got no sense about women. So I tell Clopha that I will choose a wife for him, if he wants one. And when the time comes, I'll choose wives for the other boys, too. Wives are too important a matter to be left to young men.

"'My foot!' Clopha say. 'I go marry Marie without your blessing, then.'

" 'You go do more than that,' I tell him. 'You go marry with my curse. Remember, I got the devil on a string. My curse is something to fear. And you see if Marie Eymard go marry together with you when she find out you don't bring her so much as a stick of furniture or a woven blanket or a chicken to start life with.'

"Well, you think that be the end of it. But my sons are hardheaded boys. They argue this way and that. And then I have an idea, me, how I can shut their mouths for once and all. I offer my sons a bet."

He stops and holds the fiddle up to his ear and plucks the strings in turn, listening intently. "Better," he says. He lays the fiddle on the table, pulls a lump of rosin from his pocket, and goes to work on the bow.

"The bet," he says, "is this. I will fiddle and my sons will dance. If I stop fiddling before they all stop dancing, I go bless their marriages and play at their weddings. If not, Clopha and Louis come to New Orleans with me to read anything that needs to be read, and Aristile, 'Tit Paul, and Télémaque go tend the shrimp boats and help Octavie with the hogs and the chickens and the cotton."

'Dres Petitpas grins under his moustache. "It is a good bet I make, eh? I cannot lose.

"My sons go off behind the hog pen and talk for a while, and when they come back, they tell me that they will take my bet—on two conditions. One, they will dance one after another, so I must fiddle out five in a row. Two, I will provide a partner for them—one partner, who must dance as long as I fiddle.

"Now I am proud of my five sons, because this shows they are smart as well as strong. They know I can play the sun up and down the sky. They know I can play until the cows come home and long after the chickens come to roost. They know nobody human can dance as long as I can play." He looks away from the bow and straight at me. "They don't know you."

I turn my head away. I don't know how long I can dance. All night, for sure, then paddle home after and dance in the cabin while I do my chores. Maybe the next night, too. I might could do what I guess 'Dres Petitpas wants. But I won't. I won't show my face to the people of Pierreville, my white face and pink eyes and white, white hair. I won't go among the ducks and risk their pecking—not for anybody and for sure not for 'Dres Petitpas.

"I see you at the Doucet *fais-do-do*," he says. "I see you dance like a leaf in the wind, like no human girl I ever seen. I go to a man I know, a hairy, sharp-tooth man, and he tell me about a little swamp owl girl dances all night long at the loup-garous' ball. I think this girl go make a good partner for my boys. What you say, *hein*? You come dance with my five strong sons?"

My heart is sick inside me, but I can't be angry at the loup-garou who betrayed me. 'Dres Petitpas is a hard man to say no to. But I do. I say, "No."

"I don't ask you to dance for nothing," 'Dres Petitpas coaxes me. "I go give you land to raise cotton on and a mule to plow it with."

"No."

"You greedy girl, you," he says, like it's a compliment. "How you like to marry one of my sons, then? Any one you like. Then you be important lady, nobody dare call you swamp owl girl or little white slug."

I jump up and go for him, so angry the blood burns like ice in my veins. I stop when I see he's holding Tante Eulalie's fiddle over his head by the neck.

"Listen, *chère*. You don't help me, I take this fiddle and make kindling out of it, and I break that loom and that wheel, and then I burn this cabin to ash. What you say, *chère*: yes or no? Say 'yes' now, and we have a bargain. You help me win my bet and I give you land and a mule and a husband to keep you warm. That is not so bad a bargain, *hein?*"

It sticks in my throat, but I have no choice. "Yes," I say.

"That's good," Murderes Petitpas says, and he tucks Tante Eulalie's fiddle under his chin and draws the bow across the strings. It sounds a note, strong and sweet. "The contest is set for Saturday night—that's three nights from now. We start after supper, end when the boys get tired. Make a real *fais-do-do*, eh? Put the children down to sleep?" He laughs with the fiddle, a skip of notes. "Might could take two-three days. You understand?"

I understand very well, but I can't help trying to find a way out. "I do not know if I can dance for three days and nights."

"I say you can, and I say you will. I got your fiddle, me."

"I cannot dance in the sun."

A discord sounds across the strings. "Little white slug don't like sun, eh? No matter. We make the dance in Doucet's barn. You know where it at already." Tante Eulalie's fiddle mocks me with one of the tunes he played that night. Despite myself, my feet begin to move, and he laughs. "You a dancing fool, *chère*. I win my bet, my sons learn who's boss, and I go be a rich man on the radio."

He's fiddling as he speaks and moving toward the door. I'm dancing because I can't help it, with tears of rage stinging the back of my nose and blurring my eyes. I don't let them fall till he's gone, though. I have that much pride.

The rest of that night is black, black, and the next two days, too. There are knocks at my door, but I do not answer them. I am too busy thinking how I will make Murderes Petitpas sorry he mess with me. I take my piece of blue cloth off the loom and sew a dancing dress for myself, with Tante Eulalie's lace to the neck and cuffs. Early the third morning, I make a gris-gris with Tante Eulalie's gold ring. I sleep and wash myself and put on the dress and braid my hair in a tail down my back and hang the gris-gris around my neck. Then I get in my pirogue and paddle through the maze of the swamp to the warm lights of the Doucets' farm

It is very strange to tie my pirogue to the wharf and walk up to the barn in the open. Under my feet, the dirt is warm and smooth, and the air smells of flowers and spices and cooking meat. The barn doors are open and the lantern light shines yellow on the long tables set up outside and the good people of Pierreville swarming around with plates and forks, scooping jambalaya and gumbo, dirty rice and fried okra, red beans and grits from the dishes and pots.

At first they don't see me and then they do, and all the gumbo ya-ya of talk stops dead. I walk toward them through a quiet like the swamp at sunset. My heart beats so hard under my blue dress that I think everybody must see it, but I keep my chin up. The people are afraid, too. I can smell it on them, see it in their flickering eyes that will not meet mine, hear it in their whispers: *Haunt. Devil. Look at her eyes— like fireballs. Unnatural.*

A woman steps in front of me. She is wiry and faded, with white-streaked hair in stiff curls around her ears and a flowery dress made up of store-bought calico. "I am Octavie Petitpas," she says, her voice tight with fear. "You come to dance with my sons?"

I see 'Dres Petitpas grinning his yellow-tooth grin over her head. "Yes, ma'am."

"Your partner's here, boys," 'Dres Petitpas shouts. "Time to dance!"

The fiddler turns to five men standing in an uneven line—his five sons. The first must be Clopha the reader, thin as his father is wide, with lines of worry across his forehead. Aristile and 'Tit Paul are big like their father, with trapped, angry eyes.

Louis is a little older than me, with a mustache thin as winter grass. Télémaque is still a boy, all knees and elbows.

I walk up to Clopha and hold out my hand. He looks at it, then takes it with a sigh. His hand is cold as deep water.

We all troop into the Doucets' barn, Clopha and me and 'Dres and every soul from St. Mary's parish who can find a place to stand. 'Dres climbs up on a trestle table, swings his fiddle to his shoulder, and starts to play "Jolie Blonde." He's grinning under his black mustache and stamping with his foot: he's having a good time, if nobody else is.

Clopha and I start to dance. I know right away that he will not last long. He has already lost the bet in his heart, him, already lost his Marie, who I can see watching us, her hands to her mouth and tears wetting her cheeks like a heavy rain. It is hard work dancing with Clopha. I think his father tricks him so often that he is like Old Boudreaux, who doesn't know how to win. This makes Clopha heavy and slow. I have to set the pace, change directions, twirl under his lax arm without help or signal. He plods through five, six, seven tunes, and then he stumbles and falls to his knees, shaking his head heavily until Marie Eymard comes and helps him up with a glare that would burn me black, if it could.

Then it is Aristile's turn.

Aristile is strong, him, and he is on fire to beat me. My head barely reaches his heart, and he crushes me to him as if to smother me. Half the time, I'm dancing on tiptoe. The other, I'm thrown here and there by his powerful arms, my shoulders aching as he puts me through my paces like a mule. It's wrestling, not dancing, but I dance with wolves, me, and I am stronger than I look. Six songs, seven, eight, nine, and then the tunes all run together under our flying feet. I do not even notice that Aristile has fallen until I find myself dancing alone. Then I blink at the sun pouring in through the barn door while two men carry Aristile to a long bench along the wall. I see a girl in pink kneel beside him with a cup and a cloth for his red face, and then I go up to 'Tit Paul and the music carries us away.

'Tit Paul is even more angry than his brother, and bigger and taller. He cheats. When we spin, he loosens his grip on my waist and wrist, hoping to send me flying into the crowd. I cling to him like a crab, me, pinching his shirt, his cuff, his thick, sweaty wrist. The dance is a war between us, each song a battle, even the waltzes. I win them all, and also the war, when 'Tit Paul trips over his own dragging feet and falls full length in the dust, barrel chest heaving, teeth bared like a mink. I feel no pity for him. I think some day 'Tit Paul will find a way to shove his father's curse back into his throat.

The music doesn't stop, so I don't either, two-stepping alone as men carry 'Tit Paul to the bench where he, too, is comforted by a dark-haired girl. Through the barn doors, I see that it is dark again outside. I have danced, as 'Dres Petitpas has fiddled, for a night and a day. I am a little tired.

I dance up to Louis and hold out my hand.

Louis, who understands numbers, dances carefully, making me do all the work of turning, twisting, threading the needles he makes with his arms. From time to time, he speeds up suddenly, stumbles in my way so I must skip to keep from falling, throws me off balance whenever he can. After a time, his father sees what he's up to and shouts at him, and the spirit goes out of Louis like water draining out the hole in a bucket. There is a girl to give him water and soft words when he falls, too, a thin child with her hair in braids. I feel no pity for Louis, either, who is sly enough to beat his father at his own game when he's older.

It's light again by now, and I have danced for two nights and a day. I feel that my body is not my own but tied by the ears to Murderes Petitpas's fiddle bow. As long as he plays, I will dance, though my feet bleed into the barn floor and my eyes sting with the dust. 'Dres launches into "La Two-Step Petitpas," and I dance up to Télémaque who is still a child, and all I think when I hold out my hand is how glad I am Octavie gave her husband no more sons.

Télémaque, like me, is stronger than he looks. He has watched me dance with his four brothers, and he has learned that I cannot be tripped and I cannot be flung. He gives me a sad, sweet smile and limps as he dances, like he's a poor cripple boy I'd be ashamed to beat. I think it is a trick lower than any of Louis's, and I turn my face from him and let myself be lost in the stream of music. The bow of 'Dres Petitpas lifts my feet; his fingers guide my arms; his notes swirl me up and down and around as a paddle swirls the waters of the bayou. Around me, I feel something like a thunderstorm building, clouds piling, uneasy with lightning, the air growing thicker and thicker until I gasp for breath, dancing in the middle of the Doucets' barn with Télémaque limp at my bleeding feet and Murderes Petitpas triumphant on his table and his neighbors around us, growling and muttering.

"The last one down!" he crows. "What you say now, Octavie?"

Octavie Petitpas steps out from the boiling cloud of people, and if she looked worn before, now she looks gray as death.

"I say you are a fine fiddler, Murderes Petitpas. There ain't a man in the whole of Louisiana, maybe even the world, could do what you done. Or would want to."

"I am a fine fiddler," 'Dres says. "Still, I can't win my bet without my little owl girl, eh?" He waves his bow arm toward the five brothers sitting on the bench with their gray-faced sweethearts. "There they are, girl. Take your pick, you. Any one you want for your husband, and land and a mule, just like I promised. Murderes Petitpas, he keep his word, *hein?*"

I touch Tante Eulalie's lace at my neck for luck, and the little bulge of the grisgris hanging between my breasts and I say, "I do not want your land or your mule, 'Dres Petitpas. I do not want to marry any of your five sons. They have sweethearts of their own, them, nice Cajun girls with black eyes and rosy cheeks who will give them nice black-eyed babies."

An astonished wind of whispers blows through the crowd.

I go on. "I make you a bet now, Murderes Petitpas. I bet I can dance longer than you can. Dance with me, and if I win, you will give your blessing on your sons' marriages and return what you stole from me."

His eyes narrow under his broad-brimmed hat, and his fingers grip the neck of his fiddle. "No," he says. "I make no more bets, me. I have what I want. I will not dance with you."

"If you do not dance, Murderes Petitpas, everybody will think you are afraid of a little white-skin, pink-eye swamp girl, with her bare feets all bloody. What you afraid of, *hein?* You, who fiddle the devil out of hell and back down again?"

"I ain't afraid," says 'Dres through his flat yellow teeth. "I just ain't interested. You don't want to marry together with one of my sons, you go away back to the swamp. We got no further business together."

Louis gets to his feet and limps up beside me. "I say you do, Pap. If you win, you get my word I don't go run away first chance I see."

"And my word I don't go with him," says Télémaque, joining him.

Aristile comes up on the other side of me. "And mine."

"And mine," says 'Tit Paul.

"And you got my word not to make your life a living hell for taking my sons from me out of pure cussedness," says Octavie.

'Dres Petitpas looks down on the pack of us. His face is red as fire and his eyes glow hot as coals. "I see you boys still got some learning to do. I take your bet, swamp owl girl. You bring up a fiddler to play for us, and I dance the sun around again."

Everybody get real quiet, and Octavie says, "'Dres, you know there ain't no other fiddler in St. Mary's parish."

"That's it, then. I don't dance without music. The bet's off."

Someone in the crowd laughs. I'd laugh myself if this was a story I was hearing, about Young 'Dres Petitpas and how he owns all the music in St. Mary's parish.

Then another voice speaks out of the crowd. "I will play for this dance," says my friend Ulysse.

I spin around to see him in a store-bought suit, with his wild, black hair all slicked down with oil, looking innocent as a puppy in a basket.

"I have an accordion," he says, and gives me a sharp-toothed smile, and I know, just then, that I love him.

Another man turns up with a washboard and a spoon, and he and Ulysse jump up on the table as 'Dres Petitpas climbs down. Ulysse strikes up a tune I've heard a thousand times: *"T'es Petite et T'es Mignonne,"* which is Tante Eulalie's special tune for me. It gives my weary feet courage, and I dance up to Murderes Petitpas and take hold of his hand.

That is when the good people of Pierreville discover that Murderes Petitpas cannot dance. He has two left feet and he can't keep time, and he may know what a Window or a Cajun Cuddle or a Windmill looks like from above, but he for sure doesn't know how to do them. We stumble and fumble this way and that around the floor while the storm breaks at last in a gale of laughter. I am laughing, too, in spite of the pain in my feet, like dancing on nails or needles. I don't care if he falls first or I do. I've won already, me. The good people of Pierreville have seen 'Dres Petitpas for what he is. His sons will marry whoever they want, and he will not dare say a word against it.

Scree, scraw goes the accordion; *thunk-whoosh* goes the washboard, with Ulysse's hoarse voice wailing above it all, and I'm dancing like the midges above the water at dusk, with 'Dres stumbling after me. Somehow my feet don't hurt so much now, and my legs are light, and I enjoy myself. It is still dark outside the barn when 'Dres falls to his knees and bends his head.

As the accordion wheezes into silence, Octavie runs to her husband and puts her arms around his shoulders. His sons are kissing their sweethearts, and everybody's talking and fetching more food and slapping Ulysse and the washboard player on the back and pretending that I don't exist.

I step up to Octavie and I say, "Miz Petitpas, I'll take my fiddle now, my Tante Eulalie's fiddle your husband took from me."

She looks up and says, "Eulalie? Old Eulalie Favrot, that run away to the swamp? You kin to Eulalie Favrot?"

I nod. "Tante Eulalie take me in when I'm a baby, raise me like her own."

Octavie stands up and waves to an ancient lady in a faded homespun dress. "Tante Belda, you come here. This here's Eulalie Favrot's girl she raised. What you think of that?"

The ancient lady brought her face, wrinkled as wet cloth, right up to my lace collar so she can squint at it better. "That 'Lalie's wedding lace," she says. "I know it anywhere, me. How she keeping, girl?"

"She catch a cough this winter and die," I say.

"I sure am sorry to hear that," the ancient lady says. "'Lalie is my cousin, god-mother to my girl, Denise. She marry Hercule Favrot back in the 'teens sometime. Poor Hercule. He lose his shrimp boat and his nets to 'Dres Petitpas because of some *couyon* bet they make. Hercule take to drink, him, beat 'Lalie half to death. One morning she find him floating in the duck pond, dead as a gutted fish. 'Lalie go away after the funeral, nobody know where. She never have no children."

"She have me," I say. "Can I have her fiddle back now?"

Someone brings me a plate of food while I wait, but I am too tired to eat. My legs shake and my feet burn and sting. I think maybe I should sit down, but I can't move my legs, and how will I get home before light? I feel tears rising in my eyes, and then there is an arm around my waist and a voice in my ear.

"Cadence, *chère*," Ulysse says. "Miz Petitpas bring your fiddle. Take it, you, and I carry you home to sleep."

The plate disappears from my hands and Tante Eulalie's fiddle and bow appear in its place. Ulysse picks me up in his arms like I'm a little child, and I put my head against the tight weave of his store-bought suit and let him carry me out of the Doucets' barn.

The moon's getting low, and there's a chill in the air says dawn isn't far away. Ulysse sets me in my pirogue, crawls in after, casts off, and starts to paddle. I see the Doucets' wharf get small behind us, and the people of Pierreville standing there, watching us go. The ancient lady that once was the prettiest girl in the parish waves her handkerchief to us as we slip among the cypress trees and the lights of the Doucets' farm disappear behind Spanish moss and leaves.

We do not speak as we glide through the waterways. The music echoes in my ears, accordion and washboard and fiddle all together as they play them at the loup-garous' ball. I hum a little, quietly. The sun rises and Ulysse throws me his jacket to put over my head. When we get to my cabin, Ulysse carries me and my fiddle inside and closes the door.

Not long after, we are married together, Ulysse and me, with Tante Eulalie's gold ring. We still live in the swamp, but we visit Pierreville to hear the gossip and go to a *fais-do-do* now and then. Ulysse always brings his accordion and plays if they ask him. But I keep my dancing for the loup-garous' ball and for my husband in our own cabin. We dance to the music of our voices singing and the fiddling of our eldest daughter, 'Tit 'Lalie.

And Murderes Petitpas?

Old 'Dres Petitpas fiddles no more, him. He says he fiddle himself dry in those two days and two nights. He won't go out into the swamp either, but sits on his front porch and sorts eggs from Octavie's chickens and tells his grandchildren big stories about what a fine fiddler he used to be. Aristile has got Old Boudreaux's fiddle now, and you can hear him playing with his wife's brother and two cousins on the radio. But Aristile Petitpas ain't the only fiddler in St. Mary's parish, not by a long shot. There's plenty of fiddlers around these days, and singers and accordion players and guitar players. They play Cajun and zydeco, waltzes and two-steps and the new jit-terbugs, and they play them real fine. But there's none them can fiddle the devil out of hell, like 'Dres Petitpas did one time.

ELIZA GRISWOLD

Monkey

Eliza Griswold is a writer who focuses on conflict, human rights, and religion. Her reportage and analyses have appeared in The New Yorker, The New York Times Magazine, Harper's *magazine, and* The New Republic, *among other publications. She was a 2007 Nieman Fellow at Harvard University and is the recipient of the first Robert I. Friedman Award for international investigative reporting. Her first book of poems,* Wideawake Field, *was recently published by Farrar, Straus and Giroux.*

Her brief but powerful poem "Monkey" was originally published in The New Yorker *February 5.*

—E.D.

The soldiers are children and the monkey's young.
He clings to my leg, heart against calf—
a throat filling, refilling with blood.
Last week, the children ate his mother—
dashed her head against the breadfruit.
A young girl soldier laughs,
tears the baby from my leg
and hurls him toward the tree.
See, she says, you have to be rough.
When she was taken, the girl's
heart, too, pulsed in her throat.

REGGIE OLIVER

Mr. Poo-Poo

Reggie Oliver has been a professional playwright, actor, and theater director since 1975. Besides being a writer of original plays, he has translated the dramatic works of Feydeau, de Maupassant and others. Out of the Woodshed, *his biography of Stella Gibbons, author of* Cold Comfort Farm, *was published by Bloomsbury in 1998. His other publications include three volumes of ghost stories:* The Dreams of Cardinal Vittorini, The Complete Symphonies of Adolf Hitler, *both published by Haunted River Press, and* Masques of Satan, *published by Ash Tree. He lives near Aldeburgh, Suffolk, with his wife, the artist and actress, Joanna Dunham.*

"Mr. Poo-Poo" was first published in At Ease with the Dead, *edited by Barbara and Christopher Roden, and reprinted a few months later in Oliver's collection* Masques of Satan.

—E.D.

Across the rugged, dusty surface of Io, the inhabited satellite of Jupiter, a delegation of creatures was approaching. They were strange beings, two-legged, but short and squat, clad in some sort of iridescent material; their heads sprouted tentacles of a vaguely octopoid kind and their eyes were large, lidless, and saucerlike.

"Who are these folk, Zarkon?" I asked.

"They are the Minikoits, Captain Lysander," said Zarkon, "and they have lived on Io longer than any of us. Whence or how they came here, none knows, not even they."

"They are strange beings indeed. I have seen none like them. And what are their intentions?" I asked.

"Their ways are dark, Captain. Who knows whether they mean well or ill? I say to you only this: beware, for they have strange powers."

The little group halted a few yards from us and two of them stepped forward.

"Greetings," said the first Minikoit in a curious, metallic voice.

"Greetings, O stranger men," said the second, in a similar tone but with a perceptible South London accent.

"All right, cut!" said the Assistant Floor Manager. She listened hard to her cans, then she said, "Right. Keep V. T. running. We're going again straight away."

That was in the days when most television drama was shot in the studio. The director would be up in the control box and the Assistant Floor Manager would relay his instructions conveyed to her through "cans" (earphones). The program in question was the long-running BBC science fiction series *Jupiter 5*. Believe it or not, it still has a cult following, it sells well on DVD, and I am frequently asked to attend conventions of *Jupiter 5* fans.

"Okay," said the A. F. M. "We're going again. First positions, please! And, Second Minikoit, you got your line slightly wrong. It's 'Greetings, O strangers,' not 'Greetings, O stranger men.' Okay?"

The second Minikoit took off his tentacled head. Underneath he was glistening with sweat. "Sorry," he said in his normal voice. "Sorry, everyone."

"And can you please not take your head off! It holds things up. We're running late as it is. Makeup, can you please come and help—sorry—er—"

"Nicky," said the man who had taken his head off.

"Nicky! Right. Makeup, if you could please help Nicky put his head back on. The rest of you, first positions, please!"

"Sorry," said Nicky. "Sorry, everyone!"

"Okay!" said the A. F. M. "Can we move it, please! We're running behind time!" In those days we were always behind time.

In the recording break I was approached by Nicky, his Minikoit head tucked tidily under his arm. He was small and stocky, with blunt, swarthy features and a wide mouth that cut his flat head almost in half when he grinned. He looked as if he would have to shave twice a day. I thought in my snobbish way that he might be rather shy about addressing one of the "stars" of *Jupiter 5*, but this was not the case. There was a touch of obsequiousness about him, but he was not shy at all.

"You take your part very well," he said. I thanked him with what I hoped was distant, if uncondescending, cordiality, but he was one of those people on whom such nuances are lost. I am now rather ashamed of the airs I gave myself in those days, in spite of the fact that, in light of what happened later, I wish I had been a good deal frostier toward him.

His idea of a conversation was to ask me a question, listen to the answer without apparently taking much of it in, then, on the strength of this continued familiarity, ask me another, slightly more personal, one. He managed to extract from me the information that I was thirty-five, lived in a small house in Queen's Park, was married to a stage designer called Anne, and had two daughters, Isobel and Kitty, aged seven and five respectively. In self-defense I asked him some questions about himself in return. Nicky was in his mid-thirties, unmarried, and lived in a flat in Stoke Newington. His chief occupation, he told me, was as an "entertainer," but he supplemented his earnings from this by doing extra work and "small parts" on television. "Small parts" could be taken in two ways, because it was fairly obvious that he had landed the role of "2nd Minikoit" more because of his height—which was barely five foot three—than his acting ability.

Throughout the recording break he stuck to me so that I longed for some relief: for the director to need to have a word with me, or for the makeup girl to come and fuss with the unbecoming silver eye shadow that I wore as Captain Lysander of the Third Star Fleet. Just before the resumption of recording ended our conversation, he requested permission to ask me "a personal question." I shrugged my shoulders and braced myself for the ordeal.

He said, "Have you been born again through the Blood of Jesus?"

I am no good at smart replies, and anyway this sort of question always reduces me to near idiocy. I cannot remember what I said in answer to him; I only know that it was sheer babble, and that I was at last delivered from him by Makeup, who never feel they have done their job until they have powdered your nose with a soft brush before every scene. Max Factor never smelled sweeter.

At the end of the day's shooting I decided to get away quickly, rather than hobnob in the BBC bar, as I usually did in the vain hope of enhancing my career. I wanted to avoid Nicky at all costs. I had made good time and was just leaving the foyer of Television Center when I heard the scamper of feet behind me. It was Nicky. He asked if I had time for a drink and a chat, and I said that I had to get back to my wife and children. It was one of those lies which turn into the truth as you speak it. My eyes moistened at the prospect: I needed them.

Nicky did not seem particularly downcast by my rebuff. He said he understood, and that I was "very lucky to have a wife and kids." Then he handed me a card, saying, "I forgot to give you this."

By this time we were on the road outside Television Center, facing the White City tube station. I thanked him hurriedly and, in a reckless moment, hailed a taxi to take me home to Queen's Park. In the taxi I read the card. On it was his name, Nicky Beale, his address and telephone number, and, in bold red lettering, the following:

MR. POO-POO
ALL ROUND CHILDREN'S ENTERTAINER
FOR THAT SPECIAL KIDS' PARTY—
"IT'S GOT TO BE MR. POO-POO!"

Two months passed and my memories of Nicky faded. Then my daughter Isobel's eighth birthday arrived. Like most men, I always allow myself to be surprised by these events, but my wife Anne was prepared. She had consulted Isobel, who insisted that a full-scale children's party for all her friends was necessary—complete with an entertainer. Anne told me that she was organizing the food, the invitations, and the presents for the other children, and she was deputizing me to find the children's entertainer. It was not a task I relished, but it was little enough compared with what she had taken on.

As usual I put it off till almost the last moment, despite constant reminders from Anne and Isobel. When finally I had absolutely no excuses for further delay I found that I had no idea how to begin to find a children's entertainer. It was then that I remembered the card that Nicky Beale had given me, so, taking the line of least resistance, I rang his number.

He seemed quite unsurprised to hear from me, and I was pleased to find that he was brisk and businesslike on the phone. He promised a magic act, some organized games—prizes extra—and a cartoon show to wind up. The price he named was well within the budget prescribed by Anne.

I began to feel rather proud of myself, but when I announced to Anne that I had secured the services of Mr. Poo-Poo for Isobel's party she seemed disappointed.

"Couldn't you get hold of *Kidzexperience*?"

"What on earth is *Kidzexperience*?"

"Oh, darling, I told you all about her. You never listen, do you? It's this amazing young children's entertainer. She does a fantastic mime act dressed as a clown; then she gets the children doing all these weird creative things with bits of cutout colored paper."

"Sounds rather dreary to me."

"Oh, no! She's absolutely *the* latest thing. Everybody is having her for their kids' parties. She's done Royalty and everything." If my wife has a fault it is that she is a dedicated follower of fashion.

"Well, we've got Mr. Poo-Poo instead."

I don't think she was entirely reconciled to Mr. Poo-Poo, but she seemed mollified when I told her how little he was charging for his services.

If children knew how much their parents suffer to create and run their parties, would they grant them a dispensation? I doubt it. The tradition, reinforced by their peers, had somehow acquired the iron inevitability of Christmas and funerals. Much as I disliked the whole business, I have to concede that it could have been worse. Anne is a gifted organizer, and, besides having me to assist her, she had an able and willing subordinate in Magda, our Romanian au pair.

Magda was small, round, and dark. Looking at her, friends of ours invariably concluded that she came "of peasant stock" because that was what their preconceptions told them she looked like, but, as a matter of fact, she was the daughter of a minor civil servant and quite well educated. She had a decent command of English, which she was rapidly burnishing at night school. In the performance of her duties she was efficient, and the children seemed to like her. Despite Magda's being obviously very capable, my wife's attitude to her was vaguely pitying. She invariably referred to her, though of course never in her presence, as "poor Magda" because, like all beautiful women, Anne looked on physical inadequacies as an insuperable disadvantage in life. Magda, though not exactly ugly, was squat, full-breasted, and her upper lip was adorned with the whisper of an incipient mustache. Her best feature was a pair of large dark brown eyes, which in unguarded moments had a mournful expression, as if brooding on centuries of tragic Balkan history.

On the day of the party she was in her liveliest mood, and it was she who answered the door to Mr. Poo-Poo. Seeing them together in the hall I was at once struck by the strange similarity between the two of them. They were, to within a centimeter or so, of a height, both squat and swarthy, both with pronounced features that were rather too big for their faces. This vision of the pair stayed with me, but it was only later that it acquired a sinister aspect.

I began to feel rather nervous about Mr. Poo-Poo's performance, knowing that if it fell below a certain standard Anne (and Isobel) would hold me responsible, but I was reassured by the efficiency with which Nicky set up his props in the drawing room. When the children filed in after tea, they were in a good frame of mind because they had been fed extremely well.

Mr. Poo-Poo acquitted himself capably. His size was a distinct advantage because the children regarded him almost as one of them. He began with a magic act which was colorful and competent. Once or twice during the games that followed, he was in danger of losing control, but Magda always stepped in at exactly the right moment to restore order. There might have been some restlessness during the slightly antiquated cartoon show that rounded off the entertainment but, by this time, all the children were too exhausted to contrive serious disruption.

When it was over I congratulated Nicky on his performance. He smiled and shook my hand, but I could tell that his mind was on other things. His eyes kept straying toward Magda, who was helping him to pack up his equipment. I had noticed that she had watched his performance with great concentration, and now, while they tidied things away, they began chatting together as if they had been performing the same task for years. She helped carry his paraphernalia down to his car. On her return I commented that they seemed to have got on.

Magda said, "Maybe I go out with Poo-Poo." When I reported this remark to Anne she pursed her lips but made no comment.

It soon became clear that Nicky's intentions toward Magda were very formal and traditional. I cannot say that I had serious misgivings at first about the courtship, but certain aspects of it struck me as odd. When an arrangement had been made for Nicky to "take her out" he would arrive in his car and wait in it outside our house. Unless Magda had already joined him at the exact time appointed for their meeting he would hoot twice on his horn—"that's why he's called Mr. Poo-Poo," remarked Isobel astutely—but he would never, despite several invitations, come inside the house and wait for Magda there. The hooting business irritated me perhaps more than it should have done. I became absurdly worried about what the neighbors might think, but at the back of my mind was the sense that this peremptory summons of his fiancée signified a taste for power.

Further evidence of this emerged in the following weeks when I began to notice that, at odd moments of repose, Magda could be observed reading something called a Good News Bible, and that certain passages had been highlighted in brilliant orange or green. Knowing Magda to have come from a Catholic family, I inquired about this. Her reply was characteristically short and to the point.

"I join Mr. Nicky Poo-Poo's church," she said.

It made sense. His questioning of me about my faith when we had first met suggested that his own was of an intense and Evangelical kind. He therefore "belonged to a church" with all that that implied in terms of allegiance. It was necessary that anyone proposing to become one flesh with Mr. Poo-Poo should also become one flesh with his church. I suspected that conversion, being "born again," and the lustral properties of the Blood of Jesus were going to play their part. Still, I did not worry unduly. Each to his own, I thought, and this attitude might have been appropriate in other circumstances; but I had reckoned without the very peculiar qualities of Mr. Poo-Poo.

In due course, as I had rather expected, Magda told us that she intended to marry Mr. Poo-Poo, as we all now called him without even thinking of his real name, Nicky Beale. My wife Anne was a great deal more surprised than I by this turn of events, and a great deal more anxious. It had nothing to do with losing an au pair, the luxury of which we were beginning to regard as something of an extravagance. She thought that Magda was entering into the marriage for the wrong reasons, and had several serious talks with her on the subject, from which she came away baffled.

"She absolutely refutes the idea that she's marrying him to stay in England," said Anne, "and I think I sort of believe her. She says he's a good man. She says, 'I will live with him very well,' a typical Magda remark. She says his church is good and full of good people who take care of each other, and I have no doubt that it is, but what I don't get is the impression that she is in love with Mr. Poo-Poo, or, for that matter, that she is a fully fledged convert to his religion."

"What about her family in Romania?" I asked.

"I don't think she cares much for any of them. She's a bit vague on the subject, but I gather her father is several kinds of bastard. Oh, she's absolutely determined to go through with this, and there is nothing I can do to stop her."

My daughters, Kitty and Isobel, were thrilled by the idea of the marriage. For several weeks after the news was broken to them their favorite game was called "Mr. and Mrs. Poo-Poo," which, out of a strange childish delicacy, they never played or discussed in Magda's presence. In it Isobel took the role of the husband. Kitty, as Mrs. Poo-Poo, would find herself in need of a cake, or a kitten, or a colored handkerchief, and was just on the point of going out to the shops when Isobel in the role of Mr. Poo-Poo would inform her that there was no need. He would then wave his magic wand and produce the required object from a hat or a sleeve. Needless to say they were delighted to hear that they were going to be bridesmaids. I, in the inevitable absence of Magda's family, had been asked to give the bride away.

As the day approached both Anne and I noticed an appreciable lowering of Magda's spirits. She would not explain her change of mood, and indignantly resisted the suggestion that she was having doubts about the marriage. I don't think, anyway, that the explanation was as simple as that. On her evenings out she was fetched by her fiancé less frequently than before, but she never left the house without her Good News Bible. Suspicion that she was undergoing some kind of program of instruction was confirmed by the sight of a pile of books in her bedroom. They were paperbacks with luridly colored covers and bore titles such as *Challenge to the Ungodly*, *Weapons of Spiritual Warfare*, *Armageddon and Antichrist*, and *End Time Prophecies*. Once I overheard her talking to Nicky on the phone.

"No, Nicky," she was saying, "I miss this Bible Study because my bus is late, not because I do not want to come." Then, with a burst of defiance, she said, "But how do you know? You were not there!" A long silence followed in which she was obviously listening to his instructions. She began to say, "Yes, Nicky . . . Yes, Nicky" in a dull monotone. I did not like the note of submissiveness in her voice. Anne and I had always appreciated her lack of servility, her simple, forthright views, her strong sense of self-worth. I had the feeling that this last was being deliberately and systematically eroded, but whether by Mr. Poo-Poo or his Church, I could not say. Perhaps they were acting in concert.

By this time the marriage was only a week away, and all thoughts of dissuading her from going through with it had to be set aside. When the day came we did our best to be cheerful about it. The costs of the nuptial celebrations were to be defrayed by the church, but I paid for a car to take myself and Anne, Magda, and her bridesmaids, my daughters, all the way from Queen's Park to the Peniel Gospel Church in Stoke Newington. Magda was all in white, which did not suit her. There was something grotesque about this dark, stocky little woman, veiled and puffed in muslin and tulle with her bouquet of orange blossom. She looked like a battered meringue.

The Peniel Gospel Church in Stoke Newington was a large Victorian Gothic church which had been taken over by Mr. Poo-Poo's sect when it proved to be surplus to Anglican requirements. Inside, pews had been torn out, carpets laid, and sound systems installed. The entrance of the bride was greeted by a lively number played on guitars, fiddles, electric keyboards, and several tambourines banged by a number of children, who were enthusiastic, uncoordinated, and overweight. This was evidently a church event, rather than a family one. Conducting the ceremony was the leader of Mr. Poo-Poo's church. His name was Jim Rundle, and he was known to all as Pastor Jim. He was a big man with a face that might have been solidly handsome before corpulence took its toll, and he wore a shiny suit over a pink vest and dog collar. After joining the couple with a fairly conventional form of words, Pastor Jim delivered a sermon, eloquent in parts but overlong and repetitive. I was interested to hear what he would say about the bride and groom.

"Nicky here," he said, "has been a faithful laborer in our vineyard for over three years. He really loves the Lord and His Word, and we really praise You, Lord, that he has brought our sister Magda here out of the darkness into new birth through the Blood of Jesus."

At this there were loud murmurs from all around us of "Amen" and "Praise the Lord." Anne and I looked at one another. We took the implication that Magda's life before her conversion had been one of "darkness" rather amiss. Perhaps we shouldn't have done, but in the long run I was more disconcerted by the curiously impersonal terms in which he referred to the couple, as if their whole identity were tied up in their salvation.

After the service there was a reception in the large, naked church hall next to the church. There were mounds of sandwiches and cakes. To drink there was orange juice and tea; alcohol had no role to play. I was approached by Pastor Jim, who greeted me warmly and thanked me for my small part in the ceremony. I could see that he was anxious to communicate to me that I would not be called upon to make a speech on behalf of the bride, and that there would be nothing so pagan as a toast. I indicated my relief that this was the case, though I had prepared something.

I asked why Nicky's parents were not present at the wedding, and Pastor Jim explained that they had fallen out with their son when he had joined the Peniel Gospel Church. He did not explain further except to say, "They're very worldly people."

What he meant by this I could not say, but his description made me feel immense sympathy toward them. I had a vision, almost certainly inaccurate, of cheerful, champagne-sipping sophisticates: I was worldly myself; perhaps they were like me. There was a little pause while Pastor Jim and I both thought our own thoughts, and when he spoke again it was almost as if he were making a confession.

He said, "This is a day of great rejoicing for us here, you know. The fact is, we were beginning to be a little worried about Nicky. He's a good lad, and very close to Christ, but he was extremely anxious to marry. Perhaps a little too anxious, if you understand my meaning, but then I think that text of Paul's—'It is better to marry than to burn'—was very much one that spoke to his heart. I think some of the young women in the congregation found his attentions a little needy, if you know what I mean. So Magda here is a real gift from God. They seem well suited, don't they? And, of course, he helped to bring her to Christ, so it's a double blessing, isn't it?"

Very soon Anne, the children, and I wanted to leave the celebrations. When we said good-bye to Magda, still in wedding cake white, there were tears in her eyes.

For over a month we heard nothing from the Poo-Poos, not even a postcard from wherever they had honeymooned. Magda became an inhabitant of the past, and not even Isobel and Kitty mentioned her after a couple of weeks. Then, at about eleven one sultry August evening, someone was ringing our doorbell, repeatedly, violently. It woke the children. I answered the door, taking care to keep the chain on. Through the gap in the door I looked down on a pair of dark frightened eyes in a dead-white face. It was Magda.

"I come in, please?" she said. She came in. She was wearing a flimsy mackintosh and carried a large plastic bag full of her belongings. As soon as she saw Anne she started to cry. I elected to put the children back to bed—they had crept to the top of the stairs to witness this dramatic scene—while my wife handled Magda.

I got Isobel and Kitty back into their room, but they were full of wonder and excitement. When it comes to the lives of others, children do not differentiate between tragedy and comedy: it is all drama and excitement to them.

"Why was Magda crying?" asked Isobel.

"I think she was just very tired," I said.

Having pondered this, Isobel said, "We want ask her what it's like being married to Mr. Poo-Poo."

"We want ask her," said Kitty, who was at the stage when she toed her elder sister's party line religiously.

"Perhaps she'll tell you tomorrow," I said. "But just now she's very very tired."

"Then why is she talking to Mum in the spare room?" asked Isobel.

This was unanswerable, so I read them a story until they fell asleep.

After that, I went downstairs, made myself and Anne a cup of tea, and, when Anne didn't come, drank them both myself. I watched television listlessly for a while and then went to bed. I was still not asleep when Anne came in shortly after one o'clock. She sat down heavily on the bed with the words, "Your Mr. Poo-Poo is an absolute monster."

"He's not *my* Mr. Poo-Poo," I said, but she ignored this and began to undress. I asked, "What has he been doing? Knocking her about or something?"

"No. Not exactly. But he makes demands." There was a moment when Anne hesitated before breaking Magda's confidence. "You won't tell anyone else?"

"Good God, no!"

"He wants it all the time, apparently. I won't go into details—they're too horrible—but he wants it at least once a night, and sometimes he'll demand it in the middle of the day if he's at home. I mean Magda's a perfectly healthy, normal girl, but she just can't stand it. And he won't take no for an answer."

"You mean he rapes her?"

"Not strictly speaking, but to all intents. He puts her under such pressure. She's terrified of him."

"Good God!"

"I know, and she has begun to find him physically repulsive. Yes, of course he never was a thing of beauty, but I genuinely think there was some sort of a mutual attraction at first. She wasn't just looking for a meal ticket. And he's pretty horrible in other ways, too. He likes to control everything she does: when she does the washing, when she cleans the flat, what she buys at the shops, even what she wears. He's incredibly mean with money, and sometimes, when he's out doing a whole day of TV-extra work, he locks her in the flat so she can't get out at all."

"How did she get away?"

"Fire escape."

Anne and I discussed the situation into the early hours and decided, though we could barely afford it, to reemploy Magda as an au pair and let her stay until she could find somewhere else to go. Kitty and Isobel were for some reason delighted, but I noted that the relationship between them and Magda was different from what it had been. She had become more their servant than their nanny, but their tyranny was light. Despite all our protests they insisted on calling Magda "Mrs. Poo-Poo," which she bore stoically, even cheerfully.

Two days later, at six in the evening, the telephone rang, and I answered it in the hallway.

"Is Magda there?" said a voice I had half expected. It was Mr. Poo-Poo. I hesitated. "Before you commit the sin of lying," he went on, "I ought to say, I have been watching the house. I do know she's there."

I asked him what he wanted.

"I want to speak to Magda."

"She may not want to speak to you."

"She is my wife," said Mr. Poo-Poo. By this time Magda had appeared at the top of the stairs. Covering the mouthpiece of the phone I asked her if she wanted to speak to her husband. She shook her head violently, then made a curious gesture with her right hand as if she were warding off some evil.

"She doesn't want to speak to you," I said.

"I'm not giving up. She has gone astray and I must call her back. But just tell her this. Tell her that she is running the risk of eternal hellfire. Tell her. Hell is not a joke." Then he rang off.

Magda came downstairs.

"What did my husband say?" she asked. I mumbled something. "He talk about hell?" I nodded. Magda looked at me defiantly. "I tell you," she said, "I do not give this about Mr. Poo-Poo's hell!" and she snapped her fingers. It was a typical Magda reaction—forthright, bold, uncomplicated—but her voice had cracked as she spoke.

The following day, at exactly the same time, the telephone rang again. Mr. Poo-Poo was a creature of method. He said he wanted to speak to Magda, and I said that I would not let him speak to Magda unless she wanted to speak to him. He asked if I had passed on to her his message about hell, and I said yes, because after a fashion I had.

"I am only warning her of what will come to pass," said Mr. Poo-Poo. "That is the punishment, you see, that God has reserved for the evildoer. I have been told what will happen. Ours is a charismatic church, and there are those who speak in tongues, and there are those who have visions laid on them. This woman in our church, Mrs. Harris—but we call her Sister Bernice—she had a vision laid on her about the End Times, the coming Judgment, and about hell. Sister Bernice is very close to Christ, and her message is a warning from Jesus about the wages of sin. She said she had a vision of hell. She said it's like a great pit, all dark, and miles deep. Like thousands of miles. And there's this thing in the pit which is built up high, so high, but it never reaches out of the darkness; and this thing is like a great house or a block of flats, only it's made of sticks. Little sticks, like twigs. It's made of millions of twigs, and there are all these rooms in it, and thousands of passages, all twig. And in the little twig rooms live the damned. And they can move from one room to another through the passages, but they can never get out. They can climb up the twig stairs and along the passages, but they can never get out if they go up or down or sideways. The damned are always living there, but then someone starts a fire. And it's like panic, and everyone is running along these passages made of sticks to escape, but the passages start burning and falling into each other. And people are burning, and like frying and bubbling up—Sister Bernice said she saw all this in her vision— but there's no fainting or dying because people there are dying forever, and there's no relief from the pain because there's no anesthetics in hell. And they run and run and there's just more little rooms and passages, all made of twigs and sticks. And they all burn in the end. Pastor Jim says that in like the olden days, the born again Christians used to put a cat in like a wicker basket, and put it over a fire. And I know that's supposed to be cruel, but the cat was like the symbol of the devil, and the screams of the cat was like reminding them of the sounds the damned might make in hell, and how the cat was caught in the burning basket like forever and—"

At this point I managed to summon up enough willpower to put down the phone.

I told no one in the house about Mr. Poo-Poo's call, but the following day I found the number of the Peniel Gospel Church in the phone book, rang it, and asked to speak to Pastor Jim. He was aware of the situation. Despite a great deal of talk about him "understanding exactly" how I felt, it was clear that he was fully behind Mr. Poo-Poo. I told him about Mr. Poo-Poo's obsession with hell. Pastor Jim was unsympathetic.

"I realize that to a liberal intellectual like yourself the word 'hell' is either a joke or a swear word," said Pastor Jim—filling the phrase "liberal intellectual" with all the withering contempt that those who are neither habitually feel toward those whom they consider to be both—"but to us simple folk who live in the real world it is a very

serious thing. Eternal damnation is no joke, believe you me. I am not going to criti-
cize anyone who loves his wife so much that he wants to save her from being
damned to all eternity."

Like most arguments based firmly on false premises, this was hard to answer, so I
didn't. That evening I waited for the telephone to ring, but it did not. The following
morning I noticed that a letter had come for Magda. The envelope was handwritten
in pale purple ballpoint. It did not look like a masculine hand, but the post code was
Stoke Newington, so I stood by Magda as she opened it. Inside was a single, lined
sheet of paper that looked as if it had been torn from a notebook. On it was written:

"At the prayer meeting last night, many of us spoke in tongues, and I had laid on
me this word of prophesy:

"The Day of Judgment is nigh. If you don't return, you'll burn.

"Sister Bernice."

"This Sister Bernice, I know her," said Magda. "She is not right in the head"; and
she tore up the paper.

The following day three letters came from Stoke Newington, the addresses handwritten in brown felt-tip pen. In Magda's envelope was a plain piece of paper on
which was scrawled: "It is better to marry than to burn. I Corinthians 7 v. 9." The
other two envelopes were addressed to my daughters Kitty and Isobel. As they too
obviously came from Mr. Poo-Poo I opened them, fearing the worst; but the contents simply baffled me. Inside each envelope was a piece of paper on which had
been drawn, in the same brown felt-tip pen, a crisscross of lines. I could not think
what they meant, except, I suppose, they might possibly be intended to represent a
heap of sticks or twigs.

During the next week our family seemed to be afflicted by lethargy and ill luck.
Neither Anne nor I wanted to attribute this to anything other than one of those periodic downturns of fortune to which everyone is subject. It was exacerbated by my
own irritability at losing a job of which I had been almost certain. I preferred to
brood in private rather than share my frustration, but this only increased the tension.
The children began to have nightmares, to which they were not normally prone.
Magda was taciturn and stoic. Both Anne and I noticed that the electric lights in the
house were dimmer than they should be, and that a more than usual number of light
bulbs were expiring. An electrician was called in but could offer no explanation or
remedy.

Then, on the Saturday morning—it was late August—we woke to see a sky of
heavy unbroken cloud. It was as if a great grey eiderdown had been stretched across
London. It brooded over the red brick, late-nineteenth-century bank clerk's houses
of Queen's Park, creating a strange, stuffy, indoor effect, as confined and cluttered as
a Victorian parlor. The drapery of clouds hung low, moving slowly across the scene,
but releasing not a drop of water, and the pressure of the atmosphere held our heads
in a steady, aching grip, like a pair of tongs applied to the temples. In the afternoon
I remember looking out from our landing window onto the garden below and longing for rain. All the foliage seemed dull and dusty under the gray sky. My attention
was drawn to a brown patch in the middle of the lawn, about a foot or so in diameter. From where I was I could not make it out. It might have been an animal had it
not been so immobile—a dead animal? The unfamiliar thing annoyed me, so I went
downstairs and into the garden to investigate.

It was not an animal, living or dead, and it was not something which should have
filled me with fear, but it did. It was a neat pile of dead twigs and sticks, arranged in
a little tumulus as if in preparation for a bonfire. I picked up the lot, disregarding the

thorns on some of the twigs which made me bleed, and crammed it into a dustbin; then I went indoors to phone Mr. Poo-Poo.

He was out, so I shouted instead into his answering machine until the thing beeped and terminated my call. I cannot remember all that I said, but I am sure I was incoherent, and must have sounded mad. I did tell him to stop threatening us.

I have no idea how I spent the rest of the day, but I do remember that the weather had not broken by the time we went to bed. I fell into a thick, heavy sleep which was interrupted only a couple of hours later by the sound of thunder. This might have been a relief had it not been punctuated by the screams of our children. Anne, for some unaccountable reason, was still wrapped in sleep, so I leapt out of bed and ran to their room.

Kitty and Isobel were sitting bolt upright and staring at the window opposite them. The curtains had been opened since we said good-night. In the small second before I turned toward what they were looking at out of the window I was aware of a sudden and complete silence. There was no thunder, no distant noise of London traffic, nothing. When I looked at the window I saw through it what I could not, should not have seen.

In a pale lusterless light I saw that a great structure was raised that went up miles high and went down miles below into the infinite darkness. It was a great tower of Babel, like those depicted in old paintings, or books of Bible stories, except that it was not made of stone, it was made of a great network of twigs and sticks. Trapped in this monstrous basket weave of chambers and crooked corridors was an infinite number of living creatures, some human, some mammalian, some birdlike, but all of them pale, naked, hairless, and featherless with open, haunted eyes. I thought some saw me and stretched out feeble, attenuated limbs toward me in supplication— because they were not only trapped, they were beginning to burn. In a hundred places, then a thousand, then a million, flames began to flicker. Parts of the structure started to crumble and collapse as the flames took hold. The creatures struggled in their tangles of burning sticks and let out silent cries. They tried to claw their way from one web of burning wreckage to another, but they did nothing but fall, and fall on other burning creatures. Now the whole structure seemed alight and full of agony and chaos, but still it held to its monstrous height and depth. I tried to call out—on what? on a merciful God?—but no sound came. Then there was a bang and a flash, a great roar of rain, and the vision vanished, to be replaced by darkness and the sparkle of drops and rivulets of rain on the window. Isobel and Kitty began to scream again and I ran to comfort them.

The following morning I found Magda standing in the hall with her bags packed. She said, "I am doing no good here. I go back to Mr. Poo-Poo." I somehow knew that all Anne's and my protests would have no effect.

"I prefer to go to Mr. Poo-Poo than go to hell," she said.

Anne said, "You don't really believe that do you, Magda?" Magda shrugged her shoulders. I said that the least we could do was to drive her back to Stoke Newington, so she rang Mr. Poo-Poo to inform him of her return. From what I could gather by standing near the phone as Magda spoke to him, Mr. Poo-Poo was not in the least surprised by her decision. He said he would wait in for her.

When we arrived at Mr. Poo-Poo's flat in Stoke Newington, I having followed Magda's curt, precise instructions, she told me to park on the other side of the road from the house where his flat was situated. She got out of the car without a word, her belongings in a suitcase that we had given to her as a leaving present.

I did not drive off immediately. From my car I watched Magda cross the street and ring the front door bell. There was a long wait, then the door was opened wide by Mr. Poo-Poo. He was wearing a buff cardigan and a pair of green trousers very well pressed, with a crease at the front as sharp as a knife. He had put on weight. There was no expression on his face and he offered her no greeting. She entered the dark hall with bowed head, carrying her suitcase unaided. Then he closed the street door behind her.

We heard no more of either of them. Occasionally, with a twitch of guilt, Anne would say, "I wonder how the Poo-Poos are getting on." I think she used the name deliberately, so that Nicky and Magda Beale would somehow cease to be real people. She was relegating them to a comic mythology of the past because there was, after all, nothing we could do about them, or so we told ourselves.

Just over a year later, one dark, rainy evening in November, I went to fetch my second daughter Kitty from a children's party in Notting Hill Gate. When I rang the bell I was confronted by the usual harassed mother who said, "Come in. You're a little early. The entertainer is still doing his stuff."

I could hear that a raucous time was being had in the big drawing room off the main hall. I would have preferred to have sat peacefully in the hall, and perhaps chatted with the lady of the house, but she had not the time nor the patience for this. She chivvied me into the sitting room, where I joined a small knot of other attendant parents.

Our offspring, seated on the white shag pile carpet in front of us, were watching an old-fashioned Punch and Judy show, never a form of theater that has appealed to me. Mr. Punch, hugging a great stick in his stumpy little arms, was smashing Judy about with tremendous vigor, and the children were responding with squeals of delight. Emblazoned on the red-and-white-striped awning that hung down from the puppet stage were the words:

MR. POO-POO

It is extraordinary how the body takes over at moments like these. Before my conscious mind had digested this information, it seemed to me, my heart was knocking and the sour taste of fear was in my mouth. Why? I was in no way threatened. Did I imagine that Kitty, sitting in the front row of the audience, was being corrupted? Punch and Judy was certainly a new addition to Mr. Poo-Poo's repertoire as an entertainer, and it was one at which he had gained a ghastly expertise.

"That's the way to do it!" shrieked Mr. Poo-Poo through his swozzle, as Mr. Punch gave Judy another tremendous crack with the bludgeon. The children cried out with joy. The strange inhuman distortion of Mr. Poo-Poo's voice brought to mind the mechanized, metallic tones of the Minikoits in *Jupiter 5*.

To the right and behind the puppet stage a woman was sitting very still and upright on a dining chair, her back to the wall. At her feet was a child asleep in a carrycot. I wondered who she was. The au pair of the house? Then I recognized Magda. She had not been easy to identify, because everything about her had changed; all color had gone from her face and clothing, and even the darkness of her lustrous eyes had lost its intensity.

I smiled at her and she pretended not to see me, but I was sure she had. The moment I endeavored to make eye contact she had looked away and then down at the child. Evidently it was hers, because I recognized that intense gaze of concentrated love with which a mother looks at her own baby. For a moment it wiped the gloom from her face. She twitched at the blankets of the baby's cot but otherwise made no movement. Above her the little proscenium of Mr. Poo-Poo's puppet stage gaped like the mouth of Hell.

ELIZABETH HAND

Winter's Wife

Elizabeth Hand is a longtime reviewer for the Washington Post Book World, The Village Voice, *and* DownEast *magazine, among others, and she writes a regular column for* The Magazine of Fantasy & Science Fiction. *A multiple-award-winning author, her most recent works include the psychological thriller* Generation Loss, *a novella,* Illyria, *and a short story collection,* Saffron and Brimstone: Strange Stories. *Hand has just finished writing* Wonderwall, *a young adult novel about Arthur Rimbaud. She lives in Maine with her two teenage children and her partner, U.K. critic John Clute.*

"Winter's Wife" was published in Gardner Dozois and Jack Dann's outstanding anthology, Wizards.

—E.D.
—K.L. & G.G.

Winter's real name was Roderick Gale Winter. But everyone in Paswegas County, not just me and people who knew him personally, called him Winter. He lived in an old schoolbus down the road from my house, and my mother always tells how when she first moved here he scared the crap out of her. It wasn't even him that scared her, she hadn't even met him yet; just the fact that there was this creepy-looking old schoolbus stuck in the middle of the woods with smoke coming out of a chimney and these huge piles of split logs around and trucks and cranes and heavy equipment, and in the summer all kinds of chainsaws and stuff, and in the fall deer and dead coyotes hanging from this big pole that my mother said looked like a gallows, and blood on the snow, and once a gigantic dead pig's head with tusks which my mother said was scarier even than the coyotes. Which, when you think of it, does sound pretty bad, so you can't blame her for being freaked out. It's funny now because her and Winter are best friends, though that doesn't mean so much as it does other places, like Chicago where my mother moved here from, because I think everyone in Shaker Harbor thinks Winter is their friend.

The schoolbus, when you get inside it, is sweet.

Winter's family has been in Shaker Harbor for six generations, and even before that they lived somewhere else in Maine.

"I have Passamaquoddy blood," Winter says. "If I moved somewhere else, I'd melt."

He didn't look like a Native American, though, and my mother said if he did have Indian blood it had probably been diluted by now. Winter was really tall and skinny, not sick skinny but bony and muscular, stooped from having to duck through the door of the schoolbus all those years. He always wore a gimme cap that said WINTER TREE SERVICE., and I can remember how shocked I was once when I saw him at Town Meeting without his hat and he had almost no hair. He'd hunt and butcher his own deer, but he wouldn't eat it—he said he'd grown up dirt poor in a cabin that didn't even have a wooden floor, just pounded earth, and his family would eat anything they could hunt, including snake and skunk and snapping turtle. So he'd give all his venison away, and when people hired him to butcher their livestock and gave him meat, he'd give that away too.

That was how my mother met him, that first winter fifteen years ago when she was living here alone, pregnant with me. There was a big storm going on, and she looked out the window and saw this tall guy stomping through the snow carrying a big paper bag.

"You a vegetarian?" he said when she opened the door. "Everyone says there's a lady from away living here who's going to have a baby and she's a vegetarian. But you don't look like one to me."

My mother said no, she wasn't a vegetarian, she was a registered certified massage therapist.

"Whatever the hell that is," said Winter. "You going to let me in? Jesus Q. Murphy, is that your woodstove?"

See, my mother had gotten pregnant by a sperm donor. She had it all planned out, how she was going to move way up north and have a baby and raise it—him, me—by herself and live off the land and be a massage therapist and hang crystals in the windows and there would be this good energy and everything was going to be perfect. And it would have been, if she had moved to, like, Huntington Beach or even Boston, someplace like that, where it would be warmer and there would be good skate parks, instead of a place where you have to drive two hours to a skate park and it snows from November till the end of May. And in the spring you can't even skate on the roads here because they're all dirt roads and so full of pot holes you could live in one. But the snowboarding is good, especially since Winter let us put a jump right behind his place.

But this part is all before any snowboarding, because it was all before me, though not much before. My mother was living in this tiny two-room camp with no indoor plumbing and no running water, with an ancient woodstove, what they call a parlor stove, which looked nice but didn't put out any heat and caused a chimney fire. Which was how Winter heard about her, because the volunteer fire department came and afterwards all anyone was talking about at the Shaker Harbor Variety Store was how this crazy lady from away had bought Martin Weed's old rundown camp and now she was going to have a baby and freeze to death or burn the camp down—probably both—which probably would have been okay with them except no one liked to think about the baby getting frozen or burned up.

So Winter came by and gave my mother the venison and looked at her woodpile and told her she was burning green wood, which builds up creosote which was why she had the chimney fire, and he asked her who sold her the wood, which she told him. And the next day the guy who sold her the wood came by and dumped off three cords of seasoned wood and drove off without saying a word, and the day after that two other guys came by with a brand-new woodstove which was ugly but very efficient and had a sheath around it so a baby wouldn't get burned if he touched it. And the day after *that* Winter came by to make sure the stove was hooked up right, and he went to all the cabin's windows with sheets of plastic and a hair dryer and covered them so the cold wouldn't get in, and then he showed my mother where there was a spring in the woods that she could go to and fill water jugs rather than buy them at the grocery door. He also gave her a chamber pot so she wouldn't have to use the outhouse, and told her he knew of someone who had a composting toilet they'd sell to her cheap.

All of which might make you think that when I say "Winter's wife" I'm referring to my mom. But I'm not. Winter's wife is someone else.

Still, when I was growing up, Winter was always at our house. And I was at his place, when I got older. Winter chops down trees, what they call wood lot management—he cuts trees for people, but in a good way, so the forest can grow back and be healthy. Then he'd split the wood so the people could burn it for firewood. He had a portable sawmill—one of the scary things Mom had seen in his yard—and he also mills wood so people can build houses with the lumber. He's an auctioneer, and he can play the banjo and one of those washboard things like you see in old movies. He showed me how to jump-start a car with just a wire coat hanger, also how to carve wood and build a treehouse and frame a window. When my mother had our little addition put on with a bathroom in it, Winter did a lot of the carpentry, and he taught me how to do that too.

He's also a dowser, a water witch. That's someone who can tell where water is underground, just by walking around in the woods holding a stick in front of him. You'd think this was more of that crazy woo-woo stuff my mother is into, which is what I thought whenever I heard about it.

But then one day me and my friend Cody went out to watch Winter do it. We were hanging out around Winter's place, clearing brush. He let us use the hill behind the schoolbus for snowboarding, and that's where we'd built that sweet jump, and Winter had saved a bunch of scrap wood so that when spring came we could build a half-pipe for skating too.

But now it was spring and since we didn't have any money really to pay Winter for it, he put us to work clearing brush. Cody is my age, almost fourteen. So we're hacking at this brush and swatting blackflies and I could tell that at any minute Cody was going to say he had to go do homework, which was a lie because we didn't have any, when Winter shows up in his pickup, leans out the window and yells at us.

"You guys wanna quit goofing off and come watch someone do some real work?"

So then me and Cody had an argument about who was going to ride shotgun with Winter, and then we had another argument about who was going to ride in the truck bed, which is actually more fun. And then we took so long arguing that Winter yelled at us and made us both ride in the back.

So we got to the place where Winter was going to work. This field that had been a dairy farm, but the farm wasn't doing too good and the guy who owned it had to sell it off. Ms. Whitton, a high school teacher, was going to put a little modular house on it. There'd been a bad drought a few years earlier, and a lot of wells ran dry. Ms. Whitton didn't have a lot of money to spend on digging around for a well, so she hired Winter to find the right spot.

"Justin!" Winter yelled at me as he hopped out of the truck. "Grab me that hacksaw there—"

I gave him the saw, then me and Cody went and goofed around some more while Winter walked around the edge of the field, poking at brush and scrawny trees. After a few minutes he took the hacksaw to a spindly sapling.

"Got it!" Winter yelled, and stumbled back into the field. "If we're going to find water here, we better find a willow first."

It was early spring, and there really weren't any leaves out yet, so what he had was more like a pussy willow, with furry gray buds and green showing where he'd sawn the branch off. Winter stripped the buds from it until he had a forked stick. He held the two ends like he was holding handlebars, and began to walk around the field.

It was weird. 'Cause at first, me and Cody were laughing—we didn't mean to, we couldn't help it. It just looked funny, Winter walking back and forth with his arms out holding that stick. He kind of looked like Frankenstein. Even Ms. Whitton was smiling.

But then it was like everything got very still. Not quiet—you could hear the wind blowing in the trees, and hear birds in the woods, and someone running a chainsaw far off—but still, like all of a sudden you were in a movie and you knew something was about to happen. The sun was warm, I could smell dirt and cow manure and meadowsweet. Cody started slapping blackflies and swearing. I felt dizzy, not bad dizzy but like you do when the school bus drives fast over a high bump and you go up on your seat. A few feet away Winter continued walking in a very straight line, the willow stick held out right in front of him.

And all of a sudden the stick began to bend. I don't mean that Winter's arms bent down holding it: I mean the stick itself, the point that stuck straight out, bent down like it was made of rubber and someone had grabbed it and yanked it toward the ground. Only it wasn't made of rubber, it was stiff wood, and there was no one there—but it still bent, pointing at a mossy spot between clumps of dirt.

"Holy crap," I said.

Cody shut up and looked. So did Ms. Whitton.

"Oh my god," she said.

Winter stopped, angling the stick back and forth like he was fighting with it. Then it lunged down and he yelled "Whoa!" and opened his hands and dropped it. Me and Cody ran over.

"This is it," said Winter. He pulled a spool of pink surveyor's tape from his pocket and broke off a length. I stared warily at the willow stick, half expecting it to wiggle up like a snake, but it didn't move. After a moment I picked it up.

"How'd you do that?" demanded Cody.

"I didn't do it," said Winter evenly. He took the stick from my hand, snapped off the forked part and tossed it; tied the surveyor's tape to what remained and stuck it in the ground. "Wood does that. Wood talks to you, if you listen."

"No lie," I said. "Can you show me how to do that sometime?"

"Sure," said Winter. "Can't today, got a towing job. But someday."

He and Ms. Whitton started talking about money and who had the best rates for drilling. The next time my mom drove past that field, the drill rig was there hammering at the ground right where Winter's stick had pointed, and the next time I ran into Ms. Whitton in the hall at school she told me the well was already dug and all geared up to pump a hundred gallons a minute, once she got her foundation dug and her house moved in.

Not long after that, Winter announced he was going to Reykjavik.

It was after school one day, and Winter had dropped by to shoot the breeze.

"What's Reykjavik?" I asked.

"It's in Iceland," said my mother. She cracked the window open and sat at the kitchen table opposite Winter and me. "Why on earth are you going to Reykjavik?"

"To pick up my wife," said Winter.

"Your wife?" My eyes widened. "You're married?"

"Nope. That's why I'm going to Iceland to pick her up. I met her online, and we're going to get married."

My mother looked shocked. "In *Iceland*?"

Winter shrugged. "Hey, with a name like mine, where else you gonna find a wife?"

So he went to Iceland. I thought he'd be gone for a month, at least, but a week later the phone rang and my mom answered and it was Winter, saying he was back safe and yes, he'd brought his wife with him.

"That's incredible," said Mom. She put the phone down and shook her head. "He was there for four days, got married, and now they're back. I can't believe it."

A few days later they dropped by so Winter could introduce us to her. It was getting near the end of the school year, and me and Cody were outside throwing stuff at my treehouse, using the open window as a target. Sticks, a Frisbee, a broken yo-yo. Stuff like that.

"Why are you trying to break the house?" a woman asked.

I turned. Winter stood there grinning, hands in the pockets of his jeans, his gimme cap pushed back so the bill pointed almost straight up. Beside him stood a woman who barely came up to his shoulder. She was so slight that for a second I thought she was another kid, maybe one of the girls from school who'd ridden her bike over or hopped a ride in Winter's truck. But she didn't have a kid's body, and she sure didn't have a kid's eyes.

"Justin." Winter squared his shoulders and his voice took on a mock-formal tone. "I'd like you to meet my wife. Vala, this is Justin."

"Justin." The way she said my name made my neck prickle. It was like she was turning the word around in her mouth; like she was tasting it. "*Gleour mig ao kynnast per.* That's Icelandic for 'I am glad to meet you.'"

She didn't really have an accent, although her voice sounded more English than American. And she definitely didn't look like anyone I'd ever seen in Maine, even though she was dressed pretty normal. Black jeans, a black T-shirt. Some kind of weird-looking bright blue shoes with thick rubber soles, which I guess is what people wear in Iceland; also a bright blue windbreaker. She had long straight black hair done in two ponytails—one reason she looked like a kid—kind of slanted eyes and a small mouth and the palest skin I've ever seen.

It was the eyes that really creeped me out. They were long and narrow and very very dark, so dark you couldn't even see the pupil. And they weren't brown but blue, so deep a blue they were almost black. I've never seen eyes that color before, and I didn't really like seeing them now. They were cold—not mean or angry, just somehow *cold*; or maybe it was that they made *me* feel cold, looking at them.

And even though she looked young, because she was skinny and her hair didn't have any gray in it and her face wasn't wrinkled, it was like she was somehow pretending to be young. Like when someone pretends to like kids, and you know they don't, really. Though I didn't get the feeling Vala didn't like kids. She seemed more puzzled, like maybe we looked as strange to her as she did to me.

"You haven't told me why you are trying to break the house," she said.

I shrugged. "Uh, we're not. We're just trying to get things through that window."

Cody glanced at Vala, then began searching for more rocks to throw.

Vala stared at him coolly. "Your friend is very rude."

She looked him up and down, then walked over to the tree house. It was built in the crotch of a big old maple tree, and it was so solid you could live in it, if you wanted to, only it didn't have a roof.

"What tree is this?" she asked, and looked at Winter.

"Red maple," he said.

"Red maple," she murmured. She ran her hand along the trunk, stroking it, like it was a cat. "Red maple . . ."

She turned and stared at me. "You made this house? By yourself?"

"No." She waited, like it was rude of me not to say more. So I walked over to her and stood awkwardly, staring up at the bottom of the treehouse. "Winter helped me. I mean, your husband—Mr. Winter."

"Mr. Winter." Unexpectedly she began to laugh. A funny laugh, like a little kid's, and after a moment I laughed too. "So I am Mrs. Winter? But who should be Winter's proper wife—Spring, maybe?"

She made a face when she said this, like she knew how dumb it sounded; then reached to take my hand. She drew me closer to her, until we both stood beside the tree. I felt embarrassed—maybe this was how they did things in Iceland, but not here in Maine—but I was flattered, too. Because the way she looked at me, sideways from the corner of her eyes, and the way she smiled, not like I was a kid but another grownup . . . it was like she knew a secret, and she acted like I knew it, too.

Which of course I didn't. But it was kind of cool that she thought so. She let go of my hand and rested hers against the tree again, rubbing a patch of lichen.

"There are no trees in Iceland," she said. "Did you know that? No trees. Long long ago they cut them all down to build houses or ships, or to burn. And so we have no trees, only rocks and little bushes that come to here—"

She indicated her knee, then tapped the tree trunk. "And like this—lichen, and moss. We have a joke, do you know it?"

She took a breath, then said, "What do you do if you get lost in a forest in Iceland?"

I shook my head. "I dunno."

"Stand up."

It took me a moment to figure that out. Then I laughed, and Vala smiled at me. Again she looked like she was waiting for me to say something. I wanted to be polite, but all I could think was how weird it must be, to come from a place where there were no trees to a place like Maine, where there's trees everywhere.

So I said, "Uh, do you miss your family?"

She gave me a funny look. "My family? They are happy to live with the rocks back in Iceland. I am tired of rocks."

A shadow fell across her face. She glanced up as Winter put his hands on her shoulders. "Your mother home, Justin?" he asked. "We're on our way into town, just wanted to say a quick hello and introduce the new wife—"

I nodded and pointed back to the house. As Winter turned to go, Vala gave me another sharp look.

"He tells me many good things about you. You and he are what we would call *feogar*—like a father and his son, Winter says. So I will be your godmother."

She pointed a finger at me, then slowly drew it to my face until she touched my chin. I gasped: her touch was so cold it burned.

"There," she murmured. "Now I will always know you."

And she followed Winter inside. When they were gone, Cody came up beside me.

"Was that freaky or what?" he said. He stared at the house. "She looks like that weird singer, Boink."

"You mean Björk, you idiot."

"Whatever. Where is Iceland, anyway?"

"I have no clue."

"Me neither." Cody pointed at my chin. "Hey, you're bleeding, dude."

I frowned, then gingerly touched the spot where Vala had pressed her finger. It wasn't bleeding; but when I looked at it later that night I saw a red spot, shaped like a fingerprint. Not a scab or blister or scar but a spot like a birthmark, deep red like blood. Over the next few days it faded, and finally disappeared; but I can still feel it there sometimes even now, a sort of dull ache that gets worse when it's cold outside, or snowing.

That same month, Thomas Tierney returned to Paswegas County. He was probably the most famous person in this whole state, after Stephen King, but everyone up here loves Stephen King and I never head anyone say anything good about Thomas Tierney except after he disappeared, and then the only thing people said was good riddance to bad rubbish. Even my mom, who gets mad if you say something bad about anyone, even if they hit you first, never liked Thomas Tierney.

"He's one of those people who thinks they can buy anything. And if he can't buy it, he ruins it for everyone else."

Though the truth was there wasn't much that he wasn't able to buy, especially in Paswegas. People here don't have a lot of money. They had more after Tierney's telemarketing company moved into the state and put up its telephone centers everywhere, even one not too far from Shaker Harbor, which is pretty much the end of nowhere. Then people who used to work as fishermen or farmers or teachers or nurses, but who couldn't make a living at it anymore, started working for International Corporate Enterprises. ICE didn't pay a lot, but I guess it paid okay, if you didn't mind sitting in a tiny cubicle and calling strangers on the phone when they were in the middle of dinner and annoying them so they swore at you or just hung up.

Once when she heard me and Cody ranking on people who worked at ICE, my mom took us aside and told us we had to be careful what we said, because even if we hated the company it gave people jobs and that was nothing to sneeze about. Of course a lot of those people who worked for ICE ended up not being able to afford to live here anymore, because Tierney gave all his friends from away the expensive jobs, and then they bought land here, which used to be cheap, and built these big fancy houses. So now normal people can't afford to live here, unless they were lucky enough to already own a house or land, like my mom and Winter.

But then Tierney got caught doing something bad, sneaking money from his company or something, and ICE got bought by a bigger company, and they shut down all their operations in Maine, and all the people who worked there got thrown out of work and a lot of them who did own their own houses or land got them taken away because they couldn't afford to pay their bills anymore. Then people *really* hated Thomas Tierney; but it didn't do any good, because he never even got in trouble for what he did, I mean he didn't go to jail or anything, and he didn't lose his money or his house down in Kennebunkport or his yacht or his private airplane.

As a matter of fact, the opposite happened: he bought the land next to Winter's. Winter dropped by the day he found out about it.

"That sumbitch bought old Lonnie Packard's farm!" he yelled.

Me and Cody looked at each other and sort of smirked, but we didn't say anything. I could tell Cody wanted to laugh, like I did—who the hell actually says "sumbitch?"—but at the same time it was scary, because we'd never seen Winter get mad before.

124 ⤕ Elizabeth Hand

"I can't blame Lonnie," Winter went on, shifting from one foot to the other and tugging at his cap. "He had to sell his lobster boat last year cause he couldn't pay his taxes, and then he had that accident and couldn't pay the hospital. And it's a salt farm right there on the ocean, so he never got much out of it except the view."

Cody asked, "Why didn't he sell it to you?"

Winter whacked his palm against the wall. "That's what I said! I told Lonnie long time ago, ever he wanted to sell that land I'd take it. But yesterday he told me, 'Winter, your pockets just ain't that deep.' I said, 'Well Lonnie, how deep is deep?' And he pointed out there at the Atlantic Ocean and said, 'You see that? You go out to the Grand Banks and find the deepest part, and I'm telling you it ain't deep as Thomas Tierney's pockets.'"

So that was that. Tell you the truth, I didn't give much thought to it. Where we snowboarded in the woods was safely on Winter's property, I knew that; besides which it was late spring now, and me and Cody were busy working on that half-pipe behind Winter's house and, once it was done, skating on it.

Sometimes Winter's wife would come out and watch us. Winter had made her a bench from a hunk of oak, laid slats across it and carved her name on the seat, VALA with carved leaves and vines coming out of the letters. The bench was set up on a little rise, so that you could look out across the tops of the trees and just catch a glimpse of the ocean, silver-blue above the green. Vala was so tiny she looked like another kid sitting there, watching us and laughing when we fell, though never in a mean way. Her laugh was like her eyes: there was a kind of coldness to it, but it wasn't nasty, more like she had never seen anyone fall before and every time it happened (which was a lot) it was a surprise to her. Even though it was warmer now, she always wore that same blue windbreaker, and over it a sweatshirt that I recognized as one of Winter's, so big it was like a saggy dress. It could get wicked hot out there at the edge of the woods, but I never saw her take that sweatshirt off.

"Aren't you hot?" I asked her once. She'd brought some water for us and some cookies she'd made, gingersnaps that were thin and brittle as ice and so spicy they made your eyes sting.

"Hot?" She shook her head. "I never get warm. Except with Winter." She smiled then, one of her spooky smiles that always made me nervous. "I tell him it's the only time winter is ever warm, when he is lying beside me."

I felt my face turn red. On my chin, the spot where she had touched me throbbed as though someone had shoved a burning cigarette against my skin. Vala's smile grew wider, her eyes too. She began to laugh.

"You're still a boy." For a moment she sounded almost like my mother. "Good boys, you and your friend. You will grow up to be good men. Not like this man Tierney, who thinks he can own the sea by buying salt. There is nothing more dangerous than a man who thinks he has power." She lifted her head to gaze into the trees, then turned to stare at me. "Except for one thing."

But she didn't say what that was.

I had always heard a lot about Thomas Tierney, and even though I had never seen him, there were signs of him everywhere around Shaker Harbor. The addition to the library; the addition to the school; the big old disused mill—renamed the ICE Mill— that he bought and filled with a thousand tiny cubicles, each with its own computer and its own telephone. The ICE Mill employed so many people that some of them drove two hours each way to work—there weren't enough people around Shaker Harbor to fill it.

But now it was empty, with big FOR SALE signs on it. Winter said it would stay empty, too, because no one in Paswegas County could afford to buy it.

"And no one outside of Paswegas County would *want* to buy it," he added. "Watch that doesn't drip—"

I was helping Winter varnish a crib he'd made, of wood milled from an elm tree that had died of the blight. He wouldn't say who it was for, even when I asked him outright, but I assumed it was a present for Vala. She didn't look pregnant, and I was still a little fuzzy about the precise details of what exactly might make her pregnant, in spite of some stuff me and Cody checked out online one night. But there didn't seem much point in making a trip to Iceland to get a wife if you weren't going to have kids. That's what Cody's dad said, anyway, and he should know since Cody has five brothers and twin sisters.

"I think they should make the mill into an indoor skate park," I said, touching up part of the crib I'd missed. "That would be sweet."

We were working outside, so I wouldn't inhale varnish fumes, in the shadow of a tower of split logs that Winter sold as firewood. I had to be careful that sawdust didn't get onto the newly varnished crib, or bugs.

Winter laughed. "Not much money in skate parks."

"I'd pay."

"That's my point." Winter shoved his cap back from his forehead. "Ready to break for lunch?"

Usually Winter made us sandwiches, Swiss cheese and tomato and horseradish sauce. Sometimes Vala would make us lunch, and then I'd lie and say I wasn't hungry or had already eaten, since the sandwiches she made mostly had fish in them— not tuna fish, either—and were on these tiny little pieces of bread that tasted like cardboard.

But today Winter said we'd go into town and get something from Shelley's Place, the hot dog stand down by the harbor. It was warm out, mid-August; school would start soon. I'd spent the summer hanging out with Cody and some of our friends, until the last few weeks when Cody had gone off to Bible Camp.

That's when Winter put me to work. Because along with the crib, Winter had started building a house—a real house, not an addition to the schoolbus. I helped him clear away brush, then helped build the forms for the foundation to be poured into. Once the concrete cured, we began framing the structure. Sometimes Vala helped, until Winter yelled at her to stop, anyway. Then she'd go off to tend the little garden she'd planted at the edge of the woods.

Now I didn't know where Vala was. So I put aside the can of varnish and hopped into Winter's pickup, and we drove into town. Most of the summer people had already left, but there were still a few sailboats in the harbor, including one gigantic yacht, the *Ice Queen*, a three-masted schooner that belonged to Thomas Tierney. According to Winter she had a crew of ten, not just a captain and mate and deckhands but a cook and housekeeper, all for Tierney; as well as a red-and-white striped mainsail, not that you'd ever have any trouble telling her apart from any of the other boats around here.

When he saw the *Ice Queen*, Winter scowled. But there was no other sign of Tierney, not that I could see. A few summer holdovers stood in line in front of Shelley's little food stand, trying to act like they fit in with the locals, even though the only other people were contractors working on job sites.

And Lonnie Packard. He was at the very front of the line, paying for a hot dog with onions and sauerkraut wrapped in a paper towel. It was the first time I'd seen

Lonnie since I'd heard about him selling his farm to Thomas Tierney, and from the look on Winter's face, it was the first time he'd seen him, too. His mouth was twisted like he wasn't sure if he was going to smile or spit something out, but then Lonnie turned and nodded at him.

"Winter," he said. He pronounced it "Wintah" in this exaggerated way he had, like he was making fun of his own strong accent. "How's it hanging?"

Winter poked at the bill of his cap and gave his head a small shake. "Not bad." He looked at Lonnie's hot dog, then flashed me a sideways grin. "Now *that* looks like lunch. Right, Justin?"

So that's how I knew Winter wasn't going to stay pissed about Lonnie selling his farm, which was kind of a relief.

But Lonnie didn't look relieved. He looked uncomfortable, although Lonnie usually looked uncomfortable. He was a big rough-faced guy, not as tall as Winter but definitely plus-sized, with a bushy brown beard and baggy jeans tucked into high rubber fisherman's boots, which kind of surprised me since I knew he'd had to sell his boat. Then I remembered all the money he must have gotten from Thomas Tierney; enough to buy another boat, probably. Enough to buy anything he wanted.

"Gotta run," said Lonnie. "Got you an assistant there, eh, Winter?"

"Justin does good work," said Winter, and moved up to the window to place our order. For a moment Lonnie stared at him like he was going to say something else, but Winter was already talking to Shelley.

Instead Lonnie glanced at me again. It was a funny look, not like he was going to speak to me, more like he was trying to figure something out. Lonnie's not stupid, either. He puts on that heavy accent and acts like he's never been south of Bangor, but my mother said he actually has a law degree and fishes just because he likes it better than being a lawyer, which I think I would, too. I waited to see if he was going to talk to me, but instead he turned and walked quickly to where a brand-new SUV was parked in one of the spots reserved for fishermen, got inside and drove off. I watched him go, then angled up beside Winter to get my food.

Shelley gave me a quick smile and went back to talking to Winter. "See you're putting a house up by your place," she said, and handed him a paper towel with two hot dogs on it, a container of fried clams for Winter, and two bottles of Moxie. Winter nodded but didn't say anything, just passed her some money.

"Regular housing boom going on down there," Shelley added, then looked past us to the next customer. "Can I help you?"

We drove back to Winter's place and ate, sitting outside on a couple of lawn chairs and listening to woodpeckers in the pine grove. The air smelled nice, like sawdust and varnish and fried clams. When I was almost done, Vala stepped out of the schoolbus and walked over to me.

"*Ertu búinn?*" she said teasingly. "Are you finished? And you didn't save any for me?"

I looked uncertainly at Winter, still chewing.

"Mmm mm," he said, flapping his hand at me. "None for her! Nothing unhealthy!"

"Hmph." Vala tossed her head, black ponytails flying. "Like I'd eat that—it's nothing but grease."

She watched disapprovingly as the last fried clam disappeared into Winter's mouth, then looked at me. "Come here, Justin. I want to show you something."

"Hey!" Winter called in mock alarm as Vala beckoned me toward the edge of the woods. "He's on the clock!"

"Now he's off," retorted Vala, and stuck her tongue out. "Come on."

Vala was strange. Sometimes she acted like my mother, grumpy about me forgetting to take my shoes off when I went into the school bus, or if me and Cody made too much noise. Other times, like now, she acted more like a girl my own age, teasing and unpredictable.

The way she looked changed, too. I don't mean her clothes—she pretty much wore the same thing all the time—but the way that sometimes she would look old, like my mom does, and other times she'd look the same age as me and my friends. Which creeped me out, especially if it was one of those times when she was acting young, too.

Fortunately, right now she was acting young but looking older, like someone who would be married to Winter. For one thing, she was wearing his clothes, a pair of jeans way too big for her and cuffed up so much you couldn't even see her shoes, and that baggy sweatshirt, despite it being so hot.

"I said come," she repeated, and whacked me on the shoulder.

I stood hastily and followed her, wondering if everyone in Iceland was like this, or if it was just Vala.

Under the trees everything was green and gold and warm; not hot like out in the full sun, but not cool, either. It made me sweat, and my sweat and the dim light made the mosquitoes come out, lots of them, though they never seemed to bother Vala, and after a few minutes I ignored them and (mostly) forgot about them. The ground was soft and smelled like worms, a good smell that made me think of fishing, and now and then we'd go by a kind of tree that smelled so good I'd stop for a second, a tree that Winter calls Balm of Gilead, because its buds smell like incense.

Winter owned a lot of land, more than a hundred acres. Some of it he cut for firewood or lumber, but not this part. This part he left wild, because it joined up with Lonnie's land—Thomas Tierney's land, now—and because it was old-growth forest. People think that all the woods in Maine are wild and old, but most of it isn't much older than what you'd find someplace like New Jersey—the trees were cut hundreds or maybe a thousand years ago by the Passamaquoddy or other Indians, and when those trees grew back they were cut by Vikings, and when those trees grew back they were cut by the English and the French and everyone else, all the way up till now.

So there's actually not a lot of true virgin forest, even if the trees look ancient, like what you see in a movie when they want you to think it's someplace totally wild, when it's really, like, trees that are maybe forty or fifty years old. Baby trees.

But these trees weren't like that. These were old trees—wolf trees, some of them, the kind of trees that Winter usually cuts down. A wolf tree is a big crooked tree with a huge canopy that hogs all the light and soil and crowds out the other trees. Wolf trees are junk trees, because they're crooked and spread out so much they're not much good for lumber, and they overwhelm other, smaller trees and keep them from growing up tall and straight so they can be harvested.

When I was little I'd go with Winter into the woods to watch him work, and I was always afraid of the wolf trees. Not because there was anything scary about them—they looked like ordinary trees, only big.

But I thought wolves lived in them. When I said that to Winter once, he laughed.

"I thought that too, when I was your age." He was oiling his chain saw, getting ready to limb a wolf tree, a red oak. Red oaks smell terrible when you cut them, the raw wood stinks—they smell like dog crap. "Want to know the real reason they call them that?"

I nodded, breathing through my mouth.

"It's because a thousand years ago, in England and around there, they'd hang outlaws from a tree like this. Wolf's-head trees, they called them, because the outlaws were like wolves, preying on weaker people."

Where the wolf trees grew here, they had shaded out most other trees. Now and then I saw an old apple tree overgrown with wild grape vines, remnants of Lonnie's family farm. Because even though this was old-growth forest, birds and animals don't know that. They eat fruit from the farm then poop out the seeds—that's how you get apple trees and stuff like that in the middle of the woods.

I was getting hot and tired of walking. Vala hadn't said anything since we started, hadn't even looked back at me, and I wondered if she'd forgotten I was even there. My mother said pregnancy makes women spacey, more than usual even. I was trying to think of an excuse to turn back, when she stopped.

"Here," she said.

We'd reached a hollow on the hillside above the farm. I could just make out the farmhouse and barn and outbuildings, some apple trees and the overgrown field that led down to the ocean. There was no real beach there, just lots of big granite rocks, also a long metal dock that I didn't remember having seen before.

It was still a pretty spot, tucked into the woods. A few yards from the farmhouse, more trees marched down to a cliff above the rocky beach. Small trees, all twisted from the wind: except for three huge white pines, each a hundred feet tall.

Winter called these the King's Pines, and they were gigantic.

"These trees are ancient," he'd told me, pointing up at one. "See anything up there?"

I squinted. I knew bald eagles nested near the ocean, but I didn't see anything that looked like a nest. I shook my head.

Winter put his hand on my shoulder and twisted me till I was staring almost straight up. "There, on the trunk—see where the bark's been notched?"

I saw it then, three marks of an axe in the shape of an arrow.

"That's the King's Mark," said Winter. "Probably dating back to about 1690. That means these were the King's Trees, to be used for masts in the king's naval fleet. See how high up that mark is? That's how old these trees are. Over three hundred years ago, this was a big tree. And it was probably at least three hundred years old then."

Now, with Vala, I could see the King's Pines jutting out above the other trees, like the masts of a schooner rising from a green sea. I figured that's what Vala was going to show me, and so I got ready to be polite and act like I already didn't know about them.

Instead she touched my arm and pointed just a few feet away, toward a clearing where trees had grown around part of the pasture.

"Whoa," I whispered.

In the middle of the clearing was a bush. A big bush, a quince, its long thin branches covered with green leaves and small red flowers—brilliant red, the color of valentines, and so bright after the dim woods that I had to blink.

And then, after blinking, I thought something had gone wrong with my eyes; because the bush seemed to be *moving*. Not moving in the wind—there wasn't any wind—but moving like it was breaking apart then coming back together again, the leaves lifting away from the branches and flickering into the air, going from dark green to shining green like metallic paint, and here and there a flash of red like a flower had spun off, too.

But what was even more bizarre was that the bush made a noise. It was *buzzing*, not like bees but like a chainsaw or Weedwhacker, a high-pitched sound that got louder then softer then louder again. I rubbed my eyes and squinted into the overgrown field, thinking maybe Thomas Tierney had hired someone to clean up and that's what I was hearing.

There was no one there, just tall grass and apple trees and rocks, and beyond that the cliff and open sea.

"Do you see what they are?"

Vala's voice was so close to my ear that I jumped; then felt my skin prickle with goosebumps at her breath, cold as though a freezer door had opened. I shook my head and she touched my sleeve, her hand cold through the cloth, and led me into the clearing, until the bush rose above us like a red cloud.

"See?" she murmured.

The bush was full of hummingbirds—hundreds of them, darting in and out as though the bush were a city, and the spaces between the leaves streets and alleys. Some hovered above the flowers to feed, though most flew almost too fast to see. Some sat on the branches, perfectly still, and that was the weirdest thing of all, like seeing a raindrop hanging in the air.

But they didn't stay still; just perched long enough that I could get a look at one, its green green wings and the spot of red on its throat, so deep a red it was like someone had crushed its tiny body by holding it too hard. I thought maybe I could hold it too, or touch it, anyway.

So I tried. I stood with my palm open and held my breath and didn't move. Hummingbirds whizzed around like I was part of the quince, but they didn't land on me.

I glanced at Vala. She was doing the same thing I was, this amazed smile on her face, holding both arms out in front of her so she reminded me of Winter when he was dowsing. The hummingbirds buzzed around her, too, but didn't stop. Maybe if one of us had been wearing red. Hummingbirds like red.

Vala wasn't wearing red, just Winter's grubby old gray sweatshirt and jeans. But she looked strange standing there, eerie even, and for a second I had this weird feeling that I wasn't seeing Vala at all, that she had disappeared and I was standing next to a big gray rock.

The feeling was so strong that it creeped me out. I opened my mouth, I was going to suggest that we head back to Winter's house, when a hummingbird flickered right in front of Vala's face. Right in front of Vala's *eye*.

"Hey!" I yelled; and at the same instant Vala shouted, a deep grunting noise that had a word in it, but not an English word. Her hand flashed in front of her face, there was a greenish blur and the bird was gone.

"Are you okay?" I said. I thought the hummingbird's sharp beak had stabbed her eye. "Did it—?"

Vala brought her hands to her face and gasped, blinking quickly. "I'm sorry! It frightened me—so close, I was surprised—"

Her hands dropped. She gazed at the ground by her feet. "Oh no."

Near the toe of one rubber shoe, the hummingbird lay motionless, like a tiny bright green leaf.

"Oh, I am sorry, Justin!" cried Vala. "I only wanted you to see the tree with all the birds. But it scared me—"

I crouched to look at the dead hummingbird. Vala gazed back into the woods.

"We should go," she said. She sounded unhappy, even nervous. "Winter will think we got lost and get mad at me for taking you away. You need to work," she added, and gave me tight smile. "Come on."

She walked away. I stayed where I was. After a moment I picked up a stick and tentatively prodded at the dead bird. It didn't move.

It was on its back and it looked sadder that way. I wanted to turn it over. I poked it again, harder.

It still didn't budge.

Cody doesn't mind touching dead things. I do. But the hummingbird was so small, only as long as my finger. And it was beautiful, with its black beak and the red spot at its throat and those tiny feathers, more like scales. So I picked it up.

"Holy crap," I whispered.

It was heavy. Not heavy like maybe a bigger bird would have been, a sparrow or chickadee, but *heavy*, like a rock. Not even a rock—it reminded me of one of those weights you see hanging from an old clock, those metal things shaped like pine cones or acorns, but when you touch them they feel heavy as a bowling ball, only much smaller.

The hummingbird was like that—so little I could cradle it in my cupped palm, and already cold. I guessed that rigor mortis had set in, the way it does when you hang a deer. Very gently I touched the bird's wing. I even tried to wiggle it, but the wing didn't move.

So I dropped the bird into my cupped palm and turned it onto its stomach. Its tiny legs were folded up like a fly's, its eyes dull. Its body didn't feel soft, like feathers. It felt hard, solid as granite; and cold.

But it looked exactly like a live hummingbird, emerald green where the sun hit it, beak slightly curved; a band of white under the red throat. I ran my finger along its beak, then swore.

"What the frig?"

A bright red bead welled up where the dead bird's beak had punctured my skin, sharp as a nail.

I sucked my finger, quickly looked to make sure Vala hadn't seen me. I could just make her out in the distance, moving through the trees. I felt in my pocket till I found a wadded-up Kleenex, wrapped the hummingbird in it and very carefully put it into my pocket. Then I hurried after Vala.

We walked back in silence. Only when the skeletal frame of the new house showed brightly through the trees did Vala turn to me.

"You saw the bird?" she asked.

I looked at her uneasily. I was afraid to lie, but even more afraid of what she might do if she knew what was in my pocket.

Before I could reply, she reached to touch the spot on my chin. I felt a flash of aching cold as she stared at me, her dark eyes somber but not unkind.

"I did not mean to hurt it," she said quietly. "I have never seen a bird like that one, not so close. I was scared. Not scared—startled. My reaction was too fast," she went on, and her voice was sad. Then she smiled, and glanced down at my jeans pocket.

"You took it," she said.

I turned away, and Vala laughed. In front of the house, Winter looked up from a pile of two-by-sixes.

"Get your butt over here, Justin!" he yelled. "Woman, don't you go distracting him!"

Vala stuck her tongue out again, then turned back to me. "He knows," she said matter-of-factly. "But maybe you don't tell your friend? Or your mother."

And she walked over to kiss Winter's sunburned cheek.

I muttered, "Yeah, sure;" then crossed to where I'd left the varnish. Vala stood beside her husband and sighed as she stared at the cloudless sky and the green canopy of trees stretching down to the Bay. A few boats under sail moved slowly across the blue water. One was a three-masted schooner with a red-striped mainsail: Thomas Tierney's yacht.

"So Vala," said Winter. He winked at his wife. "You tell Justin your news yet?"

She smiled. "Not yet." She pulled up the sweatshirt so I could see her stomach sticking out. "Here—"

She beckoned me over, took my hand and placed it on her stomach. Despite the heat, her hand was icy cold. So was her stomach; but I felt a sudden heat beneath my palm, and then a series of small thumps from inside her belly. I looked at her in surprise.

"It's the baby!"

"*Eg veit*," she said, and laughed. "I know."

"Now don't go scaring him off, talking about babies," said Winter. He put his arm around his wife. "I need him to help me finish this damn house before it snows."

I went back to varnishing. The truth is, I was glad to have something to do, so I wouldn't think about what had happened. When I got home that evening I put the hummingbird in a drawer, wrapped in an old T-shirt. For a while I'd look at it every night, after my mother came in to give me a kiss; but after a week or so I almost forgot it was there.

A few days later Cody got back from Bible Camp. It was September now. Labor Day had come and gone, and most of the summer people. School started up. Me and Cody were in eighth grade, we were pretty sick of being with the same people since kindergarten, but it was okay. Some days we skated over at Winter's place after school. It was getting crowded there with the piles of split firewood and all the stacks of lumber for the new house, and sometimes Winter yelled at us for getting in the way.

But mostly everything was like it usually was, except that Vala was getting more pregnant and everyone was starting to think about winter coming down.

You might not believe that people really worry about snow all the time, but here they do. My mother had already gotten her firewood from Winter back in August, and so had most of his other regular customers. Day by day, the big stacks of split wood dwindled, as Winter hauled them off for delivery.

And day by day the new house got bigger, so that soon it looked less like a kid's drawing of a stick house and more like a fairy tale cottage come to life, with a steep roof and lots of windows, some of them square and some of them round, like portholes, and scallop-shaped shingles stained the color of cranberries. I helped with that part, and inside, too, which was great.

Because inside—inside was amazing. Winter did incredible things with wood, everyone knew that. But until now, I had only seen the things he made for money, like furniture, or things he made to be useful, like the cabinets he'd done for my mother.

Now I saw what Winter did for himself and Vala. And if the outside of the little house looked like a fairy tale, the inside looked like something from a dream.

Winter usually carved from pine, which is a very soft wood. But he'd used oak for the beams, and covered them with faces—wind-faces with their mouths open to blow, foxes and wolves grinning from the corners, dragons and people I didn't recognize but who Vala said were spirits from Iceland.

"*Huldufolk*," she said when I asked about them. "The hidden people."

But they weren't hidden here. They were carved on the main beam that went across the living room ceiling, and on the oak posts in each corner, peeking out from carved leaves and vines and branches that made the posts look almost like real trees. There were *huldufolk* carved into the cupboards, and on benches and cabinets and bookshelves, and even on the headboard that Winter had made from a single slab of chestnut, so highly polished with beeswax that the entire bedroom smelled like honey.

So even though the house looked small from the outside, when you got inside you could get lost, wandering around and looking at all the wonderful carven things. Not just carved so the wood resembled something new, but so that you could see what was *inside* the wood, knots and whorls turned to eyes and mouths, the grain sanded and stained till it felt like soft, the way skin might feel if it grew strong enough to support walls and ceilings and joists, while still managing to remain, somehow, skin, and alive.

It was the most amazing house I've ever seen. And maybe the most amazing thing wasn't that it made me want to live in it, but that after spending hours working on it, I began to feel that the house lived in *me*, the way the baby lived inside Vala.

Only of course I could never tell anyone that, especially Cody. He would think I'd gone nuts from inhaling varnish fumes—even though I wore a dust mask, like Vala wore a fancy ventilating mask that made her look like Darth Vader.

She was working inside, too, building a stone fireplace. She found rocks in the woods and brought them up in a wheelbarrow. Big rocks, too, I was amazed she could lift them.

"Don't tell Winter," she whispered to me when I found her once, hefting a huge chunk of granite from the edge of the woods. "He'll just worry, and yell at me. And then *I* will yell at *you*," she added, and narrowed her spooky blue-black eyes.

Once the rocks were all piled inside she took forever, deciding which one would go where in the fireplace. When I made a joke about it she frowned.

"You do not want to make rocks angry, Justin." She wasn't kidding, either. She looked pissed off. "Because rocks have a very, very long memory."

It was early morning, just after seven on a Saturday. My mom had dropped me off at Winter's place on her way to see a client. It was a beautiful day, Indian summer, the leaves just starting to turn. I could see two sailboats on the water, heading south for the winter. I would rather have been skating with Cody, but Winter was anxious to get the inside of his house finished before it got too cold, so I said I'd come over and help trim up some windows.

Winter was outside. Vala, after yelling at me about the rocks, had gone up to the bedroom to get something. I yawned, wishing I'd brought my iPod, when upstairs Vala screamed.

I froze. It was a terrifying sound, not high-pitched like a woman's voice but deep and booming. And it went on and on, without her taking a breath. I started for the steps as Winter raced in. He knocked me aside and took the stairs two at a time.

"*Vala!*"

I ran upstairs after him, through the empty hall and into the bedroom. Vala stood in front of the window, clutching her face as she gazed outside. Winter grabbed her shoulders.

"Is it the baby?" he cried. He tried to pull her toward him, but she shook her head, then pushed him away so violently that he crashed against the wall.

"What is it?" I ran to the window. Vala fell silent as I looked out across the yellowing canopy of leaves.

"Oh no." I stared in disbelief at the cliff above the bay. "The King's Pines—"

I rubbed my eyes, hardly aware of Winter pushing me aside so he could stare out. "*No!*" he roared.

One of the three great trees was gone—the biggest one, the one that stood nearest to the cliff-edge. A blue gap showed where it had been, a chunk of sky that made me feel sick and dizzy. It was like lifting my own hand to find a finger missing. My chin throbbed and I turned, so the others wouldn't see me crying.

Winter pounded the windowsill. His face was dead white, his eyes so red they looked like they'd been smeared with paint. That frightened me more than anything, until I looked up and saw Vala.

She had backed against the wall—an unfinished wall, just gray sheetrock, blotched where the seams had been coated with putty. Her face had paled, too; but it wasn't white.

It was gray. Not a living gray, like hair or fur, but a dull mottled color, the gray of dead bark or granite.

And not just her face but her hands and arms: everything I could see of her that had been skin, now seemed cold and dead as the heap of fireplace rocks downstairs. Her clothes drooped as though tossed on a boulder, her hair stiffened like strands of reindeer moss. Even her eyes dulled to black smears, save for a pinpoint of light in each, as though a drop of water had been caught in the hollow of a stone.

"Vala." Winter came up beside me. His voice shook, but it was low and calm, as though he were trying to keep a frightened dog from bolting. "Vala, it's all right—"

He reached to stroke the slab of gray stone wedged against the wall, reindeer moss tangling between his fingers; then let his hand drop to move across a rounded outcropping.

"Think of the baby," he whispered. "Think of the girl. . . ."

The threads of reindeer moss trembled, the twin droplets welled and spilled from granite to the floor; and it was Vala there and not a stone at all, Vala falling into her husband's arms and weeping uncontrollably.

"It's *not* all right—it's *not* all right—"

He held her, stroking her head as I finally got the nerve up to speak.

"Was it—was it a storm?"

"A storm?" Abruptly Winter pulled away from Vala. His face darkened to the color of mahogany. "No, it's not a storm—"

He reached for the window and yanked it open. From the direction of the cliff came the familiar drone of a chainsaw.

"It's Tierney!" shouted Winter. He turned and raced into the hall. Vala ran after him, and I ran after her.

"No—you stay here!" Winter stopped at the top of the stairs. "Justin, you wait right here with her—"

"No," I said. I glanced nervously at Vala, but to my surprise she nodded.

"No," she said. "I'm going, and Justin too."

Winter sucked his breath through his teeth.

"Suit yourself," he said curtly. "But I'm not waiting for you. And listen—you stay with her, Justin, you understand me?"

"I will," I said, but he was already gone.

Vala and I looked at each other. Her eyes were paler than I remembered, the same dull gray as the sheetrock; but as I stared at her they grew darker, as though someone had dropped blue ink into a glass of water.

"Come," she said. She touched my shoulder, then headed out the door after her husband. I followed.

All I wanted to do was run and catch up with Winter. I could have, too—over the summer I'd gotten taller, and I was now a few inches bigger than Vala.

But I remembered the way Winter had said *You stay with her, Justin, you understand me?* And the way he'd looked, as though I were a stranger and he'd knock me over, or worse, if I disobeyed him. It scared me and made me feel sick, almost as sick as seeing the King's Pine chopped down; but I had no time to think about that now. I could still hear the chainsaw buzzing from down the hill, a terrible sound, like when you hear a truck brake but you know it's not going to stop in time. I walked as fast as I dared, Vala just a few steps behind me. When I heard her breathing hard I'd stop, and try to keep sight of Winter far ahead of us.

But after a few minutes I gave up on that. He was out of sight, and I could only hope he'd get down to the cliff and stop whoever was doing the cutting, before another tree fell.

"Listen," said Vala, and grabbed my sleeve. I thought the chainsaw was still running, but then I realized it was just an echo. Because the air grew silent, and Vala had somehow sensed this before I did. I looked at her and she stared back at me, her eyes huge and round and sky-blue, a color I'd never seen them before.

"There is still time," she whispered. She made a strange deep noise in the back of her throat, a growl but not an animal growl; more like the sound of thunder, or rocks falling. "Hurry—"

We crashed through the woods, no longer bothering to stay on the path. We passed the quince bush shimmering through its green haze of feeding hummingbirds. Vala didn't pause but I slowed down to look back, then stopped.

A vehicle was parked by the farmhouse, the same new SUV I'd seen that day down at Shelley's hot dog stand: Lonnie Packard's truck. As I stared, a burly figure came hurrying through the field, the familiar orange silhouette of a chainsaw tucked under his arm. He jumped into the SUV, gunned the engine and drove off.

I swore under my breath.

"Justin!" Vala's anxious voice came from somewhere in the woods. "Come on!"

I found her at the head of the trail near the cliff. Through a broken wall of scrawny, wind-twisted trees I could just make out the two remaining pines, and the bright yellow gash that was the stump of the one that had fallen. The sharp scent of pine resin and sawdust hung in the air, and the smell of exhaust fumes from the chainsaw.

But there was no other sign of Lonnie, obviously, or of anyone else.

"Look," said Vala in a hoarse whisper. She clutched me and pulled me toward her, her touch so cold it was like I'd been shot up with novocaine. My entire arm went numb. "There! The boat—"

She pointed down to the boulder-strewn beach where the dock thrust into the bay. At the end of the dock bobbed a small motorboat, a Boston Whaler. Further out, the hulking form of the *Ice Queen* rose above the gray water, sails furled.

She was at anchor. Several small forms moved across the deck. I squinted, trying to see if I recognized any of them. A frigid spasm shot through my ribs as Vala nudged me, indicating the rocks below.

"Is that him?" she hissed. "This man Tierney?"

I saw Winter loping across the beach toward the dock, jumping from one boulder to the next. On the shore, right next to the end of the dock, stood two men. One was tall, wearing an orange life vest and a blaze-orange watch cap and high rubber boots. The other was shorter, white-haired, slightly heavyset, wearing sunglasses and a red-and-white windbreaker, striped like the *Ice Queen*'s sails.

"That's him," I said.

Vala fixed her intense sky-blue gaze on me. "You're sure?"

"Yeah. I've seen his picture in the newspaper. And online."

She stood at the top of the trail and stared down. An angry voice rose from the rocks—Winter's—then another voice joined in, calmer, and a third, calm at first then laughing. I heard Winter curse, words I couldn't believe he knew. The third man, Tierney, laughed even harder.

I glanced at Vala, still staring at what was below us. One of her hands grasped the branch of a birch tree beside the path. She seemed to be thinking; almost she might have been daydreaming, she looked so peaceful, like somehow she'd forgotten where she was and what was happening. Finally she shook her head. Without looking back at me, she snapped the branch from the tree, dropped it, and started down the trail toward the beach.

I started after her, then hesitated.

The branch lay across the narrow path at my feet. Where Vala had touched them, the leaves had shriveled and faded, from yellow-green to the dull gray of lichen, and the white birch bark had blackened into tight charred-looking curls.

I tried to lift the branch. It was too heavy to move.

"It's *my* land now." Thomas Tierney's voice echoed from the cliff-face. "So I suggest you get the hell off it!"

I looked down to see Vala's small form at the bottom of the trail, hopping lightly from one boulder to the next as she headed for the dock. I scrambled down the path after her.

But I couldn't go as fast. For some reason, maybe because first Winter and then Vala had raced down before me, rocks had tumbled across the narrow trail. Not big rocks, but enough of them that I had to pick my way carefully to keep from falling.

Not only that: in spots a white slick of frost covered the ground, so that my feet slipped and once I almost fell and cracked my head. I stopped for a minute, panting. As I caught my breath I looked away from the beach, to where the cliff plunged into a deep crevice in the granite.

There, caught in the gigantic crack so that it looked as though it had grown up from the rocks, was the fallen pine. It tilted over the water, black in the shadow of the cliff, its great branches still green and strong-looking, the smell of pine sap overpowering the smell of the sea. In its uppermost branches something moved, then lifted from the tree and flew out above the bay—a bald eagle, still mottled brown and black with its young plumage.

I couldn't help it. I began to cry. Because no matter how strong and alive the tree looked, I knew it was dead. Nothing would bring it back again. It had been green when no one lived here but the Passamaquoddy, it had seen sailors come from far across the sea, and tourists in boats from Paswegas Harbor, and maybe it had even seen the *Ice Queen* earlier that morning with her red-and-white striped mainsail and Thomas Tierney on the deck, watching as Lonnie Packard took a chainsaw to its great trunk and the tree finally fell, a crash that I hadn't heard.

But Vala had.

You stay with her, Justin, you understand me?

I took a deep breath and wiped my eyes, checked to make sure I could still see Vala on the rocks below, then continued my climb down. When I finally reached the bottom I still had to be careful—there were tidal pools everywhere between the granite boulders, some of them skimmed with ice and all of them greasy with kelp and sea lettuce. I hurried as fast as I could toward the dock.

"*You don't own those trees.*" Winter's voice rang out so loudly that my ears hurt. "Those are the King's Pines—no man owns them."

"Well, I own this land," retorted Tierney. "And if that doesn't make me the god-damn king, I don't know what does."

I clambered over the last stretch of rocks and ran up alongside Vala. Winter stood a few yards away from us, towering above Thomas Tierney. The other man stood uneasily at the edge of the dock. I recognized him—Al Alford, who used to work as first mate on one of the daysailers in Paswegas Harbor. Now, I guessed, he worked for Tierney.

"King?" Vala repeated. *"Hann er klikkapor."* She looked at me from the corner of her eyes. "He's nuts."

Maybe it was her saying that, or maybe it was me being pissed at myself for crying. But I took a step out toward Tierney and shouted at him.

"It's against the law to cut those trees! It's against the law to do any cutting here without a permit!"

Tierney turned to stare at me. For the first time he looked taken aback, maybe even embarrassed or ashamed. Not by what he'd done, I knew that; but because someone else—a kid—knew he'd done it.

"Who's this?" His voice took on that fake nice tone adults use when they're caught doing something, like smoke or drink or fight with their wives. "This your son, Winter?"

"No," I said.

"Yes," said Vala, and under her breath said the word she'd used when I first met her: *feogar.*

But Winter didn't say anything, and Tierney had already turned away.

"Against the law?" He pulled at the front of his red-and-white windbreaker, then shrugged. "I'll pay the fine. No one goes to jail for cutting down trees."

Tierney smiled then, as though he was thinking of a joke no one else would ever get, and added, "Not me, anyway."

He looked at Al Alford, and nodded. Al quickly turned and walked—ran, practically—to where the Boston Whaler rocked against the metal railing at the end of the dock. Tierney followed him, but slowly, pausing once to stare back up the hillside—not at the King's Pines but at the farmhouse, its windows glinting in the sun where they faced the cliff. Then he walked to where Alford waited by the little motorboat, his hand out to help Tierney climb inside.

I looked at Winter. His face had gone slack, except for his mouth: he looked as though he were biting down on something hard.

"He's going to cut the other ones, too," he said. He didn't sound disbelieving or sad or even angry; more like he was saying something everyone knew was true, like *It'll snow soon* or *Tomorrow's Sunday.* "He'll pay the twenty thousand dollar fine, just like he did down in Kennebunkport, he'll wait and do it in the middle of the night when I'm not here. And the trees will be gone."

"No he will not," said Vala. Her voice was nearly as calm as Winter's. There was a subdued roar as the motorboat's engine turned over, and the Boston Whaler shot away from the dock, toward the *Ice Queen.*

"No," Vala said again, and she stooped and picked up a rock. A small gray rock, just big enough to fit inside her fist, one side of it encrusted with barnacles. She straightened and stared at the ocean, her eyes no longer sky-blue but the pure deep gray of a stone that's been worn smooth by the sea, with no pupil in them; and shining like water in the sun.

"*Skammastu þeî, Thomas Tierney. Farthu til fjandanns!*" she cried, and threw the rock toward the water. "*Farthu! Låttu þeog hverfa!*"

I watched it fly through the air, then fall, hitting the beach a long way from the waterline with a small thud. I started to look at Vala, and stopped.

From the water came a grinding sound, a deafening noise like thunder; only this was louder than a thunderclap and didn't last so long, just a fraction of a second. I turned and shaded my eyes, staring out to where the Boston Whaler arrowed toward Tierney's yacht. A sudden gust of wind stung my eyes with spray; I blinked, then blinked again in amazement.

A few feet from the motorboat a black spike of stone shadowed the water. Not a big rock—it might have been a dolphin's fin, or a shark's, but it wasn't moving.

And it hadn't been there just seconds before. It had never been there, I knew that. I heard a muffled shout, then the frantic whine of the motorboat's engine being revved too fast—and too late.

With a sickening crunch, the Boston Whaler ran onto the rock. Winter yelled in dismay as Alford's orange-clad figure was thrown into the water. For a second Thomas Tierney remained upright, his arms flailing as he tried to grab at Alford. Then, as though a trapdoor opened beneath him, he dropped through the bottom of the boat and disappeared.

Winter raced toward the water. I ran after him.

"Stay with Vala!" Winter grabbed my arm. Alford's orange life vest gleamed from on top of the rock where he clung. On board the *Ice Queen*, someone yelled through a megaphone, and I could see another craft, a little inflated Zodiac, drop into the gray water. Winter shook me fiercely. "Justin! I said, *stay with her—*"

He looked back toward the beach. So did I.

Vala was nowhere to be seen. Winter dropped my arm, but before he could say anything there was a motion among the rocks.

And there was Vala, coming into sight like gathering fog. Even from this distance I could see how her eyes glittered, blue-black like a winter sky; and I could tell she was smiling.

The crew of the *Ice Queen* rescued Alford quickly, long before the Coast Guard arrived. Winter and I stayed on the beach for several hours, while the search-and-rescue crews arrived and the Navy Falcons flew by overhead, in case Tierney came swimming to shore, or in case his body washed up.

But it never did. That spar of rock ripped a huge hole in the Boston Whaler, a bigger hole even than you'd think; but no one blamed Alford. All you had to do was take a look at the charts and see that there had never been a rock there, ever. Though it's there now, I can tell you that. I see it every day when I look out from the windows at Winter's house.

I never asked Vala about what happened. Winter had a grim expression when we finally went back to his place late that afternoon. Thomas Tierney was a multimillionaire, remember, and even I knew there would be an investigation and interviews and TV people.

But everyone on board the *Ice Queen* had witnessed what happened, and so had Al Alford; and while they'd all seen Winter arguing with Tierney, there'd been no exchange of blows, not even any pushing, and no threats on Winter's part—Alford testified to that. The King's Pine was gone, but two remained; and a bunch of people from the Audubon Society and the Sierra Club and places like that immediately filed a lawsuit against Tierney's estate, to have all the property on the old Packard Farm turned into a nature preserve.

Which I thought was good, but it still won't bring the other tree back.

One day after school, a few weeks after the boat sank, I was helping to put the finishing touches on Winter's house. Just about everything was done, except for the fireplace—there were still piles of rocks everywhere and plastic buckets full of mortar and flat stones for the hearth.

"Justin." Vala appeared behind me, so suddenly I jumped. "Will you come with me, please?"

I stood and nodded. She looked really pregnant now, and serious.

But happy, too. In the next room we could hear Winter working with a sander. Vala looked at me and smiled, put a finger to her lips then touched her finger to my chin. This time, it didn't ache with cold.

"Come," she said.

Outside it was cold and gray, the middle of October but already most of the trees were bare, their leaves torn away by a storm a few nights earlier. We headed for the woods behind the house, past the quince bush, its branches stripped of leaves and all the hummingbirds long gone to warmer places. Vala wore her same bright blue rubber shoes and Winter's rolled-up jeans.

But even his big sweatshirt was too small now to cover her belly, so my mother had knit her a nice big sweater and given her a warm plaid coat that made Vala look even more like a kid, except for her eyes and that way she would look at me sometimes and smile, as though we both knew a secret. I followed her to where the path snaked down to the beach, and tried not to glance over at the base of the cliff. The King's Pine had finally fallen and wedged between the crack in the huge rocks there, so that now seaweed was tangled in its dead branches, and all the rocks were covered with yellow pine needles.

"Winter has to go into town for a few hours," Vala said, as though answering a question. "I need you to help me with something."

We reached the bottom of the path and picked our way across the rocks, until we reached the edge of the shore. A few gulls flew overhead, screaming, and the wind blew hard against my face and bare hands. I'd followed Vala outside without my coat. When I looked down, I saw that my fingers were bright red. But I didn't feel cold at all.

"Here," murmured Vala.

She walked, slowly, to where a gray rock protruded from the gravel beach. It was roughly the shape and size of an arm.

Then I drew up beside Vala, and saw that it really *was* an arm—part of one, anyway, made of smooth gray stone, like marble only darker, but with no hand and broken just above the elbow. Vala stood and looked at it, her lips pursed; then stooped to pick it up.

"Will you carry this, please?" she said.

I didn't say anything, just held out my arms, as though she were going to fill them with firewood. When she set the stone down I flinched—not because it was heavy, though it was, but because it looked exactly like a real arm. I could even see where the veins had been, in the crook of the elbow, and the wrinkled skin where the arm had bent.

"Justin," Vala said. I looked up to see her blue-black eyes fixed on me. "Come on. It will get dark soon."

I followed her as she walked slowly along the beach, like someone looking for sea glass or sand dollars. Every few feet she would stop and pick something up—a hand, a foot, a long piece of stone that was most of a leg—then turn and set it carefully into my arms. When I couldn't carry anymore, she picked up one last small rock—a clenched fist—and made her way slowly back to the trail.

We made several more trips that day, and for several days after that. Each time, we would return to the house and Vala would fit the stones into the unfinished fireplace, covering them with other rocks so that no one could see them. Or if you did see one, you'd think maybe it was just part of a broken statue, or a rock that happened to *look* like a foot, or a shoulder blade, or the cracked round back of a head.

I couldn't bring myself to ask Vala about it. But I remembered how the Boston Whaler had looked when the Coast Guard dragged it onshore, with a small ragged gash in its bow, and a much, much bigger hole in the bottom, as though something huge and heavy had crashed through it. Like a meteor, maybe. Or a really big rock, or like if someone had dropped a granite statue of a man into the boat.

Not that anyone had seen that happen. I told myself that maybe it really was a statue—maybe a statue had fallen off a ship, or been pushed off a cliff or something.

But then one day we went down to the beach, the last day actually, and Vala made me wade into the shallow water. She pointed at something just below the surface, something round and white, like a deflated soccer ball.

Only it wasn't a soccer ball. It was Thomas Tierney's head: the front of it, anyway, the one part Vala hadn't already found and built into the fireplace.

His face.

I pulled it from the water and stared at it. A green scum of algae covered his eyes, which were wide and staring. His mouth was open so you could see where his tongue had been before it broke off, leaving a jagged edge in the hole of his screaming mouth.

"*Loksins,*" said Vala. She took it from me easily, even though it was so heavy I could barely hold it. "At last . . ."

She turned and walked back up to the house.

That was three months ago. Winter's house is finished now, and Winter lives in it, along with Winter's wife.

And their baby. The fireplace is done, and you can hardly see where there is a round broken stone at the very top, which if you squint and look at it in just the right light, like at night when only the fire is going, looks kind of like a face. Winter is happier than I've ever seen him, and my mom and I come over a lot, to visit him and Vala and the baby, who is just a few weeks old now and so cute you wouldn't believe it, and tiny, so tiny I was afraid to hold her at first but Vala says not to worry—I may be like her big brother now but someday, when the baby grows up, she will be the one to always watch out for me. They named her Gerda, which means Protector; and for a baby she is incredibly strong.

NATHALIE ANDERSON

Troll

"Troll" is the second of Nathalie Anderson's poems that we've reprinted from The Journal of Mythic Arts. *This poem, which begs to be read aloud, stayed with us with its grumbling antihero and droll, ferocious wordplay ("She's the mange in your manger"). Anderson is the author of the collections* Following Fred Astaire *and* Crawlers. *Her poems have appeared in* Denver Quarterly, Nimrod, The Paris Review, *and* Prairie Schooner, *among others. Anderson was the librettist for two operas* The Black Swan *and* Sukey in the Dark. *She is the Poet in Residence at the Rosenbach Museum and Library, and teaches at Swarthmore College.*

—K.L. & G.G.

Troll under her bridge, raw from clawing up
her rankling, swollen green with grudgery,
feeling on her spine each splintery plank,
each trip trap tramp, each neat little goat's hoof.
She's a cat-fit rash for rocketing, back
always up, hackles always bristling. She's
the worm in your apple, thorn in your flesh.

When troll meets troll at day's end, what ecstasies
of grumbling. Says this: "One drove before me
gratingly slow, and the last parking place
filched thievishly. Had the gall to ask then
for directions: TROLL FACE! TROLL FACE! One
won't ask again. I'm the fly in your ointment,
snake in your grass, skeleton at your feast."

"Uh-huh," says that: "I've claimed my window seat
when two come giggling, want seats together,
want me to trade: TROLL TONGUE! TROLL TONGUE! Two
won't ask again. I'm the stick in your craw, boil
on your backside, edge on your teeth." "Uh-huh,"
says this: TROLL FIST! "Uh-huh," says that: TROLL FANG!
Back and forth the bad blood, the belly-aching.

And where do they get off, those billy-goats,
calling themselves gruff? Here they come again,

traipsing so innocent, with their butt-heads,
their daggers, their bull-dozer shoulders. Ha!
Dunk her or drown her, she pops right back up
with her havoc and hoodoo. She's the mange
in your manger, iceberg in your bath.

She's your nil wind. She's your own weevil star.

WILLIAM BROWNING SPENCER

The Tenth Muse

William Browning Spencer has been back in Austin for over a year now after a brief sojourn in the Midwest, the inspiration for "The Tenth Muse." In 2006, Subterranean Press published his short story collection The Ocean and All Its Devices, *which received a starred review in* Publishers Weekly *(his third starred review in a row from that magazine).*

He's written screenplays based on his own fiction, including a screenplay for Zod Wallop, *and is now back working on his new novel,* My Sister Natalie: Snake Goddess of the Amazon.

"The Tenth Muse" was first published in Subterranean *issue #6, edited by William Schafer.*

—E.D.

1

I listened to my agent's voice on the phone, not wishing to pick up the receiver immediately for fear Max was seeking another loan. Traditionally, it tends to be the other way around: writers borrow, or attempt to borrow, money from their agents. My agent, however, was Max Felwin, who was, by turns, impecunious and rich, his fortunes falling and rising as a result of drugs, frequent marriages, and manic states. When he was down on his luck, he would hit up some of his clients for a loan.

If he was calling me for a loan, then he was in big trouble, indeed, and his mind had slipped back a decade or so to a time when my financial health and prospects were happier. My last novel had sold three thousand copies. I carried photocopies of the reviews (excellent) in my pocket as a talisman against complete ego collapse, but money would have been more eloquent praise.

"Marsh," he said to the answering machine, "I've been talking to Priest over at *American Promise*, and he's committed to a piece, a three- or four-parter, first North

American serial rights, and I'm thinking there's a book in it too. This is for a Morton Sky piece *with* an interview. I—"

That's when I picked up the receiver. "Morton Sky doesn't give interviews," I said.

"Marsh," Max said, "I knew you were there." I could tell by the sound of his voice that he was in his hearty, triumphant mode. "And I knew you'd say that! Sure, he doesn't give interviews! If he gave interviews, we'd be in trouble, because the world would no doubt have grown sick of his pompous proclamations long ago. But he has remained blessedly silent, and—"

I made an interrupting sound which he brushed aside with a laugh.

"I've got you an interview, Marsh. I did that *before* talking to Priest. Give me some credit."

"Why would—"

"Maybe because you were his next door neighbor."

"I was a kid. He never noticed me at all."

"Your father was his friend. You have memories in common. Besides, you're a huge fan."

"We tried that before."

"That's right, we did. But he's older, and I got lucky, got the old fart on the phone, and he sounded sort of weakened, not the same old thundering windbag, and he said, 'Marshall Harrison?' and I said, 'Yes, Harrison,' and I was going to explain what that meant, but he said, 'All right,' so we settled on a time. I was stunned. I had this whole sales pitch ready to go, and it was good, but I didn't need it. And get this, you're invited to stay at the house while you conduct the interview. He said there isn't a decent motel in town, so you might as well stay with him."

I needed the money, but that wasn't my sole motivation for flying the next morning from my home in Austin, via a disorienting stopover in Dallas, to Kansas City, renting a car, and aiming that car east on 152. I was curious about what Morton Sky had to say, and, in truth, I couldn't resist this opportunity to contemplate my past through the patina of accrued wisdom and regret. I'd always intended to return to Empire to see if it made any more sense now then it had when I was ten. This was my chance. The aging, almost irrelevant Morton Sky and his overly venerated relic of a novel would serve as the catalyst for deeper philosophical concerns.

And I'd write about my father and mother, remarkable people, volatile people. My father was, for a while, famous himself, having written a collection of poetry, *Imploding*, that captured the spirit of the late sixties with such passion and anarchic wit that it sold several hundred thousand copies, an extraordinary feat for a book of poetry, an *unheard* of feat for a book of poetry that was rigorously metrical and assumed an educated, literary background on the part of its readers.

My father wrote *Imploding* when we were living in Durham, where he taught literature courses at Duke University.

I remember the students, ragged and exotic to my child's eyes, who sat at his feet while he declaimed, waving his arms, standing on a coffee table. My father knew everything and could grab, from the air, any secret a book had ever held, any dead author's words, any thought the mind of man had formulated in the face of the terror and beauty of the world. My father was the spokesman for all that was important. I couldn't have articulated that when I was a kid, but I know it is what I thought, because I still think it, reflexively, and it requires an effort of willed objectivity to think otherwise.

My mother is a more elusive shape in my mind, because she is still alive, and I am older.

When we moved to Empire and rented the house next to Morton Sky, Marshall Harrison was the celebrity author, and Morton Sky was an odd, morose man tending to his dying grandmother who had been ill for years and who expired a month after our arrival.

If I could portray my father in juxtaposition to Sky, I might have something quite powerful, something worthy of a book.

On the plane, I'd tried to read *The Resolution of My Dread,* the only novel Morton Sky had ever written, but I couldn't get beyond Jenny's description of Main Street. I don't know why, on first reading, I (and the rest of America) hadn't paused to wonder at narrator Jenny's eleven-year-old voice, slangy, naive, and yet peppered with words like "elucidate" and "lambent" and "benign." This female Huck Finn with a thesaurus stuck in her throat should have created a convulsion of disbelief, but she didn't. Instead, America fell in love with her.

On publication in the spring of 1976, the novel leapt onto the *New York Times* best seller list, where it resided for eighty-two weeks. It has, even more impressively, achieved classic status, never going out of print, required reading in many high schools and progenitor of an equally famous movie. It still sells a quarter of a million copies a year.

Critically, the novel has followed the inevitable arc of such popular phenomena, first lavished with praise by reviewers who marveled at its authenticity, then applauded for its success, later venerated in critical studies, and finally disdained by younger critics who, having been bludgeoned by its thousand imitators, see nothing original in it and wonder how an earlier generation could have been so smitten by such a formulaic account of coming-of-age angst.

What can I say? I had loved the book; I was a little embarrassed by it now. There are certain novels that you only get if you come upon them at the right time, when your life is poised over a chasm of change. I was seventeen when I read the book. There are a lot of us who came upon *Resolution* at just that age.

On highway 291, I stopped at a gas station, filled the rented Buick up, and bought a soda inside, where coffee cups and bumper stickers certifying that I had visited Harry Truman's home in Independence were to be had for a pittance.

I passed on the souvenirs, got back in the Buick, and drove on into the Heartland. I turned the radio on and REO Speedwagon jumped out, freed from someone's attic. The Midwest liked to hang back a little, politically, theologically, musically, maybe twenty years behind the parade in case something went wrong up ahead. If the present went belly-up, they'd have a shorter run back to the fifties.

2

I arrived in Empire in the late afternoon, the last stretch of road flanked by tall rows of corn. Farms and crops gave way to houses with manicured lawns, and the speed limit shifted from 55 to 35 to 25 quickly enough to guarantee a steady stream of speeding-ticket revenue from incoming motorists lulled by the monotony of corn and soybean vistas. I passed the old Moose Lodge, saw it was sporting the same ancient sign, much the worse for wear, and then I entered the downtown area, where slow time continued to have its way. There was a McDonald's that hadn't been there before, and a big Bank of America building that had replaced Art's American Five & Dime, but the Empire Barbershop remained, and I knew it would look the same inside. The courthouse, although shrunken and diminished by time, retained its dignity and managed to convey a certain admirable stoicism.

Driving slowly, I peered into several empty storefronts and tried to locate the movie theater I had frequented but could find no trace of it. A yellow dog took its time getting across the street as the July sun sucked the finish from the dozen or so cars and trucks parked along Main; no parking meters existed to count the hours. Empire wasn't close enough to K. C. to be adopted by well-heeled commuters, and it was wearing away, drifting into stuporous old age.

In other words, it was much the same as it had been when my family arrived here.

Downtown consisted of two parallel streets and eight or nine blocks, so I made the tour in about five minutes and then drove around some until I located Emory Street. Halfway down the second block, on the left, was Morton Sky's house, a large faux-Victorian edifice with a black, wrought-iron fence surrounding it and a lawn that hadn't seen a lawn mower in months.

I had been surprised to learn that Sky had never moved. I had known he was still in Empire, that fact being something the press always noted, as proof of the author's abiding love for his town, or proof of his humility, or proof of his fear of the larger world. Well, no one agreed on just what it was proof of, but it was one of the few solid facts the press had, so they can be forgiven for hoping it was a fact that carried some truth or revelation within.

What I hadn't realized until Max gave me the address was that Sky had not only remained in Empire, he had remained in the family home, and, if he had made any repairs to it in the years since I'd been gone, time had unraveled them again.

To the left of Sky's house was a newer house, a small, tidy white house of two stories with purple shutters and a porch full of bright, multicolored flowers in pots. And to the right of Sky's house was a vacant lot. I imagined I saw the faint outlines of the house that my father had rented in the spring of 1974 and in which we had lived until February of '75 when it burned down.

It had been a big house, although not as big as the house next door. In Durham, we'd lived in a modest ranch house, and my older brother Andrew and I were fascinated by the new dimension of a second floor. We would race each other up the stairs, banging into the wall at the landing and pushing off it for the last flight of steps that brought us to the second floor hallway. Looking up, I'd see the soles of my brother's tennis shoes—he always won—and beyond his shoulders I'd see the attic's trapdoor, and I'd stop running. I was naturally wary of that door.

Three weeks after we were settled in our house, I ran up the stairs alone; I'd almost reached the top when that trapdoor flew open, and my father hung suspended in front of me like some ghastly magic trick, his face twisted, hands clawing at his throat, and before I could scream, something exploded, a loud reverberating *crack!* that shook the ceiling, and my father fell to his knees, the rope descending beside him to lie in coils by his side. My mother rushed out of their bedroom at the end of the hall and ran to him, screaming, "You sonofabitch! You stupid sonofabitch!" She fell on him, fists flying, screaming. Then she was lifting the rope from around his neck—I saw the red burn mark and blood on his pale throat—hugging him, sobbing deeply, while my father said nothing at all. I can't remember if we went to the emergency room that night or not. Sometimes we did, and sometimes we didn't. Not all the trips were prompted by my father's destructive proclivities. My mother was overly fond of sleeping pills.

"Christ, Louise! Sleeping pills!" my father would shout at her slumped form, there on the passenger seat. Andrew and I always sat in the back seat, saying nothing, dragged out of sleep, groggy. I suppose it would have been bad parenting to leave us alone at three in the morning. My father would lean over the steering wheel, concentrating, speeding to the hospital, which, conveniently, was only two miles away. "Fucking sleeping pills," he'd mutter, as though he were offended more by her method than her intention.

I didn't get out of the car. I didn't knock on Morton Sky's door and avail myself of his hospitality. I'd arrived a day early, and I had a reserved room waiting for me in a bed-and-breakfast in the neighboring town of Cale. I thought I'd revisit some places; see what memories I might revive, and take notes for the philosophical and thematic underpinnings that would transform my article into something more than a sighting of the great man breaking the surface of his silence.

3

"Much of my past," I wrote, "is a matter of hearsay. This is true, to a lesser or greater degree, of every human being." I admired this opening while finishing off the last of a glazed donut and a cup of coffee. I hadn't slept well in the small bedroom of my Victorian B & B in Cale. With its glut of ancient chairs and trunks and dowdy lamps, the room could have been serving as storage space for the effects of some long-dead relative, space that had been hastily adapted to accommodate an unexpected guest. I am sensitive to dust and mold, and I spent the night coughing and sneezing and exhausting an entire box of Kleenex.

I'd risen early, dressed and gone driving around Cale until I came upon Dale's Donuts and Coffee where a couple of parked cars suggested it might already be open in the first gray glimmer of dawn. It was.

I sat at a small table next to the front window. This was Main Street again, but a slightly more prosperous one than that of Empire. All the customers seemed to know the waitress, and good-natured banter reached my ears until I lost myself in my writing.

Before leaving for Empire, I'd called my mother to inform her of the proposed interview with Morton Sky. My mother had remarried in 1988. That husband, a man of great decency and no discernible personality, passed on six years ago, and my mother now resided in an assisted-living apartment in Greensboro, North Carolina.

I was hoping she'd talk about our time in Empire, although I knew it was unlikely. In the past, whenever I'd tried to get her to talk about Empire, she'd refused.

She surprised me this time. On learning that I'd be interviewing Morton Sky, she said, "There were always some who said your father wrote that book. After all, what did Morton Sky know about writing? He didn't know anything about life or literature. But, of course, the people who suggested your father wrote the book didn't know anything about your father. Really, why would he do such a thing? Why would he waste his time writing another man's book?"

I'd never given any thought to the ridiculous notion that my father had written *The Resolution of My Dread*. It was not a book he would have liked at all, the sentiment too easy, the narrator's cynicism nothing more than adolescent attitude.

"I just read the book recently," my mother continued. This came as a surprise to me. I'd always assumed she'd read it when it came out, and that we had never talked about it for obvious reasons.

"They have a little library here," she said, "and I saw Morton Sky's book. I'd never cared to read it, didn't care for the title, but I took it and I read it right through."

The line was silent. I waited. Finally, I spoke, "Mom?"

"Well." She hesitated. "It wasn't a good book. But, I swear, some of the sentences, some of the language, it brought Marshall back, like he was in the room with me. There were tears in my eyes when I finished that book. Your father and I fought all the time, but we were close—we loved each other—and I know the sound of him, and it's in that book, not all the time, but sometimes. I think he must have helped with it. I can't really see it. Your father was a selfish man. If you were a pretty coed, he might give you some extra attention, but a man like Morton Sky? It seems unlikely. Well . . . they did a lot of drinking together; he was over there drinking a lot, sometimes all night. I guess he must have helped with Sky's novel. You might ask Mr. Sky about that, although when I saw him on television— that was decades ago—he didn't seem the sort of man who would give credit to another."

I drove back to the bed-and-breakfast, collected my stuff, paid my bill, and drove to Empire.

I visited the Empire Gazette, the Empire Library, the police station, Ronnie's American Restaurant (where I ate lunch), the Empire Barbershop (where I got a haircut), Thompson's Auto Repair & Tires (nothing; the car was a rental). I called Jill Withers from Greta's Bar & Grill. Since I'd called her from Austin, she'd had time to think about meeting me. There was new reluctance in her voice. She thought maybe we *shouldn't* meet. "I don't know anything about him. I was just a kid when we lived next door."

I explained to her that I intended to write about my own boyhood in Empire, something to surround and give thematic substance to the interview, and that all I would ask of her is shared memories of that time. Our houses had flanked Sky's three-story ruin. The house Jill's parents had rented had been replaced by the new, purple-shuttered dwelling that I'd seen on Emory Street. If she had some thoughts on how she had perceived the man in the house next door that would be terrific, but I wasn't asking for anything that would compromise Mr. Sky's privacy, and if she didn't want to say anything at all about him, I'd respect that. "It will be good just seeing you," I said. "It's been a long time. I didn't expect you to still be in town. Calling your mother was a long shot."

"I'm just back," she said. And, letting me know she wasn't a fool, added, "I guess I could see you, but we ain't long lost pals, you know." I laughed and told her the drinks would be on me.

I wouldn't have recognized her. Nor she, me, I'm sure. Which was what you'd expect. I'd been ten years old then; Jill had been eleven. In 1974, her hair was red, as red as a firecracker on the Fourth, with freckles splashed across the bridge of her nose and her eyes blue and fierce with life.

Her hair had turned blonde since then, the roots brown. Her eyes, outlined in black mascara, had faded from blue to gray, as though what she'd seen in the intervening years had leached the color from them.

She had described herself over the phone ("frizzy blonde hair, blue jeans, a Tigers

T-shirt and the only woman in town who ain't fat") and that was the woman I waved at, and she came over, studied me, and sat down with a sigh.

"Marshall Harrison," she said. "Been a while, huh?"

"It has," I said. "You are looking well, Ms. Withers."

She waved the compliment away with a faint frown, rooted through her purse, and found a pack of cigarettes. "You can call me Jill. After all, we go back a long way. I'm gonna smoke," she said. "Want one?"

"I don't smoke," I said. It sounded priggish, a declaration of moral superiority. In Austin, *no one* smoked, not in a restaurant or bar; it was against the law, and I saw myself telling her that and the look she would send me.

The waitress came, and we both ordered beers. Jill didn't want anything to eat. A cheap date.

She took a long swallow of beer and slapped the mug down with a sigh of satisfaction. "I've only been back in town a week. When Mom told me there was a call for me, I figured it was my ex with some new line of bullshit. Instead it's you from a million years ago. I *do* remember. You and your brother . . . ?"

"Andrew," I said.

"Yeah, Andrew. I remember we used to hang out a lot, kid's stuff, comic books, swimming. . . . That was about a century ago."

A different century, I thought. *It really was a different century.*

She looked around the bar. "Maybe I could get work here. I need something, that's for sure. Living with Mom's the reason I ran off with an idiot like Lonnie in the first place. Now I'm back—and in a *trailer park*. There's a moral in there somewhere."

I can't take any credit for getting her to talk about Sky. In fact, most of the people I'd encountered that day had something to say about the man. The waitress at Ronnie's American Restaurant said Mr. Sky had never gotten over his grandmother's death ("She raised him, you know"), and that's why he didn't write another book. Bobby Thompson over at the auto repair said, "The man hit the ball out of the park on his first swing. He quit because he knew there was nowhere to go but down." Two customers over at the barbershop had nearly come to blows over my question. "He ain't writing," the one said, "because he's high on heroin, thinks Reagan is still the president, has a dope dealer drives out from St. Louis every other week with a briefcase full of heroin and a couple of hookers."

The other was outraged. "A man like that wouldn't go near heroin. If you could read, you might read his book, and then you'd know something of his character. He hasn't written another book because there aren't any people to write it *for*, just a bunch of assholes like you, TV-addicted, celebrity-gossiping assholes who wouldn't know a good book if it bit them on the ass."

They shoved each other some and knocked over a pile of magazines (*Sports Illustrated, People,* and *Missouri Fish & Game* among them), but the head barber, clearly the authority figure, said that the both of them were going to have to get used to bowl haircuts from their wives because they sure as hell weren't going to get any haircuts in his establishment if they couldn't act like civilized humans, and that quieted them immediately, with the one shaking his head in disgust and banging out the door.

When it came to Morton Sky, everyone had an opinion, but no one had anything much in the way of facts or even interesting anecdotes. Morton Sky had his groceries delivered to the house, and he didn't interact much with the town that he'd made famous. I was supposed to arrive at his doorstep at 7:00 that night, and the afternoon was rapidly fading away, so if Jill Withers didn't have anything substantive,

I'd have to create the atmosphere for this interview out of the weak fumes of my own recollections.

Jill said, "I had a crush on your father. He was the handsomest man I'd ever seen.

"Maybe he knew about it. I mean, knew I had a crush, because he always took time to ask how I was doing, and he always talked to me like I was an adult. He used to call me his Muse, remember?"

I remembered it as soon as she said it.

"That reminds me," she said. "I haven't thought of it in years, but at the time I think it creeped me out some. I had come by to see you, I don't remember what for, and your dad and Morton Sky were sitting out back of your house, on that stone bench where there used to be a white gazebo, and your dad called me over. 'Here comes my Muse,' he said. He rattled off some Greek names, other Muses, I guess, and I knew that a Muse was a goddess that inspired artists, so even though he was kidding, I was flattered, and I blushed. I could feel my face, hot and red. Then I looked at Morton Sky, and he was staring at me like he'd never seen me before, and he said, 'That's what I need. I need a Muse,' but he wasn't joining in a joke. He had a serious, desperate look, and your dad said, still joking, 'Stop looking at my Muse that way! Get your own.' But even then, Morton Sky didn't laugh. He looked away from me, and I thought he might cry or something, and I went on off to find you."

She said she hadn't thought much of it at the time, but now . . . well, if Morton Sky had ever looked at her daughter that way she would have made a point of *never* letting her daughter near that man again.

I thought I'd leave that anecdote out. A creepy look did not a pedophile make, and it would be unfair to the man to portray him as exhibiting some vague, unhealthy interest in a child, when Jill, a child, could have easily misinterpreted the man's expression. Besides, Morton Sky may have radiated weirdness, but I'd never felt he was dangerous. You wanted dangerous? My *parents* were dangerous. My brother and I knew better than to get between them when they were fighting.

<h2 style="text-align:center">4</h2>

Early that day, at the Empire Gazette, a newspaper that was still put together with hot wax, column-wide strips of typeset copy, and a plastic roller, I had been redirected to the library for its archives, and in the library, I'd found myself leaning over an eyepiece and staring at a halftone of my father who was smiling into the camera. Despite the halftone's rough resolution, my father's good looks shone through. I had heard people say he looked like Errol Flynn, meaningless back then because I didn't know who that actor was, but now the comparison seemed accurate. The headline read: *Poet Marshall Harrison Dies in Fire.*

On a jump page there was a photo of me, my mother, and my brother Andrew, all of us standing in front of the fire-ravaged house (a scorched chimney and some black remnants of the frame) and squinting into the camera like tourists documenting a visit to some decaying shrine. *Why would anyone take a photo like that? And why would we cooperate?* My brother towered over me and seemed to be scowling. I was smiling with what looked like childish exuberance. I know I was intent on hiding, at any cost, the knowledge within me, and perhaps I thought that a smile was the best disguise.

Jill said, "I'm sorry about the fire and your dad. I cried and cried. I thought I'd go crazy, and it wasn't like I was family, like I had the right to go off like I did. My mom took me to Dr. McLachlan so that he could give me some pills to calm me down, and she wouldn't let me go the funeral, said it was unhealthy. It's a long time coming, but I want to say I'm sorry for your loss."

"Thank you."

"They never did learn what started the fire, did they?"

"My father drank; he smoked a lot in bed," I said, but I didn't really answer her question. The truth was, the investigators had thought it might be arson, because of the extreme heat, the way the metal bookcases were surreally twisted and an empty wine bottle had melted flat like something in a Salvador Dali painting. But they never discovered a source for all that heat, and the investigation went nowhere. The heat turned my father's body into a cinder beyond the reach of the limited forensics they had at the time. Pieces of his grandfather's ancient revolver were found in the debris, and he could have shot himself with that gun—as he had threatened to do on more than one occasion—but the fierce blaze destroyed any hope of ever learning what actually happened.

I had been awakened by ripping and snapping sounds and my brother's shouts. He was in the room, in his underwear, shaking me by the shoulders, telling me to get up. Groggily, I reached for my jeans, which lay on the floor.

"No time!" he shouted. "The house is on fire."

I was aware of smoke in the room, smoke tickling my throat. A tremendous crash came from below us, shaking the house, and I was wide awake, with panic in my lungs. I ran down the hall, and somehow I was in front of him, and I saw flames at the foot of the stairs, and I leaned over the banister and looked into the open door of my father's study. He was lying on the cot that he sometimes napped on when he was, as he put it, recharging his batteries. I couldn't see his face for the smoke. A circle of flames surrounded the cot—*just like the students who used to sit at his feet*—and I saw blood on one of the pillows, a splash of blood, and more blood on the sheet tangled at his feet.

I shouted for my father to get up, but his stillness was absolute. I would have tried to reach him, to shake him back to consciousness, back to life, but a roar from the flames at the foot of the stairs made me turn away from this horror, and I saw flames racing toward me, leaping and snapping as they ascended the stairs like hounds in a killing frenzy.

I turned, and my brother and I ran back down the hall to my parents' bedroom where we roused my mother, who awoke, listless and confused.

"A *fire*?" she said, as though the word itself were one she'd never heard.

My brother was in charge, and a good thing that. He made us go out in the hall again and run through the smoke to my bedroom, my mother screaming, "Where's your father? Where's your father?" Andrew shoved open the window, and we were able to lean out, grab the thick branch of the maple tree, and swing over to the trunk. My mother was an athletic woman, an avid tennis player and hiker, and the descent would normally have been no problem for her, but she was in one of her overmedicated periods, and, after successfully gaining the trunk of the tree, she slipped, fell through branches that slowed her fall, and broke her ankle when she hit the ground.

I looked at my watch, saw that it was almost 7:00, and told Jill I would have to go.

"Thanks for coming," I said. "You can't think of anything else about Morton Sky?"

"No. I guess it's not so much loyalty that protects Sky from gossip. He just keeps out of the way, so there's nothing for gossip to feed on. It wasn't that way with his grandmother."

"What do you mean?"

Jill leaned forward. "Now that I think of it, that's something the town never *did* talk about. That's common knowledge that nobody cared to share."

"What's that?"

"Well, everyone agreed that Sky's grandmother was a witch. People would cross the street rather than walk by her door. My own grandmother was scared to death of her."

It was time to go. She asked me to call her before I left town. I said I would. Maybe we could get together for another drink before I left.

5

I pressed the doorbell, but I couldn't hear it ring within, so I took the big brass knocker in my hand and banged it three times. Some flakes of green paint fell from the door, and I waited a minute and knocked some more, and more of the door's dying paint job fluttered to the ground. Someone was coming. I heard the steady thump of shoes, and the door swung inward, and I was looking at Morton Sky, a really old Morton Sky sporting a brown tweed jacket over what looked like a striped pajama top. The fashion statement was completed with gray sweatpants and black dress shoes over white socks.

He regarded me from under hooded eyes. "No solicitors," he said. "Can't you read the sign?"

I looked around for a sign but didn't see one.

"There used to be a sign," he said.

"I'm Marshall Harrison," I said. "We had an appointment. I'm here to interview you."

Sky smiled. His teeth were long and yellow; his eyelids drooped, causing him to appear rueful, puzzled, and sly, all at the same time.

"Marshall!" He clapped his hands, the gesture mechanical, an imperfect attempt to show his real delight or a parody of that delight. He opened the door wider and backed up, ushering me into a gloomy corridor, the floor covered with an oriental rug so dirty and ill-used that various stains had triumphed over the original pattern, creating a more modern asymmetrical design.

He had already turned his back and was walking away, stooped at the shoulders, one finger held up in a gesture that, I assumed, indicated I should follow him.

He turned his head to look back at me. "Didn't recognize you. Guess New York changes a man from the inside out." He turned away and marched on.

I followed him. I had used the same book jacket photo for years now; maybe it was time for a new one. .

"I live in Austin, Texas, not New York," I said.

He laughed and didn't look back. "As long as you're living, right?"

I didn't have a clue what that meant, but it did remind me of the early years when Morton Sky gave interviews. He had a pompous, overly fastidious way of saying things and a fondness for inscrutable epigrams. Humility, a virtue America loves to discover in its icons, was not Sky's long suit. His manner, in the recorded interviews that I had watched, showed a man who was dealing with fools and had just about reached the limits of his patience.

America had loved him in spite of the arrogance of his demeanor, but maybe—this just occurred to me—Max had been right in suggesting that the man's welcome would have worn thin had he chosen to stay in the limelight.

I entered a large room with several sofas, lots of overstuffed chairs, a host of bookcases, a massive antique wardrobe, a worn green carpet, and a hanging chandelier in which small, flame-shaped bulbs glowed wanly. No lamps were turned on, and the room was filling up with shadows and certain to grow darker as the light that glowed behind the window shades receded, following the sun over the horizon.

"Please have a seat," my host said, waving at a sofa. "I'll fetch us something to drink." And he disappeared down another hallway.

I waited, sitting on the sofa. I noticed that the bookcase closest to me held nothing but copies of *The Resolution of My Doom*, various foreign editions of the book and the numerous American editions and paperback reprints. I recognized the tan spines of the first edition, four rows, and it occurred to me that the contents of the bookcase would fetch a tidy sum. I counted the first editions and made a note to look up the going rate for a well-preserved, jacketed copy.

I was feeling a little woozy, not drunk, but tired. Drinking after a sleepless night and before an interview. What was I thinking? I closed my eyes, just the briefest respite . . .

"Hello, Marshall. Dropped off, did you? I do that all the time." Sky was holding a silver tray upon which resided two wine glasses and a bottle of wine. He put the tray down on an end table, turned the wine glasses right side up, and filled both of them.

He offered one to me, and I took it.

Holding his own filled wine glass, he eased himself into a bulky brown arm chair. I expected dust to rise from the frayed and dirty fabric, and perhaps it did. It was too dark to tell.

The years hadn't treated Morton Sky well. He had been handsome once, but age had exaggerated the features that had made him so, causing me to doubt any youthful good looks that could morph into this dissolute, watery-eyed fat man. His size gave him the aspect of a hulking ruin that might succumb to gravity at any moment and crumble before my eyes.

I sipped the wine, neither of us saying anything. *Not very good wine*, I thought. Perhaps the bitterness was something that only connoisseurs could learn to love.

I decided to break the silence with a requisite bit of flattery, explaining how I was a big fan of his book, which I had read when I was seventeen, years after we'd moved from Empire. Only then, I told him, did I realize that I had lived next door to a genius. It is impossible to overflatter a writer, so I poured it on.

He didn't answer. He might have been asleep, his chin resting on his chest, lips pursed and swollen, eyes lost in the shadows of his prominent brow. His big hands clutched the arms of the chair, and I could hear his breathing, a slow rasp.

"Mr. Sky—" I began.

He coughed. "Didn't recognize you," he said. "You look different without the mustache."

He seemed to recede. I was hideously tired. I shouldn't have indulged in those afternoon beers. I had never had a mustache. He was saying something else, muttering to himself.

"Don't want to kill you, but I'm no pharmacist. Ten pills for half a bottle. That seemed right." He held his own wine glass up, still filled to the brim. "I'll be right back," he said. "I just need to pour this out. Wouldn't do to drink it, and I might. I find I'm very absentminded these days."

With some effort he got up, and he was slowly making his way toward the hall when I blacked out.

6

I awoke with a jolt. I had been falling. My heart was racing, and I was sweating profusely.

Morton Sky was leaning forward, his face a foot from mine, the network of exploded capillaries that scrawled across his nose and cheeks like a map of bad living, his eyes blue and stupidly inquisitive.

"It worked," he said, and smiled.

I tried to stand but could not. I looked down. I wasn't on the sofa. My wrists were bound with duct tape to the wooden armrests of a straight-backed chair. My right arm was bare where my shirt sleeve had been rolled up. A drop of blood glistened darkly on my forearm.

I couldn't see my feet, but they too were bound. I looked at Sky again, and he was holding up a syringe, looking at the liquid that remained within.

His eyes moved back to my face.

"Epinephrine," he said. "Stuff you get in those little asthma inhalers. I know, you don't have to tell me, it's a little risky. But you don't look like a man with a weak heart, and I couldn't wait around all night, could I?"

My heart was beating as though it might sprout wings and fly. If I opened my mouth to scream, my heart would fly out. I was sick to my stomach, buzzing with nausea. I was going to die.

Morton Sky stood up, turned and walked back to the armchair he had been sitting in earlier. He sat down, slapped his hands on his knees, leaned forward, smiled, and said, "Okay, ask me anything."

"Why . . ." Too many words crowded my mind.

Morton Sky was oblivious to my confusion. "I never really thought you were dead, Marshall. I don't know why you came back, but I was glad to hear it. I've got something of yours."

He stood up abruptly and walked out of the room again.

He returned with another silver tray, this one holding a dozen tiny burning candles floating in the oil of oversized shot glasses.

He set this tray down, and returned to the armchair. "So ask me why I haven't written another book," he said, wiggling slightly before settling comfortably in the chair and giving me his full attention, as a parent might grant an audience with a child. "Go on, that's what everyone asks."

I said nothing.

He shouted: "Ask me!"

"Why didn't you write another book?" I said. My insides were dancing, but I thought, *No need to ask now. I know the answer: you lost your mind.*

"That's a good question," he said. "I did so well with that first book. I could have made quite a lot of money with another book. Even if the book was vilified by the reviewers, everyone would have to own a copy, wouldn't they? And here's what's really interesting, although it may come as no surprise to you . . ." He paused for dramatic effect, and then he leaned forward, shouting, "I *did* write another book!" He leaned back, composed himself, and spoke in a softer voice, "Quite a few more books, actually."

He got up and strode to the dark, looming shape of the wardrobe. He swung it open. I still couldn't see what was within, but Sky must have anticipated that. He reached out and flipped a wall switch which turned on a standing lamp to the right and in front of the wardrobe. I stared at stacked reams of paper, bound in bundles by thick brown rubber bands. The manuscripts rose to within two feet of the wardrobe's ceiling. Two feet and the wardrobe would be completely filled.

He let me stare at this manifestation of his industry for several minutes, and then he turned the lamp off again. He went back, got the tray of burning candles, and began arranging them around me. He placed one on the floor directly in front of me, and then, following some painstaking methodology known only to him, placed the others around me in a circle, with some of the candles in clumps, others spaced several feet apart. He arose from the last candle, surveyed his work, nodded, and walked to yet another bookcase, from which he withdrew an oversized book that looked to be bound in worn red leather. He opened it and looked up at me. "I am going to give you back something of yours. Can you guess what?"

I couldn't. I realized now that, in his eroded mental state, he thought I was my father.

"I'm not very good at this. Gran always said, 'You can teach a conjure, but those without the gift will be prenticed all their lives.'"

He began to read. What he read sounded like Latin, and it rose and fell in strange, unvarying cadences. I was unable to translate any of it, despite my two years of high school Latin, but I confess my mind was elsewhere. I was distracted by my racing heart, which had sped up even more when I saw the long, curved knife that hung from a cord around his neck. It dangled, naked and bright, over his pajama-striped belly, and I was pretty sure it was a new addition to his fashion accessories. Surely he wasn't wearing it when he opened the door.

All I knew was this: a sharp—it looked *very* sharp—knife doesn't bode well when the lunatic wearing it is chanting Latin and the audience (i.e., me) is tied to a chair.

He put the book down on the floor, slipped out of his jacket and let it drop to the floor. He unbuttoned his pajama top and tossed that away, too, revealing new proof of his madness, had any been required. Half circles of lurid red dots, wounds, some fresher than others, covered his chest and stomach. Scattered amid these red half-circles were dozens of livid scratch marks.

He clutched the knife, still dangling from the chain around his neck, turned his wrist outward and administered a quick, downward stroke. A five-inch vertical line of blood appeared, ending just above his navel. He held the knife against the wound, and blood flowed over the blade. Now he bowed his head to lift the chain from over his head.

Jesus I thought. *Kill yourself! Please just kill yourself*.

He lifted the knife, and I saw his eyes, and I was out of luck, so far out of luck, but maybe, maybe, not tortured, okay, just *not tortured. Please*.

And this is where the chance of selling this piece to *American Promise*, a magazine that prides itself on its rationality, pretty much goes out the window.

Still muttering something, Sky shook the knife blade over the bound book, and I watched as small drops of blood spotted the moldering cover. Instantly, the creature was with us, within the circle. I don't know what Morton Sky was doing at that moment, because I couldn't take my eyes off the thing.

It was, I want to say, insectile, but that suggests a remote and alien creature, an unknowable intelligence, and much of this thing's horror lay in its familiarity. It emitted a stink of yearning, of sewn-together desires, perverse and vile and yet *shared*.

It moved toward me while my mind tried to comprehend what it was—and, somehow, what it *meant*.

It wore a kind of ghostly shroud, like a translucent, hooded raincoat, which obscured its actual form. It was no bigger than a child, but not a child, more like a dog standing on its hind legs, and it moved with ragged, illogical speed, a motion that filled me with vertiginous nausea. The creature glided to the book, prodded it with a clawed finger and turned toward me. Jill's face appeared, the red-haired, eleven-year-old Jill, and my gasp of recognition called the whole of her into being, and she was standing in front of me, but not Jill, never for a moment a plausible illusion. She was translucent, and the thing within her moved with its own logic. But she was gathering substance as though—and only later, on reflection, did I think this—some feedback from my emotions, my thoughts, fine-tuned the simulacrum.

The Jill thing came up to me, extended a finger, touched my bare arm just above the elbow, and I felt an excruciating pain. Slowly, while I writhed in agony, she drew her finger down, toward my thumb, and a line of blood followed the track of her nail. Then she drew back, blinked, and hissed. Abruptly she turned away and moved quickly toward Sky who had backed beyond the circle of candles.

He watched her approaching, and he cringed, a big man trying to squeeze himself into some other reality, anywhere not here, bent forward as though he'd been punched in the stomach, his arms out in front of him, the fingers of his hands splayed. This was an overwrought performance, exaggerated gestures from a silent film. You had to be there to appreciate its accuracy.

He pointed a trembling finger at me. "There's your master," he whispered. She did not turn to follow his finger, nor did she give any indication that she had heard him. She came on.

When she reached him, her arm shot out, and she clutched his naked forearm and pulled him close. Her head darted and turned, with inhuman speed, and her mouth opened, and she bit him on the pallid, trembling flesh of his upper arm. He shrieked. Immediately she released him, and I saw the mark of her teeth, a black semicircle in the gloom. Blood ran down his arm. She spoke. "Right now!" she said. "Now!" Her voice was a whisper, but loud enough to fill my head, vicious, full of unholy need.

And Sky staggered toward her, whimpered, and she spun him toward the hallway, and into the hallway, and his whimpering came back to me, rapidly diminishing, as they climbed the stairs to the second floor.

I listened, still and attentive, and I heard nothing but my own heart for long minutes, and then, finally, I heard something, faint but unmistakable, a sound like no other, the precise, authoritative *thak, thak, thak* of an electric typewriter.

I looked at my own bloodied arm and saw that the clawed nail that had slid through my flesh had also cut the duct tape cleanly, as a razor might. I yanked my arm back; I writhed in agony as my heart beat faster, and my wrist came away, free, throwing me backwards with the chair. My head hit one of the candles as I came down, and I felt the flame bite my ear, and I smelled my burning hair. But my arm was free, and that was all that mattered. I quickly tore the tape from my other wrist and both ankles. I stood up alive. I turned and started for the door.

I stopped. I was not going to climb those stairs. I was not going to risk my life for Morton Sky who had, I believed, hijacked my father's Muse by occult means and, possibly, murdered my father. But I was going to satisfy my curiosity regarding Sky's literary efforts. I walked to the wardrobe and, bending forward, I dragged one of the bound manuscripts from the middle of the pile, causing the others to spill around me, a literary avalanche. I fanned the pages with my thumb, satisfying myself that I held typewritten pages, just as Sky had said, and then I walked to the front door and let myself out, closing the door behind me.

I called Jill Withers from my cell phone on the way out of town. Something had come up, I said, and I had to leave immediately. This news didn't devastate her.

"So did you learn why he never wrote another book?" she asked.

I gave her the generic answer: "Success was more than he could handle."

I suppose she sensed my reluctance to pursue the subject. She thanked me for calling, wished me luck, and said that she had a cousin in Austin and would look me up if she ever got down that way.

7

She hasn't called. Almost three years have gone by, so I don't expect she will. A little over eighteen months ago, Morton Sky lost his life when his house burned down. Who knows what exorcism he was attempting? Every newspaper, every magazine, every television news station dusted off his bio, and the resurrected hype and conjecture surrounding his famous book caused a new spike in its sales. No one noted that the house next to Sky's had burned down years before, carrying off another writer, famous once himself. Surely some of Empire's old-timers marked this coincidence, but the reporters, with access to famous writers and celebrities ready to testify to *Resolution*'s impact on their lives, didn't seek out Empire's anonymous residents.

The day I left Empire, I drove to Kansas City and checked into a Best Western to wait it out until my flight the next evening. I studied my wounded forearm in the shower; stitches might have been a good idea, but I saw no signs of infection. *Supernatural creatures*, I thought, *are probably germ-free.*

I lay down on the bed, and I woke on top of the bedspread, shivering in my jockey shorts, at 3:15 in the morning. I turned up the thermostat, which had been set to 65, and crawled under the sheets, but I couldn't fall asleep again, so I got the manuscript I'd taken from Sky's wardrobe stash, plumped up the pillows behind me, and turned on the nightstand lamp. The first page was a blank sheet of paper. "Chapter 1" was centered at the top of the next page. The text (double-spaced, courier) began: "My name is Lisa Anne Jenkins. If I had someone handy, I'd just talk to her or even him. I wouldn't write this down. If you are reading this, you are probably going to use it against me later. Don't take umbrage, that's just the way it will be."

Umbrage, indeed.

Word for word, except for the heroine's name, this was the opening of *The Resolution of My Dread.* I flipped through the manuscript and quickly confirmed what I'd guessed: except for name changes, this was the same book Morton Sky had written in 1975.

On some of the manuscript pages, I found rust-brown smears (blood, I assumed). One page near the end of the manuscript contained a bloody handprint.

A bad day, I thought.

I lay in bed and stared at the ceiling. I thought of all the typed pages, each page its own arduous, sacred task (no word-processing magic to call upon). I thought of the wardrobe, tall and wide and jammed with dozens of *Resolution* clones, all created on an electric typewriter. Perhaps, every day of his life, Morton Sky thought he was writing something new, something powerful, revolutionary, and imbued with fire and passion.

Until he read what he'd written.

Maybe the creature that drove him no longer graced him with any inward light. I had heard it command him, in that uncanny, imperious voice, and the urgency I heard was undeniable, but what she (it) had uttered, I realized, was: "*Write* now!"

The thing had turned on him, and he had tried to give it back to the man he'd stolen it from, but the one he could have returned it to was dead, and I was not a suitable substitute, even if the same blood flowed in my veins.

All this was long ago. My agent, Max Felwin, is gone. A woman he refused to marry shot him dead, the price he paid for trying to change his ways.

I had called him the day after my return from Empire. He had been gracious when I told him I couldn't write—or even talk about—the interview with Sky. He was used to projects that failed to materialize, having dealt with writers and editors for almost fifty years.

I am compelled to add something to this narrative, which isn't to be published until after my death, at which time you are all free to question my sanity. I have no reputation to preserve, and I'm not interested in posterity's good opinion. I write to hear these words in my own mind, to stand back and read them later and judge their truth from a distance.

This month, in the mail, I received the galleys for a book of my father's collected essays. These are essays my father wrote for various magazines and journals after the success of *Imploding*.

I was sure I had read all these pieces. They are not his best work, being the rants of a man who had let his celebrity status lull him into sloppy prose and self-importance. But there is an essay, the first in the book, that I had never read before.

"My Suicides" filled me with a growing sense of dread and revelation. I could hear Andrew's voice saying, "I wish he'd just do it right!" after another of my father's failed attempts.

In the essay, my father describes the various ways in which he tried to kill himself, with alcohol, drugs, and by his own hand. He even speaks, with humor, of his failed attempt to hang himself, although he fails to note that his youngest child was present for this performance. He writes frankly, without self-pity or melodrama, about his mental illness, its various diagnoses and the delusions it inspired.

He writes these lines:

I had called Calliope my Muse, because *Imploding* aspired to epic poetry, but later I strove for something more personal and Polyhymnia, the Muse of sacred poetry, befriended me. In my drunkenness, my drug stupors, my derangements, I didn't understand that I was summoning something more ancient, a banished sister whose atavistic heart burned with rage and terrible need, a tenth Muse that was nameless and moved without mercy through the darkest night. The Muse that offered the shotgun to Hemingway, the arsenic to Chatterton, the ocean to Hart Crane, the river to Virginia Woolf, the pills to Jack London, and the pistol to Robert E. Howard. This is the Muse of oblivion, of negation and obsession, and her voice is as sweet as any of her sisters.

For the first time, I felt my father's absence, and I wept.

JEFFREY FORD

The Drowned Life

"The Drowned Life" is Jeffrey Ford's ninth story to appear in this anthology. The story was originally published in the premiere volume of Jonathan Strahan's annual anthology, Eclipse One: New Science Fiction and Fantasy *(Night Shade Books). Ford's most recent books include the novels* The Girl in the Glass *(winner of the Edgar Award) and* The Shadow Year, *as well as a collection named after this story. He is a professor of writing and early American literature at Brookdale Community College in New Jersey.*
                                                                —K.L. & G.G.

It came trickling in over the transom at first, but Hatch's bailing technique had grown rusty. The skies were dark with daily news of a pointless war and genocide in Africa, poverty, AIDS, desperate millions in migration. The hot air of the commander-in-chief met the stone cold bullshit of congress and spawned water spouts, towering gyres of deadly ineptitude. A steady rain of increasing gas prices, grocery prices, medical costs, drove down hard like a fall of needles. At times the mist was so thick it baffled the mind. Somewhere in a back room, Liberty, Goddess of the Sea, was tied up and blindfolded—wires leading out from under her toga and hooked to a car battery. You could smell her burning, an acid stink that rode the fierce winds, turning the surface of the water brown.

Closer by, three sharks circled in the swells, their fins visible above chocolate waves. Each one of those slippery machines of Eden stood for a catastrophe in the secret symbolic nature of this story. One was *Financial Ruin*, I can tell you that—a stainless-steel beauty whose sharp maw made Hatch's knees literally tremble like in a cartoon. In between the bouts of bailing, he walked a tightrope. At one end of his balancing pole was the weight of the bills, a mortgage like a Hydra, whose head grew back each month for a house too tall and too shallow, taxes out the ass, failing appliances, car payments. At the other end was his job at an HMO, denying payment to people with legitimate claims. Each conversation with each claimant was harrowing for him, but he was in no position to quit. What else would he do? Each poor sap denied howled with indignation and unallied pain at the injustice of it all. Hatch's practiced façade, his dry, "Sorry," hid indigestion, headaches, sweat, and his constant, subconscious reiteration of Darwin's law of survival as if it were some golden rule.

Beyond that, the dog had a chronic ear infection, his younger son, Ned, had recently been picked up by the police for smoking pot and the older one, Will, who had a severe case of athlete's foot, rear-ended a car on route 70. "Just a tap. Not a scratch," he'd claimed, and then the woman called with her dizzying estimate.

Hatch's wife, Rose, who worked twelve hours a day, treating the people at a hospital whose claims he would eventually turn down, demanded a vacation with tears in her eyes. "Just a week, somewhere warm," she said. He shook his head and laughed as if she was kidding. It was rough seas between his ears and rougher still in his heart. Each time he laughed, it was in lieu of puking.

Storm Warning was a phrase that made surprise visits to his consciousness while he sat in front of a blank computer screen at work, or hid in the garage at home late at night smoking one of the Captain Blacks he'd supposedly quit, or stared listlessly at Celebrity Fit Club on the television. It became increasingly difficult for him to remember births, first steps, intimate hours with Rose, family jokes, vacations in packed cars, holidays with extended family. One day Hatch did less bailing. "Fuck that bailing," he thought. The next day he did even less.

As if he'd just awakened to it, he was suddenly standing in water up to his shins and the rain was beating down in a strong southwester. The boat was bobbing like the bottom lip of a crone on Thorazine as he struggled to keep his footing. In his hands was a small plastic garbage can, the same one he'd used to bail his clam boat when at eighteen he worked the Great South Bay. The problem was Hatch wasn't eighteen anymore, and though now he was spurred to bail again with everything he had, he didn't have much. His heart hadn't worked so hard since his 25th anniversary when Rose made him climb a mountain in Montana. Even though the view at the top was gorgeous—a basin lake and a breeze out of heaven—his T-shirt jumped with each beat. The boat was going down. He chucked the garbage can out into the sea and *Financial Ruin* and its partners tore into it. Reaching for his shirt pocket, he took out his smokes and lit one.

The cold brown water was just creeping up around Hatch's balls as he took his first puff. He noticed the dark silhouette of Captree Bridge in the distance. "Back on the bay," he said, amazed to be sinking into the waters of his youth, and then, like a struck wooden match, the entire story of his life flared and died behind his eyes.

Going under was easy. No struggle, but a change in temperature. Just beneath the dark surface, the water got wonderfully clear. All the stale air came out of him at once—a satisfying burp followed by a large translucent globe that stretched his jaw with its birth. He reached for its spinning brightness but sank too fast to grab it. His feet were still lightly touching the deck as the boat fell slowly beneath him. He looked up and saw the sharks still chewing plastic. "This is it," thought Hatch, "not with a bang but a bubble." He herded all of his regrets into the basement of his brain, an indoor oak forest with intermittent dim light bulbs and dirt floor. The trees were columns that held the ceiling and amid and among them skittered pale, disfigured doppelgangers of his friends and family. As he stood at the top of the steps and shut the door on them, he felt a subtle tearing in his solar plexus. The boat touched down on the sandy bottom and his sneakers came to rest on the deck. Without thinking, he gave a little jump and sailed in a lazy arc ten feet away, landing, with a puff of sand, next to a toppled marble column.

His every step was a graceful bound, and he floated. Once on the slow descent of his arc, he put his arms out at his sides and lifted his feet behind him so as to fly. Hatch found that if he flapped his arms, he could glide along a couple of feet above the bottom, and he did, passing over coral pipes and red seaweed rippling like human hair in a breeze. There were creatures scuttling over rocks and through the sand—long antennae and armor plating, tiny eyes on sharp stalks and claws continuously practicing on nothing. As his shoes touched the sand again, a school of striped fish swept past his right shoulder, their blue glowing like neon, and he followed their flight.

He came upon the rest of the sunken temple, its columns pitted and cracked, broken like the tusks of dead elephants. Green vines netted the destruction—two wide marble steps there, here a piece of roof, a tilted mosaic floor depicting the Goddess of the Sea suffering a rash of missing tiles, a headless marble statue of a man holding his penis.

2

Hatch floated down the long empty avenues of Drowned Town, a shabby, but quiet city in a lime green sea. Every so often, he'd pass one of the citizens, bloated and blue, in various stages of decomposition, and say, "Hi." Two gentlemen in suits swept by but didn't return his greeting. A Drowned mother and child, bulging eyes dissolving in trails of tiny bubbles, dressed in little more than rags, didn't acknowledge him. One old woman stopped, though, and said, "Hello."

"I'm new here," he told her.

"The less you think about it the better," she said and drifted on her way.

Hatch tried to remember where he was going. He was sure there was a reason that he was in town, but it eluded him. "I'll call Rose," he thought. "She always knows what I'm supposed to be doing." He started looking up and down the streets for a pay phone. After three blocks without luck, he saw a man heading toward him. The fellow wore a business suit and an overcoat torn to shreds, a black hat with a bullet hole in it, a closed umbrella hooked on a skeletal wrist. Hatch waited for the man to draw near, but as the fellow stepped into the street to cross to the next block, a swift gleaming vision flew from behind a building and with a sudden clang of steel teeth meeting took him in its jaws. *Financial Ruin* was hungry and loose in Drowned Town. Hatch cowered backward, breast stroking to a nearby dumpster to hide, but the shark was already gone with its catch.

On the next block up, he found a bar that was open. He didn't see a name on it, but there were people inside, the door was ajar, and there was the muffled sound of music. The place was cramped and narrowed the further back you went, ending in a corner. Wood paneling, mirror behind the bottles, spinning seats, low lighting and three deadbeats—two on one side of the bar and one on the other.

"Got a pay phone?" asked Hatch.

All three men looked at him. The two customers smiled at each other. The bartender with a red bow tie, wiped his rotted nose on a handkerchief, and then slowly lifted an arm to point. "Go down to the grocery store. They got a pay phone at the deli counter."

Hatch had missed it when the old lady spoke to him, but he realized now that he heard the bartender's voice in his head, not with his ears. The old man moved his mouth, but all that came out were vague farts of words flattened by water pressure. He sat down on one of the bar stools.

"Give me something dry," he said to the bartender. He knew he had to compose himself, get his thoughts together.

The bartender shook his head, scratched a spot of coral growth on his scalp, and opened his mouth to let a minnow out. "I could make you a Jenny Diver . . . pink or blue?"

"No, Sal, make him one of those things with the dirt bomb in it . . . they're the driest," said the closer customer. The short man turned his flat face and stretched a grin like a soggy old doll with swirling hair. Behind the clear lenses of his eyes, shadows moved, something swimming through his head.

"You mean a Dry Reach. That's one dusty drink," said the other customer, a very pale, skeletal old man in a brimmed hat and dark glasses. "Remember the day I got stupid on those? Your asshole'll make hell seem like a backyard barbecue if you drink too many of them, my friend."

"I'll try one," said Hatch.

"Your wish is my command," said the bartender, but he moved none too swiftly. Still, Hatch was content to sit and think for a minute. He thought that maybe the drink would help him remember. For all of its smallness, the place had a nice relaxing current flowing through it. He folded his arms on the bar and rested his head down for a moment. It finally came to him that the music he'd heard since entering was Frank Sinatra. "The Way You Look Tonight," he whispered, naming the current song. He pictured Rose, naked, in bed back in their first apartment, and with that realization, the music went off.

Hatch looked up and saw that the bartender had turned on the television. The two customers, heads tilted back, stared into the glow. On the screen there was a news show without sound but the caption announced *News from the War*. A small seahorse swam behind the glass of the screen but in front of the black and white imagery. The story was about a ward in a makeshift field hospital where army doctors treated the wounded children of the area. Cute little faces stared up from pillows, tiny arms with casts listlessly waved, but as the report obviously went on, the wounds got more serious. There were children with missing limbs, and then open wounds, great gashes in the head, the chest, and missing eyes, and then a gaping hole with intestines spilling out, the little legs trembling and the chest heaving wildly.

"There's only one term for this war," said the old man with the sunglasses. "Clusterfuck. Cluster as in cluster and fuck as in fuck. No more need be said."

The short man turned to Hatch, and still grinning, said, "There was a woman in here yesterday, saying that we're all responsible."

"We are," said the bartender. "Drink up." He set Hatch's drink on the bar. "One Dry Reach," he said. It came in a big martini glass—clear liquid with a brown lump at the bottom.

Hatch reached for his wallet, but the bartender waved for him not to bother. "You must be new," he said.

Hatch nodded.

"Nobody messes with money down here. This is Drowned Town . . . think about it. Drink up, and I'll make you three more."

"Could you put Sinatra back on," Hatch asked sheepishly. "This news is bumming me out."

"As you wish," said the bartender. He pressed a red button under the bar. Instantly, the television went off, and the two men turned back to their drinks. Sinatra sang "Let's take it nice and easy," and Hatch thought, "Free booze." He sipped his drink and could definitely distinguish its tang from the briny sea water. Whether he liked the taste or not, he'd decide later, but for now he drank it as quickly as he could.

The customer further from Hatch stepped around his friend and approached. "You're in for a real treat, man," he said. "You see that little island in the stream there?" He pointed at the brown lump in the glass.

Hatch nodded.

"A bit of terra firma, a little taste of the world you left behind upstairs. Remember throwing dirt bombs when you were a kid? Like the powdery lumps in homemade brownies? Oh, and the way they'd explode against the heads of your victims. Well you've got a dollop of high grade dirt there. You bite into it, and you'll taste your life left behind—bright sun and blue skies."

"Calm down," said the short man to his fellow customer. "Give him some room."

Hatch finished the drink and let the lump roll out of the bottom of the glass into his mouth. He bit it with his molars but found it had nothing to do with dirt. It was mushy and tasted terrible, more like a sodden meatball of decay than a memory of the sun. He spit the mess out and it darkened the water in front of his face. He waved his hand to disperse the brown cloud. A violet fish with a lazy tail swam down from the ceiling to snatch what was left of the disintegrating nugget.

The two customers and the bartender laughed, and Hatch heard it like a party in his brain. "You got the tootsie roll," said the short fellow and tried to slap the bar, but his arm moved too slowly through the water.

"Don't take it personally," said the old man. "It's a Drowned Town tradition." His right ear came off just then and floated away, his glasses slipping down on that side.

Hatch felt a sudden burst of anger. He'd never liked playing the fool.

"Sorry, fella," said the bartender, "but it's a ritual. On your first Dry Reach, you get the tootsie roll."

"What's the tootsie roll?" asked Hatch, still trying to get the taste out of his mouth.

"Well, for starters, it ain't a tootsie roll," said the man with the outlandish grin.

3

Hatch marveled at the myriad shapes and colors of seaweed in the grocery's produce section. The lovely wavering of their leaves, strands, tentacles, in the flow soothed him. Although he stood on the sandy bottom, hanging from the ceiling were rows of fluorescent lights, every third or fourth one working. The place was a vast concrete bunker, set up in long aisles of shelves like at the Super Shopper he'd trudged through innumerable times back in his dry life.

"No money needed," he thought. "And free booze, but then why the coverage of the war? For that matter why the tootsie roll? *Financial Ruin* has free rein in Drowned Town. Nobody seems particularly happy. It doesn't add up." Hatch left the produce section, passed a display of starfish, some as big as his head, and drifted off, in search of the deli counter.

The place was enormous, row upon row of shelved dead fish, their snouts sticking into the aisle, silver and pink and brown. Here and there a gill still quivered, a fin twitched. "A lot of fish," thought Hatch. Along the way, he saw a special glass case that held frozen food that had sunk from the world above. The hot dog tempted him, even though a good quarter had gone green. There was a piece of a cupcake with melted sprinkles, three french fries, a black Twizzler, and a red and white Chinese takeout bag with two gnarled rib ends sticking out. He hadn't had any lunch, and his stomach growled in the presence of the delicacies, but he was thinking of Rose and wanted to talk to her.

Hatch found a familiar face at the lobster tank. He could hardly believe it, Bob Gordon from up the block. Bob looked none the worse for wear for being sunk, save for his yellow complexion. He smoked a damp cigarette and stared into the tank as if staring through it.

"Bob," said Hatch.

Bob turned and adjusted his glasses. "Hatch, what's up?"

"I didn't know you went under."

"Sure, like a fuckin' stone."

"When?" asked Hatch.

"Three, four weeks ago. Peggy'd been porking some guy from over in Larchdale. You know, I got depressed, laid off the bailing, lost the house, and then eventually I just threw in the pail."

"How do you like it here?"

"Really good," said Bob and his words rang loud in Hatch's brain, but then he quickly leaned close and these words came in a whisper, "It sucks."

"What do you mean?" asked Hatch, keeping his voice low.

Bob's smile deflated. "Everything's fine," he said, casting a glance to the lobster tank. He nodded to Hatch. "Gotta go, bud."

He watched Bob bound away against a mild current. By the time Hatch reached the deli counter, it was closed. In fact, with the exception of Bob, he'd seen no one in the entire store. An old black phone with a rotary dial sat atop the counter with a sign next to it that read: Free Pay Phone. NOT TO BE USED IN PRIVACY!

Hatch looked over his shoulder. There was no one around. Stepping forward he reached for the receiver, and just as his hand closed on it, the thing rang. He felt the vibration before he heard the sound. He let it go and stepped back. It continued to ring, and he was torn between answering it and fleeing. Finally, he picked it up and said, "Hello."

At first he thought the line was dead, but then a familiar voice sounded. "Hatch," it said, and he knew it was Ned, his younger son. Both of his boys had called him Hatch since they were toddlers. "You gotta come pick me up."

"Where are you?" asked Hatch.

"I'm at a house party behind the 7-Eleven. It's starting to get crazy."

"What do you mean it's starting to get crazy?"

"You coming?"

"I'll be there," said Hatch, and then the line went dead.

He stood at the door to the basement of his brain and turned the knob, but before he could open it, he saw way over on the other side of the store, one of the silver sharks, cruising above the aisles up near the ceiling. Dropping the phone, he scurried behind the deli counter, and then through an opening that led down a hall to a door.

4

Hatch was out of breath from walking, searching for someone who might be able to help him. For ten city blocks he thought about Ned needing a ride. He pictured the boy, hair tied back, baggy shorts and shoes like slippers, running from the police. "Good grief," said Hatch and pushed forward. He'd made a promise to Ned years earlier that he would always come and get him if he needed a ride, no matter what. How could he tell him now, "Sorry kid, I'm sunk." Hatch thought of all the things that could happen in the time it would take him to return to land and pick Ned up at the party. Scores of tragic scenarios exploded behind his eyes. "I might as well be bailing," he said to the empty street.

He heard the crowd before he saw it, faint squeaks and blips in his ears and eventually they became distant voices and music. Rounding a corner, he came in sight of a huge vacant lot between two six-story brownstones. As he approached, he could make out there was some kind of attraction at the back of the lot, and twenty or so Drowned Towners floated in a crowd around it. Organ music blared from a speaker on a tall wooden pole. Hatch crossed the street and joined the audience.

Up against the back wall of the lot, there was an enormous golden octopus. Its flesh glistened and its tentacles curled, unfurled, created fleeting symbols dispersed by schools of tiny angel fish constantly circling it like a halo. The creature's sucker disks were flat black as was its beak, its eyes red, and there was a heavy, rusted metal collar squeezing the base of its lumpy head as if it had shoulders and a neck. Standing next to it was a young woman, obviously part fish. She had gills and her eyes were pure black like a shark's. Her teeth were sharp. There were scales surrounding her face and her hair was some kind of fine green seaweed. She wore a clamshell brassiere and a black thong. At the backs of her heels were fan-like fins. "My name is Clementine," she said, "and this beside me is Madame Mutandis. She is a remarkable specimen of the Midas Octopus, so named for the beautiful golden aura of her skin. You see the collar on the Madame and you miss the chain. Notice, it is attached to my left ankle. Contrary to what you all might believe, it is I who belong to her and not she to me."

Hatch looked up and down the crowd he was part of—an equal mixture of men and women, some more bleached than blue, some less intact. The man next to him held his mouth open, and an eel's head peered out as if having come from the bowels to check the young fish woman's performance.

"With cephalopod brilliance, nonvertebrate intuition, Madame Mutandis will answer one question for each of you. No question is out of bounds. She thinks like the very sea itself. Who'll be first?"

The man next to Hatch stepped immediately forward before anyone else. "And what is your question?" asked the fish woman. The man put his hands into his coat pockets and then raised his head. His message was horribly muddled, but by his third repetition Hatch as well as the octopus got it— "How does one remove an eel?" Madame Mutandis shook her head sac as if in disdain while two of her tentacles unfurled in the man's direction. One swiftly wrapped around his throat, lurching him forward, and the other dove into his mouth. A second later, the Madame released his throat and drew from between his lips a three-foot eel, wriggling wildly in her suctioned grasp. The long arm swept the eel to her beak, and she pierced it at a spot just behind the head, rendering it lifeless. With a free tentacle, she waved forward the next questioner, while brushing gently away the man now sighing with relief.

Hatch came to and was about to step forward, but a woman from behind him wearing a kerchief and carrying a beige pocketbook passed by, already asking, "Where are the good sales?" He wasn't able to see her face, but the woman with the question, from her posture and clothing, seemed middle aged, somewhat younger than himself.

Clementine repeated the woman's question for the octopus. "Where are the good sales?" she said.

"Shoes," said the woman with the kerchief. "I'm looking for shoes."

Madame Mutandis wrapped a tentacle around the woman's left arm and turned her to face the crowd. Hatch reared back at the sudden sight of a face rotted almost perfectly down the middle, skull showing through on one side. Another of the octopus's tentacles slid up the woman's skirt between her legs. With the dexterity of a hand, it drew down the questioner's underwear, leaving them gathered around her ankles. Then, wriggling like the eel it removed from the first man's mouth, that tentacle slithered along her right thigh only to disappear again beneath the skirt.

Hatch was repulsed, fascinated, aroused, as the woman trembled and the tentacle wiggled out of sight. She turned her skeletal profile to the crowd, and that bone grin widened with pleasure, grimaced in pain, gaped with passion. Little spasms of sound escaped her open mouth. The crowd methodically applauded until finally the object of the Madame's attentions screamed and fell to the sand, the long tentacle retracting. The fish woman moved to the end of her chain and helped the questioner up. "Is that what you were looking for?" she asked. The woman with the beige pocketbook nodded and adjusted her kerchief before floating to the back of the crowd.

"Ladies and gentlmen?" said the fish woman.

Hatch noticed that no one was too ready to step forth after the creature's last answer, including himself. His mind was racing, trying to connect a search for a shoe sale with the resultant . . . what? Rape? Or was what he witnessed consensual? He was still befuddled by the spectacle. The gruesome state of the woman's face wrapped in ecstasy hung like a chandelier of ice on the main floor of his brain. At that moment, he realized he had to escape from Drowned Town. Shifting his glance right and left, he noticed his fellow drownees were as still as stone.

The fish woman's chain must have stretched, because she floated over and put her hand on his back. Gently, she led him forward. "She can tell you anything," came Clementine's voice, a whisper that made him think of Rose and Ned and Will, even the stupid dog with bad ears. He hadn't felt his feet move, but he was there, standing before the shining perpetual motion of the Madame's eight arms. Her black parrot beak opened, and he thought he heard her laughing.

"Your question?" asked Clementine, still close by his side.

"My kid's stuck at a party that's getting crazy," blurted Hatch. "How do I get back to dry land?"

He heard murmuring from the crowd behind him. One voice said, "No." Another two said, "Asshole." At first he thought they were predicting the next answer from Madame Mutandis, but then he realized they were referring to him. It dawned that wanting to leave Drowned Town was unpopular.

"Watch the ink," said Clementine.

Hatch looked down and saw a dark plume exuding from beneath the octopus. It rose in a mushroom cloud, and then turned into a long black string at the top. The end of that string whipped leisurely through the air, drawing more of itself from the cloud until the cloud had vanished and what remained was the phrase 322 *Bleeter Street* in perfect, looping script. The address floated there for a moment, Hatch repeating it, before the angel fish veered out of orbit around the fleshy golden sac and dashed through it, dispersing the ink.

The fish woman led Hatch away and called, "Next." He headed for the street, repeating the address under his breath. At the back of the crowd, which had grown, a woman turned to him as he passed and said, "Leaving town?"

"My kid . . ." Hatch began, but she snickered at him. From somewhere down the back row, he heard, "Jerk," and "Pussy." When he reached the street, he realized that the words of the drowned had crowded the street number out of his thoughts. He remembered Bleeter Street and said it six times, but the number . . . Leaping forward, he assumed the flying position, and flapping his arms, cruised down the street, checking the street signs at the corners and keeping an eye out for sharks. He remembered the number had a 3, and then for blocks he thought of nothing but that last woman's contempt.

5

Eventually, he grew too tired to fly and resumed walking, sometimes catching the current and drifting in the flow. He'd seen so many street signs—presidents' names, different kinds of fish, famous actors and sunken ships, types of clouds, waves, flowers, slugs. None of them was Bleeter. So many store fronts and apartment steps passed by and not a soul in sight. At one point, tiny starfish fell like rain all over town, littering the streets and filling the awnings.

Hatch had just stepped out of a weakening current and was moving under his own volition when he noticed a phone booth wedged into an alley between two stores. Pushing off, he swam to it and squeezed himself into the glass enclosure. As the door closed, a light went on above him. He lifted the receiver, placing it next to his ear. There was a dial tone. He dialed and it rang. Something shifted in his chest and his pulse quickened. Suffering the length of each long ring, he waited for someone to pick up.

"Hello?" he heard; a voice at a great distance.

"Rose, it's me," he screamed against the water.

"Hatch," she said. "I can hardly hear you. Where are you?"

"I'm stuck in Drowned Town," he yelled.

"What do you mean? Where is it?"

Hatch had a hard time saying it. "I went under, Rose. I'm sunk."

There was nothing on the line. He feared he'd lost the connection, but he stayed with it.

"Jesus, Hatch. . . . What the hell are you doing?"

"I gave up on the bailing," he said.

She groaned. "You shit. How am I supposed to do this alone?"

"I'm sorry, Rose," he said. "I don't know what happened. I love you."

He could hear her exhale. "OK," she said. "Give me an address. I have to have something to put into Mapquest."

"Do you know where I am?" he asked.

"No, I don't fucking know where you are. That's why I need the address."

It came to him all at once. "322 Bleeter Street, Drowned Town," he said. "I'll meet you there."

"It's going to take a while," she said.

"Rose?"

"What?"

"I love you," he said. He listened to the silence on the receiver until he noticed in the reflection of his face in the phone booth glass a blue spot on his nose and one on his forehead. "Shit," he said and hung up. "I can take care of that with some ointment when I get back," he thought. He scratched at the spot on his forehead and blue skin sloughed off. He put his face closer to the glass, and then there came a pounding on the door behind him.

Turning, he almost screamed at the sight of the half-gone face of that woman who'd been goosed by the octopus for her shoe sale query. He opened the door and slid past her. Her Jolly Roger profile was none too jolly, he noticed. As he spoke the words, he surprised himself with doing so—"Do you know where Bleeter Street is?" She jostled him aside in her rush to get to the phone. Before closing the door, she called over her shoulder, "You're on it."

"Things are looking up," thought Hatch as he retreated. Standing in the middle of the street, he looked up one side and down the other. Only one building, a darkened store front with a plate glass window behind which was displayed a single pair of sunglasses on a pedestal, had a street number—621. It came to him that he would have to travel in one direction, try to find another address and see which way the numbers ran. Then, if he found they were increasing, he'd have to turn around and head in the other direction, but at least he would know. Thrilled at the sense of purpose, he swept a clump of drifting seaweed out of his way, and moved forward. He could be certain Rose would come for him. After thirty years of marriage they'd grown close in subterranean ways.

Darkness was beginning to fall on Drowned Town. Angle-jawed fish with needle teeth, a perpetual scowl, and sad eyes, came from the alleyways and through the open windows of the apartments. Each had a small phosphorescent jewel dangling from a downward curving stalk that issued from the head. They drifted down the shadowy street like fireflies, and although Hatch had still to see another address, he stopped in his tracks to mark their beautiful effect. It was precisely then that he saw *Financial Ruin* appear from over the rooftops down the street. Before he could even think to flee, he saw the shark swoop down in his direction.

Hatch turned, kicked his feet up, and started flapping. As he approached the first corner, and was about to turn, he almost collided with someone just stepping out onto Bleeter Street. To his utter confusion, it was a deep-sea diver, a man inside a heavy rubber suit with a glass bubble of a helmet and a giant nautilus shell strapped to his back feeding air through two arching tubes into his suit. The sudden appearance of the diver wasn't what made him stop, though. It was the huge chrome gun in his hands with a barbed spear head as wide as a fence post jutting from the barrel. The diver waved Hatch behind him as the shark came into view. Then it was a dagger-toothed lung, a widening cavern with the speed of a speeding car. The diver pulled the trigger. There was a zip of tiny bubbles, and *Financial Ruin* curled up, thrashing madly with the spear piercing its upper pallet and poking out the back of its head. Billows of blood began to spread. The man in the suit dropped the gun and approached Hatch.

"Hurry," he said, "before the other sharks smell the blood."

6

Hatch and his savior sat in a carpeted parlor on cushioned chairs facing each other across a low coffee table with a tea service on it. The remarkable fact was that they were both dry, breathing air instead of brine, and speaking in a normal tone. When they'd entered the foyer of the stranger's building, he hit a button on the wall. A sheet of steel slid down to cover the door, and within seconds the sea water began to exit the compartment through a drain in the floor. Hatch had had to drown into the air and that was much more uncomfortable than simply going under, but after some extended wheezing, choking, and spitting up, he drew in a huge breath with ease. The diver had unscrewed the glass globe that covered his head and held it beneath one arm. "Isaac Munro," he said and nodded.

Dressed in a maroon smoking jacket and green pajamas, moccasins on his feet, the silver-haired man with drooping mustache sipped his tea and now held forth on his situation. Hatch, in dry clothes the older man had given him, was willing to listen, almost certain Munro knew the way back to dry land.

"I'm in Drowned Town, but not of it. Do you understand?" he said.

Hatch nodded, and noticed what a relief it was to have the pressure of the sea off him.

Isaac Munro lowered his gaze and said, as if making a confession, "My wife Rotzy went under some years ago. There was nothing I could do to prevent it. She came down here, and on the day she left me, I determined I would find the means to follow her and rescue her from Drowned Town. My imagination, fired by the desire to simply hold her again, gave birth to all these many inventions that allow me to keep from getting my feet wet, so to speak." He chuckled and then made a face as if he were admonishing himself.

Hatch smiled. "How long have you been looking for her?"

"Years," said Munro, placing his tea cup on the table.

"I'm trying to get back. My wife Rose is coming for me in the car."

"Yes, your old neighbor Bob Gordon told me you might be looking for an out," said the older man. "I was on the prowl for you when we encountered that cutpurse Leviathan."

"You know Bob?"

"He does some legwork for me from time to time."

"I saw him at the grocery today."

"He has a bizarre fascination with that lobster tank. In any event, your wife won't make it through, I'm sorry to say. Not with a car."

"How can I get out?" asked Hatch. "I can't offer you a lot of money, but something else perhaps."

"Perish the thought," said Munro. "I have an escape hatch back to the surface in case of emergencies. You're welcome to use it if you'll just observe some cautionary measures."

"Absolutely," said Hatch and moved to the edge of his chair.

"I take it you'd like to leave immediately?"

Both men stood and Hatch followed through a hallway lined with framed photographs that opened into a larger space; an old ball room with peeling flowered wallpaper. Across the vast wooden floor, scratched and littered with, of all things, old leaves and pages of a newspaper, they came to a door. When Munro turned around, Hatch noticed that the older man had taken one of the photos off the wall in the hallway.

"Here she is," said Isaac. "This is Rotzy."

Hatch leaned down for a better look at the portrait. He gave only the slightest grunt of surprise and hoped his host hadn't noticed, but Rotzy was the woman at the phone booth, the half-faced horror mishandled by Madame Mutandis.

"You haven't seen her, have you?" asked Munro.

Hatch knew he should have tried to help the old man, but he thought only of escape and didn't want to complicate things. He felt the door in front of him was to be the portal back. "No," he said.

Munro nodded and then reached into the side pocket of his jacket and retrieved an old-fashioned key. He held it in the air but did not place it in Hatch's outstretched palm. "Listen carefully," he said. "You will pass through a series of rooms. Upon entering each room, you must lock the door behind you with this key before opening the next door to exit into the following room. Once you've started you can't turn back. The key only works to open doors forward and lock doors backward. A door cannot be opened without a door being locked. Do you understand?"

"Yes."

Munro placed the key in Hatch's hand. "Then be on your way and godspeed. Kiss the sky for me when you arrive."

"I will."

Isaac opened the door and Hatch stepped through. The door closed and he locked it behind him. He crossed the room in a hurry, unlocked the next door and then passing through, locked it behind him. This process went on for twenty minutes before Hatch noticed that it took fewer and fewer steps to traverse each room to the next door. One of the rooms had a window, and he paused to look out on some watery side street falling into night. The loneliness of the scene spurred him forward. In the following room he had to duck down so as not to skin his head against the ceiling. He locked its door and moved forward into a room where he had to duck even lower.

Eventually, he was forced to crawl from room to room, and there wasn't much room for turning around to lock the door behind him. As each door swept open before him, he thought he might see the sky or feel a breeze in his face. There was always another door but there was also hope. That is until he entered a compartment so small, he couldn't turn around to use the key but had to do it with his hands behind his back. His chin against his chest. "This has got to be the last one," he thought, unsure if he could squeeze his shoulders through the next opening. Before he could insert the key into the lock on the tiny door before him, a steel plate fell and blocked access to it. He heard a swoosh and a bang behind him and knew another metal plate had covered the door going back. He was trapped.

"How are you doing, Mr. Hatch?" he heard Munro's voice say. By dipping one shoulder he was able to turn his head and see a speaker built into the wall.

"How do I get through these last rooms?" Hatch yelled. "They're too small and metal guards have fallen in front of the doors."

"That's the point," called Munro, "you don't. You, my friend are trapped, and will remain trapped forever in that tight uncomfortable place."

"What are you talking about? Why?" Hatch was frantic. He tried to lunge his body against the walls but there was nowhere for it to go.

"My wife, Rotzy. You know how she went under? What sunk her? She was ill, Mr. Hatch. She was seriously ill but her health insurance denied her coverage. You, Mr. Hatch, personally said No."

This time what flared before Hatch's inner eye was not his life, but all the many pleading, frustrating, angry voices that had traveled in one of his ears and out the other in his service to the HMO. "I'm not responsible," was all he could think to say in his defense.

"My wife used to tell me, 'Isaac, we're all responsible.' Now you can wait, as she waited for relief, for what was rightly due her. You'll wait forever, Hatch."

There was a period where he struggled. He couldn't tell how long it lasted, but nothing came of it, so he closed his eyes, made his breathing more steady and shallow, and went into his brain, across the first floor to the basement door. He opened it and could smell the scent of the dark wood wafting up the steps. Locking the door behind him, he descended into the dark.

7

The woods were frightening, but he'd take anything over the claustrophobia of Munro's trap. Each dim light bulb he came to was a godsend, and he put his hands up to it for the little warmth it offered against the wind. He noticed that the creatures prowled around the bulbs like waterholes. They darted behind the trees, spying on him, pale specters whose faces were like masks made of bone. One he was sure was his cousin Martin, a malevolent boy who'd cut the head off a kitten. He'd not seen him in over thirty years. He also spotted his mother-in-law, who was his mother-in-law with no hair and short tusks. She grunted orders to him from the shadows. He kept moving and tried to ignore them.

When Hatch couldn't walk any further, he came to a clearing in the forest. There, in the middle of nowhere, in the basement of his brain, sat twenty yards of street with a brownstone situated behind a wide sidewalk. There were steps leading up to twin doors and an electric light glowed next to the entrance. As he drew near, he could make out the address in brass numerals on the base of the banister that led up the right side of the front steps.

He stumbled over to the bottom step and dropped down onto it. Hatch leaned forward, his elbows on his knees and his hands covering his face. "That's not me," he said, "it's not me," and he tried to weep till his eyes closed out of exhaustion. What seemed a second later, he heard a car horn and looked up.

"There's no crying in baseball, asshole," said Rose. She was leaning her head out the driver's side window of their SUV. There was a light on in the car and he could see both their sons were in the backseat, laughing and pointing at Hatch.

"How'd you find me?" he asked.

"The Internet," said Rose. "Will showed me Mapquest has this new feature where you don't need the address anymore, just a person's name, and it gives you directions to wherever they are in the continental United States."

"Oh, my god," he said and walked toward Rose to give her a hug.

"Not now Barnacle Bill, there's some pale creeps coming this way. We just passed them and one lunged for the car. Get in, Mr. Drowned Town."

Hatch got in and saw his sons. He wanted to hug them but they motioned for him to hurry and shut the door. As soon as he did, Rose pulled away from the curb.

"So, Hatch, you went under?" asked his older son, Will.

Hatch wished he could explain but couldn't find the words.

"What a pile," said Ned.

"Yeah," said Will.

"Don't do it again, Hatch," said Rose. "Next time we're not coming for you."

"I'm sorry," he said. "I love you all."

Rose wasn't one to admonish more than once. She turned on the radio and changed the subject. "We had the directions, but they were a bitch to follow. At one point I had to cut across two lanes of traffic in the middle of the Holland Tunnel and take a left down a side tunnel that for more than a mile was the pitchest pitch black."

"Listen to this, Hatch," said Ned and leaned into the front seat to turn up the radio.

"Oh, they've been playing this all day," said Rose. "This young woman soldier was captured by insurgents and they made a video of them cutting her head off."

"On the radio, you only get the screams, though," said Will. "Check it out."

The sound, at first, was like from a musical instrument, and then it became human—steady, piercing shrieks in desperate bursts that ended in the gurgle of someone going under.

Rose changed the channel and the screams came from the new station. She hit the button again and the same screaming. Hatch turned to look at his family. Their eyes were slightly droopy and they were very pale. Their shoulders were somehow out of whack and their grins were vacant. Rose had a big bump on her forehead and a rash across her neck, but at least they were together.

"Watch for the sign for the Holland Tunnel," she said amid the dying soldier's screams as they drove on into the dark. Hatch kept careful watch, knowing they'd never find it.

DON TUMASONIS

The Swing

Don Tumasonis, a resident of Scandinavia for most of his adult life, has had his writing likened by critics to that of so many well-known authors that it came as something of a relief (not to mention shock!) when he recently discovered another writer's work being likened to his own. While this does not settle the nagging question of the urquelle—*that original scribbler from whom all others obviously derive their style and inspiration—it does provide Tumasonis with the hope that perhaps after all, he is not like anybody else.*

A slow writer, plodding and methodical, he views himself as a sort of louche slacker who writes only when the spirit infrequently moves him, crushed as he normally is by the bearable lightness of being. The clear result of such sloth is only a handful of published stories—thirteen, to be exact—which have nonetheless done rather well for themselves. Two have won International Horror Guild awards, several have appeared in year's best anthologies on both sides of the Atlantic, and one was optioned for filming.

"The Swing" was first published in the Ash-Tree Press anthology At Ease with the Dead, *edited by Barbara and Christopher Roden.*

—E.D.

There was hell to pay after.

The police were called in. They in turn called in the county sheriff. That led to the state police. In the end, a kidnapping suspected, strings were pulled and the FBI arrived.

When the crime crews searched the area of the disappearance—and they did this thoroughly—several objects were found that were traced back to Ginny: dental braces, one filling, a gold-plated necklace chain, several metal buttons, and a buckle or two. In other words, anything metallic she had on her.

Of course, fingers of suspicion pointed one way only. We five—Mike Dater, Bobby Kraulin, Gordon Dater, Gilb Deuch, and myself—were the obvious suspects, twelve years old or not. Days of grilling ensued; we each of us stuck to our mutually inconsistent stories. Psychiatrists came in; leading questions were asked, and terms for perversions not suspected by myself or the others were bandied about until our pubescent, pre-Internet ignorance was apparent even to the most hardened investigators. We were let go, but were marked thereafter throughout the neighborhood. My own family was the first to pack up and go. We went to Colorado.

For years after, and even now, I suppose, I remained obsessed by the events of a single hour. I went to university, served in the military, got married, lived abroad, and never a day went by without my reflecting over what had happened near the church of Saint Christina. A full twenty years elapsed before I even dared to go back where it all had taken place, back to that small Upstate town of Oratio, named after a somewhat less than heroic general of the Revolutionary War, who, defying orders at Saratoga, had almost lost the day for the colonial rebels, and then, amazingly, had a place of honor at Washington's inauguration.

It goes to show that no matter how much you fuck up, there's always a second chance if you're well enough connected. People might not forgive, but they are much prone to forgetting—something I was counting on during what was to be my single visit back to a place where I had no intention of contacting any former companions left behind in ignominy. I was, after all, looking for answers, not recriminations.

In all likelihood, few of any neighbors remaining would be able to connect my adult features with those of the youth of decades before. I was not about to court that possibility, however, and therefore decided to restrict almost all of my short stay to the vicinity of the archives and library of the Historical Society in the larger city of Porchester, of which Oratio was an outlying appendage. I avoided the small township itself, except for one hour, more of which later.

Fixated as I was throughout the years, I had touched all the obvious bases, and many less known, in a vain effort to come up with some explanation. Microgravity? Got it. Mathematical simulation? Been there, done that. Classical mechanics?—no one knew better his Mach, his Wirkus, Rand and Ruina, or for that matter his Case and Swanson, than I. For what they used to call a score of years, I pursued all rational avenues of inquiry, with no result. Wherefore my reluctant trip back to the city of Porchester, and its formerly rural satellite of Oratio, where I grew up.

I had a belief, in no way justifiable, that the key to explaining what had happened to us years before lay buried in the records of the city's Historical Society, and their archives of local history that ran back almost to the revolution, when Porchester was first incorporated. Granted, they were well known for having a deep and broad collection of local manuscript materials and unpublished documents, whereas Oratio, a cultural sump, had preserved almost nothing regarding its own past.

But really, I was going only on feeling, an idea that something might be found, a feeling somewhat weaker than a hunch, more like an intuition, but there nonetheless. So almost immediately after landing by plane from New York and checking into my mohotel, I took a taxi to the city, and the Porchester Historical Society.

Its headquarters in the old center was located in a distinguished large white Federal building, the former home of the city's first mayor, wealthy from corruption. The wide sweep of its portico, with grand white pillars that stretched up two tall stories to support a coffered ceiling, gave it the look of a Roman temple. Its appearance had always intimidated me on my trips to the city as a boy, keeping me from ever investigating what was, beyond doubt, one of the city's oldest and most intriguing structures.

Walking into the building was walking into an unknown past. The noise of busy outside traffic was suddenly gone, and a quiet unusual in these times pervaded. Cell phones–off territory—you felt that immediately. The interior air, on that late spring day, was cool and a bit stuffy, and the lighting of the large hall dim. A lot of brasswork gleamed, reflecting electric lights that had replaced the candles of long ago. Music— Vivaldi or Monteverdi, I think—was pumped in softly from hidden speakers.

Following a sign, I made my way up the stairs to the library on the second floor. The librarian was long-legged and good-looking. Her hair was long, too, and fine, and she removed her glasses when she talked to me. I also noticed a wedding ring, and left it at that. After using some time to idly and discreetly flirt with me while I filled out the visitors' register, she gave up, and moved on to the matter at hand.

There was a problem in framing my request for research materials. I couldn't very well start by saying a lost friend—literally so—had vanished under highly unusual circumstances that had focused attention on my possible complicity in her disappearance, not unless I was willing to chance gossip of my return spreading back to the small town of my birth, just across the canal from the city. There was no point in stirring up any remaining reservoirs of ill-feeling; my intention was to maintain anonymity throughout my visit.

Instead, I made up some story about wanting to study the Indian presence in Oratio, not mentioning that I had grown up there. This led to dragging out old deeds, rolls of cadastral maps, diaries, and other papers, none of which in any likelihood had seen daylight for a hundred years or more. I could see nonetheless that the librarian—whose name was Marion Reade—perhaps alerted by my unwillingness to play, was game to the fact that something more was going on than I had told her. She herself was obviously a player: players recognize players, so she knew that I had something serious in mind that obviated the desire to flirt, with its concomitant potential of a short affair, and given that she really was attractive, what could *that* possibly be?

Whatever she thought, I devoted the better part of the next two days to the boxed materials—all relating to Oratio—that, at my request, she took out one after the other from the collection. Some were so dusty, it was unlikely that they had ever been examined at any time since initial storage. I had no clear idea of what I was searching for, having only that gut feeling that something might be found here.

Fortunately, someone industrious had been through the holdings at one time, leaving a rough record of their work in the form of lined sheets of paper, two or three to each large archival box I had signed for. These abbreviated lists told, in a general way, what each box held. I had already, using these as an aid, gone carefully through the contents of eighteen boxes, and was beginning to wonder if there was anything here to be found. So much so that when storage box Ib-23Ya, a rectangular affair with edges reinforced with metal strips like an old-fashioned cardboard suitcase, was placed on my desk, I watched the librarian's hips gently sway as she walked away, instead of immediately lifting the flat cover and going through the folders.

My indolence vanished when I looked at the yellowing paper listing the contents of Ib-23Ya. There, past *Oratio/records of births, 1902–1912* and *Oratio/viii: Marriages 1915–20*, amongst lists of protocols of town meetings and the like, was this intriguing entry: *Oratio/xxxii: Westman bequest Papers, commonplace book Oratio history & folklore, correspondence 1932–1954.*

This was more promising than anything I had seen up to then, and I felt a trace of excitement building as I riffled through the manila folders, the weak yet definite scent of something less than ordinary awaiting. It is a developed sense that every researcher knows; the sudden anticipation of something big coming up. My fingers fumbled with the string that, looped around two paper buttons in an infinity pattern, had held the flap of the file's pocket shut for years.

Once I had things out in the open, I found yet another lined sheet of paper showing the contents of the file, as expected, but with some added detail. According to the anonymous addenda, Benjamin Westman had been a resident of Oratio, who for a hobby had collected folklore and stories from the older residents of the town in the days before it became a de facto suburb of Porchester City. He had been an intimate of the artist of the fantastic, Terrence Hinley, which acquaintance placed him on the fringes of the Farnsworth group. Born in 1902, Westman served in the Army during the First War, before taking a job with Porchester Gas and Electric. Declared indigent in 1952, he was remanded to a Veteran's Hospital, where he died, a patient in the psychiatric ward, in 1958.

From the pile of documents and prehistoric copies printed in the negative on photographic stock, I pulled out a small clothbound notebook. There was no title on the blank cover label. Opening to the first page, I scanned down a list, which was penned in a large neat hand in real ink, not ballpoint: *On Onondaga games. The Medicine-Man. On the Oratio pond. On Halacker's Stage Inn. Indian tortures. The meeting place. Settlers' games. Ladders. Swamp dwellers. Ropes. See-saws. Elemental. Will-o-the-Wisps. Inscribed stones. Swings. Disappearances.*

I stopped on the last word, and looked again. Bingo. I must have started, since, when I looked up the librarian gave a questioning half-smile from where she sat by the tall windows at the other side of the room. I weakly smiled back, only to immediately drop my gaze as soon as was polite to the notebook's pages, which I had, without looking, already opened.

More than half—actually, most—of the pages were torn out and missing. Why? Then again, the man ended up mad—didn't he? What was left? A few pages of random notes, all of which I include here for the sake of completeness, as the surviving quasi-scholarly legacy of Westman:

> Missing picture from Veronese Christina cycle, showing her on swing by Lake Bolsena. Putative death by drowning wrong. Theodoric's daughter.
>
> Montenegrin rope swing, with lashing around the lower portion stiffening it for a seat, mounted from a step, since it is so high off the ground. Halacker's public house rumored to once have had old print or picture on its walls of similar local device.
>
> Sam Patch, the Jumping Man, on his way to meeting with Fate in Rochester, stopped here. Asked if he would venture the then-existing swing (perhaps for a leap while in motion?), he looked it over, and reportedly blanched, leaving with some uncharacteristic mumbled excuse about its being 'women's work.' Some things evidently can not be done as well as others.
>
> Hebron Wells, age 98, resident in Oratio since birth in 1846: "I reckon I'm the oldest fellar there is around. These parts, anyways. Could tell ya lot more, if it weren't for my memory being shot and all. But the swing. Yep, I remember that. Or *them*. There's always been one around. My granpaw, he fought in 1812, he used to tell us that old squaw man Allen, the one with the mill and three wives—all at the same time, ha!—said the Indians used to meet there. Have parties. Near the pond, back where the farm is now, by that new church. Don't know what they did though—I forget, see? Used to remember. Wait. No. But, yes—now I got it—that swing, it was on a tree, like. A rope, that's what they used, the settlers who took over. That was just after the tribe was moved out, or was shot out, ha! Someone cut it down, afore granpaw's time. Put back up again, right quick, he said. This was all before he was even born, my granpaw. So there's always been something there. I remember girls too, pretty ones. Wyllys, Henderson, there's one, Karina, she was called. Yup, I remember them, all pretty girls. Damn! Can't remember what happened to them. Pretty. Pretty."
>
> Tanganyika natives on long swing, see photograph in *National Geographic*. Large lake in background.
>
> The blanket toss, as practiced by the Seneca groups; not in *HRAF*. Little-known variant of the Eskimo *nulakataq*. First interpreted (wrongly) as a game.

A number of cured hides well-stitched together used, held tautly by a group of men. Generally, a girl on the verge of womanhood thrown into the air. The purported heights reached, as consistently related by European eyewitnesses — trappers, missionaries, military, and the like — in all reasonableness would not satisfy today's standards of proof. Claim being that the girl, directed by an old woman, would look to find or see some thing (impending threat? — unsure), as predicted by that same older person, perhaps from a dream. Generally, the threat should be of a supernatural nature; or rather, the instrument of the toss was not lightly resorted to for any mundane or individual affairs or advantage; such use was seen as facetious, and insulting to the gods. The important thing, all the reports concur, was that utmost care was exercised to ensure the medicine woman's young protégé would not be *seen*.

[pages missing]

and yet, common to all of these is the widely shared feeling of being in a state of transcendence, not unlike that experienced at the moment of sexual climax, the rush of certain opiates and their natural or synthetic derivatives, or subjectively reported experiences of near death. Possibly the feeling of euphoria, and the temptation to let go stem from the feeling of falling through space at the end of each swing cycle, when the rider moves neither forward nor back, but is, if only for less than a second, suspended without gravity in time.

Every neighborhood has its secrets.

The Danes say *huske* for a swing; they use its homonym *huske*, for 'remember.' Are these related? Memory, and being up there? Memory of what? Look these up.

Then this last thing: a half page near the end of the notebook, the top part torn out, with names, and dates, and nothing more:

Hypatia Ames 1803
Abigail Wakeman 1823
Harriet Burr 1843
Bethia Wyllys 1883
Ann Henderson 1903
Karina O'Reilly 1923

That was the sum remaining of Wakeman's notes. The rest of the file encompassed local traditions as collected from residents, old recipes, newspaper clippings and cutouts, letters, some press photos, movie tickets, a prize medal from a grade school, and more ephemera and plain junk, none of which seemed directly connected with what was left of the jottings in the notebook. I found none of the missing pages. A look through those archival sign-in books from the years since his bequest suggested nothing: the visitors' requests to examine the Society's materials were too general to see what precise files had been examined.

I arranged for photocopies to be made of the notebook, and after these were finished and I had paid for them, I thanked the librarian, regretting silently lack of world enough or time, and left.

That evening, in my room, I looked through the white pages of the local telephone book out of curiosity, to see how many of my old neighbors and acquaintances were still around. I remembered every name, every house — childhood impressions are that strong. When I saw that everyone was gone except for one cousin of a friend, I was struck by the irony of all my precautions against being recognized again. In a country of essentially rootless people, always recreating their own past, there was hardly any need to worry about seeing anyone you knew after twenty years—the mobility being such as it is. I had been free all along to present myself as whoever I cared to be, to act out any role I chose for myself.

I had planned to spend a very short time in Oratio the next day, around noon, before leaving to pick up my luggage from the so-called hotel where I was staying, close by the airport. It would leave me with a little over an hour to check in for my flight back to JFK.

A taxi took me from the hotel to a place about a mile from Saint Christina's parish church. I would walk the rest of the way, along the main road from the city, to take in the changes—of which, it turned out, there were many.

A superhighway cut under the road; strip development had run rampant, and the heavily trafficked way was spoiled by cheap discount stores, automotive parts dealers, drive-in banks and eateries, model shops, and the like. A sign on one of the fast food outlets—*George Pappas—Home of the Famous $6.99 Garbage Plate*— gives a fair idea of what was there. Litter and debris of a car civilization covered the curbs, and after twenty years there were still no sidewalks or bike paths. Off on the tree-lined streets, filled with older wood-sided homes, life seemed unchanged, impervious, by all appearances, to the commerce-generated wreckage just a few steps away.

The last quarter mile to the church sloped gently downhill towards the west, and I could see that the church side of the road was under *development*, as scenic vandalism and crimes against habitat are called these days. There was a clear view down to the new church. Of the old one, there was not a trace. Homes that had lined the stretch between were gone, torn down to make way for construction. Mounds of stone and dirt were piled up all around, seemingly at random. Bulldozers and other earth-moving machinery were at work as I closed the final distance. Something big was being built.

When I came to where the old buildings and the school's swing had been, there was nothing left, except the few trees that had been closest to the road, and the parking lot on which the swing's patch of land behind the old school had abutted. The swing was gone, and all had been neatly planted over with grass, apparently years before.

The new church was open, so I went inside. One old man was in there, on his knees praying. Everything was changed. The interior, once a traditional nave, was now hemispherically disposed, a church in the half-round, with seats like a theater around an altar at the side. The choir loft was closed down, but there was something like a bandstand next to the pulpit, with a small organ, and a guitar on a stand.

The noticeboard, one of those with black rolls of latitudinal felt for inserting white plastic letters, showed three Masses on Sunday, down from the seven of twenty years back. The Christina wall reliefs I had known as a youth were gone. I left through the doors by the bell tower and went into the adjacent former school, now labeled "St. Christina's Apostolic Life Center," whatever those last words might have meant. Perhaps something to fit in with the "Healing Masses" I had seen announced on the church bulletin board.

I walked down the long, empty hallway of what once had been my school, with the classrooms—now conference rooms and a library—off to either side, before coming to the office of my former principal, a stern, then-fiftyish nun who at times was the object of my wet dreams. Her glass-fronted office, where she had once exercised old-fashioned discipline with a wooden ruler, was now that of the "life center" secretary, one Mrs. Gianfranco, according to the anodized nameplate by the door. I knocked, and was motioned in by a trim woman of about forty, who was on the telephone.

"Yes, Deacon Mike will be available for counseling on Thursday at seven o'clock. . . . Evening, yes. You're welcome, Mrs. Miller."

Putting the receiver down, she threw me an official smile, but the message in the brown Italian eyes, framed by some impossible retro hair puffball dyed black, was *Go ahead, buster, try to make my day.*

Carefully, I introduced myself, but in the middle of explaining why I had come by, another call came on her telephone, and she left me hanging, shoving over a copy of the current parish newsletter, while she engaged another parishioner in the intricacies of diaconal scheduling.

Leafing through the brochure, I saw to my surprise that the present pastor was the Right Reverend Eugene Mwebya-Mubangizi. When Mrs. Gianfranco—whom I assumed the woman to be—put down the telephone a second time, I commented on the ethnicity of the current vicar.

"Oh, yes, Father Mwebya-Mubangizi has been with us a number of years now. God sent him to us from Africa."

I must have lifted my eyebrows, since she added, "Holy Mother Church is running short of priests, you know, so we have to take what we can get."

"I see. Look, I'm an old parishioner"—and throwing caution aside, I gave her my real name—"and I've come back to look around. I've been away for twenty years, and just wanted to see how—things turned out. Nostalgia. You miss things, places. What happened to the old school building? I see it's gone now."

"Oh, it's been that way for years. The siding wasn't worth repairing, and they weren't using it anyway, so they took it down, along with the old rectory. Reverend Eugene—he hated the buildings, actually—sold the land to a developer, and was able to renovate the church and build a new rectory."

She said this in a pleasant way, but there was a certain beadiness to her glance, as if she had already, during the short time of our meeting, weighed me up in a cunning way, to see if I could offer anything to her advantage. She had obviously rejected the notion, and now her pleasantries were running on fumes. I already missed Marion, fleeting as our acquaintance had been.

"Glad to hear St. Christina's picked up some cash. By the way, do you know anything about what happened to the swing—the big old one in back of the school?"

Before I had finished, the look in her eyes told me that I had drawn a blank.

"I've been here four whole years, and I don't remember any swing. Perhaps it was taken down before I or Father Gene came here."

I nodded, noticing at the same time a large photograph, with the lady sitting before me and an impressively large black priest at the center of a group of women. From the way he had his arm around her, it was unlikely that St. Christina's would be the object of any clerical child-abuse investigation in the near future. Clearly, Mrs. Gianfranco had taken her own adage of "taking what we can get" to heart.

"Perhaps I could walk around, just look. It would be nice if I could find—a bit of the swing, or something. A memento, a keepsake, you know."

"I doubt there's anything left. But you're welcome to look around. The new park in back is very nice."

Mrs. Gianfranco—I wondered what her husband thought of her obviously warm relationship with the pastor, as evidenced by the picture—grandly stood up, signaling that my audience was over.

On her way to hustle me out she remembered something, caught herself, called me to stop and, rummaging about, pulled out a large oblong paperback from beneath a pile of papers on her cluttered desk.

"It's a history of the parish. We had it printed a few years ago, thought we could make some money for repairs. We still have most of them around. Maybe you can find something about your swing in it."

I took the book from her hand, and was about to thank her when she said, "That'll be fifteen dollars, please." She was smiling sweetly all the while, right up to when I slapped the bills down into her palm.

When I was almost out of the building, her voice rang down the corridor. "If you want to see the stones in the book, they're out back, leaning against the school wall."

Outside, leafing through the book, which was mostly pictures, I thought about destitute parishes in a failing Church, trying to retrench by all means available, and wondered what stones she had meant.

Nearly a third of the book was about St. Christina's sister parish in Tanzania, from whence the current pastor came, with a not-too-subtle pitch for donations. Further on, there was fulsome praise for the new construction program, showing the old buildings I had known so well in the process of being demolished. On the next page:

> During the clearance of the old buildings, a group of inscribed stones similar in size and shape to grave markers of various periods were found to have been used to line the fishpond by the Lourdes statue overlooking a rock garden by the main entrance of the old school. Although the local history group was informed, Mr. Christiansen, its chairperson, was unable to provide any information concerning these, other than that ". . . they would certainly be of great value in local historical terms, if anyone was able to find out more about them." They were cleaned and refurbished at the expense of a group of veterans in the parish, and may now be seen upon application to the Parish Life Center Secretary.

Walking to the back of the new school, still reading the book, I was unable to make out the inscriptions on the nondescript stones in the rather poor photograph of them in the midst of a group of bemused-looking construction workers. I had already gone through the entire publication without finding any picture of the swing, when I rounded the corner at the back of the school.

Seven flat stones were lined up there, neatly leaning against the institution's wall. Remarkably for these days and times, both wall and stones were graffiti-free. These last were of worn local slate, with the six names I had already half-expected, and one new to me.

Sinspella Karnbrook 1783 16 yrs
Hypatia Ames 1803 aged 12
Abigail Wakeman 1823 was fourteen
Harriet Burr 1843 of years 13
Bethia Wyllys 1883 twelve
Ann Henderson 1903 age 13
Karina O'Reilly 1923 12 years old

Anticipated, and yet a shock. My heart beat wildly, and I felt as if something dark and enormous had begun to rise out of a large, once-familiar body of water, now suddenly strange. Something whose existence had been previously unsuspected, but whose mass and rough shape were now obvious, without any sharp outline or details yet clear. Something ominous that you might not *want* to see clearly.

Recovering slightly, I backed away, not even sure I could trust those mute stones. I was hyperventilating when I turned the corner.

Trying to gather myself, trying, in spite of myself, to make some reason out of what I had just seen, I retreated across the church parking lot, to the grassy plot where the swing once towered, and stood with my back to the traffic, looking at its former site.

The parking lot stretched out before me; beyond it was a new park, carved out from what had been open fields and hedgerows. In the distance, I could see the tangle of trees and bushes surrounding the local pond, still there. Viewed with child's eyes, I had once thought it quite distant from the school. Now I saw it was in fact quite close, possibly no more than a five minute walk from the school, with the fields between now smoothed and evenly covered with neatly trimmed turf. That water where we had played hockey in winters long ago, and had caught tadpoles in spring, had at least survived, seemingly inviolate.

Mulling over what I had just seen back of the school, and the events of years past, I heard the tread of someone walking up behind me. Turning, I saw a man, of about my age and build. It wasn't long before I recognized Gilbert Deuch, broken nose as before, hair still pale blond with a strand or two of nearly indiscernible grey thrown in, his teenage frame now magically fleshed out with the weight of years, his face lined either from hard knocks or outdoor life, or both.

Looking back at me, he stood wordlessly for more than just a moment, probably, like myself, registering the changes. Finally he broke the silence, by then grown uncomfortable.

"I thought you'd come back."

A pause.

"All the others did, except Gordo Dater—he died a few years ago, cancer. But I bet he'd have come back too, if he lived any longer."

"You stayed."

"No. No, I didn't. I just didn't move as far away as the others, as far as you, for instance."

"Let me guess how you knew I was here—the Gianfranco woman?"

"She never can keep her mouth shut. Sometimes it works out to my advantage, like now. When things cooled down—let me rephrase that—when everyone had moved away from the neighborhood, I realized I could come back here if I wanted to, that there was just about nobody left who remembered. Real American. All new people. Everybody on the move. Hardly anyone's left."

"So you live here again."

"Nope. I decided even if most of the old crowd was gone, I didn't want anybody on to me, even if there was the slightest chance. I live about twenty minutes' drive from here. Don't go to church any more, the wife does. She attends here."

"Then how—"

"My wife kept her last name, and she's great pals with *administrator* Gianfranco."

He almost spat the title out.

"And she's so new . . ."

"That she has no idea. She doesn't know you from Adam, but whenever someone new comes by, she calls my wife up. She called my Margaret two minutes after you left her office. Gossip. My wife knows a little, though, and recognized your name; she called me. About when you were looking at the stones."

"You know about those."

"Everybody does, but I'm the only one who knows what they mean. Partly, at least. Excepting maybe present company."

I kept silent, and waited.

"There were some other stones, no inscriptions on them," he continued. "Some were so old they weren't even sure what they were, or from when, so they dumped them. There were probably wooden markers, too, that the Indians used, but if those were ever there, they rotted away."

Then, his pale blue eyes watching me, unflinching, he said it: "Gianfranco didn't tell you, did she, that there was a newer stone? That the veterans took away?"

From the look in his eyes, he knew she hadn't. I think he was enjoying it, or waiting to see if shock would draw something from me, something that might explain things more, add another piece to his puzzle that could solve it for him, or somehow exculpate him from whatever he felt about his own involvement. And I think he wanted me to squirm. In his own way, he always had been a bit of a prick. But I had my own hand to play, and had already expected something like this.

"You know whose name was on it?"

"I can guess," I answered.

He said nothing to that, but only nodded, still keeping his eyes on me.

"Come on, let's have a beer together at Halacker's. And talk."

I said, "I don't think so."

Then, since he kept his eyes focused on me, jaw clenched, I added, "I'm going back today. My plane's in an hour and a half. I can't stay and talk."

He looked at me, and then said, "I'll take you to the airport. Where are your bags? At a motel nearby there?"

I reluctantly gave a nod, but already found myself following him to his car: practical and not flashy, but expensive Swedish, engineered for safety, and we drove off.

For the first five minutes on the interstate, dust in the air turning the blue skies grey, he looked at the road ahead, silent. Bleached highwayside plants, sere survivors of winter's road salt kill, rustled silently in the unfelt wind as we sped past.

If Gilb was tense, he showed no obvious sign of it—his hands were loose on the wheel, not clenching it. But then he began fiddling with the rear-view mirror, and I knew from observed habit of long ago that he was angry, and barely containing himself. We were, however, close to my hotel, and whatever was bothering him was put aside as he pulled into the hostelry's drive.

Coming back to the car five minutes later with my single suitcase, I had hoped what I suspected was an impending confrontation had been put off. Faint chance. Having had time to think it over while I had been inside, he began without preamble almost immediately after we started off for the airport.

"When Ginny disappeared, a lot of people suffered. Myself included," he said.

"I know that. We all did. We all suffered."

His fists tightened on the wheel.

"You say that. But I saw what happened that day. What you did. I *know*."

"What are you trying to say? We all thought something different. We all had different stories. Something *happened*, all right, but you'd have to be a smarter man than everyone else to know, as you put it, what *happened* then."

I could see his jaw muscles tighten while he listened, and was glad the airport was only a few minutes away.

In a slow, cadenced voice that told me he was barely containing his rage, he said, "Don't give me that BS. You can bullshit the others, but you can't bullshit me." He paused while turning into the airport approach road, and then continued: "You're holding back. You found something. What?"

I deflected his question, using the politician's cheap ploy. I asked him a question in return, an inspired hunch that came to me while looking at him.

"What about yourself. It was you, wasn't it, who took the pages from the Westman book?"

"And if I did?"

"Maybe *you'd* like to share them with me?"

He said nothing; the ramp for departures was looming, and he ran the car up it without any more talk. His face, reddened during the outburst, was losing its flush and returning to its dull, flat tone again.

Watching me take my bag from the trunk, he made one last try.

"Okay, you want to know something, I'll tell you something. When they made that park in the back of the church, ten years after you left, they tried to fill the pond. Bulldozer came up on it, didn't get much further than the edge of the thicket around it. Something sliced the treads, like a razor."

"Sliced the treads? Steel treads?"

He nodded. "Not just once, either. They tried to go in three times, and the last time, a front axle sheared. The foreman went to look, started going into the thicket himself, something happened, like he stumbled; he lost a foot. Cut clean and neat in a second, right off. Never found what did it. After that, they decided to leave it, and built a bike path around it instead. Now you got something from me. So, maybe you got anything you want to tell me?"

Under the roar of jets taking off and landing, under a murky sky, he had given up; there was almost a pleading tone to his voice. On the verge of telling him something, I hesitated and decided against it—there was something about the phrasing and tenor of his words; and he was holding back: he had only told me a little, I was sure of it.

"Not this time round, I think."

He nodded slowly. He didn't offer his hand, nor did I.

Inside the airport, I checked in at the counter of a cheap carrier—the one that gives you purple potato chips. With the new security regulations in effect, I took my suitcase over to a nearby table, where an inspector asked me to undo the lock. I did as I was asked.

"Will the bag be unlocked all the way to Kennedy?" I asked her.

"Please put the bag on the table," was the curt reply.

She clearly had her instructions: no talking to the customer. Be a robot. Short, clipped sentences. Keep them at a distance. No fraternizing. Everyone a terrorist.

This is what it's come to, I felt like saying, but I held my peace.

I watched as she applied sniffer strips to the seams of my luggage, checking for explosives and chemicals. And it came to me. About time, and memory.

Sometimes, we think that people long dead died only a few years ago, and relatedly, in our ignorance, that someone still alive is dead. Or that someone dead is still alive. This applies not only to persons whom we know or have only heard of, but also to events, and processes.

The point is, things happen to people and you don't remember. It's not that a monstrous mouth opens in the middle of the sky and snatches them away. It's just that suddenly, they're gone. And you might not even remember.

I can see now that whatever had happened on the swing long before will never be known, only parts of it. It was our brush with the ineffable, and Ginny was the sacrificial victim. Something hardened inside us afterwards, that kept us separate, no longer able to say what we thought, or what was inside us. It might have been the same thing; it might have been something entirely different. The point now was that she was gone, the golden girl of our youth, and even resurrecting Gordon Dater, were that possible, would never bring back the knowledge of what really happened.

The round central hall of the city airport was new, lighted indirectly from a high dome above. Beneath it was a horrible sculptural group of what looked to be gigantic stone dildos, probably meant to be inspirational. Porchester never did, and evidently never would, get things right. I thought about fields of childhood, pain, the pond in the distance. Where I saw a smudged blur growing above it, on my longest arc through the air, years back.

We're high above, crossing the muddy grey of rivers welling up in the Pennsylvania highlands, oxbowing across a landscape nowhere untouched by some construction, road, or building. All this is apparent from the sky. There is no wilderness again.

Then I think of something else.

She was, I now realize, of Flemish extraction.

Everything points that way, given my life's worth of accumulated physiognomatic knowledge, those hints and clues built up over decades of observation, those filed-away facts of physical appearance, their stochastic interconnections. The green-blue eyes, the blondness, the delicate narrow jaw with those squarish chipmunk rami lately so sought after by modeling agencies, the slightly pursed and projecting lips—sort of duckish proto–Julia Roberts ready-to-kiss, and the cleft chin, the lynx eyes, the light freckles: they all add up to one specific locale on the planet.

Virginia couldn't say Flemish though, not around where we grew up, since that brand of ethnicity wouldn't have registered on ordinary Upstate minds. So she said German, although I suppose she could have just as well have said Dutch, which had the virtue of being slightly more exotic, though not by much.

These days, Ginny would have been hard put to explain her family background at all, since most people around can hardly find Europe on the map any more. The exception proving the rule is the case of their own national background—everyone somehow seems able to spot their grandparents' obscure, blood-drenched tribal patch on a Mercator grid, no matter how ignorant they are about the rest of the world, no matter how much that same world affects them.

"Flemish? Oh yeah, that's nice." Typical polite incomprehension masked; on to next topic.

It's what gets us into situations, not caring about anybody besides ourselves, not wanting to know anything that we don't want to think about. We all became too corporate.

Not that we didn't have resources available back then, to jog our curiosity, to knock us out of our complacency, if we had cared. The older people were sometimes like that, not afraid to put us in the way of the unusual, make us stretch our minds, let you know the world is stranger than you think. Things odd enough to get you thinking. Maybe they knew that getting kicked out of the rut was a good thing, sometimes. Making kids curious, instead of unquestioning.

Making you look at things more closely. Like my church of childhood, St. Christina's, for example. The old cigar-chomping Irish pastor known for his Sunday mid-Mass flatulence, the man who kick-started the show into a proper countryside parish, had a penchant for the unusual.

Rather than stick to the obvious, and pick a nice safe saint's name—St. John's, St. Michael's, St. Theresa's; any of them would have been all right—or some aspect of the deity—trinity, family, whatever—he plumped for the nearly unknown and probably legendary Christina, making us the laughing stock of the diocese. He probably thought it gave his church distinction, since there were no others named after that particular Christina in the entire country. Maybe he thought it would parochially toughen us—"How do you do—my Saint's named Sue"—that sort of thing.

Our Christina was one of an extremely long list of martyrs who, even pre-Vatican II, had been conveniently ignored by Rome for a long time, the hierarchy evidently embarrassed by the titillating aspects of her demise. Her legend inspired an extremely salacious cycle of paintings by Veronese. One canvas in particular, depicting her flagellation in public, would, if better known, qualify her immediately as the patron saint of S-M and bondage, but it was tucked away—still is, for all I know—in some remote little museum in the Venetian lagoon, no doubt having been deemed too prurient in content for continued display in the tourist-saturated Academy, whither it had first been banished when Christina's Torcello church was demolished.

Without question, our priest had got wind of some of this, since he had commissioned a series of ten plaques in low relief that more or less showed the same incidents Veronese had used or imagined. These sensual sculptures were placed around the walls of our church, five to each long side, in lieu of the stations of the cross. Word was that, when the bishop came on his yearly round of confirmations, he, seeing these artistic masterpieces for the first time, shook his head in disbelief, clucking and rolling his eyes heavenward at the same time. One plaque, for some reason, was removed before I could remember; I grew up with nine on the church walls, and never saw the missing one, which was probably broken.

If able, the boys of the parish living nearby would sneak into the church after hours, preferably alone, just to get an uninterrupted look at the silky marble skin, cruelly torn by strips of twisted iron representing thongs of Roman whip, blackened tangles frozen in midlash.

Not to go into detail, but I now realize sex is a powerful didactic tool. Maybe it wasn't being used enough when I grew up, which might explain a lot these days. But all this searching after fact, after the event—maybe the priest's intention was realized in me some way. Sex, the prod of learning. Not that it matters any more.

That leaves the matter of the swing.

It started, as far as I recall, with the burst, the burn of hormonal fires on the cusp of adolescence. It was the last year of grade, or grammar, school, as the first eight years were then called. We were twelve, most of our class, with a few already thirteen. Playmates of the other sex, once innocently regarded, now became the objects of unrequited desire, appraised with thoughtful looks. Each visit to the church would have eyes wandering from the tribulations of its patron saint to the budding bodies of the smooth-skinned girls around us. Furtive touching of marble flesh stoked thoughts that were impure.

My pals—Bobby Kraulin, Gilb Deuch, the Dater Bros—that band of boys, myself included, living nearest the church, who formed an inner core at the parish school—schemed and fantasized together to find some way to see, to comprehend, with deeper intimacy, those suddenly attractive but now much more mysterious classmates at the verge of womanhood. We wouldn't have known what to do if confronted with actual carnality, but that ignorance did not obviate the lust that drove our dreams.

Living just around the corner from my house, Ginny was the focus of my own imaginings. I would endlessly extol her merits, as I conceived them, to my friends, when we verbally undressed absent victims, weighing corporal pros and cons like hardened old roués. Never realizing that the sought after had little to do with the physicality of things.

I can see more easily now that I was attracted to Ginny precisely because she was unbound by local codes, or any codes, for that matter. She said what she thought, and was unsparing with words in a friendly fashion. Maybe it was something Flemish, in the genes. She had sniffed along the borders of what growing up as a young woman in America then entailed, and wasn't having any of it. She would rather have continued as she had been, one of the gang, an honorary guy.

· The problem was that regardless of how she perceived herself, we boys saw her differently. Already she was a creature apart, becoming in spite of herself the unknown *other*—herself impossibly attempting a state of arrest, trying to stop the then inevitable course of things, resisting. We, in our turn, were constantly after her with sly remarks, plucking, always plucking at her and her self-esteem, perhaps in the hope that she would somehow unravel. The unraveling would be, I sensed, in some form of sexual surrender.

Eventually things came to a head. Our old wooden parish church and combined school was an L-shaped building set close to the main road, the classroom leg running parallel to the thoroughfare. Once a new brick church was consecrated, its white-painted forerunner fell into semi-disuse. Importantly, it screened, and made invisible to any cars going by, an enormous swing set.

The swing's metal frame was the highest I have ever seen, and the most solid. It could never be built today because of safety rules in an overregulated society, but obviously, once upon a time, it was seen as a good thing.

A long, horizontal pole high above the ground rested on six main supports, three at either end meeting to form the skeletons of steep half-pyramids. A couple of additional poles below the middle of the high horizontal were set up like columns to keep the chief element from sagging. Between these a crossbar was welded, making a frozen trapeze, from which you could hang by your legs, or do chin-ups. The whole was vaguely like a giant old style tent frame bare of canvas.

To put it another way, this was not your ordinary *buranko*. The thing was made from heavy pipes of massive diameter, further rigidity obtained by sinking the legs down into rough concrete foundations. No one knew how deep those ran. The apex must have stood at least eighteen feet, more like twenty. But all things seem bigger to children.

Except for the very last foot or so near the top, the swing hung from no flimsy chains or rope; whoever had built the monster had permanence in mind, with each seat depending from two lines of heavy metal rods, each half a yard long, linked to one another by eyebolts welded shut. These were connected to the top frame by several heavy links of iron that looked more suitable for the anchor of some giant seagoing freighter than for a playground swing. The seats themselves were of some extinct species of thick black vinyl, formula long lost, reminiscent of heat-coagulated asphalt on lost summer roads, at its gleaming, chewable best.

The giant frame had been there as long as anyone could remember. Rumor was that it had been set up by "veterans"—of which war, was never specified. We approached it with awe. It was in fact dimensioned for adults—most children below our age had difficulty even getting up on the seats, so high off the ground. Once up, we lacked the weight to build momentum. We were too small to gain any real altitude unaided, by thrusting our feet alone—again, a sign that the set wasn't made for kids. On the other hand, most adults avoided it, and mothers disliked it, telling their children to stay away or to be very careful. Something about it intimidated, most likely memories from their own childhoods.

To make any headway, you needed at least two others to push from behind. With the concerted efforts of those involved you could attain some serious height—at least in relative terms. On this swing, anchored to the bedrock, you could oscillate to your heart's content, taking it higher than you ever thought possible, and the thing would never shake. We sneered at the flimsier sets at the public school down the road.

No one had ever even dreamed of taking our swing to the max, though—it was all too frightening—seeing the ground drop away from your feet, the rush of acceleration upward—to dare tempt fate by pumping further, into a wider arc. No one ever came near taking the swing to its limit. We were just too scared. All except one person, that is.

I can't remember what exactly started it off. There had been the usual flirting after school, the veiled insinuations, the constant sly probing. The gang of us—four or five boys, and Ginny—were outside her house after school, shooting the breeze, saying nothing at all, and everything. The air was as thick as plum pudding, heavy with unrealized dreams and wishful, rummish, sodden desire.

In the end, she broke the mood.

"Going in. Change. Be out soon. See you."

It was so unexpected, abrupt, that we stood there wondering what she was up to. Not many minutes later, we knew.

Virginia—it was impossible to think of her as Ginny in her new outfit—came out wearing a slinky black number she must have stolen from her smaller but older sister. The skirt was short, showing her pool-bronzed legs and already shapely thighs. We were suddenly boys in the presence of a woman—how had we even dared carry on the way we had only moments ago?

Standing there, the gap separating her *knowledge* from our childhood stretching rapidly by the light-year, I suddenly had a thought. Whether it was inspired by art books around the house, I don't remember. I must, by then, have seen in reproduction the rococo reveries of Fragonard and Boucher, faux milkmaids in Arcady with swains, aristocratic serving girls on revelatory—*swings*. Whatever I may precisely have thought, I know I suggested we all go over to the empty parish school yard, and try out—the swing. I do remember thinking how desperate I was to put things back on equal footing, to shrink the chasm that the simple act of putting on adult clothing had created.

I walked behind Virginia on the four-minute stroll, letting Bobby Kraulin do point honors and chat with her, while I watched from behind. It was obvious—to anyone who looked—that Ginny had nothing on underneath, the dress was that tight. I suddenly knew that I wanted her high on the swing, kicking her legs, losing herself. I wanted to *see*. Not necessarily her long bare legs, or secrets hidden beyond. Faint hope that. But see *everything*. Everything inexpressible. That's what I wanted. And I think the others did too.

The graying school custodian waved at us, as he shuffled across Mercerport Road to the church-provided house where he lived with his family. When we arrived behind the old building, the large tarmacked playground that doubled as the church parking lot on Sundays was abandoned. Fields, fallow, mostly brilliant green weeds, stretched back of the place, where the park is now, past the looming bell tower, the new brick church, and adjacent school and convent, out to the hedgerows, until it all ended in distant forest, the far-off pond at one corner shimmering through its surrounding thicket in the late spring haze. Summer vacation was about to start.

I think I was the first one up. With Bobby and Gilb providing propulsion, I went as high as I could go, until fear took over. I saw over the tops of the trees to the north on my forward arcs, I was that high up. I was afraid of letting go, of losing my grip on the metal rods I held in my hands, and flying endlessly away. Some of our older brothers told us that if we swung high enough, we might be able to see the lake, Ontario, five miles north, or even Canada across it.

I never got that high, yelling in near panic to the others to stop their pushing. What had happened was, on the highest part of my last full forward swing, I saw a blur in the air, far away in the direction of the pond, a smudged patch that seemed to grow or move close while I looked at it. It scared me — I thought I was getting vertigo, afraid I would pass out, afraid I would let go.

Later, when we all, except Ginny, had had our turn, we sat enthusing, as boys will, in the grass before the swing. We had forgotten, in our exuberance, the main object of our little trip — to get Ginny on the swing. That's how exciting it was being up there, up on it. You forgot everything else; after, it would take some while for the adrenalin to cool.

Ginny, however, had not forgotten. Although momentarily ignored, she was still there. She maintained her distance, leaning with one shoulder against the time-pitted dark metal of one upright, regarding us in a cool manner, as if we were children — which we were.

"If you had only gone higher — you could've gone even with the top, a couple of more swings!" Bobby said to Gilb Deuch, my nearest neighbor on the street.

"Naw, it was *unstable*. If I kept going, I coulda been thrown."

We blinked. That wasn't talking our talk, that was showing off. For Virginia. *Unstable*, for Christ's sake.

"What," I asked, "what if you kept on going, *round* the top?"

We had all fantasized about this before. Opinion was divided. Some of us thought the top links from which the seats ultimately hung would break. Others thought the stunt could be done, but that you would be shaken off, with nasty results, once you had reached 360°, a full loop. Certainly, the problem facing other swings — shakiness, that they were likely to tip if pushed hard — was not a problem here: the church swing was like granite. The empty speculation went on, until Ginny — tan arms crossed over her breast, index finger held casually out, pointing nowhere, poised as if to tap one bare shoulder, probably disgusted at our shallow blather — calmly said, "I'll go over. I can do it."

She stopped us cold with that simple statement. It was getting near dinner time; mothers would soon be calling from across the street, using that loud and idiosyncratic local chirp, substituting for a whistle — invented and spread, as most odd habits were, by the Dater Bros — to herd their offspring home. It would have been easy to ignore Ginny, to break up, to head back.

No one did.

We all watched as she mounted the nearest seat, the rest of us just standing there, looking. She pulled the hem of the dress higher, up over her golden thighs with fine blonde hairs barely visible, to free her legs.

And it was so still you could have heard our hearts beat. None of us moving, she turned, so her hair swung like an ocean wave, and she looked at us askant. It came back to us then—this was the moment we had tacitly planned and anticipated.

Finally, wordlessly, two of us began to push from behind—I think it was Gilb and one of the Dater Bros—as she gained speed and momentum. She quickly rose up like a huge pendulum, perfectly snapping her legs at the apex of each forward arc, taut and straight like a diver, for maximum gain. She was soon higher than any of us had ever been before, but was not yet level with the high crossbar. ·

"What's wrong? Can't you push any harder? What's wrong?" she yelled down to us.

The truth was, we weren't tall enough, muscled enough, any of us, to push the seat, with Virginia on it, any further.

"Can't go any higher; not with you guys pushing me!" Ginny cried.

"I'm not doing this any more," Gilb muttered, and he dropped out from behind. Mike, I think it was, gave up too. The support team had failed. Virginia quickly started losing momentum—she was a slim girl, and her kicks, artful as they were, did not allow her to maintain her height. We thought it was all done, when we heard a voice, a deep, gravelly man's voice, say, "Move back, boys, I'll take over."

It was someone none of us had ever seen before, and after, none of us could agree how he had looked. There was something undefined about him, that made his appearance hard to pin down.

I was certain then that he was very tall, swarthy, with lank black hair, dark eyes, and dressed in black or dark grey. But Bobby had a totally opposite image of the guy, and Gilb disagreed with both of us. The Daters weren't even sure if anyone else was there at all, although they thought there might have been, they claimed afterwards. There were five widely differing opinions, which didn't help things very much, later on.

In my view, at least, the stranger smoothly caught the swing with our friend, our goddess, our temptress-in-the-making, and pushed it till it soared, higher and higher, until we were certain it would go over the top with one or two more shoves. I remember Ginny whooshing by on one swoop, her jaw clenched, her knuckles white around the hanging rods. There was, however, no fear in her eyes. She kept them open throughout, looking towards the horizon.

On the final shove, I'm not sure what happened. Just as the creaking swing was about to go vertical, Virginia—almost upside down, about to do what no one had ever done before—may have taken her body out of the plane of motion. She might have loosened her grip, flying out into space, just before the apogee. She might have even made it to the zenith, poised for a moment, before the descent. I don't know, nor did anyone else there that day know. It all happened so quickly.

The only thing I noticed—and I think the Dater brothers did, too—was a short piercing cry—a sudden earsplitting burst—not a scream, but something like one, cut off immediately after. But it didn't sound like Ginny at all. It had come from somewhere else, far off. Anyway, that's what I thought. The Daters thought something else. Regardless.

She was there, above, and then she was gone.

The empty swing noisily fell straight down in jumbled clattering swags of iron rods, looped over both sides of the upper frame.

I looked to Gordon. His mouth was open in astonishment as, I suppose, was mine.

I looked for the dark stranger who had pushed the swing into its frighteningly ever-accelerating rush, and he was gone too, no sign of him anywhere, in spite of the clear wide views in every direction.

And that was that.

A few weeks after Ginny disappeared, I walked over to the pond, to a point at the marge of its surrounding thicket of trees and brush, to about where I guessed I had seen the blur high up. I was still shaken by what had happened; I walked carefully. I hadn't told any of the others I was going there. I hadn't told them what I had seen. It was my first time in the fields alone.

By a sort of stile at a corner formed by two hedgerows and the pond, right about where I guessed I had seen the ripple in the air, I looked in towards the water. There, not far out, at about boy height—my height—was something like a swarm of mayflies, except these weren't moving: they were frozen there in the air, in spite of a slight breeze on that hot day. And they weren't blacks and translucencies; they were a reddish brown. Small bumps formed on my thin arms, in spite of the heat.

I wanted to run, but doing what I still think was the bravest thing I had ever done in my life, the war included, I picked up a large stone, and threw it. There was a loud crack, a shattering sound, like the noise some glassy tooth—if it was really big—might make if it was snapped by a rock. And the swarm of dried blood—because that is what I think it was, held by some unseen matrix—was gone, with only dozens of expanding rings in the pond's water, showing where invisible things falling had hit, disappearing into the dark and leafy depths.

Then I ran, ran as fast as I could, stumbling wildly over the furrowed fields, home.

Cloudless eve, sun still, and the plane is coming into New York. I see all of Manhattan far below to starboard, Brooklyn, Queens, blocks and buildings like a street map, bronze evening waters surrounding, dark forests of Jersey behind.

Sometimes we do or see things, the meaning of which escapes us until much later. Other times we never comprehend at all.

Ginny was brave, and whatever happened to her, she didn't go down without a fight. We were wrong, we boys. Wrong to have done what we did. Men see something else. A woman should have been with her, and then—maybe—the two would have *seen*, seen together. Seen as in generations past, with periodicity, come back and tell the tribe, or whoever occupies the land. And then and only then go back, to be taken away, in payment for knowledge given. But we've broken that connection now, and I wonder what lies ahead.

Each time I meet a new woman, I ask her, have you ever, when a child, thought of swinging as high as you were able, seeing far and as much as you could, and then letting go, flying through the air forever?

Everyone had.

SONYA TAAFFE

Follow Me Home

Sonya Taaffe has a confirmed addiction to myth, folklore, and dead languages. Poems and short stories of hers have been shortlisted for the SLF Fountain Award, honorably mentioned in The Year's Best Fantasy and Horror, *and reprinted in* The Alchemy of Stars: Rhysling Award Winners Showcase, The Best of Not One of Us, Fantasy: The Best of the Year 2006, *and* Best New Fantasy. *A respectable amount of her work can be found in* Postcards from the Province of Hyphens *and* Singing Innocence and Experience *(Prime Books). She is currently pursuing a Ph.D. in Classics at Yale University. Her livejournal is* Myth Happens *(http://sovay.livejournal.com/).*

"Follow Me Home" was originally published in Lone Star Stories, *edited by Eric T. Marin, in the February issue.*

—E.D.

You dream the wire where your hanging flesh
tatters to bloody flags in the sun,
the battlefield stink like a butcher's sewer
and the shop-display of no man's land
garlands the mud with boots, cloth, corpses
pared to a clench-jawed grin; a knife-blade
speckles troutlike with rust, a china head
rattles like a dice-cup with the glass eyes within,
dainties discarded in a drawer at home
where letters tied with red ribbon leaf-drift
now. A clock-tick, a ratsfoot whisper,
and I dream the night before the last came
stained with earth like a sexton and another
man's hand: the shell-casings, the shrapnel
I picked from a flooded ditch, a watch-face
splintered to half past ten and in the sunset
soaked to Mars; the beheaded, the detonated,
the flayed, the impaled, gathered in my wake
like a murder to the gallows, pilgrims to the cross,
a cluster of bullets like bruises in my hand.
The mortar-flares. The silence. The wasted land.
The same dream kicks and sways with the wind

each night by graveside or candlelight: I plant
red poppies and dog roses and the children play
with blind dolls and pocketknives, crying rhymes
at crows; for the dead I could not harrow,
for the words I never wrote, for the last letter
I unfolded with your smile on my face—
blasted, blown open, unsurprised.

LAIRD BARRON

The Forest

Laird Barron's work has appeared in places such as The Magazine of Fantasy & Science Fiction, SCIFICTION, *and* The Del Rey Book of Science Fiction and Fantasy. *It has also been reprinted in numerous year's best anthologies. His debut collection,* The Imago Sequence and Other Stories, *was recently published by Night Shade. Mr. Barron is an expatriate Alaskan currently at large in Washington State.*

"The Forest" was originally published in Inferno: New Tales of Terror and the Supernatural, *edited by Ellen Datlow.*

—E.D.

After the drive had grown long and monotonous, Partridge shut his eyes and the woman was waiting. She wore a cold white mask similar to the mask Bengali woodcutters donned when they ventured into the mangrove forests along the coast. The tigers of the forest were stealthy. The tigers hated to be watched; they preferred to sneak up on prey from behind, so natives wore the masks on the backs of their heads as they gathered wood. Sometimes this kept the tigers from dragging them away.

The woman in the cold white mask reached into a wooden box. She lifted a tarantula from the box and held it to her breast like a black carnation. The contrast was as magnificent as a stark Monet if Monet had painted watercolors of emaciated patricians and their pet spiders.

Partridge sat on his high, wooden chair and whimpered in animal terror. In the daydream, he was always very young and powerless. The woman tilted her head. She came near and extended the tarantula in her long, gray hand. "For you," she said. Sometimes she carried herself more like Father and said in a voice of gravel, "Here is the end of fear." Sometimes the tarantula was a hissing cockroach of prehistoric girth, or a horned beetle. Sometimes it was a strange, dark flower. Sometimes it was an embryo uncurling to form a miniature adult human that grinned a monkey's hateful grin.

The woman offered him a black phone. The woman said, "Come say good-bye and good luck. Come quick!" Except the woman did not speak. Toshi's breathless voice bled through the receiver. The woman in the cold white mask brightened then dimmed like a dying coal or a piece of metal coiling into itself.

Partridge opened his eyes and rested his brow against window glass. He was alone with the driver. The bus trawled through a night forest. Black trees dripped with fog.

The narrow black road crumbled from decades of neglect. Sometimes poor houses and fences stood among the weeds and the ferns and mutely suggested many more were lost in the dark. Wilderness had arisen to reclaim its possessions.

Royals hunted in woods like these. He snapped on the overhead lamp and then opened his briefcase. *Stags, wild boar, witches. Convicts.* The briefcase was nearly empty. He had tossed in some traveler's checks, a paperback novel and his address book. No cell phone, although he left a note for his lawyer and a recorded message at Kyla's place in Malibu warning them it might be a few days, perhaps a week, that there probably was not even phone service where he was going. Carry on, carry on. He had hopped a redeye jet to Boston and once there eschewed the convenience of renting a car or hiring a chauffeur and limo. He chose instead the relative anonymity of mass transit. The appeal of traveling incognito overwhelmed his normally staid sensibilities. Here was the first adventure he had undertaken in ages. The solitude presented an opportunity to compose his thoughts—his excuses, more likely.

He'd cheerfully abandoned the usual host of unresolved items and potential brushfires that went with the territory—a possible trip to the Andes if a certain Famous Director's film got green-lighted and if the Famous Director's drunken assertion to assorted executive producers and hangers-on over barbequed ribs and flaming daiquiris at the Monarch Grille that Richard Jefferson Partridge was the only man for the job meant a blessed thing. There were several smaller opportunities, namely an L.A. documentary about a powerhouse high school basketball team that recently graced the cover of *Sports Illustrated*, unless the documentary guy, a Cannes Film Festival sweetheart, decided to try to bring down the Governor of California instead, as he had threatened to do time and again, a pet crusade of his with the elections coming that fall, and then the director would surely use his politically savvy compatriot, the cinematographer from France. He'd also been approached regarding a proposed documentary about prisoners and guards at San Quentin. Certainly there were other, lesser engagements he'd lost track of, these doubtless scribbled on memo pads in his home office.

He knew he should hire a reliable secretary. He promised himself to do just that every year. It was hard. He missed Jean. She'd had a lazy eye and a droll wit; made bad coffee and kept sand-filled frogs and fake petunias on her desk. Jean left him for Universal Studios and then slammed into a reef in Maui learning to surf with her new boss. The idea of writing the want ad, of sorting the applications and conducting the interviews and finally letting the new person, the stranger, sit where Jean had sat and handle his papers, summoned a mosquito's thrum in the bones behind Partridge's ear.

These details would surely keep despite what hysterics might come in the meanwhile. Better, much better, not to endure the buzzing and whining and the imprecations and demands that he return at once on pain of immediate career death, over a dicey relay.

He had not packed a camera, either. He was on vacation. His mind would store what his eye could catch and that was all.

The light was poor. Partridge held the address book close to his face. He had scribbled the directions from margin to margin and drawn a crude map with arrows and lopsided boxes and jotted the initials of the principles: Dr. Toshi Ryoko; Dr. Howard Campbell; Beasley; and Nadine. Of course, Nadine—she snapped her fingers and here he came at a loyal trot. There were no mileposts on the road to confirm the impression that his destination was near. The weight in his belly sufficed. It was a fat stone grown from a pebble.

Partridge's instincts did not fail him. A few minutes before dawn, the forest receded and they entered Warrenburgh. Warrenburgh was a loveless hamlet of crabbed New England shop fronts and angular plank and shingle houses with tall, thin doors and oily windows. Streetlights glowed along Main Street with black gaps like a broken pearl necklace. The street itself was buckled and rutted by poorly tarred cracks that caused sections to cohere uneasily as interleaved ice floes. The sea loomed near and heavy and palpable beneath a layer of rolling gloom.

Partridge did not like what little he glimpsed of the surroundings. Long ago, his friend Toshi had resided in New Mexico and Southern California, did his best work in Polynesia and the jungles of Central America. The doctor was a creature of warmth and light. *Rolling Stone* had characterized him as "a rock star among zoologists" and as the "Jacques Cousteau of the jungle," the kind of man who hired mercenaries to guard him, performers to entertain his sun-drenched villa, and filmmakers to document his exploits. This temperate landscape, so cool and provincial, so removed from Partridge's experience of all things Toshi, seemed to herald a host of unwelcome revelations.

Beasley, longstanding attendant of the eccentric researcher, waited at the station. "Rich! At least you don't look like the big asshole *Variety* says you are." He nodded soberly and scooped Partridge up for a brief hug in his powerful arms. This was like being embraced by an earthmover. Beasley had played Australian rules football for a while after he left the Army and before he came to work for Toshi. His nose was squashed and his ears were cauliflowers. He was magnetic and striking as any character actor, nonetheless. "Hey, let me get that." He set Partridge aside and grabbed the luggage the driver had dragged from the innards of the bus. He hoisted the suitcases into the bed of a '56 Ford farm truck. The truck was museum quality. It was fire engine red with a dinky American flag on the antenna.

They rumbled inland. Rusty light gradually exposed counterchange shelves of empty fields and canted telephone poles strung together with thick, dipping old-fashioned cables. Ducks pelted from a hollow in the road. The ducks spread themselves in a wavering pattern against the sky.

"Been shooting?" Partridge indicated the .20 gauge softly clattering in the rack behind their heads.

"When T isn't looking. Yeah, I roam the marshes a bit. You?"

"No."

"Yah?"

"Not in ages. Things get in the way. Life, you know?"

"Oh, well, we'll go out one day this week. Bag a mallard or two. Raise the dust."

Partridge stared at the moving scenery. Toshi was disinterested in hunting and thought it generally a waste of energy. Nadine detested the sport without reserve. He tasted brackish water, metallic from the canteen. The odor of gun oil and cigarette smoke was strong in the cab. The smell reminded him of hip waders, muddy clay banks, and gnats in their biting millions among the reeds. "Okay. Thanks."

"Forget it, man."

They drove in silence until Beasley hooked left onto a dirt road that followed a ridge of brambles and oak trees. On the passenger side overgrown pastures dwindled into moiling vapors. The road was secured by a heavy iron gate with the usual complement of grimy warning signs. Beasley climbed out and unlocked the gate and swung it aside. Partridge realized that somehow this was the same ruggedly charismatic Beasley, plus a streak of gray in the beard and minus the spring-loaded tension and the whiskey musk. Beasley at peace was an enigma. Maybe he had quit the bottle for good this time around. The thought was not as comforting as it should have been. If this elemental truth—Beasley the chronic drunk, the lovable, but damaged brute—had ceased to hold, then what else lurked in the wings?

When they had begun to jounce along the washboard lane, Partridge said, "Did T get sick? Somebody—think Frank Ledbetter—told me T had some heart problems. Angina."

"Frankie . . . I haven't seen him since forever. He still working for Boeing?"

"Lockheed-Martin."

"Yah? Good ol' L&M. Well, no business like war business," Beasley said. "The old boy's fine. Sure, things were in the shitter for a bit after New Guinea, but we all got over it. Water down the sluice." Again, the knowing, sidelong glance. "Don't worry so much. He misses you. Everybody does, man."

Toshi's farm was more of a compound lumped in the torso of a great, irregular field. The road terminated in a hardpack lot bordered by a sprawl of sheds and shacks, gutted chicken coops and labyrinthine hog pens fallen to ruin. The main house, a Queen Anne, dominated. The house was a full three stories of spires, gables, spinning iron weathercocks, and acres of slate tiles. A monster of a house, yet somehow hunched upon itself. It was brooding and squat and low as a brick and timber mausoleum. The detached garage seemed new. So too the tarp and plastic-sheeted nurseries, the electric fence that partitioned the back forty into quadrants and the military drab shortwave antenna array crowning the A-frame barn. No private security forces were in evidence, no British mercenaries with submachine guns on shoulder slings, nor packs of sleek, bullet-headed attack dogs cruising the property. The golden age had obviously passed into twilight.

"Behold the Moorehead Estate," Beasley said as he parked by slamming the brakes so the truck skidded sideways and its tires sent up a geyser of dirt. "Howard and Toshi bought it from the county about fifteen years ago—guess the original family died out, changed their names, whatever. Been here in one form or another since 1762. The original burned to the foundation in 1886, which is roughly when the town—Orren Towne, 'bout two miles west of here—dried up and blew away. As you can see, they made some progress fixing this place since then."

Partridge whistled as he eyed the setup. "Really, ah, cozy."

There were other cars scattered in the lot: a Bentley; a Nixon-era Cadillac; an archaic Land Rover that might have done a tour in the Sahara; a couple of battered pickup trucks and an Army surplus jeep. These told Partridge a thing or two, but not enough to surmise the number of guests or the nature of Toshi's interest in them. He had spotted the tail rotor of a helicopter poking from behind the barn.

Partridge did not recognize any of the half dozen grizzled men loitering near the bunkhouse. Those would be the roustabouts and the techs. The men passed around steaming thermoses of coffee. They pretended not to watch him and Beasley unload the luggage.

"For God's sake, boy, why didn't you catch a plane?" Toshi called down from a perilously decrepit veranda. He was wiry and sallow and vitally ancient. He dressed in a bland short sleeve button-up shirt a couple of neck sizes too large and his omnipresent gypsy kerchief. He leaned way over the precarious railing and smoked a cigarette. His cigarettes were invariably Russian and came in tin boxes blazoned with hyperbolic full-color logos and garbled English mottos and blurbs such as, "Prince of Peace!" and "Yankee Flavor!"

"The Lear's in the shop." Partridge waved and headed for the porch.

"You don't drive, either, eh?" Toshi flicked his hand impatiently. "Come on, then. Beasley—the Garden Room, please."

Beasley escorted Partridge through the gloomy maze of cramped halls and groaning stairs. Everything was dark: from the cryptic hangings and oil paintings of Mooreheads long returned to dust, to the shiny walnut planks that squeaked and shifted everywhere underfoot.

Partridge was presented a key by the new housekeeper, Mrs. Grant. She was a brusque woman of formidable brawn and comport; perhaps Beasley's mother in another life. Beasley informed him that "new" was a relative term as she had been in Campbell's employ for the better portion of a decade. She had made the voyage from Orange County and brought along three maids and a gardener/handyman who was also her current lover.

The Garden Room was on the second floor of the east wing and carefully isolated from the more heavily trafficked byways. It was a modest, L-shaped room with low, harshly textured ceilings, a coffin wardrobe carved from the heart of some extinct tree, a matching dresser, and a diminutive brass bed that sagged ominously. The portrait of a solemn girl in a garden hat was centered amidst otherwise negative space across from the bed. Vases of fresh cut flowers were arranged on the window sills. Someone had plugged in a rose-scented air freshener to subdue the abiding taint of wet plaster and rotting wood; mostly in vain. French doors let out to a balcony overlooking tumbledown stone walls of a lost garden and then a plain of waist-high grass gone the shade of wicker. The grass flowed into foothills. The foothills formed an indistinct line in the blue mist.

"Home away from home, eh?" Beasley said. He wrung his hands, out of place as a bear in the confined quarters. "Let's see if those bastards left us any crumbs."

Howard Campbell and Toshi were standing around the bottom of the stairs with a couple of other elder statesmen types—one, a bluff aristocratic fellow with handlebar mustaches and fat hands, reclined in a hydraulic wheelchair. The second man was also a corn-fed specimen of genteel extract, but clean-shaven and decked in a linen suit that had doubtless been the height of ballroom fashion during Truman's watch. This fellow leaned heavily upon an ornate blackthorn cane. He occasionally pressed an oxygen mask over his mouth and nose and snuffled deeply. Both men stank of medicinal alcohol and shoe polish. A pair of bodyguards hovered nearby. The guards were physically powerful men in tight suit-jackets. Their nicked up faces wore the perpetual scowl of peasant trustees.

Toshi lectured about a so-called supercolony of ants that stretched six thousand kilometers from the mountains of Northern Italy down along the coasts of France and into Spain. According to the reports, this was the largest ant colony on record; a piece of entomological history in the making. He halted his oration to lackadaisically introduce the Eastern gentlemen as Mr. Jackson Phillips and Mr. Carrey Montague and then jabbed Campbell in the ribs, saying, "What'd I tell you? Rich is as suave as an Italian prince. Thank God I don't have a daughter for him to knock up." To Partridge he said, "Now go eat before cook throws it to the pigs. Go, go!" Campbell, the tallest and gravest of the congregation, gave Partridge a subtle wink. Meanwhile, the man in the wheelchair raised his voice to demand an explanation for why his valuable time was being wasted on an ant seminar. He had not come to listen to a dissertation and Toshi damned-well knew better . . . Partridge did not catch the rest because Beasley ushered him into the kitchen whilst surreptitiously flicking Mr. Jackson Phillips the bird.

The cook was an impeccable Hungarian named Gertz, whom Campbell had lured, or possibly blackmailed, away from a popular restaurant in Santa Monica. In any event, Gertz knew his business.

Partridge slumped on a wooden stool at the kitchen counter. He worked his way through what Gertz apologetically called "leftovers." These included sourdough waffles and strawberries, whipped eggs, biscuits, sliced apples, honeydew melon, and chilled milk. The coffee was a hand ground Columbian blend strong enough to peel paint. Beasley slapped him on the shoulder and said something about chores.

Partridge was sipping his second mug of coffee, liberally dosed with cream and sugar, when Nadine sat down close to him. Nadine shone darkly and smelled of fresh cut hayricks and sweet, highly polished leather. She leaned in tight and plucked the teaspoon from his abruptly nerveless fingers. She licked the teaspoon and dropped it on the saucer and she did not smile at all. She looked at him with metallic eyes that held nothing but a prediction of snow.

"And . . . action," Nadine said in a soft, yet resonant voice that could have placed her center stage on Broadway had she ever desired to dwell in the Apple and ride her soap-and-water sex appeal to the bank and back. She spoke without a trace of humor, which was a worthless gauge to ascertain her mood anyhow, she being a classical Stoic. Her mouth was full and lovely and inches from Partridge's own. She did not wear lipstick.

"You're pissed," Partridge said. He felt slightly dizzy. He was conscious of his sticky fingers and the seeds in his teeth.

"Lucky guess."

"I'm a Scientologist, Grade Two. We get ESP at G-2. No luck involved."

"Oh, they got you, too. Pity. Inevitable, but still a pity."

"I'm kidding."

"What . . . even the cultists don't want you?"

"I'm sure they want my money."

Nadine tilted her head slightly. "I owe the Beez twenty bucks, speaking of. Know why?"

"No," Partridge said. "Wait. You said I wouldn't show—"

"—because you're a busy man—"

"That's the absolute truth. I'm busier than a one-armed paper hanger."

"I'm sure. Anyway, I said you'd duck us once again. A big movie deal, fucking a B-list starlet in the South of France. It'd be something."

"—and then Beasley said something on the order of—"

"Hell yeah, my boy will be here!—"

"—come hell or high water!"

"Pretty much, yeah. He believes in you."

Partridge tried not to squirm even as her pitiless gaze bore into him. "Well, it was close. I canceled some things. Broke an engagement or two."

"Mmm. It's okay, Rich. You've been promising yourself a vacation, haven't you? This makes a handy excuse; do a little R&R, get some *you* time in for a change. It's for your mental health. Bet you can write it off."

"Since this is going so well . . . How's Coop?" He had noticed she was not wearing the ring. Handsome hubby Dan Cooper was doubtless a sore subject, he being the hapless CEO of an obscure defense contractor that got caught up in a federal dragnet. He would not be racing his classic Jaguar along hairpin coastal highways for the next five to seven years, even assuming time off for good behavior. Poor Coop was another victim of Nadine's gothic curse. "Condolences, naturally. If I didn't send a card . . ."

"He *loves* Federal prison. It's a country club, really. How's that bitch you introduced me to? I forget her name."

"Rachel."

"Yep, that's it. The makeup lady. She pancaked Thurman like a corpse on that flick you shot for Coppola."

"Ha, yeah. She's around. We're friends."

"Always nice to have friends."

Partridge forced a smile. "I'm seeing someone else."

"Kyla Sherwood—the Peroxide Puppet. Tabloids know all, my dear."

"But it's not serious."

"News to her, hey?"

He was boiling alive in his Aspen-chic sweater and charcoal slacks. Sweat trickled down his neck and the hairs on his thighs prickled and choroused their disquiet. He wondered if that was a massive pimple pinching the flesh between his eyes. That was where he had always gotten the worst of them in high school. His face swelled so majestically people thought he had broken his nose playing softball. What could he say with this unbearable pressure building in his lungs? Their history had grown to epic dimensions. The kitchen was too small to contain such a thing. He said, "Toshi said it was important. That I come to this . . . what? Party? Reunion? Whatever it is. God knows I love a mystery."

Nadine stared the stare that gave away nothing. She finally glanced at her watch and stood. She leaned over him so that her hot breath brushed his ear. "Mmm. Look at the time. Lovely seeing you, Rich. Maybe later we can do lunch."

He watched her walk away. As his pulse slowed and his breathing loosened, he waited for his erection to subside and tried to pinpoint what it was that nagged him, what it was that tripped the machinery beneath the liquid surface of his guilt-crazed, testosterone-glutted brain. Nadine had always reminded him of a duskier, more ferocious Bettie Page. She was thinner now, probably going gray if not for the wonders of modern cosmetics. Her prominent cheekbones, the fragile symmetry of her scapulae through the open-back blouse, registered with him as he sat recovering his wits with the numb intensity of a soldier who had just clambered from a trench following a mortar barrage.

Gertz slunk out of hiding and poured more coffee into Partridge's cup. He dumped in some Schnapps from a hip flask. "Hang in there, my friend," he said drolly.

"I just got my head beaten in," Partridge said.

"Round one," Gertz said. He took a hefty pull from the flask. "Pace yourself, champ."

Partridge wandered the grounds until he found Toshi in D-Lab. Toshi was surveying a breeding colony of cockroaches: *Pariplenata americana*, he proclaimed them with a mixture of pride and annoyance. The lab was actually a big tool shed with the windows painted over. Industrial-sized aquariums occupied most of the floor space. The air had acquired a peculiar, spicy odor reminiscent of hazelnuts and fermented bananas. The chamber was illuminated by infrared lamps. Partridge could not observe much activity within the aquariums unless he stood next to the glass. That was not going to happen. He contented himself to lurk at Toshi's elbow while a pair of men in coveralls and rubber gloves performed maintenance on an empty pen. The men scraped substrate into garbage bags and hosed the container and applied copious swathes of petroleum jelly to the rim where the mesh lid attached. Cockroaches were escape artists extraordinaire, according to Toshi.

"Most folks are trying to figure the best pesticide to squirt on these little fellas. Here you are a cockroach rancher," Partridge said.

"Cockroaches . . . I care nothing for cockroaches. This is scarcely more than a side effect, the obligatory nod to cladistics, if you will. Cockroaches . . . beetles . . . there are superficial similarities. These animals crawl and burrow, they predate us humans by hundreds of millions of years. But . . . beetles are infinitely more interesting. The naturalist's best friend. Museums and taxidermists love them, you see. Great for cleansing skeletal structures, antlers and the like."

"Nature's efficiency experts. What's the latest venture?"

"A-Lab—I will show you." Toshi became slightly animated. He straightened his crunched shoulders to gesticulate. His hand glimmered like a glow tube at a rock concert. "I keep a dozen colonies of dermestid beetles in operation. Have to house them in glass or stainless steel—they nibble through anything."

This house of creepy-crawlies was not good for Partridge's nerves. He thought of the chair and the woman and her tarantula. He was sickly aware that if he closed his eyes at that very moment the stranger would remove the mask and reveal Nadine's face. Thinking of Nadine's face and its feverish luminescence, he said, "She's dying."

Toshi shrugged. "Johns Hopkins . . . my friends at Fred Hutch . . . nobody can do anything. This is the very bad stuff; very quick."

"How long has she got?" The floor threatened to slide from under Partridge's feet. Cockroaches milled in their shavings and hidey holes; their ticktack impacts burrowed under his skin.

"Not long. Probably three or four months."

"Okay." Partridge tasted breakfast returned as acid in his mouth.

The technicians finished their task and began sweeping. Toshi gave some orders. He said to Partridge, "Let's go see the beetles."

A-Lab was identical to D-Lab except for the wave of charnel rot that met Partridge as he entered. The dermestid colonies were housed in corrugated metal canisters. Toshi raised the lid to show Partridge how industriously a particular group of larvae were stripping the greasy flesh of a small mixed breed dog. Clean white bone peeked through coagulated muscle fibers and patches of coarse, blond fur.

Partridge managed to stagger the fifteen or so feet and vomit into a plastic sink. Toshi shut the lid and nodded wisely. "Some fresh air, then."

Toshi conducted a perfunctory tour, complete with a wheezing narrative regarding matters coleopteran and teuthological, the latter being one of his comrade Howard Campbell's manifold specialties. Campbell had held since the early seventies that One Day Soon the snail cone or some species of jellyfish was going to revolutionize neurology. Partridge nodded politely and dwelt on his erupting misery. His stomach felt as if a brawler had used it for a speed bag. He trembled and dripped with cold sweats.

Then, as they ambled along a fence holding back the wasteland beyond the barn, he spotted a cluster of three satellite dishes. The dishes' antennas were angled downward at a sizable oblong depression like aardvark snouts poised to siphon musty earth. These were lightweight models, each no more than four meters across and positioned as to be hidden from casual view from the main house. Their trapezoidal shapes didn't jibe with photos Partridge had seen of similar devices. These objects gleamed the yellow-gray gleam of rotting teeth. His skin crawled as he studied them and the area of crushed soil. The depression was over a foot deep and shaped not un-like a kiddy wading pool. This presence in the field was incongruous and somehow sinister. He immediately regretted discarding his trusty Canon. He stopped and pointed. "What are those?"

"Radio telescopes, obviously."

"Yeah, what kind of metal is that? Don't they work better if you point them at the sky?"

"The sky. Ah, well, perhaps later. You note the unique design, eh? Campbell and I . . . invented them. Basically."

"Really? Interesting segue from entomological investigation, doc."

"See what happens when you roll in the mud with NASA? The notion of first contact is so glamorous, it begins to rub off. Worse than drugs. I'm in recovery."

Partridge stared at the radio dishes. "UFOs and whatnot, huh. You stargazer, you. When did you get into that field?" It bemused him how Toshi Ryoko hopscotched from discipline to discipline with a breezy facility that unnerved even the mavericks among his colleagues.

"I most assuredly haven't migrated to that field—however, I will admit to grazing as the occasion warrants. The dishes are a link in the chain. We've got miles of con-ductive coil buried around here. All part of a comprehensive surveillance plexus. We monitor everything that crawls, swims, or flies. Howard and I have become en-amored of astrobiology, cryptozoology, the occulted world. Do you recall when we closed shop in California? That was roughly concomitant with our lamentably over-publicized misadventures in New Guinea."

"Umm." Partridge had heard that Campbell and Toshi disappeared into the back country for three weeks after they lost a dozen porters and two graduate students in a river accident. Maybe alcohol and drugs were involved. There was an investigation and all charges were waived. The students' families had sued and sued, of course. Partridge knew he should have called to offer moral support. Unfortunately, associ-ating with Toshi in that time of crisis might have been an unwise career move and he let it slide. *But nothing slides forever, does it?*

"New Guinea wasn't really a disaster. Indeed, it served to crystallize the focus of our research, to open new doors. . . ."

Partridge was not thrilled to discuss New Guinea. "Intriguing. I'm glad you're go-ing great guns. It's over my head, but I'm glad. Sincerely." Several crows described broad, looping circles near the unwholesome machines. Near, but not too near.

"Ah, but that's not important. I imagine I shall die before any of this work comes to fruition." Toshi smiled fondly and evasively. He gave Partridge an avuncular pat on the arm. "You're here for Nadine's grand farewell. She will leave the farm after the weekend. Everything is settled. You see now why I called."

Partridge was not convinced. Nadine seemed to resent his presence—she'd al-ways been hot and cold when it came to him. What did Toshi want him to do? "Ab-solutely," he said.

They walked back to the house and sat on the porch in rocking chairs. Gertz brought them a pitcher of iced tea and frosted glasses on trays. Campbell emerged in his trademark double-breasted steel-blue suit and horn-rim glasses. For the better part of three decades he had played the mild, urbane foil to Toshi's megalomaniacal iconoclast. In private, Campbell was easily the dominant of the pair. He leaned against a post and held out his hand until Toshi passed him a smoldering cigarette.

"I'm glad you know," he said, fastening his murky eyes on Partridge. "I didn't have the nerve to tell you myself."

Partridge felt raw, exhausted, and bruised. He changed the subject. "So . . . those guys in the suits. Montague and Phillips. How do you know them? Financiers, I presume?"

"Patrons," Campbell said. "As you can see, we've scaled back the operation. It's difficult to run things off the cuff." Lolling against the post, a peculiar hybrid of William Burroughs and Walter Cronkite, he radiated folksy charm that mostly diluted underlying hints of decadence. This charm often won the hearts of flabby dilettante crones looking for a cause to champion. "Fortunately, there are always interested parties with deep pockets."

Partridge chuckled to cover his unease. His stomach was getting worse. "Toshi promised to get me up to speed on your latest and greatest contribution to the world of science. Or do I want to know?"

"You showed him the telescopes? Anything else?" Campbell glanced to Toshi and arched his brow.

Toshi's grin was equal portions condescension and mania. He rubbed his spindly hands together like a spider combing its pedipalps. "Howard . . . I haven't, he hasn't been to the site. He has visited with our pets, however. Mind your shoes if you fancy them, by the way."

"Toshi has developed a knack for beetles," Campbell said. "I don't know what he sees in them, frankly. Boring, boring. Pardon the pun—I'm stone knackered on Dewar's. My bloody joints are positively gigantic in this climate. Oh—have you seen reports of the impending Yellow Disaster? China will have the whole of Asia Minor deforested in the next decade. I imagine you haven't—you don't film horror movies, right? At least not reality horror." He laughed as if to say, *You realize I'm kidding, don't you, lad? We're all friends here.* "Mankind is definitely eating himself out of house and home. The beetles and cockroaches are in the direct line of succession."

"Scary," Partridge said. He waited doggedly for the punch line. Although, free association was another grace note of Campbell's and Toshi's. The punch line might not even exist. Give them thirty seconds and they would be nattering about engineering E. coli to perform microscopic stupid pet tricks or how much they missed those good old Bangkok whores.

Toshi lighted another cigarette and waved it carelessly. "The boy probably hasn't the foggiest notion as to the utility of our naturalistic endeavors. Look, after dinner, we'll give a demonstration. We'll hold a séance."

"Oh, horseshit, Toshi!" Campbell scowled fearsomely. This was always a remarkable transformation for those not accustomed to his moods. "Considering the circumstances, that's extremely tasteless."

"Not to mention premature," Partridge said through a grim smile. He rose, upsetting his drink in a clatter of softened ice cubes and limpid orange rinds and strode from the porch. He averted his face. He was not certain if Campbell called after him because of the blood beating in his ears. Toshi did clearly say, "Let him go, let him be, Howard. . . . She'll talk to him. . . ."

He stumbled to his room and crashed into his too-short bed and fell unconscious.

Partridge owed much of his success to Toshi. Even that debt might not have been sufficient to justify the New England odyssey. The real reason, the motive force under the hood of Partridge's lamentable midlife crisis, and the magnetic compulsion to heed that bizarre late-night call, was certainly his sense of unfinished business with Nadine. Arguably, he had Toshi to thank for that, too.

Toshi Ryoko immigrated to Britain, and later the U.S., from Okinawa in the latter sixties. This occurred a few years after he had begun to attract attention from the international scientific community for his brilliant work in behavioral ecology and prior to his stratospheric rise to popular fame due to daredevil eccentricities and an Academy Award nominated documentary of his harrowing expedition into the depths of a Bengali wildlife preserve. The name of the preserve loosely translated into English as, "The Forest that Eats Men." Partridge had been the twenty-three-year-old cinematographer brought aboard at the last possible moment to photograph the expedition. No more qualified person could be found on the ridiculously short notice that Toshi announced for departure. The director/producer was none other than Toshi himself. It was his first and last film. There were, of course, myriad subsequent independent features, newspaper and radio accounts—the major slicks covered Toshi's controversial exploits, but he lost interest in filmmaking after the initial hubbub and eventually faded from the public eye. Possibly his increasing affiliation with clandestine U.S. government projects was to blame. The cause was immaterial. Toshi's fascinations were mercurial and stardom proved incidental to his mission of untangling the enigmas of evolutionary origins and ultimate destination.

Partridge profited greatly from that tumultuous voyage into the watery hell of man-eating tigers and killer bees. He emerged from the crucible as a legend fully formed. His genesis was as Minerva's, that warrior-daughter sprung whole from Jupiter's aching skull. All the great directors wanted him. His name was gold—it was nothing but Beluga caviar and box seats at the Rose Bowl, a string of "where are they now" actresses on his arm, an executive membership in the Ferrari Club and posh homes in Malibu and Ireland. Someday they would hang his portrait in the American Society of Cinematography archives and blazon his star on Hollywood Boulevard.

There was just one glitch in his happily-ever-after: Nadine. Nadine Thompson was the whip-smart Stanford physiologist who had gone along for the ride to Bangladesh as Toshi's chief disciple. She was not Hollywood sultry, yet the camera found her to be eerily riveting in a way that was simultaneously erotic and repellant. The audience never saw a *scientist* when the camera tracked Nadine across the rancid deck of that river barge. They saw a woman-child—ripe, lithe and lethally carnal.

She was doomed. Jobs came and went. Some were comparative plums, yes. None of them led to prominence indicative of her formal education and nascent talent. None of them opened the way to the marquee projects, postings, or commissions. She eventually settled for a staff position at a museum in Buffalo. An eighty-seven-minute film shot on super-sixteen millimeter consigned her to professional purgatory. Maybe a touch of that taint had rubbed off on Partridge. Nadine was the youthful excess that Hollywood could not supply, despite its excess of youth, the one he still longed for during the long, blank Malibu nights. He carried a load of guilt about the whole affair as well.

Occasionally, in the strange, hollow years after the hoopla, the groundswell of acclaim and infamy, she would corner Partridge in a remote getaway bungalow, or a honeymoon seaside cottage, for a weekend of gin and bitters and savage lovemaking. In the languorous aftermath, she often confided how his magic Panaflex had destroyed her career. She would forever be "the woman in that movie." She was branded a real-life scream queen and the sexpot with the so-so face and magnificent ass.

Nadine was right, as usual. "The Forest that Eats Men" never let go once it sank its teeth.

He dreamed of poling a raft on a warm, muddy river. Mangroves hemmed them in corridors of convoluted blacks and greens. Creepers and vines strung the winding waterway. Pale sunlight sifted down through the screen of vegetation; a dim, smoky light full of shadows and shifting clouds of gnats and mosquitoes. Birds warbled and screeched. He crouched in the stern of the raft and stared at the person directly before him. That person's wooden mask with its dead eyes and wooden smile gaped at him, fitted as it was to the back of the man's head. The wooden mouth whispered, "You forgot your mask." Partridge reached back and found, with burgeoning horror, that his skull was indeed naked and defenseless.

"They're coming. They're coming." The mask grinned soullessly.

He inhaled to scream and jerked awake, twisted in the sheets and sweating. Red light poured through the thin curtains. Nadine sat in the shadows at the foot of his bed. Her hair was loose and her skin reflected the ruddy light. He thought of the goddess Kali shrunk to mortal dimensions.

"You don't sleep well either, huh," she said.

"Nope. Not since Bangladesh."

"That long. Huh."

He propped himself on his elbow and studied her. "I've been considering my options lately. I'm thinking it might be time to hang up my spurs. Go live in the Bahamas."

She said, "You're too young to go." That was her mocking tone.

"You too."

She didn't say anything for a while. Then, "Rich, you ever get the feeling you're being watched?"

"Like when you snuck in here while I was sleeping? Funny you should mention it. . . ."

"Rich."

He saw that she was serious. "Sometimes, yeah."

"Well you are. Always. I want you to keep that in mind."

"Okay. Will it help?"

"Good question."

The room darkened, bit by bit. He said, "You think you would've made it back to the barge?" He couldn't distance himself from her cry as she flailed overboard and hit the water like a stone. There were crocodiles everywhere. No one moved. The whole crew was frozen in that moment between disbelief and action. He had shoved the camera at, who? Beasley. He had done that and then gone in and gotten her. Blood-warm water, brown with mud. He did not remember much of the rest. The camera caught it all.

"No," she said. "Not even close."

He climbed over the bed and hugged her. She was warm. He pressed his face into her hair. Her hair trapped the faint, cloying odor of sickness. "I'm so fucking sorry," he said.

She didn't say anything. She rubbed his shoulder.

That night was quiet at the Moorehead Estate. There was a subdued dinner and afterward some drinks. Everybody chatted about the good old days. The real ones and the imaginary ones too. Phillips and Montague disappeared early on and took their men-at-arms with them. Nadine sat aloof. She held on to a hardback—one of

Toshi's long-out-of-print treatises on insect behavior and ecological patterns. Partridge could tell she was only pretending to look at it.

Later, after lights out, Partridge roused from a dream of drowning in something that wasn't quite water. His name was whispered from the foot of the bed. He fumbled upright in the smothering dark. "Nadine?" He clicked on the lamp and saw he was alone.

It rained in the morning. Toshi was undeterred. He put on a slicker and took a drive in the Land Rover to move the radio telescopes and other equipment into more remote fields. A truckload of the burly, grim laborers followed. The technicians trudged about their daily routine, indifferent to the weather. Campbell disappeared with Phillips and Montague. Nadine remained in her room. Partridge spent the morning playing poker with Beasley and Gertz on the rear porch. They drank whiskey—coffee for Beasley—and watched water drip from the eaves and thunderheads roll across the horizon trailing occasional whip-cracks of lightning. Then it stopped raining and the sun transformed the landscape into a mass of illuminated rust and glass.

Partridge went for a long walk around the property to clear his head and savor the clean air. The sun was melting toward the horizon when Beasley found him dozing in the shade of an oak. It was a huge tree with yellowing leaves and exposed roots. The roots crawled with pill bugs. Between yawns Partridge observed the insects go about their tiny business.

"C'mon. You gotta see the ghost town before it gets dark," Beasley said. Partridge didn't bother to protest. Nadine waited in the jeep. She wore tortoiseshell sunglasses and a red scarf in her hair. He decided she looked better in a scarf than Toshi ever had, no question. Partridge opened his mouth and Beasley gave him a friendly shove into the front passenger seat.

"Sulk, sulk, sulk!" Nadine laughed at him. "In the garden, eating worms?"

"Close enough," Partridge said and hung on as Beasley gunned the jeep through a break in the fence line and zoomed along an overgrown track that was invisible until they were right on top of it. The farm became a picture on a stamp and then they passed through a belt of paper birches and red maples. They crossed a ramshackle bridge that spanned an ebon stream and drove into a clearing. Beasley ground gears until they gained the crown of a long, tabletop hill. He killed the engine and coasted to a halt amid tangled grass and wildflowers and said, "Orren Towne. Died circa 1890s."

Below their vantage, remnants of a village occupied the banks of a shallow valley. If Orren Towne was dead its death was the living kind. A score of saltbox houses and the brooding hulk of a Second Empire church waited somberly. Petrified roofs were dappled by the shadows of moving clouds. Facades were brim with the ephemeral light of the magic hour. Beasley's walkie-talkie crackled and he stepped aside to answer the call.

Nadine walked partway down the slope and stretched her arms. Her muscles stood forth in cords of sinew and gristle. She looked over her shoulder at Partridge. Her smile was alien. "Don't you wish you'd brought your camera?"

The brain is a camera. What Partridge really wished was that he had gone to his room and slept. His emotions were on the verge of running amok. The animal fear from his daydreams had sneaked up again. He smelled the musk of his own adrenaline and sweat. *The brain is a camera and once it sees what it sees there's no taking it back*. He noticed another of Toshi's bizarre radio dishes perched on a bluff. The antenna was focused upon the deserted buildings. "I don't like this place," he said. But she kept walking and he trailed along. It was cooler among the houses. The earth was trampled into concrete and veined with minerals. Nothing organic grew and no birds sang. The subtly deformed structures were encased in a transparent resin that lent the town the aspect of a waxworks. He thought it might be shellac.

Shadows fell across Partridge's path. Open doorways and sugar-spun windows fronted darkness. These doors and windows were as unwelcoming as the throats of ancient wells, the mouths of caves. He breathed heavily. "How did Toshi do this? Why did he do this?"

Nadine laughed and took his hand playfully. Hers was dry and too warm, like a leather wallet left in direct sunlight. "Toshi only discovered it. Do you seriously think he and Howard are capable of devising something this extraordinary?"

"No."

"Quite a few people spent their lives in this valley. Decent farming and hunting in these parts. The Mooreheads owned about everything. They owned a brewery and a mill down the road, near their estate. All those busy little worker bees going about their jobs, going to church on Sunday. I'm sure it was a classic Hallmark. Then it got cold. One of those long winters that never ends. Nothing wanted to grow and the game disappeared. The house burned. Sad for the Mooreheads. Sadder for the people who depended on them. The family circled its wagons to rebuild the mansion, but the community proper never fully recovered. Orren Towne was here today, gone tomorrow. At least that's the story we hear told by the old-timers at the Mad Rooster over cribbage and a pint of stout." Nadine stood in the shade of the church, gazing up, up at the crucifix. "This is how it will all be someday. Empty buildings. Empty skies. The grass will come and eat everything we ever made. The waters will swallow it. It puts my situation into perspective, lemme tell you."

"These buildings should've fallen down. Somebody's gone through a lot of trouble to keep this like—"

"A museum. Yeah, somebody has. This isn't the only place it's been done, either."

"Places like this? Where?" Partridge said. He edged closer to the bright center of the village square.

"I don't know. They're all over if you know what to look for."

"Nadine, maybe . . . Jesus!" He jerked his head around to peer at a doorway. The darkness inside the house seemed fuller and more complete. "Are there people here?" His mind jumped to an image of the masks that the natives wore to ward off tigers. He swallowed hard.

"Just us chickens, love."

A stiff breeze rushed from the northwest and whipped the outlying grass. Early autumn leaves skated across the glassy rooftops and swirled in barren yards. Leaves fell dead and dry. Night was coming hard.

"I'm twitchy—jet lag, probably. What do those weird-looking rigs do?" He pointed at the dish on the hill. "Toshi said they're radio telescopes he invented."

"He said he invented them? Oh my. I dearly love that man, but sometimes he's such an asshole."

"Yeah. How do they work?"

Nadine shrugged. "They read frequencies on the electromagnetic spectrum."

"Radio signals from underground. Why does that sound totally backwards to me?"

"I didn't say anything about radio signals."

"Then what did you say?"

"When we get back, ask Toshi about the node."

"What are you talking about?" Partridge's attention was divided between her and the beautifully grotesque houses and the blackness inside them

"You'll see. Get him to show you the node. That'll clear some of this stuff up, pronto."

Beasley called to them. He and the jeep were a merged silhouette against the failing sky. He swung his arm overhead until Nadine yelled that they would start back in a minute. She removed her shades and met Partridge's eyes. "You okay, Rich?" She refused to relinquish her grip on his hand.

"You're asking *me*?"

She gave him another of her inscrutable looks. She reached up and pushed an unkempt lock from his forehead. "I'm not pissed, in case you're still wondering. I wanted you to see me off. Not like there're any more weekend rendezvous in the stars for us."

"That's no way to talk," he said.

"Just sayin'." She dropped his hand and walked away. In a moment he followed. By the time they made the summit, darkness had covered the valley. Beasley had to use the headlights to find the way home.

Gertz served prawns for dinner. They ate at the long mahogany table in the formal dining room. Jackson Phillips begged off due to an urgent matter in the city. Beasley packed him and one of the muscle-bound bodyguards into the helicopter and flew away. That left six: Toshi; Campbell; Nadine; Carrey Montague and the other bodyguard; and Partridge. The men wore suits and ties. Nadine wore a cream-colored silk chiffon evening gown. There were candles and elaborate floral arrangements and dusty bottles of wine from the Moorehead cellar and magnums of top dollar French champagne from a Boston importer who catered to those with exclusive tastes and affiliations. Toshi proposed a toast and said a few words in Japanese and then the assembly began to eat and drink.

Somewhere in the middle of the third or fourth course, Partridge realized he was cataclysmically drunk. They kept setting them up and he kept knocking them down. Toshi or Campbell frequently clapped his back and clinked his glass and shouted "*Sic itur ad astra!*" and another round would magically appear. His head was swollen and empty as an echo chamber. The winking silverware and sloshing wineglasses, the bared teeth and hearty laughter came to him from a sea shell.

Dinner blurred into a collage of sense and chaos, of light and dark, and he gripped his glass and blinked dumbly against the shattering flare of the low-slung chandelier and laughed uproariously. Without transition, dinner was concluded and the men had repaired to the den to relax over snifters of Hennessy. They lounged in wing-backed leather chairs and upon opulent leather divans. Partridge admired the vaulted ceiling, the library of towering lacquered oak bookcases, and the impressive collection of antique British rifles and British cavalry sabers cached in rearing cabinets of chocolate wood and softly warped glass. Everything was so huge and shiny and far away. When the cigar and pipe smoke hung thick and the men's cheeks were glazed and rosy as the cheeks of Russian dolls, he managed, "I'm supposed to ask you about the node."

Campbell smiled a broad and genial smile. "The node, yes. The node, of course, is the very reason Mr. Phillips and Mr. Montague have come to pay their respects. They hope to buy their way into Heaven."

"He's right, he's right," Mr. Carrey Montague said with an air of merry indulgence. "Jack had his shot. Didn't he though. Couldn't hack it and off he flew."

"I was getting to this," Toshi said. "In a roundabout fashion."

"Exceedingly so," Campbell said.

"Didn't want to frighten him. It's a delicate matter."

"Yes," Campbell said dryly. He puffed on his pipe and his eyes were red around the edges and in the center of his pupils.

"Shall I. Or do you want a go?" Toshi shrugged his indifference.

"The node is a communication device," Campbell said through a mouthful of smoke. "Crude, really. Danforth Moorehead, the Moorehead patriarch, developed the current model. Ahem, the schematic was delivered to him and he effected the necessary modifications, at any rate. Admittedly, it's superior to the primitive methods— scrying, séances, psychedelic drugs, that nonsense. Not to mention some of the more gruesome customs we've observed in the provincial regions. Compared to that, the node is state of the art. It is a reservoir that filters and translates frequency imaging captured by our clever, clever radio telescopes. It permits us to exchange information with our . . . neighbors."

Partridge dimly perceived that the others were watching him with something like fascination. Their eyes glittered through the haze. "With who? I don't—"

"Our neighbors," Campbell said.

"Oh, the things they show you." Carrey Montague sucked on his oxygen mask until he resembled a ghoul.

Partridge swung his head to look from face to face. The men were drunk. The men seethed with restrained glee. No one appeared to be joking. "Well, go on then," he said dreamily. His face was made of plaster. Black spots revolved before him like ashen snowflakes.

"I told you, Richard. Mankind can't go on like this."

"Like what?"

Toshi chuckled. "Assuming we don't obliterate ourselves, or that a meteorite doesn't smack us back to the Cambrian, if not the Cryptozoic, this planet will succumb to the exhaustion of Sol. First the mammals, then the reptiles, right down the line until all that's left of any complexity are the arthropods: beetles and cockroaches and their oceanic cousins, practically speaking. Evolution is a circle—we're sliding back to that endless sea of protoplasmic goop."

"I'm betting on the nuclear holocaust," Campbell said.

Partridge slopped more brandy into his mouth. He was far beyond tasting it. "Mmm hmm," he said intelligently and cast about for a place to inconspicuously ditch his glass.

"NASA and its holy grail—First Contact, the quest for intelligent life in the universe . . . all hogwash, all lies." Toshi gently took the snifter away and handed him a fresh drink in a ceramic mug. This was not brandy; it was rich and dark as honey in moonlight. "Private stock, my boy. Drink up!" Partridge drank and his eyes flooded and he choked a little. Toshi nodded in satisfaction. "We know now what we've always suspected. Man is completely and utterly alone in a sea of dust and smoke. Alone and inevitably slipping into extinction."

"Not quite alone," Campbell said. "There are an estimated five to eight million species of insects as of yet unknown and unclassified. Hell of a lot of insects, hmm? But why stop at bugs? Only a damned fool would suppose that was anything but the tip of the iceberg. When the time of Man comes to an end *their* time will begin. And be certain this is not an invasion or a hostile occupation. We'll be dead as dodos a goodly period before they emerge to claim the surface. They won't rule forever. The planet will eventually become cold and inhospitable to any mortal organism. But trust that their rule will make the reign of the terrible lizards seem a flicker of an eyelash."

"You're talking about cockroaches," Partridge said in triumph. "Fucking cockroaches." That was too amusing and so he snorted on his pungent liquor and had a coughing fit.

"No, we are not," Campbell said.

"We aren't talking about spiders or beetles, either," Toshi said. He gave Partridge's knee an earnest squeeze. "To even compare them with the citizens of the *Great Kingdom* . . . I shudder. However, if I *were* to make that comparison, I'd say this intelligence is the ur-progenitor of those insects scrabbling in the muck. The mother race of idiot stepchildren."

Campbell knelt before him so they were eye to eye. The older man's face was radiant and distant as the moon. "This is a momentous discovery. We've established contact. Not us, actually. It's been going on forever. We are the latest . . . emissaries, if you will. Trustees to the grandest secret of them all."

"Hoo boy. You guys. You fucking guys. Is Nadine in on this?"

"Best that you see firsthand. Would you like that, Rich?"

"Uhmm-wha?" Partridge did not know what he wanted except that he wanted the carousel to stop.

Campbell and Toshi stood. They took his arms and the next thing he knew they were outside in the humid country night with darkness all around. He tried to walk, but his legs wouldn't cooperate much. They half-dragged him to a dim metal door and there was a lamp bulb spinning in space and then steep, winding concrete stairs and cracked concrete walls ribbed with mold. They went down and down and a strong, earthy smell overcame Partridge's senses. People spoke to him in rumbling nonsense phrases. Someone ruffled his hair and laughed. His vision fractured. He glimpsed hands and feet, a piece of jaw illumed by a quivering fluorescent glow. When the hands stopped supporting him, he slid to his knees. He had the impression of kneeling in a cellar. Water dripped and a pale overhead lamp hummed like a wasp in a jar. From the corner of his eye he got the sense of table legs and cables and he smelled an acrid smell like cleaning solvents. He thought it might be a laboratory.

—Crawl forward just a bit.

It was strange whatever lay before him. Something curved, spiral shaped, and darkly wet. A horn, a giant conch shell—it was impossible to be certain. There was an opening, as the *external os* of a cervix, large enough to accommodate him in all his lanky height. Inside it was moist and muffled and black.

—There's a lad. Curl up inside. Don't fight. There, there. That's my boy. Won't be long. Not long. Don't be afraid. This is only a window, not a doorway.

Then nothing and nothing and nothing; only his heart, his breathing, and a whispery static thrum that might've been the electromagnetic current tracing its circuit through his nerves.

Nothingness grew very dense.

Partridge tried to shriek when water, or something thicker than water flowed over his head and into his sinuses and throat. Low static built in his ears and the abject blackness was replaced by flashes of white imagery. He fell from an impossible height. He saw only high velocity jump cuts of the world and each caromed from him and into the gulf almost instantly. Fire and blood and moving tides of unleashed water. Bones of men and women and cities. Dead, mummified cities gone so long without inhabitants they had become cold and brittle and smooth as mighty forests of stone. There loomed over everything a silence that held to its sterile bosom countless screams and the sibilant chafe of swirling dust. Nadine stood naked as ebony in the heart of a ruined square. She wore a white mask, but he knew her with the immediacy of a nightmare. She lifted her mask and looked at him. She smiled and raised her hand. Men and women emerged from the broken skyscrapers and collapsed bunkers. They were naked and pallid and smiling. In the distance the sun heaved up, slow and red. Its deathly light cascaded upon the lines and curves of cyclopean structures. These were colossal, inhuman edifices of fossil bone and obsidian and anthracite that glittered not unlike behemoth carapaces. He thrashed and fell and fell and drowned.

Nadine said in his ear, *Come down. We love you.*

The cellar floor was cool upon his cheek. He was paralyzed and choking. The men spoke to him in soothing voices. Someone pressed a damp cloth to his brow.

—Take it easy, son. The first ride or two is a bitch and a half. Get his head.

Partridge groaned as gravity crushed him into the moldy concrete.

Someone murmured to him.

—They are interested in preserving aspects of our culture. Thus Orren Towne and places, hidden places most white men will never tread. Of course, it's a multifaceted project. Preserving artifacts, buildings, that's hardly enough to satisfy such an advanced intellect. . . .

Partridge tired to speak. His jaw worked spastically. No sound emerged. The concrete went soft and everyone fell silent at once.

Partridge stirred and sat up. He tried to piece together how he ended up on the back porch sprawled in a wooden folding chair. He was still in his suit and it was damp and clung to him the way clothes do after they have been slept in. The world teetered on the cusp of night. Parts of the sky were orange as fire and other parts were covered by purple-tinted rain clouds like a pall of cannon smoke. Partridge's hair stood in gummy spikes. His mouth was swollen and cottony. He had drooled in his long sleep. His body was stiff as an old plank.

Beasley came out of the house and handed him a glass of seltzer water. "Can't hold your liquor anymore?"

Partridge took the glass in both hands and drank greedily. "Oh you're back. Must've been a hell of a party," he said at last. He had slept for at least sixteen hours according to his watch. His memory was a smooth and frictionless void.

"Yeah," Beasley said. "You okay?"

Partridge was not sure. "Uh," he said. He rolled his head to survey the twilight vista. "Beasley."

"Yeah?"

"All this." Partridge swept his hand to encompass the swamped gardens and the decrepit outbuildings. "They're letting it fall down. Nobody left from the old days."

"You and me. And Nadine."

"And when we're gone?"

"We're all gonna be gone sooner or later. The docs . . . they just do what they can. There's nothing else, pal." Beasley gave him a searching look. He shook his shaggy head and chuckled. "Don't get morbid on me, Hollywood. Been a good run if you ask me. Hell, we may get a few more years before the plug gets pulled."

"Is Montague still here?"

"Why do you ask?"

"I heard someone yelling, cursing. Earlier, while I slept."

"Huh. Yeah, there was a little fight. The old fella didn't get his golden ticket. He wasn't wanted. Few are. He shipped out. Won't be coming back."

"I guess not. What was he after?"

"Same thing as everybody else, I suppose. People think Toshi is the Devil, that he can give them their heart's desire if they sign on the dotted line. It ain't so simple."

Partridge had a wry chuckle at that. "Damned right it's not simple, partner. I'm still selling my soul to Tinsel Town. No such luck as to unload the whole shebang at once." Partridge shook with a sudden chill. His memory shucked and jittered; it spun off the reel in his brain and he could not gather it fast enough to make sense of what he had seen in the disjointed frames. "Lord, I hate the country. Always have. I really should get out of here, soon."

"My advice—when you get on that bus, don't look back," Beasley said. "And keep your light on at night. You done with that?"

"Um-hmm." He could not summon the energy to say more right then. The strength and the will had run out of him. He put his hand over his eyes and tried to concentrate.

Beasley took the empty glass and went back into the house. Darkness came and the yard lamps sizzled to life. Moths fluttered near his face, battened at the windows and Partridge wondered why that panicked him, why his heart surged and his fingernails dug into the arm rests. In the misty fields, the drone of night insects began.

He eventually heaved to his feet and went inside and walked the dim, ugly corridors for an interminable period. He stumbled aimlessly as if he were yet drunk. His thoughts buzzed and muttered and were incoherent. He found Toshi and Campbell in the den crouched like grave robbers over a stack of shrunken, musty ledgers with hand-sewn covers and other stacks of photographic plates like the kind shot from the air or a doctor's X-ray machine. The den was tomb-dark except for a single flimsy desk lamp. He swayed in the doorway, clinging to the jam as if he were in a cabin on a ship. He said, "Where is Nadine?"

The old men glanced up from their documents and squinted at him. Toshi shook his head and sucked his teeth. Campbell pointed at the ceiling. "She's in her room. Packing. It's Sunday night," he said. "You should go see her."

"She has to leave," Toshi said.

Partridge turned and left. He made his way up the great central staircase and tried a number of doors that let into dusty rooms with painters cloth draping the furniture. Light leaked from the jamb of one door and he went in without knocking.

"I've been waiting," Nadine said. Her room was smaller and more feminine than the Garden Room. She sat lotus on a poster bed. She wore a simple yellow sundress and her hair in a knot. Her face was dented with exhaustion. "I got scared you might not come to say good-bye."

Partridge did not see any suitcases. A mostly empty bottle of pain medication sat on the night stand beside her wedding ring and a silver locket she had inherited from her great-grandmother. He picked up the locket and let it spill through his fingers, back and forth between his hands.

"It's very late," she said. Her voice was not tired like her face. Her voice was steady and full of conviction. "Take me for a walk."

"Where?" He said.

"In the fields. One more walk in the fields."

He was afraid as he had been afraid when the moths came over him and against the windows. He was afraid as he had been when he pulled her from the water all those years ago and then lay in his hammock bunk dreaming and dreaming of the crocodiles and the bottomless depths warm as the recesses of his own body and she had shuddered against him, entwined with him and inextricably linked with him. He did not wish to leave the house, not at night. He said, "Sure. If you want to."

She climbed from the bed and took his hand. They walked down the stairs and through the quiet house. They left the house and the spectral yard and walked through a gate into the field and then farther into heavier and heavier shadows.

Partridge let Nadine lead. He stepped gingerly. He was mostly night blind and his head ached. Wet grass rubbed his thighs. He was soaked right away. A chipped edge of the ivory moon bit through the moving clouds. There were a few stars. They came to a shallow depression where the grass had been trampled or had sunk beneath the surface. Something in his memory twitched and a terrible cold knot formed in his stomach. He whined in his throat, uncomprehendingly, like a dog.

She hesitated in the depression and pulled her pale dress over her head. She tossed the dress away and stood naked and half hidden in the fog and darkness. He did not need to see her, he had memorized everything. She slipped into the circle of his arms and he embraced her without thinking. She leaned up and kissed him. Her mouth was dry and hot. "Come on," she muttered against his lips. "Come on." Her hands were sinewy as talons and very strong. She grasped his hair and drew him against her and they slowly folded into the moist earth. The soft earth was disfigured with their writhing and a deep, resonant vibration traveled through it and into them where it yammered through their blood and bones. She kissed him fiercely, viciously, and locked her thighs over his hips and squeezed until he gasped and kissed her back. She did not relinquish her fistful of his hair and she did not close her eyes. He stared into them and saw a ghost of a girl he knew and his own gaunt reflection which he did not know at all. They were sinking.

Nadine stopped sucking at him and turned her head against the black dirt and toward the high, shivering grass. There was no breeze and the night lay dead and still. The grass sighed and muffled an approaching sound that struck Partridge as the thrum of fluorescent lights or high-voltage current through a wire or, as it came swiftly closer, the clatter of pebbles rolling over slate. Nadine tightened her grip and looked at him with a sublime combination of glassy terror and exultation. She said, "Rich—"

The grass shook violently beneath a vast, invisible hand and a tide of chirring and burring and click-clacking blackness poured into the depression from far-flung expanses of lost pasture and haunted wilderness, from the moist abyssal womb that opens beneath everything, everywhere. The cacophony was a murderous tectonic snarl out of Pandemonium, Gehenna, and Hell; the slaughterhouse gnash and whicker and serrated wail of legion bloodthirsty drills and meat-hungry saw teeth. The ebony breaker crashed over them and buried them and swallowed their screams before their screams began.

After the blackness ebbed and receded and was finally gone, it became quiet. At last the frogs tentatively groaned and the crickets warmed by degrees to their songs of loneliness and sorrow. The moon slipped into the moat around the Earth.

He rose alone, black on black, from the muck and walked back in shambling steps to the house.

Partridge sat rigid and upright at the scarred table in the blue-gray gloom of the kitchen. Through the one grimy window above the sink, the predawn sky glowed the hue of gunmetal. His eyes glistened and caught that feeble light and held it fast like the eyes of a carp in its market bed of ice. His black face dripped onto his white shirt which was also black. His black hands lay motionless on the table. He stank of copper and urine and shit. Water leaked in fat drops from the stainless steel goose-neck tap. A grandfather clock ticked and tocked from the hall and counted down the seconds of the revolutions of the Earth. The house settled and groaned fitfully, a guilty pensioner caught fast in dreams.

Toshi materialized in the crooked shadows near the stove. His face was masked by the shadows. He said in a low, hoarse voice that suggested a quantity of alcohol and tears, "Occasionally one of us, a volunteer, is permitted to cross over, to relinquish his or her flesh to the appetites of the colony and exist among them in a state of pure consciousness. That's how it's always been. These volunteers become the inter-preters, the facilitators of communication between our species. They become undy-ing repositories of our civilization . . . a civilization that shall become ancient history one day very soon."

Partridge said nothing.

Toshi said in his hoarse, mournful voice, "She'll never truly die. She'll be with them until this place is a frozen graveyard orbiting a cinder. It is an honor. Yet she waited. She wanted to say good-bye in person."

Partridge said nothing. The sun floated to the black rim of the horizon. The sun hung crimson and boiling and a shaft of bloody light passed through the window and bathed his hand.

"Oh!" Toshi said and his mouth was invisible, but his eyes were bright and wet in the gathering light. "Can you *imagine* gazing upon constellations a hundred million years from this dawn? Can you imagine the wonder of gazing upon those constella-tions from a hundred million eyes? Oh, imagine it, my boy. . . ."

Partridge stood and went wordlessly, ponderously, to the window and lingered there a moment, his mud-caked face afire with the bloody radiance of a dying star. He drank in the slumbering fields, the distant fog-wreathed forests, as if he might never look upon any of it again. He reached up and pulled the shade down tight against the sill and it was dark.

PAUL PARK

Fragrant Goddess

Paul Park's "Fragrant Goddess" first appeared in The Magazine of Fantasy & Science Fiction's *annual October/November double issue. With the publication of* The Hidden World, *Park has just completed his alternate history series that began with* A Princess of Roumania. *Park teaches at Williams College in Massachusetts.*

—K. L. & G. G.

He was familiar with the house, of course, having seen it in photographs and once in person a dozen years before. He didn't remember it being so huge. He and Sabine had come up the walkway between these same bronze foo dogs, the male with its paw on a bronze ball. Then—still—the windows had been brown with sticky paper, opaque, as Jeremy had pointed out. No one had lived there for many years. The house had been abandoned after Arkady Ferson's death in the early 1970s. There was a suggestion he'd been murdered, a possibility that intrigued Sabine far more than Ferson's small connection with the subject of Jeremy's dissertation. Now the front door stood open and Sabine, he imagined, waited for him inside.

Or else she was watching him from the front windows or the shelter of the porch—he didn't like that idea. The stone walk was a long one. His leg hurt. As he approached, he thought she might be calculating all the ways he'd changed. He saw himself diminishing as he got bigger. He was kind of bald. He wasn't in great shape. And of course he limped. Which would she notice first?

"Boo!"

She was perched along the back of the female dog, motionless, invisible, in clear sight. Now she scrambled down, and any consolation that the years might also have treated her unkindly was already gone. In the bright sunlight she seemed radiant to him, dressed in an Indian printed smock above her knees. It fastened with a string around her neck. She hugged him, and he was aware of her smell, which came back suddenly—the same lavender perfume mixed with the same sweat. He felt her naked arms around his neck, aware also of his damp, uncomfortable suit. This was the third time he was in Seattle and he'd never seen a drop of rain—how small she was! He had forgotten.

Her face was close by his. She'd never been a beautiful woman, he remembered with surprise. Her features had always been too big for her small face. But she had always seemed beautiful—a European trick perhaps—and younger than she was. At twenty-six she'd looked like a teenager, especially at a distance. It was the language of her body—"gamine," he supposed. Now, as she separated from him and scampered barefoot up the stairs, she looked twenty-six or so.

He followed her through the line of fat white Ionic columns to the front door. He'd read a little bit about the house, knew, for example, there was a fine Tiffany window over the staircase, and the walls had been hand-painted by . . . someone, some marginally famous turn-of-the-century decorative artist—he'd not been interested in any of those things until he'd had to imagine Sabine living here.

She made a little pirouette in the cavernous, dark entranceway. "I'm so excited to see you," she said, her accent still thick. When he'd first met her, she'd scarcely spoken any English. Now she was fluent, obviously, and his French was rusty. So they turned naturally to a language they'd never spoken with each other. "I can't wait to show you," she said. She ran up the double stairway to the landing and stood below the window, a floral pattern of green and crimson glass. She wore an ankle bracelet, he noticed, and the bottoms of her feet were dark.

"Tell me again how this happened," he said.

"I told you on the phone! When Scott and I first moved out here, we bought a house in Fremont—you know? But his parents were living too close by. Once we came by here and there was a real estate sign—I'd told him how I'd knocked on the door with you—do you remember? I had always remembered this place. Always I used to drive past when I had the chance, and when the sign came, Scott said it was an opportunity. But I suppose it was a gift for me—do you know Arkady Ferson also lived in Belgium? We bought it from the Lightbearers Foundation—do you like it?" she asked, as if she were talking about the dress she wore, and which she was modeling for him under the dappled light, and which he did like very much. It was blue and red and left her arms exposed. He could see the soft hair in her armpits. And she didn't have to bother with a bra or anything like that.

Once he had shared a cab with her down Fifth Avenue, thirty blocks in rush hour from the University Club to her apartment—a cold, rainy night, and they had kissed and groped each other the entire way. Her wet shirt had been unbuttoned to her waist. Why hadn't she asked him to come up? No, it was because he had to continue on crosstown. He was meeting Joanna and her parents at some Chinese restaurant on Ninth. All the way there he'd been sniffing himself guiltily, and he was already late, and Joanna was already pissed off. *She has no idea how virtuous I am*, he'd thought as he'd washed his face and hands in the cramped restaurant bathroom. The lavender smell had already dissipated, to be replaced, with any luck, by the scent of Joanna's perfume, the musk oil she used to wear in those days. Sabine had met Scott right after that.

He stood below her on the stairs. She was smiling, and she raised her left hand to her mouth to hide her big teeth—an endearing gesture that he remembered now. Did she ever think about that taxi ride? Was she thinking about it now? He couldn't help himself: "You must be awfully rich!"

"Well, no—I don't think so. I mean yes and no—I suppose we are. We have to work, of course."

Just out of law school when she'd married him, Scott was now the head litigator for a timber company. A novice when Jeremy had known him, now he was some kind of A player, which even on the West Coast stood for something. Since the accident, of course, Jeremy no longer played.

Had he told her about the accident? He'd mentioned the divorce, he knew. And the tenure decision. When she'd met him he had already been working on his dissertation, his book on Leonardo Fioravanti. Some things hadn't changed, at least.

But it was squash that had brought them together, at the club where he'd given lessons all through graduate school. The North American Open had been in Seattle that year. During the break after the Women's C quarterfinal, he and Sabine had climbed the hill to Arkady Ferson's old house. Jeremy had wondered if any of the Lightbearers still lived there. He was already out of the A draw.

Now Sabine was talking to him and he realized he wasn't listening. But he followed her from room to room. ". . . I leave the door unlocked and it is best I do. You know it is the Asian art museum inside the park, and many times people think this house is part of the museum. So they come right into the front hall. I don't like them to call me or ring the bell. But I keep a feather duster beside the door, and if I am downstairs I pick it up. That way they can think I am the maid, something like that. *S'il vous plaît,*" she said, turning, hands on hips, knees together. "*La patronne n'est pas à la maison.* It is mostly Chinese people who come in."

He laughed and she laughed too, hiding her teeth. There was a skylight above the staircase. It filled the upper floor with brightness and shining dust motes. Jeremy wondered if the Lightbearers had ever sealed it up. Or was it only sections of the house that they'd kept dark?

"You said you had something for me."

"La, la, la. It is a surprise."

She showed him her office and her exercise room. It was lined with mirrors and filled with low-tech wooden equipment. Nothing like the machines at the racquet club, they looked like Scandinavian toys for gifted children. When he asked about them, she lay down on one to demonstrate. But then she sat up suddenly, blushing, radiant. "I should wear a different dress," she said.

Because of the mirrors. "It's beautiful," he said.

Embarrassed, she pointed toward the open window. "I like the roofs best of all. Come with me. Can you, with your leg?"

"It doesn't hurt."

"You will have to take your shoes off."

And so they climbed onto the asphalt and tar. It was like an entire country up there, with mountains and flat places, and the skylight a reflecting pool. "I spend more time here than in the house," she said—hard to believe. But on the steepest shingles there were marks of little trails, like goat paths in the Alps.

Following her, he passed a cereal bowl and an empty juice glass balanced on a ledge. He found her squatting on the ridgepole, three stories above the street. He climbed atop a dormer and stood up. He could see the whole neighborhood of mansions, gardens, and big trees. There was a tower in the park across the street. "People come here to make love," she said. "No, in the cars in that parking lot or by the curb. I don't know why. Look, you can see them—"

He saw nothing. He was watching her. "Sometimes I like to think about them, shut up in their little cars," she said.

And the taxi ride? "What about Scott?" he asked.

She laughed, hid her mouth. "I hope he has a mistress. Poor man! But you will see—tonight he is going to St. Louis for his business."

Before Scott she had married an American in Brussels where she was from, a Wall Street type. Once in the United States, he had treated her badly. That was the time Jeremy had known her best, when he was already living with Joanna. She had used to come to lessons close to tears. Squash had started as a way of keeping hold of her first husband, who had not deserved her.

Now she squatted above Jeremy, knees apart. "What about Joanna?" she asked.

He shrugged. The subject was unavoidable. And then suddenly Joanna came back to him, an image of her face, her coarse hair and freckled skin. Her beautiful thick eyebrows, the hair on her arms and upper lip. The surprised expression on her face, when he'd seen her the last time. He looked out toward the tower in the park.

Sabine said, "Once I was up here and it started to rain. But the window slid down and I was trapped outside. So I saw a little man walking there along that street and I had to call out. I told him to go into the house and I led him upstairs with the sound of my voice—la, la, la! Isn't that ridiculous? He was just anyone!"

What did she mean by this little story, told in this bright tone? He made a calculation: She must not have heard about Joanna's death. No reason she should have. They'd never met, after all.

He turned back to look at her—smiling, squatting above him on the roof. No reason to bring up something that might cast a pall—literally, he supposed. No—figuratively. No—literally. It was not something he wanted to discuss.

He said, "After the accident I couldn't forgive her. I thought I could, but I couldn't. I broke my pelvis. I guess I told you."

"She was driving?"

"Yes, but it wasn't her fault. It was on the Merritt Parkway. There was a big rainstorm. I looked up at her from the stretcher—she was soaking wet. We'd put off having children until my job was permanent—just as well. She was always careful that way."

"I did not wish to make you sad. So, and Fioravanti?"

Jeremy smiled. "I'm surprised you remember. That was the problem, wasn't it? No publications. Or else not enough—no book, at least."

Once more Sabine tried to change the subject. "I used to love to watch you play."

And in a little bit, "It's not so wonderful sometimes, having children. Sometimes you feel like an impostor, I suppose. I look at Sophie and think I'm not her mother."

"I wasn't even competing anymore," Jeremy said. Embarrassed, he put his hand over his bald spot. "We've all lost something," he said—a fatuous remark. But she smiled, wrinkled up her nose.

"Très distingué. But we must not let you get a sunburn for your interview! And besides, I have not shown you what I found!"

"What did you find?" In fact, he was eager to know. That was why he was here, after all, not to reminisce about old happy times.

"I found it downstairs. You will see!"

She'd mentioned it on the phone when he had called. Something about Ferson and Fioravanti—his obsession. Now she hid her mouth again; her hand was dark with asphalt. She was laughing at him, he thought. Stringing him along. She didn't move to go until a couple of minutes later—"Oh, damn! There is Sophie, home from school. She won't like her crazy mother up here. Quick, we must get down."

Carrying a book bag, a girl was walking down the street under the big trees. Sabine crouched out of sight, and then she slid down the shingles toward the back of the house. There she ran along the narrow lip of the roof, thirty feet above the garden, until she came to a small dormer—not the window they had climbed up through. Jeremy followed her more carefully, and by the time he dropped down into her bathroom, Sabine was already filling up a small brass tub, dipping her feet in. "Please, sit here and wash your feet. I had this made expressly. Scott thinks it is some kind of bidet. You must use a loofah and some almond soap."

He sat beside her on the tub's wooden rail, scrubbing first one foot, then the other. Their thighs touched. Then she slipped away, scuffing her feet along a towel on the floor, leaving dark streaks. "Sophie! Sophie!" she called. "*Il y a quelqu'un . . .* There is someone you must meet."

Later, at the conference hotel, lying awake past midnight, Jeremy tried to recompose the afternoon into an erotic history. He needed to calm down and get some rest. His interview was early and he needed this job—a tenure-track position at Butler College. And so he tried to imagine sexual intercourse on the burning rooftop or in the bathroom. That would have been more comfortable, spread out on those fluffy towels.

But even in his own fantasy he was disturbed by small, fleeting memories of Joanna, her hair coarse and wild as she turned, her expression of surprise as he attempted to embrace her. No, he didn't want to think about that: back to business. He spat on his palms, got to work. Nose to the grindstone. Hand to the plow. So—the bathroom, then. But there was Sophie outside the door. When he and Sabine had gone downstairs she'd looked at him without a hint of suspicion. And then Scott had shown up, glad to see him, full of old times. Sabine had prepared a meal earlier that day, and now she just had to heat it up in the enormous kitchen. Already she seemed distracted. And she resisted when he asked her to show him the basement— that was the reason he had come, of course. Not to see how rich she was. He persisted. She refused. What was there to see? A bunch of carpeted rooms without any light fixtures. Locks on all the doors.

Scott laughed. "She's got her little temple down there. No men allowed."

Sabine dried her hands on a towel. "There is not so much from the Lightbearers' time. Some books and so."

"But you mentioned something."

"Yes, of course. Just one thing. What do you think? Here—I will walk you out."

He had to get back for the Renaissance Studies dinner. She led him out into the entranceway again. Then she picked up from the mantelpiece what looked like a spice bottle with a screw-on cap. "You see I remember what you told me all those years ago."

He took the bottle. There was some black liquid at the bottom of it, a thick black sludge. Confused, he held it up. She seemed proud of herself. But he felt stupid. "I'd like to see the books," he said, finally. "Anything. You're sure you couldn't show me the downstairs?"

That, suddenly, was the wrong thing to say. "You're not even paying attention! 'Fragrant Goddess'—you see I remember. I kept it for you. I knew you would call one day. But you are never satisfied. Always you want more."

Now, in his hotel bed, Jeremy saw what she meant. He was unsatisfied. He wanted more.

He wanted to walk down the dark stairs into her temple, her inner sanctum, as Scott had described it. Fragrant Goddess—was she kidding him? But there was some crude Cyrillic script on the label. Something scrawled in pencil. Was this a joke she had whipped up in her kitchen, with its copper pots and pans?

If so, where had she found the recipe? What was she hiding? Some books and so—what books?

Down in the Lightbearers' labyrinth, Sabine was waiting for him in the dark. She was lying on her back before the private altar in her temple. But as Jeremy fumbled through the little rooms of his small fantasy, inevitably he found himself grabbing hold of other ghosts, old men long dead. And this was another kind of delusion: Perhaps in Ferson's library there were some undiscovered papers, some new information about Leonardo Fioravanti, the Bolognese alchemist and surgeon who had tormented Jeremy all these years.

In Naples he had discovered the cause of syphilis, the French pox. Though spread through lechery, the root of it was cannibalism, as he determined by feeding pig meat to a pig, dog meat to a dog, hawk meat to a hawk, and watching them die of the disease. Fioravanti had the cure, though, for it and many other illnesses. Taken both internally and as a salve, his nostrums reduced fevers, knitted broken bones, cured heartsickness, took away all pain, even in hopeless cases, Jeremy thought. "Theriac" was one, made from snake's blood. "Scorpion's Oil" was another. "Fragrant Goddess" was a third, the strongest of all. It was a remedy Fioravanti had learned from a slave, a woman from the Spanish Netherlands whom he had liberated after the siege of "Africa," a town on the Tunisian coast.

To Jeremy he was a Protean, elusive figure. Because of the lies he told in print and even in his private correspondence, he seemed to represent a new phase in the history of masculine self-invention. This was what Jeremy's book was about. And because he wanted to dramatize the social difference between doctors and empirics in the late Renaissance, Jeremy had tried (or at least lately he was trying) to alternate chapters of conventional historiography with passages of historical fiction. Theory and argument gave way to invented narrative in different sections of the book—an invented secret history of Fioravanti's life, a substitute for the actual *Secret History* the alchemist had claimed to write, which was of course lost. In these fictional passages, however, Jeremy was beginning to see caricatures of his old professors and other long-standing experts in his field. And in the main figure of the drama, a caricature of himself.

Men staggered into middle age so damaged and so hurt, so guilty, Jeremy thought, every one of them was looking for a magic balm to heal them without any need for introspection or forgiveness. In its multiple drafts, his manuscript now told the story of Jeremy's disaffection, his distrust of academic knowledge, and his embrace, Fioravanti-style, of experience, lies, and sensory information. Now the book was seven hundred pages, and even in his overheated dreams, it was impossible for Jeremy to imagine an academic press would ever touch it.

Impossible, also, to concentrate on the task at hand. Instead of Sabine in her temple, which just a few minutes before he had been decorating with embroidered pillows and silk brocades, bronze statuettes of Hindu deities and clouds of incense smoke, as well as (God help him!) mirrors and exercise equipment while she lay flat on her back on the narrow bench, skirt rucked up, knees out to the side—now it was Arkady Ferson he imagined, an old man sitting stiffly on his stool in the same room.

Arkady Ferson had lived in that house. He had haunted that basement. That had been his refuge, his own inner sanctum, away from the light. Jeremy had seen a photograph (a timed exposure?) of an old man on a stool, a white-haired old man in a dark room. Now suddenly it was obvious that in his pose and gestures he was mimicking the famous engraving of Leonardo Fioravanti from the frontispiece of the *Autobiography*—maybe there was room for Ferson in his book! Why not? Surely no discussion of empiricism was complete without trying to reproduce, as Ferson had claimed, the alchemist's results. No discussion, also, of charlatanism or fraud.

All of us had broken bones to heal, fevers to bring down—Arkady Ferson, originally from St. Petersburg, had understood that much at least. He had come to Seattle in the 1950s. With his followers he had moved into the big white house and published a series of occult treatises, including two at least on Fioravanti: If illness was a symptom of divine rage, then secret knowledge was God's grace. The adept would begin to glow like a metal vessel in the process of distilling—a metaphor that Ferson took quite literally, hence the sealed windows and the chambers without light.

So: a nut job, obviously. A dead end. But Fioravanti, too, had been despised and hated by his peers, had died in poverty.

Jeremy didn't want to think about that. He really needed the Butler job. And so to distract himself he returned to his sexual fantasy, determined to organize it in a more efficient way: He would go to the house the next morning, after his triumphant interview. Sabine would have left the door unlocked. Scott was in St. Louis.

But Jeremy wouldn't climb the stairs or go to search for her up on the roof. He would find the basement, and he would bring a flashlight, and in a warren of little rooms he would find a hidden chamber, a closet really, and on dusty shelves there would be a complete set of the 1609 edition of Fioravanti's works. Maybe there would even be a diary—Alexander would help him with the Russian translations. . . .

No, no, no. In his hotel bedroom, Jeremy dried his hands on the bedsheets and turned over onto his side. "It is incredible how virtuous I am," he told himself.

Drained of his last erotic impulse, he gave himself up. In the bottom of Sabine's house, in a crystal—no, a carved, hinged, wooden case, he would find the only copy of the master's *Secret History*, handwritten, never published, though referred to often in the *Autobiography*—the repository of all his alchemical wisdom.

And he would hear Sabine behind him. "What are you doing here?" And he would turn off the flashlight, leaving them in darkness. He would turn toward her, and both of them would glow with secret knowledge or nostalgia or desire. "You're beautiful," he'd say. So many regrets. Memories like ghosts. Ah, God, he thought, suddenly sleepy—was it possible that a ghost could move through time, haunting and changing and poisoning the past?

On the tenth of September the seawall was broken in three places after a bombardment lasting thirteen days. Don Juan de Vega, the Spanish viceroy of Sicily, entered the town at four o'clock. There was a slaughter, of course, of the men who'd taken refuge in the mosque.

But by the western wall, near the gardens of Aphrodisium that had given the city its name, all was quiet at the end of the afternoon. Giordano Orsini had allotted the poor neighborhoods to his men. Fires burned there overnight. The Spanish captains had reserved for themselves the mansions of the African governors and the Turkish corsairs.

The richest house in that western district belonged to Brambarac, the African commander. Don Garcia de Toledo chose this house to sleep in. But in the evening when he arrived, he was disturbed to find the roof had collapsed during the bombardment. The upper walls were broken in. Don Garcia stood between the great stone lions at the gate. He sent his men to find another house close by.

Late as usual, and unaware of this change of plans, Leonardo Fioravanti arrived after dark. He had been working in the barracks outside the city, where there was an infirmary. For three weeks since the beginning of the siege, he had spent every hour of daylight in that place, setting broken bones, irrigating gunshot wounds with quinta essenza and balsamo artificiato. Despite all efforts, many soldiers and sailors had died under his hands.

Stinking, weary, and discouraged, he came at last to the lion gate. He had walked in darkness through the deserted roads, and everything was dark. Later he would write of this campaign to say that it was worth a dozen courses in the university. He would boast of his miraculous cures. But at that moment he perceived no benefit. He stood with his hand on the stone haunch of the female lion, surveying the broken building, its black, gaping windows along the front. There were no stars or moon. Torchlight came obliquely from other houses, and the sound of muffled cries.

But in the dark building nevertheless there was a glimmer of candlelight. Maybe Don Garcia was there after all, he thought, in some undamaged section of the palace. So the surgeon persevered up the long flagged path, climbed the long stone steps. And he had been wrong to think that even the front part of the house was nothing but collapsed rubble behind a more-or-less intact facade. For when he looked through the empty door, the yawning wooden casements, he saw the first-floor ceilings were still whole, and there was even a staircase leading nowhere. This he glimpsed in the candlelight, a single tiny flame that hesitated by the stairs. Then it disappeared, but not before he had seen the imprint of a small naked foot in the dust—surely a woman's footprint!

"Captain!" he shouted, and then drew his sword. Who was this in the ruined house of Brambarac? News of this prince had even spread to Naples, the splendor of his gardens, the richness of his tables, and the beauty of his many wives and concubines. Maybe one of these still haunted the wrecked mansion.

Though the surgeon still hovered in the doorway, his mind moved boldly through the darkness, following the flame—she might be a Christian woman from Antwerp or Ghent or Brussels, stolen from her family by El Draghut the Corsair, then sold as a slave in the disgusting bagnios of Algiers. Now she was homeless and without refuge in this city of infidels. How grateful she would be to any rescuer or protector, a girl scarcely grown (if you could judge by the size of her footprint), yet skilled in all the lecherous arts.

Shouts came from up the street. The surgeon stepped over the threshold. Sword outstretched, he shuffled into the darkness, following the place in his mind where he had seen the candle flame. Among the piles of rubble he poked his way toward the back staircase. And as he moved, he imagined he saw some light back there, an orange glow reflected from a secret source—perhaps a fire burning in an inner court. Instead, behind the broken staircase he found a wooden stairs descending to the cellars.

And at the turning of the stairs he saw her—just a glimpse before she disappeared. And he was mistaken to have thought she was carrying a candle. But there was a light that glowed around her and around her hands especially, a dim, orange light.

He put up his sword, slid it back into its sheath. Part of him was too weary for this adventure. In the battle on the beach, he had taken a thrust from an African knight— that was weeks ago, and yet the wound hadn't healed. Walking downstairs was painful, and he managed it a single step at a time, descending into darkness—where was she? She had vanished ahead.

But he could hear her voice ahead of him, a little singsong murmur gathering him on. At the second turning he went forward like a blind man, both hands outstretched. There was a stone corridor, and a stone chamber at the end of it, and what looked like a fire burning there; he couldn't tell. The witch was waiting with her back turned. She was wrapped in strips of cloth, and there was cloth over her face and hair. The light glowed around her. Limping, he reached for the cloth around her shoulders, stripped it away. Already he understood something was wrong; when she turned toward him he let out a cry. For this was no Christian beauty from the harem of Brambarac, melting with shy gratitude for her deliverance. But she was old, older than he, thirty-one or -two at least, with coarse wild hair and a spot on her dark cheek. Her eyebrows were thick and tufted, and there was hair on her upper lip. She stank of some musky perfume, an oil smeared on her body to hide her rottenness; he wasn't fooled. Limping forward, he grasped hold of her thick neck, crushing her throat before she could make a sound or summon her familiar. He pulled her down onto the floor, pressed the weight of his body into her as she flailed and thrashed—ah, God, would it ever end?

Jeremy started awake. Horrified, he sat up in bed.

Heart pounding, he put his hands to his face.

Once he had listened to a lecture on the science of dreams. In it, the professor had claimed that the central figure in a dream, or else the dominating sequence of events, could have no meaning. No, it was the furniture, the incidental details that were able to teach us something about ourselves. Now, awake, Jeremy saw the truth of this. In his dream-state he had grasped something his waking self had missed.

Fearfully, hesitantly, he closed his eyes again. He allowed himself to imagine the stone cellar in Brambarac's ruined palace—this time as a set devoid of actors. There was a series of stone apertures halfway up the wall. And there were bottles, old apothecary bottles with glass stoppers and hand-printed labels—oh, it was obvious. It wasn't Sabine who had mixed up some poisonous sludge as a joke to mock at him and his obsessions. Why hadn't he believed her? She had given him a bottle of Arkady Ferson's Fragrant Goddess, prepared by him and described in his 1969 treatise, the veracity of which Jeremy had always rejected out of hand.

But Ferson must have hidden some of it before he died. Naked, Jeremy jumped out of bed and searched the wastebasket where he had dropped the bottle the previous night. He twisted open the crusted lid, smelled some of the foul liquid. Was it possible the old man had dosed himself with this? Even at the time there had been speculation he'd been poisoned, murdered by some other cult member in a squabble over the foundation's vanished funds. No one had been prosecuted for the crime.

Jeremy resealed the bottle, studied the label. *Dushistaia Boginia,* it said in Cyrillic letters. Fragrant Goddess. Leonardo Fioravanti had told the story many times, how in Palermo in the 1580s he had cured the wife of the governor of Sicily. In the middle of the street she had vomited up a hairy, mottled mass as big as a baby. Afterward she'd been in perfect health.

That was after a single dose. If you read between the lines, it was obvious the elixir contained both arsenic and mercury—effective poisons, as Fioravanti himself had pointed out. The precise recipe, along with its various palliatives, he claimed to have recorded in the *Secret History.* He did not publish them in the *Autobiography,* or any of his other books. Dying in poverty in Rome, why should he bequeath to an ungrateful world the secret of these miraculous cures, discovered and refined with so much difficulty?

Why indeed? But there was no time for Jeremy to think about these things. He was already late. He showered, put on his suit, went downstairs for his interview at nine o'clock.

The search committee had a room at the conference. He knocked on the door of a sixth-floor suite in the same hotel. Besides some armchairs and the woman he was supposed to meet, there was a bed with a shiny quilt and a mountain of pillows.

Often he was good at interviews, but not this morning. He found himself distracted by a notion that was almost entirely a fantasy—was it possible that Arkady

Ferson had discovered or acquired the *Secret History*, used its formulae to make a batch of Fragrant Goddess and the other cures? No, it was not possible—the manuscript had never been found. There was no reason, independent of Fioravanti's claims, to assume it had ever existed. And surely, if it had come into his possession, in Brussels or St. Petersburg, perhaps, Ferson would have boasted of it, written about it in his idiotic treatises, sold it when he was short of cash.

Still, at the same time was it credible that Ferson would have drunk the contents of the screw-top bottle if he hadn't at least thought his recipe was genuine? But what an idiot! These ancient manuscripts, discovered at long last, always turned out to be forgeries. What had Sabine said? "Some books and so."

Okay, so maybe Ferson had discovered something, purchased something that turned out to be a fake. Then maybe he had poisoned himself out of stupidity or else despair. Or else he had died of natural causes—that was obviously a possibility, and the screw-top bottle had been prepared as something to impress the Lightbearers, one of a long sequence of frauds: Ferson and Fioravanti were one of a kind! And if Ferson hadn't said anything about the manuscript, it was for the same reason Fioravanti had destroyed it or never written it—the desire for alchemical or secret knowledge, the conviction that secrecy was a prerequisite for holiness or truth. These men weren't professionals like Jeremy, who even now was plotting out an article on this entire subject, a publishable article that would enable him to ace his interview with Butler College, which at this exact same moment he was in the process of blowing with his disjointed and distracted answers to the most basic questions—the woman was looking at him as if he'd lost his mind. They sat in circular armchairs and she stared at him. Had she heard anything about him, any rumor of misconduct? She was attractive, too, in a sharp sort of way, her blond hair pulled back. Sensible skirt. He'd like to have her on this bed with all the pillows. Had anyone slept in it the previous night?

His interview lasted forty-five minutes. When it was over and the door had closed behind him, he scarcely remembered what he'd said. Maybe he had made self-deprecating jokes. Maybe he'd discussed his thesis, summarizing it poorly, because his mind was elsewhere and (it now occurred to him) whole sections had to be rewritten. He stood in the hallway looking at an immense potted plant, thinking that if a man was lucky, his secret history would die with him, the submerged causes and poisonous events. His autobiography would not include them, or anything else that made him special or unique. All that could be pieced together, as if by policemen or detectives searching for clues. That was true for Fioravanti, and Arkady Ferson, and Jeremy as well.

He limped along the blue carpet toward the elevator. Someone passed him, a woman hurrying toward the interview he'd just left. Doubtless she'd do better; she was younger, certainly. Just out of graduate school.

He took the elevator to the ground floor and limped out into the street. Another glorious June day. Where had everything gone wrong? People passed him and they couldn't tell. How could they know? A man in a suit: How could they tell that everything was finished, gone, done? How could they know that it was only just a matter of time before it all fell apart, and he was punished as he deserved? Things had started out so well.

But Fioravanti, too, had had this experience—in Naples, Venice, and Madrid, his career had followed the same trajectory. He had acquired aristocratic patrons, stunned the city with his cures. But then the doctors and professors had conspired to drive him out, ruin him—it was always the same. In Jeremy's case, it was Joanna who had broken him—quite literally on the Merritt Parkway. He'd never been the same after that. He'd taken a medical leave of absence. That was when his thesis had gone wrong, his teaching, too. She had broken him and then abandoned him. Now she was dead. The police, when they'd come to talk to him, had been like children or like stupid undergraduates, never asking the right questions.

In the pocket of his coat, his fingers closed around Arkady Ferson's bottle. He pulled it out, examined the penciled script. Then he turned uphill toward the art museum and Sabine's house. As he climbed, he labored to put these thoughts behind him, all these ways of blaming others for his own mistakes. They were part of the secret history, which had never been recorded, or else had been destroyed, and which in any case was even less reliable than what you saw on the outside, where fraud could be challenged and ascertained.

He came into the neighborhood of prosperous houses, bigger and bigger as he climbed uphill. At the top he came to Sabine's house with its bronze guardians. He'd stopped only once, on Broadway, to buy a flashlight in a Walgreens near the Jimi Hendrix statue. Now he stood between the foo dogs with Ferson's bottle in one hand and the flashlight in the other; he limped up the steps. And the door was unlocked, and the house was in shadow, and he moved through the atrium to the stairwell at the back of the house, under the Tiffany window.

"*Qui est là? Sophie, est-ce que c'est toi?*" But he found the doors and climbed down into the Lightbearers' domain, where Arkady Ferson had lived out his fraudulent life, met his fraudulent end.

He switched on his flashlight, made the turning of the stairs. Then he was in among the small dark rooms, some with mattresses still on the floor. This is where the Lightbearers had lived, indulged their superstitions and their mad old master. This was where Sabine had followed in their footsteps; she had always been interested in astrology and things like that. Low ceilings, cheap particleboard smelling of mildew, but even so he could make out a scent of lavender and incense—it led him on. Sabine, of course, was behind him at the top of the stairs. "Who are you down there? I will call the police!"—who indeed? It wasn't the first time someone had made that threat.

Small dusty objects skewered by the flashlight's trembling beam. Where was he? What did he expect to find? Sabine was behind him. He could hear her footsteps.

And then he came to the end, a square room with a single entrance. Stone walls ahead, the foundation wall. An industrial carpet. A four-poster bed with a canopy. A bookcase. Some books and so.

Sabine was behind him. She was at the door. Brave girl—"What are you doing here? Why are you here?"

Holding up the light, he turned to look at her. He couldn't tell if she could see his face. Maybe she thought she'd recognized him, but now she wasn't sure. But it was possible she could see some of his secret essence, because he'd scared her. He was not what he pretended and she knew it; she looked terrified. He painted her face, stroked her body with the light. She was dressed in a white shirt and blue jeans, cowboy boots. A gold necklace. Gold earrings. Yellow hair pulled back. She squinted, held up her hand.

"You're beautiful," he said. Nothing else—he didn't have to say anything else. But he came toward her, smiling, the bottle in one hand, the flashlight in the other. Her old friend; she had kissed him once. Did she remember?

The flashlight gave him an advantage and he turned it off, leaving them in darkness. Then he dropped it and the bottle too, stepped toward her with his hands held out. He saw nothing as he reached out toward her. But then he could hear her fumbling for the door. He jumped forward and she closed the door on him and closed the bolt.

The darkness made him dizzy. He fell to the floor onto his hands and knees, groping for the light. He dug his fingers into the heavy carpet. Had the Lightbearers locked Arkady Ferson in here, shut him up like an animal until he died? The flashlight had rolled away someplace, was nowhere to be found. But his hand fell on the screw-top bottle. He sat up cross-legged with the bottle in his lap.

Maybe Sabine was already calling the police. Maybe he didn't have much time. But he had always been a quick study. In the darkness he was already developing the skills of a blind man, whose other senses grow to compensate; his ears were ringing. His fingertips, stroking the glass bottle, picking at the lid, were perfectly sensitive to texture and to temperature. And he could smell Sabine's lavender perfume, which masked a darker, musky odor.

As he waited, it occurred to him he did see something after all, a little gathering of light in the far corner of the wall.

EILEEN GUNN

Up the Fire Road

Originally published in Jonathan Strahan's appropriately eclectic anthology
Eclipse One, *"Up the Fire Road" is that rare and happy event: a new story
by Eileen Gunn. Gunn's first collection of stories,* Stable Strategies and
Others, *was a finalist for a couple of awards and received the Sense of Gen-
der Award from The Japanese Association of Feminist Science Fiction and
Fantasy. Gunn is the sometime editor and publisher of the science fiction
Web site* The Infinite Matrix, *a board member of the Clarion West Writers
Workshop. She lives in Seattle and is at work on a biography of Avram
Davidson.*

—K. L. & G. G.

Andrea

The main thing to understand about Christy O'Hare is he hates being bored.
Complicated is interesting, simple is dull, so he likes to make things complicated.

Used to be the complications were more under his control. Like one time
he went down to Broadway for coffee, but the coffee place was closed. So he hitched
a ride downtown, but the driver was headed for Olympia on I-5, so Christy figured
he'd go along for the ride and get his coffee at that place in Oly that has the great
huevos. He ended up thumbing to San Francisco and coming back a week later
with a tattoo and a hundred bucks he didn't have when he left home. I think he was
more interested in doing something that would make a good story than he was in
getting a cup of coffee. But I did wonder where the hell he was.

He's not a bad guy. I don't agree with what my mother said about him being a
selfish son of a bitch. But Christy is the star of his own movie, and it's an action flick.
If life is dull, just hook up with him for a while. And if life seems slow and meaningless, go somewhere where you depend on him to get you back.

Like the ski trip. It's not that he *wanted* us to get lost on Mt. Baker, where we could
have died of exposure, but ordinary cross-country skiing, on groomed trails, with
parking lots and everything, is just so crowded and boring. Starting out way too late
makes things more interesting. Drinking a pint of Hennessy and smoking a couple
joints makes things *much* more interesting and gives the Universe a head start.

That's how we found ourselves, last year, four miles up a fire road as the sun was setting. Early March: warm days, cold nights. Slushy snow, pitted with snowshoe tracks, turning to ice as the temperature dropped. Did we bring climbing skins for our skis? Of course not. Did we bring a headlamp, or even a flashlight? Nope.

"We've got an hour of visibility," I said. "Let's get back."

"It's all downhill. Won't take long. There's a trail that cuts off to the hot-spring loop about half a mile ahead. We can go back that way, and stop by the hot spring." He extended the flask to me. "Here, babe, take a drink of this."

I pushed it away. "It'll be dark by then," I said. "How will we find our way out?"

"The hot spring is just off the main road, the paved one that we drove up. We can walk back down the road to our truck in the dark. No problem."

As it turned out, the hot spring was a lot farther away than that, but it was a natural enough mistake, because we didn't have a map. We didn't have much food, either, just a couple of power bars, and we didn't have a tent or even a tarp, and we didn't have dry clothes. Oh, yeah—we had the cell phone, but its battery needed a charge.

By the time we found the hot spring, it was dark. There was a moon, but it was just a crescent, and it wasn't going to last more than an hour or two before dipping below the trees. I was starting to shiver.

"We got plenty of time," Christy said. "Let's warm up in the hot spring, then we can take our time getting back to the road, 'cause you'll be warmer."

Well, it made a certain amount of sense. Of course, we didn't have any towels or anything, but our clothes were wool, so they'd keep us pretty warm, even though they were wet with sweat from climbing up the fire road. All I had to do was get my body temperature up a bit, and I'd be fine for a couple of hours.

It was slippery and cold getting down to the hot spring. It wasn't anything fancy, like Scenic or Bagby. No decking, no little hand-hewn log seats, just a couple of dug-out pools near a stream, with flat stones at one side, so you don't have to walk in the mud.

We took off our skis, took off our clothes, put our boots back on without tying the laces, and moving gingerly and quickly, in the cold air and the snow, climbed down to the spring, shed our boots, and started to get into the water.

Hotter than a Japanese bath. We dumped some snow in, tested again. Still hot, but tolerable. Soon we were settled in and accustomed to the heat. It sure felt good—I was so tired—but adrenaline kept me alert. We still had a ways to go to get back to the truck.

That's when I saw the old guy, watching us from behind a tree, the moonlight making his outline clear. Creepy, I thought.

I whispered to Christy, "There's somebody watching us. Don't look like you're looking. Over to my left, past the big fir."

Christy liked that, I could tell: it suddenly made things even more interesting. He liked danger. He liked the idea of someone watching us get naked. He sidled around for a better look, and tried not to look like he was looking.

Then he froze. "It's not a guy," he said. "It's a bear."

"What do we do?"

"Stay here and hope it goes away."

"Do bears like hot springs?" I asked.

"Fuck if I know. I don't think so."

I kept my eye on the figure in the forest. It still looked a lot more like a guy than a bear to me. It came closer. It obviously could see us. It waved a mittened hand,

and resolved into a guy with a big beard and a fur hat. "How you folks doing tonight," it said.

"Whattaya know," said Christy, "a talking bear."

Christy

I met Andrea at Burning Man. She was welding together a giant sheet-metal goddess robot with glowing snakes for hair. She was wearing a skirt made of old silk ties, and nothing else. No shoes, no shirt. Great service, though.

I lost my heart to her. I would do whatever she wanted. It's been that way ever since. She wanted a baby, and now she's got one. Doesn't need me anymore. Neither of the women do—her or Mickey. The babies need me, though. I'll stand by my kids, if their mothers will let me.

I'm not going to say that Andrea lies, but what happened on Mt. Baker wasn't my fault. I didn't even want to go skiing that day. It was dark and rainy in the morning, and it was a long drive to Mt. Baker. That's why we got there so late: she kept changing her mind about going. And if I hadn't been stoned, I wouldn't have misjudged the distance to the hot spring.

She's always saying that it's my fault when I screw up. Sure, I screw up, but why assign blame like that? Everybody screws up—even Andrea screws up sometimes. That's why I like skiing cross-country: because, when you screw up, you can recover. Usually, anyway.

You can make more mistakes, going cross-country, like finding yourself in the middle of fucking nowhere without a sandwich. But sometimes you get a chance to see stuff that most people, in their safe little lives, never even dream of.

Like the sasquatch. Where would you ever see a sasquatch, if you didn't go cross-country skiing? Or a talking bear, either. Whatever.

I figured it would calm Andrea down if she thought it was a talking bear, because that's an idea she's familiar with: *ursus fabulans*, the talking bear. We all know the talking bear. Even the Romans knew the talking bear. *Introit tabernum ursus et cervesiam imperavit*, as the book says. A bear goes into a bar and orders a beer.

But I knew it was a sasquatch—I'm not an idiot, Mt. Baker is crawling with them—and I wanted, naturally enough, to find out more. Besides, we were sitting there in the hot spring, facing a long, cold, dark walk back down the side of the mountain to the truck. The sasquatch asked us, real friendly, how we were doing. I saw no problem with partaking of his hospitality, you know? Maybe the sasquatch had a nice little cabin somewhere, or a warm cave with a fire already going. Maybe the sasquatch had a treasure and would bestow it upon us if he took a shine to us.

So I said, well, man, my sister's not feeling so good, and we sure could use a place to sleep tonight. You know any place around here, any place warm? Andrea looked at me hard when I called her my sister, but she didn't say anything. She's cool, Andrea. We didn't want to tell the sasquatch our whole story. Everybody needs to keep some truths to themselves. It's the only way.

And the sasquatch invited us back to his place. Polite as can be. Seemed like a good man, this sasquatch.

We leaped out of the hot spring, and got dressed real fast. It was colder now. We were all warmed up, so the hot spring was not a dumb idea, no matter what Andrea thought.

Skiing behind the sasquatch, she gave me a what-the-fuck? look. It was so dark, I couldn't see her face, but Andrea can do the what-the-fuck? look with her entire body.

I gave her a shrug that said *later*. Of course, Andrea was gonna have to rethink what I told her, and she was gonna have to ask why, and she was gonna have to just fuck with me on it, but she knew enough not to do any of those things while we were following a sasquatch through a frigid forest in the middle of the night.

We skied in the dark for maybe a half hour or so: it was slow going. The sasquatch, I noticed, had furry webbed feet that worked like snowshoes. Obviously, sasquatches evolved in the snow, like yeti. That's part of my theory. I'm just learning about this stuff. I found a couple of Web sites that have been helpful.

So, we were climbing on some kind of a narrow path. Climbing is relatively easy on my mountaineering skis, even without skins, but going down you don't have the control you'd have with steel edges. It was steep and it's icy. I was hoping we could get out of there in the morning without having to sidestep all the way down. When we came to the sasquatch's cave, it didn't look like anything was there at all—just a wall of granite with a row of doug firs in front of it. But somehow there was a gap in the rock, and the sasquatch gestured us in.

Inside, of course, it was bare ground, so we took off the skis and carried them in. No sense leaving them out there, risking that it would snow during the night and cover them up. I've done it, can you tell? Even if you know exactly where you put your skis, it's scary, out in the middle of nowhere, you don't see 'em.

The squatch struck a spark and lit a funny little oil lamp, and me and Andrea looked around inside the cave.

Back from the mouth of the cave, the ground sloped down and the roof was higher than I could see, in the dark. It seemed big inside, even though we couldn't see. I wonder if humans have some kind of sonar, like bats or dolphins.

We followed the wall, and not far from the entrance, we came to a house made of logs and rocks. We went by several sets of doors and windows, like some old tourist motel, right in the cave.

We went in one of the doors and entered a big room. The floor was covered with the skins of deer and mountain sheep. No bearskins, I noticed. There was a strong musky smell, like raccoon or bear. Sasquatch, I bet.

There was another lamp, and there were big piles of balsam boughs, which I knew were comfortable to sleep on, and they smelled good. The sasquatch had a pretty nice place. Cold, though.

The sasquatch soon had a little fire going in a fireplace, and there must have been a way for the smoke to get out, because the room didn't fill with smoke. There was a pot of water on the fire, and, criminy, the squatch even had a bunch of those heavy, handmade pottery mugs, like the kind you find cheap at the Goodwill. What, did he carry those things all the way into the woods? Sasquatches shop at thrift stores?

Soon we were drinking fir-tip tea, which was good, if somewhat redundant in the mountains.

After a couple cups of tea, Andrea went outside to take a leak, and I got the sasquatch alone. I dug in my pack and pulled out the Hennessy, of which there was still a little left, and offered the sasquatch some. He took a pull, I took a pull, and pretty soon I was breaking out the grass. While I was rolling a couple fat joints, I told the sasquatch that I thought my sister had the hots for him.

He took this a good bit cooler than I might have expected. I mean, Andrea is a good-looking woman. I wondered what sasquatch chicks looked like, that he was so unimpressed. Or maybe there was just no accounting for taste.

I told the sasquatch that when Andrea came back inside, I could set it up for him with her. I told him this all had to be aboveboard. But I could tell, I said, that he was a stable fellow—solid, responsible—and my sister was ready to settle down and have kids. This last part was true, actually: Andrea and I had had The Conversation, though we didn't come to any conclusion, or at least not one that made her shut up about it.

The sasquatch just nodded at what I said, and I took this as agreement. We smoked a joint on it.

Andrea

When I came back into the room, the old guy was warming up some kind of a soup he had in a pot near the fire.

"You folks are probably pretty hungry, eh?"

He and Christy had been smoking that homegrown Christy carried with him. Pretty punk stuff.

"Yeah," I said. "We didn't bring much to eat."

"Well, honey, let me tell you." He patted my shoulder, left his hand there just a little too long, y'know? "You and your brother shouldn't go off skiing like this without bringing some emergency rations. You're lucky you ran into me. I'll take care of you."

Yeah, I thought, I'm sure.

But he was nice enough, and the soup was okay, though Lord knows what was in it. Roots and stuff. No meat. There was something potatolike, but it wasn't a potato. I didn't ask, because I didn't want to make the old guy feel bad. I've eaten a lot of weird stuff—a little more wouldn't hurt me.

He had these handmade wooden bowls to eat out of. I'd seen bowls like that before. Very rustic, kind of Zen, you know? I took some meditation classes in Berkeley, and the monks, they had bowls kind of like that.

The cave was warming up a bit from the fire, but I wouldn't have called it warm. The old guy noticed I was shivering, and put an arm around me. Christy moved away. Bastard.

"What's your name?" I asked. He said something, but I didn't catch it. It came out kind of funny, like he was clearing his throat at the same time.

"What?" I said.

"Call me Mickey," he said.

"Like the mouse?" I asked.

"Like the mouse," he said.

After supper, I left Christy and the old man talking, and lay down on a pile of balsam branches. I was tired, and it was soft and kind of cozy.

In the middle of the night, I heard a noise in my sleep, and I opened my eyes. Was it a noise I dreamed, or a noise in the real world? It took me a while to wake up. The oil lamps were out, but the fire was still burning, and by its dim light, I could see the old man moving across the room. He was wearing some kind of a tall hat. Other people came up behind him. It was very dark and shadowy, and completely silent. I wondered a bit if I was dreaming, but it didn't seem to be a dream.

Where was Christy? He wasn't next to me. One of those people looked like him.

I got up from the pile of branches and slipped my boots back on. I stood there in the dark, very quietly, thinking they couldn't see me.

The old man came closer to me, and the group moved with him. Yes, that was Christy there, in the tall hat.

The people moved so strangely, like they weren't used to walking upright, and the cave was so dim, lit with a faint orange glow that seemed to come from within the people themselves that I thought again that it was a dream. They were carrying ropes of twisty brown vines with yellow and orange berries on them, like swags of tinsel from a Christmas tree, and they encircled me, looping strands of vines over my head. It wasn't scary, though, it was like an interesting slow-motion dream. I felt that I could duck out of the vines and run away if I wanted, or wake up from it, but I didn't want to. The berries seemed to give off a dim light, and I was able to see better, like my eyes were getting used to the dark.

The people were all dressed in rags that looked like dead oak leaves. Their garments fluttered, although there was no movement of the air. I tried to talk to them, but they couldn't seem to understand what I was saying. I'm not sure there was any sound coming out of my mouth. The visitors looped the vines around me and Christy and the old man and pulled them tight, bringing us closer and closer, until we were bound together as if we were sticks in a ball of twine.

Then, suddenly, as if a bubble had popped, the room was dark again. The visitors disappeared, and then the orange berries went out quietly, one by one, and the vines bound us less and less until they were gone. We sank onto the balsam boughs, Christy on one side of me, and Mickey on the other.

Christy fell asleep right away. I was feeling dizzy, but I wasn't falling asleep. It was like being stoned, maybe because I'd been asleep already. Mickey was staring at me intently. He didn't seem so much like an old man, just like another human being who was concerned about me.

"I'm okay," I said. "I'm just a bit out of breath."

He ran this hand down the center of my back to just below my waist, and pulled me toward him. He kissed me very lightly on the lips, and I could feel my whole body respond to those two points of contact, his hand and his lips. Now he didn't seem like an old man at all.

Christy

I can tell you that nobody was more surprised than I was to find out that the squatch was a girl. How could I have thought the squatch was a bear or an old guy? It must have been some trick of the light. But she had looked like a guy—how was I to know?

And of course, when I found myself in bed with this beautiful girl, what could I do? I was putty in her hands, just like with Andrea. Obviously she had targeted me right from the beginning, there at the pool. She didn't say anything about that, but she didn't have to. I could tell.

So Mickey was there, she was willing, and I was certainly able. That was just how it goes sometimes: the right moment, the right two people. Andrea was asleep next to us, but I knew that this was okay, that she wouldn't wake up. I mean, she was out cold.

All I can say is we had a blast. Mickey was hot, she was juicy, she was gorgeous, and boy did she give good head.

Afterward, when all the other people appeared, it was strange but familiar to get up and join them. Mickey gave me a tall hat. It was a sort of a wedding, I think, but I was not a one hundred percent cooperative bridegroom. I just walked around in a fog, and then Andrea woke up and she walked around, too, with me and with Mickey, and I thought that made everything okay. The three of us being together like that, I mean Andrea must have known, when she woke up and saw us. But I thought, what would Andrea do, now that Mickey and I had this thing going?

The other people, they had ropes of bittersweet, which I thought was odd. I'd never seen real bittersweet in the Northwest. They have something else here that they call bittersweet, the stuff with the little purple flowers and the red fruit, but I call it nightshade. Where I grew up, the bittersweet has orange berries with little yellow shells that cover them. Beautiful, but it strangles everything that comes near it. My mom used to have me busting my butt out there in the back field, cutting bittersweet away from the trees, because it would just take over, climb all the trees and overwhelm them. It was real pretty in the wintertime, though, with the yellow and orange berries sticking up in the snow. So I loved seeing those people with the bittersweet vines, even though I knew that if it took hold, they'd never get rid of it.

Andrea was dancing faster and faster, sort of pulling us along in this frenzy. The visitors roped her in with the bittersweet, her and me and Mickey, all together, until we fell on the bed of balsam branches, all hot and sweaty, and I had a brief thought that maybe we could get a threesome going, and I was getting a hard-on, and then I was coming and falling into a deep sleep at the same time. You know, a lot of that night is just a blur to me. That was some weed, I'll tell you. I don't remember any more.

The next morning, the three of us were like old married people, chewing on roots around the fire, eating some kind of a porridge of seeds. Andrea and Mickey, they seemed pretty friendly, in spite of what went on last night. So things were okay in that area. I didn't notice the musky smell anymore. Probably that was what I smelled like myself at this point.

There was a thing about caves that I actually hadn't thought through: they're dark. If you stay in your cave, the sun might as well never have come up. I needed to get out of the dark, get outside, take a dump, and prepare for a long ski out, maybe through the woods, the way we'd come up. I hoped there was a forest road nearby, but my guess was the sasquatch was a deep-woods guy, as far from civilization as he could get.

And we needed to get going pretty soon too.

So I put on my parka, and went out to the mouth of the cave, and you know what? It was raining, raining hard. Water was flowing in the snow, down the slots of our tracks, down the slope of the mountain, down through the trees, down to the hot spring, down to the road, which was, by my guess, a couple thousand feet below us. Staying over had not been a very good idea, if getting home soon was our goal.

But I'll tell you what I do when something doesn't work out: I go with the flow. I let life keep happening. I keep an eye out for opportunity.

And, to my mind, the opportunity at this point was to find out about the treasure. Easiest thing would be to get the info directly from Mickey, not poke around in acres of rock. Might involve smoking a few more joints, a bit more bonding. I could handle that. Andrea would find something to keep her busy.

Andrea

Mickey wasn't bad in bed. He was younger than I had thought, and he gave good head. He was a lot gentler than Christy too. Christy likes it kind of rough and fast. Not that there was anything wrong with that, but Mickey was a gentleman, and quite attractive in a way. Kind of hairy, though. Some guys are just, like, bears if they don't wax it all off, but I'd never slept with a guy who was as hairy as Mickey.

So he was talking afterward, real quiet, the way some guys do, just trying to find out a little about you, and maybe trying to impress you a bit with who they are. He mentioned this workshop that he had. To hear him tell it, he could make anything he wanted, which I guess explains about the bowls and the cups. Well, what he said was "it" could make anything he needed, but he was a little vague about what "it" was. Didn't trust me, I guess. But he said he'd bring me something nice, something that was useful. I wondered what he meant, because if he could have anything he needed, why would he be living in a cave?

Maybe "it" was the secret treasure that Christy told me about. I asked if it could make money. But Mickey said he didn't need money. I guess that made sense to me: having what you need is not the same thing as having money. Because the only thing that you *need* about money is the ability to turn it into something else.

So the next day, Mickey gave me a silk undershirt. It was warm and light, and I could wear it without Christy wondering what it was and where it came from. It was kind of a weird color, not olive-green, not an earth tone, but something that could be described as either of those things. Mickey said it was a wedding present, that we were now, the three of us, bound to one another.

I noticed that Christy has a new wool hat, because he'd lost his old one when we skied up to the cave. I wondered if Mickey had given it to him, also as a wedding present. I bet that was true. I wondered what else it could make.

In the days after our first night together, I didn't see any of the other people who were there that night. It was like there wasn't anybody in the cave but the three of us. I figured there were other caves with the other people in them, or maybe they lived farther back in our cave. I asked Mickey where his neighbors went, they seemed so nice. He said something about they were "respecting our privacy." Okay, okay. If he didn't want to give me a straight answer, he didn't have to.

So I thought I'd take a look farther back in the cave, and just see if there was any sign of people living back there, plus maybe that was where the warehouse was. Maybe they were all together in a workshop there, making pottery and knitting hats and tie-dyeing shirts, like some ancient hippie cult. I mean, anything seemed possible.

I got one of the oil lamps, which are pretty bright, and I walked back in the cave, which got narrower as I went back. It wasn't scary, as it would have been when we first came to the cave. It was a bit damp, sure, but it wasn't dripping, and there didn't seem to be any animals or big spiders moving around. When I got way to the back, the cave was much more like a tunnel than the big room it seemed like out near the front.

On one of the walls, I noticed some painting, right on the rock. A large group of dancing figures, one with a tall hat, just like the one Mickey had worn at our wedding. They were carrying garlands of red-orange berries with yellow casings. Bittersweet.

The figures had recognizable faces. There was Mickey, there was Christy, there was me. And there was my mother. Had my mother been there at the wedding? I didn't remember her being there, for sure, and it seemed so unlikely that she would have just appeared there in the woods and gone away without taking me back with her.

Had Mickey come back here and painted this scene? I was touched, really. It was sweet, in a mystical sort of way. I stood there looking at the drawings for a little while, and my oil lamp started guttering. The figures had looked so lifelike, and now they started to move. My mother turned to look at me, and she seemed to be speaking. What was she saying? The oil lamp guttered more, and went out.

I stood there in the dark, not knowing which way to move, and for the first time I was afraid. I heard my mother's voice. "Calm down, Andrea," she said. "You never get anywhere by panicking." I waited for a minute, and took a few deep breaths. The darkness did not seem so deep. Was my mother there with me or not?

As I stood debating the question, it became clear that there was a dull light coming from a part of the darkness, and I thought that maybe that was the direction from which I'd come. "Go ahead," said my mother's voice. "Trust yourself." Well, that certainly sounded like my mother. All that new-age crap. I walked toward the dim light, and as I walked the light got stronger. Soon I was back at the front of the cave again.

Christy and Mickey weren't anywhere to be seen. I looked out the front of the cave, and it was fucking pouring down rain. Where had they gone? Mickey's little house was empty. I yelled out a bit, calling Christy's name. Everything seemed so much like a dream. Was I on some kind of strange drug? Was I in the woods at all? Was I at my mom's house, and having some kind of a psychotic episode? I thought I was past that kind of thing, really.

The fire was still going, and I lit a couple of the oil lamps from it. Just about the time I was starting to get worried, Christy and Mickey came out of the back of the cave. Christy had an oil lamp. I wondered where they had been, since I hadn't seen any light back there at all. They looked funny, but I couldn't put my finger on why. Christy had his hand on Mickey's shoulder, but he moved it when he saw me.

"Andrea! There you are!" he said, as though he'd been looking for me. I know that lying tone.

"Where'd you go? I was worried," I said.

"Everything's fine. Just go with the flow, babe. Just go with the flow."

That's good advice if you've got a flow to go with. Christy did, Christy always did, but he wasn't going to tell me about it.

Mickey had started poking at the fire, stirring it up, and was putting the big pot on the hook over it, and tossing stuff in the pot. I thought maybe I could help with that, and pretty soon we were working together on chopping up stuff and it was starting to smell pretty good. Christy didn't make himself useful, but then he never does, you know?

I asked Mickey about the paintings I'd seen in the back of the cave. He said maybe we should go back there while the stew was cooking, and he squeezed my shoulder. Christy was nodding off anyway, so we slipped away easily, grabbing a lamp on the way out.

Walking toward the back of the cave, I noticed more pictures and some strange writing, like lines and circles. I asked Mickey what it meant.

"Instructions and rules, mostly. Stuff you need to know to raise your kids right."

"Do you have kids?"

"Mmmmph." It was a yes, I thought.

"Where are they? Are they grown up?"

He made some more noises. "Old enough. Scattered."

Poor guy, I thought. Getting old up here in the mountains, and his kids off somewhere, probably don't visit. I wondered if they even know he's living in a cave now.

"That was nice, last night," I said. "I was wondering about the pictures in the cave of us dancing." Mickey didn't say anything, he just kept leading me deeper into the cave. "Haven't we already gone past the painting I was talking about?"

"It's a circular path," said Mickey. "We'll come by it again." We walked, and it did seems as though we were going uphill and around a curve.

This isn't what I thought it was like, but I have to agree that it did look as though the picture was coming up again.

"There!" I said. "There's the picture." We stopped, because I made us stop. Mickey would have continued on by.

"See that?" He nodded. "That's us there, isn't it?" He nodded again. "And there, toward the back, that's my mother." He nodded again.

"Okay," I said. "How did my mother get there?"

"Your mother is a very strong soul," said Mickey. "Whatever has been done to her, she has fought back, and has entered the realm from which there is movement back and forth."

"I don't understand," I said. "Do you know my mother?"

Mickey kissed me. "And you are also a very strong soul. I am sure I am seeing your mother in you."

"Was she here? Do you know my mother? What is she doing in the cave?"

"We need to keep walking, just past here," said Mickey. He moved a curtain aside as we passed, and there was a small room cut into the rock. We stopped and went inside, and he was so nice and gentle, and he has a deliciously masculine scent.

Christy

So we figured to stay for a few days. Seemed like the easiest thing to do. A lot pleasanter than walking down the mountain in the mud.

Mickey was totally great, and Andrea seemed to be okay with what was going down, whatever she thought. She never said a word to me about it.

Mickey and I had a lot of chances to get together, and we took advantage of them. She was a total delight. Not to say that Andrea wasn't neat, but it's the unexpected treat that is sweetest, isn't it? Even Andrea would understand that.

Andrea and Mickey seem to be becoming friends too, which is more than I could have hoped for. They went off for long walks into the cave together, and they always came back hand in hand and smiling. I wondered sometimes if they were talking about me, but Andrea had no idea, and Mickey seemed to live on another planet when it came to fucking.

The few days became a week, and the rain continued. It was a lot of work, just to get water and roots and dry wood for fuel. I always liked to camp out, but then I had those packets of freeze-dried shit. The week became several, and then a month. But I will never complain about rainy weather again. It was the happiest time of my life, at least to date: two women, both of them great in bed, and each of them devoted to me.

Though, clearly, Mickey was a lot more devoted than Andrea. This is completely understandable, and I don't fault Andrea for it in the least. She was much more the modern woman, with her complaints and, let's face it, her neurotic shit. There are consequences for that, is all. I totally support her in her struggle for getting a handle on what goes on between men and women, I just think she's taking her own sweet time at it.

I asked Mickey a few times about the people who were there that first night. Who were they? Where are they? How come they don't come around at all, and she said they were giving us the time we needed to create our family, our oneness. And this made sense, though I did feel I was getting the shut-up explanation. I mean, it's no skin off my ass if her friends don't want to come around and see us. Really. What do I care?

But they never did come around during the daytime. Or even at night, except that once. And we were there for, well, it was nearly six weeks, I think. We stayed—and I would have stayed longer, let me be clear about it—until Andrea started throwing up and said she thought she was pregnant.

I tried to convince her that this was no problem. Lots of women give birth at home, away from hospitals, but she wasn't hearing any of this. She said she had to go home, she had to get hold of her mother, and she had to have some answers. Naturally, I thought the answers thing meant she'd finally decided that it wasn't okay about me and Mickey, but that wasn't what Andrea meant at all.

Turned out she'd been stewing on this wonky idea that her mother was some kind of alien or something, and that she was in like psychic communication with her. Fuck. Andrea's mother is the least psychic middle-aged woman I have ever met. She's all business, she's an accountant or something, and she always treats me as though I had a communicable disease, which I'm quite sure I don't have, and if I did, she'd be the last person I'd give it to.

When Andrea told me she was pregnant and wanted to go home, I confess I had to think about it for a little. Not that I wouldn't have taken her home, but I needed to think about what I would say to Mickey, and whether I would want to come back to the cave after taking Andrea home. On the other hand, Andrea and her child were my responsibility too, and it's funny how, well, connected I felt to her, knowing it was my kid she was pregnant with.

When I talked to Mickey, it turned out she was very cool with it and didn't seem surprised or hurt. Kind of the ideal woman.

And then she told me that she might be pregnant too. As you might imagine, this was both a pleasure and a shock. Two babies? I was always aware that unprotected sex could create a baby: I was completely with that program. But I confess I hadn't considered the idea that unprotected sex could create two babies in a month.

Okay, okay, it was dumb of me. I hadn't thought it through, okay? But I can tell you I was pretty proud of myself. Or at least that was my first reaction. And then I thought, well, I am going to have to get a job.

But the women, Andrea and Mickey, were so much more practical. With them, it was always, what am I going to do now? Andrea was for going home to her mother, and Mickey was for staying there in the cave and giving birth all alone by herself.

This was a little too close to the mama-bear-baby-bear thing for me, but Mickey seemed so at home with the idea, it seemed to make sense to me as a solution. Only it wasn't one, was it?

So when Andrea told me that she wanted to go back to the city, I figured I'd take her there and then come back to be with Mickey. After all, Andrea has her mother, right? And Mickey hasn't got anybody, since her friends—her supposed friends, the useless twats—never come around.

I tell this to Mickey, figuring it'll make her feel better. Instead, she goes all weird on me. Like, we've never fought. We've never even disagreed. But all of a sudden, she's like, "How could you?" As if I'm some monster because I want to stay with her.

"Andrea will need you," she says. "How could you leave her at a time like this?"

"Her mother will take care of her," I say, wondering what the big deal is. "Her mother will, in fact, take much better care of her than I could."

"That old bat?" says Mickey. "She can scarcely feed herself. She can barely walk and chew gum at the same time. Look what happened to Andrea, under her care."

"What? What happened to Andrea?"

"She was running wild, and Lord knows what all. She got involved with *you*."

My feelings were hurt, but I wasn't inclined to let her know that. "So did you."

"That's different. I can take care of myself. I know what I want and how to get it.

But Andrea just sleepwalks through life, accepting whatever is handed to her, not taking charge. Somebody needs to take charge."

"Excuse me for not grasping your point here, but what's your point? If I'm such a dolt, how come you want me to take care of Andrea and the baby?"

"That's a very good question, Christy. But I'm not going to answer it just now. You just get her out of here and get her back to Seattle safely. Can you do that?"

Yeah, I could do that, and I did. But the price of that is I was shut out of Mickey's life. She made it clear she wanted me out, and I didn't need to come back.

Andrea

As we left, I was not sure whether I was going home or leaving it, going out into a strange and dangerous world. I wasn't anxious to go back to the city with Christy. Would he and I stay together? I didn't want to be with him, but I had to worry about having a baby by myself and taking care of it.

I understood Christy better than I ever had before, but I didn't like what I understood. Never had, I guess, but when it was just me, it didn't seem so important, as long as life was interesting. Maybe I hate being bored almost as much as Christy.

We slogged down the side of the mountain, carrying our skis. It was a pleasant enough spring day, a little overcast. The snow was long gone, and the trees were starting to bud green. There was skunk cabbage poking up in the wet places, and some little white flowers here and there. What were they? I couldn't remember. As we walked, everything that had happened in the past six weeks seemed like an extended dream.

It was a hassle getting down to the car, because the fire road in some places was pretty soggy. When we got down to the main road and looked for our car, of course it was gone. "Forest Service towed it, babe," said Christy. Well, duh. We started walking, and after a few miles we got a lift from a guy in a pickup truck.

"Mud skiing?" the guy says when he stops, nodding at our skis. A humorist.

Christy says, "We been up the mountain for a while."

"Whoa," said the guy. "Are you those two skiers vanished a month ago? You're alive?"

"Six weeks ago," said Christy, "but who's counting? I think we're alive."

"Rescue copters were over here for three days, combing the area. How do you feel? Need water? Something to eat? You want me to drive you to a hospital?"

"I just want to get my car back, man. I need to get my girlfriend here to her mom's house. She's pregnant. My girlfriend, I mean."

"I think I better take you to the sheriff's office. They'll know what to do. Where you been, anyway?"

"Ripvanwinkleville," said Christy.

Great. The sheriff's office. I hope Christy's not packing out any of that homegrown.

Christy

When we got back, I figured I had to do something fast to support me and Andrea and the baby. I mean, Andrea wasn't going to be able to bring in much from waitressing after a few months.

I figured there should be a book in there somewhere, if I could just find somebody to write it. Any real writer would jump at the chance. So I got hold of this guy

I knew at *The Stranger.* We'd talked about doing this Hunter Thompson thing once, over a pitcher or two of margaritas, but nothing ever came of it. He wasn't against the idea, but he said it would be easier to sell the book if it was a news story first. He said if the story had legs, it would walk, and then he'd write the book. First he had to finish a book on hiking in Peru, anyway. But he thought his friend Darla could help with the news story.

Darla was kind of a mistake—all she knew was the confession market. So the story broke in *News of the World,* and everybody thought it was a big joke. I guess I can't blame them. That headline wouldn't have been my first choice: "He fathered a bigfoot baby . . . and became a deadbeat dad."

I got phone calls and e-mail from all my old buddies, who basically figured I'd pulled off a scam of some kind. I mean, it's nice to be congratulated, but if it's your life and not a scam, it's a little embarrassing.

It wasn't my idea to contact Maury. That was Darla, came up with that. I had had my sights on Oprah, actually. A lovely woman, a bit matronly, but clearly someone who could converse on a higher plane, who would not judge me because I had left my little one behind with a loving parent. I could hear her: she would extend her generous hand to me, and she would say, "You sharing your story here with us today has brought us all a bit closer to an understanding of our relationship to the wilderness." That's how I wanted to tell my story.

But Darla couldn't get the Oprah people to even return her calls, so she went on this Web site and sent my story to the Maury show. So we don't hear from them, and we don't hear from them, and we don't hear from them. They are really into deadbeat dads there, which isn't my story, in my opinion. But like Darla said, we didn't have time to wait for them to do a show on bigfoot babies. I had to fit into the story they were doing.

So, anyway, I went to the show, and they had a woman up there and three deadbeat dads. Maury talked for a while, and the woman cried, and then the deadbeat dads talked. And then I interrupted, and I took the dads to task for not taking better care of their kids. I really pitched into them. I was like, I'd give anything to get back to my kid and take care of him or her. And this was true, or it seems true when I think about it. Anyway, I did my stuff, and pretty soon I was sitting up there with the deadbeat dads, and we were all crying and Maury was comforting us.

The part I didn't understand was that not only did Mickey not want to spend any time with me, but neither did Andrea. She was into the whole idea of having a baby, but not into the idea of me anymore.

So then, Maury kind of jumped all over me, y'know? He asked how come if I was such a good dad I wasn't supporting my kid either?

Even the deadbeat dads joined in. I think this is the result of all those therapy programs at prisons. We've raised a whole generation of ex-cons who are in touch with their sensitive sides.

It was rough—Oprah, like I said, would have been a much better choice—but I stood up for myself, and Maury even said I was making a good case for parental responsibility in the abstract, if not in actuality. Eventually, we all hugged, and I got out of there alive.

The Maury people liked how I handled it, and they did a follow-up show a few weeks later, where they had me working with this psychic who said she could lead me to the cave again, but she couldn't. We got a couple of TV shows out of it, including one where people who've been cheated by psychics confront the cheats. And then I met this guy that wanted to do a film script. When he finished it, he said, he was hoping they could get Ben Stiller or Luke Wilson to play me. I always liked Owen Wilson better than Luke, but apparently he wasn't available or something.

Andrea

Well, it's like I thought, Christy always lands on his feet.

We had a hard time getting along after we got back to Seattle. Before, we had mostly the same opinions about things, but now, it seemed like whatever he wanted to do was totally screwed. I don't know why, but I just didn't want to go along with his schemes. Me being pregnant made a difference, for sure. Christy was completely sure it's his baby, but how could he be so sure of that? I didn't rub his nose in it, but I think he knew there was something going on between me and Mickey. He would believe what he wanted to believe, just like he would tell the stories that get him the biggest reaction from other people, when you got right down to it, whether he believed them or not.

He wasn't a bad dad, though. He's very into the baby, and he doesn't seem to care whose it is. When I was pregnant, he was always bugging me to eat right, and exercise, and all this stuff. And once little Baker had arrived, Christy was all over me with baby-care advice from the shopping channel.

But, give me a break, I knew how to take care of a baby. I used to be a babysitter. It's no big deal. Just keep them breathing and don't drop them.

And of course my mother was delighted. She certainly didn't think it was Christy's baby. When Baker was born, she took one look at him and she said, "We've got to talk." And of course, when we sat down to talk, which was, with one thing and another, a month later, she wormed the whole story out of me, just as you have.

"I knew it," she said. "I knew it. I had a dream."

The thing that I wondered about was the story that Christy told—about him and the bigfoot baby. I mean, I'm the one that should have been on Oprah or something, technically. Mickey threw us out of the cave, after all—so didn't that make *him* the deadbeat dad? I mean, really, if Mickey is Baker's dad?

It's kind of soon to tell, but there's something about Baker that is *so* not like Christy.

So I watched the Maury show. It's not something I'd ordinarily do, but I had to watch it, when he said he'd be on it.

It was a show on deadbeat dads, and while "deadbeat" probably does describe Christy pretty well, I didn't figure that he was completely aware of that. So I thought there would be some acknowledgment by Christy of just where he went wrong, you know?

So I tuned in, and it wasn't like Christy was actually on the show: Christy was in the audience. Why did I believe him, I thought. Had again.

And then, when he spoke up from the audience, and accused those young guest guys, I thought, what?! He wasn't telling this straight. What was going on? And then I realized that he was talking about Mickey.

He even mentioned his name: he even called him Mickey. But he was talking about him like he was a girl. This I didn't understand. Christy embroiders, you know, but he doesn't usually tell bald-faced lies. It's too easy to get caught, for one thing, telling bald-faced lies. Christy is smarter than that.

And he was crying like she broke his heart and stole his baby. Mickey? Hey! It's my heart that was broken. I'm the one who got seduced and abandoned. Mickey's the deadbeat dad, not you, I thought. And I've got the baby.

So after the show, I went to the Maury people. I told them Christy was taking advantage of them. They weren't interested in that story. And why should they be? They had a good story already in Christy. But I said, you're on a roll here. If they kept it going, maybe they could bring Mickey in too.

They liked that idea. "Do you know where she is?" the guy asked.

"He's a he!" I said. "Mickey is a he. I ought to know. He got me pregnant. I don't know why Christy is pretending he's a girl. This is my story, and he swiped it!"

I would have thought they'd be surprised by this, but it turned out they're used to this kind of a story. If it's a love triangle, they can keep bringing people back until the cows come home. If it's got a bi angle, they love that too.

So I met with them again, with a story doctor. Very professional, very slick. They do this hundreds of times a season. Kind of creepy, actually.

I had little Baker with me, 'cause I was nursing him, and they glommed onto him. "So this is Bigfoot's baby?" they asked. For Pete's sake, he's just a baby, I said. Leave him out of this.

So the deal was, they were not going to tell Christy that I was going to be on the show, or Mickey, if they could find him. They kept calling Mickey "she."

Christy

What did I look like, I wondered. Wardrobe had tried to spiff me up a bit, with a haircut and some clothes that weren't too bad. They even shaved me, sort of, with a razor that left me with a nice even stubble.

I wasn't expecting Andrea. They had made her up to look very wholesome and earth-mother-y, with a peasant skirt and embroidered blouse, like some sort of old-country woman headed for the market. Her hair was wound into a braid, and the braid was curled into a large round bun at the back. I felt like I'd been set up. Where was the hot babe with the welding gun who had won my heart at Burning Man? This was a mom!

They brought us out like the contestants in some old game show, sitting on chairs in front of the audience.

Then Maury came out and he introduced us, and he started asking us questions about where we live and how we met. Pretty soon we started talking, and I didn't think it would amount to all that, or that we could talk about it in public.

Then they started showing the videos of the kid. I mean, babies are babies, and we're hardwired to find them cute. But gee whiz, the audience went a little wild at the baby video. I admit, Baker is a cute kid. I looked a lot like that when I was a toddler. I can show you the photos.

And then they said they had photos of the other baby, but they ran videos of some bear cub instead. The audience was confused, but game. It was a tease, I thought. They don't have any photos, because they've never been able to find Mickey, because I've never been able to find Mickey. Cute little cub, though.

And then they brought out Andrea's mother.

Andrea

So my mother was on the show, which I wouldn't have agreed to if anybody had asked me. And she and Maury, I swear, they tag-teamed me, and pretty soon I was telling the unexpurgated version.

I said, which I had never said out loud to anyone, even Christy, that I didn't think the baby is Christy's. My mom said, basically, that she certainly hoped not, and that Christy was an aimless good-for-nothing.

Christy acted like he was outraged, and he threw himself off the chair and onto the floor and kicked his heels a lot and yelled. Since he knew perfectly well how my mother feels about him, I felt this was a little stagy, but I think it's something that men have to do on the Maury show.

I said that I was just a bit annoyed that my own mother would rather see me with a fatherless kid from some hookup with a grizzly halfway up a volcano than for me to have a baby with Christy.

But my mom just looked at me and said, "That's the way it is."

Maury was still in control, though, whatever my mother thought, and he started talking to my mom about her entirely misspent youth. And she told this perfect stranger—she doesn't even watch his show—stuff she had never told me in my entire life. My mother told Maury that she used to hike on Mt. Baker, and that she, in fact, had had her own fling with the sasquatches, way back before I was born.

She made it sound like a picnic of some kind. No long weeks in a cave. It was summer, and the weather was warm and sunny. It was like some fantasy romance. The love sasquatches. I don't know why I got so angry about that.

But I was pretty incensed by it all. My mom had always been so tight with the details about my dad that I assumed he was some kind of criminal. And now I find out he's a sasquatch, and on network television. If I were a typical Maury guest, I'd be jumping up and down and crying.

But I know that doesn't work with my mom. So I just ask her: was Mickey my father?

She said, "Honey, I don't know. It was a long time ago. Life was different then, before I took the accounting course. I didn't always keep track of stuff."

There was a lot of yelling from the audience, some of them laughing and some of them scolding her.

And then they brought out Mickey.

Christy

I don't know how they do this stuff. I certainly didn't have anything to do with it. They didn't ask me for any advice or help. But somehow they found Mickey, or maybe Mickey just decided to allow herself to be found.

Either way, she walked out onto the stage at the Maury Show and paused. She looked great. Elegant, all spiffed up in some kind of classy New York clothes. She looked like Candice Bergen, maybe, or that woman who lives in Connecticut and does the magazine—Martha Stewart. Older, you know, and maybe a little authoritative, but still pretty great-looking. I guess I hadn't thought about it, but maybe Mickey does that craft stuff too, like Martha—that's how she gets all those hats and bowls and coffee cups and stuff.

They told me later that, to the studio audience, Mickey looked like a sasquatch. Some people screamed, other people laughed. But I wasn't paying a lot of attention to the audience reaction at the time.

Of course, I wanted to run to Mickey, but Maury gestured to me and Andrea to stay in our seats. He went over to her, rather cautiously, I thought, and guided her to a seat next to Andrea's mother, who looked at Mickey speculatively.

Andrea looked at Mickey too. Tears welled up in her eyes, and she said to me and the studio audience, "He's lost weight."

I swear, I thought at the time, "She's not even seeing the same person I'm seeing." I said, "Looks to me like she gained about ten pounds, but I figure, she had a baby, she's going to gain a little weight."

Andrea looked at me intently for the first time, like she was actually listening to me. "What are you talking about?"

I said, "Well, you gained weight."

Andrea gave me the evil eye. I said, "I'm talking about Mickey, that's who. She had the baby, and she's still carrying a few extra pounds. But it's nothing to me. She looks great. You look great. Jeez."

Then Andrea said to me, right on camera in front of the TV audience, "Mickey is a man, you idiot."

I was surprised, but I was not going to put up with being treated that way. Idiot. Huh. I said, "I understand how you could have thought that, but the fact is that she's a girl. I found out for myself in the traditional manner."

Of course by now, there were more people in the audience screaming and laughing. I've done some street theater, and this happens—people act out, and certainly on the Maury show the audience is encouraged to act out. I've found that the best way to deal with it is to ignore it.

And then Maury turned to me and Andrea, and he looked sort of sad. "Christy and Andrea," he said, "is this your friend Mickey?" We each nodded. "And you each say you've slept with Mickey?" We each nodded. Andrea's mother just shrugged, and then she nodded too.

"Well, you've shown us here today that not everyone is seduced by Hollywood's ideal of beauty . . ." I was about to object to that statement, when I saw Mickey sort of focus on Maury. He did kind of a double take, then said, ". . . though of course you . . . you would carry it to a . . . new standard." He shook his head a little, like there was something wrong with his eyes.

Then Maury pulled himself together and held up a manila envelope. "I've got the tests right here," he said. The Maury show is very supportive with the paternity test thing, and I was looking forward to the results. Maury tore the envelope open and pulled out the lab report.

At that point, Mickey stood up and said, "I don't think we need to hear this." She gestured with one hand, and an opening appeared in the floor of the stage right in front of us. It looked like it led into a cave, and it sure was dark down there.

Then people started coming out of it, people with tall hats and clothing that looked like it was made from dead oak leaves. They were carrying bittersweet vines and two babies, neither of whom looked to me like a bear cub, though I've been told that, to the audience, they both looked like bear cubs.

The people in hats danced with Mickey and Maury and Andrea's mother, and they handed the babies about while they danced. Maury danced, but Andrea and I did not dance. We watched, slightly paralyzed, while Mickey and Andrea's mother entangled themselves in the bittersweet, and then entangled Maury. Then they all danced down into the trapdoor with the babies, even Maury.

But Maury looked a little worried, just a tiny bit. As he descended down into the floor, he looked right at the cameraman and said, "Keep it rolling, Anthony." He disappeared into the cave, wrapped in bittersweet. Maury was a pro, I thought, and I respected that.

Andrea and I were left sitting on the sound stage, looking at the audience. I'm sure you've seen the clip on YouTube.

M. T. ANDERSON

The Gray Boy's Work

"The Gray Boy's Work" was originally published in the young adult anthology The Restless Dead, *edited by Deborah Noyes. This is M. T. Anderson's second appearance in this series, following "Watch and Wake" in the eighteenth volume—a story not coincidentally also published in an anthology,* Gothic, *edited by Deborah Noyes. Anderson's novel* The Astonishing Life of Octavian Nothing, Traitor to the Nation *recently won a National Book Award, while his satirical science fiction novel* Feed *was a National Book Award finalist and winner of the L.A.* Times Book Prize. *His vampire novel* Thirsty *and his middle-reader pastiche* The Game of Sunken Places *are both recommended to readers of this anthology. He lives outside of Boston.*

—K. L. & G. G.

When the man returned from the war, he came the last part of the voyage in a farmer's oxcart, half asleep. He brought with him an angel or a goddess seated captive beside him.

His children spied him from afar and they ran to the cart crying, "Father! It's Father!" and "Pa!" The man was shivering in the February weather and was barely able to lift his hand. The angel beside him was an Angel of Victory, and she had on her head a lantern with a candle sputtering within it. She was blindfolded.

The man's wife ran out of the house laughing with joy, and she went to his side. Even before he was lowered to the ground, she was embracing him. Their voices were small in the wide, cold fields beneath the mountains. The clouds that day were yellow and thick. The wind blew hard past the family, now reunited, and past their house and barn.

The man's eldest son, Ezra, was shy of his father, and he stood back while the other two children jumped and called their greetings. Ezra felt great relief, for his father was home and God had touched the valley with His forefinger; and the boy smiled to see his brother and sister hopping in pride and affection.

The father, set down on the ground, could not stand, and looked to Ezra for aid. Ezra's mother paid the farmer who had brought the father home on the cart.

Ezra went and stood beside his father. It felt good to offer his father an arm, a shoulder. Ezra had not seen his father for nearly two years. The father took the boy's arm and said, "You are a good boy." The mother on one side and the son on the other, they walked the father to his house. The angel followed behind, dragging her vestments through the brown snow.

The mother said to the father, "You won some great victory." She smiled and pressed his hand to her mouth.

The father did not answer.

"We saw the signs in the sky," the woman explained. "On Christmas Eve there was chariots come out of the mountains."

Jesse, the youngest son, hopped and exclaimed that there had been angels in the air playing upon Instruments of Music.

"I told the children, the trombones celestial mean just one thing," said the mother. "Triumph in New Jersey."

There was a space of white silence then, for the father looked at his children with his mouth open wide. "We won," he agreed at last. They saw that his eyes were wet.

He said, "I did not think to ever see you again in this life."

And the man held his children to him one by one, and the two young ones pranced about him. He asked to sleep, and they took him to his bed and laid him down; and they were quiet as they could be, considering their excitement at his return.

He slept heavily, with Victory seated beside him, her blindfolded face cast down.

Despair had been in the house for some months because the family had not known whether their father was alive or dead. Each day, they said their prayers for his safe return, dawn, noon, and night. But with so many months passing, and no word, they had come to a silence about it all, and finally, their prayers themselves were silent. There was work to be done, the mother said, and another day to be got through. The mother and sister baked without a word in the early morning, and the two boys scattered out to the barn, where they milked and gathered eggs; the first sunlight fell across the red mountains, and Despair sat at the table with her frown and her fangs and her hair in her eyes and watched them all.

Now, while the man slept his first sleep in his own house, Despair rose from her seat and greeted Victory. They sat together and took each other's hands. Their breath mingled by the kitchen table.

They seemed to be acquainted.

The mother watched with careful eyes the angels' soft civility.

The father slept long. Through the night, little Esther slept curled against him. She was so young she could barely remember him from when he had left for the war.

Ezra was glad for his father's sleep, because it gave him time to get all things in order for his father. Ezra wanted the barn and all of the things that had been in his care for near two years to be perfect. So while the man slept through the morning, Ezra groomed the horse and hung the tools and got the Bits, as he called his sister and his brother, to help him sweep.

Ezra saw the Apples' boy Lem walking by the stream that morning and said to him, "My father is back." Lem Apple's father had not gone to fight for the cause of the country in the war. Lem Apple stared at Ezra.

Ezra said, "He's back," and shrugged like it was nothing. "Guess he's a hero. Fought with General Washington. They won at New Jersey."

Lem Apple gaped, nodded, and kept on walking.

Victory knelt before the mother. The mother reached into the angel's lantern and pried free the candle.

She took it to the hearth, trimmed the wick, and lit it once more in the fire.

"That's better, ain't it?" she said, twisting the candle back into its socket. "Now there's a flame in your head again."

Victory smiled.

When the man awakened, he turned and saw that they had prepared the noon meal for him. He rolled off the bed and walked to the table. The woman put soup in front of him. Ezra stood across the room and watched him.

The father ate noisily and said nothing. The children did not eat. They studied their father carefully. Esther, the little girl, and Jesse, the youngest boy, sat, but they did not bother with their food. Ezra folded his hands in front of him.

They waited as long as they could, and then Jesse said, "Father, you kill any Englishmen?"

The father ate his soup and said, "We all killed some."

The mother gave another bowl to Despair. Despair was left-handed with her spoon.

"You want to see the barn?" Ezra asked. "I took real good care of it."

"I reckon you did," said the father. "You're a little man."

Ezra did not reply.

The father looked at his son. He said, "I know. You ain't little."

Ezra turned his eyes down and ate his soup.

The man had left for the war when the first call was on the land, when the redcoats had taken Boston and the people rose from all of the farms, the hills, and the villages to chase them out. One day, omens had walked across the family's fields, hand in hand, singing like glass about Necessity.

"What are they?" Ezra asked.

"They're omens," said his father.

Ezra said, "They're in the beans."

His father nodded and knocked at the dirt with his spade; he put his hand up to his brow so he could squint at the singing. Then he went across the field to talk to them. Ezra watched his father greet them and nod. And later that night, when the omens had passed over all the town, all the villagers and farmers had come together on the Green. They had gone shouting to the doctor's house, because word said that the doctor was a Tory and a redcoat-lover, and was for the king. The farmers yelled for him until he came to his front door. Then they took him and dragged him through dung, and they fed him dirt while his stuck-up daughters cried. The doctor tried to fight his neighbors with one arm, but he was not a strong man and there were forty or fifty men against him. Then the villagers threw him to the ground before the meetinghouse, and someone said, "You get out of the village before nightfall tomorrow or it won't go easy with you."

No one had seen him since.

Two days after that, Ezra's father had left to join the Patriots outside of Boston. The family heard from him when he was there and then in New York. He couldn't write, himself. The family got letters he'd had friends write for him when he reenlisted. After that, there was the silence, and months turned into a year, and no word came to the family; and Despair had arrived, eating their stew, coughing through the night, sucking softly at the white parts of their arms.

The mountains were big and pewter in the afternoon. Ezra said to his father, "You want I should show you the barn?"

The father replied, "Your mother and I got to have a walk first."

"Where you got to walk?" asked Esther.

"I got to walk with your mother," the father repeated. He gave his wife a look. They went out together. They left the children by the fireplace.

Ezra went outside to get more wood. He brought in several armloads and stacked them. He put another log on the fire so when they got back, it would still be going high. He took good care of the family. They would notice when they returned. They would comment on how, when his father was gone, Ezra watched out for the rest of them.

His little brother Jesse sat at the table and stared. He hadn't spoken or moved for some time. Ezra was tired of people just watching other people, so he said, "What ails?"

Jesse shook his head.

Ezra said, "What's the trouble?"

In a voice that was sure and that was hard as rocks, Jesse said, "Father run away. He run away from the camp before General Washington ever led that New Jersey battle."

In his stomach, Ezra felt something like a fear of dropping. He lay down the poker by the fire. He knew that it was true.

"No," he said.

Jesse held up his hands.

Ezra asked, "How do you know that?"

"I just know. That's what they're talking about. I know." He sighed. "He run away."

Despair started laughing. Jesse and Ezra turned to her. She smiled at them both.

When the man and the woman came back from their walk, the woman frowned and the man had no look at all on his face. They held each other's hands. Their children stood in the mud of the dooryard and watched them come up from the river.

The parents walked up and stood among their children.

"Now I'll look at that barn," said Ezra's father.

Ezra did not stir.

"Ezra," said the father, "let's look at that barn."

Ezra did not move. "You run away," he said to his father. "You didn't fight the battle."

"I fought battles."

"How many redcoats you kill?"

"I don't know."

"How can you not know?"

"I don't."

"How? If you killed them, how can't you know?"

"Breed's Hill," growled the father. "Battles. Boston Neck. Dorchester Heights. Long Island. Kip's Bay."

"If you killed redcoats, how's it you can't know how many?"

The father reached out and grabbed the boy's collar and dragged the boy toward him. The father's teeth were clenched. He said, "I can't know"—giving the boy a solid shake—"I can't know because when you fight in a battle, you're in lines, with lead and grapeshot filling the whole air, and everything is on fire, and your musket don't aim at nothing, and the redcoats come on at you, rank after rank, and you may see some of them fall down through the smoke, screaming, but there's a man you love's brains on your arm and his face is down by your feet, so you don't take so careful notice of which phantom got hit by which deadly part of the air." The father shook his son again.

"In battle," he said, "you load and you fire into the smoke, and you pray that the battle is already over."

He let his son go.

Ezra stumbled back. The boy straightened his smock. He looked his father in the eye.

And Ezra said, "You're a deserter."

"I fought for two years. Near enough."

"You run away. General Washington fought that battle without you."

"If you knew what that camp was like . . . the winter camp . . . If you saw that . . ." Ezra's voice choked. "I told the Apple boy Lem that you was a hero."

"Ezra!" said the mother.

The boy was thrilled that his father looked scared now. The boy said, "I told Lem Apple that you was a hero. I guess I told him lies."

"Ezra," said the mother, "you get inside the barn. Father, you come—"

"I don't need orders from a woman," said the man; but he went inside the house all the same.

Ezra went to the barn to do chores. He was glad not having to look at his father. He was glad of being alone.

The father lay on his bed, talking to his littlest daughter. "Esther," he said, "you're my Esther. When I left home, your feet, they made tiny mouse footprints. I always said, 'Where did that mouse get into the house? Where's that little mouse?' "

She looked at her father with large oval eyes.

He took some of her hair in his hand. "Did your brother tell you about the time he rolled you down the roof?"

There was a knock on the door. The woman answered it. It was the neighbors, the Apples, come with a friend of theirs from the next village over. They wanted to speak to the father. They were full of joy. They held their hats against their stomachs and did not know whether to sit or stand.

"Sir," said one, "we hear you fought next to General George Washington."

The father smiled faintly.

Some minutes later, Ezra came in from the barn to find them all sitting around the table. Despair hung in one corner of the house, smeared in webbing. Her eyes blinked white. Victory stood facing the fire.

". . . So we chased them across the river," the father was saying. "And we threw into it all their furniture, all their tents . . ."

Ezra stood with his arms crossed.

His father said, "Later, they burned most of New York. I don't rightly know who burned it. They did. We did. Someone burned it."

Ezra watched his father. The father's eyes did not meet his son's.

"Mr. Brainerd," said the Apple husband, pointing at his friend from the next village, "Mr. Brainerd here fought down in New York. You know each other?"

The father rubbed his mouth with his hand and kept rubbing.

"It's a pleasure to meet you, sir," said Mr. Brainerd.

"It is a pleasure," said the father.

"I reckon I seen you about the camp."

The father nodded, with his hand still on his mouth.

"That was truly a time," said Mr. Brainerd. "That was a time. Your tales do bring it back. I wish I could've fought alongside you at New Jersey. I was sent away for my leg."

The father agreed carefully, "It was truly a time."

The son still watched, his face clean of emotion.

"I missed the tales," said the son.

"I can tell you another time," said his father.

The son glared. The father could not abide his son's look and stood up to fix something, anything. "We got any . . . we got any cake," he asked his wife, "we could give them a piece of?"

"Well," said the wife, "I believe we got—"

"He run away," announced Ezra.

Everyone looked at Ezra.

"He run away. From the camp."

The father made a move to throw a cup. He set it down instead and turned away to touch the wall.

The guests watched him.

The father turned halfway toward them, as if to speak, then faced the wall again. He lay both of his hands on the plaster.

The Apples looked at each other. Mr. Brainerd smacked his lips.

Ezra went to the fire and made like he was propping it up.

The wife went to stand by her husband. She put her arm around him.

"I reckon," said one of the Apples, "that we've stayed long enough."

They rose to leave.

As they opened the door, the father turned toward them. He said, "We et candles. We boiled our own shoes to make a broth. Mr. Brainerd, you tell them."

"You're lucky to be alive, sir," said Mr. Brainerd. "Lucky you're not hanged. I got to get back over the mountain."

"We boiled shoes. I et leather."

Mr. Apple said, "This is your own . . . your . . ." He waved his hand.

"There was smallpox," said the father. "Men dying. Most of the men. Tell them. I prayed for mercy. I never had the smallpox. A man in my tent, he had it. They wouldn't move me."

"Sir," said Mr. Apple, "we have a great many chores."

"The snow was high and we didn't have no shoes after a time. We was drilling barefoot in the snow. Men were dying. Boys were covered in sores. There wasn't any food."

His wife said, "He is still a hero."

"I fought two years for this country," said the father. "Congress called, and I went."

"That's right," said Mr. Apple, rattling the latch. "Good day, then."

Ezra watched this all unfold. He watched the Apples and their friend leave. The mother sat.

The father still spoke, but now to the closed door, where the winter was.

"I seen men's arms," said the father. "I seen men's arms in a stack where they been sawed." He put his hands over his eyes. "And I thought to myself, 'I want to be able to hold my children when I get home.'"

Ezra, lying on his mattress in the loft, could hear his parents talk. He listened to hear if there would be anything that might change something somehow.

At one time, his mother said, "Ezra brought in more wood," and the father made a noise that meant, "So he did." They busied themselves making a fire to keep the cottage warm through the night.

At another time the father said, "That fence up to the Mastersons' got to be repaired."

And at another time, the mother said, "We smoked our own pig this year," and the father said, "Had a fine flavor at supper."

There was no word of desertion.

Still, Ezra lay waiting for some argument that would free his father of the charge.

The next morning, Despair wore the blindfold, and Victory had the fangs. Ezra found them sitting in the barn when he went out to tend to the animals.

The boy stood in the darkness of dawn and looked at Victory. The door of the broken lantern upon her head creaked closed as she turned to look back at him. Her eyes were not the eyes of a person, but were golden.

"Miss," he said, "you took off the blindfold."

She shook her head slowly.

He did not like talking to someone with fangs.

"I got to feed all the animals," he said. "Could you go outside?"

The angels rose to their feet. Their garments were dusted with straw from where they had slept. Ezra stepped backward. They were as tall as he was. The barn was dark and cold. He backed against the wall. He watched the golden eyes and they watched him.

For a time, they did not move. He said, "Pardon me, Miss Victory. Miss Despair."

"You mistook," whispered Victory. "She ain't Despair. She's Prayer."

Victory and Prayer turned. Prayer stumbled toward the door, blinded, legs straight, feeling her way with her paws.

The door closed behind them.

Ezra made sure that they were gone before he knelt by the cows.

That morning, the plains between the mountains were purple with the cold.

The boy and his father walked along the edge of a field. The boy said, "I know the paddock fence up near the Mastersons' wants mending."

The father nodded.

"I was set to do it," said the boy. "I would've done it this week."

They walked on for a ways. Their old hide shoes crackled on the frozen dirt.

Suddenly the boy said, "I'm set to do it today."

"What?"

"Mend the paddock fence."

The father nodded, but said, "Can't today. Too cold to work with wood."

"I'll do it," said the boy. "This instant." He turned away from his father and started walking quickly back to the house and the barn for tools.

"Ezra," said the father, "you can't today. It's all frozen. The wood. The sap. You can't."

The boy walked faster. The father watched him go.

Some minutes later, Ezra passed his father. He was headed for a small stand of trees. He carried an ax.

Ezra went among the trees. Their bark was gray or black. The breeze was frigid in the copse.

The boy could feel the father enter the copse behind him. The boy did not turn to face his father. He tugged on branches. He reflected that he was engaged in his own work, come what might.

He found a limb that he thought would be fine for the paddock fence. His father could not complain of it. It was a fine limb.

The boy began to strike at it with his ax. The father stood off some ways and watched.

The wood was resilient with the cold. The ax bounced back. The boy struck harder. It made no difference. The ax did nothing.

"Ezra," said the father, saying his son's name softly. "You don't have to show me."

The boy kept smacking the tree limb. The ax did nothing but chip the bark and then spring away.

"Ezra."

The boy looked up, and saw that Victory and Prayer walked across the field.

He lowered the ax.

Behind them was a boy of Ezra's age.

The procession—two angels, one boy—reached the copse. The father did not look at the three who approached. He waited, as if for a catastrophe; he studied a place where a tree had been torn out of the ground; his whole face scowled with anger and concern.

His son walked to his side. Father and son stood together.

Victory and Prayer parted. The boy behind them limped forward. He was gray and did not have the flesh of the living. He could not walk straight, as something had happened to his leg.

"Get away with you," said the father. "We don't want you here."

"Who is he?" asked the son.

"I'm a hired hand," said the gray boy in a gentle, rasping voice. "I do work of all kinds."

"Where are you from?" asked the son. "I don't know you."

The gray boy gestured to the father. "He knows me," said the gray boy. "I come from under the mountain."

Victory smiled.

"Get away with you," said the father.

"I am here to help," said the gray boy. "These excellent spirits will convey me to your house, where I shall receive my first meal. Once I have eaten of your food, then I am bound to work."

"We don't wish you to stay," said the father, but the angels and the boy had turned already and were walking out of the copse.

They walked across the field. The father and son stood by the stone wall and watched the gray boy limp toward their home.

When the father and the son returned to the house in a few hours, the gray boy was carrying stones. Victory walked behind the gray boy, her hands folded near her stomach. She smiled as he staggered lamely beneath the weight of the stones.

"I'll set it down here," said the gray boy.

He fell to his knees and dropped the stone on the ground near a wall made of rocks. He had built the wall with impossible speed.

The father could not even bring himself to look at the gray boy. He pinched at his eyes with his fingers and walked into the house.

His wife was directing the making of butter. "Sprinkle in the salt," she said to little Esther. "Just so. And lay the carrot across it." When she saw her son and husband come in, she announced, "There's another one of them come. A gray boy."

The father said nothing.

Ezra said, "We already seen him."

"He says he'll aid 'round the house," the mother noted. "That's welcome."

Jesse and Ezra watched each other's faces. Jesse went outside.

The mother said, "He already split shingles for the barn roof and builded some fashion of wall. He's quick. I don't think he's of this world."

Ezra followed his brother.

When the two of them were alone in the barn, with the animals shifting all around them in the darkness, Jesse whispered, "I know who he is."

"Who?" asked Ezra.

"The gray boy."

"I meant, who is he?"

"He's a boy got killed in Father's regiment. Come for something."

Ezra fit his thumbnail into a crack in the wall. He worked his thumb up and down the crack.

"We don't need Father here," said Ezra. "It's ours now." He pointed at a trough. "I built that." He pointed at the hay. "We brought that hay in. It was about to rain for a week, and we got it all in on time."

Jesse perched on a rail. He drew his knees up to his chin. He teetered there and listened to his brother.

Ezra said, "The fields gave it all to us. I stood there every day and prayed to the hills."

Jesse nodded, breathing through his mouth. Finally, he said, "What'd you ask for?"

"That I'd get through a day," said Ezra. "That there wouldn't be no fire or drought." Ezra knocked absently on the wall. He finished, "I prayed that he would come home."

Later in the afternoon, when the father and the son were working in the yard, they saw neighbors walk slowly by. The neighbors were there to gawk at the deserter, the man who had abandoned General Washington's camp.

The father and the son lifted stones onto the wall and nestled them so the stones wouldn't rock uneasily.

The minister went by. He did not greet the father. He did not even look directly at the father. He greeted the son—"Good day, sir! You are well, I hope! Woodpile looks most impressive!"—as one would greet a man who owned a broad farm and who worked it diligently every day.

"Thank you, sir," said the son.

The father lowered his head. He kept on picking up stones.

The minister walked on.

The son, suddenly, laughed at his stooping father's back. It was a harsh, short laugh.

The father threw down his stone and walked away.

The son felt a sickness in his arms, a weakness, as if he had just been rebuked.

The father stalked across the dooryard toward the barn. His lips were slewed to one side. His shoes scraped on the frozen ground.

The gray boy stumbled around the corner of the barn. He held the pieces of the ax in his hands.

"I tried to mend the fence," he said to the father. "I tried to cut some branches." He started crying. "It broke. The ax broke into splinters." The head had come off the haft.

The father took the pieces from the gray boy. "Go inside," he said.

"Back at home I had a little ax for play."

"I reckon you did."

The gray boy wiped his eyes with his dirty wrists. He stared at the father. He turned and went inside.

When Ezra went into the house a few minutes later, wringing out his hands to warm them, he found the gray boy sitting by the fire on a stool, drinking cream out of a bowl.

"What's he doing there?" said Ezra.

"Leave him be," said Ezra's mother. "He's upset."

The gray boy looked at Ezra like he planned to kill him.

Glaring at Ezra, hunched over his bowl, the gray boy lapped the cream. His tongue was gray, too, and a full foot long.

Later that night, Ezra's mother asked the gray boy to fetch some squash up out of the cellar. The gray boy said politely that it would be most agreeable to do so. He stepped across Prayer's tail and swung open the trapdoor in the floor.

They all, shuffling around the cottage, had to step across Prayer's tail.

When the gray boy returned, he had two squash in his hands. The mother went to cut the first of them, then threw down the knife in anger.

The squash had rotted. Its insides were black, dry, and fibrous.

The second the boy had brought up was the same. She went down to find another and discovered that the lot of them had rotted.

Ezra witnessed all of this.

He watched from the table. He watched the gray boy apologize: "Ma'am, I must have jinxed the squash. It was me, surely." Ezra saw his mother tell the gray boy not to be ridiculous, that a body doesn't jinx squash. The gray boy apologized again, sneaking looks at Ezra.

The girl Esther told the gray boy to stop apologizing and go out into the yard with her. They went outside, the gray boy's lame leg clattering against the door frame.

Ezra and his father watched each other.

"I know what you believe," said Ezra's father. "You believe he's a dead boy from my regiment. You reckon he's come to haunt me."

Ezra looked his father in the eye.

"That ain't what he is," said Ezra's father. "He's something much worse, because he won't ever go away. He'll be with you always."

"I don't want to sleep near him. He gave me a look."

"Both of you need to stop that," said the mother.

The father said, "I don't know what I've done to us all. But I did it because I . . ." He would not say anything further. He rose and put on his coat and his hat. He went outside.

Ezra lay his head down on the table but did not close his eyes.

In the late afternoon, snow began to fall over the valley. Ezra stood near the pigs and looked up at the sky. The snow had not been announced by wind. The pigs were not comfortable with the snow. They stood near the door and dipped their heads as if expecting the blow of the ax.

Ezra shooed the pigs toward their pen. He was worried that it would be too cold in the barn. He thought he should maybe get the Bits and lead some of the animals into the house.

Jesse walked into the barn, a scarf around most of his face. He walked over to Ezra.

"The gray boy ruined the beans," he said. "Mother asked him to cut some beans from the cellar and they're all over with webs and blight."

Ezra frowned and nodded.

Together, they walked to the house.

Inside, the gray boy was crying before an audience. Ezra's mother petted the gray boy's head. Little Esther and the father watched from the other side of the table.

"I'm too hurt to do anything," said the gray boy. "It's my leg. It ruins everything for you."

"Now, that's nonsense," Ezra's mother said. "Your leg don't ruin anything."

Ezra took a seat next to his father. His father inclined his head to welcome Ezra. Ezra saw his father's mouth.

They watched the gray boy nestle his head up against Ezra's mother's bosom. The gray boy wiped his eyes and stared at Ezra and the father. The gray boy's face was stark and unsmiling. Neither was it wet with tears. For the mother's sake, the gray boy made a fake sound like sobs.

Ezra and his father both put their hands on their laps. They looked at one another, united for a moment in their hatred of the crippled child's tyranny.

Ezra's father reached out and put his hand on Ezra's shoulder.

At his father's touch, Ezra remembered that he was supposed to hate his father. He sat with his father's hand weighing on his shoulder like an unuseful ornament. He could not, for a moment, remember his fury with his father. The hand lay there; Ezra tried to recall why it should not.

While he waited to remember his anger, he picked up the hand like a clod of dirt and dumped it from him.

The father was startled.

Ezra watched his father get angry. He started to cower; he could tell that his father's anger would be great.

Victory came climbing out of the loft, with a rope tied to Prayer's arm. Victory looked down upon them all from the loft, her body raked to the side by the tug of the rope.

The father rose from his seat. Ezra pushed his own chair backward. He put his palm on the edge of the table, ready to stand.

"I am tired," said the father to Ezra, "of your looks. I'm tired of your airs. I only been back two days, and I'm tired of you not saying—" He could not continue. He rapped once on the table like a spirit.

Ezra rose warily. He watched as his father tried to collect words and failed.

Failing, the father paced across the room, edging around the mother and the gray boy, and seized a red plate from the cabinet.

He hurled it at Ezra. It broke against the table and splinters of it hit the chair.

Ezra saw that his father was a little man. He saw that his father was a little man who danced across the room to get a piece of crockery to smash. He was a little man who had to stage and act out his own fit like a schoolgirl.

Ezra's mother had her arms around the gray boy, her mouth open. Esther was starting to cry; Jesse had turned away and was looking at something else.

Ezra did not think anything was funny, but he smiled anyway, thinking of his father as a schoolgirl who had run away and now pranced around the room looking for crockery to smash. "I hate you," he said.

His father's shoulders were low. "Of course you do," he said.

"I'm going to take care of the sheep."

"You should," said the father.

Esther said Ezra's name and held out her hand.

Ezra left the house.

Up on the hillside, the snow churned in great tides, driven by the darkness of night. Ezra made his way along the path.

Jesse came running behind him. "I'll help," said Jesse.

"There ain't no need to," said Ezra.

"You can't drive sheep alone," said Jesse.

They walked in silence. Sometimes the wind rose and they held on to their hats.

They reached a hut made of rough piled stones on the hilltop. The door was closed, and three sheep were milling uneasily inside. Ezra let them amble by him. He and Jesse clucked to them and started to drive them down the hill.

"He didn't mean it," said Jesse.

They had made it only a hundred yards or so when one of the sheep spooked at something by the wall and ran off to the side. The other two sheep did not notice, blinded as they were by the snow.

Jesse ran after the one. He called her name and scampered away over stones and hummocks.

The mountains were no longer clear. The only forms were the folds of the air limned by the snow.

Ezra kept on down the hillside after the other two, who blinked at the great flakes that fell on their eyelashes.

The two sheep came to the gate and stile. Ezra had left the gate open. The sheep ran through the gate, past the figure of a boy.

Ezra stopped.

It was not Jesse.

The gray boy stood on the path, his lamed foot crooked on the ground.

Ezra went to stalk past the boy.

"I am from under the mountain," said the gray boy.

"Could you kindly step—"

"I've sailed on rivers of ice."

The boy reached out and threw Ezra to the ground.

Ezra's arm was hurt on the stone wall; his back was hurt on the frozen dirt. He lay and tried to get up. Sore, he rose.

The gray boy had not moved.

Ezra leaped past the gray boy, but the gray boy's hands seized him and tossed him to the side. Ezra's ribs hit the gate, and he stumbled. This time he did not fall. The gray boy was strong and did not move.

"Get out of the way," said Ezra. "The sheep are running."

The gray boy's mouth opened, and his tongue snaked out slowly. The snow blew between them.

Ezra turned and ran back up the hill, calling Jesse's name. He did not know what was happening.

The gray boy kept pace with him.

Ezra was amazed. Even with the limp, the gray boy ran at his speed.

The gray boy took Ezra's arms and began to steer him.

"Jesse!" hollered Ezra.

He fell to his knees so he would not be led. The gray boy stopped and dragged him across the ground. Ezra struggled, but the gray boy had him; Ezra's face scraped over frost and stone.

They were headed for the hut. Snow slanted across Ezra's eyes. He did not have a lantern, and it was almost dark.

They reached the hut. Ezra jammed his leg against the stone wall. The gray boy threw Ezra into the darkness.

Ezra yelled for help. He called for Jesse and Esther and for his father.

The gray boy said, "Your father asked me to do this. He wishes you to learn. You hurt him." He slammed the wooden door, and the latch fell into place. "I am the boy he always wanted. I am not afraid."

"Let me be," demanded Ezra.

"Prayer brought me," said the boy. "And Victory."

Ezra was alone in the shed. The wind blew between the stones.

He called his brother's name. The gale from the mountains was huge, however, much vaster than his breath. He could feel the weight of the falling snow.

He heard the scrape of the gray boy's limp, circling the hut.

He backed against the wall next to the door. If the gray boy came in, he would offer an ambush. But now he could not hear any movement outside, other than the wind.

He stood alone in the hut. The snow fell over the mountains.

He wished to relax his arms, but he could not, because the cold was so heavy all around him. The air felt thick like water.

After a time, he squatted. He drew his knees up to his chest, hoping in that way to keep some of his heat clutched to him.

He did not know when his family would come for him. He did not know if they would come at all. The gray boy may have spoken the truth: his father might be sitting grimly in the house, waiting for a lesson to be learned out in the sheep shed.

Ezra beat on the old door. The door was so unfair, he could not conceive of it as solid. He rammed his shoulder against it. It did not yield.

Snow, he knew, was now piling on the other side of the door. He battered the planks and screamed. Nothing stirred. No one came.

After a while, he sat again. His senses were of no use to him.

He did not trust the darkness. Anything could be in the darkness. He imagined the arms that his father had seen stacked; he imagined revenants that sought their arms. They could be looking with eyes of accusation at the son of the traitor. They hung trailing around him. He thought he felt them. He did not fear ghostly retribution; but he feared the weight of their sadness, the infinite sadness that comes of an infinite blank and them dead forever.

The darkness seemed many-handed, groping.

He squatted near the door. He pressed his fingers between his thighs to keep them warm. He wrapped them together as fists.

Later, he breathed upon them.

He felt that time had smeared. He could no longer reckon by hours.

He remained in one place. He altered his squat. He hunkered.

He had seen men with frostbite. There was a man who lived in the next village whose face was a mask and whose hands were lopped stumps, pollarded like trees, cut back to the branch.

Ezra shook out his hands, hoping to unsettle the ice in them. He could not feel much. His breath itself was getting cold.

He sat immobile.

He imagined the gray boy standing with his father on the field of battle. He imagined his father and mother taking in the gray boy as their own son. He imagined himself dead, wandering through the frozen pastures with snow blown through his face and his chest and his legs, and he watched the new family labor in the barn, which did not seem to be his. He pictured the gray boy in his place growing old.

After some time, the world no longer rendered meaning to him. He thought about the house and the fireplace in the house, but there no longer seemed to be a difference between one thing and another thing. He could not tell the difference between the house and the hearth and the fire. They seemed to be of one substance. He knew that there was a difference between touching the stone of the fireplace and touching the fire itself, but it seemed to him, everything burned to the touch. The ground beneath him burned. The walls burned.

The sky burned, as it was said it would burn in the hour of Last Things.

The snow came down out of the sky upon him. He could see nothing.

He heard his father call, "I will search the shed!"

Ezra made a noise that he thought would identify him.

He heard his father call his name. His father was by the door.

There was a voice from down the hill. It was the gray boy. "I cannot climb there on my own. Come lift me, sir."

Ezra made a noise, but it was too soft.

"Up here," said his father.

"I cannot walk there," said the gray boy. "But that was not the way he ran. He ran toward the mountains."

Ezra turned to his side and tried slapping the planks of the door. His hands were not solid. The cold had melted them.

"Come down this path," said the gray boy. "I am not mistaken. I saw him light out for the hills."

Ezra was terrified by his own silence. The father was hesitating; not opening the door. The father was going to remove himself.

Ezra swayed his body. He pictured his father in the cart; his own leaping joy at the sight of his father; the desire to touch the man again, simply to touch him, and know him real.

Ezra slammed his head into the door.

"I'll be down," said the father, "soon as I check the shed."

"He ran off to the mountain," said the gray boy, "reviling you as he ran."

Ezra battered the door with his blunt and senseless palms.

"You hear . . . ?"

"I heard he called you coward."

"So he may have," said the father.

"Follow me," said the gray boy.

"You lie," said the father outside the door, suddenly sounding certain. "I know you lie."

And Ezra, seeing the father smile in the cart, smile to be home, beat at the door with his limbs.

He no longer knew what he saw.

Light—he knew that—and the hands reaching out to take him.

There was snow all around him, white and gentle as it fell.

The mother; the father. Victory was there, and Prayer. Out of all their mouths came scrolls, unfurled commentary, but he could not read. Jesse's scroll was golden.

The snow fell over the pastures, and a family was together in the night. Everyone pointed at things that meant so much to him; his own face, among them.

They hugged him. They cried. They had been searching the way to the mountains for hours.

They lifted him up and carried him.

In the sky above the valley and the mountains an eagle flew with yellow eyes, and its talons dragged the legend and the compass rose through the storm.

In the morning, Ezra awoke to find he could not see. He reached up and touched a blindfold. He was lying next to the fire. He fumbled in the grit around him.

"Rest," said his mother. "The angels put the blindfolds on you and your father while you were asleep. They're gone."

Ezra sat up.

"Sad you didn't get the fangs instead," said Jesse. "You could've opened oysters with your mouth."

Blindfolded, Ezra and his father ate a slow breakfast together at the table. When Ezra felt his father reaching for the ewer, he reached out his own hand and took his father's wrist. His father paused, then patted his son's arm. For a long time, they remained like that.

Ezra's father asked, "Is he smiling?"

"Neither of you's smiling," said Ezra's mother. She laughed and touched the father's cheek.

"Where's the gray boy?" Ezra asked.

"Up in the sheep shed," said Jesse. "He says he won't come down. He says people don't understand how hard it is to live with a leg like his."

After breakfast, father and son went out into the dooryard together. They moved slowly, with their hands outstretched. Together, father and son felt their way across the snow. They touched rock wall and empty hayrick. They ran their fingers across the wood of the barn.

They could feel the sun on their faces.

They spent the long morning after that snowfall together, stumbling, catching each other's arms; and they thanked God for the blindfolds upon them, which hid, so they might see all anew.

CATHERYNNE M. VALENTE

The Seven Devils of Central California

Catherynne M. Valente is a prolific writer whose dense and recursive poetry and prose can be found in The Journal of Mythic Arts, Clarkesworld Magazine, Jabberwocky, Lone Star Stories, Fantasy Magazine, Interfictions, The Book of Voices, *and* Salon Fantastique, *among other magazines and anthologies. Her story "Urchins, While Swimming" received the Million Writers Award for best online short fiction in 2006 and her novel* The Orphan's Tales: In the Night Garden *received the James Tiptree, Jr. Award. "The Seven Devils of Central California" appeared in the Summer issue of the relatively new Web site* Farrago's Wainscot. *Valente lives in Cleveland, Ohio.*

—K. L. & G. G.

I. The Devil of Diverted Rivers

Put out your tongue:
I taste of salt. Salt and sage
and silt—
dry am I, dry as delving.

My fingers come up
through the dead sacrament-dirt;
my spine humps along the San Joaquin—
remember me here, where water was
before Los Angeles scowled through,
hills blasted black
by the electric hairs of my forearms.

Pull the skin from my back and there is gold there,
a second skeleton,
carapace smeared to glitter in the skull-white sun.
There is a girl sitting there
between the nugget-vertebrae
who came all the way from Boston
when her daddy hollered Archimedes' old refrain—

Eureka, baby, eureka, little lamb,
I'll have you a golden horse
and a golden brother
and golden ribbons for your golden hair,
just you pack up your mama and come on over Colorado,
not so far, not so.

They flooded out her daddy's valley
when she was seventeen
and skinny as a fork.
Crouched down she was,
rooting potatoes out of the ground,
brushing beetles from her apron,
and the wind sounded like an old Boston train.

I am waiting for you to stop in your thrum,
for you to pause and look toward Nevada:
I am holding back the waters
with the blue muscles of my calves,
waiting for you.
All the way down to the sea,
one of these mornings bright as windows,
I'll come running like a girl
chasing golden apples.

I deny you, says the city below.
I deny you, says the dry riverbed, full of bones.
I deny you, say the mute, fed fields far off from the sea.

II. The Devil of Imported Brides

Look here: my fingernails show through
the lace and dried orange blossoms of a dress
I never wore.

You can see them up on the ridgeline like a fence
severed by earthquake:
yellow and ridged, screw-spiraled, broken,
brown moons muddy and dim.

The roots of the Sierras are blue and white:
the colors of stamped letters, posted,
flapping over the desert like rag-winged vultures,
gluey nose pointed east. All around the peaks
the clack of telegraphs echo
like woodpeckers:

Would like a blonde, but not particular.
Must be Norwegian or Swede, no Germans.
Intact Irish wanted,
must cook better than the ranch hands.
Don't care if she's ugly enough

to scare the chickens
out of their feathers,
but if she ain't brood-ready,
she goes right back to Connecticut
or the second circle of hell
or wherever it is
spit her out.

Look here: my horns spike up sulfurous through
a veil like mist on the fence posts. My tail rips the lace;
thumps black on the floor of an empty silver mine.
Never was a canary in the dark
with a yellow like my eyes. Sitting
in the cat-slit pupil with her bill of sale
stuffed in her mouth—

Why, hullo, Molly! Doesn't your hair look nice!
If you glisten it up enough
he'll be sure to love you real and true,
not for the silver nuggets you pull out of the rock
like balls from the Christmas box,
not for the crease-eyed boys he pulls from you
like silver nuggets, but for the mole on your little calf,
and the last lingering tilt to your voice,
that remembers Galway.

It was the seventh babe killed her,
and I sat up in her bloody bed,
orange blossoms dead on the pillow,
the clacking of brass-knockered codes
so loud in my ears
I flew down to the mine,
deeper than delving,
just for silence.

It is cold down here,
what silver is left
gnarls and jangles.
I put my hands up through the mountains
like old gloves with their fingers torn,
and wait.

I deny you, says the father of seven, bundled against the stove.
I deny you, says the silver, hanging in the earth
like a great chandelier.
I deny you, say the mountain towns, minding their own.

III. The Devil of Fruit Pickers

Strawberries and nickels
and the sun high as God's hat.
My old callused feet stamp down

the green vines and leaves of Fresno,
my throat of bone whistling still
for water.

My wings are tangled in grapevine
and orange-bark,
pearwood and raw almonds,
green skin prickles my shoulder blades,
lime-flesh and rice-reeds,
soybean pods and oh,
the dead-leaved corn. I can hardly fly
these days.

But I burrow, and stamp,
and how the radishes go up in my path.

Between the wings rides Maria,
born in Guadalajara with strong flat feet,
fishy little mouth scooped clean
by her father with fingers like St. Stephen.
This was before the war, of course.
Her black hair flies coarse as broom-bramble,
bags of oranges belted at her waist,
singing while I dance, riding me like her own
sweat-flanked horse.

She saved her nickels, and picked her berries,
bent over,
bent over,
bent over in the fields till her back was bowed
into the shape of an apple-sack,
and nothing in her but white seeds and sunburn.

She curled up into me,
dry as an old peapod,
and how we ride now,
biding our time,
over the dust and cows,
over all her nickels in a neat bank-row.

Watch our furrows, how we draw them,
careful as surveyors,
careful as corn-rows.

I deny you, say the strawberries, tucked tight into green.
I deny you, say the irrigation ditches, glimmering gold.
I deny you, say the nickels, spent into air.

IV. The Devil of Gold Flake

My hair runs underneath the rivers,
gold peeling from my scalp. I remember
the taste of a thousand rusted pans

pulling out ore like fingernails at the quick.
I lie everywhere;
I point at the sea.

All along my torso are broken mines,
like buttons on a dress. The state built
a highway through them,
a gray rod to straighten my back. The driller-shacks
shudder dusty and brown,
slung with wind-axes and bone-bowls:
my stomach dreams of the ghosts of gold.

They suck at my skin,
hoping for a last gurgle of metal,
tipping in for the final bracelet and brick—
there must be something left in me,
there must be something—why do I not give it to them,
selfish creature, wretched mossy beast?

Underneath the deepest drill
hunches Annabella, the miner's wife,
who sifted more gold
than her coarse-coated man,
so deft and delicate were her fingers
round that old, beaten pan. He brought her
from St. Louis, already pregnant—and manners
make no comment there—already heavy with gold.
She smelled of the Mississippi
and steam-fat oatmeal cakes,
even after the oxen died, and with blood in her hair,
she crossed half of Wyoming on foot.

But the boulders loved her,
watched her every day from a high blue perch.
They wriggled at her, her yellow dress
gone brown with creek-silt, her bustle
and wire hoops collapsed on the grass.
While she knelt with gold in her knuckles,
they snapped to attention,
slid laughing to the creek-bed—she doesn't blame
the poor things, even now.
Her babies left cabbages and peppermints
at the creek for years after.

I felt the highway roll smooth and hot
over my ox-drenched head,
and the only gold I allowed to ooze up from my scalp
were the broken dashes marking lanes
like borders on an old map
showing a river like a great hand flattening the page.

But I confess:
I am an old wretched beast, and my tail,

waiting in the spangled dust,
is made of quartz-shot boulders
clapped in moss.

I deny you, say the desiccated lodes.
I deny you, say our great-grandchildren, with such clean hands.
I deny you, says the highway, blithe and black.

V. The Devil of Mine Canaries

Watch the sun peek out over the Siskiyous
with their lavish snow like ladies' bonnets—
see my feathers, how bright, how brave!
I open my wings over the thin green
boyish arms of the Russian River,
yellow as sulfur, yellow as gas,
wide as any Italian angel.

What is a devil
but death and wind?
I come golden as a mine shaft,
and how black, how ever black,
come my eyes!

Who remembers where they got the songbirds?
Bought from Mexico, from Baja with shores
like sighs? They got the cages
out of their wives' bustles, wrangled
to hand and wing. *Pretty bird, pretty bird!*
Don't be afraid of the dark.

Yella-Girl loved her miner, thought
her black demon,
white eyes showing clam-shy through the dust,
was the greatest raven born since Eden.
She pecked cornmeal from his palm,
stood guard at his bedknob,
little golden sentinel. She'd draw the gold
for him, she thought, like to like.

For birds, the angry gases
have a strange color:
pink, almost pretty (Pretty bird, pretty bird!)
curling up from the dark like beckoning.
Yella-Girl seized up in mid-stroke,
falling onto a carpet of jaundiced feathers
half a leg deep. She fell thinking
of her miner, of corn in his black hand,
and I stood up
out of the canary-grave,
body crawling with pretty, pretty birds,

beaks turned out
like knives.

I deny you, says the buried mine, long stopped up.
I deny you, say the crows, too big to tame.
I deny you, says the miner, a new bird swinging at his side like a lunchbox.

VI. The Devil of Acorn Mash

I am hard to see.
You will have to look carefully.

Carefully down,
at your well-shod feet
to see the shallows in the rock,
where she and her son,
light beating their black hair like blankets,
worked rough-husked black oak acorns
into mash and meal,
bread and pancakes.
Like horse hooves driven into
the granite, the hollows still breathe.

These are my footprints.
I have already passed this way
and gone.

I deny you, says the forest, full again.
I deny you, say endless feet.
I deny you, says the treeless plain, flat and brown.

VII. The Devil of the Railroad

If I just try, I can taste bitter tang
of the golden tie bent over my toe
somewhere in Kansas,
like the memory of licking clean a copper plate.

But here at my head,
between the Santa Lucias and two crescent bays,
ribboned and rawboned, bonneted in iron,
coal-shod and steam-breathed, I taste
corn-freight and cattle, pallets of tomatoes
and stainless-steel screwdrivers, and there, behind my tongue,
the phosphorescent traces
of silver forks and weak tea shaking on linen,
burning the air where they no longer
drink themselves down to calm nerves like baling wire,
to spear Pacific salmon before the conductor ever sighted blue.

Out of the slat-cars come thousands of horns,
honest black and brown,

bull-thick, tossing in the heat.
In the slick, wet turn of my silver-steel against the rail
Li-Qin sings a little song, full of round golden vowels.
She wore gray shapeless things, hammering ties,
taking her tooth-shattering turn at the drill,
laying rail with bloody, sun-smashed hands
while the pin against wood sounded her name over and over
like a command to attention:
Li-Qin, Li-Qin, Li-Qin!
She had tea from thrice-used bags
and a half bowl of rice at the end of the day,
one grain of sugar dissolving in her cup
like snow.

With her hair bound back she plied the drill
until it slipped like splashed water,
hammered into her heart,
laying track for the train to bellow through her,
bloodred as cinnabar on the wooden stays.

There is a car swinging back and forth
between a shipment of umbrellas to San Francisco
and swordfish packed in ice for Santa Barbara.
I have such a tail, you know, enough to bring them all
from the mountains and the sea.
With silver forks and weak tea
they sit at a long table with a cloth of cobwebs,
clinking their cups as I rattle them through the desert:

a Boston goblin with drowned lips violet,
a bridal imp, her veil torn and burning,
a gnomish grandmother,
sucking tea through slices of strawberries,
an old, wretched, bustleless beast, smug as a river,
a yellow bird, brimstone-wings folded around
a little urchin in deerskin, her hands full of acorns,
and a demon in gray with a huge flayed heart
hanging in her breast like a pendant.

I brought them on my tail,
my endless black tail,
like a dragon out of books older than any of us,
I brought them like freight,
like wagons,
like horses,

and we are coming to dance on the shore
by the great golden bridge,
we are coming to remember ourselves
to the tide,
to sing at the moon until it cracks,
to stamp our hooves under so many crinoline dresses,

to stamp our hooves under so many rags,
to stamp our hooves on the earth like pickaxes,
and sunder California along every wrinkle,
send her gleaming
into the sea.

I deny you, shudders the sky, whole and inviolate.
I deny you, whispers the unwilling sea.
I deny you, trembles the fault line.

The sun dips deep into salt and foam,
and a long engine whistle
breaks the blue
into seven pieces.

TED CHIANG

The Merchant and the Alchemist's Gate

Ted Chiang's science fiction short stories have won the Hugo Award, three Nebulas, the Campbell Award, the Sturgeon Award, and two Locus Awards, among others. "The Merchant and the Alchemist's Gate" originally appeared in The Magazine of Fantasy & Science Fiction, *and has also been published in a limited edition by Subterranean Press. Chiang lives in Bellevue, Washington.*

—K. L. & G. G.

O mighty Caliph and Commander of the Faithful, I am humbled to be in the splendor of your presence; a man can hope for no greater blessing as long as he lives. The story I have to tell is truly a strange one, and were the entirety to be tattooed at the corner of one's eye, the marvel of its presentation would not exceed that of the events recounted, for it is a warning to those who would be warned and a lesson to those who would learn.

My name is Fuwaad ibn Abbas, and I was born here in Baghdad, City of Peace. My father was a grain merchant, but for much of my life I have worked as a purveyor of fine fabrics, trading in silk from Damascus and linen from Egypt and scarves from Morocco that are embroidered with gold. I was prosperous, but my heart was troubled, and neither the purchase of luxuries nor the giving of alms was able to soothe it. Now I stand before you without a single dirham in my purse, but I am at peace.

Allah is the beginning of all things, but with Your Majesty's permission, I begin my story with the day I took a walk through the district of metalsmiths. I needed to purchase a gift for a man I had to do business with, and had been told he might appreciate a tray made of silver. After browsing for half an hour, I noticed that one of the largest shops in the market had been taken over by a new merchant. It was a prized location that must have been expensive to acquire, so I entered to peruse its wares.

Never before had I seen such a marvelous assortment of goods. Near the entrance there was an astrolabe equipped with seven plates inlaid with silver, a water clock that chimed on the hour, and a nightingale made of brass that sang when the wind blew. Farther inside there were even more ingenious mechanisms, and I stared at them the way a child watches a juggler, when an old man stepped out from a doorway in the back.

"Welcome to my humble shop, my lord," he said. "My name is Bashaarat. How may I assist you?"

"These are remarkable items that you have for sale. I deal with traders from every corner of the world, and yet I have never seen their like. From where, may I ask, did you acquire your merchandise?"

"I am grateful to you for your kind words," he said. "Everything you see here was made in my workshop, by myself or by my assistants under my direction."

I was impressed that this man could be so well versed in so many arts. I asked him about the various instruments in his shop, and listened to him discourse learnedly about astrology, mathematics, geomancy, and medicine. We spoke for over an hour, and my fascination and respect bloomed like a flower warmed by the dawn, until he mentioned his experiments in alchemy.

"Alchemy?" I said. This surprised me, for he did not seem the type to make such a sharper's claim. "You mean you can turn base metal into gold?"

"I can, my lord, but that is not in fact what most seek from alchemy."

"What do most seek, then?"

"They seek a source of gold that is cheaper than mining ore from the ground. Alchemy does describe a means to make gold, but the procedure is so arduous that, by comparison, digging beneath a mountain is as easy as plucking peaches from a tree."

I smiled. "A clever reply. No one could dispute that you are a learned man, but I know better than to credit alchemy."

Bashaarat looked at me and considered. "I have recently built something that may change your opinion. You would be the first person I have shown it to. Would you care to see it?"

"It would be a great pleasure."

"Please follow me." He led me through the doorway in the rear of his shop. The next room was a workshop, arrayed with devices whose functions I could not guess—bars of metal wrapped with enough copper thread to reach the horizon, mirrors mounted on a circular slab of granite floating in quicksilver—but Bashaarat walked past these without a glance.

Instead he led me to a sturdy pedestal, chest high, on which a stout metal hoop was mounted upright. The hoop's opening was as wide as two outstretched hands, and its rim so thick that it would tax the strongest man to carry. The metal was black as night, but polished to such smoothness that had it been a different color, it could have served as a mirror. Bashaarat bade me stand so that I looked upon the hoop edgewise, while he stood next to its opening.

"Please observe," he said.

Bashaarat thrust his arm through the hoop from the right side, but it did not extend out from the left. Instead, it was as if his arm were severed at the elbow, and he waved the stump up and down, and then pulled his arm out intact.

I had not expected to see such a learned man perform a conjuror's trick, but it was well done, and I applauded politely.

"Now wait a moment," he said as he took a step back.

I waited, and behold, an arm reached out of the hoop from its left side, without a body to hold it up. The sleeve it wore matched Bashaarat's robe. The arm waved up and down, and then retreated through the hoop until it was gone.

The first trick I had thought a clever mime, but this one seemed far superior, because the pedestal and hoop were clearly too slender to conceal a person. "Very clever!" I exclaimed.

"Thank you, but this is not mere sleight of hand. The right side of the hoop precedes the left by several seconds. To pass through the hoop is to cross that duration instantly."

"I do not understand," I said.

"Let me repeat the demonstration." Again he thrust his arm through the hoop, and his arm disappeared. He smiled, and pulled back and forth as if playing tug-a-rope. Then he pulled his arm out again, and presented his hand to me with the palm open. On it lay a ring I recognized.

"That is my ring!" I checked my hand, and saw that my ring still lay on my finger. "You have conjured up a duplicate."

"No, this is truly your ring. Wait."

Again, an arm reached out from the left side. Wishing to discover the mechanism of the trick, I rushed over to grab it by the hand. It was not a false hand, but one fully warm and alive as mine. I pulled on it, and it pulled back. Then, as deft as a pickpocket, the hand slipped the ring from my finger and the arm withdrew into the hoop, vanishing completely.

"My ring is gone!" I exclaimed.

"No, my lord," he said. "Your ring is here." And he gave me the ring he held. "Forgive me for my game."

I replaced it on my finger. "You had the ring before it was taken from me."

At that moment an arm reached out, this time from the right side of the hoop. "What is this?" I exclaimed. Again I recognized it as his by the sleeve before it withdrew, but I had not seen him reach in.

"Recall," he said, "the right side of the hoop precedes the left." And he walked over to the left side of the hoop, and thrust his arm through from that side, and again it disappeared.

Your Majesty has undoubtedly already grasped this, but it was only then that I understood: whatever happened on the right side of the hoop was complemented, a few seconds later, by an event on the left side. "Is this sorcery?" I asked.

"No, my lord, I have never met a djinni, and if I did, I would not trust it to do my bidding. This is a form of alchemy."

He offered an explanation, speaking of his search for tiny pores in the skin of reality, like the holes that worms bore into wood, and how upon finding one he was able to expand and stretch it the way a glassblower turns a dollop of molten glass into a long-necked pipe, and how he then allowed time to flow like water at one mouth while causing it to thicken like syrup at the other. I confess I did not really understand his words, and cannot testify to their truth. All I could say in response was, "You have created something truly astonishing."

"Thank you," he said, "but this is merely a prelude to what I intended to show you." He bade me follow him into another room, farther in the back. There stood a circular doorway whose massive frame was made of the same polished black metal, mounted in the middle of the room.

"What I showed you before was a Gate of Seconds," he said. "This is a Gate of Years. The two sides of the doorway are separated by a span of twenty years."

I confess I did not understand his remark immediately. I imagined him reaching his arm in from the right side and waiting twenty years before it emerged from the left side, and it seemed a very obscure magic trick. I said as much, and he laughed. "That is one use for it," he said, "but consider what would happen if you were to step through." Standing on the right side, he gestured for me to come closer, and then pointed through the doorway. "Look."

I looked, and saw that there appeared to be different rugs and pillows on the other side of the room than I had seen when I had entered. I moved my head from side to side, and realized that when I peered through the doorway, I was looking at a different room from the one I stood in.

"You are seeing the room twenty years from now," said Bashaarat.

I blinked, as one might at an illusion of water in the desert, but what I saw did not change. "And you say I could step through?" I asked.

"You could. And with that step, you would visit the Baghdad of twenty years hence. You could seek out your older self and have a conversation with him. Afterward, you could step back through the Gate of Years and return to the present day."

Hearing Bashaarat's words, I felt as if I were reeling. "You have done this?" I asked him. "You have stepped through?"

"I have, and so have numerous customers of mine."

"Earlier you said I was the first to whom you showed this."

"This Gate, yes. But for many years I owned a shop in Cairo, and it was there that I first built a Gate of Years. There were many to whom I showed that Gate, and who made use of it."

"What did they learn when talking to their older selves?"

"Each person learns something different. If you wish, I can tell you the story of one such person."

Bashaarat proceeded to tell me such a story, and if it pleases Your Majesty, I will recount it here.

The Tale of the Fortunate Rope-Maker

There once was a young man named Hassan who was a maker of rope. He stepped through the Gate of Years to see the Cairo of twenty years later, and upon arriving he marveled at how the city had grown. He felt as if he had stepped into a scene embroidered on a tapestry, and even though the city was no more and no less than Cairo, he looked upon the most common sights as objects of wonder.

He was wandering by the Zuweila Gate, where the sword dancers and snake charmers perform, when an astrologer called to him. "Young man! Do you wish to know the future?"

Hassan laughed. "I know it already," he said.

"Surely you want to know if wealth awaits you, do you not?"

"I am a rope-maker. I know that it does not."

"Can you be so sure? What about the renowned merchant Hassan al-Hubbaul, who began as a rope-maker?"

His curiosity aroused, Hassan asked around the market for others who knew of this wealthy merchant, and found that the name was well known. It was said he lived in the wealthy Habbaniya quarter of the city, so Hassan walked there and asked people to point out his house, which turned out to be the largest one on its street.

He knocked at the door, and a servant led him to a spacious and well-appointed hall with a fountain in the center. Hassan waited while the servant went to fetch his master, but as he looked at the polished ebony and marble around him, he felt that he did not belong in such surroundings, and was about to leave when his older self appeared.

"At last you are here!" the man said. "I have been expecting you!"

"You have?" said Hassan, astounded.

"Of course, because I visited my older self just as you are visiting me. It has been so long that I had forgotten the exact day. Come, dine with me."

The two went to a dining room, where servants brought chicken stuffed with pistachio nuts, fritters soaked in honey, and roast lamb with spiced pomegranates. The older Hassan gave few details of his life: he mentioned business interests of many varieties, but did not say how he had become a merchant; he mentioned a wife, but said it was not time for the younger man to meet her. Instead, he asked young Hassan to remind him of the pranks he had played as a child, and he laughed to hear stories that had faded from his own memory.

At last the younger Hassan asked the older, "How did you make such great changes in your fortune?"

"All I will tell you right now is this: when you go to buy hemp from the market, and you are walking along the Street of Black Dogs, do not walk along the south side as you usually do. Walk along the north."

"And that will enable me to raise my station?"

"Just do as I say. Go back home now; you have rope to make. You will know when to visit me again."

Young Hassan returned to his day and did as he was instructed, keeping to the north side of the street even when there was no shade there. It was a few days later that he witnessed a maddened horse run amok on the south side of the street directly opposite him, kicking several people, injuring another by knocking a heavy jug of palm oil onto him, and even trampling one person under its hooves. After the commotion had subsided, Hassan prayed to Allah for the injured to be healed and the dead to be at peace, and thanked Allah for sparing him.

The next day Hassan stepped through the Gate of Years and sought out his older self.

"Were you injured by the horse when you walked by?" he asked him.

"No, because I heeded my older self's warning. Do not forget, you and I are one; every circumstance that befalls you once befell me."

And so the elder Hassan gave the younger instructions, and the younger obeyed them. He refrained from buying eggs from his usual grocer, and thus avoided the illness that struck customers who bought eggs from a spoiled basket. He bought extra hemp, and thus had material to work with when others suffered a shortage due to a delayed caravan.

Following his older self's instructions spared Hassan many troubles, but he wondered why his older self would not tell him more. Who would he marry? How would he become wealthy?

Then one day, after having sold all his rope in the market and carrying an unusually full purse, Hassan bumped into a boy while walking on the street. He felt for his purse, discovered it missing, and turned around with a shout to search the crowd for the pickpocket. Hearing Hassan's cry, the boy immediately began running through the crowd. Hassan saw that the boy's tunic was torn at the elbow, but then quickly lost sight of him.

For a moment Hassan was shocked that this could happen with no warning from his older self. But his surprise was soon replaced by anger, and he gave chase. He ran through the crowd, checking the elbows of boys' tunics, until by chance he found the pickpocket crouching beneath a fruit wagon. Hassan grabbed him and began shouting to all that he had caught a thief, asking them to find a guardsman. The boy, afraid of arrest, dropped Hassan's purse and began weeping. Hassan stared at the boy for a long moment, and then his anger faded, and he let him go.

When next he saw his older self, Hassan asked him, "Why did you not warn me about the pickpocket?"

"Did you not enjoy the experience?" asked his older self.

Hassan was about to deny it, but stopped himself. "I did enjoy it," he admitted. In pursuing the boy, with no hint of whether he'd succeed or fail, he had felt his blood surge in a way it had not for many weeks. And seeing the boy's tears had reminded him of the Prophet's teachings on the value of mercy, and Hassan had felt virtuous in choosing to let the boy go.

"Would you rather I had denied you that, then?"

Just as we grow to understand the purpose of customs that seemed pointless to us in our youth, Hassan realized that there was merit in withholding information as well as in disclosing it. "No," he said, "it was good that you did not warn me."

The older Hassan saw that he had understood. "Now I will tell you something very important. Hire a horse. I will give you directions to a spot in the foothills to the west of the city. There you will find within a grove of trees one that was struck by lightning. Around the base of the tree, look for the heaviest rock you can overturn, and then dig beneath it."

"What should I look for?"

"You will know when you find it."

The next day Hassan rode out to the foothills and searched until he found the tree. The ground around it was covered in rocks, so Hassan overturned one to dig beneath it, and then another, and then another. At last his spade struck something besides rock and soil. He cleared aside the soil and discovered a bronze chest, filled with gold dinars and assorted jewelry. Hassan had never seen its like in all his life. He loaded the chest onto the horse and rode back to Cairo.

The next time he spoke to his older self, he asked, "How did you know where the treasure was?"

"I learned it from myself," said the older Hassan, "just as you did. As to how we came to know its location, I have no explanation except that it was the will of Allah, and what other explanation is there for anything?"

"I swear I shall make good use of these riches that Allah has blessed me with," said the younger Hassan.

"And I renew that oath," said the older. "This is the last time we shall speak. You will find your own way now. Peace be upon you."

And so Hassan returned home. With the gold he was able to purchase hemp in great quantity, and hire workmen and pay them a fair wage, and sell rope profitably to all who sought it. He married a beautiful and clever woman, at whose advice he began trading in other goods, until he was a wealthy and respected merchant. All the while he gave generously to the poor and lived as an upright man. In this way Hassan lived the happiest of lives until he was overtaken by death, breaker of ties and destroyer of delights.

"That is a remarkable story," I said. "For someone who is debating whether to make use of the Gate, there could hardly be a better inducement."

"You are wise to be skeptical," said Bashaarat. "Allah rewards those he wishes to reward and chastises those he wishes to chastise. The Gate does not change how he regards you."

I nodded, thinking I understood. "So even if you succeed in avoiding the misfortunes that your older self experienced, there is no assurance you will not encounter other misfortunes."

"No, forgive an old man for being unclear. Using the Gate is not like drawing lots, where the token you select varies with each turn. Rather, using the Gate is like taking a secret passageway in a palace, one that lets you enter a room more quickly than by walking down the hallway. The room remains the same, no matter which door you use to enter."

This surprised me. "The future is fixed then? As unchangeable as the past?"

"It is said that repentance and atonement erase the past."

"I have heard that too, but I have not found it to be true."

"I am sorry to hear that," said Bashaarat. "All I can say is that the future is no different."

I thought on this for a while. "So if you learn that you are dead twenty years from now, there is nothing you can do to avoid your death?" He nodded. This seemed to me very disheartening, but then I wondered if it could not also provide a guarantee. I said, "Suppose you learn that you are alive twenty years from now. Then nothing could kill you in the next twenty years. You could then fight in battles without a care, because your survival is assured."

"That is possible," he said. "It is also possible that a man who would make use of such a guarantee would not find his older self alive when he first used the Gate."

"Ah," I said. "Is it then the case that only the prudent meet their older selves?"

"Let me tell you the story of another person who used the Gate, and you can decide for yourself if he was prudent or not."

Bashaarat proceeded to tell me the story, and if it pleases Your Majesty, I will recount it here.

The Tale of the Weaver Who Stole from Himself

There was a young weaver named Ajib who made a modest living as a weaver of rugs, but yearned to taste the luxuries enjoyed by the wealthy. After hearing the story of Hassan, Ajib immediately stepped through the Gate of Years to seek out his older self, who, he was sure, would be as rich and as generous as the older Hassan.

Upon arriving in the Cairo of twenty years later, he proceeded to the wealthy Habbaniya quarter of the city and asked people for the residence of Ajib ibn Taher. He was prepared, if he met someone who knew the man and remarked on the similarity of their features, to identify himself as Ajib's son, newly arrived from Damascus. But he never had the chance to offer this story, because no one he asked recognized the name.

Eventually he decided to return to his old neighborhood, to see if anyone there knew where he had moved to. When he got to his old street, he stopped a boy and asked him if he knew where to find a man named Ajib. The boy directed him to Ajib's old house.

"That is where he used to live," Ajib said. "Where does he live now?"

"If he has moved since yesterday, I do not know where," said the boy.

Ajib was incredulous. Could his older self still live in the same house, twenty years later? That would mean he had never become wealthy, and his older self would have no advice to give him, or at least none Ajib would profit by following. How could his fate differ so much from that of the fortunate rope-maker? In hopes that the boy was mistaken, Ajib waited outside the house and watched.

Eventually he saw a man leave the house, and with a sinking heart recognized it as his older self. The older Ajib was followed by a woman that he presumed was his wife, but he scarcely noticed her, for all he could see was his own failure to have bettered himself. He stared with dismay at the plain clothes the older couple wore until they walked out of sight.

Driven by the curiosity that impels men to look at the heads of the executed, Ajib went to the door of his house. His own key still fit the lock, so he entered. The furnishings had changed, but were simple and worn, and Ajib was mortified to see them. After twenty years, could he not even afford better pillows?

On an impulse, he went to the wooden chest where he normally kept his savings, and unlocked it. He lifted the lid, and saw the chest was filled with gold dinars.

Ajib was astonished. His older self had a chest of gold, and yet he wore such plain clothes and lived in the same small house for twenty years! What a stingy, joyless man his older self must be, thought Ajib, to have wealth and not enjoy it. Ajib had long known that one could not take one's possessions to the grave. Could that be something that he would forget as he aged?

Ajib decided that such riches should belong to someone who appreciated them, and that was himself. To take his older self's wealth would not be stealing, he reasoned, because it was he himself who would receive it. He heaved the chest onto his shoulder, and with much effort was able to bring it back through the Gate of Years to the Cairo he knew.

He deposited some of his newfound wealth with a banker, but always carried a purse heavy with gold. He dressed in a Damascene robe and Cordovan slippers and a Khurasani turban bearing a jewel. He rented a house in the wealthy quarter, furnished it with the finest rugs and couches, and hired a cook to prepare him sumptuous meals.

He then sought out the brother of a woman he had long desired from afar, a woman named Taahira. Her brother was an apothecary, and Taahira assisted him in his shop. Ajib would occasionally purchase a remedy so that he might speak to her. Once he had seen her veil slip, and her eyes were as dark and beautiful as a gazelle's. Taahira's brother would not have consented to her marrying a weaver, but now Ajib could present himself as a favorable match.

Taahira's brother approved, and Taahira herself readily consented, for she had desired Ajib, too. Ajib spared no expense for their wedding. He hired one of the pleasure barges that floated in the canal south of the city and held a feast with musicians and dancers, at which he presented her with a magnificent pearl necklace. The celebration was the subject of gossip throughout the quarter.

Ajib reveled in the joy that money brought him and Taahira, and for a week the two of them lived the most delightful of lives. Then one day Ajib came home to find the door to his house broken open and the interior ransacked of all silver and gold items. The terrified cook emerged from hiding and told him that robbers had taken Taahira.

Ajib prayed to Allah until, exhausted with worry, he fell asleep. The next morning he was awoken by a knocking at his door. There was a stranger there. "I have a message for you," the man said.

"What message?" asked Ajib.

"Your wife is safe."

Ajib felt fear and rage churn in his stomach like black bile. "What ransom would you have?" he asked.

"Ten thousand dinars."

"That is more than all I possess!" Ajib exclaimed.

"Do not haggle with me," said the robber. "I have seen you spend money like others pour water."

Ajib dropped to his knees. "I have been wasteful. I swear by the name of the Prophet that I do not have that much," he said.

The robber looked at him closely. "Gather all the money you have," he said, "and have it here tomorrow at this same hour. If I believe you are holding back, your wife will die. If I believe you to be honest, my men will return her to you."

Ajib could see no other choice. "Agreed," he said, and the robber left.

The next day he went to the banker and withdrew all the money that remained. He gave it to the robber, who gauged the desperation in Ajib's eyes and was satisfied. The robber did as he promised, and that evening Taahira was returned.

After they had embraced, Taahira said, "I didn't believe you would pay so much money for me."

"I could not take pleasure in it without you," said Ajib, and he was surprised to realize it was true. "But now I regret that I cannot buy you what you deserve."

"You need never buy me anything again," she said.

Ajib bowed his head. "I feel as if I have been punished for my misdeeds."

"What misdeeds?" asked Taahira, but Ajib said nothing. "I did not ask you this before," she said. "But I know you did not inherit all the money you gained. Tell me: did you steal it?"

"No," said Ajib, unwilling to admit the truth to her or himself. "It was given to me."

"A loan, then?"

"No, it does not need to be repaid."

"And you don't wish to pay it back?" Taahira was shocked. "So you are content that this other man paid for our wedding? That he paid my ransom?" She seemed on the verge of tears. "Am I your wife then, or this other man's?"

"You are my wife," he said.

"How can I be, when my very life is owed to another?"

"I would not have you doubt my love," said Ajib. "I swear to you that I will pay back the money, to the last dirham."

And so Ajib and Taahira moved back into Ajib's old house and began saving their money. Both of them went to work for Taahira's brother the apothecary, and when he eventually became a perfumer to the wealthy, Ajib and Taahira took over the business of selling remedies to the ill. It was a good living, but they spent as little as they could, living modestly and repairing damaged furnishings instead of buying new. For years, Ajib smiled whenever he dropped a coin into the chest, telling Taahira that it was a reminder of how much he valued her. He would say that even after the chest was full, it would be a bargain.

But it is not easy to fill a chest by adding just a few coins at a time, and so what began as thrift gradually turned into miserliness, and prudent decisions were replaced by tight-fisted ones. Worse, Ajib's and Taahira's affections for each other faded over time, and each grew to resent the other for the money they could not spend.

In this manner the years passed and Ajib grew older, waiting for the second time that his gold would be taken from him.

"What a strange and sad story," I said.

"Indeed," said Bashaarat. "Would you say that Ajib acted prudently?"

I hesitated before speaking. "It is not my place to judge him," I said. "He must live with the consequences of his actions, just as I must live with mine." I was silent for a moment, and then said, "I admire Ajib's candor, that he told you everything he had done."

"Ah, but Ajib did not tell me of this as a young man," said Bashaarat. "After he emerged from the Gate carrying the chest, I did not see him again for another twenty years. Ajib was a much older man when he came to visit me again. He had come home and found his chest gone, and the knowledge that he had paid his debt made him feel he could tell me all that had transpired."

"Indeed? Did the older Hassan from your first story come to see you as well?"

"No, I heard Hassan's story from his younger self. The older Hassan never returned to my shop, but in his place I had a different visitor, one who shared a story about Hassan that he himself could never have told me." Bashaarat proceeded to tell me that visitor's story, and if it pleases Your Majesty, I will recount it here.

The Tale of the Wife and Her Lover

Raniya had been married to Hassan for many years, and they lived the happiest of lives. One day she saw her husband dine with a young man, whom she recognized as the very image of Hassan when she had first married him. So great was her astonishment that she could scarcely keep herself from intruding on their conversation. After the young man left, she demanded that Hassan tell her who he was, and Hassan related to her an incredible tale.

"Have you told him about me?" she asked. "Did you know what lay ahead of us when we first met?"

"I knew I would marry you from the moment I saw you," Hassan said, smiling, "but not because anyone had told me. Surely, wife, you would not wish to spoil that moment for him?"

So Raniya did not speak to her husband's younger self, but only eavesdropped on his conversation and stole glances at him. Her pulse quickened at the sight of his youthful features; sometimes our memories fool us with their sweetness, but when she beheld the two men seated opposite each other, she could see the fullness of the younger one's beauty without exaggeration. At night, she would lie awake, thinking of it.

Some days after Hassan had bid farewell to his younger self, he left Cairo to conduct business with a merchant in Damascus. In his absence Raniya found the shop that Hassan had described to her, and stepped through the Gate of Years to the Cairo of her youth.

She remembered where he had lived back then, and so was easily able to find the young Hassan and follow him. As she watched him, she felt a desire stronger than she had felt in years for the older Hassan, so vivid were her recollections of their youthful lovemaking. She had always been a loyal and faithful wife, but here was an opportunity that would never be available again. Resolving to act on this desire, Raniya rented a house, and in subsequent days bought furnishings for it.

Once the house was ready, she followed Hassan discreetly while she tried to gather enough boldness to approach him. In the jewelers' market, she watched as he went to a jeweler, showed him a necklace set with ten gemstones, and asked him how much he would pay for it. Raniya recognized it as one Hassan had given to her in the days after their wedding; she had not known he had once tried to sell it. She stood a short distance away and listened, pretending to look at some rings.

"Bring it back tomorrow, and I will pay you a thousand dinars," said the jeweler. Young Hassan agreed to the price and left.

As she watched him leave, Raniya overheard two men talking nearby.

"Did you see that necklace? It is one of ours."

"Are you certain?" asked the other.

"I am. That is the bastard who dug up our chest."

"Let us tell our captain about him. After this fellow has sold his necklace, we will take his money, and more."

The two men left without noticing Raniya, who stood with her heart racing but her body motionless, like a deer after a tiger has passed. She realized that the treasure Hassan had dug up must have belonged to a band of thieves, and these men were two of its members. They were now observing the jewelers of Cairo to identify the person who had taken their loot.

Raniya knew that since she possessed the necklace, the young Hassan could not have sold it. She also knew that the thieves could not have killed Hassan. But it could not be Allah's will for her to do nothing. Allah must have brought her here so that he might use her as his instrument.

Raniya returned to the Gate of Years, stepped through to her own day, and at her house found the necklace in her jewelry box. Then she used the Gate of Years again, but instead of entering it from the left side, she entered it from the right, so that she visited the Cairo of twenty years later. There she sought out her older self, now an aged woman. The older Raniya greeted her warmly, and retrieved the necklace from her own jewelry box. The two women then rehearsed how they would assist the young Hassan.

The next day, the two thieves were back with a third man, whom Raniya assumed was their captain. They all watched as Hassan presented the necklace to the jeweler.

As the jeweler examined it, Raniya walked up and said, "What a coincidence! Jeweler, I wish to sell a necklace just like that." She brought out her necklace from a purse she carried.

"This is remarkable," said the jeweler. "I have never seen two necklaces more similar."

Then the aged Raniya walked up. "What do I see? Surely my eyes deceive me!" And with that she brought out a third identical necklace. "The seller sold it to me with the promise that it was unique. This proves him a liar."

"Perhaps you should return it," said Raniya.

"That depends," said the aged Raniya. She asked Hassan, "How much is he paying you for it?"

"A thousand dinars," said Hassan, bewildered.

"Really! Jeweler, would you care to buy this one too?"

"I must reconsider my offer," said the jeweler.

While Hassan and the aged Raniya bargained with the jeweler, Raniya stepped back just far enough to hear the captain berate the other thieves. "You fools," he said. "It is a common necklace. You would have us kill half the jewelers in Cairo and bring the guardsmen down upon our heads." He slapped their heads and led them off.

Raniya returned her attention to the jeweler, who had withdrawn his offer to buy Hassan's necklace. The older Raniya said, "Very well. I will try to return it to the man who sold it to me." As the older woman left, Raniya could tell that she smiled beneath her veil.

Raniya turned to Hassan. "It appears that neither of us will sell a necklace today."

"Another day, perhaps," said Hassan.

"I shall take mine back to my house for safekeeping," said Raniya. "Would you walk with me?"

Hassan agreed, and walked with Raniya to the house she had rented. Then she invited him in, and offered him wine, and after they had both drunk some, she led him to her bedroom. She covered the windows with heavy curtains and extinguished all lamps so that the room was as dark as night. Only then did she remove her veil and take him to bed.

Raniya had been flush with anticipation for this moment, and so was surprised to find that Hassan's movements were clumsy and awkward. She remembered their wedding night very clearly; he had been confident, and his touch had taken her breath away. She knew Hassan's first meeting with the young Raniya was not far away, and for a moment did not understand how this fumbling boy could change so quickly. And then of course the answer was clear.

So every afternoon for many days, Raniya met Hassan at her rented house and instructed him in the art of love, and in doing so she demonstrated that, as is often said, women are Allah's most wondrous creation. She told him, "The pleasure you give is returned in the pleasure you receive," and inwardly she smiled as she thought of how true her words really were. Before long, he gained the expertise she remembered, and she took greater enjoyment in it than she had as a young woman.

All too soon, the day arrived when Raniya told the young Hassan that it was time for her to leave. He knew better than to press her for her reasons, but asked her if they might ever see each other again. She told her, gently, no. Then she sold the furnishings to the house's owner, and returned through the Gate of Years to the Cairo of her own day. When the older Hassan returned from his trip to Damascus, Raniya was home waiting for him. She greeted him warmly, but kept her secrets to herself.

I was lost in my own thoughts when Bashaarat finished this story, until he said, "I see that this story has intrigued you in a way the others did not."

"You see clearly," I admitted. "I realize now that even though the past is unchangeable, one may encounter the unexpected when visiting it."

"Indeed. Do you now understand why I say the future and the past are the same? We cannot change either, but we can know both more fully."

"I do understand; you have opened my eyes, and now I wish to use the Gate of Years. What price do you ask?"

He waved his hand. "I do not sell passage through the Gate," he said. "Allah guides whom he wishes to my shop, and I am content to be an instrument of his will."

Had it been another man, I would have taken his words to be a negotiating ploy, but after all that Bashaarat had told me, I knew that he was sincere. "Your generosity is as boundless as your learning," I said, and bowed. "If there is ever a service that a merchant of fabrics might provide for you, please call upon me."

"Thank you. Let us talk now about your trip. There are some matters we must speak of before you visit the Baghdad of twenty years hence."

"I do not wish to visit the future," I told him. "I would step through in the other direction, to revisit my youth."

"Ah, my deepest apologies. This Gate will not take you there. You see, I built this Gate only a week ago. Twenty years ago, there was no doorway here for you to step out of." My dismay was so great that I must have sounded like a forlorn child. I said, "But where does the other side of the Gate lead?" and walked around the circular doorway to face its opposite side.

Bashaarat walked around the doorway to stand beside me. The view through the Gate appeared identical to the view outside it, but when he extended his hand to reach through, it stopped as if it met an invisible wall. I looked more closely, and noticed a brass lamp set on a table. Its flame did not flicker, but was as fixed and unmoving as if the room were trapped in clearest amber.

"What you see here is the room as it appeared last week," said Bashaarat. "In some twenty years' time, this left side of the Gate will permit entry, allowing people to enter from this direction and visit their past. Or," he said, leading me back to the side of the doorway he had first shown me, "we can enter from the right side now, and visit them ourselves. But I'm afraid this Gate will never allow visits to the days of your youth."

"What about the Gate of Years you had in Cairo?" I asked.

He nodded. "That Gate still stands. My son now runs my shop there."

"So I could travel to Cairo, and use the Gate to visit the Cairo of twenty years ago. From there I could travel back to Baghdad."

"Yes, you could make that journey, if you so desire."

"I do," I said. "Will you tell me how to find your shop in Cairo?"

"We must speak of some things first," said Bashaarat. "I will not ask your intentions, being content to wait until you are ready to tell me. But I would remind you that what is made cannot be unmade."

"I know," I said.

"And that you cannot avoid the ordeals that are assigned to you. What Allah gives you, you must accept."

"I remind myself of that every day of my life."

"Then it is my honor to assist you in whatever way I can," he said.

He brought out some paper and a pen and inkpot and began writing. "I shall write for you a letter to aid you on your journey." He folded the letter, dribbled some candle wax over the edge, and pressed his ring against it. "When you reach Cairo, give this to my son, and he will let you enter the Gate of Years there."

A merchant such as myself must be well versed in expressions of gratitude, but I had never before been as effusive in giving thanks as I was to Bashaarat, and every word was heartfelt. He gave me directions to his shop in Cairo, and I assured him I would tell him all upon my return. As I was about to leave his shop, a thought occurred to me. "Because the Gate of Years you have here opens to the future, you are assured that the Gate and this shop will remain standing for twenty years or more."

"Yes, that is true," said Bashaarat.

I began to ask him if he had met his older self, but then I bit back my words. If the answer was no, it was surely because his older self was dead, and I would be asking him if he knew the date of his death. Who was I to make such an inquiry, when this man was granting me a boon without asking my intentions? I saw from his expression that he knew what I had meant to ask, and I bowed my head in humble apology. He indicated his acceptance with a nod, and I returned home to make arrangements.

The caravan took two months to reach Cairo. As for what occupied my mind during the journey, Your Majesty, I now tell you what I had not told Bashaarat. I was married once, twenty years before, to a woman named Najya. Her figure swayed as gracefully as a willow bough and her face was as lovely as the moon, but it was her kind and tender nature that captured my heart. I had just begun my career as a merchant when we married, and we were not wealthy, but did not feel the lack.

We had been married only a year when I was to travel to Basra to meet with a ship's captain. I had an opportunity to profit by trading in slaves, but Najya did not approve. I reminded her that the Koran does not forbid the owning of slaves as long as one treats them well, and that even the Prophet owned some. But she said there was no way I could know how my buyers would treat their slaves, and that it was better to sell goods than men.

On the morning of my departure, Najya and I argued. I spoke harshly to her, using words that it shames me to recall, and I beg Your Majesty's forgiveness if I do not repeat them here. I left in anger, and never saw her again. She was badly injured when the wall of a mosque collapsed, some days after I left. She was taken to the bimaristan, but the physicians could not save her, and she died soon after. I did not learn of her death until I returned a week later, and I felt as if I had killed her with my own hand.

Can the torments of Hell be worse than what I endured in the days that followed? It seemed likely that I would find out, so near to death did my anguish take me. And surely the experience must be similar, for like infernal fire, grief burns but does not consume; instead, it makes the heart vulnerable to further suffering.

Eventually my period of lamentation ended, and I was left a hollow man, a bag of skin with no innards. I freed the slaves I had bought and became a fabric merchant. Over the years I became wealthy, but I never remarried. Some of the men I did business with tried to match me with a sister or a daughter, telling me that the love of a woman can make you forget your pains. Perhaps they are right, but it cannot make you forget the pain you caused another. Whenever I imagined myself marrying another woman, I remembered the look of hurt in Najya's eyes when I last saw her, and my heart was closed to others.

I spoke to a mullah about what I had done, and it was he who told me that repentance and atonement erase the past. I repented and atoned as best I knew how; for twenty years I lived as an upright man, I offered prayers and fasted and gave alms to those less fortunate and made a pilgrimage to Mecca, and yet I was still haunted by guilt. Allah is all-merciful, so I knew the failing to be mine.

Had Bashaarat asked me, I could not have said what I hoped to achieve. It was clear from his stories that I could not change what I knew to have happened. No one had stopped my younger self from arguing with Najya in our final conversation. But the tale of Raniya, which lay hidden within the tale of Hassan's life without his knowing it, gave me a slim hope: perhaps I might be able to play some part in events while my younger self was away on business.

Could it not be that there had been a mistake, and my Najya had survived? Perhaps it was another woman whose body had been wrapped in a shroud and buried while I was gone. Perhaps I could rescue Najya and bring her back with me to the Baghdad of my own day.

I knew it was foolhardy; men of experience say, "Four things do not come back: the spoken word, the sped arrow, the past life, and the neglected opportunity," and I understood the truth of those words better than most. And yet I dared to hope that Allah had judged my twenty years of repentance sufficient, and was now granting me a chance to regain what I had lost.

The caravan journey was uneventful, and after sixty sunrises and three hundred prayers, I reached Cairo. There I had to navigate the city's streets, which are a bewildering maze compared to the harmonious design of the City of Peace. I made my way to the Bayn al-Qasrayn, the main street that runs through the Fatimid quarter of Cairo. From there I found the street on which Bashaarat's shop was located.

I told the shopkeeper that I had spoken to his father in Baghdad, and gave him the letter Bashaarat had given me. After reading it, he led me into a back room, in whose center stood another Gate of Years, and he gestured for me to enter from its left side.

As I stood before the massive circle of metal, I felt a chill, and chided myself for my nervousness. With a deep breath I stepped through, and found myself in the same room with different furnishings. If not for those, I would not have known the Gate to be different from an ordinary doorway. Then I recognized that the chill I had felt was simply the coolness of the air in this room, for the day here was not as hot as the day I had left. I could feel its warm breeze at my back, coming through the Gate like a sigh.

The shopkeeper followed behind me and called out, "Father, you have a visitor."

A man entered the room, and who should it be but Bashaarat, twenty years younger than when I'd seen him in Baghdad. "Welcome, my lord," he said. "I am Bashaarat."

"You do not know me?" I asked.

"No, you must have met my older self. For me, this is our first meeting, but it is my honor to assist you."

Your Majesty, as befits this chronicle of my shortcomings, I must confess that so immersed was I in my own woes during the journey from Baghdad, I had not previously realized that Bashaarat had likely recognized me the moment I stepped into his shop.

Even as I was admiring his water clock and brass songbird, he had known that I would travel to Cairo, and likely knew whether I had achieved my goal or not.

The Bashaarat I spoke to now knew none of those things. "I am doubly grateful for your kindness, sir," I said. "My name is Fuwaad ibn Abbas, newly arrived from Baghdad."

Bashaarat's son took his leave, and Bashaarat and I conferred; I asked him the day and month, confirming that there was ample time for me to travel back to the City of Peace, and promised him I would tell him everything when I returned. His younger self was as gracious as his older. "I look forward to speaking with you on your return, and to assisting you again twenty years from now," he said.

His words gave me pause. "Had you planned to open a shop in Baghdad before today?"

"Why do you ask?"

"I had been marveling at the coincidence that we met in Baghdad just in time for me to make my journey here, use the Gate, and travel back. But now I wonder if it is perhaps not a coincidence at all. Is my arrival here today the reason that you will move to Baghdad twenty years from now?"

Bashaarat smiled. "Coincidence and intention are two sides of a tapestry, my lord. You may find one more agreeable to look at, but you cannot say one is true and the other is false."

"Now as ever, you have given me much to think about," I said.

I thanked him and bid farewell. As I was leaving his shop, I passed a woman entering with some haste. I heard Bashaarat greet her as Raniya, and stopped in surprise. From just outside the door, I could hear the woman say, "I have the necklace. I hope my older self has not lost it."

"I am sure you will have kept it safe, in anticipation of your visit," said Bashaarat.

I realized that this was Raniya from the story Bashaarat had told me. She was on her way to collect her older self so that they might return to the days of their youth, confound some thieves with a doubled necklace, and save their husband. For a moment I was unsure if I were dreaming or awake, because I felt as if I had stepped into a tale, and the thought that I might talk to its players and partake of its events was dizzying. I was tempted to speak, and see if I might play a hidden role in that tale, but then I remembered that my goal was to play a hidden role in my own tale. So I left without a word, and went to arrange passage with a caravan.

It is said, Your Majesty, that Fate laughs at men's schemes. At first it appeared as if I were the most fortunate of men, for a caravan headed for Baghdad was departing within the month, and I was able to join it. In the weeks that followed I began to curse my luck, because the caravan's journey was plagued by delays. The wells at a town not far from Cairo were dry, and an expedition had to be sent back for water. At another village, the soldiers protecting the caravan contracted dysentery, and we had to wait for weeks for their recovery. With each delay, I revised my estimate of when we'd reach Baghdad, and grew increasingly anxious.

Then there were the sandstorms, which seemed like a warning from Allah, and truly caused me to doubt the wisdom of my actions. We had the good fortune to be resting at a caravanserai west of Kufa when the sandstorms first struck, but our stay was prolonged from days to weeks as, time and again, the skies became clear, only to darken again as soon as the camels were reloaded. The day of Najya's accident was fast approaching, and I grew desperate.

I solicited each of the camel drivers in turn, trying to hire one to take me ahead alone, but could not persuade any of them. Eventually I found one willing to sell me a camel at what would have been an exorbitant price under ordinary circumstances, but which I was all too willing to pay. I then struck out on my own.

It will come as no surprise that I made little progress in the storm, but when the winds subsided, I immediately adopted a rapid pace. Without the soldiers that accompanied the caravan, however, I was an easy target for bandits, and sure enough, I was stopped after two days' ride. They took my money and the camel I had purchased, but spared my life, whether out of pity or because they could not be bothered to kill me I do not know. I began walking back to rejoin the caravan, but now the skies tormented me with their cloudlessness, and I suffered from the heat. By the time the caravan found me, my tongue was swollen and my lips were as cracked as mud baked by the sun. After that I had no choice but to accompany the caravan at its usual pace.

Like a fading rose that drops its petals one by one, my hopes dwindled with each passing day. By the time the caravan reached the City of Peace, I knew it was too late, but the moment we rode through the city gates, I asked the guardsmen if they had heard of a mosque collapsing. The first guardsman I spoke to had not, and for a heartbeat I dared to hope that I had misremembered the date of the accident, and that I had in fact arrived in time.

Then another guardsman told me that a mosque had indeed collapsed just yesterday in the Karkh quarter. His words struck me with the force of the executioner's ax. I had traveled so far, only to receive the worst news of my life a second time.

I walked to the mosque, and saw the piles of bricks where there had once been a wall. It was a scene that had haunted my dreams for twenty years, but now the image remained even after I opened my eyes, and with a clarity sharper than I could endure. I turned away and walked without aim, blind to what was around me, until I found myself before my old house, the one where Najya and I had lived. I stood in the street in front of it, filled with memory and anguish.

I do not know how much time had passed when I became aware that a young woman had walked up to me. "My lord," she said, "I'm looking for the house of Fuwaad ibn Abbas."

"You have found it," I said.

"Are you Fuwaad ibn Abbas, my lord?"

"I am, and I ask you, please leave me be."

"My lord, I beg your forgiveness. My name is Maimuna, and I assist the physicians at the bimaristan. I tended to your wife before she died."

I turned to look at her. "You tended to Najya?"

"I did, my lord. I am sworn to deliver a message to you from her."

"What message?"

"She wished me to tell you that her last thoughts were of you. She wished me to tell you that while her life was short, it was made happy by the time she spent with you."

She saw the tears streaming down my cheeks and said, "Forgive me if my words cause you pain, my lord."

"There is nothing to forgive, child. Would that I had the means to pay you as much as this message is worth to me, because a lifetime of thanks would still leave me in your debt."

"Grief owes no debt," she said. "Peace be upon you, my lord."

"Peace be upon you," I said.

She left, and I wandered the streets for hours, crying tears of release. All the while I thought on the truth of Bashaarat's words: past and future are the same, and we cannot change either, only know them more fully. My journey to the past had changed nothing, but what I had learned had changed everything, and I understood that it could not have been otherwise. If our lives are tales that Allah tells, then we are the audience as well as the players, and it is by living these tales that we receive their lessons.

Night fell, and it was then that the city's guardsmen found me, wandering the streets after curfew in my dusty clothes, and asked who I was. I told them my name and where I lived, and the guardsmen brought me to my neighbors to see if they knew me, but they did not recognize me, and I was taken to jail.

I told the guard captain my story, and he found it entertaining, but did not credit it, for who would? Then I remembered some news from my time of grief twenty years before, and told him that Your Majesty's grandson would be born an albino. Some days later, word of the infant's condition reached the captain, and he brought me to the governor of the quarter. When the governor heard my story, he brought me here to the palace, and when your lord chamberlain heard my story, he in turn brought me here to the throne room, so that I might have the infinite privilege of recounting it to Your Majesty.

Now my tale has caught up to my life, coiled as they both are, and the direction they take next is for Your Majesty to decide. I know many things that will happen here in Baghdad over the next twenty years, but nothing about what awaits me now. I have no money for the journey back to Cairo and the Gate of Years there, yet I count myself fortunate beyond measure, for I was given the opportunity to revisit my past mistakes, and I have learned what remedies Allah allows. I would be honored to relate everything I know of the future, if Your Majesty sees fit to ask, but for myself, the most precious knowledge I possess is this:

Nothing erases the past. There is repentance, there is atonement, and there is forgiveness. That is all, but that is enough.

JOYCE CAROL OATES

Valentine, July Heat Wave

Joyce Carol Oates is one of the most prolific and respected writers in the United States today. Oates has written fiction in almost every genre and medium. Her keen interest in the Gothic and psychological horror has spurred her to write dark suspense novels under the name Rosamond Smith, to write enough stories in the genre to have published five collections of dark fiction, the most recent The Female of the Species: Tales of Mystery and Suspense, *and to edit* American Gothic Tales. *Oates's short novel* Zombie *won the Bram Stoker Award, and she has been honored with a Life Achievement Award by the Horror Writers Association.*

Oates's most recent novels are The Stolen Heart, Missing Mom, *and* Blood Mask. *Oates has been living in Princeton, New Jersey, since 1978, where she teaches creative writing. She and her husband Raymond J. Smith ran the small press and literary magazine* The Ontario Review. *Smith died early this year.*

"Valentine, July Heat Wave" was originally published in the March/April issue of Ellery Queen's Mystery Magazine, *edited by Janet Hutchings.*

—E. D.

My calculated estimate is *Eight days should be about right.*

Not that I am a pathologist, or any kind of "naturalist." My title at the university is professor of humanities. Yet a little research has made me fairly confident *Eight days during this heat should be about right.*

Because I have loved you, I will not cease to love you. It is not my way (as I believe you must know) to alter. As you vowed to be *my wife*, I vowed to be *your husband*. There can be no alteration of such vows. This, you know.

You will return to our house, you will return to our bedroom. When I beckon you inside you will step inside. When I beckon you to me you will come to me. You will judge if my estimate has been correct.

Eight days! My valentine.

The paradox is: Love is a live thing, and live things must die.

Sometimes abruptly, and sometimes over time.

Live things lose life: vitality, animation, the pulse of a beating heart and coursing blood carrying oxygen to the brain, the ability to withstand invasion by predatory organisms that devour them. Live things become, in the most elemental, crudest way of speaking, dead things.

And yet, the paradox remains: In the very body of death, in the very corpse of love, an astonishing new life breeds.

This valentine I have prepared for you, out of the very body of love.

You will arrive at the house alone, for that is your promise. Though you have ceased to love me (as you claim) you have not ceased to be an individual of integrity and so I know that you would not violate that promise. I believe you when you've claimed that there is no other man in your life: no other "love." And so, you will return to our house alone.

Your flight from Denver is due to arrive at 3:22 P.M. You've asked me not to meet you at the airport and so I have honored that wish. You've said that you prefer to rent a car at the airport and drive to the house by yourself and after you have emptied your closets, drawers, shelves of those items of yours you care to take away with you, you prefer to drive away alone, and to spend the night at an airport hotel where you've made a reservation. (Eight days ago when I called every airport hotel and motel to see if you'd made the reservation yet, you had not. At least, not under your married name.) When you arrive at the house, you will not turn into the driveway but park on the street. You will stare at the house. You will feel very tired. You will feel like a woman in a trance of—what?

Guilt, surely. Dread. That sick sense of imminent justice when we realize we must be punished, we will get what we "deserve."

Or maybe you will simply think: *Within the hour it will be ended. At last, I will be free!*

Sometime before 4:00 P.M. you will arrive at the house, assuming the flight from Denver isn't delayed. You had not known you were flying into a Midwestern heat wave and now you are reluctant to leave the air-conditioned interior of the car. For five weeks you've been away and now, staring at the house set back some distance from the street, amid tall, aging oaks and evergreens, you will wish to think *Nothing seems to have changed.* As if you have not noticed that at the windows, downstairs and upstairs, venetian blinds seem to have been drawn tightly shut. As if you have not noticed that the grass in the front lawn is overgrown and gone to seed and in the glaring heat of the summer sun patches of lawn have begun to burn out.

On the flagstone walk leading to the front door, a scattering of newspapers, fliers. The mailbox is stuffed with mail no one seems to have taken in for several days though you will not have registered *Eight days!* at this time.

Perhaps by this time you will concede that, yes, you are feeling uneasy. Guilty, and uneasy.

Knowing how particular your husband is about such things as the maintenance of the house and grounds: the maintenance of neatness, orderliness. The exterior of the house no less than the interior. Recognizing that appearances are trivial, and yet: Appearances can be signals that a fundamental principle of order has been violated.

At the margins of order is anarchy. What is anarchy but brute stupidity!

And so, seeing uneasily that the house seems to be showing signs of neglect, quickly you wish to tell yourself *But it can have nothing to do with me!* Five weeks you've been away and only twice, each time briefly, you have called me, and spoken with me. Pleading with me *Let me go, please let me go* as if I, of all people, required pleading-with.

My valentine! My love.

You will have seen: my car parked in the driveway, beside the house. And so you know (with a sinking heart? with a thrill of anticipation?) that I am home. (For I might have departed, as sometimes, admittedly, in our marriage I did depart, to work in my office at the university for long, utterly absorbed and delirious hours, with no awareness of time.) Not only is the car in the driveway, but I have promised you that I would be here, at this time; that we might make our final arrangements together, preparatory to divorce.

The car in the driveway is in fact "our" car. As the house is "our" house. For our property is jointly owned. Though you brought no financial resources to our marriage and it has been entirely my university income that has supported us yet our property is jointly owned, for this was my wish.

As you are *my wife*, so I am *your husband*. Symmetry, sanctity.

This valentine I've designed for you, in homage to the sanctity of marriage.

On the drive from the airport, you will have had time to think: to rehearse. You will repeat what you've told me and I will try to appeal to you to change your mind but of course you will not change your mind *Can't return, not for more than an hour* for that is the point of your returning: to go away again. You are adamant, you have made up your mind. *So sorry please forgive if you can* you are genuine in your regret and yet adamant.

The house, our house: 119 Worth Avenue. Five years ago when we were first married you'd thought that this house was "beautiful"—"special." Like the old residential neighborhood of similarly large houses on wooded lots, built on a hill overlooking the university arboretum. In this neighborhood known as University Heights most of the houses are solidly built brick with here and there a sprawling white colonial, dating back to the early decades of the twentieth century. Our house is dark red brick and stucco, two stories and a third part-story between steep shingled roofs. Perhaps it is not a beautiful house but certainly it is an attractive, dignified house with black shutters, leaded-glass windows, a screened veranda, and lifting from the right-hand front corner of the second floor a quaint Victorian structure like a turret. You'd hurried to see this room when the real estate agent showed us the house but were disappointed when it turned out to be little more than an architectural ornament, impractical even as a child's bedroom.

On the phone you'd murmured *Thank God no children.*

Since you've turned off the car's motor, the air-conditioning has ceased and you will begin to feel a prickling of heat. As if a gigantic breath is being exhaled that is warm, stale, humid, and will envelop you.

So proud of your promotion, Daryll. So young!

How you embarrassed me in the presence of others. How in your sweetly oblivious way you insulted me. Of course you had no idea. Of course you meant well. As if the fact that I was the youngest "senior" professor in the humanities division of the university at the time of my promotion was a matter of significance to me.

As my special field is Philosophy of Mind so it's "mind" that is valued, not trivial attributes like age, personality. All of philosophy is an effort of the mental faculties to discriminate between the trivial and the profound, the fleeting and the permanent, the many and the One. Pride is not only to be rejected on an ethical basis but on an epistemological basis, for how to "take pride" in one's self?—in one's physical being, in which the brain is encased? (Brain being the mysterious yet clearly organic repository of "mind.") And how to "take pride" in what is surely no more than an accident of birth?

You spoke impulsively, you had no idea of the crudeness of your words. Though in naïveté there is a kind of subtle aggression. Your artless blunders made me wince in the presence of my older colleagues (for whom references to youth, as to age, were surely unwelcome) and in the presence of my family (who disapproved of my marrying you, not on the grounds that you were too young, but that you were but a departmental secretary, "no match" intellectually for me which provoked me to a rare, stinging reply *But who would be an intellectual match for me? Who, and also female?*)

Yet I never blamed you. I never accused you. Perhaps in my reticence. My silences. My long interludes of utter absorption in my work. Never did I speak of the flaws of your character and if I speak of them now it is belatedly and without condemnation. Almost, with a kind of nostalgia. A kind of melancholy affection. Though you came to believe that I was "judgmental"—"hypercritical"—truly you had no idea how I spared you. Many times.

Here is the first shock: the heat.

As you leave the car, headed up the flagstone path to the front door. This wall of heat, waves of heat shimmering and nearly visible rushing at you. "Oh! My God." Several weeks away in mile-high Denver have lulled you into forgetting what a midsummer heat wave in this sea-level Midwestern city can be.

Stale humid heat. Like a cloud of heavy, inert gas.

The heat of my wrath. The heat of my hurt. As you are my wife I spared you, rarely did I speak harshly to you even when you seemed to lose all control and screamed at me *Let me go! Let me go! I am sorry I never loved you please let me go!*

That hour, the first time I saw your face so stricken with repugnance for me. Always, I will remember that hour.

As if, for the five years of our cohabitation, you'd been in disguise, you'd been playing a role, and now, abruptly and without warning, as if you hadn't known what you would say as you began to scream at me, you'd cast aside the disguise, tore off the mask and confronted me. *Don't love you. It was a mistake. Can't stay here. Can't breathe. Let me go!*

I was stunned. I had never imagined such words. I saw your mouth moving, I heard not words but sounds, strangulated sounds, you backed away from me, your face was contorted with dislike.

I told you then: I could not let you go. Would not let you go. For how could I, you are *my wife.*

Remembering how on a snowy morning some months before, in late winter, you'd entered my study in my absence and propped up a valentine on the windowsill facing my desk. For often you did such things, playful, childlike, not seeming to mind if I scarcely noticed or, noticing, paid much attention. The valentine came in a bright red envelope, absorbed in my work somehow I hadn't noticed. Days passed and I did not notice (evidently) and at last you came into my study to open the envelope for me laughing in your light rippling way (that did not sound accusing, only perhaps just slightly wounded) and you drew out of the red envelope a card of a kind that might be given to a child, a kitten peeking out of a watering can and inside a bright red TO MY VALENTINE. And your name. And I stared at this card not seeming to grasp for a moment what it was, a "valentine," thrust into my face for me to admire.

Perhaps I was abrupt with you then. Or perhaps I simply turned away. Whereof one cannot speak, there one must be silent. The maddened buzzing of flies is a kind of silence, I think. Like all of nature: the blind devouring force to which Schopenhauer gave the name *will*.

Your promise was, at the time of our marriage, you would not be hurt. You would not be jealous of my work, though knowing that my work, as it is the best part of me, must always take priority over my personal life. Freely you'd given this promise, if perhaps recklessly. You would not be jealous of my life apart from you, and you would not be hurt. Bravely pledging *I can love enough for both of us!*

And yet, you never grasped the most elemental logistics of my work. The most elemental principles of philosophy: the quest for truth. Of course, I hardly expected you, lacking even a bachelor's degree from a mediocre land-grant university, to understand my work which is understood by very few in my profession, but I did expect you, as my wife, to understand that there can be no work more exacting, exhausting, and heroic.

But now we are beyond even broken promises. Inside our house, your valentine is waiting.

As a younger man only just embarked upon the quest of truth, I'd imagined that the great work of my life would be a definitive refutation of Descartes, who so bluntly separated "mind" and "body" at the very start of modern philosophy, but unexpectedly in my early thirties my most original work has become a corroboration and a clarification of the Cartesian position: that "mind" inhabits "body" but is not subsumed in "body." For the principles of logic, as I have demonstrated by logical argument, in a systematic geometry in the mode of Spinoza, transcend all merely "bodily" limitations. All this, transmuted into the most precise symbols.

When love dies, can it be revived? We will see.

On the front stoop you will ring the doorbell. Like any visitor.

Not wishing to enter the house by the side door, as you'd done when you lived here.

Calling in a low voice my name: "Daryll?"

How strange, *Daryll* is my name. My given name. Yet I am hardly identical with *Daryll* and in the language of logic it might even be claimed that I am *no thing* that is *Daryll* though I am simultaneously *no thing* that is *not-Daryll*. Rather, *Daryll* is irrelevant to what I am, or what I have become.

No answer. You will try the door knocker. And no answer.

How quiet! Almost, you might think that no one is home.

You will take out your house key, carried inside your wallet, in your purse. Fitting the key into the lock you will experience a moment's vertigo, wishing to think that the key no longer fits the lock; that your furious husband has changed the locks on the doors, and expelled you from his life, as you wish to be expelled from his life. But no, the lock does fit. Of course.

Pushing open the door. A heavy oak door, painted black.

Unconsciously you will have expected the interior of the stolid old dark brick house to be coolly air-conditioned and so the shock of overwarm, stale air, a rancid-smelling air seems to strike you full in the face. "Hello? Daryll? Are you . . ."

How weak and faltering, your voice in your own ears. And how your nostrils are pinching at this strange, unexpected smell.

Rancid-ripe. Sweet as rotted fruit, yet more virulent. Rotted flesh?

Please forgive!

Can't return. Not for more than an hour.

It was my fault, I had no idea . . .

. . . from the start, I think I knew. What a mistake we'd both made.

Yes I admit: I was flattered.

. . . young, and ignorant. And vain.

That you, the most brilliant of the younger professors in the department . . .

Tried to love you. To be a wife to you. But . . .

Just to pack my things. And what I can't take with me, you can give to Goodwill. Or throw out with the trash.

. . . the way they spoke of you, in the department. Your integrity, your genius. And stubborn, and strong . . .

If I'd known more! More about men. Like you I was shy, I'd been afraid of men, I think. A virgin at twenty-five . . .

No. I don't think so.

Even at the beginning, no. Looking back at it now, I don't think I ever did, Daryll. It was a kind of . . .

. . . like a masquerade, a pretense. When you said you thought you loved me. Wanting so badly to believe . . .

Please, Daryll? Can you? Forgive?

. . . only just time enough to pack a few things. The divorce can be finalized by our lawyers, we won't need to meet again.

The most brilliant young philosopher of his generation, they said of you. And he is ours . . .

This masquerade. "Marriage."

So badly I wanted to be your wife. I am so ashamed!

Daryll? Can you forgive me?

Standing in the doorway of the living room you will see to your astonishment that sheets—bedsheets?—have been carefully drawn over the furniture, like shrouds. One of the smaller Oriental rugs has been rolled up and secured with twine as if in preparation for being hauled away. Books have been removed from the shelves that cover most of two walls of the living room and these books have been neatly placed in cardboard boxes. At the windows, blinds have been tightly drawn shut. Flies buzz and bat against the slats. There's a green twilit cast to the air as if the house has sunk beneath the surface of the sea.

The smell: What is it? You think *Something that has spoiled, in the kitchen?*

You will not venture into the kitchen at the rear of the house.

Though you enter the dining room, hesitantly. Seeing on the long oaken table a row of manila folders each neatly marked in black ink: FINANCES, BANK RECORDS, IRS & RECEIPTS, LAST WILL AND TESTAMENT.

You will begin now to be frightened. Panic like flames begins to lick at you.

And that sound: murmurous and buzzing as of muffled voices behind a shut door.

"Daryll? Are you—upstairs?"

Telling yourself *Run! Escape!*

Not too late. Turn back. Hurry!

Yet somehow you will make your way to the stairs. The broad front staircase with the dark cranberry carpeting, worn in the center from years of footsteps predating your own. Like a sleepwalker you grip the banister, to steady your climb.

Is it guilt drawing you upstairs? A sick, excited sense of what you will discover? What it is your duty, as *my wife*, to discover?

You will be smiling, a small fixed smile. Your eyes opened wide yet glassy as if unseeing. And your heart rapidly beating as the wings of a trapped bird.

If you faint . . . Must not faint! Blood is draining from your brain, almost you can feel darkness encroaching at the edges of your vision; and your vision is narrowing, like a tunnel.

At the top of the stairs you pause, to clear your head. Except you can't seem to clear your head. Here, the smell is very strong. A smell confused with heat, shimmering waves of heat. You begin to gag, you feel nausea. Yet you can't turn back, you must make your way to the bedroom at the end of the corridor.

Past the charming little turret room with the bay window and cushioned window seat. The room you'd imagined might somehow have been yours, or a child's room, but which proved to be impracticably small.

The door to the bedroom is shut. You press the flat of your hand against it feeling its heat. Even now thinking almost calmly *No. I will not. I am strong enough to resist.*

You dare to grasp the doorknob. Dare to open the door. Slowly.

How loud the buzzing is! A crackling sound like flame. And the rancid-rot smell, overwhelming as sound that is deafening, passing beyond your capacity to comprehend.

Something brushes against your face. Lips, eyes. You wave it away, panicked. "Daryll? Are you—here?"

For there is motion in the room. A plane of something shifting, fluid, alive and iridescent-glittering: yet not human. In the master bedroom, too, venetian blinds have been drawn at every window. There's the greeny undersea light. It takes you several seconds to realize that the room is covered in flies. The buzzing noise you've been hearing is flies. Thousands, millions?—flies covering the ceiling, the walls. And the carpet, which appears to be badly stained with something dark. And on the bed, a handsome four-poster bed that came with the house, a Victorian antique, there is a seething blanket of flies over a humanoid figure that seems to have partly melted into the bedclothes. Is this—who is this? The face, or what had been the face, is no longer recognizable. The skin has swollen to bursting like a burnt sausage and its hue·is blackened and no longer does it have the texture of skin but of something pulpy, liquefied. Like the manic glittering flies that crawl over everything, this skin exudes a dark iridescence. The body has become a bloated balloon body, fought over by masses of flies. Here and there, in crevices that had once been the mouth, the nostrils, the ears, there are writhing white patches, maggots like churning frenzied kernels of white rice. The throat of the humanoid figure seems to have been slashed. The bloodied steak knife lies close beside the figure, where it has been dropped. The figure's arms, covered in flies, are outstretched on the bed as if quivering, about to lift in an embrace of welcome. Everywhere, dark, coagulated blood has soaked the figure's clothing, the bedclothes, the bed, the carpet. The rot-smell is overwhelming. The carrion-smell. Yet you can't seem to turn away. Whatever has drawn you here has not yet released you. The entire room is a crimson wound, a place of the most exquisite mystery, seething with its own inner, secret life. *Your husband* has not died, has not vanished but has been transmogrified into another dimension of being, observing you through a galaxy of tiny unblinking eyes: the buzzing is his voice, multiplied by millions. Flies brush against your face. Flies brush against your lips, your eyelashes. You wave them away, you step forward, to approach the figure on the bed. *My valentine! My love.*

DONALD MEAD

A Thing Forbidden

Donald Mead writes historical fantasy, traditional fantasy, and his own brand of alternate history that he calls "historical shift." His first story, "iKlawa," was published in 2006 by The Magazine of Fantasy & Science Fiction.

Mead credits much of his success to his hometown critique group. He hopes to see their names in these same pages someday. When he's not writing, he can often be found at the Codex Web site: a group of rebel, neo-pro writers who love to discuss the markets and complain about response times. Mead lives in Bloomington, Illinois, and works in the finance department of a car manufacturer.

"A Thing Forbidden" was originally published in The Magazine of Fantasy & Science Fiction's *April issue, edited by Gordon Van Gelder.*

—E. D.

Christ's dead eyes opened and he gave me a blood-soaked stare.

My yelp was swallowed up by the lingering chords of the hymn. I grabbed Mrs. Mora's arm and pointed at the wooden crucifix that hung at the front of the sanctuary.

She gave it a look and shrugged. "A lot of things are going to be different in a Catholic church, Virginia. Our cross has Christ nailed to it. You might think it's distasteful, but it reminds us of His suffering for our sins."

I regarded the crucifix again. Christ sagged, eyes closed. Maybe it was just the mountains come-a-calling, although the horror had never before followed me into church. That always had been my safe place. My breathing eased as we sat.

Mrs. Mora tucked the hymnal away and handed me several loose sheets of paper. "Have you been following along?" She touched her finger to one of the sheets. "We're here."

I nodded and took the sheets, giving Christ a quick glance.

I fought the urge to yank off the thin black scarf Mrs. Mora had given me to wear over my hair—over my hat, really. I didn't know women wore scarves in Catholic church, and I had so wanted to make a good impression with my little round hat fixed up with flowers and feathers. It matched perfectly with my calico hooped skirt and jacket. But when Mrs. Mora saw it, she had insisted I wear "a modest scarf." She had even wanted me to take off my hat, which I couldn't do since it was fixed with pins and held my curls up.

Mama had helped me with the hat that morning. She put her love into it despite the circumstances. "Please come with us to the Methodist service at the fort," she had said. "One Christian is as good as another in God's eyes."

"You know the vow I made in the mountains, Mama." I smiled, but the look she returned held only anguish.

Papa had hitched up the carriage for me; I couldn't ride horseback in a hooped skirt. He didn't answer when I said good-bye.

People in the front pews rose and shuffled into the center aisle, led by a man in a dark jacket and matching trousers. His thick black hair was tied back and stuffed down his collar.

They lined up in front of the priest. Father O'Rourke seemed almost dwarfish standing before the man in the dark jacket. I guessed the Spanish cowboy—*vaqueros* Mrs. Mora called them—stood six and a half feet tall.

Father O'Rourke retrieved a plate of wafers from the altar. He took one and held it up. "*Corpus Domini nostri Jesu Christi custodiat animam tuam in vitam aeternam. Amen.*"

He placed the wafer in the man's mouth.

I looked at the papers again—Mrs. Mora's handwritten translations. *May the Body of our Lord Jesus Christ preserve your soul unto everlasting life. Amen.*

The man turned away and the next in line, a much shorter vaquero, just a bit taller than Father O'Rourke, stepped forward.

Mrs. Mora nudged me and gave me an impish smile. "So many men."

I felt myself flush and looked away. The church was filled with men—women sprinkled among them like cactus flowers. Many were Spanish, but there were also Irish, German, and American immigrants.

Mrs. Mora leaned closer. "There's so much work to be done. Jobs are bringing men from everywhere. Some people are getting rich." She poked me to make me look at her. "How old are you? Old enough to marry?"

I shook my head. "Sixteen."

"But soon," she said. "And your pick of men."

I looked forward to keep from laughing. "When I write to my cousins in Springfield, I tell them to forget Illinois and come to California. They could get a good man in no time."

"And things will only get better once we become a state," said Mrs. Mora. "I hope they send more priests. So many souls to save. So many baptisms."

People in the next pew stood and moved to the aisle.

"What should I do when it's our turn?"

Mrs. Mora reddened. "Oh, nothing this time. The Holy Eucharist is for Catholics only. But you won't have long to wait to receive the body of Christ. Were you a Christian before . . . ?" Her voice became strained. "Before you joined the Donner train?"

"Yes. Methodist."

"Oh, that's good." She released a pent-up breath. "You won't have to be baptized— just a profession of faith and confession. Then you can consume the body—I mean, join in the Eucharist."

Mrs. Mora looked down and fiddled with the hymnal.

I patted her hand. "It's all right. I know it's not really flesh."

She looked at me and gave a distressed smile. "But, Virginia, it's symbolic only for Protestants. Not in the Catholic faith. Once the bread has been sanctified by the priest, it is very much the body of Christ. You consume His flesh, drink His blood, and accept His divinity."

Father O'Rourke's voice filled the tiny sanctuary. "*Quod ore sumpsimus, Domine, pura mente capiamus.*"

I looked at the translation to fight a stab of panic. *What has passed our lips as food, Lord, may we possess in purity of heart.*

"But you won't taste flesh or blood or bone," Mrs. Mora said. "It still tastes like bread. It's part of the miracle of the Eucharist. Sister Rosa was supposed to explain all of this."

I shook my head. The Sister was probably just as concerned for my sensitivity as Mrs. Mora.

I looked at the crucifix. *This is your first test, isn't it? But you can't test me like you did Job. After the mountains, you know I can withstand anything.*

I cocked my head. Christ's face seemed different. I squinted, trying to see through the haze of incense. His eyes were open again, and the crown of thorns was gone. His beard was longer, and his face was even more gaunt than before.

I forced down a scream and tugged on Mrs. Mora's dress. "Do you see anything wrong with the crucifix? Look at the face."

She studied it for a moment. "No one knows how Christ actually looked. You see a lot of different faces on crucifixes."

She couldn't see it, but that wasn't her fault. You had to battle Satan before you could recognize his devices. The Enemy had followed me from the mountains and had taken the feral face of that awful Hessian, Louis Keseberg.

I stiffened as the wooden head swiveled to look at me. His lips moved and a whisper found my ears. "It's too late for you, Virginia. You've tasted unsanctified flesh. You belong to my army, not His. And our battle for California is about to begin."

I grew dizzy and closed my eyes. *The battle's long over. You should've stayed buried in the mountains.*

A bang at the back of the sanctuary caused me to open my eyes. I looked back, along with the rest of the parishioners, to see a young ranch hand in filthy work clothes standing by the open doors. He fought labored breathing. "They found gold at Sutter's Mill!"

I lifted my skirt and dodged a pile of horse manure. Sutter's Fort wasn't nearly as modern as Springfield, and I missed the conveniences of gas lighting and street sweepers. But the warm sunny winters more than compensated for rough living.

A man, unkempt, smelly, and toting a basket of otter furs, smiled as he walked by. Papa was right—there were endless ways to make a living in California, depending on how hard you were willing to work and what unpleasantries you were able to endure. I used to worry about having lost all of the cattle, but not anymore. A year had passed since our rescue from the mountains, and Papa's work at Sutter's Mill had afforded us a house next to Hock Farm.

It was a good thing Captain Sutter was a Christian. All these men streaming in from the States with pockets full of money—it was a troublesome combination. But the Captain didn't allow alcohol to be sold at the fort, and he was most intolerant of gambling and women who made gain of their loose virtue.

I stopped and looked back at the worn paddock that was used for morning muster on sunny days. Odd. There were usually soldiers coming, going, or sitting in front of the barracks having a smoke. If I didn't fend off at least one marriage proposal during a visit I considered it a wasted trip. Today—nothing.

I ducked into Mackey's Store.

A wide brown dress topped with a bun of blond hair was busy shelving canned beans. Doris turned and smiled. "Virginia. Your mother was in just this morning. Did she forget something?"

I shook my head and glanced around. "Where's Mackey?"

"Gone!"

She wheeled and returned to stacking. The cans clacked as she put her weight into her work. "Damn fool! Off with a bunch of men to find their fortune. Can you believe it? Not three days after some kid finds gold up in the hills and the whole valley's gone loco."

She stopped and looked at me. I noticed her eyes were puffy and red. "Forgetting that the good solid work that brought him out here paid for this place along with our wagons and horses."

Doris turned to the counter where some loose tobacco lay next to an open tin can. She wiped her hands on her apron. "And for what? To chase a dream? California's about hard work, not easy riches."

"Is that where all the soldiers are?"

She nodded and started sweeping up tobacco with her hand.

"But who's guarding the fort? What if there's trouble? What if someone gets stranded in the mountains again?"

She dumped tobacco into the can and closed the lid. "Well, there you have it, girl. A man can be as dumb as a horse. Dangle a carrot in front of his eyes and he'll go right off a cliff. Guess it's up to you and me. I'm as strong as any man, and Lord knows you have history tracking around those mountains."

I shivered. "I hope it doesn't come to that. I don't ever want to go back into the mountains again. Can't Captain Sutter do something? Order the men back to work?"

"The Captain's up at the mill trying to keep squatters off his property—mostly his own men. Isn't that a dandy? He hires these men, clothes and feeds them, and then they turn on him. It's devil's gold. Brings out the worst in folks. A lot of them are so-called Christians. And what do you think is going to follow?"

I shrugged.

"Every slacker, sinner, charlatan, and shyster is going to come riding over the mountains to get a share of that gold. And every harlot in the country will be hot on their heels."

My own heels pounded the boardwalk. I had stayed too long at Mackey's just to hear bad news, and now I was in danger of being late to the Catholic ladies' social.

So it would be a war. The horrible vision in church had been right, but God wasn't defenseless. I'd seen it in the mountains.

I must have been too deep in thought. I came upon a man, his back turned, and had to skid to a halt to avoid a collision.

He turned and greeted me with a toothy grin and vacant eyes. "The end of the world is at hand."

"Keseberg!"

His grin faded, and although his dust-covered, reeking body was only a few feet away, he squinted as if he needed glasses. "Virginia Reed?"

"You know it's me! You tried to convince the party to hang my father back in the Sierra Nevadas! Did the mountains scatter your brains?"

His eyes drifted as mine sometimes did when those awful memories took hold. "Why didn't they listen? We should've hanged him." He babbled a couple of words in German.

I considered launching myself at him, but his fleas kept me at bay. "If they had, no one would've ridden ahead to the fort and brought back help. How many more would've died? How many more would you have eaten?"

His eyes shifted to me. "I only did what was necessary to survive. We all did."

"That's a lie! You murdered Levinah Murphy. Captain Sutter's men found her jewelry in your pockets and her body butchered in your cabin!"

"Missus Murphy." His eyes wandered again. "Funny, her meat was actually sweet to the taste."

My hand lashed.

Keseberg staggered back and rubbed his cheek. "I underestimate your strength, young one. But it's a bit hypocritical, don't you think?"

"What's that supposed to mean?" My voice cracked with rage.

His smile deepened. "Virginia. Half the party died in the Sierra Nevadas. The Donners are still up there—their scattered bones, anyway."

"Shut your mouth!"

"Weren't the Donners your friends? Didn't you all come from Illinois in the same wagon train?"

I could only give a strangled hiss.

"And what did you feel when you placed their flesh on the fire and ate it? You hate me because you can't bear your own guilt."

I glanced around. The dirt street and boardwalks were still empty. "Turn your other cheek, Keseberg. My Christian attitude just ran out."

Keseberg laughed. "Why are you acting so righteous? Who are you trying to impress?" He glanced at the fort's muster hall where the Catholic ladies were meeting. "Were you going to that Catholic *sitzung*? You still think you saw God in the mountains? How arrogant! The rest of us met the devil and you met God. Well, don't waste your time—the Catholics don't take cannibals."

"I never did. I never did!" Fury was making me light-headed so I turned and stalked down the boardwalk. It was too late to make a dignified entrance to the meeting, and I was too angry to make good company.

Keseberg called after me. "The end of the world is at hand! California will eat her whole!"

I spotted a work-hand as I rode up to the church. He was set to chopping away at the brush creeping up on the north wall. The poor man was overmatched, with nothing but a tomahawk he must have bought before coming over the mountains. He hacked away as if he could hold back nature. Two miles from the fort, nature was still in charge.

I gave a start when he turned. It was Father O'Rourke, sweat soaking through the chest and armpits of his white shirt.

He smiled. "Thought I heard a horse. I was hoping it was Charles Murphy coming to help me with this overgrowth. How are you, Virginia?"

He had a singsong accent just like Papa's—straight from Ireland.

I dismounted and tied Jeebers to the picket fence that bordered the church grounds. "I'm fine, Father. And I'll be glad to help."

He looked me up and down. "Not in that nice dress you're not."

He took off his work gloves and sat on the church stoop. I joined him.

"Did you bring a letter from your father?"

I shook my head. "Papa's being stubborn."

"He's Irish Protestant, isn't he?"

"Yes."

There was a strange sadness in the Father's eyes. "I'll still need his permission to continue with your conversion. Otherwise, you'll have to wait until you're older."

"I'll work on him," I said, brushing road dust off my dress. "I thought you were a work-hand when I first rode up."

He glanced at the overgrowth. "Lost my trunk on the voyage to New York. It had all of my frocks in it. The Church was in such a hurry to get more priests into California, I didn't have time to get new ones. The one I use now is borrowed from Father Rodriguez."

"Maybe Missus Mora could make you a new one."

He shook his head. "I left my measurements with a priest in New York. He'll send some new ones along soon enough." He looked at me. "Speaking of Missus Mora, she said you didn't come to the Catholic ladies meeting yesterday. If you want to show God your commitment, you'll have to try harder than that."

"I had a run-in with Louis Keseberg. I should've ignored him, but I let him bait me. He said I was a cannibal, same as him." I looked into the Father's eyes. "I slapped him, and I'm truly repentant."

I had the impression he was holding back a laugh. "There'll be plenty of confessions in your future. No one is without sin. We'll worry about penance after you become a Catholic."

"Do you think I'm a cannibal, Father?"

"No, lass. If you say you're not, then I believe you."

"Do you believe in the devil? A real flesh-and-bone monster who wants to destroy God's creation?"

He gave me a long look. "You have to ask? I'm a priest."

"That's good. Because I do too. He did horrible things up in the mountains. I saw it. And I think he's here among us in California."

"You're talking about this gold find, aren't you?"

I nodded.

He looked over my shoulder toward the mountains. "On that we agree, lass. I've seen sensible men leave their jobs and families and go traipsing off with nothing more than a mule and a pick. All in search of a golden idol."

"But I've seen God too. I've seen Him beat the devil."

He smiled. "This part of the story I've heard from Patrick Breen."

"And none better to tell it," I said. "Every night while we were stuck in the mountains, Mama and I would go to Mister Breen's cabin—mind you, we'd run out of food weeks earlier and were down to eating tree bark and tallow. He'd pull out his Bible and find a verse that gave us enough strength to face another day. Then he'd end the night with a prayer, but not any 'thank you kindly, Lord' everyday prayer. He'd belt out a thank you so full of happiness it would scare the wolves away from the cattle bones. And he'd wail about the sinfulness of mankind as to make you wish you could crawl under a rock. By the time he'd finish, we were so full of Spirit the skin hanging off our bones and the barren state of our bellies were no longer a burden."

"And that's when you made your vow? That's when you decided to become a Catholic?"

"Yes. Mister Breen was Catholic, and I thought if being a Catholic made you that strong, so strong you could stand up to starvation while others had taken to eating the dead, then that was the religion for me."

"I have great respect for Mister Breen," Father O'Rourke said. "An Irishman cut from the old cloth like my own pap. He'd be so proud of you now."

"It does my heart good that you say so, Father. But the true nature of my visit is this Eucharist business."

He raised an eyebrow.

"I'm told it's the consumption of the flesh of Christ."

Understanding seemed to take hold in his face. "Put your heart at rest, lass. It's not cannibalism."

"But it is the eating of His flesh, isn't it? No symbolism in the Catholic faith. 'Take, eat. This is my body,' He said."

His smile now looked practiced. "It's consumption of His spiritual flesh, not His physical flesh. It is a gift He left us to experience His divine nature on Earth. Don't fret."

"But I do fret, Father, I made another vow to God in the mountains—that I would never eat human flesh. I don't make such vows lightly."

"Nor should you, lass. But it's not cannibalism."

"Did God's son come to us in the flesh?"

He nodded, no longer smiling.

"When you bless the bread, is it just bread or is it Christ?"

"It is Christ. But, Virginia, to become a Catholic, at some point you must partake in the Eucharist."

I looked away. "My vows are at odds."

Father O'Rourke put his work gloves back on and stood. "Then you must choose."

I liked Saturdays. The school at Sutter's Fort was closed on the weekend, and on sunny days Papa would let me take Jeebers to the Sacramento River and I'd fish the day away. Funny—Captain Sutter tried to name it Sutter's River when he was building the fort so many years ago. Mrs. Mora told me the Spanish would have none of that. They told the Captain their ancestors had named it nearly a hundred years earlier, and that was that.

But today was no day for fishing. I got out of bed, put on a dress, and went to look for Mama. I found her hoeing in the garden.

"About time you woke up. Get a hoe and start at the far side of that row of beans."

I picked up a hoe, but I started on the closer end of the row.

If she noticed, she didn't say anything. Her face was well shaded by a straw bonnet, and she kept her eyes on her work, pounding away at weeds and dirt clods. The hem of her blue dress was tinged brown with dust.

"Mama?"

"Hm?"

"You remember back in the mountains, right at Christmastime?"

She didn't look up. "You know I don't like talking about the mountains."

"I know, but this is important. Do you remember? It was right after Betsy Donner died. I thought you'd be too sad to even remember Christmas, but the next day, you put on your best smile and cooked us a Christmas meal."

"I don't remember." Her voice was strange, hollow. She kept hoeing.

"How could you not remember? We hadn't eaten proper food in weeks, and we were living off tallow that made us sick half the time. And this Christmas meal comes out of nowhere like a gift from heaven."

She worked faster and began to move away.

I threw down my hoe and marched in front of her.

She stopped and looked at me. Her eyes were wide and her face frozen.

"That Christmas stew, Mama. The onions were mostly rotten and the broth was made from boiled leather, but where did that meat come from?"

"Tripe from the oxen." Her words were a tremble, just above a whisper.

"It wasn't tripe!" I grabbed her hoe and yanked it out of her hands and threw it aside. She stepped back and tried to hide a grimace and welling tears with her hands.

"There was blood-meat in that stew, Mama. Where'd it come from?"

"Oh, honey. You've got to understand. We were going to die. I had to."

I couldn't stop my own tears. "What did you do, Mama?" I grabbed her shoulders. "What did you do to me?"

"It was Billy. I'm so sorry . . . sorry." She took a long suck of air and sobbed.

I let her go. "Billy?"

She dropped her hands and nodded, still crying. "I remembered where he'd died in the fall. I didn't have to dig through much snow since the wolves had done most of the work for me. They'd made off with most of the meat, but there was a clump of flesh left that was good for eating." She looked me in the eyes. "It was Christmas, Virginia. I had to make it special."

"Billy?" I started to laugh.

Mama looked at me, sniffling. When my laughing didn't stop, she planted her fists on her hips. "Have you gone crazy, girl? I just told you the most god-awful secret I kept buried in my heart and all you can do is laugh."

I recovered enough to fetch Mama's hoe and hand it back to her. "I just found out I ate my own pony." I picked up my hoe. "I feel like the weight of the world's been lifted off my shoulders."

Mama wiped her nose, gave me a cross look, and went back to work. "I suppose this has something to do with this Catholic nonsense you've taken up. Did that priest tell you to go and scare the dickens out of your mother?"

"It does have something to do with this *Catholic* business, and no, Father O'Rourke wouldn't ask anyone to do such a horrible thing. It's just . . ."

"What?"

"Nothing. I mean, I'm sorry for scaring you, and you did the right thing putting poor old Billy in the stew. I loved him, but there was no sense in us starving while the wolves were getting fat."

We worked away in silence for a little while.

"Your papa and I had a little talk this morning before he set off for the mill."

I stopped hoeing. "And?"

"Well, we both agreed that you're becoming a young lady now, and that you're not likely to let go of this Catholic vow of yours."

I held my breath.

"You're old enough to make this decision on your own. He wrote a letter for the priest and put it on the table."

I dropped my hoe and charged for the house. I heard Mama call after me. "You can't finish your hoeing first?"

I didn't answer. I found the letter and ran to the stable for Jeebers. Mama was still in the garden gawking at me as I rode by. "I'll be back in an hour, I promise." I dug my heels into Jeebers and shouted, "Thank you, Mama! And tell Papa I love him!"

"Virginia Reed! Stop riding that horse like a man!"

"I'm sorry, Sister Beatrice." I really wasn't sorry. Not even Catholic yet and I was piling up sins like an undertaker piling up gold teeth.

I dismounted and pushed my dress down to cover my legs. I'd forgotten about putting on riding trousers under my dress when I started out. Had there been soldiers about when I rode into the fort, I would've dismounted at the gate and led Jeebers in by the rein. Marriage proposals were one thing; I could brush those off by the bushel. But I didn't know what I'd do if a soldier tried to encourage some sort of base behavior from me. Maybe I'd run away. Maybe I'd slap him like I did Louis Keseberg.

As it was, the soldiers were still neglecting their duties and out digging for gold. All I had to endure was a cross Sister Beatrice.

I held tight to Jeebers even though he was in no mood for wandering. I'd given him quite a ride from home. "I'm trying to find Father O'Rourke. No one answered at his cabin so I came to the fort hoping he was here." I knew he sometimes held meetings with the Sisters at their dormitory on the fort grounds, and I didn't want to ride the extra miles to the church if I could help it.

The Sister's eyes blazed. "I should speak to your mother about your poor habits. Half the men around here haven't seen an unmarried woman for over a year. If they catch a glimpse of you with your dress hiked up over your knees . . ."

"Please, Sister Beatrice. I have to find the Father. My papa is letting me join the church."

The Sister worked her jaw in silence and gave me a cold stare. "Well, everyone is looking for the Father. He's at church, so you've got two miles to practice ladylike riding."

"Thank you." I led Jeebers toward the fort's gate. I was in too much of a hurry for *ladylike* riding, so I'd have to mount up out of the Sister's sight.

Something tickled my interest. I turned. "Sister?"

"Yes?"

"What did you mean when you said everyone was looking for the Father?"

"I mean that Louis Keseberg was looking for him all morning. Louis said he needed to be baptized a Catholic right away. Said he was dying or some such nonsense, and wanted to leave this world as a Christian." The Sister rolled her eyes. "He looked perfectly healthy to me."

"Louis Keseberg?"

She nodded. "That's why Father O'Rourke is at the church. He and Louis went out there for a baptism."

I patted Jeebers's neck to help calm my nerves. "Are they alone?"

"Yes." She paused and shook her head. "I mean no. Sister Rosa should be there this time of day. It's her turn to clean the church."

I didn't care if Sister Beatrice saw my bare legs. I ignored her yells as I kicked Jeebers into a gallop.

I saw rising smoke as I neared the church, and I was afraid I'd find nothing but charred timbers. When I arrived, the church was safe and sound. The smoke was coming from behind the building.

I tied off Jeebers, picked up a stout branch good for hitting, and ran around back.

There was Louis Keseberg, sitting on a log, as pleased as a cat with a mouse. He whistled a tune as he roasted a piece of meat at the end of a stick over a fire, which he must have built from the remnants of the church's construction. Two daggers were propped on a log next to him, both forged of black steel that glinted razor-sharp. Their hilts looked of ivory, carved in the shape of some tormented soul in the last throes of life. They gave me a chill.

A groan caused me to turn toward the back wall of the church. There was Father O'Rourke, tied and lying on the ground. Blood leaked from his forehead, and there were red splatters on his white vestments. His eyes slowly drifted in my direction. "Run, Virginia. Get to the fort." His voice was weak and raspy.

Keseberg quit his whistling and turned to look at me. "Ah, Virginia. Fate decreed you would come, although I'm often a Doubting Thomas. Come have lunch with me." He withdrew the meat from the fire and poked at it with his finger.

My heart raced and I gripped my branch with both hands. "Keseberg, what have you done?" My voice sounded strange—high and shrill.

"It's not so much what I've done, but what you're going to do. You wanted to join God's army since the mountains—indeed, you were meant to join, but Mister Breen got in the way. He may have put this Catholic obsession in your head, but fate won't be denied."

I took a step forward and raised the branch. He was a good twenty feet away and could reach those knives before I got a lick at him. "God's army? You've been hand in hand with the devil all this time, haven't you?"

Keseberg extended the meat back into the flames. "God . . . the devil. Really competing gods. Don't you find it ironic that they both require cannibalism of their soldiers? Maybe it's more than ironic. In any case, *my* god was quite upset that you denied him in the mountains. It seems there's something very special in you, though for the life of me, I can't see it."

He examined the meat again and turned to me. "It's time for you to join, Virginia."

My breath caught as I got a good look at the meat. I had seen its like before. I looked at Father O'Rourke, but other than a nasty gash on the forehead, he seemed fine.

"Run, lass," he said. "Stop thinking about it."

Keseberg laughed. "She won't run." Quick as a snake, he snatched up one of the knives and pointed it toward the Father, who lay about ten feet away. "She knows what I'll do to you if she does."

I forced myself to breathe. I had left all my tears in the mountains, but I had hate to burn. I imagined it showed in my eyes. "Where's Sister Rosa?"

Keseberg kept the knife poised at Father O'Rourke. "Where does one make a sacrifice? On the altar, my dear."

I ran to the church's back door.

"Don't look, Virginia," Father O'Rourke said. "It's horrible."

I opened the door and entered. It was horrible. For all the sharpness of those knives, Keseberg had been savage with the Sister's innards. I had once seen a sheep carcass after coyotes had finished with it. Very similar. Keseberg had even used part of the Sister's offal as a garland around the crucifix.

Father O'Rourke probably expected wailing when I came back outside, but I was sure Keseberg knew better. He now stood over the Father with the knife ready to strike. "Throw the branch on the fire, Virginia."

Keseberg was still too far away for me to make a charge. He had it all figured out. I glanced at the log he had been sitting on as I walked to the fire. The other knife was gone. I tossed the branch in the flames, and it began to crackle. "Afraid of a sixteen-year-old girl?"

"The mountains made you strong, Virginia, and I like all of the advantages." Keseberg stepped around the sitting log and approached. The roasted piece of Sister Rosa was in his other hand. He presented it. "Join."

Father O'Rourke rolled on his side to face us. "Don't do it, Virginia. It's forbidden—a terrible sin."

Keseberg gave a soulless laugh. "Her strength works against her now, Priest. Her spirit sustained her in the mountains, but now she'll sacrifice herself to save you."

"Hold it steady." I grabbed his arm to stop him from moving, although my shaking wasn't improving matters.

He pointed the knife at my heart. "Turn back now and it will cost both your lives."

I knew there was no turning back.

"*Corpus Domini nostri Jesu Christi . . .*"

May the body of our Lord Jesus Christ . . .

I looked back at Father O'Rourke. A blessing for Satan's feast?

Keseberg's voice turned harsh. "A wasted prayer, Priest. You can't sanctify this meat. The knives I used came straight from Satan's heart. It can't be blessed."

". . . *custodiat animam tuam in vitam aeternam.*"

. . . preserve your soul unto everlasting life.

"No hesitation, Virginia," Keseberg said. "Now is the time."

I still held his arm. I pulled it closer.

"Amen," Father O'Rourke said.

Maybe Keseberg was right. Father O'Rourke's blessing couldn't overcome the evil of the knives . . .

. . . had he been trying to bless the meat.

I bit deeply, and my mouth filled with the taste of buttered crust and stone-baked bread.

Keseberg howled and staggered back. He dropped his knife to hold his wrist and dangling hand. Bone and vessels were severed cleanly, following the shape of my mouth. Blood spouted to his heart's rhythm.

I shoved him, and he went toppling over a log.

He looked up at me. His feral look was gone and his eyes were wide. "Stay away!"

I leaped on him. Grabbing his shoulder with one hand, I forced his head back with the other. His screaming ended as I bit through his windpipe and part of his throat—this time, earthy rye. My mouth was so full of bread I couldn't swallow. I put my lips to a broken, pumping artery in his neck.

The sweetest of wines.

The voice of Father O'Rourke rose behind me. "*Corpus tuum, Domine, quod sumpsi, et Sanguis quem potavi, adhaereat visceribus meis.*"

May Your body, Lord, which I have eaten and Your blood which I have drunk, cleave to my very soul.

I turned to him, sated. "Look, Father. Look. I've chosen."

HOLLY BLACK

A Reversal of Fortune

Author of the young adult novels including, most recently, Ironside, *as well as the best-selling* Spiderwick Chronicles, *Holly Black lives with her husband, Theo, in a Tudor Revival house in Amherst, Massachusetts. "A Reversal of Fortune" was originally published in Ellen Datlow and Terri Windling's anthology* The Coyote Road: Trickster Tales, *and we suggest that readers who enjoy this tale of a deal with the devil look for these just-as-engaging stories by Black, also published in 2008: "The Coat of Stars" (So Fey), "Paper Cuts Scissors" (Realms of Fantasy), and "The Poison Eaters" (The Restless Dead).*

—K. L. & G. G.

Nikki opened the refrigerator. There was nothing in there but a couple of shriveled oranges and three gallons of tap water. She slammed it closed. Summer was supposed to be the best part of the year, but so far Nikki's summer sucked. It sucked hard. It sucked like a vacuum that got hold of the drapes.

Her pit bull, Boo, whined and scraped at the door, etching new lines into the battered wood. Nikki clipped on his leash. She knew she should trim his nails. They frayed the nylon of his collar and gouged the door, but when she tried to cut them, he cried like a baby. Nikki figured he'd had enough pain in his life and left his nails long.

"Come on, Boo," she said as she led him out the front door of the trailer. The air outside shimmered with heat and the air conditioner chugged away in the window, dribbling water down the aluminum siding.

Lifting the lid of the rusty mailbox, Nikki pulled out a handful of circulars and bills. There, among them, she found a stale half bagel with the words "Butter me!" written on it in gel pen and the crumbly surface stamped with half a dozen stamps. She sighed. Renee's crazy postcards had stopped making her laugh.

Boo hopped down the cement steps gingerly, paws smearing sour cherry tree pulp and staining his feet purple. He paused when he hit their tiny patch of sun-withered lawn to lick one of the hairless scars along his back.

"Come *on*. I have to get ready for work." Nikki gave his collar a sharp tug.

He yelped and she felt instantly terrible. He'd put on some weight since she'd found him and was looking better, but he still was pretty easily freaked. She leaned down to pat the solid warmth of his back. His tail started going and he turned his massive face to lick her cheek.

Of course that was the moment her neighbor, Trevor, drove up in his gleaming black truck. He parked in front of his trailer and hopped out, the plastic connective tissue of a six-pack threaded between his fingers. She admired the way the muscles on his back moved as he walked to the door of his place, making the raven tattoo on his shoulder ripple.

"Hey," she called, pushing Boo's wet face away and standing up. Why did Trevor pick this moment to be around, when she was covered in dog drool, hair in tangles, wearing her brother's gi-normous T-shirt? Even the thong on one of her flip-flops had ripped out so she had to shuffle to keep the sole on.

The dog raised his leg and pissed on a dandelion just as Trevor turned around and gave her a negligent half wave.

Boo rooted around for a few minutes more and then Nikki tugged him inside. She pulled on a pair of low-slung orange pants and a black T-shirt with the outline of a dachshund on it. Busy thinking of Trevor, she cut through the self-service car wash that stood between the trailer park and the highway. As she waded through the streams of antifreeze-green cleanser and gobs of snowy foam bubbles, Nikki realized she still wore her broken flip-flops.

There were a couple of people waiting on the bench by the bus stop, the stink of exhaust from the highway not appearing to bother them one bit. Two women with oversized glasses were chatting away, their curled hair wilting in the heat. An elderly man in a black and white hound's-tooth suit leaned on a cane and grinned when she got closer.

Nikki took a deep breath of the sour cherry spatter mixed with the car wash liquids that make the Jersey summers smell like a chemical plant of rotten fruit. She tried to decide if the bus was going to come before she ran back for some sandals.

Just then, Nikki's brother Doug's battered gray Honda pulled into the trailer park. He'd bought the car two weeks ago even though he didn't have a job; he anticipated a big winning in another month and seemed to think he was already made of money.

Nikki ran over to the car and rapped on the window.

Doug jumped in his seat, then scowled when he saw her. His beard glimmered with grease as he eased himself out of the car. He was a big guy to begin with, and over four hundred pounds now. Nikki was just the opposite—skinny as a straw no matter what she ate.

"Can you take me to work?" she asked. "It's too hot to take the bus."

He shook his head and belched, making the air smell like a beach after the tide went out and left the mussels to bake in the sun. "I got some more training to do. Spinks is coming over to do gallon-water trials."

"Come on," she said. It sucked that he got to screw around when she had to work. "Where were you anyway?"

"Chinese buffet," he said. "Did fifty shrimp. Volume's okay, I guess. My speed blows, though. I just slow down after the first five to eight minutes. Peeling is a bitch and those waitresses are always looking at me and giggling."

"Take me to work. You are going to puke if you eat anything else."

His eyes widened and he held up a hand, as if to ward off her words. "How many times do I have to tell you? It's a 'reversal of fortune' or a 'Roman incident.' Don't *ever* say puke. That's bad luck."

Nikki shifted her weight, the intensity of his reaction embarrassing her. "Fine. Whatever. Sorry."

He sighed. "I'll drive you, but you have to take the bus home."

"Deal!" Nikki shouted, running for the house. She kicked off her flip-flops and picked up some sandals, then ran back. Sitting in the cracked backseat of his car, she brushed a tangle of silvery wrappers off the leather. A pack of gum sat in the grimy brake well and she pulled out a piece.

"Good for jaw strength," Doug said.

"Good for fresh breath," she replied, rolling her eyes. "Not that you care about that."

He looked out the window. "Gurgitators get groupies, you know. Once I'm established on the competitive eating circuit, I'll be meeting tons of women."

"There's a scary thought," she said as they pulled onto the highway.

"You should try it. I'm battling the whole 'belt of fat' thing—my stomach only expands so far—but the skinny people can really pack it in. You should see this little girl that's eating big guys like me under the table."

"If you keep emptying out the fridge, I might just do it," Nikki said. "I might have to."

Nikki walked through the crowded mall, past skaters getting kicked out by rent-a-cops and listless homemakers pushing baby carriages. At the beginning of summer, when she'd first gotten the job, she had imagined that Renee would still be working at the T-shirt kiosk and Leah would be at Gotheteria and they would wave to each other across the body of the mall and go to the food court every day for lunch. She didn't expect that Renee would be on some extended road-trip vacation with her parents and that Leah would ignore Nikki in front of her new black-lipsticked friends.

If not for Boo, she would have spent the summer waiting around for the bizarre postcards Renee sent from cross-country stops. At first they were just pictures of the Liberty Bell or the Smithsonian with messages on the back about the cute guys she'd seen at a rest stop or the number of times she'd punched her brother using the excuse of playing Padiddle—but then they started to get loonier. A museum brochure where Renee had given each of the paintings obscene thought balloons. A ripped piece of a menu with words blacked out to spell messages like "Cheese is the way." A leaf that got too mangled in the mail to read the words on it. A section of newspaper folded into a boat that said, "Do you think clams get seasick?" And, of course, the bagel.

It bothered Nikki that Renee was still funny and still having fun while Nikki felt lost. Leah had drifted away as though Renee was all that had kept the three of them together, and without Renee to laugh at her jokes, Nikki couldn't seem to be funny. She couldn't even tell if she was having fun.

Kim stood behind the counter of The Sweet Tooth candy store, a long string of red licorice hanging from her mouth. She looked up when Nikki came in. "You're late."

"So?" Nikki asked.

"Boss's son's in the back," Kim said.

Kim loved anime so passionately that she convinced their boss to stock Pocky and lychee gummies and green tea and ginger candies with hard surfaces but runny, spicy insides. They'd done so well that the Boss started asking Kim's opinion on all the new orders. She acted like he'd made her manager.

Nikki liked all sweets equally—peanut butter taffy, lime-green foil-wrapped "alien coins" with chocolate discs inside, gummy geckos and gummy sidewinders and a whole assortment of translucent gummy fruit, long strips of paper dotted with sugar dots, shining and jagged rock candy, hot-as-Hell atomic fireballs, sticks of violet candy that tasted like flowery chalk, giant multicolored spiral lollipops, not to mention chocolate-covered malt balls, chocolate-covered blueberries and raspberries and peanuts, and even tiny packages of chocolate-covered ants.

The pay was pretty much crap, but Nikki was allowed to eat as much candy as she wanted. She picked out a coffee toffee to start with because it seemed breakfast-y.

The boss's son came out of the stockroom, his sleeveless T-shirt thin enough that Nikki could see the hair that covered his back and chest through the cloth. He scowled at her. "Most girls get sick of the candy after a while," he said, in a tone that was half grudging admiration, half panic at the profits vanishing through her teeth.

Nikki paused in her consumption of a pile of sour gummy lizards, their hides crunchy with granules of sugar. "Sorry," she said.

That seemed to be the right answer, because he turned to Kim and told her to restock the pomegranate jelly beans.

Nikki's stomach growled. While his back was turned, she popped another lizard into her mouth.

It was pouring when Nikki finished her shift. Rain slicked her skin and plastered her hair to her neck as she waited for the bus in front of Macy's. By the time it finally came, she was soaked and even more convinced that her summer was doomed.

Nikki pushed her way into one of the few remaining seats, next to an old guy that smelled like a sulfurous fart. It took her a moment to realize he was the hound's-tooth suit-and-cane guy from the bus stop that morning. He'd probably been riding the bus this whole time. Still jittery from sugar, she could feel the headache-y start of a post-candy crash in her immediate future. Nikki tried to ignore the heavy wetness of her clothes and to breathe as shallowly as possible to avoid the old guy's stink.

The bus lurched forward. A woman chatting on her cell phone stumbled into Nikki's knee.

"'Scuse me," the woman said sharply, as though Nikki were the one that fell.

"I'm going to give you what you want," the man next to her whispered. Weirdly, his breath was like honey.

Nikki didn't reply. Nice breath or not, he was still a stinky, senile old pervert.

"I'm talking to you, girl." He touched her arm.

She turned toward him. "You're not supposed to talk to people on buses."

His cheeks wrinkled as he smiled. "Is that so?"

"Yeah, trains too. It's a mass-transportation thing. Anything stuffed with people, you're supposed to act like you're alone."

"Is that what you want?" he asked. "You want everyone to act like you're not here?"

"Pretty much. You going to give me what I want?" Nikki asked, hoping he would shut up. She wished she could just tell freakjobs to screw themselves, but she hated that hurt look that they sometimes got. It made her think of Boo. She would put up with a lot to not see that look.

He nodded. "I sure am."

The 'scuse-me woman looked in their direction, blinked, then plopped her fat ass right on Nikki's lap. Nikki yelped and the woman got up, red-faced.

"What are you doing there?" the 'scuse-me lady gasped.

The old pervert started laughing so hard that spit flew out of his mouth.

"Sitting," Nikki said. "What the hell are you doing?"

The woman turned away from Nikki, muttering to herself.

"You're very fortunate to be sitting next to me," the pervert said.

"How do you figure that?"

He laughed again, hard and long. "I gave you what you wanted. I'll give you the next thing you want too." He winked a rheumy eye. "For a price."

"Whatever," Nikki muttered.

"You know where to find me."

Mercifully, the next stop was Nikki's. She shoved the 'scuse-me woman hard as she pushed her way off the bus.

Doug sat on the steps of the trailer, his hair frizzy with drizzle. He looked grim.

"What's going on?" Nikki asked. "Only managed to eat half your body weight?"

"Boo's been hit," he said, voice rough. "Trevor hit your dog."

For a moment, Nikki couldn't breathe. The world seemed to speed up around her, cars streaking along the highway, the wind tossing wet leaves across the lot.

She thought about the raven tattoo on Trevor's back and wished someone would rip it off along with his skin. She wanted to tear him into a thousand pieces.

She thought about the old pervert on the bus.

I'll give you the next thing you want too.

You know where to find me.

"Where's Boo now?" Nikki asked.

"At the vet. Mom wanted me to drive you over as soon as you got home."

"Why was he outside? Who let him out?"

"Mom came home with groceries. He slipped past her."

"Is he oka—?"

Doug shook his head. "They're waiting for you before they put him down. They wanted to give you a chance to say good-bye."

She wanted to throw up or scream or cry, but when she spoke, her voice sounded so calm that it unnerved her. "Why? Isn't there anything they can do?"

"Listen, the doctor said they could operate, but it's a couple thousand dollars and you know we can't afford it." Doug's voice was soft, like he was sorry, but she wanted to hit him anyway.

Nikki looked across the lot, but the truck wasn't in front of Trevor's trailer and his windows were dark. "We could make Trevor pay."

Doug sighed. "Not going to happen."

Now she felt tears well in her eyes, but she blinked them back. She wouldn't grieve over Boo. She'd save him. "I'm not going anywhere with you."

"You have to, Nikki. Mom's waiting for you."

"Call her. Tell her I'll be there in an hour. I'm taking the bus." Nikki grabbed the sleeve of Doug's jacket, gripping it as hard as she could. "She better not do anything to Boo until I get there." Tears slid down her cheek. She ignored them, concentrating on looking as fierce as possible. "You better not either."

"Calm down. I'm not going to—" Doug said, but she was already walking away.

Nikki got on the next bus that stopped and scanned the aisles for the old pervert. A woman with two bags of groceries cradled to her chest looked up at Nikki, then abruptly turned away. A youngish man stretched out on the long backseat shifted in his sleep, his fingers curled tightly around a bottle of beer. Three men in green coveralls conversed softly in Spanish. There was no one else.

Nikki slid into her seat, wrapping her arms around her body as though she could hold in her sobs with sheer pressure. She had no idea what to do. Looking for a weird old guy that could grant wishes was pathetic. It was sad and stupid.

If there was some way to get the money, things might be different. She thought of all the stuff in the trailer that could be sold, but it didn't add up to a thousand dollars. Even sticking her hand into the till at The Sweet Tooth was unlikely to net more than a few hundred.

Outside the window, the strip malls and motels slid together in her tear-blurred vision. Nikki thought of the day she'd found Boo by the side of the road, dehydrated and bloody. With all those bite marks, she figured his owners had been fighting him against other dogs, but when he saw her he bounded up as dumb and sweet and trusting as if he'd been pampered since he was a puppy. If he died, nothing would ever be fair again.

The bus stopped in front of a churchyard, the doors opened, and the old guy got on. He wore a suit of shiny sharkskin and carried a cane with a silver greyhound instead of a knob. He still stank of rotten eggs, though. Worse than ever.

Nikki sat up straight, wiping her face with her sleeve. "Hey."

He looked over at her as though he didn't know her. "Excuse me?"

"I've been looking for you. I need your help."

Sitting down in the seat across the aisle, he unbuttoned the bottom button on his jacket. "That's magic to my ears."

"My dog." Nikki sank her fingernails into the flesh of her palm to keep herself calm. "Someone hit my dog and he's going to die. . . ."

His face broke into a wrinkled grin. "And you want him to live. Like I've never heard that one before."

He was making fun of her, but she forced a smile. "So you'll do it."

He shook his head. "Nope."

"What do you mean? Why not?"

A long sigh escaped his lips, like he was already tired of the conversation. "Let's just say that it's not in my nature."

"What is that supposed to mean?"

He shifted the cane in his lap and she noticed that what she had thought of as a greyhound appeared to have three silver heads. He scowled at her, like a teacher when you missed an obvious answer and he knew you hadn't done the reading. "You have to give me something to get something."

"I've got forty bucks," she said, biting her lip. "I don't want to do any sex stuff."

"I am not entirely without sympathy." He shrugged his thin shoulders. "How about this—I will wager my services against something of yours. If you can beat me at any contest of your choosing, your dog will be well and you'll owe me nothing."

"Really? Any contest?" she asked.

He held out his hand. "Shake on it and we've got a deal."

His skin was warm and dry in her grip.

"So, what's it going to be?" he asked. "You play the fiddle? Or maybe you'd like to try your hand at jump rope?"

She took a long look at him. He was slender and his clothes hung on him a bit, as though he'd been bigger when he'd bought them. He didn't look like a big eater. "An eating contest," she said. "I'm wagering that I can eat more than you can."

He laughed so hard she thought for a moment he was having a seizure. "That's a new one. Fine. I'm all appetite."

His reaction made her nervous. "Wait—" she said. "You never told me what you wanted if I lost."

"Just a little thing. You won't miss it." He indicated the door of the bus with his cane. "Next stop is yours. I'll be by tomorrow. Don't worry about your dog for tonight."

She stood. "First tell me what I'm going to lose."

"You'll overreact," he said, shaking his head.

"I won't," Nikki said, but she wasn't sure what she would do. What could he want? She'd said "no sex," but he hadn't made any promises.

The old guy held out his hands in a conciliatory gesture. "Your soul."

"What? Why would you want that?"

"I'm a collector. I have to have the whole set—complete. All souls. They're going to look *spectacular* all lined up. There was a time when I was close, but then there were all these special releases and I got behind. And forget about having them mint-in-box. I have to settle for what I can get these days."

"You're joking."

"Maybe." He looked out the window, as if considering all those missing souls. "Don't worry. It's like an appendix. You won't even miss it."

Nikki walked home from the bus stop, her stomach churned as she thought over the bargain she'd made. Her soul. The devil. She had just made a bargain with the devil. Who else wanted to buy souls?

She stomped into the trailer to see her mom on the couch, eating a piece of frozen pizza. Doug sat next to her, watching a car being rebuilt on television. Both of them looked tired.

"Oh, honey," her mother said. "I'm so sorry."

Nikki sat down on the shag rug. "You didn't kill Boo, did you?"

"The vet said that we could wait until tomorrow and see how he's doing, but he wasn't very encouraging." Long fingers stroked Nikki's hair, but she refused to be soothed. "You have to think what would be best for the poor dog. You don't want him to suffer."

Nikki jumped up and stalked over to the kitchen. "I don't want him to die!"

"Go talk to your sister," their mother said. Doug pushed himself up off the couch.

"Show me how to train for an eating contest," Nikki told him when he tried to speak. "Show me right now."

He shook his head. "You're seriously losing it."

"Yeah," she said. "But I need to win."

The next morning, after her mother left for work, Nikki called herself out sick and started straightening up the place. After all, the devil was the most famous guest she'd ever had. She'd heard of him, and what was more, she was pretty sure he knew a lot of people she'd be impressed by.

He knocked on the door of the trailer around noon. Today, he wore a red double-breasted suit with a black shirt and tie. He carried a gnarled cane in a glossy brown, like polished walnut.

Seeing her looking at it, he smiled. "Bull penis. Not too many of these around anymore."

"You dress like a pimp," Nikki said before she thought better of it.

His smile just broadened.

"So are you *a* devil or *the* devil?" Nikki held the screen door open for him.

"I'm a devil to some." He winked as he walked past her. "But I'm the devil to you."

She shuddered. Suddenly the idea of him being the supernatural seemed entirely too real. "My brother's in the back waiting for us."

Nikki had set up on the picnic table in the common area of the trailer park. She walked onto the hot concrete and the devil followed her. Doug looked up from where he carefully counted out portions of sour-gummy frogs onto paper plates. He looked like a giant, holding each tiny candy between two thick fingers.

Nikki brushed an earwig and some sour cherry splatter off a bench and sat down. "Doug's going to explain the rules."

The devil sat down across from her and leaned his cane against the table. "Good. I'm starving."

Doug stood up, wiping sweaty palms on his jeans. "This is what we're going to do. We have a bag of 166 sour-gummy frogs. That's all we could get. I divided them into sixteen plates of ten and two plates of three, so you each have a maximum of eighty-three frogs. If you both eat the same number of frogs, whoever finishes their frogs first wins. If you have a . . . er . . . reversal of fortune, then you lose, period."

"He means if you puke," Nikki said.

Doug gave her a stern look, but didn't say anything.

"We need not be limited by your supply," said the devil. A huge tarnished silver platter appeared on the table. It scuttled over to Nikki on chicken feet and she saw that it was heaped with sugar-studded frogs.

The candy on the paper plates looked dull in comparison with what glimmered on the table. Nikki picked up an orange-and-black gummy candy poison dart frog and put it regretfully down. It just seemed dumb to let the devil supply the food. "You have to use ours."

The devil shrugged. With a wave of his hand, the dish of frogs disappeared, leaving nothing behind but a burnt-sugar smell. "Very well."

Doug put a plastic pitcher of water and two glasses between them. "Okay," he said, lifting up a stopwatch. "Go!"

Nikki started eating. The salty sweet flavor flooded her mouth as she crammed in candy.

Across the table, the devil lifted up his first paper plate, rolling it up and using the tube to pour frogs into a mouth that seemed to expand. His jaw unhinged like a snake. He picked up a second plate.

Nikki swallowed frog after frog, ignoring the cloying sweetness, racing to catch up.

Doug slid a new pile in front of Nikki and she started eating. She was in the zone. One frog, then another, then a sip of water. The sugar scraped her throat raw, but she kept eating.

The devil poured a third plate of candy down his throat, then a fourth. At the seventh plate, the devil paused with a groan. He untucked his shirt and undid the button on his dress pants to pat his engorged belly. He looked full.

Nikki stuffed candy in her mouth, suddenly filled with hope.

The devil chuckled and unsheathed a knife from the top of his cane.

"What are you doing?" Doug shouted.

"Just making room," the devil said. Pressing the blade to his belly, he slit a line in his stomach. Dozens upon dozens of gooey half-chewed frogs tumbled into the dirt.

Nikki stared at him, paralyzed with dread. Her fingers still held a frog, but she didn't bring it to her lips. She had no hope of winning.

Doug looked away from the mess of partially digested candy. "That's cheating!"

The devil tipped up the seventh plate into his widening mouth and swallowed ten frogs at once. "Nothing in the rules against it."

Nikki wondered what it would be like to have no soul. Would she barely miss it? Could she still dream? Without one, would she have no more guilt or fear or fun? Maybe without a soul she wouldn't even care that Boo was dead.

The devil cheated. If she wanted to win, she had to cheat too.

On her sixth plate, Nikki started sweating, but she knew she could finish. She just couldn't finish before he did.

The devil cheated. If she wanted to win, she had to cheat too.

She had to beat him in quantity. She had to eat more sour-gummy frogs than he did.

"I feel sick," Nikki lied.

"Don't *you know*." Doug shook his head vigorously. "Fight it."

Nikki bent over, holding her stomach. While hidden by the table, she picked up one of the slimy, chewed-up frogs that had been in the devil's stomach and popped it in her mouth. The frog tasted like sweetness and dirt and something rotten.

The nausea was real this time. She choked and forced herself to swallow around the sour taste of her own gorge.

Sitting up, she saw that the devil had finished all his frogs. She still had two more plates to go.

"I win," the devil said. "No need to keep eating."

Doug sank fingers into his hair and tugged. "He's right."

"No way." Nikki gulped down another mouthful of candy. "I'm finishing my plates."

She ate and ate, ignoring how the rubbery frogs stuck in her throat. She kept eating. Swallowed the last sour-gummy frog, she stood up. "Are you finished?"

"I've been finished for ages," said the devil.

"Then *I* win."

The devil yawned. "Impossible."

"I ate one more frog than you did," she said. "So I win."

He pointed his cane at Doug. "If you cheated and gave her another frog, we'll be doing this contest over and you'll be joining us."

Doug shook his head. "It took me an hour to count out those frogs. They were exactly even."

"I ate one of the frogs from your gut," Nikki said. "I picked it up off the ground and I ate it."

"That's disgusting!" Doug said.

"Five-second rule," Nikki said. "If it's in the devil for less than five seconds, it's still good."

"That's *cheating*," said the devil. He sounded half admiring and half appalled, reminding her bizarrely of her Boss's son at The Sweet Tooth.

She shook her head. "Nothing in the rules against it."

The devil scowled for a moment, then bowed shallowly. "Well done, Nicole. Count on seeing me again soon." With those words, he ambled toward the bus station. Pausing in front of Trevor's trailer, he pulled out a handful of envelopes from the mailbox and kept going.

Nikki's mother's car pulled into the lot, Boo's head visible in the passenger side window. His tongue lolled despite the absurd cone-shaped collar around his neck.

Nikki hopped up on top of the picnic table and shrieked with joy, leaping around, the sugar and adrenaline and relief making her giddy.

She stopped jumping. "You know what?"

Doug looked up at her. "What?"

"I think my summer is starting not to suck so much."

Doug sat down on a bench so hard that she heard the wood strain. The look he gave her was pure disbelief.

"So," Nikki asked, "you want to get some lunch?"

MAGGIE SMITH

Village Smart

Maggie Smith is the author of Lamp of the Body *and* Nesting Dolls. *Her poems appear or will be featured soon in* Massachusetts Review, Quarterly West, Gulf Coast, *and* Green Court.

"Village Smart" was originally published in Mid-American Review *Vol. XXVII, #2.*

—*E. D.*

It's what they call the devil, as in *cunning*.
When his cloven heart is hungry, he finds a way to feed it.
For every child sewn up into a sack and drowned,
candy-dipped in pitch, cut and seasoned, there is one
untouched but waiting. Name your first son Sorrowful
if you must. At least you have a son. If the devil comes
to claim him, carve the eyes and tongue from a deer
to prove the deed done. What will you tell your son
about this world? That children can be unzipped
from the bellies of beasts? No one is out of danger.
Darkness threads a needle as fast as light. As the devil eats,
bones pile under the table. Bread cries out in the oven
for fear of burning. A heart nestles among red apples.

VERONICA SCHANOES

Rats

Veronica Schanoes's story "Rats" was first published in Interfictions: An Anthology of Interstitial Writing (one of whose editors, Delia Sherman, also has a story in this volume). Schanoes, whose work has appeared in Lady Churchill's Rosebud Wristlet, Trunk Stories, and Jabberwocky, often uses fairy tales to surprising results. A New Yorker by birth and desire, Schanoes is a professor at Queen's College in New York City.

—K. L. & G. G.
—E. D.

What I am about to tell you is a fairy tale and so it is constantly repeating. Little Red Riding Hood is always setting off through the forest to visit her granny. Cinderella is always trying on a glass slipper. Just so, this story is constantly reenacting itself. Otherwise, Cinderella becomes just another tired old queen with a palace full of pretty dresses, abusing the servants when the fireplaces haven't been properly cleaned, embroiled in a love-hate relationship with the paparazzi. Beauty and Beast become yet another wealthy, good-looking couple. They are only themselves in the story and so they only exist in the story. We know Little Red Riding Hood only as the girl in the red cloak carrying her basket through the forest. Who is she during the dog days of summer? How can we pick her out of the mob of little girls in bathing suits and jellies running through the sprinkler in Tompkins Square Park? Is she the one who has cut her foot open on the broken beer bottle? Or is she the one with the translucent green water gun?

Just so, you will know these characters by their story. As with all fairy tales, even new ones, you may well recognize the story. The shape of it will feel right. This feeling is a lie. All stories are lies, because stories have beginnings, middles, and endings, narrative arcs in which the end is the fitting and only mate for the beginning—yes, that's right, we think upon closing the book. Yes, that's the way. Yes, it had to happen like that. Yes.

But life is not like that—there is no narrative causality, there is no foreshadowing, no narrative tone or subtly tuned metaphor to warn us about what is coming. And when somebody dies it is not tragic, not inevitably brought on as a fitting end, not a fabulous disaster. It is stupid. And it hurts. It's not all right, Mommy! sobbed a little girl in the playground who had skinned her knee, whose mother was patting her and lying to her, telling her that it was all right. It's not all right, it hurts! she said. I was there. I heard her say it. She was right.

But this is a fairy tale and so it is a lie, perhaps one that makes the stupidity hurt a little less, or perhaps a little more. You must not expect it to be realistic. Now read on. . . .

Once upon a time.

Once upon a time, there was a man and a woman, young and very much in love, living in the suburbs of Philadelphia. Now, they very much enjoyed living in the suburbs and unlike me and perhaps you as well they did not at all regret their distance from the graffiti and traffic, the pulsing hot energy, the concrete harmonic wave reaction of the city. But happy as they were with each other and their home, there was one source of pain and emptiness that seemed to grow every time they looked into each other's eyes, and that was because they were childless. The house was quiet and always remained neat as a shot of bourbon. Neither husband nor wife ever had to stay at home nursing a child through a flu—neither of them ever knew what the current bug going around was. They never stayed up having serious discussions about orthodonture or the rising cost of college tuition, and because of this, their hearts ached.

"Oh," said the woman. "If only we had a child to love, who would kiss us and smile, and burn with youth as we fade into old age."

"Oh," the man would reply. "If only we had a child to love, who would laugh and dance, and remember our stories and family long after we can no longer."

And so they passed their days. Together they knelt as they visited the oracles of doctors' offices; together they left sacrifices and offerings at the altars of fertility clinics. And still from sunup to sundown, they saw their faces reflected only in the mirrors of their quiet house, and those faces were growing older and sadder with each glance.

One day, though, as the woman was driving back from the supermarket with the trunk of the station wagon—bought when they were first married and filled with dewy hope for a family—laden with unnaturally bright, unhealthily glossy fruits, vegetables, and even meat, she felt a certain quickening in her womb as she drove over a pothole, and she knew by the bruised strawberries she unpacked from the car that at last their prayers were answered and she was pregnant. When she told her husband he was as delighted as she and they went to great lengths to ensure the health and future happiness of their baby.

But even as the woman visited doctors, she and her husband knew the four shadows were lurking behind, waiting, and would come whether invited or not, so finally they invited the four to visit them. It was a lovely Saturday morning and the woman served homemade rugelach while the four shadows bestowed gifts on the child growing in her mother's womb.

"She will have an ear for music," said the first, putting two raspberry rugelach into its mouth at once.

"She will be brave and adventurous," said the second, stuffing three or four chocolate rugelach into its pockets to eat later.

But the third was not so kindly inclined—if you know this story, you know that there is always one. But contrary to what you may have heard, it was invited just as much as the others were, because while pain and evil cannot be kept out, they cannot come in without consent. In any case, there is always one. This is the way the story goes.

"She shall be beautiful and bold—adventurous and have a passion for music and all that," said the third. "But my gift to your child is pain. This child shall suffer and she will not understand why; she will be in pain and there will be no rest for her; she will suffer and suffer and she will always be alone in her suffering, world without end." The third scowled and threw a piece of raisin rugelach across the room. Some people are like that. Shadows too. The rugelach fell into a potted plant.

Sometimes cruelty cannot help itself, even when it has been placated with an invitation and excellent homemade pastry, and then what can you do?

You can do this: you can turn for help to the fourth shadow, who is not strong enough to break the evil spell—it never is, you know; if it were, there would be no story—but it can, perhaps, amend it.

So as the man and woman sat in shock, but perhaps not as much shock as they might have been had they never heard the story themselves, the fourth approached the woman, who had crossed her hands protectively over her womb.

"Now, my dear," it began, spraying crumbs from the six apricot rugelach it was eating. "Uncross your hands—it looks ill-bred and it does no good, you know. What's done is done, and I cannot undo it: you must bite the bullet and play the cards you're dealt. My gift is this: your daughter, on her seventeenth birthday, will prick herself on a needle and find a—a respite, you might say—and after she has done that, she will be able to rest, and eventually she will be wakened by a kiss, a lover's kiss, and she will never be lonely again."

And the soon-to-be parents had to be content with that.

After the woman gave birth to her daughter she studied the baby anxiously for signs of suffering, but the baby just lay, small, limp, and sweating in her arms, with a cap of black fuzz like velvet covering her head. She didn't cry, and hadn't, even when the doctor had smacked her, partially out of genuine concern for this quiet, unresponsive, barely baby, and partially out of habit, and partially because he liked to hit babies. She just lay in her mother's arms with her eyes squeezed shut, looking so white and soft that her mother named her Lily.

Lily could not tolerate her mother's milk—she could nurse only a little while before vomiting. She kept her eyes shut all day, as if even a little light burned her painfully. After she was home for a few days, she began to cry, and then she cried continuously and loudly, no matter how recently she had been fed or changed. She could only sleep for an hour at a time and she screamed otherwise, as though she were trying to drown out some other more distressing noise.

One afternoon, when Lily was a toddler, her mother lay her down for a nap and after ten or fifteen minutes dropped the baby-raising book she was reading in a panic. Lily's crying had stopped suddenly, and when her mother looked into her room, there was Lily smashing her own head against the wall, over and over, with a look of relief on her two-year-old face. When her mother rushed to stop her, she started screaming again, and she screamed all the while her mother was washing the blood off the wall.

She had night terrors and terrors in the bright sunshine and very few friends. She continued to hit her head against the wall. She tried to hit herself with a hammer and when she was prevented from doing so she laid about her, smashing her mother's hand. When her mother went to the emergency room to have her hand set and put in a cast the nurses clucked their tongues and told each other what a monster her husband must be.

When she got home she found Lily curled in a ball under the dining-room table, gibbering with fear of rats, of which there were none, and she would allow only her mother to speak to her.

Lily did love music. She snuck out of the house late at night and got rides into the city to hear bands play, and she loved her father's recordings of Bach and Chopin as well. Back when she was three or four, Chopin had been the only thing that could get her to lie down and sleep. Chopin and phenobarbitol. She wrote long reviews of new records for her school paper that were cut for reasons of space. As she got older, she got better and better at forcing the burning, gnawing rats under her skin on the people around her. But she still felt alone because they could just walk away from her but she could not rip her way out of her skin her brain her breath although she tried so hard, more than once, but her mother caught her, put her back together, sewed her up, every single time but not once could she clean Lily so well that she didn't feel the corrosion and corruption sliding through her veins, her lymph nodes, her brain, so that she didn't feel the rats burrowing through her body.

Lily ran away to New York City when she was sixteen and a half and in what her parents loathed, she found a kind of peace—in the neon lights and phantasmagoric graffiti that blotted out what was in her eyes and especially in the loud noises and the hard fast beats coming from CBGB that drowned out the rats clawing through her brain much better than her own screaming ever had, it was like banging her head against the wall from the inside. She knew there was something wrong with her— she talked to other people who loved the bands she saw because the fast and loud young and snotty sound wired them, jolted them full of electricity and sparks, but Lily just sped naturally and all she wanted was to make it stop.

On her seventeenth birthday, Lily went home with a skinny man who played bass and shot heroin. Lily watched him cook the powder in some water over his lighter and stuck her arm out. "Show me how," she told him.

"You have easy veins," he told her, because her veins were large and close to the surface of her skin, fat and filled with rats. They showed with shimmering clarity, veiled only by the fleshy paper of her lily-white skin.

He shot her up and just after the needle came away from her skin—it stopped. It really stopped, not just the rat-pain that she knew about, but the black tarpits of her thinking and feeling—they stopped too. It stopped, and God, it felt so good and free that she didn't mind the puking, it even felt fine, because everything else had stopped, and she could finally get some sleep, some real sleep.

The next morning she woke up and felt like shit again. And it was worse, because for a while she'd felt fine. Just fine.

We should all get to feel just fine sometimes.

So Lily found some kind of respite on a needle's tip and the marks it left were less obvious than the old dull hard scars on her wrists that she rubbed raw when she needed a fix. She worked as a stripper, using feathers, black gloves, and fetish boots to hide all kinds of scars, and sometimes in a midtown brothel. So she was often flush, and if she was still a holy terror, a mindfuck and a half, now she was flush, and had some calmer periods and a social circle, even if they did sometimes ignore her. She wrote pieces on music for underground papers, and once every two weeks her mother came to visit and bought her groceries and took her out to lunch and apologized when she threw cutlery at waiters and worried and worried over how thin Lily was becoming.

You can't stay high all the time, but you can try.

Lily knew she was getting thin. She would stare in the mirror and not see herself, and when she could put the rats to sleep she wasn't quite sure who she was or how she would know who she was.

Who are you? asked the caterpillar, drawing on his hookah. Keep your temper.

The rats were eating her from the inside out and she was dissolving, she was real only under her mother's eyes—the power of her mother's gaze held her bones together even as her ligaments and skin slowly liquefied, dissipating in a soft-focus movie dissolve.

Dissolve.

Fade in. We are in London with Lily, far enough away from her mother that she could dissolve entirely. Lily had heard that there was something happening in London, something that could shut down the banging slamming violence in her skull even better than the noise at CBs, some kind of annihilation.

There was.

Look at Lily at the Roxy, if you can recognize her. Can you find her? She is in the bathroom, shooting herself up with heroin and water from the toilet. She is out front sitting by the stage, sitting on the stage, sitting at the bar, throwing herself against the wall so violently that she breaks her own nose. The rats are still following her, snapping and snarling at anybody who comes near, and when nobody comes near, they turn on themselves, begin to eat themselves, gnaw on their own soft bellies.

Can you recognize Lily? When her face and form began to dissolve in the mirror, she panicked and knew she had to take some drastic action before she blinked and found only a mass of rats where her reflection should be, a feeding frenzy. In London the colors were bright like the sun when you have a hangover, so bright it hurt to look at them. The clothing was made to be noticed, to cause people to shrink back and flinch away. Lily wanted to look like that. She bleached her hair from chestnut brown to white blond and left dark roots showing. She back-combed it so a frizzy mess stood out around her head like a halo: Saint Lily, Our Lady of the Rats. She drew large black circles around both eyes, coloring them in carefully. She outlined her lips even more carefully, and the shine on them is blinding. Her black clothing was covered in bright chrome like a 1950s car.

She was visible then. She could see herself when she looked in the mirror, bright and blond, outlined in black. Covered in rats.

Her mother thought she looked like a corpse.

Everyone can see her now, everyone who matters, anyway. She is out and about and she is sleeping with the young man playing bass, well, posing with the bass, onstage. He is wearing tight black jeans, no shirt, and a gold lamé jacket. He is a year older than her. Neither of them is out of their teens. They are children. Despite everything, their skin looks new and shiny.

She had been frightened of him the first time they met. Now she was visible but that came with a certain price as well. Usually the rats kept everyone at arm's length if that close, so that no matter how desperately she threw herself at people they shied away. They knew enough to be frightened by the rats, even if they couldn't see them, even if they didn't know they were there. They told themselves, told each other, that they avoided her because she was nasty, the most horrible person in the world, a liar, a selfish bitch, and she was, she knew she was, but really they were afraid of the rats.

But the rats stood aside when Chris came near. They drew back at his approach, casting their eyes down and to the side as if embarrassed by their own abated ferocity. There was something familiar about him, but Lily was too confused by the rats' unusual behavior to think much about what it was. Chris was slight with skin so pale that Lily longed to bruise him and watch the spreading purple, skin that had sharp lines etched into it by smoke and sleeplessness, and zits all over his face. One of them was infected. When he spoke she could barely understand him, his voice was so deep and the vowels so impenetrable.

When she shot him up he said it was his first time but she knew better from the way he brought his sweet blue veins up so that they almost floated above the surface of his sheer skin. When they fucked later that night she could tell that it was his first time.

Lily didn't have much curiosity left—it hurt too much to be awake and she tried to dull herself as much as possible. But while they were kissing for the first time she felt a chill that startled her into wakening and she looked over his shoulder and saw what was so familiar about her Chris (she knew he was hers and she his now). Over his shoulder she saw his rats—just a few, younger than hers, but growing and mating and soon the two of them would be locked together, breaking skin with needles and teeth, surrounded by flocks of rats that could no longer be distinguished or separated out, just a sea of lashing tales and sharp teeth and clutching claws. But she wouldn't be alone, he would see them too, and he wouldn't be alone, she would see them too, their children, their parents, their rats.

Do you recognize this story yet? Perhaps you've seen the T-shirts on every summer camp kid on St. Mark's Place as they fantasize about desperation and hope that self-destruction holds some kind of romance.

Do you recognize this story yet? Perhaps you've read bits of interviews here and there: she was nauseating, she was the most horrible person in the world, she was a curse, a dark plague sent to London on purpose to destroy us, she turned him into a sex slave, she destroyed him, say the middle-aged men and occasional women who look back twenty-five years at a schizophrenic teenage girl with a personality disorder shooting junk—because here and now we still haven't figured out a way to make that kind of illness bearable, who'd wanted to die since she was ten because she hurt so much, and what they see is a frenzied harpy. She destroyed him.

And her? What about her?

Can we not weep for her?

Look again at those photographs and home movies and look at how young they were. Shiny. Not old enough ever to have worried about lines on her face, or knees that ached with the damp, or white hairs—every ache and twinge is a fucking blessing and don't you forget it.

Do you recognize this story yet?

Don't you already know what happens next?

Kiss kiss kiss fun fun lies: Yes oh yes we're having fun. I'm so happy!

Kiss kiss kiss fight fight fight. He hit her and she wore sunglasses at night. She trashed his mother's apartment. He left her and turned back at the train station. He was running by the time he got back to the squat they had been sharing—he had a vision of Lily sprawled on the floor dying—not alone, please, anything but alone. He lifted her head up onto his lap; her heart was beating still but her lips were turning blue. His mum had been a nurse and he knew how to make her breathe again.

Kiss.

On tour with the band, away from Lily, he became a spitting wire, destroying rooms, grabbing pretty girls from the audience, shitting all over them, smashing himself against any edge he could find, carving his skin so that he became a pustule of snot and blood and shit and cum where oh where was his Lily Lily I love you.

The band broke up. He could fuck up but he couldn't play. They moved to New York and bopped around Alphabet City. They tried methadone and they need so much they stopped bothering and anyway methadone only stopped the craving for heroin; it didn't give her any respite. When they were flush they spent money like it was going out of style, on smack, on makeup, on clothing, on presents for each other.

She bought him a knife.

If there is a knife in the story, somebody will have to get stabbed by the end.

Lily knows that she can't stand much more of this, much more of herself, much more of her jonesing, much more of the endless days trapped in a gray room in a gray city, and even though it's all gray the city still hurts her eyes it's a kind of neon gray. The effort it takes just to open her eyes in the morning (afternoon), just to get dressed, is too much and if she could feel desire anymore, if she could want anything, all she would want would be to stop fighting, stop moving, to sink back and let herself blur and dissolve under warm blankets.

But the smack-sickness shakes her down and she has to move.

Even her rats are weak, she can see. They are staggering and puking. Sometimes they halfheartedly bite one another. She wants to die, but her Chris takes too good care of her, except when he hits her, for that to happen.

When they were curled up together under the covers back in London, which is already acquiring the coloring of a home in her quietly bleeding memory, Lily had asked Chris how much he loved her. More than air, he said. More than smack. Would you douse yourself in gasoline and set yourself on fire if I needed you to? she asked. Yes, he said. Would you set me on fire if I needed you to? she asked. Not that, he said. I love you, I couldn't live without you, don't, don't, don't leave me alone. Not that. Anything but alone.

The regular chant of lovers.

If I needed you to? she pressed. Wouldn't you do it if I needed you to?

He couldn't. He wouldn't.

Then you don't really love me at all, she told him, if you don't love me enough to help me when I need it.

So he had to say yes. And he had to promise.

Now, in piercing gray New York City she puts the knife in his hand and reminds him of his promise. He pushes her away. No. But he doesn't drop the knife. Perhaps he's forgotten to. She reminds him again and somehow she finds energy and drive she hasn't had in months to scream and berate and plead in a voice like fingernails on a blackboard. She hits him with his bass and scratches at his sores. A man keeps his promises, she tells him. A real man isn't scared of blood.

She winds up shaking and crying to herself on the bathroom floor when Chris comes in, takes her head on his lap and stabs her in the gut, wrenching the knife up toward her breasts. He goes on stabbing and sawing and stroking her forehead until she stops breathing.

The last things she sees are the expression of blank, loving concern on his face and the rats swarming in as her blood spreads across the bathroom tiles.

He watches the rats gnaw on the soft flesh of her stomach and crawl through her body in triumph until finally he watches them lie down and die, exposing their little bellies to the ceiling. The next morning, he remembers nothing.

The police find him sitting bolt upright in bed, staring straight ahead, with the knife next to him. They take Lily away in a body bag. No more kisses.

He is dying now, he thinks. Her absence is slowly draining his blood away. His rats are all dead and their corpses appear everywhere he looks.

You know the rest of the story. He dies a month later of an overdose procured for him by his mother. Why are you still reading? What are you waiting for? The kiss? But he kissed her already, don't you remember? And she woke up, and afterward she was never alone.

They were children, you know. And there still are children in pain and they continue to die and for the people who love them that is not romantic. Their parents and friends don't know what is going to happen ahead of time. They have no narrator. When these children die all that is left is a blank, an absence, and friends and parents lose the ability to see in color. The future takes on a different shape and they go into shock, staring into space for hours. They walk out into traffic and they don't see the trucks, don't hear the horns. A mist lifts and they find that they have pinned the messenger to the wall by his throat. They find themselves calling out names on streets in the dead of night. Walking up the block becomes too hard and they turn back. They can't hear the doctor's voice.

Death is not romantic; it is not exciting; it is no poignant closure and it has no narrative causality. There are even now teenagers—children—slicing themselves and collapsing their veins and refusing to eat because the alternative is worse, and their deaths will not be a story. Instead there will be an empty place in the future where their lives would have been. Death has no narrative arc and no dignity, and now you can silkscreen these two kids' pictures on your fucking T-shirt.

JACK M. HARINGA

A Perfect and Unmappable Grace

By day, Jack M. Haringa teaches English to high school juniors and seniors at an independent school in New England. By night, he writes fiction and literary criticism and performs feats of freelance copyediting. On weekends and holidays, he is also the coeditor, with S. T. Joshi, of Dead Reckonings, *a critical review journal of horror, dark fantasy, and suspense literature. Jack lives with his wife and son in Worcester, Massachusetts.*

"A Perfect and Unmappable Grace" was originally published in Bander-snatch, *edited by Paul G. Tremblay and Sean Wallace.*

—E. D.

A rapping, distant and muffled. Then pounding. A shout. Blankets tangling around thin ankles, hand fumbling for the watch. More pounding. Is that a four? Fingers drop the timepiece, skim the table for wire and glass. Papers, magazines sliding to the floor. The spectacles cling to his ears. Stone. Stone.

"Stone!"

He shoves his arms into the robe, yanks the bedroom door open. The hall light casts spindly shadows up the staircase. Shuffling to the edge of the landing, listening.

"Open the damn door, Stone."

Bare feet seek their way from riser to riser. He knows the voice, hears others behind it. *Why didn't they use the bell,* he wonders. The bell grinds as a prelude to more pounding, but muffled by a coat hung across its box.

"I'm coming. Stop it. I'm coming." Softer, "Idiots."

The predawn cold drafts under the door and across his bare toes, bringing the hour into focus at last. He has barely finished sliding back the last bolt when the door swings inward, and he must dance back to avoid skinned knuckles, a broken foot. Three men stand at the threshold, propping up a fourth.

"You'll wake the dead, and my neighbors with them. Can you not telephone? Make an appointment like normal men of business?" His hands flitter at the visitors, then up to his head to smooth the halo of gray, unruly from sleep.

"No time for niceties, Doctor." One man steps in, his hat brim so low the hall light reveals only a sharp chin, a thin twist of mouth, the point of a nose.

Stone steps aside, leaving room for the other two ambulatory men to haul their groaning companion into the foyer. They look like a vaudeville act, one tall and one short flanking a boneless drunk. The middle man's coat opens to reveal a stained shirt, garish in the hall light until they trudge to the back of the house with him.

Stone leans out the door to see if any lights have appeared in the windows across the street, but there is nothing. A light rain patters through the pines to his left. Beneath them ticks a large engine, disembodied in the moonless night. To his right a field of shadowy stones dark even in day.

"This is an emergency." Stone turns to find the man has removed his hat. He looks remarkably clean-shaven for this hour, but his eyes are bloodshot and underscored with purplish circles. "See what you can do, but do it fast."

"Why can't you shoot one another in the daytime?" Stone mutters, closing the door and bolting it.

He moves past the waiting room and into a pantry, slips a record from its sleeve and onto the turntable. The needle lands lightly on the disk, and Adderley teases the first notes of "Bohemia After Dark" from his horn. Stone's fingers tap at his breast, following Kenny Clarke's beats, as he drifts back into the hall to the door under the stairs.

By the time he reaches the basement, the wounded man has stopped groaning. They've splayed him on a table, one arm outstretched to the wall as if in supplication, the other clutched to his chest. His hands are already bluing, but his face has taken on the hue of a farm-fresh egg. The two who carried him have moved to opposite corners of the room and like defeated boxers stare sullenly at their shoes, their hands, anywhere but at the center of the ring. The music is softer here but still insistent, and the third man, Bromberg, slaps his hat against his thigh.

"Why always with the *schwartze* music, Stone?" He looks to the ceiling for the hidden speakers.

"It calms the patient," he explains. "Steadies the nerves." He snaps gloves on his unflinching hands, trades his bathrobe for a lab coat, slips his bare feet into a cold pair of rubber-soled shoes. Bromberg turns away from the table, gestures to his men who slouch to him.

Stone peels the gunsel's shirt from his bloody skin. Two wounds seep black blood across the man's abdomen, one just below the solar plexus and another three inches to the left of his navel. Stone shakes his head, shrugs, clears his throat. Reaching under the table he pulls up a mask and the hiss of gas fills the rests between jazz notes. The mask fits smoothly over the gunsel's face, and the man's shallow breaths slow. Over to the sink, collecting sponges and a rinse bottle in a kidney tray, back to the table. Cleaning away the thick blood and visceral fluid to the soft touch of Horace Silver on the ivories. Revealing skin now approaching the shade of a ripe Bosc pear.

He makes preliminary probes at the wounds, checks the man's pulse, shakes his head again. He does not bother to touch any instruments.

"Mr. Bromberg?" Stone looks up, and the three men pull apart guiltily. Bromberg approaches the table slowly, raises an eyebrow. "This man, he is dead already. He is just not yet aware of the fact."

"Do something for him." Bromberg will not meet Stone's eyes.

"Do what? He should have been brought to a hospital. In Newark, perhaps? Or Elizabeth? Somewhere closer to the action as you say, yes? Not driven through the country to my home. Even if I were equipped to treat him, it is too late."

"Doctor," anger in his voice as he works the brim of his hat in his frustrated hands, then softening, "Eddie, please. There has to be something."

"So it is 'Eddie' tonight? All right, Samuel. Do you see the color of the blood there? A rupture in the intestine, sepsis inevitable. And here, this wound leads straight to the liver. What shall we put in its place? I do not have an extra available." Stone turns to a tray and fills a syringe. "He is already in shock. The best I can do is make it painless."

"And after that?" Bromberg looks up now, his eyes clear of whatever had held them down—disgust, sentiment, remorse?

"After that, my . . . other services are available."

Bromberg nods once to Stone. Smooths his hat and sets it low over his brow. His men drift across the room silently, each giving a furtive glance to their former companion before following their boss up the stairs.

Stone finds the envelope on the kitchen table. Within it a packet of mimeographed sheets, a reel of tape, a smaller envelope holding five worn bills. False dawn lightens the sky now, revealing impressions in the dirt of his driveway as the only external evidence of Bromberg's visit. He bolts the door again, considers and rejects the notion of climbing the stairs to his bedroom. The body will wait, secure in the basement's enormous cooler. A repeated click and hiss reminds him the music has fallen silent.

Back in the pantry he draws a thick 78 from a browning sleeve and places it on the turntable. A piano, lonely in the echo of a poor recording space, emerges above the spit and crackle. Stone sings to himself as he turns into the kitchen to make coffee.

"*Zeigt sich der Tod einst, mit Verlaub,*" he murmurs, thinking of poor Mileva, "*und zupft mich: 'Brüderl, kumm!', /da stell ich mich im Anfang taub /und schau mich gar nicht um.*"

He chuckles, pours coffee, sobers when he draws the papers out of the envelope. A concertina wheezes accompaniment on the record as he starts to read. *If Death should come, indeed,* he thinks, rapidly turning the pages. *They say the Old Man wasn't dumb at the end, though the stupid nurse spoke no German.* The papers are dense with scribbles and formulae, crabbed writing in two languages. He runs a fingertip over the dense blot of an atomic doodle.

Scooping the money and reel into the pocket of his robe, he stands to refill his cup. Back through the hall, checking the basement door, then mounting the stairs to his office. He fits the reel on the player, loops the tape to the second spool. Headphones press his still-wild hair to his skull. He closes his eyes and presses play.

"Unity," says a voice.

That night he dreams of Burgholzi's dark and narrow halls, of ice baths and the taste of rubber. Mileva's face wavering at the end of his bed, growing thinner as she whispers "Tete" over and over to him. Eating parfaits in the refectory, a view over the gardens and their shuffling haunts, his brother straightening his tie and saying farewell. The old microscope they allowed him, a seething drop of water trapped in the slide, a mystery unfolding under the battering of a strobe. A tower of journals collapse over him with an electric crackle.

He starts awake in the dark, scratching at his temples, the bedclothes in a twist around his feet. From the desk in the next room, the ungainly clatter of the telephone. Bromberg on the line.

Stone is able to repair two of the three more men Bromberg brings him that week. The third is dead before they even get him to the basement.

They have come before midnight, interrupting Stone at the reel-to-reel with a desperate grinding of the bell. He answers the door still clutching a sheaf of mimeo pages, sounds muted with the echo of that gruff, pure voice. They shove past him, barreling through the foyer and down the steps.

Stone takes one look at the man on the table and shakes his head. There is a tidy hole above his right temple, a ragged exit behind his left ear. Stone imagines the gunsel sitting in a car or at a table in a Brooklyn eaterie, shocked to see a man with a gun in the doorway. He still wears an expression of puzzled surprise.

"Samuel, this is beyond . . ." Stone begins, but the gangster cuts him off. It is the first time Bromberg has pulled a gun in Stone's home, the first time he has even shown he carries one. He waves it wildly, threatening the speakers from which the Prez leaps in. Stone steps cautiously to the bench, flicks a switch that cuts the music off in mid-solo.

"*Schvag!* You know who I work for?" Bromberg is ranting, his breath short gulps, blood leaking from the sleeve of his jacket. "I can have you shipped back to Zurich in a fucking box, Eddie. A fucking box."

Whatever war is being waged in the New York streets, it is taking a toll on Bromberg's conscience, his consciousness unwilling to hear that voice yet. "Look at all this shit in here. I paid for all this, every last lens and drop of formaldehyde. And what I do to get those *shtik dreck* papers you want. And now? *Kuck ind faall*, is all you tell me? *Gonif! Momzer!*"

The edges of his thin lips have turned purple, his too-wide eyes twitch in their sockets. Stone can almost smell the bennies on his breath, beneath the sour scent of drying adrenaline.

"Samuel. Sam. Sammy." Stone holds his hand out to Bromberg, coaxing him to the operating table. The gangster's heart is as raw as the back of the dead man's head. He lays his other hand on the corpse's chest, hears Bromberg shuffle forward. "Look at this boy. Who is he to you? Is he still here? You tell me."

"Not gone! Not! My niece, my sister's girl, this is her husband. What do I say to her? He can't be gone."

"Put down the gun, Sammy. Who are you going to shoot here? You have too much brain, too much soul for this *shtarker* business." Stone takes Bromberg's hand, guides it to close the young man's eyes, smooth his face. "Look at him, Samuel. Not at the wound, but at the beauty. The ratios. Look at the unity of his features. The symmetry. When nature speaks to us in the language of mathematics, we hear God's voice."

Bromberg cannot seem to stop stroking the boy's face. His breath hitches high in his chest, and Stone pulls a stool from the bench to place behind him. Bromberg sinks to the seat, his hand still on the dead man's cheek. Stone takes the gun from a limp hand, eases the suit jacket off to expose a raw wound in his forearm.

"There is a mistake being made." Stone's voice is soft but clear as he pours whiskey into a tumbler, presses the drink into the hand of Bromberg's uninjured arm. He cleans the wound, applies procaine, begins to sew. "Many mistakes, of course, but the great mistake now is we look out, not in. A dog orbits the earth, we look for holes in space, we listen to the howl of distant stars in hopes of hearing a divine whisper."

Bromberg may or may not be listening to the words. The voice quiets him at least, even if the meaning is lost. Stone sings softly, "*Doch sagt er: /'Lieber Valentin, mach keine Umständ, geh!' /da leg ich meinen Hobel hin /und sag der Welt ade.*"

"What's that song?" Bromberg mumbles. The adrenaline has burned through him. "You sing it so often."

"A little German tune my mother sang to me. This part is a carpenter being called by death:

"If Death should come to take me off
And twitch me, 'Brother, come!'

I'd not so much as turn around,
But stand there, deaf and dumb.
But if he said, 'Dear Valentine,
Allow me, after you!'
Why, then I'd put my plane away
And bid the world adieu."

Bromberg is crying now. Stone wraps a bandage lightly over the sutures and drapes the suit coat back over his shoulder. He stands beside the operating table again, gazing at the boy, who looks even younger now with eyes closed and expression blank. Bromberg looks up but says nothing.

"Numbers and nature. Nature and numbers. Fibonacci knew. Mendel had an inkling. Binet and even starstruck Kepler. It's no accident that Fuchs's first name was Lazarus. Immortality must come from within, not without, in a body of perfect unity. All forces together." Bromberg is lost, but Stone forges on. "The mystic rhythms are internal, Samuel; they are the secret voice of the heavens in our blood. The music of the spheres can only be heard by the cerebral hemispheres, our eternal cranial convergence of harmonies. God's symphony sings in ourselves, not in the stars. The Old Man was right about many things, but he spent too long looking up."

Stone stops, allows a smile to brush his lips. He turns to the two men in the shadows, snaps his fingers at them. "Wrap your friend in a winding sheet. Mr. Bromberg will be taking this one home with him."

He leaves the three gangsters in the silent glare of the operating room.

Stone cannot sleep that night or the next. He buries himself in papers, the blue of the mimeos smudging his fingertips, shirtfront, even the corners of his mouth. He wonders distantly how much of the ink he has ingested in licking his fingertips to turn the pages. On his journey through the notes he is joined only by the proxy voices of men who poison themselves to find beauty: Long Tall Dex, "Sweets" Edison, Bird, Prez.

For a week he does not see or hear from Bromberg. He can imagine the niece's grief, her anger, but cannot conceive of Bromberg's guilt or how he will react to it. There will be revenge, no doubt, and more blood in the streets of the Heights, or Hackensack, or wherever it is Bromberg prowls. He has never felt guilt, has always been the deceived and not the deceiver. He saw it in Mileva's eyes at the end of every visit she made to Burgholzi, perhaps in the slump of Hans's shoulders. Bromberg's remorse will shroud him even as he seeks revenge.

And so Stone is not surprised to receive a call on the eighth day. He does not expect the strange marriage of panic and elation in Bromberg's voice.

"Be ready, Stone. I heard you. I kept hearing you, even after I left. And then today, there she was. Right in the middle of the fucking street. I'm on my way."

The sun is still setting when he hears the crush of tires in the driveway. Through the parlor window he sees Bromberg emerge from the absurdly long Lincoln Mark IV, the chrome of its rocket-inspired fins catching the last orange rays. It is black, of course, funereal in its presence. Bromberg opens the rear door and leans in, pulls back with a woman in his arms. There are no gunsels to help him tonight.

She has been covered with a light blue blanket that reaches from hairline to ankle. Her dark brown hair holds auburn streaks; her feet are bare. Stone runs his hands through his hair, unlocks the door, ushers them inside.

Bromberg's expression shifts from tense to exultant and back again as he bears the woman down the hall and into the basement. Stone hurries to keep up, pausing only to place the needle back on its rest and stop the turntable.

The woman looks small on the operating table, superimposed as she is on the images of the countless men who have bled and wept and died there. Stone considers that a woman has never laid on that table under his care, has never ventured into this basement in the years he has owned the house. He hesitates at the foot of the stairs, watching the dark, thin gangster fuss over her.

"She fell out of the sky, Eduard. Out of the *sky*. Right in front of me."

"You mean she's a suicide? She jumped?" Stone feels disappointed at this banality.

"No, no. From the sky she came. I know it sounds like *mishegas*, but it's true. And you must look at her. Perfection. Measure it. Get your instruments." Bromberg keeps rolling forward on the balls of his feet then dropping back to his heels. His fingers move incessantly along the hem of the blanket that hangs over the table. He looks like some child magician eager to reveal a trick.

Stone draws a tray with him to the table, inhales in preparation for a sigh. Stops. He sniffs again, licks his lips. The lightest scent of lilac underscored with citrus fills his nostrils. It is the smell of his childhood garden in Zurich, down to the slight damp of the Sihl not far away.

"You smell the sea, too? The Zatoka Gdanska? And lemonade? Just like in summer when I was a boy." Bromberg takes the edge of the blanket at the woman's brow and lifts it slowly. Stone cannot help but hold his breath.

Her skin is a blend of copper and gold, entirely flawless. Slight epicanthic folds shape her eyes; her lips are full and deeply red, though Stone sees no trace of makeup; her cheekbones are high and well defined. She does not breathe.

Stone leans closer and Bromberg follows. Each takes a wrist, but neither can find a pulse. Stone puts his head gently to her soft, cool breast, hears no stirring within. Feels for rhythm in the chest, the ankle, the throat. Nothing. Gently rolls her onto her side, sees no contusions to indicate impact, feels no broken bones. On to her arms, legs, and toes to seek evidence of injection. Cannot smell anything over the persistent olfactory memories of Valentinstrasse.

"Out of the sky she fell, Eduard, I tell you truly." Bromberg drifts to the bench and pours a drink. Stone considers for a moment taking the gangster's gun and killing him with it, wonders where the thought originates.

"Extraordinary," Stone whispers, looking at the woman's face again.

"How did she die?" Bromberg wonders aloud.

"I see nothing to indicate a fall but for some pieces of gravel in her hair." He looks at his instruments, shakes his head. "Further examination is needed."

"I will watch."

Stone expects such a response and only shrugs. He draws the blanket completely off her body, leaving her naked. "Where are her clothes, Samuel?"

"She fell naked. From the sky." Stone looks up to find Bromberg transfixed by the woman's body, his eyes racing up and down her from feet to throat again and again. He tries to bring the glass to his lips and misses. Whiskey spills down the front of his suit, staining his tie, but he takes no note of it, continues until the glass is empty. Bromberg's eyes jerk from side to side, trying to take in the entirety of the woman. He breathes more heavily, almost panting, and flecks of white spittle cling to the corners of his mouth.

"I'm sorry. I'm so sorry. So so so so so so sorry. So. So." Bromberg begins to shake, his trembling swiftly becomes a vibration beyond any seizure Stone has ever witnessed. As drawn as he is to the woman's exposed skin before him, he feels he must bear witness to whatever it is that is happening to the gangster.

Bromberg shudders and falls to the cold floor, but Stone makes no move to help him. He watches Bromberg thrash for just over a minute before the man grows still, blood seeping from his eyes, nose, and ears. The last sound he makes is a long sibilance.

Stone traces a finger along the woman's arm. He is mindful not to try to apprehend all of her at once, to take each part of her in turn. This will take him the rest of his days, he knows. He lifts one of her eyelids tentatively, feeling something like fear at the thought of her eye. He gasps when he sees it. A thousand formulae rush across his retina, reflected from the vermilion nautilus of her iris.

He steps back, gives thanks, breathes deep, and loses himself in her infinite curves.

LUCY KEMNITZER

The Boulder

Lucy Kemnitzer's contemporary Icelandic folktale "The Boulder" first appeared in Fantasy Magazine, Issue 6, *one of the last print issues before it became a Web site. Kemnitzer is a sometimes teacher of at-risk adolescents and an aspiring writer of what she calls hard science fiction (what hard science fiction fans call soft). Much of what she has written is available on her Web site. She co-authored a story with S. N. Dyer published in* Asimov's. *She lives in California.*

—K. L. & G. G.

1. The farmer and the archaeologist

An archaeologist visiting a farm in southwestern Iceland was warned about a large moss-covered boulder that lay in a sloping field below the farm buildings. "Don't look straight at it; don't go too close to it; and most of all, don't speak about it anywhere within earshot of it."

The archaeologist wasn't expecting to hear a story like that here. The farmer was literate in four languages and subscribed to several learned journals devoted to current events, the sciences, and agricultural technology. The farmer dropped the subject, going on to talk about family tradition regarding the placement of buildings in the old days. He was sure that in former times, the main house and outbuildings had been located lower on the slope. The archaeologist didn't ask questions, but thought that his friend, a folklorist, might find it interesting to explore the subject.

And, "Remember," the farmer repeated before leaving to tend to his greenhouse, "pay attention to that boulder, and don't be standing in its way."

Just as the farmer said, there were the unmistakable signs of former buildings in a flat stretch on the lower slope of the field. *The main house was here,* he thought, pacing off a quadrangle somewhat larger than the average American condominium living room. *Here's some more of it.* He was following places where bits of stone lay that must have been carted from miles away, and tufts of grass that were markedly different in color, reflecting centuries later where the staves and daub of the former building nurtured the soil in a particular way. Once you knew what to look for, the hearth in particular was obvious. Depending on how old the house turned out to be, it may have been quite a substantial household.

Later in the day—the sun had no intention of setting for long at this season—the archaeologist checked his watch, picked up his notebooks, and mounted the hill to join the farmer for a meal as he had been invited to do. He gave the boulder a sideways glance as he went past, not, he told himself, because he was intimidated by the superstitions of others, but because he needed to keep his main gaze on the cow-trodden uneven ground before him. The boulder was pretty large, and covered with lichen.

The farmer was just logging off his computer when the archaeologist came to the door. "So frustrating," the farmer said. "I have been trying to do a search on this tomato wilt. Only some of the plants in the one greenhouse have been infected, but I want to be sure that it doesn't spread. But nothing is working today on the Web, and I don't know why. Do you know anything about search engines?"

The archaeologist had to acknowledge that he didn't.

"The computer screen gives me a headache. I delegate all that kind of thing to these youngsters who grew up with it."

"A conservative man," said the farmer. "No wonder you prefer to study the past."

"It's not that I don't use modern methods," the archaeologist said. "It's only that I take advantage of the presence of graduate students to save myself from headaches."

He liked to walk around in the country and look at the lay of the land. The only thing he liked nearly as well was identifying bits of debris sifted out of the back dirt. He could always identify a bit of bone even as small as his little fingernail, and he could date most metal items he would find in Iceland within a generation or two by eye alone. He liked it when his crew members were stumped and called him in to the rescue. Of course he insisted on careful lab analysis to confirm his judgment. He was rarely wrong.

The farmer lived with a collection of oddly related people, in-laws and cousins, of whom three were present for this meal, a young woman and her silent child, and an old man with the enlarged knuckles of advanced arthritis. They all had the same thin high noses and glacier-colored eyes, but the farmer and the child shared a friendlier smile than their relatives. The farmer brought to the table a bowl of potatoes and fish soup. The crowning glory of the meal was a tomato and onion salad, the tomatoes from his own greenhouses, the onions from the garden outside. But the child was more interested in the bowl of rennet custard topped with canned peaches from America. His mother took him away with the dishes as soon as the meal was over.

"What you were telling me before, about the boulder," the archaeologist ventured. "Can you tell me what makes the boulder so dangerous?"

"It's just a vicious piece of rock," the farmer said. "It takes offense easily and has demonstrated wicked behavior in the past. I suppose you want to hear the story. It has its quaint aspects: huldur folk. But for me it's an everyday menace, and a murderous robber."

"Of course I want to hear," said the archaeologist. "I'm interested in anything that might cast a light on the history of this farm."

"I thought so. You academic types take a perverse pleasure in superstitions. But what is superstition to you is personal history to me."

Of course the archaeologist had heard stories of the huldur folk before.

"I will start with my own experience," said the farmer. "This is the part I know is true because I saw it with my own eyes."

The old man snorted as the farmer poured coffee. The farmer grimaced and sat back in his chair to tell the story.

"Now I had heard the stories about that rock all my childhood," the farmer began. "My family has lived in this farm for several generations, and they knew the family that lived here before. But it was when I returned from school in Reykjavik that I had my own run-in with it. When I first set about to build the greenhouses, I thought the best place would be right about there on the slope, because the exposure is good and the slope is gentle there. Very little grading to be done. And the drainage is excellent there. I've never seen a landslide on that part of the slope. The only obstacle was that boulder, which my father warned me should not be moved. I thought, *Nonsense, it's only an old story to scare the children into staying close to the house.* So I got my brother and a couple boys from around here, because nobody else from the farm would have anything to do with it, and we took a tractor and some chain and set out to move the thing. It's not so big that it couldn't be done. Just because the old folks had been so scornful of our efforts, we were extra careful to place the chains scientifically and to treat the damned thing respectfully: we didn't want even a scratch for the old folks to be able to point to and say the huldur folk had marked us. But in spite of our best efforts, the boulder waited until everything was set and I put the tractor into gear, and then it leaped backward, rolling upslope thirty feet, dragging the tractor and me behind it. I broke my collarbone in hanging on. It rolled uphill, and it rolled right over my brother, who had been standing uphill. He disappeared before our eyes. It was sheer malice on the part of the boulder: it knew very well which of us was the better man, and that's the one it took."

"Your brother was killed?" the archaeologist took his time digesting this story. "I'm so sorry to hear that."

"Most likely he was not killed," said the farmer. "Most likely he was taken inside to live with the huldur folk. Though for us it is the same. It is as if he died fifteen years ago. I blame myself, because it was my idea, but nobody else does. Except that we keep his room for him, we go on as if he had never been."

The older man stood up. "That is not as true as the rest of what you have told, Ingvar," he said. "People don't talk to you about it, but they never forget that you gave your brother to the huldur folk out of simple foolishness and bullheadedness. It does mean that anything you say has to be corroborated by a man of known sense before it will be credited. It's a good thing you don't often have novel ideas." The old man nodded his head in farewell and stumped out of the house, calling to the small active dog by the door as he went, step by painful half step.

The farmer smiled ruefully and shrugged. "You see how it is. Every day I feel I have to make up for that. Though it was true that nobody said anything to my face about it until after old uncle came to stay with me. As I say, Ragnar was the better of us, and his loss was serious. I say this without false modesty. The men of our family are none of us worthless, but Ragnar was the best."

"You're saying the boulder had already a bad reputation before that accident?"

"Accident! I call it an attack. But yes, there are other stories. In my grandfather's time, the boulder also moved. It killed three horses at the worst possible time, when the horses were to be sold to pay off a debt. Before that, it took a child who was climbing on it. And in the old days, I think it would be in the eighteenth century but it was a different family who lived here then, it rolled down from the crest of the hill and maliciously crushed the byre that used to stand just below where the rock is now. It took two cows and the girl who was milking them that time. They say that that time the old farmer who lived here had insulted the huldur folk. I myself cannot imagine what he said."

"Is that the earliest story about the boulder?" the archaeologist asked. He had been making notes: maybe there was a pattern here. There might be some local phenomenon that was being explained with these huldur boulder stories. The folklorist would love to get her hands on this. She could get a paper out of it easily.

"Not quite. There's more, but most of it is garbled, except for the most famous story. I am surprised you do not know of it, as it concerns two of the sons of Burnt Njal. Hoskuld, the bastard, and Skarp-Hedin, the eldest—remember 'who is that man, the fifth in the line, the pale, sharp-featured man with a grin on his face and an ax on his shoulder?' Their story is the earliest one I know of having to do with that boulder."

"No, I don't know this story," said the archaeologist. Of course he knew the quote about Skarp-Hedin. He had read Njal's Saga enough times. He wished he had brought a tape recorder.

2. Skarp-Hedin and Hoskuld

The folklorist didn't get headaches from the computer screen. She had a lively e-mail correspondence with the farmer before she came up to the farm. The farmer told her she already had the whole story but he would be glad to have her visit. She drove up to the farm well after supper, taking advantage of the summer light and warmth. She knew well that the country people would be awake nearly all night at this season. As she approached the farm she saw two white-shirted boys in their early adolescence playing on a large mossy boulder. One climbed to the top and leaped off, and then the other did the same. She heard them shouting as they jumped; she couldn't make out the words.

The farmer ignored her protestations and brought out a bowl of hot potatoes and a mustard sauce accompanied by carrots and tomato wedges. The folklorist asked about the boys playing on the boulder.

"Oh, they're not real," the farmer said as nonchalantly as he might say that the carrots were not cooked. "They're just images. The boulder does that. It's not always boys. Sometimes it's girls, or an old person. We think it is to trick people into coming closer. We're not sure, because nobody approaches it."

"This is interesting," the folklorist said, willing to be made fun of if it pleased the farmer. He was deadpan as he spoke, a sure clue that he was joking. "How come I haven't heard this yet?"

"Well, you were asking about stories. That's not a story, it's an apparition."

"Oh," said the folklorist, though she didn't really see the difference.

"You did come about the story of Skarp-Hedin and Hoskuld and the boulder. Well, when Skarp-Hedin was very young, people already had mixed feelings about him. He was big and strong, and handsome in a way, but pale and fierce-looking. Some thought he would grow to be a berserk. Others thought he would use up his fierceness in viking and come back to be a competent litigator like his father. In any case he was an impetuous boy. The boulder was already known in those days as the home of huldur folk and was avoided by people of sense. In those days it was still situated at the top of the hill and the people who lived at this farm used to tell time by it. When the sun passed it, it was time for the morning meal."

The folklorist checked the tape recorder: it was running nicely. She took notes simultaneously, smiling to herself as she noticed that the farmer's diction had changed to a more stilted, old-fashioned style as he settled into the story.

"Skarp-Hedin was asking his father about the huldur folk, but Njal Thorgeirsson was a prudent man, and he said that if it was not subject to law, it was best to leave it alone. And so Skarp-Hedin asked his mother, and she said there was no honor or profit to be had from dealing with it, so it was best to leave it alone. And so he asked his brother Hoskuld and he didn't know either. But they agreed between the two of them to go and look into the mossy places, which are the windows the huldur folk use to look at the world.

"They had a hard time deciding between themselves who should take a look first. Skarp-Hedin, who was never without courage, was all for going first, because he said it was his idea to go from the first. At last Hoskuld decided he should go first because Skarp-Hedin was his father's heir and Hoskuld was not, being illegitimate. Skarp-Hedin was reluctant to let him go, but he did, saying he would watch for him."

"Humph," said the old man as he passed through the room carrying an orange from Israel. The folklorist couldn't tell what he meant other than general disparagement.

"Hoskuld climbed up on the boulder's top and lay over it, gazing into a mossy patch. Soon he whispered to Skarp-Hedin that he was seeing a beautiful world, green and blooming, with trees taller than he had ever seen, big as in the forests of Europe or Vinland. He was describing this world and the strange beasts that roamed it, deer and snakes and other wonderful things, and Skarp-Hedin was getting anxious to take his own place on the boulder. Suddenly, 'Oh! The huldur folk!' he cried out and began to disappear into the rock. But Skarp-Hedin caught him fast by the ankle and pulled, and pulled, and pulled for hours. The sun had gone all round by the west and back to the north before Skarp-Hedin managed to pull that boy out of the rock. And when he did, Hoskuld told him he had lived in that rock for several months, but he had been lame because Skarp-Hedin was holding on to his foot. But he told little of his adventures among the huldur folk, except to his blind son Amundi, who is said to have told someone the whole story. In fact," the farmer concluded, leering slightly at the thought of so provoking the folklorist, "it is said that there is to this day someone in these parts who knows the story of Hoskuld's adventures among the huldur folk. But who it is I don't know. I wish I did know, I would get that person to tell me all he knows. Perhaps it would lead to the return of my brother."

The bent old man passed through the room. The dog trotted after, clicking its long claws on the floor. The old man turned and squinted at the folklorist. "You can't give much credence to what Ingvar says in general," the old man said. "But he hasn't told you anything wrong yet."

The folklorist was used to the bluntness of country people, but this old man embarrassed her on the farmer's behalf. The farmer, though, occupied with the coffee, didn't seem bothered at all.

"Do you know any more about this old story?" the folklorist asked, aiming her question at both of the men generally.

"Ask the modernizer, here," said the old man. "Myself, I don't tell tales."

The farmer said, "Only a few fragments. I have wondered why the huldur folk of that boulder are so malicious. In other places they are dangerous, yes, but here they seem to actively wish to do us harm."

"Self-centered people always interpret events as having something to do with them," said the old man, leaving again. The dog scampered after him, but he was out the door before it caught up, and it stood there whining until the farmer got up and opened the door for it.

The folklorist thought that what the old man had said was interesting. But the farmer had been thinking along different lines. "You know usually when you hear these stories of people who visit the other world, they spend some weeks there and come back some years later. This was the other way around: Hoskuld came back after a few hours but he had lived a month with the huldur folk. I suppose that means that Ragnar must have lived to an old age, probably the end of his life by now." He stood up and crossed the room to where his computer sat on a neat table in the corner. With his back turned to the folklorist, the farmer tapped the switched-off keyboard.

The folklorist was startled again. She had put from her mind the fact that the farmer claimed to have lost his brother to the boulder. What could she possibly say to him?

The farmer returned to the table. "I must admit I have always hoped that Ragnar would return to us."

3. The archaeologist and the old man

The farmer did give the folklorist some names of people in the area who would like to talk about huldur folk in general. Most of the stories were mere scraps. Almost everyone in the neighborhood could recall admonishments: avoid this spot, always make the sign of the cross when passing that spot.

She began an inquiry into the perceived motivations of huldur folk. The neighbors were split: some thought that the huldur folk were jealous of human wealth and wished they could drive the people from the neighborhood altogether, while others thought they had a twisted sense of humor and took delight in harming people for that reason. The old man at Ingvar's farm made a point of deriding everyone's statements, though he had nothing to offer himself. When the folklorist asked him directly, he said only, "I do not make it a habit of spreading half-baked tales and suppositions."

She met with the archaeologist for lunch one day. "I'm going to put an end to it with a report of the stories. I just don't have enough to do any interpretation on it. Maybe I'll come back to it when I'm done with the big project I'm doing on traditional theories of disease."

"I hope you do," the archaeologist said. "As for the site, it's a mixed blessing. It was burned to the ground at one point. That preserves some material and obliterates other things. The old man that lives up there has been helping out quite a bit."

"What about the boulder?"

"Oh, we leave it alone, of course. We have been having our meals at the farmhouse or at the bottom of the field. Actually this is our last week until spring. Winter is coming."

The archaeologist went up to the farm the next day. He could tell before he got there that the day was going to be a difficult one: he didn't need to believe in luck or omens to figure out when he started a day out by losing in succession his pen, his memo book, his keys, wallet, and glasses, and having to change his shoes twice, that he wouldn't be at the top of his form, that his timing would be off and he would make mistakes he usually did not. His only hope as he started the day was that he would not make mistakes from which he could not recover. His consolation was that several times such difficult days as this inspired him to make leaps of intuition that led to conceptual breakthroughs in his research.

The day was as difficult as he had supposed it would be. Engaged in a heated discussion with the crew members who rode out with him, he missed the farm altogether and it was several miles before he found a good place to turn around. As he pulled up into the long drive, he saw the rest of the crew gathered in an excited clot with the old man, not at the site proper but up the slope, not far from where the boulder sat. Anxious to discover the cause of the uproar, he skidded in the rutted parking area and had to correct his parking. Meanwhile, the passengers boiled out of his car before he brought it to a complete stop, and he was the last up the hill.

The object of their excitement was an excavation apparently started during the night before. "You folks were never going to look at this section of the slope, because Ingvar steered you wrong," the old man said. "Nobody would listen to me if I said anything, so I exposed this bit for you here."

The archaeologist was stunned. His pride was offended on several counts. One, that he had not noticed this himself the many times he had climbed this hill to sit with the farmer: another, that the old man would think he would not listen to him. Another, that he was the last in his crew to see this, the very last, not counting a specialist in early house design who was sick and hadn't come today.

But the archaeologist bent down and examined what had been unearthed. The old man had certainly paid good attention to methods this summer. The dirt had not been casually thrown about but carefully deposited in labeled areas, ready to be sieved for small remains. The trench that was begun clearly showed the construction of the largish building that had once stood here.

"Do you think what I think?" the question was placed by a woman who was much older than most of the graduate students here because she had already had an extensive career as a weaver of art textiles.

"It depends on what you think," the archaeologist said.

"I think old Ragnar found us a complete pagan temple, one which was abandoned and not converted to Christian use."

"What makes you think that?" asked the archaeologist, who had been thinking about the same thing. As he had paced the building out he had seen its size and shape and orientation and its position relative to the house and outbuildings.

"Its size, shape, and position," the graduate student said, "and also the fact that I think that earth right over there is going to reveal statues of at least two gods, and probably more." The archaeologist frowned, but then he saw that the earth she was referring to was in fact heavily discolored as from the decomposition of metal.

"More likely a store of weapons," the archaeologist said. "In any case, our main task is to make both the sites secure so we can get serious in the spring."

"I'll lay a wager," the graduate student said. "If I'm right, I get first author."

"Very well," the archaeologist said; he had been intending to give her first author status on something that came out of this dig anyway.

Plans necessarily changed. This time, and for some weeks, the crew worked with flood lamps until long after dark. The air was quite chilly now and the days were getting shorter with alarming speed, but they were sleeping at the site most of the time now. Since the weather held off longer than they had a right to expect, they worked later in the year than they had intended, especially as they found what the graduate student had predicted, rare enough that the archaeologist was almost inclined to suspect a skillful forgery (the earth certainly seemed authentic, with the correct plant and animal matter at the proper depths, and no sign of disturbance). It took some care to extract and transport the statues, two of which, the size of large people, were tentatively identified as Freyr and Freya, from the pronounced genitalia and other features. There were several smaller ones as well, and other objects, none of which were surprising, not after the statues, all of the type supposed to have been destroyed in the eleventh and twelfth centuries. The archaeologist tentatively dated them at the tenth century and earlier, which is to say the temple was considerably older than the main site down the slope.

The old man worked hard beside the digging crew, and intelligently, though he was slow and made little headway due to his arthritic condition. But he scowled and stumped away every time the archaeologist approached him to talk. Finally he decided to ask the farmer more about this old man who was such a natural at archaeology but so unsociable.

"Well, in our family, friendliness is generally taken as a sign of dishonesty or incompetence," the farmer said, indicating with a shrug that he considered that he had been marked by this family prejudice himself. "But to tell the truth, I didn't really grow up with old Uncle. He kind of moved in a couple of years ago, the week of my father's funeral. He helped out a lot at that time. It was hard for me to do things in those days, as I kept thinking about how I had lost my brother through my stubbornness, and I thought my father died younger than he might have from grief over losing the better of his sons. It was Uncle really who pushed me into carrying through with the greenhouses. I had all but abandoned the project until then."

"I thought he had grown up on this land, the way he found that site for us."

"If he did, it was before my time. I never asked. You saw him. Old Ragnar is an irritable coot anyways, and he has such a low opinion of me that I hardly dare talk to him."

Now it really was the last week. There was no more pushing to be done. The ground was beginning to freeze. Already the grass crackled with frost. All the work they were doing was toward putting the sites away for the winter: double-checking the records, sheltering the opened earth from the harsh winter weather to come. The archaeologist saved a corner of his mind for stalking the old man—he was still not sure that wily old curmudgeon had not salted the site. The statues, though they looked authentic, could not be dated for some time, and the archaeologist was sure they were too good to be true.

He finally cornered the old man late in the afternoon, when the crew had gratefully left the site to enjoy kippers and tea with the farmer—they had brought the kippers and some white bread from town. The old man was working away in the corner to the left of where the statues had been recovered, carefully extracting thin corroded pieces of metal, and laying them gently in a labeled wooden box, so wrapped up in his work that he didn't notice the archaeologist's approach. The archaeologist squatted gingerly at the edge of the trench, careful not to knock the soil loose, and prepared to break the old man's gasping concentration.

But something in the old man's work commanded the archaeologist's attention, and he did not immediately call out to him. He adjusted his posture, seemingly having laid aside all the metal—even in the lowering light the archaeologist recognized them as straps once used in binding a wooden box—and lifted an object from the place where he was working. He held it higher, and squinted at it against the low rays of the sun. It was a cup.

Even dirty it was breathtaking. In design it was more eighth than ninth century: an antique before it ever got to Iceland. It was covered with a turmoil of swirling tendrils and slender grinning beasts, gold and the black of tarnished silver. The archaeologist was certain that the old man meant to keep it; but there was that about his manner that suggested he had known all along that this particular object would be here. The archaeologist cleared his throat.

"Beautiful," he said. "Thank you for finding it. The museum will no doubt put your name on the display case."

4. The old man and the farmer

The old man glared at the archaeologist with a more baleful look than ever, but he didn't say anything. He stood up painfully, and for a grotesque moment the archaeologist wondered if he intended to make a run for it, and he dreaded that he might harm the old man in tackling him, and possibly the cup too. But the old man merely stumped off up the slope to the farmhouse, swinging the cup in his hand, holding it lightly as if it were not precious. The archaeologist hurried after, but the old man was used to the slope, and in spite of his awkward gait, he reached the farmhouse well before the archaeologist.

Inside, the tag ends of the crew were drinking coffee and vodka. The farmhouse was bright and warm, the world outside the windows dark by comparison. The words the archaeologist caught as he came in behind the old man were casual, on the bawdy side. The old man found the farmer sitting at the head of the Danish table and placed the cup there before him.

"This is the source of your trouble with the boulder," the old man said abruptly. "I'll be returning the thing to them and you'll see no more trouble from it. And you'll not have me to bedevil you either, brother Ingvar."

The farmer looked from the cup to the old man, seeming to comprehend a whole story in the one utterance. He nodded his head shortly. "The trouble was then that Hoskuld or some such had taken this thing from the huldur folk? Can you come home again after it's returned?"

"Some such, but long before Burnt Njal's time. In the time of the Irish, some red-haired brat took it and gave it to the priests for their altar. It would have been easy to return the thing long ago, if people had only followed common sense. My hands are no good anymore, and I couldn't dig it by myself, or I'd have been gone a long time ago. At any rate, it's found now, and my work's done."

"Then everything will be all right and you can come home again."

The archaeologist moved closer to the table, readying himself.

"Yes, only not how you understand it. You think because I was raised here this is my home. You fail to appreciate that I have a life in that world, a family." He looked around the farmhouse. "You're so proud of your modern achievements. Your keyboard and your mouse. Your satellite dish. Your greenhouses stacked on the hill. You don't know what technology is. You just don't know."

The farmer grimaced, taking this insult as he had taken all the others.

"But I ought to tell you, Ingvar," the old man said, "you yourself have not done so badly, considering." This was apparently all the praise and all the farewell he meant to give his brother, for he reached for the cup again.

The archaeologist moved, but the old man, suddenly spry, moved faster than he did, scooping up the cup and striding out the back door. Several of the company followed but the passage through to the kitchen was narrow and some of them were drunk, so they got in each other's way, and only reached the boulder in time to see the old man's lower legs wriggling as he disappeared into the rock.

"I suppose," the archaeologist muttered grimly to the farmer, "dynamite is out of the question."

The farmer spat on the ground. "You could blow it to the heavens, if it were up to me," he said. "But the neighbors wouldn't like it. As for me, I'm going to see about my greenhouse."

TANITH LEE

The Hill

Tanith Lee was born in 1947 in North London, England, didn't learn to read until she was eight, and started to write when she was nine. "Having," she says, "virtually wrecked, single-handed, the catering world with her waitressing, the library system with her library assistance, and all types of shops with her mishandling of everything, she was set free into the world of professional writing in 1975 by DAW Books."

Tanith Lee lives with her husband John Kaiine by the sea in Great Britain and is a prolific writer of fantasy, science fiction, and horror. Her most recent books are the three books of the adult fantasy trilogy LION-WOLF: Cast a Bright Shadow, Here in Cold Hell, *and* No Flame But Mine; *the three young adult novels:* Piratica, Return to Parrot Island, *and* The Family Sea; *and* Metallic Love *(the sequel to her adult SF novel* The Silver Metal Lover). *She is currently working on a dark adult fantasy whose title she will only reveal as A.T.C.O.T.C., while researching for an even darker work concerning a rabid parallel bronze age of violence and sorcery.*

Other stories have been collected in Forests of the Night, Women as Demons, Dreams of Dark and Light, *and* Nightshades: Thirteen Journeys into Shadow. *Also hopefully soon out will be the much delayed two volumes of collected short stories:* Tempting the Gods *and* Hunting the Shadows. *Lee has twice won the World Fantasy Award for her short fiction and has had stories reprinted in several volumes of* The Year's Best Fantasy and Horror.

"The Hill" was originally published in The Mammoth Book of Monsters, *edited by Stephen Jones.*

—E. D.

Long ago, when I was about fifteen years of age, I looked out at the familiar sea, and saw that on the horizon, and without warning, it had grown into a tall and rounded hill. I mean that I saw a hill, made of the deep milky blue summer sea, standing up, far out and motionless, from the rest of the water. I stopped in astonishment. Part of my surprise was caused by the fact that no one else among the many people on the cliff path seemed to see what I did. This impossible, wondrous, terrifying thing. For if the liquid ocean could form a solid hill, surely the fabric of the world, and everything else we believe in, came into question. I confess too, I had at that time no doubts either about my eyesight or my sanity.

I. Chazen's Beasts

I am an independent woman. Daughter of a handsome, feckless father, a pretty and foolish mother, I grew up into a plain, intelligent adult. I make no bones about the intelligence, despite its limits. I have nothing else to boast of. My person is quite tall, neat, and inclined to be thin. While at the age of twenty-two, my hair had already begun to gray. Several have asked me why this happened so early; had I received some severe shock? I had to shock them by replying I had not. For, at that time, I hadn't.

I live alone, but not always in my own apartment, three rooms at the top of a large old house near London. At other times I live in the houses of my employers. I am a librarian. My task is to sort and regulate the libraries of others far less able, and normally far more wealthy than Miss Alice June Constable: myself.

The invitation to Northerham House, which I had been expecting some while, finally arrived on a late summer morning.

Used to such trips I was packed and on the train in less than five hours, reaching my destination at six o'clock that evening.

A warm strong wind was blowing as I walked up the lane. The trees shook their huge, tired green leaves, and through the rocking boughs I glimpsed the village of Northerham—which locals pronounce North'rum—below. It appeared the usual pastoral place, small houses with gardens, an inn, a pub, and a Saxon church with rambling graveyard.

The house of my employer stood off the lane, at the end of a short, curving, heavily tree-hung drive. This was no mansion either, but a pleasant two-story building with an arch over the front door and recently cut lawns. To the back extended long gardens ultimately swathed in woods. There was a scent of wallflowers, and zoos. I'd been told, in a letter from the master of the house, Professor Chazen, that by the time I arrived he would be away again on his travels. The housekeeper was off too. Only a manservant, a Mr. Swange, and a maid of all work (Doris) were in residence. Aside from that was the professor's collection of exotic beasts. All of these lived, I had been assured, among the back premises, sheds, enclosures, and pens. Chazen traveled widely, and tended to bring back curios, often of the animal kind. I can recall I had thought that his library should prove very interesting, and looked forward to reading some of the material I was to catalog.

My knocks on the front door got no reply. I therefore went round to the back by the gravel path.

A small garden cordoned off the kitchen. Washing flapped vigorously on a line and two or three hens strutted about. The kitchen door was open, but no one in sight.

I peered over the hedge, and so came face-to-face as it were with the first of the animal pens about ten yards away. Eight or nine cat creatures—large for a domestic cat certainly but smaller than most of the wild variety—were prowling or snoozing in the wire-fronted box. This container was some sixteen feet by six feet high. It's true I have never left England, but I have seen many collections and read thousands of books, and never had I seen or heard of anything quite like these cats. They were a dirtyish white in color, their fur or pelt tufted, and streaked with faint brown mottles. Their eyes glowed a pale, embered blue.

As I stared, I heard a woman's step on the gravel.

"Oh, Miss—did you knock? I never heard you—"

Doris the maid was all apologies. She led me inside and presently we were sharing the teapot at the scrubbed table. (I have never thought it necessary to keep servants at a "correct" distance. One can learn a lot from them, and in any case I am,
after all, a sort of intermittent servant myself. Besides, where needful, I can usually
assert my authority.)

"Then shall I show you the animals, miss?" inquired Doris after I had mentioned
them, some quarter of an hour later.

I was curious. Also I disapproved of the cage that held the tufted cats. I asked her
if all the cages were as restricted.

"Oh no, miss. Some are very enormous. But the cats are let out at night in summer, and in winter they're moved with the others to warmer pens in the sheds."

"Let *out*?"

"Well, there's half a mile of woods at the end of the gardens that Professor
Chazen owns with the house. They're fenced and netted right over, with small
places left to let birds and mice and suchlike in and out. His cats are noctual
really—they prefer nighttime. You may hear a bit of squawking down along the
woods after dark. Take no notice, miss."

"Noctual" having been explained (nocturnal), I envisioned nights pierced by
weird cries, as small English rodents and fowls were rent by Chazen's felines. But I
sleep well. Probably it was no worse dying like that than by the fangs of a fox, or
some neighboring tabby.

"What other beasts are there?" I asked her as she conducted me through the
hedge by the gate.

"All sorts. There's them—" (the cats) "—and some badgery things, sort of bears I
think he says—and ratty things—ugh!" (a shudder, though I noticed it was more ritual than impassioned) "snakes—great big beetles, all hairy—lizards—the professor
says they're very intelligent."

The cats growled as we passed them, lazy and bored. They had a meaty smell,
and looked healthy. Their blue eyes were neither friendly nor disarming, but Doris
clucked at them. Favorites? A sort of netted tunnel, at present closed off from the
cage, ran to the dark green woods that frothed up beyond the lawn, shrubs, and
sheds. I had been wondering how the "letting-out" was managed.

Under the shade of oak and apple trees, we skirted other imprisoned animals
some of these, as she'd told me, in huge enclosures. I recognized none of the
species. The snakes meanwhile were invisible, and the beetles shut in a large long
shed to the side. I kept up my questions, now as to where the menagerie came from.
"Oh, all sorts of countries," exclaimed Doris. "Africa—the Indies—America even.
And some of them are trained, he says, to do clever things—" but when she said this
her face fell suddenly. I considered why. Perhaps she did not like the idea of performing animals.

I began to see the netting running right over the woods, a roof and walls, glinting
as the sun sank behind us on the orchards and fields of Kent. Birds were calling and
singing in the trees, impervious or stoical about the cat tunnel leading to their sanctuary.

Our shadows long before us, Doris pointed out the padlocked gate reserved for
human entry. I saw too scattered bronze feathers and a stripe of red—which I took
for the remains of a slain pheasant—just inside the man-made boundary.

"Blett has charge of maintaining the netting," said Doris. "Or he's supposed to.
He's off on his honeymoon. Too taken up with it, if you ask me. He got sacked—
nearly got himself sacked. It was just the day the professor left. There was a great

hole in the fencing Blett'd missed. The professor didn't half take on. In a right two-and-six he was" (surprising me by her Cockney rhyming slang: two-and-six: fix). "Blett said to me the animals get restless and tear holes, trying to get out. He said things *frighten* them. I ask you, what things, *here* . . . not like the jungle, is it? But you should hear how they go on sometimes."

"The animals?"

"No, people in the village."

"Do they?"

"Really silly I calls it. So does my gentleman friend." She blushed and looked slyly at me, I, the elderly spinster. I smiled. Doris added, "It's the old ones mostly. Professor Chazen, well he doesn't go to church, doesn't believe in God, you see. And then all this stuff he's collected in the house, and the garden—the villagers like to say the professor's tempting the Devil himself."

"Do you believe in the Devil?" I asked Doris. I am a modern-minded old maid, so thought I had better let her know it.

A grim pause resulted.

"Yes," she said at last, fearfully.

I was then sorry, and chided myself.

And so found we had stopped, and stood staring at a decidedly gigantic pen.

"What's in here?"

"That's the lizards."

Roused maybe by a sympathetic awareness of her words, one of these just then emerged from a sort of bothy of twigs and stones. It straddled a piece of floor, and turned its reptillian head to see us through a swiveling, sidelong eye. It was itself very big, the size of a small spaniel, with gray scales that seemed highly polished, gleaming in the last sunlight, and purplish claws reminiscent of those of a fowl. A spiny crest, which had been lowered, now rose high. Magnified by a power of about six, one could imagine it tramping the prehistoric plains.

I preferred the lizard greatly to the furry cat-beasts. It looked soulless, dull, intemperate, and not pretty. You could mistake it for nothing that it was not.

"And these? Are they African?"

"I can't remember, miss." And then, "Oh! I must run—I left my cake in the oven—"

My first days at Northerham began as have a score of other employments.

The library was large and impressive in structure and layout; a total muddle with regard to contents. Many of the tall book stacks reared quite empty, apart from dust—one needed a ladder to ascend. Such an item had been ordered from London, it seemed, but not yet arrived. Crates massed in awkward places, savagely undone, their edges all bent nails and splinters. Some wonderful books might lie inside, unsorted and liable to be torn if not removed with extreme care.

I set to work as I always do, devising first the best system, only then unpacking. A huge old mahogany table provided help with this. In the late morning I'd lay out some appealing tome, and after lunch read for an hour at least. I am a fast reader. Little escapes me that way. And I wasn't unhappy otherwise. My room was kept clean and orderly, its bed comfortable. There was a small private bathroom next door. The view looked off down the back garden to the wood, over the pens and netting, from which, as was inevitable, uncanny warbles and squeaks would frequently sound after dark. Meals were prepared by Doris, a very good—if rather eccentric—cook. I had met Mr. Swange the first evening, when he attended the bringing in of my dinner to the dining room. Unlike rose-and-cream Doris, he was a skulking iron man with a bleak expression. As so often with manservants I've met, he treated me to a polite condescension amounting to insolence. I have generally found it useless to waste time on that. Aside from exchanging a few acid civilities, we had little to do with each other.

One of Swange's tasks was, however, to inspect the outside of the pens at sunset, and let out the corracats, as it transpired they were called.

That Swange did not like either the task or the cats was plain enough. But I became used to seeing his angular figure stalking over the back lawn as I tidied myself in my room before dinner. Sometimes he was softly cursing in the way only an aristocrat or a criminal is allowed to. My hearing is good, but I had heard all such words before, and now and then in other tongues. It meant nothing to me except that the flit of his electric torch returning was as regular as seven o'clock.

On Saturday Doris, with whom I'd kept up the teatime chat in the kitchen, asked if next day I'd be going to church. I said I would not, though would visit the church some other time, as historically it might interest me. Doris seemed sorry I wasn't a churchgoer in the theosophic sense. (Just like the professor.) It seemed Swange didn't attend either, Doris told me crisply. He preferred the new hotel at Hodcieux (pronounced locally as *Hoed-Say*) where probably he sometimes met his fancy woman, ten years his senior.

If Doris was offended by her present position in a house of atheists, she had managed herself. She stayed pleasant and obliging to me, and from what I saw, timidly flirtatious with Mr. Swange. Perhaps she respected too the shape of a pistol I had noted in his jacket when he went out to check the pens and release the corracats. We all retain means to protect ourselves, if wise. I took no offense at his gun.

As to the house, it was curiously rambling and shadowy for its size. Certain bigger rooms had been partitioned to make two or even three chambers out of one. Some of these lacked windows. Stairs went up and down, twining behind the rooms in obscure ways, to which, fairly quickly, I became accustomed. But it was something of a maze, if a tiny example.

Everywhere one came on statuettes and fetishes from foreign climes. The majority of these were exceptionally horrible to look at, leering with pointed teeth often daubed with painted blood, garlanded by carven heads (severed, obviously), and clutching in their claws clubs and other more spiky weapons. Doris, whom I had met now and then cleaning the rooms, refused to touch these icons.

"They're not to be disturbed," he" (she would mean the professor) "says. And I—well, I wouldn't *care* to touch them, Miss A."

"Whyever not? Are they so valuable?"

"He says," said she, "they can—invogle things. *Bring* things on—bad wishes, curses."

I queried inwardly what her "*invogle*" meant—*invoke*? "But they're made of wood or stone," I suggested. She said then something else I was later to recall.

"People—witches—heathen priests—can call up spirits, Professor Chazen told me. Oh, he's often given me such a turn with his tales of those places—my blood ran cold. And such bad dreams I had. He said he'd seen as much, in the dark jungles . . . they use wooden images—even animals—as a—what did he say?—a focus—can that be right? Focus . . . and they can summon the *dead*."

I refrained now from saying anything. This litany of necrotic return seemed sig-

nificant to Doris, a kind of valued other-side-of-the-coin to her religious belief. I have
noted similar fancies among pious persons before.

It was the next Thursday evening, about seven-thirty, as I was going down to drink a
glass of sherry before dinner, that I heard the crabby voice of Swange complaining to
Doris in the main hall below.

I stopped on the stairs to listen. I make no excuse for such a habit. Sometimes it's
proved a sensible precaution.

"Those damn beasts are acting oddly," I had heard Swange say.

"Oh, but—they're all so queer. You know he always says" (again, I could assume,
I thought, she referred to Chazen) "some of them have odd ways. You'd only have to
look at them twice to know it. And they often act up, don't they?"

"It's worse than usual, tonight. Plenty of them are scratch-scratching away at that
netting. As for those cats—they've having a fight fit for the *Dog and Pullet* at turn-
out time—" At which I heard Doris giggle.

Nevertheless, "Maybe it's just," she said, "the heat."

"They're from blinking *Africa*, Dorry!"

So he called her "Dorry," did he?

She said softly, I only just caught it, "Don't take on so. It won't be for much longer,
will it, de—"

She broke off as *he* hissed: "Keep it down. That old bat'll be about in a minute."

On her cue, the old bat gave a subdued cough, measured out to sound as if she
were slightly farther off up the stairs than she was, and resumed her passage down to
prove him right.

After dinner, I allowed myself half an hour of Mozart on the rather fine if out-of-
tune piano. Then I decided on a brief stroll around the grounds at the back. I'd done
this once or twice before to get some air, while it was cooler. No one made any comment. Of course, I was wanting to see if Chazen's beasts were as restive as Swange
had said.

Nothing however seemed much altered, at least to me.

The corracats had already sprinted off along their tunnel into the fenced woodland. (In their vacant daytime cage, a few clumps of fur added evidence to Swange's
account of a fight. But animals often fight, especially when cooped up.) Other animals were out of sight in the sleeping quarters of their pens. Nocturnals paced along
the perimeters, but their sentry-go activity was also quite normal, or so I thought.
Only the badger-bears, whose name I hadn't learned, seemed at all apparently disturbed. On previous walks here I had seen them lying down, grooming or playing.
Tonight all three were up in the pair of trees that grew inside their pen. Blett was
supposed, I had gathered, also to trim such enclosed trees down and back from the
wire, both here and in the wood. He had signally failed in this. The bears had
climbed as high up as they could get, to where the boughs strained against the netting roof that sealed them in. Two of the animals were cuddled together. The third,
alone in the second tree, gave the clear impression of their watchman. It uttered a
soft, brittle chittering as I went by. And six pale narrow eyes, catching the glim of a
rising half-moon, observed me with intense uneasy indifference.

I reached the edge of the caged woods, and glanced at the avenues inside. But the
woodland was black, and the trace of starlight here and there gave only misleading
information—mirages of water, a huge black clump that might be anything, and
seemed slightly to move in the windless atmosphere. Of the cats there was no sign.

They would be far off down among the trees, no doubt, as distant from the habitat of man as they could get.

I turned from the wood, and looked at the lizard enclosure. This was in the same blackness, just a trickle of starlight on a stone, a leaf—seeming to be other things—a gem, an *eye*. On other evenings, I had seen four or five of the creatures moving about. Now, despite the illusions, none was visible. They must be asleep, or hiding, in their bothy.

Returning to the house, whose curtained lampshine fell dimly on the lawn, I was struck by a peculiar something about the night.

I couldn't at first have said what it was. Certainly, as I have remarked, the evening was hot and airless. That brisk wind combing the trees on my arrival had perished days ago.

Eventually I stopped still once more. I listened. There was not a sound.

Those who live in towns and cities always suppose the countryside to be quiet. In the mechanical way it probably is, aside from the chug of a tractor or the chuffing of a periodic train. But by day *and* night a constant barrage of *natural* noises goes on. Birds flute or shrill alarms. Unseen animal movements cause rustlings and bustle. Frogs croak from ponds, insects buzz, and crickets whirr. After sunset, the volume seems increased. Dogs bark to each other from the hamlets, farms, and villages; mice and rabbits squeal; foxes offer eerie banshee screams, owls and nightjars sew up any silent seams of darkness with the stitches of their peculiar music.

Tonight, there was nothing. The motionless, empty air was heavy, and *charged*, as if before a storm. Yet the sky was very clear, deep blue with stars and lifting moonlight.

Back in the house I made myself tea. Bidding Doris good night, I went back to the library. I worked and read for another hour, then retreated to bed.

I am not unduly fanciful. Nor am I quite insensitive.

About three in the morning, according to my clock at the bedside, I woke; without a start, but fully and totally. It was as if I had not been asleep at all, so absolute was my awareness of myself and everything about me. None of the usual brief cloudiness of sleep remained. Nor had I been dreaming. My eyes had opened on the nearer of the two windows of my room.

I tend to leave my bedroom casement ajar and the curtains undrawn, when there is the privacy for it. Here I had done so. Framed between the drapes lay the sky. The moon had gone over, but the night still was not at all dark, far less so than the bedroom. I saw very clearly. Nothing was there, looking in at the window.

And yet, along with the unusual sudden waking clarity of my brain was a sort of definite knowledge that—a second or so before I opened my eyes—*something had been*.

II. Rising Up

Now and then in my later life, or rather this later middle part of life I now occupy, odd things have come my way. To say I'm always inured to such amazements would be to lie. But generally I take a (perhaps foolish) interest in them.

After the window incident, decidedly I grew more alert. (Nor did I doubt some visitor had been there. A daylight inspection from said window showed the damaged creeper outside, which bore witness to something quite hefty having *dragged* itself up the brickwork, and then slithered back.)

When I went down to breakfast that morning, Doris was in that mood she had referred to before as a two-and-six.

"Excuse me, Miss A. It's them—those cats again. Poor Mr. Swange went to get them back in their pen—as a rule they're already in the tunnel, and soon as they seen him they rush down like anything—it's when he feeds them, you see. Only to-day they wouldn't budge. Ran about along the edge of the net, and then straight back in the woods. He says they might have the rabbis—"

"The rabb—do you mean *rabies*, Doris?"

"That illness where they froth pink at the mouth, Miss A."

"Doris, that would be very serious. Has he—have you—had contact with them?"

"Oh, we weren't bitten, miss. And Mr. Swange *never* goes into the woods without the professor going with him."

I knew that with rabies, a bite wasn't necessary to cause fatal infection. Infected dogs have frequently licked a human hand before the madness became apparent in them. This hand having one small open cut, the poisonous saliva does its work. Even if not going into the woods, Swange *had* entered the cats' tunnel. A smear of fresh spit on the net—

It seemed best not to frighten Doris worse. She was already in her two-and-six.

"I'm sure it isn't rabies, Doris. How long have the animals been here, it's quite some time, isn't it?"

"About eight months for the cats, Miss A."

"Then rabies is most unlikely. Symptoms present themselves inside a few days, or weeks at the most."

Swange didn't appear. Doris seemed upset. When she produced her basket and got ready to walk down to the village, I offered to go with her. I could do, I said, with the exercise.

She cheered up on the way. Between the fields and hedgerows she chattered about her family, even adding that her "friend" and she planned one day to open a pub or hotel, and be "independent."

I left her in the village street to do her shopping for the house, and took myself over to the church. It was the typical Saxon model, its tower pointed and thatched. But outside I noticed the graveyard was excessively neglected. The old stones, ro-mantic enough in high grass, weeds, moss, and ivy, leaned, here and there the stag-nant earth actually overturned. In some spots the tilting of the slabs had become precarious, and fallen urns massed in the grass like skulls.

Then I rounded a corner. Between two massive old yew trees another little scene was going on.

From his dress, I recognized the vicar at once. He, and a group of men more roughly clad, were frowning and peering at a solid patch of chaos.

The yews were, from my point of view, quite concealing. In their shade I paused.

"This is too dreadful," said the vicar.

"Yes, sir. An' it's the same business as yesterday, sir, so it is. Plain as my nose."

"Truly, Robert. But yesterday was never so bad as this."

"Well, sir, I blame that bas—I blame that feller Blett."

The other men rumbled. It seemed they did too.

Without doubt, someone appeared to have acted the vandal here. Worked on in a coarse, uneven circle, the old graves were riven, and in places whole slabs had been heaved upward, like unnerving trapdoors. The smell of antique, hot moist earth and wetly dried death filtered through the summer air.

I considered the name, Blett. He was the man who maintained Professor Chazen's animal pens.

"But to do such a sacrilegious thing—why would *Blett* do this, in the very graveyard he cared for less than two weeks ago?"

"We seen how he cared for it. If he scythed the grass five times this year, I'm the Prince of Wales."

"I find it hard to think so ill of him." The vicar was an elderly little man of twenty-seven or eight. He plainly wanted to practice Christ's marvelous and ordinarily impossible teaching to love all men as himself. The difficulty, one could see, was constantly painful, but manfully he stayed at it. Believe or disbelieve as one may, the courage of such fragile warriors deserves to be saluted.

"Well, sir," someone patiently said, "Blett never did much about the yard here. And if he's had one sober day since I known him I'd doubt. And when he got the sack—"

"A rank drunkard he is," vowed one of the others. "And a—well, he's a bad 'un—".

"See, Vicar, he comes back after the sacking, and he spoils the graves—that were yesterday. Then last night he gets another skinful and back he comes and does worse. Allays bin a revengeful bas—a revengeful feller, Blett."

Doris had told me Blett was off on his honeymoon. Had she lied to spare me the more sordid details? I sensed Chazen too must have sacked the revengeful feller.

"Don't fret, sir," the men were now reassuring the vicar, like several kind fathers with a worried little boy. "We'll see to it. Make it proper. Then you come and bless the place over. That'll make all fine."

As they dispersed, I slunk away. Sunday fell the day after tomorrow. I hoped everything would be tidy in time for Doris's next church attendance. Though I doubted village gossip would spare her the news of a disturbance of graves.

She looked decidedly wan at lunch but volunteered nothing, so I too pretended ignorance.

During the afternoon, just as I had set a tenement of uncrated books on the mahogany sorting table, a loud crash resounded below in the core of the house, followed at once by Doris's scream.

I descended swiftly to the ground floor and found her in a gloomy, seldom-used old drawing room. Partitioned off from another bigger room, it had only one window, facing toward the back lawn, draped either side by thick brocade curtains. Dusty yellow afternoon rayed in, showing the clustering mammoths of dark furniture, and Doris with both hands still clamped to her mouth. Her broom leaned on a chair and on the floor lay her dusters and can of polish. With one more thing.

"It fell, miss—it just rocked and fell."

An example of the hideous fetish statues was in pieces on the wooden floor beyond the carpet. To my mind its breakage involved no great aesthetic loss. The head had sprawled away intact under a sideboard, where it grinned its nacred, "blood"-splotched fangs.

"I swear, Miss A—I never touched it. I never *do* touch the horrible things—I was over there, polishing that cabinet. And there's this scraping and scratching, and I looks round—and there it goes! Oh, miss!"

In countries prone to major, or minor, earth tremors, this would be a commonplace. But earthquakes are rare, if not unheard of, in Kent.

"Never mind it, Doris. Of course it wasn't your fault."

I'd noticed the single window had been opened wide, perhaps to air the mustiness of the room, for there was a quite nasty smell, dirty and distracting. The windowsill had been scored with a little mark. I went over and saw something had scratched the sill. This had a very recent look, but that might be deceiving. Doris screamed again.

"There! There!"

I glared back, and under the sideboard beheld the fetish's grinning head rattling from side to side, its fangs seeming to gnash in a flutter of something white—

"Doris, stay completely still—and silent!"

At my command she froze.

Moving forward I seized her broom and thrust its bristled end directly in under the sideboard.

Something squalled and rolled out, kicking and spitting.

It was not the severed wooden head, but one of the corracats, as I had already deduced from the flutter of its tail.

With a few more irresistible shoves, I broomed the creature back across the room and up against the wall beneath the window, the window through which it must have entered. As I did so I also ripped the nearer curtain from its rings. The heavy brocade plunged down across the cat, and in a series of moments of clawing, rolling, and wailing, it had thoroughly enmeshed itself beyond all hope of voluntary exit.

"Fetch Swange!" I shouted, guarding my well-wrapped trophy with the broom.

Doris ran out and was back with him inside five minutes.

In spite of his aversion, as I'd trusted Swange knew, or had been instructed how to cope. He had on thick gauntlets, and soon bundled the shrieking corracat outside and into its pen by the kitchen garden.

There it cowered alone, since the rest of its kind still ran free in the wood. Swange had found meanwhile, he said, another wide open place in the woodland fencing. He set to mending the hole, cursing Blett.

"That's how kitty will have got out," said Doris, explaining needlessly. "And I reckon that Blett done it before he left, to get back at us . . . to be truthful," she went on, hanging her head at the grave error of an earlier lie, "Blett isn't on honeymoon— who'd have him? No, the professor sacked him good and proper, like he said he would to Mr. Swange. Oh, I heard the professor shouting, right down in the woods— Blett and the professor were in the woods, you see. It was just after the trap came to take the professor's bags to the train—anyway, Blett must have slung his hook, as they say. Then come back later and mucked with the fences. And the professor was in such a rage. He went off without a word. But, well—" having raised her head she lowered her eyes. I had a sudden distinct impression she neither liked nor trusted Chazen, perhaps even feared him. She added softly, "I didn't want to burden you, miss, with all that tale when you'd just arrived. I thought you might think bad of us all and leave."

I smiled and told her I understood.

However, in a while I too went up to inspect the damaged barrier around the woods. Indeed it had been mutilated, but if from the outside, indicating an aggressor no longer in possession of a key to the gate, I was unsure. I pondered if Swange, or Doris, had been at all perturbed by the strange track leading, both inside the wire and out to the scene of the crime. It was a cumbersome and dragging course Blett had made—perhaps due to more than usual drunkenness. Torn leaves and smashed shrubs described it. Yet also, surely, it was too *low* a path for a man to create— though unnecessarily wide for the progress of any animal I had seen here. Had he been crawling all the way on his knees?

Doris said nothing on this. Nor did she question why the escaped cat come into the house. Maybe she put it down to mischief. But it seemed to me that a wild creature would prefer the wild, if it could have it. Only very great eagerness, or fright, would drive it into a human habitation.

Whatever the cause, for our various reasons, we three persons—Doris, Swange, and I—now seemed to generate a muted tension.

As the evening drew on, Doris was exceptionally quiet at her work. Swange had vanished, but later, as always, I noted his torch flitting back houseward through the seven o'clock dark.

He had checked the pens presumably, but not allowed the one recaptured corra-cat its routine nightly access to the woods. Presently it began to give off rapid short screeches. These went on and on. The sound was like that of a violin rasped by the bow of a madman. Inevitably, others among the animal prisoners soon added an intermittent chorus.

As I went down, once more I heard Doris speaking very low to Swange. "Couldn't you let it out, Sidney? The fence is all mended now." But apparently Sidney (were they so intimate?) could not. For the frantic cries went on, and only ceased, one and all, about eleven-thirty that night.

What woke me on this occasion was a noise at least as old as the Dark Ages; in other forms much older. It was the ominous clanging of a church bell—since Christian times a tocsin, the signal of invasion, or some worse calamity.

I'm not entirely unused to emergencies. I sprang up and put on my walking boots and buttoned my coat, which carried some extra protection, over my nightgown. Downstairs I found the lights all on, Doris huddling in her nightclothes and Swange fully dressed. From the smell of whiskey I had the feeling he might not anyway have gone to bed.

"It's in the village," he loftily told me, "that bell."

"Yes of course. The church. Hadn't we better go and see?"

"That isn't part of my work," he replied.

"Someone may need assistance."

"I'm not a village man. They can look after themselves."

I shrugged. "Well, Swange, you can let me out, if you will. I intend to find out what's happened."

Swange swore, not very foully. Doris caught his arm. "Mr. Swange! You can't let Miss A go on her own—"

"Of course he can. I'm quite well able to look after myself. Open the front door at once, man."

With an iron fist for a face, he obeyed me, and slammed the door shut again as soon as I was on the drive.

The bell was yet ringing for all it was worth, much louder and more alarming in the open air and under the hanging swags of black moonless foliage. I set off down the drive and along the lane at a brisk trot. It was generally a dawdle of twenty minutes, but I covered the ground in ten.

There were plenty of lights on in the village too, and in the church. People stood out on the street along the graveyard wall, or leaned from cottage windows. I noted the pub had opened up again too, and was now serving drinks at three twenty-five in the morning. In just over an hour the sun would rise.

As I entered the main street, the clangor of the bell suddenly ended.

The whole landscape now rang with silence. Everyone ceased to move, myself included. While from the church tower came a faint shout. The crowd repeated the message to itself and so to me. "They've got 'un—it's Jim Hardy, is it? What's he at? Has he gone off his onion?"

Presently two men and the little vicar, all in dressing gowns, appeared in the church door, supporting another man of sturdy middle years. He was dressed for the day in laborer's clothes, but all awry, his hair over his face and his coat trailing half off. As they tried to bring him out of the door, he started to roar. It seemed he would fight them all rather than leave the church. But then abruptly his legs gave. He stopped roaring, and they partly carried him up the path between the graves, to the gate in the wall, and so through groups of people to the welcoming pub.

I stood decorously with a bundle of women outside. We looked in on the lighted saloon bar. Everything that was said in there we all heard clearly enough.

After the second brandy, the man called Hardy responded to the oft-asked question "What were up with you, Jim, ringing the bell like that?"

"I see it," he said. "Plain as I see you."

"See *what*, Jim?"

"Like it says," said Jim Hardy, "in the Bible. The graves giving them up, and the dead a-walking."

It seemed Jim was a decent, hardworking laborer, who could turn his hand to various tasks, and he had been promised three days employment, with board, at a farm by Low Cob, a hamlet some thirteen miles from Northerham. There was only a single car in the village, this not owned by Jim, naturally. The cart ride he had hoped for fell through. As he was expected in Cob by five-thirty that morning he had therefore had to set out on foot in the middle hours of the night.

His road took him through the village about 2:00 A.M. The moon was sinking as he paused by the graveyard wall to light his pipe.

"That was when I seen 'em."

Unlike many older rural people, Jim Hardy was not unduly superstitious about graves. At first, he said, he thought what he was seeing was foxes or badgers, playing about there under the trees and among the tall, uncut grass. There seemed quite a few of them, a whole family, he thought, and he was asking himself what the local hunt would make of running any of them to earth on sacred ground, when something in the whole movement and method of the animals struck him as quite odd. "They were seeming," he said, shuddering, "to be slinking along slow, all of 'em, on their bellies. And in a kind of—like—a circle."

So then he'd got the notion it was *men* in the churchyard—after all, weren't these uncertain forms too big-looking for foxes? And carrying on like that—they must be up to no good. There were solid silver candle sconces in the church that were said to date back to the days of King Henry V. Though locked in a cupboard in the vestry, the church door itself was always left undone.

Jim Hardy was perfectly brave on this score. He put down his bag of work tools and selected a fine strong hammer. This in hand, he slipped through the gate, and crept by the trees and the leaning stones . . . toward the spot where the robbers were cavorting in their peculiar, lurching circle.

He took his stand where I had, between those two vast yew trees, safe from detection as he thought in their coal-black shadow.

And then one last shaft of the sinking moon struck helpfully between the graves. And he saw.

At first—as one might not—he didn't believe his eyes. "Was like a dream," he said, "like some joke som'un played on me."

But he found he couldn't move. His limbs had changed to lead, and his eyes frozen in a stare, unable to turn away. He went cold too, he told us all, as if winter snow came down on the summer land.

"They was circling, right enough, going around and around. Like *worms* they was, great, huge worms, crawling on their bellies, but their necks and heads raised up—and their *chests* raised up clear of the ground—like snakes I see in a book—and their hollow eyes—they looked at me, they looked and the eyes shone! There was white fire in them eyes, though they was all dead hollow sockets, and the broken ribs showed through their chest cases and the round bone showed through the scalp of their heads like old yeller felt caps."

His perverse acuity of description held us riveted. But having said all this, Jim Hardy lapsed. He began to shake, to stamp his feet, and to pull at something invisible in the air—I came to realize he was enacting his breaking loose from paralysis, his flight into the unlocked church, his climb up the tower, and his ringing of the harsh old bell.

From the scatter of his now gasping words, we made out that from the window above, before starting to ring, he had also seen the circle of corpses, still with heads and upper torsos raised (ribs starting through the flesh as if through unmended waistcoats), the arms and legs dragging *boneless* behind them, the glint of white hellfire in the cores of dead eye sockets, but each and all slithering round and round atop the wreckage of their undone graves, aimless or determined, he could not know which, in this ritual of their living resurrection.

The pub had become very still.

Finally the vicar, meaning well, put his slender hand gently on Jim's shoulder. Then Jim grew totally dumb. He sat rigid, only his head tilted back on the chair, his eyes fixed unblinking, locked again in the frozen stare he had described. He was very white, and his hands were very cold I should think, as if from the summer snow he had mentioned.

He would, or could, say no more. He would not move either, though they coaxed him.

Then the doctor arrived. Sent for long since, he'd been delayed by delivering a baby to the policeman's wife—which was why, of course, the policeman too had arrived with the doctor. Unfairly the doctor berated the men in the pub, saying that giving brandy had not been a sensible idea in a case of such extreme shock. The doctor informed us all too that corpses pushing out of their tombs and slithering in the churchyard by *"walking"* on their chests was all "tosh. Did any of the rest of you see anything like that? No? And does it anyway seem like the Last Day to you? Is the moon turned red as blood?" The policeman was more civilized, pleased perhaps at the healthy son with which his wife had presented him. He led the party of muttering men to inspect the ruin of the graves. Their torchlight—not electric but lit on sticks from a kitchen range—soon began to fade with the coming of dawn.

I myself went down and took a surreptitious look at the site of Jim Hardy's horror. It was the exact place, obviously, the vicar and the men had been troubled at yesterday. And there could be no doubt now, doctor or no, that the graves were fully upheaved, headstones and slabs flung headlong. The soil and other debris which had also come up, including, doubtless, pieces of bone, had poured off everywhere. The ground richly stank, the terrible odor of ancient mortal decay, and one man had turned away to vomit.

Nevertheless, no one else had seen what Jim Hardy claimed to have done.

I noted however, elsewhere in the churchyard, runnels where the grass was mashed and flattened, the ivy torn in trails, and on the old dark roots, or even in some cases quite far up the trunks over my head, were peeled green wounds. Very likely, Jim rushing in his panic, and now the nervous searchers, had caused this further damage.

III. The Apocalypse

They were tender to Jim Hardy, but the hard-tongued doctor whisked him off to the hospital.

Later the policeman, augmented by two more senior others from Hodcieux, interviewed the village, and subsequently the three of us at the house.

I have no clue what Swange said, or Doris (though I suspect it was very little). I merely told the truth, which is usually the easiest way, where one can.

The village man nodded when I said I too had afterward gone to look at the broken graves, and seen how the grass and ivy were disturbed. One of the senior officers, he who had already demanded why I had gone to the village at all in the middle of the night—my answer, to see what was wrong, made him snort—now commented sternly that for so curious and prying a woman, I appeared unnmoved. I replied that in my work, curiosity is not a fault, but that also I had learned some self-control.

(Doris told me after, with a strange momentary pride in me, that she had heard the village policeman remark to the less favorable other that I was "the best type of Englishwoman." I had gone fearlessly to the village in order to help, and confronted by horror had not lost my nerve. With the aid of such "handmaidens, young or old" the Empire had been forged. This amused me rather. My ancestry is mixed, and certainly I do not regard myself as particularly British, let alone English.)

The police departed and we were left alone.

The scalding day passed uncomfortably. The animals of Chazen's menagerie seemed all of them unsettled. The cats in the wood were shrilling, the other cat, for which at last the tunnel had been unlocked in daylight, skulked and now refused to leave the pen for the trees. Neither would the small bears come down from their high perches, even when tempted with food. The beetles, rats, and snakes kept intransigently to inner refuges of the cages from which they could not be seen. Various other species, including the lizards, appeared to have dug pits in the earth of their pens and hidden. Swange was in a stiff, cold rage. One could see it from his stalking about the lawns. He was like a guardian forced to take charge of unruly children he disliked. Later he too disappeared, as he so often did. Doris, when I met her, was pale and anxious.

By now I had abandoned my efforts on the library. Instead I'd searched among the crates of books, attempting to find anything that would throw light on those travels the professor had previously made, and so on the collections of curios, and animals, thereby accumulated.

I did locate certain texts relating at least to some of these. The corracats, for example, hailed from South Africa, where they were known to live in prides. Hunters and carrion-eaters both, sometimes they would climb trees, and in the heart of certain jungles, they were said to be the servants of a particular god, who, taking cat shape, troubled the afterlife of men.

The snakes meanwhile were allegedly capable of swallowing whole cows, which I doubted, judging not by their size alone, but from the formation of their jaws.

The beetles were especially treasured. Asian in origin, they had evolved a means of attaching gems to their hairy carapaces, sealing emeralds and rubies in; but why or how was not properly explained. Nor had I spotted any jewels cemented on Chazen's beetles.

I could find nothing written about the badger-bears, or on any other beast, apart from the lizards. There was a slim pamphlet devoted to them, slipped between the pages of another book. It seemed they could be discovered in Indonesia. Select temples maintained them as pets, and their intelligence put them under the jurisdiction of yet another god or goddess (according to the author, rather a cruel one) in whose honor they would perform funeral rites, including, of all things, "morbidly clowning, to inspire and agitate the dead."

Aside from this book, I picked up another small volume, its title being: *Raising the Dead: Ceremonies of an Elder World.*

On these pages I found engravings that depicted several of the nightmarish fetishes and icons physically represented in Chazen's house. The "instructions," if so they may be termed, were by stages stupid, insane, risible, and disgusting. On the last page of the delicious tome I came across a scrawl I recognized. It was Chazen's own handwriting, familiar to me from our earlier exchange of letters. It said only this: *The eternal and unalterable secret of animation, or reanimation, is the presence of life—how can it be any other thing than that?*

By evening, every single animal in the garden-menagerie had escaped.

Immersed in my studies, I'd ceased to hear either birdsong or wailing from the back premises of the house. Not that both had ended. The first I knew of any breakout was the very different noise of Swange shouting and swearing in the hall below. (Those who contend only women become hysterical are in error. Neither female nor male necessarily needs internal possession of a womb to lose their *head.*)

I decided to go down when Doris's high frightened voice joined his.

"What is the matter?"

"Miss A—Oh, miss—"

"Don't start telling *that* old hen," bellowed Swange. "What can *she* do? She's an old meddler. She'll only make the whole mess worse." Swange was not himself. High-colored and ranting, at his wits' end.

And it was *my* fault? I descended the last stair and trod squarely on his foot. (A slap in the face is seldom essential.) He blundered back, then in again, so I detected a past history of unfortunate developments. He collected himself just in time.

"I do beg your pardon, Mr. Swange," I said. "A misstep. At my age . . . my balance, you know. But whatever is wrong?"

He gaped, then replaced his iron mask. It was Doris who told me.

"They've all got out, miss. All those animals. They must've been that scared—you could see they were—all bristly and hiding—and digging—even the little cat in the pen, he's gone too—Oh! What shall we do?"

I asked if any were very dangerous? Could they be inveigled to return? What precisely had so alarmed them?

Doris twittered and Swange interruptively boomed, "None that dangerous, except to ducks and chickens. But they're valuable to *him.* And no, we can't lure them back—haven't I been trying? As for what they're scared of—" here he broke off. The hot metal of his face cooled to pallor. "That business in the village. What was *that?*"

"I don't know, Mr. Swange. Something certainly. But there have been incidents of grave robbery before here and there—"

"Oh, spare me, silly women! It's never that. I went and took a look myself. I spoke to some of the blokes. The graves are *empty.* No one took them, but those corpses are out and away. It's against God."

I was quite startled to find Swange after all superstitious, and at least an affiliate believer.

"Yes, I imagine God might take a poor view of such a spiritually distasteful resurrection. But what do *you* believe has happened?"

"It's Chazen. He's a bloody devil. We've meant to get away from here this twelve-month. Me and her—Doris. Saving up. The old girl at the hotel—I put it about here I'm her fancy man. But it isn't that. I've known her for years. She needs some persuasion, but I'm going to buy the place, then Dorry and me can be independent." (So Swange was indeed, incredibly, Doris's "gentleman friend"!) But Swange plunged on. "Him, with all his so-called learning and his funny ways, and all this mumbo-jumbo—*fascinates* Chazen it does, the rotten fool. The Devil himself'll carry him off, mark my words."

"So you believe the professor is responsible—"

"I *know* the bastard is. *Know* it. We have to get away—like those animals of his—cleverer than us, eh? I'd even bet Chazen might be around the place, somewhere, watching to see how it all goes. Easy enough to get his stuff put on the train and stay behind. He's at the back of this unholy filth." He gave an angry laugh, then swallowed it. Approvingly I saw he had done that because Doris had started to cry.

Beyond the window, a thick brassy dusk was quickly coming down. No bird sang or flew over the trees. From the narrow window at the back, I could see the edge of the cats' deserted pen, the netting wrenched up. And night was on its way.

"Is this the real reason why Blett left Chazen's employment?" I inquired, keeping my back turned to Swange and Doris, who were clinging together in the gloaming.

"Him, that soaker? He *helped* Chazen. Blett was loony."

"Helped him in what way?"

"You don't want to know, Miss Constable."

"I do."

"Every single one of those animals and insects—they're all to do with heathen death rites—raising the dead. And Chazen and Blett, they'd do the rituals in the woods, and now and then they'd kill one of the animals—a rat, a lizard, a bear, a cat. Meant to make the jungle magic happen. Stir it all up, after dark—"

"Ritual sacrifices."

Swange only swore, vividly now. Doris's sobs became loud.

I waited, then turned and said calmly, "What shall we do then, Mr. Swange?"

He gave me a look, but in the end, in the gathering dimness, I was only a fragile aging woman, the weaker sex, deferential at last, needing his protection. To his credit, he gave it.

"That's all right, Miss Constable. We'll be safe enough till morning if we keep inside. But we'll fasten all the doors and windows. Better start now."

I began this narrative with a reminiscence—about the day when I was barely out of childhood; the day I saw the static hill that had grown out of the fluid of the sea.

Probably it is quite apparent that, not doubting my sight or my sanity (at fifteen years it is sometimes easier not to), I was afraid. The phenomenon of the hill, to me, indicated a rent in the fabric of the organized world.

No one was with me. I've said, my father was feckless (and liked alcohol more than it cared for him), and my mother a ninny. I was alone, and the holiday people on the cliff, passing to and fro, evidently hadn't perceived anything out of the ordinary.

I began to cry—by which I mean water ran uncontrollably out of my eyes—tears, I presume, though in fact it was not like crying at all. Perhaps it was only a flag run up reading *Help! Help!*

Eventually an elderly couple, a man and lady, halted by me.

When I look back, I grasp that undoubtedly they were only a handful of years older than I am now. Not elderly then, in the precise sense, though his hair at least was gray. But generous they were. And wise.

Neither said to me demandingly, *What is it, girl*? Or worse, floodingly, *Oh, dear, dear child, whatever is wrong*?

The gentleman bowed and lifted his hat. He said, "May my wife and I be of service, young lady?"

And when I turned my streaming eyes on them, she solemnly said, "My husband is always to be trusted."

What a wonder! A sober yet gallant male, a levelheaded female who utterly approved of him. Oh, yes, others might have been suspicious. But I was not, nor had I need to be. They were as genuine as new-minted gold.

I wiped my eyes and they cleared. I said, "Look there, out at sea—that hill! It has never been there before. How *can* it be there?"

They turned and stared, as I did then, out across the blue plains of the Atlantic Ocean, to the sea-blue hill rising steeply up from it.

"Upon my word," said he, "what a thing. What do you think—?" to his wife—"Is it some island?"

"But the young lady would know if it was an island. She has told us. It was never there, before."

That they too saw it, *perused* it, discussed it, this extended to me great reassurance.

While—for the first time in my life—I found myself no longer alone. I had finally successfully communicated with two other sentient and thinking things. I am well aware those moments on the cliff secured in me forever a hopeful *liking* for strangers, and a wish toward independence and—perhaps—the desire to grow up—not into some bloom of womanhood, but straight into my middle years. It's possible, I suppose, even my hair turned gray at such an early age because of this desire, rather than because of some shock or failing.

On the cliff then we three watched the mystery of the hill. And so shortly thereafter, the three of us also observed how it started to bulge, to topple, and to change—

At midnight, it began.

The doors and windows of Northerham House had been locked and bolted. Had there been bars, such as a medieval castle or manor boasted, they would have been lowered into their slots. Swange oversaw all. That is, he followed me about, at least, to be sure the silly old maid had got things right. She had. Mr. Swange had no notion, perhaps luckily, of the number of times she had been called upon for accuracy.

Presumably he knew Doris had also fulfilled her duty. I imagine that she had.

That evening she catered for our communal meal—pretense at separation was now extraneous. We ate cold meat, pickles, hot potatoes, cheese, and biscuits, with a fine claret I think Swange had liberated from the cellar, caring not much by now for his "Master" Chazen's possessions.

Night itself descended with slight incident. But it was very overcast and black, starless, moonless and stormy, yet no thunder sounded, no lightning irritated the sky. Swange had decided every electric lamp in the house should be switched on, and this was seen to. To me then it seemed we had made of the house a livid fiery beacon. Nevertheless, all approaches—front and back—the empty sheds and enclosures, woods both fenced and adjacent to the property, the lane that led up to the drive and the drive itself, were blankly illumined by a cold, flat yellow.

Swange refused Doris's request to close the curtains.

"We must *see*," he said.

He meant *see what draws near*. He had become a sergeant in an ancient fort.

After our amalgamated meal, I went upstairs and, so far as I could, readied myself.

How should any of us know what might be abroad? A thrill of dismay went through me at the memory of the village, probably unprepared—yet even so it was by now far too late to venture into the dark. For the dark surrounded us, and we were only this small lighthouse perched on a rock.

Having gone up, I gazed from the library. From here I could see the tree-hung drive, and the curve of the lane beyond that led into Northerham.

No warning church bell sounded.

Hours were shed like heavy leaves, from a tree that did not mind whether spring would follow autumn and winter. Who, in like circumstance, has never felt the awful indifference of natural things? *They* know but too well they must first go down into the abyss. But we, the animals abroad on the world's face, accept nothing, and so struggle.

At five minutes to midnight I heard the large, always belated, library clock strike the quarter hour behind me among the book stacks. Perhaps despite myself I had been dozing a little, seated there at the window. For sure, it seemed to me that all at once everything had altered.

I got up, walked about, and looked once more from the window.

Nothing anywhere moved, not even the massed clouds above.

But again I became aware of that dense tremble of silence I had noted before. The room, the whole house, was smothered by it. It occurred to me that this silence was in fact not *merely* an absence of all sound. Human things have sharper faculties than they credit. There is nothing particularly supernatural in this, save in the most literal sense—for they are primal instincts that long ago moved in us freely, and doubtless many times saved the lives of our remotest ancestors. Now and then such talents surface again. This *silence* then was my own animal faculty, which told me unerringly the moment of terror was upon us.

I concentrated my gaze along the drive. In all that motionless light and dark of shadows and electric beams, after all—*movement*. The leaves and boughs there, low hanging to the path, were dipping, shaking. Something approached.

A twig snapped like a pistol shot. The sound seemed to splinter the night.

Out onto the drive the creature emerged. It pushed foward, in a jerky slithering. Unmistakable; it was just as Jim Hardy had recounted: a dead thing once living and mortal. Both sets of its limbs dragged bonelessly alongside and behind it, but it *walked* forward on its chest, which arched up from the driveway, so displaying the broken ribs of the body cavity among the quivering flags of mummified, clothlike skin. Some rags of hair too fluttered over its skull and down its back. Maybe, when formerly alive, it had been female. The head and neck reared craningly upward, turning a little, stiffly, as if it glanced constantly and carefully from left to right. And in the broad light of the house, the hollow black caves of its eyes flashed with a cold white sparkle.

Undeniably, it seemed to have the definite purpose of *reaching* the house. But as it drew very near, suddenly it swung itself, with a ghastly, ungainly, almost grace, away. Like any familiar or tradesman, it rounded the corner, apparently going round toward the kitchen door.

By then another of them had crawled out onto the drive, proceeding exactly as had the first of its kind. To judge by the now-continuous jostle of the lower boughs and bushes in the lane, there were many more close behind.

At this moment Doris shrieked, not once, but three times, very loudly and very near. Running out, I found her on the landing, standing there rigid, and Swange not five feet away from her. They must have retreated here from the ground floor. Now they were staring in petrified horror down the staircase, at something I could not yet see.

My eyes flew to the main door. It had stayed fast shut, as had all windows. Had the creatures then discovered some way in at the back? Was one of them already below in the hall?

Brushing by Doris, I went to the head of the staircase. And looked straight down into the face of death.

If there had been any doubt—I had had none—denial would no longer be possible. The thing that now came sliding, awkward and inexorable, with a quietly scraping thumping drumbeat up the broad stairs—was dead as any corpse could be. And if it was not as ancient and decayed as the others I'd witnessed outside, this one had been made dilapidated in other ways. Whole chunks had been wrenched from it, and certainly its eyes had been gouged out, for the pits were fairly fresh and still a little sticky with blood. Inside them nevertheless some kind of eyelight glared up at me, glittering. On the front of the head there clung a dense mane of blackish hair, though this was knotted and twisted too with blood, and with soil, and decorated with chips of what must be bone. Unlike the other corpses too, it wore clothing, or the remnants, modern enough, even to the stained and frayed silk tie still knotted round its torn throat. Beside all that, it was sufficiently fresh it ripely stank. It had the rich dirty meaty smell I had in error previously thought belonged only to the corra-cat in the drawing room.

The corpse was by now about halfway up the stairs. It showed no wish to halt its advance. And as each step was attempted and achieved, a sinister scratching sounded.

"No, Sidney," quavered Doris in a tiny whisper behind me. "Can't you see—it's *him!*"

Him? I turned to her for a split second. "*Who* is it, Doris?"

"The professor—" she whispered, before stepping back and dropping on the landing in a dead faint.

This was when Swange fired his handgun.

I spun about again to watch a vase shatter in the hall below. He had missed. Besides—if the creature were already dead, what use was there in firing at it?

And yet—do the dead walk? Do hills form from the sea? I can't say decidedly, but I will suggest, not very often.

My own little pistol was already in my hand, small and dainty as a toy, quite suitable for a silly old maid.

I raised my arm, aiming for the space between the dead man's eyes, judged the swinging of the head, and fired point-blank.

The thing on the staircase leaped. Affrontedly it reared right up, so that first it balanced on its knees and then swiftly rose to its feet—after which it tumbled slowly over backward and plummeted down to the foot of the stairs. There it writhed once, oddly as if trying to become comfortable. After that it grew immobile, and stayed so.

Swange and I also stayed where we were awhile, each one of us with our smoking gun. Doris lay motionless on the carpet behind us.

Silence had come again. It was unlike the silence I had twice been aware of. This was simply the absence of any noise.

Swange spoke very low.

"He was in the house. All the time. He came out of the old drawing room, from behind the dresser. Doris'd smelled a smell in there. We thought a rat had died in the wall. But he just came out. I said to him, Are you all right, Professor Chazen? Stupid bloody thing to say. His head like that, and crawling—he was dead, wasn't he. Doris ran straight up here, and I can tell you, I came after her. They were all round the house by then. They still are—"

I started to go down. "*Don't!*" cried Swange.

"It's all right, Mr. Swange. I just need to see—ah, yes," I said, reaching the stair-foot, standing over the corpse of my previously unmet employer, and finding what I *thought* I had in the moment he fell.

Unpleasant shrieks were beginning outside, and growls, thuds and grunting. Something slammed against the door and Swange gave a yell. But I could already make out what took place through the nearest window. "Come and look, Mr. Swange. We have some most unlikely allies."

He bounded down, and together we watched from the security behind the glass, as three corracats scrambled among the two last corpses to have reached the drive. The cats were tearing them in pieces, and as they did this, like a macabre conjuring trick, we beheld what lay behind the facade of each of the slithering undead.

Swange spoke his most blistering oath to date.

"When the corpse of the professor reared up and fell, I could see its claws," I said mildly, "poking through the chest, and another set from the lower torso. That was how they could move. They'd eaten their way in, tunneled through each corpse. Their heads were pushed up into the skull cavity. It must have been like donning a helmet, once the hindrance of any brains were either eaten or discarded."

Swange made a stifled sound.

I said, "As for seeing out, no doubt they could spy well enough from each side through chinks in the skull. And what glittered so brightly through the eyeholes of the dead when catching any light was not an eye at all, in fact only their *scales*."

Outside now the five cats were very busy, ripping away the dry old flesh to come at those same shining scales, and so to the more succulent living lizard flesh beneath. A further two cats burst from around the side of the house, involved in a vicious tug-of-war over a single dead lizard already pulled from its cadaver. Similar hunting screams came now from every direction. It seemed the cats meant to complete their hunt on all sides of the house.

Doris called feebly from above, "Sidney, Sidney—"

I went up at once and helped her to rise.

"Did Sidney shoot it?" she whimpered, pointing at Chazen's body in the hall. Though dim with faintness, her eyes strayed to my own pistol. "Or was it *you*, miss?"

I told her firmly, "I'm afraid *I* shot the vase, Doris. But Mr. Swange luckily has a steady hand. He killed the thing with one shot."

Below, Swange gave me a scowl. Then winked. "You're too hard on yourself, Miss A. You were just rattled, that was all, and no wonder. At any other time I'm sure you could shoot like a regular trooper."

No newspaper carried this story. It was, I assume, kept quiet for fear the grisly facts cause more upset than interest.

The police of course were for some days ever-present. After them came people to do with collecting and reinstating the disturbed remains—what survived of them. The graveyard was tidied and resanctified to holy ground.

The rest of Chazen's animals were rounded up and removed to a well-run zoo—aside from a pair of corracats and one snake, which eluded the searchers, and perhaps still roam the Kentish fields and woods, stealing the odd chicken or sheep. Even given the reputation of the snakes, probably no cows go missing.

Despite the bullet I had fired into the dead professor's head, experts soon enough discovered he had been killed by a savage blow to the *back* of the cranium, delivered some days earlier, and administered by a torn-up stake from the fence. Blett was the inevitable suspect. Inside a week he had been traced to a lodging house in Plymouth, and on apprehension, confessed. He had murdered Chazen in a fit of drunken wrath, fed up, he said, with Chazen's constant complaints about poor upkeep of the grounds.

Seeing what he had done, Blett had hastily dug a grave and tipped Chazen in. But this bodge was no match either for the heat or Chazen's cats. Unrealizing, Blett had bolted with drunk optimism for the coast. He had also been drunk enough, prior to the argument and homicide, deliberately to have damaged every cage and shed, in what he afterward termed "cunning ways" not immediately obvious. He intended all the precious collected animals the professor used for study (or slaughter during trials of black magic) to escape. Swange's lack of interest in the menagerie, and frequent trips to Hodcieux and the hotel, had also no doubt aided the sabotage, which went mainly undetected. Blett's subsequent fate was the usual miserable one prescribed in such circumstances. He hanged.

As for the rest, while Chazen's servants had thought he caught the train—which even Swange had ultimately doubted—the professor's body lying summer-rotting in his wood enticed the corracats to devour parts of him. For that reason they refused to return into the pen, while one that had got out through one of Blett's holes in the wood fencing followed Chazen's corpse into the house, once it was transported there. Mostly, the *freshness* of Chazen's death had stirred up the great lizards to their original function.

For these animals had really taken a role in mystic funereal rites of certain temples. The professor had never learned, beyond foolish guesswork, what this role was. But it was one of the temple's deeper mysteries.

Only some years after did I come across a volume on the sacred death practices of eastern Asia, which, in half a page, enlightened me as to why the lizards acted as they had. They were, it seemed, trained to enter the corpses of the dead, scouring out as they did so any impeding bodily matter. Then, once in full possession of a body, they would make the cadaver "dance." This dance then was the appalling reared-up slither-crawl Jim Hardy, Doris, Swange, and I had seen at firsthand. To the initiates of the temples, however, it was neither a horrific nor a profane act. Let alone the "morbid clowning" Chazen's own ignorant book claimed it to be. By showing the unopposed animal possession of every corpse, otherwise empty and lacking any motive power of its own, the "dance" displayed that the human spirit had gone far away to a place of joy and safety, where its happiness was so sure, it no longer cared what became of the cast-off flesh.

Able to get out, the lizards had quickly located Chazen's body. One served him as it had been trained to do, finally conveying its ceremonial corpse into the privacy and dark of the drawing room, through a wide-open window. (It had previously tried entry via a smaller casement without success—that of my bedroom.) The other lizards, now all questing to fulfill their purpose, found the graveyard. Perhaps a keen sense of smell assisted them, and their formerly honorable task was soon accomplished. Why did all of them return to the house? It was no doubt part of the rite to seek their temple. The house by now stood for this temple. Alas for them. None of them survived the onslaught of the corracats—nor my single pistol shot.

Ironically, no one was abroad that night in the village. The concluding journey of the lizards, in their pantomime costumes of death, went unseen. Jim Hardy therefore remains the sole village witness, and once released from hospital drank free of charge for a month on the story.

Doris and Swange are by this time long married, and thrive in their hotel at Hodcieux, which the locals pronounce Hoed-Say. I receive a postcard every year. And so have learned there are now also three little Swanges too, and one little Doris.

Chazen's house has become, I gather, a select school for young ladies. The books from the library were sold for a small fortune. I can't think why. Though decent enough, they were scarcely the best of their type I have catalogued.

And so. The hill.

The hill in the ocean became for me my credo, just as the two kind strangers who watched with me the hill's metamorphosis, channeled my unhappy youth quickly into a satisfactory, premature middle age.

I've said, we saw the impossible hill begin to bulge and topple. And then it sank sidelong—and floated with a slow swiftness, away over the horizon. Other hills very like it soon followed after. They were all the same blue as the sea, and drifted now in a lifting wind, like a fleet of ships. They were clouds.

Yes. My hill, so solid and static and inexplicable, had been a cloud, placed strangely by a freak of calm weather, darker than the upper sky and matching the color of the water, seeming therefore to be *made* of the water, upright and uncanny. A rent in the world that threatened to reveal the surrounding abysm of chaos.

We laughed, the couple and I. Less with relief than with wonder at the trick a string of coincidences of the elements had played. The gentleman thanked me too, for giving him an interesting tale to tell that night at dinner in their boardinghouse. We parted, never to meet again.

A cloud. It isn't, however, that I believe that chaos does *not* lie on all sides of us. Evidently it does, and well we know it, in our innermost hearts. But it is the *fear* of the chance of *stumbling* on that chaos that makes us start at shadows. The dead at Northerham were animated by a purely physical possession. The hill in the sea was built from a cloud the wind left to lie just long enough to deceive.

If I have any hope for anything, I trust we are eternally protected from the naked view of chaos—while in this world. And if at last we must confront it, we shall then be in some other greater form well able to contend with blasting light or shattering darkness. Like the souls of the dead who never care what is done with their cast-off flesh.

KHALED MATTAWA

Lovers: (Jaafar the Winged)

Khaled Mattawa's poem "Lovers (Jaafar the Winged)" was published in the Mid-American Review *Vol. XXVIII, #1. His poetry has appeared in* Poetry, The Kenyon Review, New England Review, Callaloo, The Iowa Review, *and* Black Warrior Review *and has been anthologized three times in* The Pushcart Prize *anthology. He is the author of two books of poetry,* Zodiac of Echoes *and* Ismailia Eclipse, *and has translated five volumes of Arabic poetry into English. He is the president of RAWI (Radius of Arab American Writers, Inc.), and teaches in the MFA Creative Writing Program at the University of Michigan, Ann Arbor.*

—*K. L. & G. G.*

Heroic acts are their own rewards, otherwise
why do them? Now the huris come and go.
You can ask for whatever you want here,
a girl who never loved you, a whore in Khyber
you'd heard about, but your faith denied.

Years later when she came before the prophet
declaring her allegiance, you could not stop
your erection. Those Ethiopian beauties
of the Najashi harem. Boys of all ages,
I had had enough of them when I asked for my first wife

whom they'd had to drag from some deep pit
in Jehenem. The angel said I can have her here,
and she'd still burn there at the same time.
It was like the old days between us, but I wasn't sure
it was her. She was charmed by my wings.

"It's true what they said about you then,"
she chuckled, having found something else
to laugh at me for. I told her my version of the story:
the famous battle—we were such a small army
before the Byzantines gathered against us.

I held the prophet's banner in my left, fighting
with my right arm which soon got lopped off.
Then I held the banner with my left and tried

to stop the bleeding. Then another horseman
chopped off my left. I held the banner with

bleeding stumps and ran toward the rear.
The same horseman chased me and cut off my head.
For a second I faced the sky, then my left eye
settled in the dust. It was such a dance, some game
you'd see played by clowns in the fair of Ukadz.

History does record everything. Sometimes
it's the victim's story that survives.
And my reward was virgins, virgins,
and every time you thrust into one of them
she returns to her virginity, her vagina

tightening up again. No blood, thank God.
When I asked for my wife I asked that
she not be a virgin. I wanted her like I had her.
She was confused about being let out of hell.
They'd cleaned her, but her eyes were pearled off

as if she had not blinked for years.
And for the first time since my death
I saw sweat, one stream rolling from under
her left ear down the side of her neck
into the top of her chest. Before it slid

between her breasts, I licked it off.
I sniffed her, the smell of burning still lingered
in her armpits, I rested my head on her chest
and remembered my one life before. When I awoke
the angels had come and taken her back.

ALEXANDER MACBRIDE

The Ape Man

Alexander MacBride's wistful short story "The Ape Man" appeared in the twenty-fifth issue of McSweeney's. It also marks his first publication. MacBride is a linguist who lives with his wife in Los Angeles.

—K. L. & G. G.

T_____'s foster mother—do you know this story? His foster mother (an ape, of course) had just lost her baby—lost it in the sense that it had died, because she was actually still carrying the little body around—it had lost its grip on her fur when she was running away from something, the bull ape, I think, and fallen down out of the trees, dozens of feet. Smashed practically to pieces, poor sweet little thing.

But so it wasn't very long after that that the apes smashed their way into the little house where T_____'s parents lived—where T_____ himself lived, for that matter, because he was just about a year old at that time. Now his mother had just died the night before, quietly, after a long illness, and the father was sitting at his little desk in despair, and the baby, that being T_____, was lying there in his little crib, crying for his mother—the mother who was lying there dead in her bed, poor woman, just as the father had found her except that he had pulled the sheet over her face.

And so the apes smashed their way in, and the big bull ape, I don't remember his name, pulverized the father, just mangled him, poor man, but before he could grab little T_____ from his crib and squeeze him to a pulp or bite out his tiny guts the ape-mother, the one whose baby had just died, rushed forward and snatched him up and dropped her own dead ape-baby in his place in the crib. And then she dashed out hooting and climbed up to the top of a tree, out of the bull ape's reach, and waited there until it was safe, waited with her new little baby, who wasn't called T_____ at that time, of course, but who got that name eventually among the apes. And from that time forward the ape-mother raised him as an ape-baby, and he grew as ape, and lived as an ape, and came to be first among all the apes. And we all know that story. I have just remembered that the ape-mother was named Kala.

But of course there was also the ape-baby, the dead ape-baby, left in the crib, left in the little house when the other apes ran off, left there with the dead mother and the dead father. And just as you would expect, just as the ape-mother loved the little human baby, the dead mother and the dead father loved the little dead ape-baby, the little ape-baby that death had stolen from his mother, that they had been given in place of their own little live baby whom the ape-mother had stolen from them. And the dead mother and the dead father raised the little dead ape as the dead do, as a dead person, and he grew as a dead person and lived as a dead person and came to be first among all the dead, just as T_____, who I suppose amounts to his brother, in a way, came to be first among the apes; just as T_____, the little living human boy, became Lord of the Apes, the little dead ape boy became Lord of the Dead. And just as T_____ eventually moved on to less archetypal activities, Opar and such, his brother, who these days we call the Ape-Man, moved on to a more ambiguous situation, out among others, out in the world, where you and I are. He's dead, of course, but being dead has never been a straightforward matter, and the things a dead person can do and the things a living person can do are in many respects the same things. And the Ape-Man has done many things.

It's been decades since T_____ died, grew very old and died, but the Ape-Man, being already dead from the beginning, is still with us, is still alive, in a way. He is always far away, standing back behind almost everything; they say there is no evil he does not have his hand in, or his finger at the very least. And T_____ was not that way of course, he was always good, but he and the Ape-Man were never enemies. Each held all the other's grief; at being dead, on the one hand, and on the other, at being alive.

Of course, there is no doubt that he is a terrible creature, and our enemy to the very last day of the world. I would never say that he is not. But I hope you will remember that once he was a tiny much-beloved little thing, a poor little dead thing, a little dead ape loved by his mother and then loved by the human dead, loved twice over. We will never be rid of him, but that thought may console us.

LIZ WILLIAMS

The Hide

Liz Williams's "The Hide" was published on the reliably excellent Web site Strange Horizons in their May 7th edition. Williams is a prolific writer whose latest novels are the Detective Inspector Chen series from Night Shade Books. "The Hide" combines a couple of familiar fantasy tropes (birds, disappearances) with an uncomfortable character in a satisfying and surprising manner. Williams has degrees in philosophy and artificial intelligence from the universities of Manchester and Sussex and a doctorate from Cambridge. She lives in Brighton, England.

—K. L. & G. G.
—E. D

The birds were white as they flew over the marsh, across the reed beds and the frosted meres, but as they drew level with the hide their shade changed, from white to black. I saw their crimson eyes, sparks in the cloudy dark, as they disappeared into the storm. Richard and I crouched in the hide and waited.

"Jude, can you see her? Can you see?" Richard whispered.

But all I could see was darkness, and the distant storm.

People lived here once. A very long time ago, when this land was called the Summer Country: named not for cowslip meadows or hazy warmth, but because it only appeared in summer, when the waters had retreated toward the Severn Estuary and the marshes were dry enough to be negotiated on foot. During all other times of year, this land—gleaming wet marshes, dense beds of dull golden reeds, and groves of alder and unpollarded willow—was the haunt only of ducks and herons, and the small people who lived along the causeways and in the lake villages.

Richard and my sister Clare and I had followed the Sweet Track the summer before, when the heat hung heavily over the water meadows, with the damselflies zooming through the kingcups that grew along the margins of the dug-out peat beds. The Track, discovered years before by an academic named Sweet, is an old road, one of the oldest in the country. I was researching it, and studying Sweet's own research, at the Moors Center, lying right in the middle of Sedgemoor.

Hard to imagine winter, in those dreaming meadows. But I knew that come September the fog would start drifting in from the Bristol Channel, smelling of salt mud and sea, hiding first the whale-humps of islands, then the arch of Brent Knoll, then the flatlands all the way to the Tor with its tower. After that would come flood and then frost, and the long, dim, damp winter.

I'd been there for six months, but Clare was living in Manchester then, working as a fundraiser for some big arts project, and this was her first visit to the area. Her New Age soul was enchanted by it all, by the faux-Arthuriana of Glastonbury and the rather more real claims of Cadbury, by the startling caverns of the Mendips and the flatlands between, where the lake villages had once stood. She and Richard had apparently met through some university bird-watching society—though I'd never known Clare to be interested in birds before. She was more enthusiastic about it in summer, perhaps, out in the wilds with a couple of bottles of beer and a blanket, and that's how we discovered the hide.

I hadn't realized it was there, although I'd been to the bird reserve a couple of times before. I must have walked right past it, but it was Clare who spotted it, as we walked along the track with the remains of a picnic in a rucksack.

"Richie! Jude! There's a causeway, in the reeds. Can we go and look?"

Moments later, she was gone. I remember feeling an odd moment of panic, as though she'd performed some unnatural conjuring trick. Then her voice came from among the russet tassels nodding several inches above our heads. "Look at this! This is so cool!"

The causeway was built of slats placed on piles, close together and easy to walk on, with the addition of a handrail, which the original Lake Village structures would not have had. Quite contemporary and not all that old, judging from the scrubbed pallor of the wood. I'd have told her all this, but I'd grown too used to the rather glazed expression that came over Clare's face whenever I talked about my work. We'd both had our noses in books as kids, but they hadn't been the same ones. She liked the myths. She was less interested in fact.

At first, I couldn't see where the causeway led. A dogleg in the middle took it out of eyesight, deep into the reeds. Clare and Richard vanished around the bend. I stood for a moment, just before the turn. The reeds swallowed sound. Distant traffic and the lowing of cattle were cut off, and the sudden rattle of a coot in the rushes made me jump. When I turned the corner, I saw that the little causeway ended in a long low structure, also raised on pilings, but with a tarpaulin roof and a laminated National Trust information sheet tacked to the wall by the door. There was nothing ancient about this place; it was not even a reconstruction like the round houses at the Bronze Age information center some miles away. It was a bird-watching hide.

As I came close to the door, I found something on the boards: a small black wing, very soft and dense. I didn't recognize the bird: this wasn't the right kind of terrain for blackbirds. Perhaps something—kestrel, maybe—had dropped it. It was clearly a recent kill; there was still a bloody fragment of meat on the bone, an electric red against the dull background of the planks. I picked it up and put it on the flat surface of the railing, not quite knowing why, as if it was a child's glove for which the owner might shortly return.

Inside, the hide was dark and still, stifling in the afternoon heat and filled with the limey odor of bird droppings. When my eyes adjusted, I saw that the floor was white with them. I looked up, but the rafters were empty. Swifts, perhaps, but I couldn't see any round hummocks of nests and they'd be in residence at this time of the year.

"Richard?" Clare's voice cut through the gloom. "Come and see!"

I went around the corner of the central notice board. Clare and Richard were standing shoulder to shoulder and I stifled an old familiar sensation. I allowed myself to wonder what would have happened if Richard had met me first—but I knew from experience that it wouldn't have made any difference.

When she saw me, Clare raised the hatch that faced out over the other side of the marsh, and fastened it with a wooden peg.

"Look."

There was a heron among the reeds, a common enough bird in this area but still alien, predatory, as startling as a pterodactyl in its blue and gray plumage. It was stalking through the shallow water at the edge of one of the reed beds and as we stared, breathless, the long beak stabbed downward and came up with a fish. Silver caught the light. The heron flipped it up and swallowed, then was gone into the reeds in search of new prey.

We kept looking for a moment, hoping it would come back. Then Clare said, "What are those?"

There were three of them, gliding over the crest of the reed beds. They had long necks, long beaks, but at first I thought they must be gulls because their wings caught a shaft of sunlight, gleaming white as they turned. Then they veered again and I saw that their wings were shadow-black, a strange trick of the light. Cormorants, perhaps. They were common along the coast and you frequently found them inland, sharing prey with the herons. They were flying west, toward the estuary.

We watched them go and then, as if some decision had been made, we filed out of the hide like obedient schoolchildren, into the hot day, and back along the track. Clare said she wanted to go back into Glastonbury and see some of the shops. She wanted to buy a crystal, or something. I just wanted a cup of tea. We headed back to where Richard had left the battered 2CV.

The car park had been empty when we'd arrived, but now there were a few more vehicles in it. One of them was a van, painted in rough red and green stripes, a homemade hippie job. As we approached the car park, a young man came around the side: typical of travelers in this part of the world, dreadlocks, mud-colored clothes, a joint held between two fingers. A dog skulked at his heels, a black and tan thing with heavy jowls and a surly look. But the young man was affable enough.

"Nice afternoon," he said. "Been out to the bird sanctuary?"

"Yes, just for a stroll. We saw a few things."

"You want to wait for evening. All the starlings come then—like a cloud. Thousands of 'em. This place is known for it."

"Starlings?" Clare asked. "Maybe we'll come back. We found the hide."

"Did you, now?" the young man said. He took a drag on the joint; sultry smoke coiled into the warm air. I thought there was a fractional sharpening of his interest, but perhaps it was only the dope. "See anything?"

"A heron," I said. He nodded, interest waning, until I added, "And some cormorants."

"You saw those?" He was staring at Clare, not me, half amused, half something else, an expression I could not identify. But that he was looking at her at all irritated me. "Black or white?"

"Black," I said, not understanding. "You don't get white ones, I thought."

"Sometimes you do." The young man spoke with assurance and I didn't know all that much about birds. I wasn't prepared to argue the toss. "How many?"

"Three. There were three of them."

"Okay. Well. Let's hope you don't see them again." I was about to ask him what he meant but he turned away, clicking his fingers at the dog, which was wandering. Richard opened the car and we drove into Glastonbury, where Richard and I spent the rest of the afternoon in one of the little cafés around the market cross while

Clare shopped. If I thought about the bird sanctuary at all, then or in the days that followed, it was simply as a fading memory of a half-pleasant, half-painful afternoon. I did not think about the cormorants at all.

For the next few months, I was busy with research in the Center and elsewhere. Richard and Clare went back up north and I tried not to wonder when I'd see Richard again. I knew I'd never be able to tell her how I'd started to feel about him, and I didn't want to. There was something behind the New Age stuff in her, something competitive and deep, something sisterly, and not in a right-on feminist way. Anyway, it was too embarrassing to talk about and God knows it wasn't as if it hadn't happened before. Perhaps she knew what was going through my head, all the same. I told myself that she seemed happy with Richard and I should be happy for them, and could not be. There should be a natural end to it, now they had returned to the north.

But when I next saw them, and summer itself was over, I found that things weren't as I'd thought.

I'd been to a conference at Lancaster, stopping off at Clare's on the way back. But when I got to her place, she wasn't there. Instead, I found Richard.

She'd been moody ever since they came back, Richard told me, over a glass of wine in a nearby bar. It was October now. At first he'd put it down to anxiety over the coming months, the time when the success or failure of Clare's fund-raising bid was going to be decided. She was snappy and short-tempered, which was new to Richard if not to me, and he'd deemed it wiser to leave her alone to get on with her work. At first, he thought this approach was a success: she was heading off to the office every morning, but three weeks or so later he had run into a colleague of Clare's, who asked how she was, given that she was on sick leave.

"I didn't want to ask her about it," Richard told me. He took a sip of his drink. "But it freaked me out. I thought—I thought she'd found someone else, but, you know, sick leave, it's not just sneaking off for an hour or two."

"Is there someone else?" I felt a cold growing elation at what he was about to say and I hated myself.

"No. I don't know. She said there wasn't, but I—I didn't believe her. I told her I did, then when she went out the next morning, I followed her. She went straight to the canal and sat on the bank. For the rest of the day, as far as I could see. I went to a pub for lunch, even, and when I came back, she was still there."

"Maybe she reckoned you'd follow her, and she thought she might as well lead you on."

"Maybe." He looked dubious. "I suppose I wouldn't have blamed her."

"Funny place to sit, the Ship Canal. It's not exactly Hawaii."

Richard looked suddenly defeated. I nearly reached out to him but stopped myself in time. "It's a shithole, Jude. They keep saying they cleaned it up for that sports bid, but it's still a murky, dirty drain. What appeal could it possibly have?"

Unless you were thinking of chucking yourself into it, I thought, but did not say, and I hated myself a little more. There was something gruesome about the idea of my sister sitting by the side of that grim channel of water, staring into gray scummy nothing, contemplating what?

"Did you follow her again?" I asked.

"A couple of times. She went back to the canal once, and then the next time she just wandered around. This was a few days ago."

"Do you think she's having some kind of breakdown?"

"I don't know. She's been worried about her work, thinks they screwed up on the funding bid, didn't have enough of the required elements. I tried talking about it last night and she said she thought she needed a break. I was wondering if she could come down to you for a few days. I know it's not exactly the weather for it, but it's not the weather for perching on the side of the bloody Ship Canal, either."

All I could see in his face was concern. I had the sense of a trap, closing. I bit back what I had so nearly told him and felt something brush my clenched hands under the table, something soft, like feathers.

"Of course she can come," I said.

Having her in the house was odd and awkward, even more so because Clare exhibited none of the signs of anxiety or depression that I'd been expecting. That made me think that the main problem lay with Richard and that, of course, gave me hope. But I told myself that I was being stupid. Clare and I went out to dinner at the local pub on the night she arrived, and when we got back to the house I bolted up to bed before we really had a chance to talk, not that we were likely to. She'd never been in the habit of opening up, after all.

I went to sleep quickly, but in the middle of the night, something woke me up. I sat up in bed, clutching at the covers. There was no one in the room, but it smelled dank, like marsh water. Worrying about damp-proofing and winter, I went back to sleep.

In the morning, Clare was gone. I sat at the kitchen table, worrying and wondering if she'd gone off like some marsh spirit, wandering the Levels in the morning mist. Twenty minutes after I'd drunk my second cup of tea, she was back, looking rosy-cheeked and cheerful, and announced that she'd been for a walk down the lane and had met a nice horse in a field. The canal-haunting woman whom Richard had described seemed to have flown like the mist itself, upward into the sunlit air.

I had to go to the Center that morning, so Clare said she'd come with me. I spent the next couple of hours going through records, while Clare—I learned at lunch— had passed the morning looking through the information section, learning about the Lake Villagers.

"I'm surprised how much is known about them," she said over soup and bread in the Center's café.

"Well, peat preserves things. If the structure's there, then you can build up guesstimates from that. I'll show you some of the computer reconstructions: I've got some on CD back at home."

"It's fascinating," Clare said. "Like a world built on water."

I stiffened, anticipating canal revelations, but all she said was, "It must have been bloody cold in the winter."

It wasn't exactly warm that afternoon. We went into Glastonbury for a cup of tea and there was a distinct sense of the year beginning to wind down, a faded quality to the light, a bite on the wind's breath.

"I keep thinking of that afternoon we spent down here," Clare said in the café. She was looking down at the table, playing with her teaspoon. "Do you remember? Everything golden and gray, and the birds in the reeds."

"That was the day we saw the cormorants."

"I've dreamed of them, you know." She spoke with a sudden rush, as if confessing something forbidden. "They keep changing. Sometimes they're black and sometimes they're white."

"Things stick in your mind," I said. "When I was a kid, we went to Tenby for a holiday—there's a fortress on a rock, just beyond the bay, and I still dream about that sometimes."

She nodded, but she looked slightly disappointed, as though she had been expecting me to say something else and I'd let her down. We did not discuss when she might be going back.

Next day, I went to the museum, but Clare did not come with me: she said she wanted to sleep in. Still nervy about signs of depression, I didn't attempt to dissuade her. When I got back to the house about midafternoon and found a note saying that she'd gone out for a walk, I wasn't worried.

But she didn't come back.

It was dark by six and I was starting to get seriously freaked out. I tried her mobile and got her answering service, left messages. I got the car out and drove into Glastonbury, wondering whether she'd gone into town. But I did not see her along the road, and she wasn't in any of the pubs. I drove back, hoping to find her at home, but the house was as dark and silent as I'd left it.

I didn't want to ring Richard, but if it turned out that something had happened to Clare, I wouldn't have been able to face myself. His landline rang and rang; I tried his own mobile and that, too, was switched off. I left more messages, tried to decide whether it was too early to call the police, and then decided that I'd rather look like an idiot than risk Clare's life. It was cold outside, with the stars hanging heavy and burning over the low black land.

The police took me seriously, though with a certain weariness, but said there was little they could do. If Clare continued to be missing, then they'd initiate a search, but until then, all they could do was keep an eye out and wait. The implication was that I should do the same.

When the doorbell rang, all my foolishness came crashing in on me. She had got lost and forgotten her key, that was all. I threw the front door open.

"Clare, I'm so—" But it wasn't Clare. It was Richard.

He didn't seem to know anything about my phone messages. He said that he was there because he had had a dream. He was disheveled, a bit stare-eyed, and he smelled dank, the sort of smell you might acquire on too close an acquaintance with the greasy waters of the Ship Canal. Both this, and the account of his dream, were completely out of character: the only thing that made me listen to him at all, rather than insisting on rest and a bath, was the fact that he knew Clare was missing.

My mind, wandering in areas that I did not understand, started to invoke further paranoia. This was all some weird game, either involving me or, worse still, directed at me. They had set it up between them, it was all planned. But then Richard started to tell me about the dream itself.

"She was walking in a dark place. She was lost, and there was a storm, but no rain. I knew that it was cold, and then I saw that she was out on the mere. You know, where we went for a walk? Where we saw the hide? And the hide was in the dream, too—I knew that if she could get to it, she'd be okay, we could pull her back. But then I saw the birds."

"The birds?" But I already knew which ones he meant.

"The cormorants, or whatever they were. Long necks, sharp beaks. They were white when I first saw them and as they flew toward her, they changed to black. Then it started to snow and the snow was black, too, like little beads of jet, and it covered her, she stood still like a statue and when I touched her, I realized she had turned to peat and she crumbled into the water."

There was a long silence after he recounted his dream, but it was just a nightmare, nothing more. Wasn't it? Richard was staring ahead into the heart of the fire as if trying to conjure its warmth back into his bones. He said, "She's out there, Jude, and we have to find her. We have to bring her back."

His eyes were burning and he looked thinner since I had last seen him, as if he'd aged in the past few days. I did not know what to make of his dream, but it was easier to leap up and go out, knowing that I'd already contacted the police and could do no more if we stayed home. Knowing that action was always easier than just sitting, with the unspoken accusation ringing in my head: it was under my care that Clare had become lost.

"Let's go, then," I said.

October had borrowed a night; when we stepped outside it felt more like the middle of January, a raw moonless landscape with the mist breathing off the ditches. A bone-coldness, seeping in even through my Barbour jacket and fisherman's sweater. I thought of Clare staring into a canal for hours at a time, and I grew colder still.

We took the car out to the bird sanctuary, driving slowly with the window down so that Richard would spot her on the road, if she should come that way. But we passed no one on the road and once we had turned into the track that led to the bird sanctuary car park, the night closed in, a clammy dark with the stars swallowed by cloud and the reed beds swimming out of the mist.

Richard was out of the car even before I'd switched the engine off, walking quickly toward the hide. I had to run to catch up with him and he did not turn to see whether I was with him or not. He was looking straight ahead, like someone possessed.

We reached the hide. As we did so, a breeze sprang up, but it didn't seem to make any difference to the mist. I thrust my hands farther into my pockets and found something brittle and sticky in there. I pulled out the black bird's wing that I'd found on the way to the hide, the last time we'd come. I remembered leaving it on the rail. There was no smell, but the bloody flesh had not clotted, it was still moist and cold as ice. I was so revolted that I nearly dropped it, but then I heard Richard's voice, calling my name, and I stuffed the thing back into my pocket and ran along the walkway.

He was standing in the entrance to the hide, clutching both sides of the door frame. His face was suffused with a kind of strange joy. He said, "Jude! It's okay. She's here."

"What? Is she all right?" I had visions of Clare collapsed, huddled against the wall in a disorientated daze, but when I pushed past him into the hide, limp with sudden relief, no one was there.

"Richard, where is she?"

"She's there," he said. He gave me an odd look, as if I was behaving like an idiot. He pointed to the shuttered window of the hide. The shutters were raised, angling out onto the reed beds. It was pitch-black in here, apart from the tiny light of my torch: I couldn't believe that he'd managed to see anything.

Then I looked through the shutter, and saw for myself.

There were more than three birds. This time, there was a flock, perhaps twenty or more, flying from east to west. I saw a smear of pale light in the east, like the gray minutes before dawn, and on the western horizon, just above the reeds, a thin red line in the sky with the storm clouds rising above it. The birds were straggling, and the ones in the east were white, but as they passed the hide, I saw the darkness melt over them, changing them to black.

Richard whispered, "Jude, can you see her? Can you see?"

The reed beds were the same, but nothing else. There was a kind of house opposite the hide, a hut on stilts. It stood in a patch of reeds, but I saw, as you see in dreams, that they were black, with crimson tips that looked like ragged bulbs of flesh. Clare stood on the balustrade that surrounded it. I leaned out, shouting.

"Clare! Clare, can you hear me?"

A shutter rattled, from across the water. A black oblong opened at Clare's shoulder, and something looked out of it. I saw myself looking at my own face, but it was changed: I looked older, lined, bitter. Across the water I saw myself raise something and wave it in mockery: something black and dripping, like the blood-drenched wing of a bird. Then the face changed and was no longer mine, was no longer anything human.

There was a splash. I looked down, and Richard was in the water, plowing through the reeds toward the opposite hut.

"Richard! Don't go, come back!" I might as well have been whispering. As the last of the birds reached the hide and changed, I saw Clare bend over the rail and reach down a hand to pull Richard up. The bird in the sky changed to black. I saw its reflection, shining white in the water below, the light breaking the water up into a thousand dazzling splinters, and the hide, the fleshy reeds, the gleam on both sides of the sky, everything was gone. I was alone, and it was night, and it was cold.

I would like to say that after I made my way home in a daze, I woke up the next day to find it had all been a dream. But Richard's rucksack was there to remind me, and Clare's belongings, and a message from the police to ask me to let them know if she appeared. She did not. There was a hunt, and they dragged the waters of the bird sanctuary. I went with them, although the place terrified me. They found nothing. They asked me a lot of questions, but I did not get the sense that I was under suspicion. The case made the papers, and after a while, the authorities and the media lost interest.

I had dreams, too. They were always the same: two dark birds, flying west. I thought a lot about the bird sanctuary, about the kind of place it might be. I thought of the people of the Summer Country, living in the liminal lands between sea and pasture, summer and winter, life and death. The area around Glastonbury was known to be the land of the dead, the Celtic lord of the dead dwelling beneath the Tor. I did not know if this was what I had seen, some kind of ancient conjured hell, filled with spirits that I, with my imperfect human sight, could only see as birds. But I gradually came to think that it was simpler than that: that just as we had gone to the hide to spy upon the life of birds, so something somewhere else had also set up a hide, to watch us, and when the time was right, to take.

TIM NICKELS

England and Nowhere

Originally from Devon, Tim Nickels is now happily exiled to Dorset where he lives with his lovely wife Charlotte and the newest little Nickels, Galina Norah, and works as an undertaker and paper conservator. His first collection, The English Soil Society, *was published by Elastic Press in 2005. However, a career high remains the acceptance of "England and Nowhere" by the legendary Des Lewis for his unfolding* Nemonymous *odyssey (Nemonyssey?): being able to submit to* Zencore! *under the cloak of an assumed name was a liberating experience.*

He tells us, "The first draft of 'England . . .' was scribbled in half an hour at a seaside flat—the same flat that leads out onto the balcony without a rail in the story. Indeed most elements—barring the obviously criminal—are true and actually happened. I spent a further five years refining the story (layering, skimming, and inserting sunbeams from that not-so-long-ago summer . . .) but the first two lines remain unchanged. As does the last."

—E. D.

There was something about the couple downstairs.

No really.

I thought they'd both been boys. Felt that stab as the blond one lay back, hands behind head; ginger-smudged armpits, smooth chest.

Huddled on that little finger of headland over the beach, they had taken out mugs of tea, sugared—one might say—with their own private chuckles. Footballs skimmed the sand below them; terriers shook their sea salt on groaning masters. All unnoticed, unheeded. They lived in each other's movie: one could imagine a cinema sun shafting to touch where their lips might have met.

He had taken his empty mug and crossed the sand track into the flat below me. She sat up; slipped her slight breasts into a bikini top, awkward arms trying to fasten it. I heard him pee—the house gave its echoes easily—and then he was out again with a kite. It was one of those big new ones you have to control with a pair of handlebars.

He'd made it to the beach when I came back onto the balcony with the binoculars. She was down there too by now—blond and boyish—very carefully laying out the kite strings for him. The balcony had no rail to lean on and I pressed elbows into ribs to stop my hands shaking.

He was older than you might think. Strong veiny forearms: all dark curls and

Mediterranean eyes. But his face was just taking on that hardness that creeps up when you're in the thirties.

The kite was flying by the time I'd come out again with another drink. She was standing by him but was careful to keep out of his way. She put something silver to her face. A movie camera. A Super 8. She was laughing. The kite was lifting him off the sand, dragging him through rock pools and the dam works of five-year-olds and their dads.

An old man, shrunken and absurd in purple Speedos—his splayed, revealed scrotum as shiny as his shaven head—was trying to adjust his hearing aid when the boy careered into him. The man looked up blankly, then continued to work his dial.

The boy kept moving.

But I remember he glanced back once or twice.

She carefully wound the kite strings when he'd finished, each string wiped free of sand with a hankie. He did some arm and shoulder exercises, jerked his head left and right, laughed and whispered in her ear when she'd finished winding. They both bent down and hunched about the beach making monkey noises, wiggling their arses, and grooming each other for nits.

Then they scrambled back up the path still giggling. When the girl reached the top, she stopped and filmed me.

Pulling the cocktail stick from my martini, I sucked off the olive and gave her a grin.

And later—in their big glass porch—she started taking more footage. The porch's roof formed my balcony floor. Both flats fronted the cul-de-sac sand track with its carpet of fir cones; the track that ended at the big white house around the point with the peacocks that you see on the postcards. Well, you don't see the peacocks on the postcards but you *do* hear their lost cries in the night like weirded-out mermaids.

I knew about their filming session because I saw her through the window when I came back from the hotel bar in the sunset and long shadows. The camera was a little thing—a cheaper Chinese model maybe or one of those the Russians made for their aborted Games. What the hell did I know. She swiveled it on a tripod as if it were the prism of a lighthouse.

As he lolled and posed on the daybed, I noticed a pretty drastic scar running up his thigh. But we've all got a few of them, whether inside or out.

And I certainly envied him his urchin curls as they fell against the pillow.

The boy went out at midnight and came back around two. I was on the balcony wide awake. Don't ask: my throat was sore and the night was clear and I'd done enough sleeping in my life. Done enough waking up and wishing I hadn't.

I looked down as he searched for a key in the luminous summer shadows. He knocked his trainers off on the door rim as he entered. They must have been pretty sandy.

A light snapped on and the girl slipped out and across the path with the tripod.

Five minutes later a great light lit up the beach—only to quickly fail and plunge the night into deeper darkness.

The sea was just beginning to take the shells.

In the breakfast sunshine I sat on a rock, popped some seaweed, and watched the limpets and cockles on the sand. In ten minutes the shell shape would disappear underneath the tide and I would only have a memory.

The artist had a punning sense of humor: I remember the shells had been placed in the shape of an ear.

I was about to cross the track to fix the first drink of the day when a woman glided by in a wheelchair. A collie dog followed closely, a chunk of driftwood in its mouth. The woman's lap held a bottle of milk and a copy of *The Western Morning News*. Those wheels were impressive: big gnarly things that you'd find on a truck. She paused in her progress and peered out across the beach; stared at the ear of shells as the tide stole them away. But the dog soon became restless and they both continued their journey around the point.

Curious, I quietly changed course and followed, padding ten yards behind. When I turned the corner the woman had disappeared.

Into the air.

As if she'd been a magician.

I took a walk and thought about the kids.

Their apartment was brightly colored inside its beach-blasted glass: blue walls, a widescreen blue canvas with further, deeper shades of blue. Found object sculptures. Rush mats. Tablets of surf wax, a couple of long boards. Yes, surf wax melted with candles into little shrines. Maybe I'd even heard some Stevie Nicks slipping up from below.

But they didn't quite fit.

Did they own or rent? I could certainly imagine her leafing through the catalogues, carefully sourcing the flat's decor—while *he* might have made do with whatever the last board bum had left behind. I fancied the boy was on first name terms with every hostel owner from here to Bali—yet I don't suppose she'd even toyed with a backpack that wasn't made of some sort of designer nothing-fluff.

Yes: scared or disdainful of water, she was too much in the shallows.

And was he too much out of his depth?

I took the path out to The Mine.

Well, we called it The Mine when we holidayed there as kids—but I'm pretty sure now it was just a glorified quarry. I can remember the gargoyled slates on the cliff top; the way they terrified my toddler sunsets.

I walked home through the lanes, enjoying the foxgloves and hart's-tongue and talking to the cows. I was working out the timing for my latest medication when I came out onto the crossroads and stopped.

It must have been twenty-five years since I'd last seen or even thought about those crossroads. The signpost was quite distinctive: the post and letters and mileages to the villages were painted in a poppy red. One of those lanes still led you down to the big barn; and back in the days of transportation the barn had ejected its livestock in favor of convicts bound for the New World. Lying there in the hay in a place of suspended animation. Neither here nor there. England and nowhere. A limbo land. *Boys in the sweating darkness; the hard walls, the pale flesh shafted by sunlight that swayed through the cow parsley; the light freckling their skin, every mole and scratch thrown up into a shining relief with nothing but themselves to feed on . . .*

I knew how they felt. I popped some pills and loped home in strange good humor, my erection fading.

Brother and sister?

That was my feeling as I thought of her taking cartridge after cartridge of Super 8. As they laughed together quietly, they might seem to share an age of time; a relaxation with self and selves not gained through romance, however passionate.

But my boy-man was dark and she was blond. He was a frayed-out beach urchin born for the surf and some hazardous sex; while the girl had nervously clutched a pair of spiky-heeled Russell & Bromleys as she tiptoed across the beach-head stream that morning.

For all her buzz-cut practicality, water certainly didn't appear to be her natural element.

I passed from countryside shadows through the scrubby fields to the coast.

I'd never seen so many butterflies; they clustered in the rough corners where the plows couldn't reach. Some of the previous season's crop burning had revealed a path I hadn't noticed before: the blackened undergrowth held no scent. I plunged on down, the ground uneven. Wasps rose angrily from their gorse bushes.

The gorse gave way to camellias, their flowers long gone. Beyond *them*, an overgrown tennis court and cypress trees; a tired-looking pavilion with a parked-up Italian sports car.

I was in the grounds of the white house.

Assuming the unhurried innocent gait of the misplaced hiker I attempted to wander casually through the tussocks, the sharp grasses spearing my thin knees. The house itself seemed in good order, one of those vaguely Arts & Craftsy jobs the Edwardians did so well. But the grounds were a forgotten jungle, as if the owner lived more inside his head than out of it.

His head?

Something glittered beside a rancid ornamental pool, a longtime stranger to frog spawn. A brooch made up of three circles. I picked it up and brushed off the dried salt. Everything was covered with it here. Three faces. Mad children?

No.

The faces of monkeys.

There was something going on in the water when I reached the beach.

A couple of boys on surf canoes had been caught on a rip and slammed into the rocks. Blood and broken bones. The helicopter from Culdrose stood by offshore but the lifeguards managed to get them up to the ambulance unaided.

Children played with the smashed fiberglass fragments, throwing them at each other as if they were splintered Frisbees.

"Someone's going to get injured," I heard a mother's voice say.

Although I couldn't see it, I smelled a bonfire.

They were eating toast in the porch when I came up from the beach. On the opposite side to the daybed were a table and two chairs. Thing is, they weren't eating at the table, they were eating in the bed. That's not strange, is it? And yet—peeping in sideways as I hosed my sandy feet off—it was as if I were a second groom at the wedding.

Uncomfortable.

Have you ever seen red and green together? Really bright red and really bright green? Do you understand? There was a buzz, a vibrant sudden disharmony, a wrongness that clashed against their previous brother-and-sister act.

I caught his Mediterranean eye: but he waved in that quick English way. The mouth swiftly wrinkled up then straightened as he turned back to study her.

Easy to say—in that blissed-out, seems-so-long-ago Cornish summer—that they were high on each other. That in the already sea-thick ionized air, their oxygen was a little too abundant.

They went out hand in hand that evening, skipping down the track to the village. The village: a post office selling shrimping nets and a tired hotel with a bar and a quiz night on Wednesdays. I lay looking up at the stars, pretty done in from my hike. I thought of the light-damaged windbreaks in the post office window; impressed by my ability to still be in awe at the wonder of it all.

Bright red, bright green:

I'd noticed that the boy—the thirtyish-year-old—kept a knackered green Renault 5 in a corner of the public car park, while my afternoon adventure had confirmed *her* little red Alfa Romeo slept under the cypress shadows along the cul-de-sac road. She wandered along there quite often, humming a funny little tune and spinning her fluffy rabbit key ring. The road was narrow. Parking was impossible unless you were In The Know. And she must have been pretty well In The Know with the white house people. They were always using their Land Rover to drag some poor tourist's vehicle back to the main road. The house was the last stop before the coastal path and its wide drive must have been tempting for the fair-weather hikers to dump their cars in.

The boy returned first. He had someone with him; not the girl, someone taller with frizzy hair who rattled. Another boy. Yes. I thought so. The newcomer had a bit of a stagger going on and was giving my neighbor—and bloody me, by now—a loud talking tour through the bars of Thailand. He was a bit odd-looking though. Sort of scrunched up. With an eye patch.

No really. Like Bowie had once.

I don't think the boy—my boy, ouch, the boy downstairs—actually spoke at all. They hung around outside for maybe twenty minutes while Thailand exhaled great plumes of hashish smoke. He said he wanted to put his tongue into somebody's ear.

They took the path down to the beach and were gone. The surf was ebbing, distant, far away. Another sound: sheep in the darkness? Surely not.

I shone my little Maglite down onto the track and realized the One-Eyed Pirate would rattle no more.

Bitch had dropped his Tic Tacs.

My boy was back with the girl in an hour. He was calm. She was gasping, breathless and intent on her camera as they scrambled up from the beach. They went inside and the old house awoke and sent up conversational vibrations. They talked till dawn, then walked slowly to the beach in a warm white misty drizzle.

They each carried a long fantastical object, green and blue. And as they planted them in the sand and walked away, I realized they were peacock feathers: the amber eyes swayed and winked at me through my shaking binoculars.

I swim through the forests: thick brown kelp like tripe, green clouds, anemones, darting fish smudges. I feel like the angel I wanted to be as a boy. I think about the Etruscan blues of Cala Domestica. The whiter whites of Fire Island. The sun shafts perfectly through the ten-foot-tall water. My eyes open, balls freezing and recessing in the cold Channel current as if I were wingless in deep space. I surface: foam-skirted rocks, the cliffs hazing away . . .

My towel lay waiting. A book and a sandwich. The pills. A can of Diet Coke with a squirt of something extra.

Shadows spun across the rocks: they were up there, the neighbors, peering down at me from an overhang. I think she smiled before they began the slide down the narrow sheep path.

Perhaps I really had heard sheep.

I hauled myself onto the rock, found my trunks, wrapped myself in the sun-warmed towel, aware of my scrawny dying little body. I'd found the little cove just last year: *my* cove, I thought, in the selfish way a child's mind slips into that of the man.

They were dressed for hiking. Expensive boots (I figured) and matching too. She carried the pack: a proper, mush-like-shit-for-the-Pole rucksack. I'd been wrong.

"We were going to pass by," he said. Soft accent—somewhere northern. "And then saw you."

"And we thought we'd come down." Hers was sharper. London or trying to be. Texting vocalized. "You're above us, aren't you."

They both had gray eyes.

You live for yourselves, right? I couldn't shake the thought. I suppose I'd written their life stories while they'd barely noticed me.

She said: "You probably think we just live for ourselves."

I nearly dropped off the rock.

"Well, we do," he said.

"Kind of," they chorused together, smiling, perfect.

Fantastic.

I wondered again whether she swam, my glance shifting from the water to my small picnic, the child-me wondering if they were hungry, the me-me pondering if they had eaten of anything but each other.

"Dan." He gave the little wave. "By the way."

My hand was still salt-clammy so I didn't offer it.

"Yes, we love swimming," she said. "Don't we, Da—" The pause was so brief as to be almost undetectable, half an eye blink at most. "Dan," she finished quickly, simply.

As she slipped to one knee and peered at the sunlit submarine sand, I realized she could have been no more than fifteen or sixteen. But she drove a car. It's hard with girls, isn't it.

"She swims like a fish." Dan was already turning away, first foot back on the track.

So there you are. She swam like a fish.

They stopped halfway up the path and she turned—the blond girl without a name—and took another little film.

Living for themselves.
Had they realized that I hadn't spoken?

I rinsed my trunks out in the basin, fascinated by my body in the long stained mirror. The sun haloed my shoulder hairs like I was an angel already. I never realized I had so many ribs.

An outdoor tap spluttered below the window. My bathroom was at the rear of the flat and I peered down into the kids' little backyard, shading my eyes. Their expedition hadn't lasted long. Dan was naked and washing out a wetsuit.

He turned the tap off. "Say again?"

Her head popped out of the French windows, clamped to a mobile: "She says she might need to move it."

"Is that all? Why are you telling me? What's it got to do with me?"

He turned the tap back on.

Her voice rose half heard, half imagined through the tap water as it spoke into the phone: "Yeah. Don't worry. Yeah. Catch you later."

She was amazing, a real gymnast. She could spin the chair on one wheel, a postage stamp turn using the impetus to throw the rubber bone fifty meters. The dog was good too, catching the toy in midair, teasing the abyss beyond the cliff edge—but always falling safely back into the long coarse sea grass.

The woman was in her fifties. She wore a dark roll-neck sweater that was a little out of place on a summer evening. She had a rug over her lap too—and by the way it fell I reckoned she had no legs at all.

Yes. Quite a magician.

Too late, she caught my eye. Christ. But she smiled. A really big grin and a wave before throwing the bone again. I smiled and raised my glass—nearly fell off the balcony—and nodded my head in that meaningless pants-down way that you'd probably do too.

Suddenly—or so it seemed—Dan and the girl were there. First they just leaned against the outside glass of the porch. Then they ventured onto the grass—unflinching, uncaring—as the collie raced around them barking deliriously. The old girl—sorry, the same-age-as-*me* girl—was roaring with laughter, tarting it up big time for the movie camera, pulling the roll-neck over her nose and doing wheelies.

She was having such a party with herself that she didn't immediately notice when the dog trotted up to the boy with the bone to throw. The woman quickly wheeled up and took the slobbery toy from Dan's fingers.

I could hear her, even in a hissy whisper. "Come on, Beth," she said, and the dog followed her down the track home to the big white house.

I slipped in for a leisurely refill. When I came out Dan was alone on their headland finger. The sea would soon be snapping at the rocks below.

He had her fluffy bunny car keys and he threw them at the sunset.

There was a firework party that night.

A couple of families had got together and made a camp above the high water mark. The display was pretty good; I think one of the dads did it for a living—he had a red boiler suit and everything. The applause echoed over as the rockets shimmered and spat.

In the gaps between the explosions, I could hear sharp laughter from the track below. And I mean sharp: derisive, brittle, ungiving.

Presently, I saw the girl walking quickly down to the beach. There were a couple of guys in Bermudas with her, young and wiry. They both wore graffitoed plaster casts on their forearms: the canoe dudes had come back to party. They were talking loudly, booming about the latest beach riot over in Rock. I could hear them even above the biggest bangers. Cracked posh voices privately honed for leadership. England and somewhere. Tongues of glory.

The porch door crashed and Dan was out and running to the promontory, standing amid the fireworks; heedless of the warning voices, the air full of shooting stars.

He came to my flat three hours later.

I heard bare feet creaking up the stairs as I lay out in my usual stellar-mesmeric position on the balcony. I never lock the front door—what the hell have I got that no one else has?—so I counted and calculated when the door was most likely to open and then peeped inside.

Yeah, it was Dan all right. Naked again, fearless and flushed. He stood in the light of the 20w economy bulb, the leg scar reaching from thigh to lower stomach. His fingernails were filthy. He stalked from room to room nursing his semi-engorged penis; trying to make sense of the artwork I'd rented with the flat. I could tell he sat on the bed for quite some time: the springs have a way about them. He was in the bathroom for a while as well—I could hear him going through the pill bottles.

Another footfall from the stairs. Lighter. The girl, chest heaving, dressed in a man's fleece that nearly covered the Bermudas. Dan came out of the bathroom and I thought they were about to kiss. But he just shook his head as she pulled the top off and gave it to him to wrap around his waist. For a moment, Dan seemed to look right at me, then he turned and they both hurried off down the stairs together.

I held the three monkeys up in my shivery fingers, turning them so they caught little pieces of moonlight.

Black-headed gulls were fighting over a ragworm breakfast, the tide sliding in an hour behind yesterday as I bent down closer to see: they told me the drugs would make my corneas swell and pop. Someone had planted hart's-tongue in the ribbed sand. Two bunches: long fleshy leaves, lightly corrugated and redolent of moist hedgerows. As unexpected here as . . . *as a second groom at a wedding,* I thought, peering in through their window as I came back; observing a scattering of hart's leaves on the daybed.

I smiled at the woman and the woman smiled back.

"Did you hear the fireworks last night? Bloody summer." She was still smiling, looking up at me as I traversed the track. The sun caught her cropped gray hair as if it were pewter. Might have been blond once. "Did I see you up at the crossroads the other day?"

God. Maybe she had.

"You know the story?"

I said nothing of course.

"All to do with the old convicts. It's a corpse way as well. And rather notorious for road accidents."

I must have raised an eyebrow.

"Oh, I mean nobody's ever died or anything." She spun the chair. "Well, well. Hear no evil, see no evil."

And speak no evil, I thought, wondering what all this was about.

She grunted good-naturedly—a gruff sort of saint—and wheeled herself home for more spells.

Sea caves: the pounding mirror of echoes and the smell; organic, salty, slippery. The uncertain discovery in the darkness: jammed pallid buoys and polystyrene. The vacated egg sacs of sharks. I squatted in the coolness, picked up the blanched quill of a cuttlefish, and rubbed it against my loosening teeth.

The caves lay on the other side of the beach. They were far below the high tide mark and submerged themselves twice a day. I admired the cleansing action of the sea most especially here. The grains rubbing and changing themselves. Changing and shrinking and wearing themselves down to nothing.

I waddled out toward the sunshine, crouching to save what was left of my head from the cave roof. A little clump of sea anemones caught my eye. They were no fools, hidden in a hollow to avoid the crushing surf of autumn. One of them had closed while trying to gorge on something that looked joyously like a methamphetamine capsule. Unable to resist, I gently released it from its captor and nibbled the end.

Salty. Minty.

Did I have any sense of moment? Of sudden crisis after the torpor of an anticipation unrecognized?

I took a stroll along the beach track that night. Actually, more like four the following morning. I carried a vermouth-free martini with me: laugh if you like, but I was still determined to burn down in style.

The track led around the head of the shore and curved naturally into the drive of the big house with its forgotten garden and cypresses. I say cypresses, but I'm not quite sure now: they just looked elegantly tall and French. Midpoint on the bend was an orange streetlight: it was slightly unexpected but I guess the council had been nabbed for public liability a few too many times.

I counted: one, two . . . *three* bats chasing insects around the streetlamp's glow; caught briefly, tiny, black. I threw an olive at the lamp but it sailed over—a pickled green beetle—uninterrupted.

Three bats. Three monkeys. Three people. The boy, the girl, the woman.

And me.

The white house had a light on.

It was in the left-hand corner, to landward. No sea view at all, I reckoned, as I filtered gin through my teeth and counted bats out there on the beach road. And the very moment I looked back—extraordinarily—the light went out. Moments later, another replaced it facing the sea. Then two lights together in the midriff of the building.

Darkness.

I was turning for home when headlamps shot out over the beach, catching a cat running up the big rusty sewerage pipe from the sea. A peacock's call rose into the night. A diesel engine rattled; gears shifted.

I slipped into the bushes by the streetlamp, lost the last of my drink as I tripped over a discarded barbecue. It was silly: the road was perfectly public. And yet—

The Land Rover was making reasonable progress, given its load. The bats sliced the air over my head as the groaning red sports car—wheel-locked, hand-braked—lurched behind on its tow rope.

I struggled out and stalked the two vehicles as they rounded the bend—but I wasn't fast enough. They were way ahead of me and I had the exaggerated caution of a drunk. Something was happening—or rather what was happening was ceasing to happen: it sounded as if the Land Rover had stopped. I tried to make my ears curl around the corner: the little convoy had obviously reached the kids' porch; a car door opened . . . quickly shut . . . one person maybe . . . muffled speech perhaps . . . porch door, opened, shut . . . gear change . . . vehicles moving off again—

I turned to look back at the lamppost. A couple of moths fluttered too close to one another and a bat took them with a single snap.

I must have stayed awake till six, lying out on the balcony in my underpants. I seemed to have run out of olives but otherwise I was doing okay. It was early July so it never really got completely dark. The Atlantic swells were coming in good and the pre-breakfast surfers would be down and waxing before seven. The A30 at Bodmin would be like a car park.

There was a noise from the flat below. A floorboard creak, the clack of plastic on plastic. A toilet seat. Up or down? Then the sound of somebody peeing, long and loud, in the hour before dawn.

And as the morning entered in earnest, a bonfire burst out from somewhere inland.

But by then I might have been dreaming.

I'd somehow rolled up in a towel and my mouth tasted like someone else's. I crawled in through the balcony door, found some juice and the last bottle of vodka; scrambled for the binoculars and was out again.

The surf: low tide, three-foot and clean, flags keeping the real hang-tenners and the weekend body boarders apart. Was Dan down there? It was hard to tell in the mass of foam and heads and flailing leashes.

I focused out beyond the crowds toward the point. There was a small group sitting astride their long boards, doing the cosmic thing. It seemed like Dan's speed—but they were too far away. It could have been a group of seals for all I could tell.

The sun shot across the ocean, seemingly intent on setting the waves alight.

Bright, bright as a bonfire.

A *bonfire*.

She was dancing when I got to the red crossroads.

Do you remember Jordan waltzing around the bonfire in Jarman's *Jubilee*? That unreal Super 8 slow motion, the flames licking in the sunlight, trying to defeat it. The girl even had a maxi dress hitched into her knickers in a semblance of a tutu. She arched and flitted through the smoke while the Fire & Rescue held off with their big hoses, fearful that they might blow her over.

"Daft maid," murmured a fireman. "Too late for the bastard in the Alfa though."

And I could see through the nearly brighter-than-day blaze that a solitary charcoal figure slumped itself in the driver's seat.

I ran.

I ran almost all the way back to the beach. My lungs were full of hot crawling crabs as I collapsed on a bench and vomited.

The lifeguards were carrying something up across the sand. Dozens of semi-naked people followed as if processing a saint's effigy through a South American village.

The body was distinctively dressed in purple Speedos. Across the short distance, I could imagine a pale dead hand clutching a hearing aid.

"How long have you got?"

The woman was suddenly there on silent wheels, her dog resting its head on my knee. She had her morning paper, her pint of milk.

I wiped my mouth, fingered my throat. Or what the surgeons had left of it.

"You have something of mine." She looked at me long and hard. "And if you hand it back I'll give you something in return."

She spoke for maybe fifteen minutes.

And when she'd finished, I reached into my pocket and gave her the brooch. She took it and called the dog and left without another word, the pinecones cracking beneath her wheels.

I must have sat there for quite some time. Staring children were shooed away.

I suppose I made quite a sight.

The girl was looking down at me.

Christ. How long had I been there?

Her camera was raised for a final sequence. I would quietly learn later—there was only ever a passing reference to the matter in court—that it was never even loaded, the Super 8 cartridges just demonstration dummies.

So their unreality was truly unreal.

You probably think we just live for ourselves. . . .

She seemed dressed for a journey, her dancing skirt now pulled down, Tic Tac's eye patch wrapped like a bracelet around her wrist. The bare arms were just beginning to turn pinkish; this blond Ariel, this . . . *creature* . . .

I knew I wouldn't forget her then: my mind's easily lost other things in its life; pretty much sapped itself of interest in anything but *Jeremy Kyle* and the morning makeovers here at the hospice. Dangling between life and death; England and nowhere.

And I do remember one thing in particular as she lowered the camera from her face that final time.

She had her father's eyes.

GARTH NIX

Sir Hereward and Mister Fitz Go to War Again

Garth Nix's tale of swords and sorcery, inspired by the work of Fritz Leiber and Robert E. Howard, was published online in the April issue of Baen's Universe *and is one of Gavin's favorite stories of the year. Nix is the author of two best-selling series, the* Abhorsen *books (of which more are promised) and* The Keys to the Kingdom, *and has just begun a third series,* The Seventh Tower. *Nix has worked in many aspects of publishing: as a sales representative, publicist, editor, and agent. He is working on a science fiction series (and an accompanying video game) and lives with his family in Sydney, Australia.*

—K. L. & G. G.

D o you ever wonder about the nature of the world, Mister Fitz?" asked the foremost of the two riders, raising the three-barred visor of his helmet so that his words might more clearly cross the several feet of space that separated him from his companion, who rode not quite at his side.

"I take it much as it presents itself, for good or ill, Sir Hereward," replied Mister Fitz. He had no need to raise a visor, for he wore a tall lacquered hat rather than a helmet. It had once been taller and had come to a peak, before encountering something sharp in the last battle but two the pair had found themselves engaged in. This did not particularly bother Mister Fitz, for he was not human. He was a wooden puppet given the semblance of life by an ancient sorcery. By dint of propinquity, over many centuries a considerable essence of humanity had been absorbed into his fine-grained body, but attention to his own appearance or indeed vanity of any sort was still not part of his persona.

Sir Hereward, for the other part, had a good measure of vanity and in fact the raising of the three-barred visor of his helmet almost certainly had more to do with an approaching apple seller of comely appearance than it did with a desire for clear communication to Mister Fitz.

The duo were riding south on a road that had once been paved and gloried in the name of the Southwest Toll Extension of the Lesser Trunk. But its heyday was long ago, the road being even older than Mister Fitz. Few paved stretches remained, but the tightly compacted understructure still provided a better surface than the rough soil of the fields to either side.

The political identification of these fallow pastures and the occasional once-coppiced wood they passed was not clear to either Sir Hereward or Mister Fitz, despite several attempts to ascertain said identification from the few travelers they had encountered since leaving the city of Rhool several days before. To all intents and purposes, the land appeared to be both uninhabited and untroubled by soldiery or tax collectors and was thus a void in the sociopolitical map that Hereward held uneasily, and Fitz exactly, in their respective heads.

A quick exchange with the apple seller provided only a little further information, and also lessened Hereward's hope of some minor flirtation, for her physical beauty was sullied by a surly and depressive manner. In a voice as sullen as a three-day drizzle, the woman told them she was taking the apples to a large house that lay out of sight beyond the nearer overgrown wood. She had come from a town called Lettique or Letiki that was located beyond the lumpy ridge of blackish shale that they could see a mile or so to the south. The apples in question had come from farther south still, and were not in keeping with their carrier, being particularly fine examples of a variety Mister Fitz correctly identified as emerald brights. There was no call for local apples, the young woman reluctantly explained. The fruit and vegetables from the distant oasis of Shûme were always preferred, if they could be obtained. Which, for the right price, they nearly always could be, regardless of season.

Hereward and Fitz rode in silence for a few minutes after parting company with the apple seller, the young knight looking back not once but twice as if he could not believe that such a vision of loveliness could house such an unfriendly soul. Finding that the young woman did not bother to look back at all, Hereward cleared his throat and, without raising his visor, spoke.

"It appears we are on the right road, though she spoke of Shumey and not Shûme."

Fitz looked up at the sky, where the sun was beginning to lose its distinct shape and ooze red into the shabby gray clouds that covered the horizon.

"A minor variation in pronunciation," he said. "Should we stop in Lettique for the night, or ride on?"

"Stop," said Hereward. "My rear is not polished sandalwood, and it needs soaking in a very hot bath enhanced with several soothing essences . . . ah . . . that was one of your leading questions, wasn't it?"

"The newspaper in Rhool spoke of an alliance against Shûme," said Mister Fitz carefully, in a manner that confirmed Hereward's suspicion that didactic discourse had already begun. "It is likely that Lettique will be one of the towns arrayed against Shûme. Should the townsfolk discover we ride to Shûme in hope of employment, we might find ourselves wishing for the quiet of the fields in the night, the lack of mattresses, ale, and roasted capons there notwithstanding."

"Bah!" exclaimed Hereward, whose youth and temperament made him tend toward careless optimism. "Why should they suspect us of seeking to sign on with the burghers of Shûme?"

Mister Fitz's pumpkin-sized papier-mâché head rotated on his spindly neck, and the blobs of blue paint that marked the pupils of his eyes looked up and down, taking in Sir Hereward from toe to head: from his gilt-spurred boots to his gold-chased helmet. In between boots and helm were Hereward's second-best buff coat, the sleeves still embroidered with the complicated silver tracery that proclaimed him as the Master Artillerist of the city of Jeminero. Not that said city was any longer in existence, as for the past three years it had been no more than a mass grave sealed with the rubble of its once-famous walls. Around the coat was a frayed but still quite golden sash, over that a rare and expensive Carnithian leather baldric and belt with two beautifully ornamented (but no less functional for that) wheel-lock pistols thrust through said belt. Hereward's longer-barreled and only slightly less orna-mented cavalry pistols were holstered on either side of his saddle horn, his saber with its sharkskin grip and gleaming hilt of gilt brass hung in its scabbard from the rear left quarter of his saddle, and his sighting telescope was secured inside its leather case on the right rear quarter.

Mister Fitz's mount, of course, carried all the more mundane items required by their travels. All three feet six and a half inches of him (four feet three with the hat) was perched upon a yoke across his mount's back that secured the two large pan-niers that were needed to transport tent and bedding, washing and shaving gear, and a large assortment of outdoor kitchen utensils. Not to mention the small but surpris-ingly expandable sewing desk that contained the tools and devices of Mister Fitz's own peculiar art.

"Shûme is a city, and rich," said Fitz patiently. "The surrounding settlements are mere towns, both smaller and poorer, who are reportedly planning to go to war against their wealthy neighbor. You are obviously a soldier for hire, and a self-evidently expensive one at that. Therefore, you must be en route to Shûme."

Hereward did not answer immediately, as was his way, while he worked at over-coming his resentment at being told what to do. He worked at it because Mister Fitz had been telling him what to do since he was four years old and also because he knew that, as usual, Fitz was right. It would be foolish to stop in Lettique.

"I suppose that they might even attempt to hire us," he said as they topped the low ridge, shale crunching under their mounts' talons.

Hereward looked down at a wasted valley of underperforming pastures filled either with sickly looking crops or passive groups of too-thin cattle. A town—presumably Lettique—lay at the other end of the valley. It was not an impressive ville, being a collection of perhaps three or four hundred mostly timber and painted-plaster houses within the bounds of a broken-down wall to the west and a dry ravine, which might have once held a river, to the east. An imposing, dozen-spired temple in the middle of the town was the only indication that at some time Lettique had seen more provident days.

"Do you wish to take employment in a poor town?" asked Mister Fitz. One of his responsibilities was to advise and positively influence Hereward, but he did not make decisions for him.

"No, I don't think so," replied the knight slowly. "Though it does make me recall my thought . . . the one that was with me before we were interrupted by that dismal apple seller."

"You asked if I ever wondered at the nature of the world," prompted Fitz.

"I think what I actually intended to say," said Hereward, "is 'Do you ever wonder why we become involved in events that are rather more than less of importance to rather more than less people?' as in the various significant battles, sieges, and so forth in which we have played no small part. I fully comprehend that in some cases the events have stemmed from the peculiar responsibilities we shoulder, but not in all cases. And that being so, and given my desire for a period of quiet, perhaps I should consider taking service with some poor town."

"Do you really desire a period of quiet?" asked Mister Fitz.

"Sometimes I think so. I should certainly like a time where I might reflect upon what it is I do want. It would also be rather pleasant to meet women who are not witch-agents, fellow officers, or enemies—or who have been pressed into service as powder monkeys or are soaked in blood from tending the wounded."

"Perhaps Shûme will offer some relative calm," said Mister Fitz. "By all accounts it is a fine city, and even if war is in the offing, it could be soon finished if Shûme's opponents are of a standard that I can see in Lettique."

"You observe troops?" asked Hereward. He drew his telescope and, carefully leaning on his mount's neck to avoid discomfort from the bony ridges (which even though regularly filed down and fitted with leather stocks were not to be ignored), looked through it at the town. "Ah, I see. Sixty pike and two dozen musketeers in the square by the temple, of no uniform equipment or harness. Under the instruction of a portly individual in a wine-dark tunic who appears as uncertain as his troops as to the drill."

"I doubt that Shûme has much to fear," said Mister Fitz. "It is odd, however, that a town like Lettique would dare to strike against such a powerful neighbor. I wonder . . ."

"What?" asked Hereward as he replaced his telescope.

"I wonder if it is a matter of necessity. The river is dry. The wheat is very thin, too thin this close to harvest. The cattle show very little flesh on their ribs. I see no sign of any other economic activity. Fear and desperation may be driving this mooted war, not greed or rivalry. Also . . ."

Mister Fitz's long, pale blue tongue darted out to taste the air, the ruby stud in the middle of what had once been a length of stippled leather catching the pallid sunlight.

"Their godlet is either asleep or . . . mmm . . . comatose in this dimension. Very strange."

"Their god is dead?"

"Not dead," said Mister Fitz. "When an other-dimensional entity dies, another always moves in quickly enough. No . . . definitely present, but quiescent."

"Do you wish to make a closer inquiry?"

Hereward had not missed the puppet's hand tapping the pannier that contained his sewing desk, an instinctive movement Mister Fitz made when contemplating sorcerous action.

"Not for the present," said Mister Fitz, lifting his hand to grasp once again his mount's steering chains.

"Then we will skirt the town and continue," announced Hereward. "We'll leave the road near those three dead trees."

"There are many trees that might be fairly described as dead or dying," remarked Fitz. "And several in clumps of three. Do you mean the somewhat orange-barked trio over yonder?"

"I do," said Hereward.

They left the road at the clump of trees and rode in silence through the dry fields, most of which were not even under attempted cultivation. There were also several derelict farmhouses, barns, and cattle yards, the level of decay suggesting that the land had been abandoned only in recent years.

Halfway along the valley, where the land rose to a slight hill that might have its origin in a vast and ancient burial mound, Hereward reined in his mount and looked back at the town through his telescope.

"Still drilling," he remarked. "I had half thought that they might dispatch some cavalry to bicker with us. But I see no mounts."

"I doubt they can afford the meat for battlemounts," said Mister Fitz. "Or grain for horses, for that matter."

"There is an air gate in the northeastern temple spire," said Hereward, rebalancing his telescope to get a steadier view. "There might be a moonshade roost behind it."

"If their god is absent, none of the ancient weapons will serve them," said Mister Fitz. "But it would be best to be careful, come nightfall. Lettique is reportedly not the only town arrayed against Shûme. The others may be in a more vigorous condition, with wakeful gods."

Hereward replaced his telescope and turned his mount to the north, Mister Fitz following his lead. They did not speak further, but rode on, mostly at the steady pace that Hereward's Zowithian riding instructor had called "the lope," occasionally urging their mounts to the faster "jag." In this fashion, several miles passed quickly. As the sun's last third began to slip beneath the horizon, they got back on the old road again, to climb out of the wasted valley of Lettique and across yet another of the shale ridges that erupted out of the land like powder-pitted keloid scars, all gray and humped.

The valley that lay beyond the second ridge was entirely different from the faded fields behind the two travelers. In the warm twilight, they saw a checkerboard of green and gold, full fields of wheat interspersed with meadows heavily stocked with fat cattle. A broad river wound through from the east, spilling its banks in several places into fecund wetlands that were rich with waterfowl. Several small hillocks in the valley were covered in apple trees, dark foliage heavily flecked with the bright green of vast quantities of emerald fruit. There were citrus groves too, stone-walled clumps of smaller trees laden with lemons or limes, and only a hundred yards away, a group of six trees bearing the rare and exquisite blue-skinned fruit known as *serqa* that was normally only found in drier climes.

"A most pleasant vista," said Hereward. A small smile curled his lip and touched his eyes, the expression of a man who sees something that he likes.

Shûme itself was a mile away, built on a rise in the ground in the northwestern corner of the valley, where the river spread into a broad lake that lapped the city's western walls. From the number of deep-laden boats that were even now rowing home to the jetties that thronged the shore, the lake was as well stocked with fish as the valley was with livestock and produce. Most of the city's buildings were built of an attractively pale yellow stone, with far fewer timber constructions than were usual for a place that Hereward reckoned must hold at least five thousand citizens.

Shûme was also walled in the same pale stone, but of greater interest to Hereward were the more recent earthworks that had been thrown up in front of the old wall. A zigzag line of revetments encircled the city, with respectably large bastions at each end on the lakeshore. A cursory telescopic examination showed several bronze demicannon on the bastions and various lesser pieces of ordnance clustered in groups at various strong points along the earthworks. Both bastions had small groups of soldiery in attendance on the cannon, and there were pairs of sentries every twenty or thirty yards along the earthen ramparts and a score or more walked the stone walls behind.

"There is certainly a professional in charge here," observed Hereward. "I expect . . . yes . . . a cavalry piquet issues from yonder orchard. Twelve horse troopers under the notional command of a whey-faced cornet."

"Not commonplace troopers," added Mister Fitz. "Dercian keplars."

"Ah," said Hereward. He replaced his telescope, leaned back a little and across, and, using his left hand, loosened his saber so that an inch of blade projected from the scabbard. "They are in employment, so they should give us the benefit of truce."

"They should," conceded Mister Fitz, but he reached inside his robe to grasp some small item concealed under the cloth. With his other hand he touched the brim of his hat, releasing a finely woven veil that covered his face. To casual inspection he now looked like a shrouded child, wearing peculiar papery gloves. Self-motivated puppets were not great objects of fear in most quarters of the world. They had once been numerous, and some few score still walked the earth, almost all of them entertainers, some of them long remembered in song and story.

Mister Fitz was not one of those entertainers.

"If it comes to it, spare the cornet," said Hereward, who remembered well what it was like to be a very junior officer, whey-faced or not.

Mister Fitz did not answer. Hereward knew as well as he that if it came to fighting, and the arts the puppet employed, there would be no choosing who among those who opposed them lived or died.

The troop rode toward the duo at a canter, slowing to a walk as they drew nearer and their horses began to balk as they scented the battlemounts. Hereward raised his hand in greeting and the cornet shouted a command, the column extending to a line, then halting within an easy pistol shot. Hereward watched the troop sergeant, who rode forward beyond the line for a better look, then wheeled back at speed toward the cornet. If the Dercians were to break their oath, the sergeant would fell her officer first.

But the sergeant halted without drawing a weapon and spoke to the cornet quietly. Hereward felt a slight easing of his own breath, though he showed no outward sign of it and did not relax. Nor did Mister Fitz withdraw his hand from under his robes. Hereward knew that his companion's molded papier-mâché fingers held an esoteric needle, a sliver of some arcane stuff that no human hand could grasp with impunity.

The cornet listened and spoke quite sharply to the sergeant, turning his horse around so that he could make his point forcefully to the troopers as well. Hereward only caught some of the words, but it seemed that despite his youth, the officer was rather more commanding than he had expected, reminding the Dercians that their oaths of employment overrode any private or societal vendettas they might wish to undertake.

When he had finished, the cornet shouted, "Dismount! Sergeant, walk the horses!"

The officer remained mounted, wheeling back to approach Hereward. He saluted as he reined in a cautious distance from the battlemounts, evidently not trusting either the creatures' blinkers and mouth-cages or his own horse's fears.

"Welcome to Shûme!" he called. "I am Cornet Misolu. May I ask your names and direction, if you please?"

"I am Sir Hereward of the High Pale, artillerist for hire."

"And I am Fitz, also of the High Pale, aide de camp to Sir Hereward."

"Welcome . . . uh . . . sirs," said Misolu. "Be warned that war has been declared upon Shûme, and all who pass through must declare their allegiances and enter certain . . . um . . ."

"I believe the usual term is 'undertakings,'" said Mister Fitz.

"Undertakings," echoed Misolu. He was very young. Two bright spots of embarrassment burned high on his cheekbones, just visible under the four bars of his lobster-tailed helmet, which was a little too large for him, even with the extra padding, one of which had come a little undone around the brow.

"We are free lances, and seek hire in Shûme, Cornet Misolu," said Hereward. "I will give the common undertakings if your city chooses to contract us. For the moment, we swear to hold our peace, reserving the right to defend ourselves should we be attacked."

"Your word is accepted, Sir Hereward, and . . . um . . ."

"Mister Fitz," said Hereward as the puppet said merely, "Fitz."

"Mister Fitz."

The cornet chivvied his horse diagonally closer to Hereward and added, "You may rest assured that my Dercians will remain true to *their* word, though Sergeant Xikoliz spoke of some feud their . . . er . . . entire people have with you."

The curiosity in the cornet's voice could not be easily denied, and spoke as much of the remoteness of Shûme as it did of the young officer's naïveté.

"It is a matter arising from a campaign several years past," said Hereward. "Mister Fitz and I were serving the Heriat of Jhaqa, who sought to redirect the Dercian spring migration elsewhere than through her own prime farmlands. In the last battle of that campaign, a small force penetrated to the Dercians' rolling temple and . . . ah . . . blew it up with a specially made petard. Their godlet, thus discommoded, withdrew to its winter housing in the Dercian steppe, wreaking great destruction among its chosen people as it went."

"I perceive you commanded that force, sir?"

Hereward shook his head.

"No, I am an artillerist. Captain Kasvik commanded. He was slain as we retreated—another few minutes and he would have won clear. However, I did make the petard, and . . . Mister Fitz assisted our entry to the temple and our escape. Hence the Dercians' feud."

Hereward looked sternly at Mister Fitz as he spoke, hoping to make it clear that this was not a time for the puppet to exhibit his tendency for exactitude and truthfulness. Captain Kasvik had in fact been killed before they even reached the rolling temple, but it had served his widow and family better for Kasvik to be a hero, so Hereward had made him one. Only Mister Fitz and one other survivor of the raid knew otherwise.

Not that Hereward and Fitz considered the rolling temple action a victory, as their intent had been to force the Dercian godlet to withdraw a distance unimaginably more vast than the mere five hundred leagues to its winter temple.

The ride to the city was uneventful, though Hereward could not help but notice that Cornet Misolu ordered his troop to remain in place and keep watch, while he alone escorted the visitors, indicating that the young officer was not absolutely certain the Dercians would hold to their vows.

There was a zigzag entry through the earthwork ramparts, where they were held up for several minutes in the business of passwords and responses (all told aside in quiet voices, Hereward noted with approval), their names being recorded in an enormous ledger and passes written out and sealed allowing them to enter the city proper.

These same passes were inspected closely under lantern light, only twenty yards farther on by the guards outside the city gate—which was closed, as the sun had finally set. However, they were admitted through a sally port and here Misolu took his leave, after giving directions to an inn that met Hereward's requirements: suitable stabling and food for the battlemounts; that it not be the favorite of the Dercians or any other of the mercenary troops who had signed on in preparation for Shûme's impending war; and fine food and wine, not just small beer and ale. The cornet also gave directions to the citadel, not that this was really necessary as its four towers were clearly visible, and advised Hereward and Fitz that there was no point going there until the morning, for the governing council was in session and so no one in authority could hire him until at least the third bell after sunrise.

The streets of Shûme were paved and drained, and Hereward smiled again at the absence of the fetid stench so common to places where large numbers of people dwelt together. He was looking forward to a bath, a proper meal, and a fine feather bed, with the prospect of well-paid and not too onerous employment commencing on the morrow.

"There is the inn," remarked Mister Fitz, pointing down one of the narrower side streets, though it was still broad enough for the two battlemounts to stride abreast. "The sign of the golden barleycorn. Appropriate enough for a city with such fine farmland."

They rode into the inn's yard, which was clean and wide and did indeed boast several of the large iron-barred cages used to stable battlemounts complete with meat canisters and feeding chutes rigged in place above the cages. One of the four ostlers present ran ahead to open two cages and lower the chutes, and the other three assisted Hereward to unload the panniers. Mister Fitz took his sewing desk and stood aside, the small rosewood and silver box under his arm provoking neither recognition nor alarm. The ostlers were similarly incurious about Fitz himself, almost certainly evidence that self-motivated puppets still came to entertain the townsfolk from time to time.

Hereward led the way into the inn, but halted just before he entered as one of the battlemounts snorted at some annoyance. Glancing back, he saw that it was of no concern, and the gates were closed, but in halting he had kept hold of the door as someone else tried to open it from the other side. Hereward pushed to help and the door flung open, knocking the person on the inside back several paces against a table, knocking over an empty bottle that smashed upon the floor.

"Unfortunate," muttered Mister Fitz, as he saw that the person so inconvenienced was not only a soldier, but wore the red sash of a junior officer and was a woman.

"I do apolog—" Hereward began to say. He stopped, not only because the woman was talking, but because he had looked at her. She was as tall as he was, with ash-blond hair tied in a queue at the back, her hat in her left hand. She was also very beautiful, at least to Hereward, who had grown up with women who ritually cut their flesh. To others, her attractiveness might be considered marred by the scar that ran from the corner of her left eye out toward the ear and then cut back again toward the lower part of her nose.

"You are clumsy, sir!"

Hereward stared at her for just one second too long before attempting to speak again.

"I am most—"

"You see something you do not like, I think?" interrupted the woman. "Perhaps you have not served with females? Or is it my face you do not care for?"

"You are very beautiful," said Hereward, even as he realized it was entirely the wrong thing to say, either to a woman he had just met or an officer he had just run into.

"You mock me!" swore the woman. Her blue eyes shone more fiercely, but her face paled, and the scar grew more livid. She clapped her broad-brimmed hat on her head and straightened to her full height, with the hat standing perhaps an inch over Hereward. "You shall answer for that!"

"I do not mock you," said Hereward quietly. "I have served with men, women . . .

and eunuchs, for that matter. Furthermore, tomorrow morning I shall be signing on as at least colonel of artillery, and a colonel may not fight a duel with a lieutenant. I am most happy to apologize, but I cannot meet you."

"Cannot or will not?" sneered the woman. "You are not yet a colonel in Shûme's service, I believe, but just a mercenary braggart."

Hereward sighed and looked around the common room. Misolu had spoken truly that the inn was not a mercenary favorite. But there were several officers of Shûme's regular service or militia, all of them looking on with great attention.

"Very well," he snapped. "It is foolishness, for I intended no offense. When and where?"

"Immediately," said the woman. "There is a garden a little way behind this inn. It is lit by lanterns in the trees, and has a lawn."

"How pleasant," said Hereward. "What is your name, madam?"

"I am Lieutenant Jessaye of the Temple Guard of Shûme. And you are?"

"I am Sir Hereward of the High Pale."

"And your friends, Sir Hereward?"

"I have only this moment arrived in Shûme, Lieutenant, and so cannot yet name any friends. Perhaps someone in this room will stand by me, should you wish a second. My companion, whom I introduce to you now, is known as Mister Fitz. He is a surgeon—among other things—and I expect he will accompany us."

"I am pleased to meet you, Lieutenant," said Mister Fitz. He doffed his hat and veil, sending a momentary frisson of small twitches among all in the room save Hereward.

Jessaye nodded back but did not answer Fitz. Instead she spoke to Hereward.

"I need no second. Should you wish to employ sabers, I must send for mine."

"I have a sword in my gear," said Hereward. "If you will allow me a few minutes to fetch it?"

"The garden lies behind the stables," said Jessaye. "I will await you there. Pray do not be too long."

Inclining her head but not doffing her hat, she stalked past and out the door.

"An inauspicious beginning," said Fitz.

"Very," said Hereward gloomily. "On several counts. Where is the innkeeper? I must change and fetch my sword."

The garden was very pretty. Railed in iron, it was not gated, and so accessible to all the citizens of Shûme. A wandering path led through a grove of lantern-hung trees to the specified lawn, which was oval and easily fifty yards from end to end, making the center rather a long way from the lantern light, and hence quite shadowed. A small crowd of persons who had previously been in the inn were gathered on one side of the lawn. Lieutenant Jessaye stood in the middle, naked blade in hand.

"Do be careful, Hereward," said Fitz quietly, observing the woman flex her knees and practice a stamping attack ending in a lunge. "She looks to be very quick."

"She is an officer of their temple guard," said Hereward in a hoarse whisper. "Has their god imbued her with any particular vitality or puissance?"

"No, the godlet does not seem to be a martial entity," said Fitz. "I shall have to undertake some investigations presently as to exactly what it is—"

"Sir Hereward! Here at last."

Hereward grimaced as Jessaye called out. He had changed as quickly as he could, into a very fine suit of split-sleeved white showing the yellow shirt beneath, with gold ribbons at the cuffs, shoulders, and front lacing, with similarly cut bloomers of yellow showing white breeches, with silver ribbons at the knees, artfully displayed through the side notches of his second-best boots.

Jessaye, in contrast, had merely removed her uniform coat and stood in her shirt, blue waistcoat, leather breeches, and unadorned black thigh boots folded over below the knee. Had the circumstances been otherwise, Hereward would have paused to admire the sight she presented and perhaps offer a compliment.

Instead he suppressed a sigh, strode forward, drew his sword, and threw the scabbard aside.

"I am here, Lieutenant, and I am ready. Incidentally, is this small matter to be concluded by one or perhaps both of us dying?"

"The city forbids duels to the death, Sir Hereward," replied Jessaye. "Though accidents do occur."

"What, then, is to be the sign for us to cease our remonstrance?"

"Blood," said Jessaye. She flicked her sword toward the onlookers. "Visible to those watching."

Hereward nodded slowly. In this light, there would need to be a lot of blood before the onlookers could see it.

He bowed his head but did not lower his eyes, then raised his sword to the guard position.

Jessaye was fast. She immediately thrust at his neck, and though Hereward parried, he had to step back. She carried through to lunge in a different line, forcing him back again with a more awkward parry, removing all opportunity for Hereward to riposte or counter. For a minute they danced, their swords darting up, down, and across, clashing together only to move again almost before the sound reached the audience.

In that minute, Hereward took stock of Jessaye's style and action. She was very fast, but so was he, much faster than anyone would expect from his size and build, and as always, he had not shown just how truly quick he could be. Jessaye's wrist was strong and supple, and she could change both attacking and defensive lines with great ease. But her style was rigid, a variant of an old school Hereward had studied in his youth.

On her next lunge—which came exactly where he anticipated—Hereward didn't parry but stepped aside and past the blade. He felt her sword whisper by his ribs as he angled his own blade over it and with the leading edge of the point, he cut Jessaye above the right elbow to make a long, very shallow slice that he intended should bleed copiously without inflicting any serious harm.

Jessaye stepped back but did not lower her guard. Hereward quickly called out, "Blood!"

Jessaye took a step forward and Hereward stood ready for another attack. Then the lieutenant bit her lip and stopped, holding her arm toward the lantern light so she could more clearly see the wound. Blood was already soaking through the linen shirt, a dark and spreading stain upon the cloth.

"You have bested me," she said, and thrust her sword point first into the grass before striding forward to offer her gloved hand to Hereward. He too grounded his blade, and took her hand as they bowed to each other.

A slight stinging low on his side caused Hereward to look down. There was a two-inch cut in his shirt, and small beads of blood were blossoming there. He did not let go Jessaye's fingers, but pointed at his ribs with his left hand.

"I believe we are evenly matched. I hope we may have no cause to bicker further?"

"I trust not," said Jessaye quietly. "I regret the incident. Were it not for the presence of some of my fellows, I should not have caviled at your apology, sir. But you understand . . . a reputation is not easily won, nor kept. . . ."

"I do understand," said Hereward.

"Come, let Mister Fitz attend your cut. Perhaps you will then join me for a small repast?"

Jessaye shook her head.

"I go on duty soon. A stitch or two and a bandage is all I have time for. Perhaps we shall meet again."

"It is my earnest hope that we do," said Hereward. Reluctantly, he opened his grasp. Jessaye's hand lingered in his palm for several moments before she slowly raised it, stepped back, and doffed her hat to offer a full bow. Hereward returned it, straightening up as Mister Fitz hurried over, carrying a large leather case as if it were almost too heavy for him, one of his standard acts of misdirection, for the puppet was at least as strong as Hereward, if not stronger.

"Attend to Lieutenant Jessaye, if you please, Mister Fitz," said Hereward. "I am going back to the inn to have a cup . . . or two . . . of wine."

"Your own wound needs no attention?" asked Fitz as he set his bag down and indicated to Jessaye to sit by him.

"A scratch," said Hereward. He bowed to Jessaye again and walked away, ignoring the polite applause of the onlookers, who were drifting forward either to talk to Jessaye or gawp at the blood on her sleeve.

"I may take a stroll," called out Mister Fitz after Hereward. "But I shan't be longer than an hour."

Mister Fitz was true to his word, returning a few minutes after the citadel bell had sounded the third hour of the evening. Hereward had bespoken a private chamber and was dining alone there, accompanied only by his thoughts.

"The god of Shûme," said Fitz, without preamble. "Have you heard anyone mention its name?"

Hereward shook his head and poured another measure from the silver jug with the swan's beak spout. Like many things he had found in Shûme, the knight liked the inn's silverware.

"They call their godlet Tanesh," said Fitz. "But its true name is Pralqornrah-Tanish-Kvaxixob."

"As difficult to say or spell, I wager," said Hereward. "I commend the short form, it shows common sense. What of it?"

"It is on the list," said Fitz. Hereward bit the edge of pewter cup and put it down too hard, slopping wine upon the table.

"You're certain? There can be no question?"

Fitz shook his head. "After I had doctored the young woman, I went down to the lake and took a slide of the god's essence—it was quite concentrated in the water, easily enough to yield a sample. You may compare it with the record, if you wish."

He proffered a finger-long inch-wide strip of glass that was striated in many different bands of color. Hereward accepted it reluctantly, and with it a fat, square book that Fitz slid across the table. The book was open at a hand-tinted color plate, the illustration showing a sequence of color bands.

"It is the same," agreed the knight, his voice heavy with regret. "I suppose it is fortunate we have not yet signed on, though I doubt they will see what we do as being purely a matter of defense."

"They do not know what they harbor here," said Fitz.

"It is a pleasant city," said Hereward, taking up his cup again to take a large gulp of the slightly sweet wine. "In a pretty valley. I had thought I could grow more than accustomed to Shûme—and its people."

"The bounty of Shûme, all its burgeoning crops, its healthy stock and people, is an unintended result of their godlet's predation upon the surrounding lands," said Fitz. "Pralqornrah is one of the class of cross-dimensional parasites that is most dangerous. Unchecked, in time it will suck the vital essence out of all the land beyond its immediate demesne. The deserts of Balkash are the work of a similar being, over six millennia. This one has only been embedded here for two hundred years—you have seen the results beyond this valley."

"Six millennia is a long time," said Hereward, taking yet another gulp. The wine was strong as well as sweet, and he felt the need of it. "A desert might arise in that time without the interference of the gods."

"It is not just the fields and the river that Pralqornrah feeds upon," said Fitz. "The people outside this valley suffer too. Babes unborn, strong men and women declining before their prime . . . this godlet slowly sucks the essence from all life."

"They could leave," said Hereward. The wine was making him feel both sleepy and mulish. "I expect many have already left to seek better lands. The rest could be resettled, the lands left uninhabited to feed the godlet. Shûme could continue as an oasis. What if another desert grows around it? They occur in nature, do they not?"

"I do not think you fully comprehend the matter," said Fitz. "Pralqornrah is a most comprehensive feeder. Its energistic threads will spread farther and faster the longer it exists here, and it in turn will grow more powerful and much more difficult to remove. A few millennia hence, it might be too strong to combat."

"I am only talking," said Hereward, not without some bitterness. "You need not waste your words to bend my reason. I do not even need to understand anything beyond the salient fact: this godlet is on the list."

"Yes," said Mister Fitz. "It is on the list."

Hereward bent his head for a long, silent moment. Then he pushed his chair back and reached across for his saber. Drawing it, he placed the blade across his knees. Mister Fitz handed him a whetstone and a small flask of light, golden oil. The knight oiled the stone and began to hone the saber's blade. A repetitive rasp was the only sound in the room for many minutes, till he finally put the stone aside and wiped the blade clean with a soft piece of deerskin.

"When?"

"Fourteen minutes past the midnight hour is optimum," replied Mister Fitz. "Presuming I have calculated its intrusion density correctly."

"It is manifest in the temple?"

Fitz nodded.

"Where is the temple, for that matter? Only the citadel stands out above the roofs of the city."

"It is largely underground," said Mister Fitz. "I have found a side entrance, which should not prove difficult. At some point beyond that there is some form of arcane barrier—I have not been able to ascertain its exact nature, but I hope to unpick it without trouble."

"Is the side entrance guarded? And the interior?"

"Both," said Fitz. Something about his tone made Hereward fix the puppet with an inquiring look.

"The side door has two guards," continued Fitz. "The interior watch is of ten or eleven . . . led by the Lieutenant Jessaye you met earlier."

Hereward stood up, the saber loose in his hand, and turned away from Fitz.

"Perhaps we shall not need to fight her . . . or her fellows."

Fitz did not answer, which was answer enough.

The side door to the temple was unmarked and appeared no different than the other simple wooden doors that lined the empty street, most of them adorned with signs marking them as the shops of various tradesmen, with smoke-grimed night lamps burning dimly above the sign. The door Fitz indicated was painted a pale violet and had neither sign nor lamp.

"Time to don the brassards and make the declaration," said the puppet. He looked up and down the street, making sure that all was quiet, before handing Hereward a broad silk armband five fingers wide. It was embroidered with sorcerous thread that shed only a little less light than the smoke-grimed lantern above the neighboring shop door. The symbol the threads wove was one that had once been familiar the world over but was now unlikely to be recognized by anyone save an historian . . . or a god.

Hereward slipped the brassard over his left glove and up his thick coat sleeve, spreading it out above the elbow. The suit of white and yellow was once again packed, and for this expedition the knight had chosen to augment his helmet and buff coat with a dented but still eminently serviceable back and breastplate, the steel blackened by tannic acid to a dark gray. He had already primed, loaded, and spanned his two wheel-lock pistols, which were thrust through his belt; his saber was sheathed at his side; and a lozenge-sectioned, armor-punching bodkin was in his left boot.

Mister Fitz wore his sewing desk upon his back, like a wooden backpack. He had already been through its numerous small drawers and containers and selected particular items that were now tucked into the inside pockets of his coat, ready for immediate use.

"I wonder why we bother with this mummery," grumbled Hereward. But he stood at attention as Fitz put on his own brassard, and the knight carefully repeated the short phrase uttered by his companion. Though both had recited it many times, and it was clear as bright type in their minds, they spoke carefully and with great concentration, in sharp contrast to Hereward's remark about mummery.

"In the name of the Council of the Treaty for the Safety of the World, acting under the authority granted by the Three Empires, the Seven Kingdoms, the Palatine Regency, the Jessar Republic, and the Forty Lesser Realms, we declare ourselves agents of the Council. We identify the godlet manifested in this city of Shûme as Pralqornrah-Tanish-Kvaxixob, a listed entity under the Treaty. Consequently, the said godlet and all those who assist it are deemed to be enemies of the World and the Council authorizes us to pursue any and all actions necessary to banish, repel, or exterminate the said godlet."

Neither felt it necessary to change this ancient text to reflect the fact that only one of the three empires was still extant in any fashion; that the Seven Kingdoms were now twenty or more small states; the Palatine Regency was a political fiction, its once broad lands under two fathoms of water; the Jessar Republic was now neither Jessar in ethnicity nor a republic; and perhaps only a handful of the Forty Lesser Realms resembled their antecedent polities in any respect. But for all that the states that had made it were vanished or diminished, the Treaty for the Safety of the World was still held to be in operation, if only by the Council that administered and enforced it.

"Are you ready?" asked Fitz.

Hereward drew his saber and moved into position to the left of the door. Mister Fitz reached into his coat and drew out an esoteric needle. Hereward knew better than to try to look at the needle directly, but in the reflection of his blade, he could see a four-inch line of something intensely violet writhe in Fitz's hand. Even the reflection made him feel as if he might at any moment be unstitched from the world, so he angled the blade away.

At that moment, Fitz touched the door with the needle and made three short plucking motions. On the last motion, without any noise or fuss, the door wasn't there anymore. There was only a wood-paneled corridor leading down into the ground and two very surprised temple guards, who were still leaning on their halberds.

Before Hereward could even begin to move, Fitz's hand twitched across and up several times. The lanterns on their brass stands every six feet along the corridor flickered and flared violet for a fraction of a second. Hereward blinked, and the guards were gone, as were the closest three lanterns and their stands.

Only a single drop of molten brass, no bigger than a tear, remained. It sizzled on the floor for a second, then all was quiet.

The puppet stalked forward, cupping his left hand over the needle in his right, obscuring its troublesome sight behind his fingers. Hereward followed close behind, alert for any enemy that might be resistant to Fitz's sorcery.

The corridor was a hundred yards long by Hereward's estimation, and slanted sharply down, making him think about having to fight back up it, which would be no easy task, made more difficult as the floor and walls were damp, drops of water oozing out between the floorboards and dripping from the seams of the wall paneling. There was cold, wet stone behind the timber, Hereward knew. He could feel the cold air rippling off it, a chill that no amount of fine timber could cloak.

The corridor ended at what appeared from a distance to be a solid wall, but closer to was merely the dark back of a heavy tapestry. Fitz edged silently around it, had a look, and returned to beckon Hereward in.

There was a large antechamber or waiting room beyond, sparsely furnished with a slim desk and several well-upholstered armchairs. The desk and chairs each had six legs, the extra limbs arranged closely at the back, a fashion Hereward supposed was some homage to the godlet's physical manifestation. The walls were hung with several tapestries depicting the city at various stages in its history.

Given the depth underground and the proximity of the lake, great efforts must have been made to waterproof and beautify the walls, floor, and ceiling, but there was still an army of little dots of mold advancing from every corner, blackening the white plaster, and tarnishing the gilded cornices and decorations.

Apart from the tapestry-covered exit, there were three doors. Two were of a usual size, though they were elaborately carved with obscure symbols and had brass, or perhaps even gold, handles. The one on the wall opposite the tapestry corridor was entirely different: it was a single ten-foot by six-foot slab of ancient marble veined with red lead, and it would have been better situated sitting on top of a significant memorial or some potentate's coffin.

Mister Fitz went to each of the carved doors, his blue tongue flickering in and out, sampling the air.

"No one close," he reported before approaching the marble slab. He actually licked the gap between the stone and the floor, then sat for a few moments to think about what he had tasted.

Hereward kept clear, checking the other doors to see if they could be locked. Disappointed in that aim as they had neither bar nor keyhole, he sheathed his saber and carefully and quietly picked up a desk to push against the left door and several chairs to pile against the right. They wouldn't hold, but they would give some warning of attempted ingress.

Fitz chuckled as Hereward finished his work, an unexpected noise that made the knight shiver, drop his hand to the hilt of his saber, and quickly look around to see what had made the puppet laugh. Fitz was not easily amused, and often not by anything Hereward would consider funny.

"There is a sorcerous barrier," said Fitz. "It is immensely strong but has not perhaps been as well thought out as it might have been. Fortuitously, I do not even need to unpick it."

The puppet reached up with his left hand and pushed the marble slab. It slid back silently, revealing another corridor, this one of more honest bare, weeping stone, rapidly turning into rough-hewn steps only a little way along.

"I'm afraid you cannot follow, Hereward," said Fitz. "The barrier is conditional, and you do not meet its requirements. It would forcibly—and perhaps harmfully—repel you if you tried to step over the lintel of this door. But I would ask you to stay here in any case, to secure our line of retreat. I should only be a short time if all goes well. You will, of course, know if all does not go well, and must save yourself as best you can. I have impressed the ostlers to rise at your command and load our gear, as I have impressed instructions into the dull minds of the battlemounts—"

"Enough, Fitz! I shall not leave without you."

"Hereward, you know that in the event of my—"

"Fitz. The quicker it were done—"

"Indeed. Be careful, child."

"Fitz!"

But the puppet had gone almost before that exasperated single word was out of Hereward's mouth.

It quickly grew cold with the passage below open. Chill, wet gusts of wind blew up and followed the knight around the room, no matter where he stood. After a few minutes trying to find a spot where he could avoid the cold breeze, Hereward took to pacing by the doors as quietly as he could. Every dozen steps or so he stopped to listen, either for Fitz's return or the sound of approaching guards.

In the event, he was midpace when he heard something. The sharp beat of hobnailed boots in step, approaching the left-hand door.

Hereward drew his two pistols and moved closer to the door. The handle rattled, the door began to move and encountered the desk he had pushed there. There was an exclamation and several voices spoke all at once. A heavier shove came immediately, toppling the desk as the door came partially open.

Hereward took a pace to the left and fired through the gap. The wheel locks whirred, sparks flew, then there were two deep, simultaneous booms, the resultant echoes flattening down the screams and shouts in the corridor beyond the door, just as the conjoining clouds of blue-white smoke obscured Hereward from the guards, who were already clambering over their wounded or slain companions.

The knight thrust his pistols back through his belt and drew his saber, to make an immediate sweeping cut at the neck of a guard who charged blindly through the smoke, his halberd thrust out in front like a blind man's cane. Man and halberd clattered to the floor. Hereward ducked under a halberd swing and slashed the next guard behind the knees, at the same time picking up one edge of the desk and flipping it upright in the path of the next two guards. They tripped over it, and Hereward stabbed them both in the back of the neck as their helmets fell forward, left-right, three inches of saber point in and out in an instant.

A blade skidded off Hereward's cuirass and would have scored his thigh but for a quick twist away. He parried the next thrust, rolled his wrist and slashed his attacker across the stomach, following it up with a kick as the guard reeled back, sword slack in his hand.

No attack—or any movement save for dulled writhing on the ground—followed. Hereward stepped back and surveyed the situation. Two guards were dead or dying just beyond the door. One was still to his left. Three lay around the desk. Another was hunched over by the wall, his hands pressed uselessly against the gaping wound in his gut as he moaned the god's name over and over.

None of the guards was Jessaye, but the sound of the pistol shots at the least would undoubtedly bring more defenders of the temple.

"Seven," said Hereward. "Of a possible twelve."

He laid his saber across a chair and reloaded his pistols, taking powder cartridges and shot from the pocket of his coat and a ramrod from under the barrel of one gun. Loaded, he wound their wheel-lock mechanisms with a small spanner that hung from a braided-leather loop on his left wrist.

Just as he replaced the pistols in his belt, the ground trembled beneath his feet, and an even colder wind came howling out of the sunken corridor, accompanied by a cloying but not unpleasant odor of exotic spices that also briefly made Hereward see strange bands of color move through the air, the visions fading as the scent also passed.

Tremors, scent, and strange visions were all signs that Fitz had joined battle with Pralqornrah-Tanish-Kvaxixob below. There could well be other portents to come, stranger and more unpleasant to experience.

"Be quick, Fitz," muttered Hereward, his attention momentarily focused on the downward passage.

Even so, he caught the soft footfall of someone sneaking in, boots left behind in the passage. He turned, pistols in hand, as Jessaye stepped around the half-open door. Two guards came behind her, their own pistols raised.

Before they could aim, Hereward fired and, as the smoke and noise filled the room, threw the empty pistols at the trio, took up his saber, and jumped aside.

Jessaye's sword leaped into the space where he'd been. Hereward landed, turned, and parried several frenzied stabs at his face, the swift movement of their blades sending the gun smoke eddying in wild roils and coils. Jessaye pushed him back almost to the other door. There, Hereward picked up a chair and used it to fend off several blows, at the same time beginning to make small, fast cuts at Jessaye's sword arm.

Jessaye's frenzied assault slackened as Hereward cut her badly on the shoulder near her neck, then immediately after that on the upper arm, across the wound he'd given her in the duel. She cried out in pain and rage and stepped back, her right arm useless, her sword point trailing on the floor.

Instead of pressing his attack, the knight took a moment to take stock of his situation.

The two pistol-bearing guards were dead or as good as, making the tally nine. That meant there should only be two more, in addition to Jessaye, and those two were not immediately in evidence.

"You may withdraw, if you wish," said Hereward, his voice strangely loud and dull at the same time, a consequence of shooting in enclosed spaces. "I do not wish to kill you, and you cannot hold your sword."

Jessaye transferred her sword to her left hand and took a shuddering breath. "I fight equally well with my left hand," she said, assuming the guard position as best she could, though her right arm hung at her side and blood dripped from her fingers to the floor.

She thrust immediately, perhaps hoping for surprise. Hereward ferociously beat her blade down, then stamped on it, forcing it from her grasp. He then raised the point of his saber to her throat.

"No you don't," he said. "Very few people do. Go, while you still live."

"I cannot," whispered Jessaye. She shut her eyes. "I have failed in my duty. I shall die with my comrades. Strike quickly."

Hereward raised his elbow and prepared to push the blade through the so-giving flesh, as he had done so many times before. But he did not, instead he lowered his saber and backed away around the wall.

"Quickly, I beg you," said Jessaye. She was shivering, the blood flowing faster down her arm.

"I cannot," muttered Hereward. "Or rather I do not wish to. I have killed enough today."

Jessaye opened her eyes and slowly turned to him, her face paper white, the scar no brighter than the petal of a pink rose. For the first time, she saw that the stone door was open, and she gasped and looked wildly around at the bodies that littered the floor.

"The priestess came forth? You have slain her?"

"No," said Hereward. He continued to watch Jessaye and listen for others, as he bent and picked up his pistols. They were a present from his mother, and he had not lost them yet. "My companion has gone within."

"But that . . . that is not possible! The barrier—"

"Mister Fitz knew of the barrier," said Hereward wearily. He was beginning to feel the aftereffects of violent combat, and strongly desired to be away from the visible signs of it littered around him. "He crossed it without difficulty."

"But only the priestess can pass," said Jessaye wildly. She was shaking more than just shivering now, as shock set in, though she still stood upright. "A woman with child! No one and nothing else! It cannot be. . . ."

Her eyes rolled back in her head, she twisted sideways and fell to the floor. Hereward watched her lie there for a few seconds while he attempted to regain the cold temper in which he fought, but it would not return. He hesitated, then wiped his saber clean, sheathed it, then despite all better judgment, bent over Jessaye.

She whispered something and again, and he caught the god's name, "Tanesh," and with it a sudden onslaught of cinnamon and cloves and ginger on his nose. He blinked, and in that blink, she turned and struck at him with a small dagger that had been concealed in her sleeve. Hereward had expected something, but not the god's assistance, for the dagger was in her right hand, which he'd thought useless. He grabbed her wrist but could only slow rather than stop the blow. Jessaye struck true, the dagger entering the armhole of the cuirass, to bite deep into his chest. Hereward left the dagger there and merely pushed Jessaye back. The smell of spices faded, and her arm was limp once more. She did not resist, but lay there quite still, only her eyes moving as she watched Hereward sit down next to her. He sighed heavily, a few flecks of blood already spraying out with his breath, evidence that her dagger was lodged in his lung though he already knew that from the pain that impaled him with every breath.

"There is no treasure below," said Jessaye quietly. "Only the godlet, and his priestess."

"We did not come for treasure," said Hereward. He spat blood on the floor. "Indeed, I had thought we would winter here, in good employment. But your god is proscribed, and so . . ."

"Proscribed? I don't . . . who . . ."

"By the Council of the Treaty for the Safety of the World," said Hereward.

"Not that anyone remembers that name. If we are remembered it is from the stories that tell of . . . god-slayers."

"I know the stories," whispered Jessaye. "And not just stories . . . we were taught to beware the god-slayers. But they are always women, barren women, with witch-scars on their faces. Not a man and a puppet. That is why the barrier . . . the barrier stops all but gravid women. . . ."

Hereward paused to wipe a froth of blood from his mouth before he could answer.

"Fitz has been my companion since I was three years old. He was called Mistress Fitz then, as my nurse-bodyguard. When I turned ten, I wanted a male companion, and so I began to call him Mister Fitz. But whether called Mistress or Master, I believe Fitz is nurturing an offshoot of his spiritual essence in some form of pouch upon his person. In time he will make a body for it to inhabit. The process takes several hundred years."

"But you . . ."

Jessaye's whisper was almost too quiet to hear.

"I am a mistake . . . the witches of Har are not barren, that is just a useful tale. But they do only bear daughters . . . save the once. I am the only son of a witch born these thousand years. My mother is one of the Mysterious Three who rule the witches, last remnant of the Council. Fitz was made by that Council, long ago, as a weapon made to fight malignant gods. The more recent unwanted child became a weapon too, puppet and boy flung out to do our duty in the world. A duty that has carried me here . . . to my great regret."

No answer came to this bubbling, blood-infused speech. Hereward looked across at Jessaye and saw that her chest no longer rose and fell, and that there was a dark puddle beneath her that was still spreading, a tide of blood advancing toward him.

He touched the hilt of the dagger in his side, and coughed, and the pain of both things was almost too much to bear; but he only screamed a little, and made it worse by standing up and staggering to the wall to place his back against it. There were still two guards somewhere, and Fitz was surprisingly vulnerable if he was surprised. Or he might be wounded too, from the struggle with the god.

Minutes or perhaps a longer time passed, and Hereward's mind wandered and, in wandering, left his body too long. It slid down the wall to the ground and his blood began to mingle with that of Jessaye and the others who lay on the floor of a god's antechamber turned slaughterhouse.

Then there was pain again, and Hereward's mind jolted back into his body, in time to make his mouth whimper and his eyes blink at a light that was a color he didn't know, and there was Mister Fitz leaning over him and the dagger wasn't in his side anymore and there was no bloody froth upon his lips. There was still pain. Constant, piercing pain, coming in waves and never subsiding. It stayed with him, uppermost in his thoughts, even as he became dimly aware that he was upright and walking, his legs moving under a direction not his own.

Except that very soon he was lying down again, and Fitz was cross.

"You have to get back up, Hereward."

"I'm tired, Fitzie . . . can't I rest for a little longer?"

"No. Get up."

"Are we going home?"

"No, Hereward. You know we can't go home. We must go onward."

"Onward? Where?"

"Never mind now. Keep walking. Do you see our mounts?"

"Yes . . . but we will never . . . never make it out the gate . . ."

"We will, Hereward . . . leave it to me. Here, I will help you up. Are you steady enough?"

"I will . . . stay on. Fitz . . ."

"Yes, Hereward."

"Don't . . . don't kill them all."

If Fitz answered, Hereward didn't hear, as he faded out of the world for a few seconds. When the world nauseatingly shivered back into sight and hearing, the puppet was nowhere in sight and the two battlemounts were already loping toward the gate, though the leading steed had no rider.

They did not pause at the wall. Though it was past midnight, the gate was open, and the guards who might have barred the way were nowhere to be seen, though there were strange splashes of color upon the earth where they might have stood. There were no guards beyond the gate, on the earthwork bastion either, the only sign of their prior existence a half-melted belt buckle still red with heat.

To Hereward's dim eyes, the city's defenses might as well be deserted, and nothing prevented the battlemounts continuing to lope out into the warm autumn night.

The leading battlemount finally slowed and stopped a mile beyond the town, at the corner of a lemon grove, its hundreds of trees so laden with yellow fruit they scented the air with a sharp, clean tang that helped bring Hereward closer to full consciousness. Even so, he lacked the strength to shorten the chain of his own mount, but it stopped by its companion without urging.

Fitz swung down from the outlying branch of a lemon tree, onto his saddle, without spilling any of the fruit piled high in his upturned hat.

"We will ride on in a moment. But when we can, I shall make a lemon salve and a soothing drink."

Hereward nodded, finding himself unable to speak. Despite Fitz's repairing sorceries, the wound in his side was still very painful, and he was weak from loss of blood, but neither thing choked his voice. He was made quiet by a cold melancholy that held him tight, coupled with a feeling of terrible loss, the loss of some future, never-to-be happiness that had gone forever.

"I suppose we must head for Fort Yarz," mused Fitz. "It is the closest likely place for employment. There is always some trouble there, though I believe the Gebrak tribes have been largely quiet this past year."

Hereward tried to speak again, and at last found a croak that had some resemblance to a voice.

"No. I am tired of war. Find us somewhere peaceful, where I can rest."

Fitz hopped across to perch on the neck of Hereward's mount and faced the knight, his blue eyes brighter than the moonlight.

"I will try, Hereward. But as you ruminated earlier, the world is as it is, and we are what we were made to be. Even should we find somewhere that seems at peace, I suspect it will not stay so, should we remain. Remember Jeminero."

"Aye." Hereward sighed. He straightened up just a little and took up the chains, as Fitz jumped to his own saddle. "I remember."

"Fort Yarz?" asked Fitz.

Hereward nodded, and slapped the chain, urging his battlemount forward. As it stretched into its stride, the lemons began to fall from the trees in the orchard, playing the soft drumbeat of a funerary march, the first sign of the passing from the world of the god of Shûme.

TERRY DOWLING

Toother

Terry Dowling is one of Australia's most awarded, acclaimed, and best-known writers of science fiction, fantasy, and horror. His short stories have been published in such anthologies as Dreaming Down Under, Wizards, Gathering the Bones, The Dark, *and* Inferno *and reprinted in many* Year's Best *volumes. They are collected in* Rynosseros, Blue Tyson, Twilight Beach, Rynemonn, Wormwood, An Intimate Knowledge of the Night, Blackwater Days, The Man Who Lost Red, Antique Futures: The Best of Terry Dowling, *and* Basic Black: Tales of Appropriate Fear.

Dowling edited Mortal Fire: Best Australian SF, The Essential Ellison, *and* The Jack Vance Treasury. *He is a musician, songwriter, and communications instructor with a doctorate in creative writing, and has been genre reviewer for* The Weekend Australian *for the past eighteen years. For more information go to: www.terrydowling.com.*

"Toother" first appeared in Eclipse One, *edited by Jonathan Strahan.*

—E. D.

As Dan Truswell gave his signature three-three knock on the door in the modest hospital tower of Everton Psychiatric Facility that Friday morning, he couldn't help but glance through the second-floor window at the new sign down in the turning circle. EVERTON PSYCHIATRIC FACILITY it said. He'd never get used to it. That was the more politically correct name for Blackwater Psychiatric Hospital, just as words like client and guest had completely replaced patient and inmate.

"Peter, it's Dan."

Dan didn't enter Peter Rait's room, of course. That wasn't their arrangement. He just waited, looking at his reflection in the small mirror Peter kept hanging outside his door, surprised not so much by the slate-gray eyes and flyaway hair but by how white that hair had become. He was fifty-nine, for heaven's sake! It was something else he'd never get used to.

Finally the door opened and Peter stood there in his pajamas.

"Careful, Doctor Dan. That's a dangerous one."

"They all are, Peter. Carla said you've been yelling. Another nightmare?"

Peter looked tired, troubled. His black hair was tousled from sleep. "They don't usually come this often now. Harry's going to phone."

"Harry Badman?" Dear industrious Harry was two years out of his life, distanced by the usual string of promotions, secondments, and strategic sidelining that marked the lives of so many career detectives in the New South Wales Police Force. "All right, Peter, so how does this dream relate?"

"Ask Harry about the teeth, Doctor Dan."

Dan's thoughts went at once to the recent desecration at Sydney's Rookwood Cemetery. "Is this about—?"

"Ask him."

"What do you have, Peter?"

"I can't say till he confirms it. Ask him. He'll know."

Dan made himself hold back the rush of questions. "It's been a while."

Peter did finally manage a smile, something of one. "It has, Doctor Dan."

Dan smiled too. "Phil knows?"

"Some of it. I'll give him an update at breakfast. But it's important. Very important."

"Tell me the rest, Peter."

"I really can't."

"There are voices?"

"God, yes. But strange." Neither of them smiled at the bathos. What internal voices weren't? "They're coming over time."

Dan frowned. This was something new. "Across years?"

"The first is from the sixties."

"More, Peter."

"Let Harry start it."

You've started it! Dan almost said, but knew to hold back, just as Peter had known how much to use as a tease.

"Listen, Peter—"

"Talk later. I'll leave you two alone."

And he closed the door. Dan, of course, looked straight into Peter's mirror again, had the good grace to laugh, then headed downstairs.

Forty-nine minutes later, as Dan sat in his office reviewing the patient database, Harry Badman phoned from Sydney. There was the inevitable small talk, the polite and awkward minimum that let them stitch up the years as best they could. Dan Truswell and Harry Badman liked one another a great deal, but their friendship had never been easy far from where their respective careers met: for Harry, pursuing the more dangerous proponents of extraordinary human behavior; for Dan, fathoming the often extraordinary reasons for it.

Finally Harry's tone changed. "I need to see you, Dan."

"It's about what happened at Rookwood last Saturday night, isn't it?"

"What have you heard?"

"What was in the news. A grave was desecrated. A recent burial." Dan said nothing about teeth. This had been one of Peter Rait's dreams after all, and it had been a while since the intense, still-young man had been "active" like this. More importantly it was Dan's way of testing Peter's special talent after all this time.

"Samantha Reid. Aged forty-one. Buried on Friday, dug up on Sunday sometime between two and four in the morning. Cold rainy night. No one saw anything. The body was hauled from the coffin and left lying beside the grave."

"So, not just a grave 'tampered with,' like the papers said. Your people are good, Harry. Why the call?"

"Things were removed from the scene. I'd like your take on it."

"Stop being coy. What was 'removed'?"

"The teeth, Dan. All the teeth."

Dan had an odd rush of emotion: revulsion, fascination, the familiar numb amazement he always felt whenever one of Peter's predictions played out like this. And there was the usual excess of rationalism as if to compensate. "What do the deceased's dental records show? Were there gold fillings?"

"Dan, *all* the teeth. And it's not the first desecration. Just the first to make the news."

Dan knew he'd been slow this time, but allowed that he was out of practice too. "There were others?"

"From secluded and disused parts of the cemetery. Much older graves."

"But recent desecrations?"

"Hard to tell conclusively. Not all were reported back then. It didn't look good for the cemetery authorities. The graves were tidied up; nothing was said. We would have assumed these earlier violations were unrelated except..." He actually paused. Had the subject been less serious, it would have been comical.

"Come on, Harry. Someone's collecting teeth. What else do you have?"

"That Rattigan murder in Darlinghurst a month back. The pensioner, remember?"

"Go on."

"She wasn't strangled like the media said."

"No?"

"She was bitten to death."

Dan was surprised to find that his mouth had fallen open in astonishment. "Bitten?"

"At least two hundred times. Increasing severity."

"These could be different crimes, Harry. What makes you think they're related?"

"Teeth fragments were found in some of the wounds. Very old teeth."

But not in very old mouths, Dan realized. "Dentures made from these older desecrations?"

"Exactly."

"Surely there was saliva DNA from whoever wore them."

"No," Harry said.

Dan grasped the implications. "So, not necessarily biting as such. Someone made dentures from these older corpse teeth and—what?—killed the Rattigan woman using some sort of handheld prosthesis?"

"Spring-loaded and vicious. All we can think of. And that's *several* sets of dentures, Dan. We've traced teeth fragments back to the occupants of three older desecrations: graves from 1894, 1906, and 1911. All female. No fragments from newer teeth—"

"Too new to shatter."

"Exactly. But there could be other teeth used, from other desecrations we don't know of. There are some very old graves there; we wouldn't necessarily be able to tell. So all we have is a major fetish angle. Something ritualistic."

"My phone number hasn't changed, Harry." The accusation hung there. *You didn't call sooner!*

"You've got your life, Dan. Annie. Phil." The barest hesitation. "Peter. I didn't want to intrude."

Dan stared at the midmorning light through his office windows and nodded to himself. "You've profiled it as what?"

"I'd rather not say. That's what this is about. Getting another take."

"Official?"

"Can be. You want the file? I'll e-mail a PDF right now. Drive up tomorrow first thing."

"See you at the Imperial Hotel at eleven."

"See you then."

Seventeen hours later they were sitting with light beers in a quiet corner of the Imperial on Bennet Street trying to make the small-talk thing work face-to-face. They did well enough for six minutes before Harry put them both out of their misery.

"You got the file okay. Anything?"

Dan set down his glass. "A question first. You kept something back on the phone yesterday. You said the Rattigan woman was bitten to death."

"That's what happened," Harry said. He looked tanned, less florid than Dan remembered; in his casual clothes he could have been another tourist visiting the local wineries.

"Her teeth were taken as well, weren't they?"

Harry barely hesitated. "How'd you know?"

Dan lifted a manila folder from the seat beside him. "The results of Net searches. Know what a toother is, Harry?"

"Tell me."

"It was a vocation, to call it that, associated with body-snatching back in the eighteenth, nineteenth centuries. Back when resurrectionists—lovely name—dug up bodies to sell to medical academies for their anatomy classes. There were people who did the same to get the teeth. Sold them to dentists to make false teeth."

"Dug up corpses?"

"Sometimes. Or did deals with resurrection men already in the trade. Mostly they'd roam battlefields and take teeth from dead soldiers."

"You're kidding."

"Not when you think about it. It was much better than getting teeth from the gibbet or the grave. Ivory and whalebone were either too expensive or decayed. No enamel coating. Teeth made from porcelain sounded wrong or were too brittle. Corpse teeth were better, soldiers' teeth usually best of all, injuries permitting. Sets of authentic Waterloo Teeth fetch quite a bit these days."

"What, dentures made from soldiers who died at Waterloo?"

Dan nodded. "Fifty thousand in a single day. Mostly young men. Supply caught up with demand with battles like that. But that's the thing. There weren't many battles on that scale. Demand outstripped supply."

"You already knew this stuff?"

"Some of it. You know what I'm like. And that's quite a file you sent. I stayed up late."

Harry had his notebook on the table in front of him. He opened it and began making notes. "Go on."

"Back then there just weren't enough corpses of executed criminals or unknown homeless to satisfy the demand. Not enough from the right age or gender, even when you had poorer people selling their own teeth. Some resurrectionists began killing people."

"And these toothers did too."

"There's little conclusive evidence that I'm aware of. But that's the point, Harry. You do a job like this, you try to make sure there isn't."

"But body-snatchers can't be doing this."

"It presents that way is all I'm saying—a similar MO. If the cemetery desecrations and the Rattigan death *are* related, as the fragments suggest, we need to allow a context for it."

Harry wrote something and looked up. "So this joker could be proceeding like a modern-day toother."

Dan shrugged. "Just putting it forward, Harry. He took the Rattigan woman's teeth. Used others to kill her. So, a psychopath possibly. A sociopath definitely, probably highly organized. A latter-day resurrectionist? Not in the sense we know it. But we only have the teeth being taken and the single recent murder. I assume there are no similar cases in the CID database?"

Harry shook his head. "The usual run of biting during domestics and sexual assault. Random mostly. Nothing like this."

"Then he may be escalating; either a loner doing his own thing or someone acquainted with the old resurrectionist methodology."

Harry started writing again. "Do you have more on that?"

"Going back a hundred, two hundred years, he'd see a likely subject, get them alone, and have an accomplice grab them while he slapped a pitch-plaster over their mouth and nose—"

Harry looked up. "A what?"

"A sticky mass of plaster mixed with pitch. Mostly used during sexual assault, but what some resurrectionists used too. Silenced your victim and incapacitated them. Suffocated them if that was the intention. All over in minutes."

Harry was suitably horrified. "They just held them till they expired?"

"Or did a traditional 'burking'—covered the mouth and nose with their hand till the victim asphyxiated."

"This actually happened?"

"It did. The biting takes it in a completely different direction, of course. Was the Rattigan woman drugged or bound?"

"Not that we can tell."

"That tends to suggest an accomplice. Someone to help restrain her. Do Sheehan's people have anything?"

"Just the fetish, ritual angle, Dan. A loner after trophies. It's early days. But you're taking it further, saying there could be an accomplice, someone getting the teeth for someone else—who then makes dentures and uses them to kill."

Dan glanced around to make sure that they weren't being overheard. They still had the bar virtually to themselves. "Just another possibility, Harry. Much less likely. And no conventional client. There's no economic reason for it now. It presents like that, is what I'm saying."

"Okay, so either a loner or a gopher for someone who originally wanted the teeth for fetishistic reasons but is escalating. He now kills people and does the extractions himself. Focusing on females?"

"Seems that way. But until we know more I'm still tempted to say a loner with a special mission."

Harry drained his glass and set it down on the table. "So why do a *new* grave? Why show his hand like this? Was he interrupted before he could finish? Did he *want* people to know?"

"He's fixated. He may have seen the Reid woman alive and wanted that particular set of teeth. Like in the Poe story."

Harry frowned. "What Poe story?"

"'Berenice.' A brother obsessed with his sister's teeth extracts them while she's in a cataleptic coma."

"Where do you get this stuff, Dan?"

"They're called books, Harry. But this guy is doing it for himself. And I definitely believe it's a he. He could be using the more traditional techniques."

"Drugs would be easier."

"They would. But he wants them fully conscious. So we're back to the ritual aspect you mentioned."

"That emblematic thing," Harry said.

"The what?"

"Two—three years back. That conversation we had at Rollo's. You said that people try to be more. Have emblematic lives."

Dan never ceased to be amazed by what Harry remembered from their conversations. "Emblematic? I said that?"

"Four beers. You said that. Make themselves meaningful to themselves, you said. Do symbolic things."

"Okay, well this is his thing, Harry. We can't be sure if he's following aspects of the old toother/resurrectionist MO but Sheehan's right. Given the special dentures he's made for himself, doing this has some powerful fetishistic or symbolic meaning for him. And he may have done this a lot: gone somewhere, seen a lovely set of teeth on someone, arranged to get them alone, then suffocated or bitten them and taken their teeth."

"That's horrible. You actually think he may have already done that and hidden the bodies?"

"Because of the desecrations, the older teeth being used, that's how I'm seeing it, and it may get worse." Dan thought of Peter Rait's voices. *They're coming over time*.

"How could it—ah! He may start removing the teeth while the victims are alive. And conscious?"

Dan deliberately left a silence, waiting for Harry to say it.

It took a five-count. "You think it's already got to that! But the coroner's report for the Rattigan woman showed the extractions were postmortem."

"Harry, I think that may have been her one bit of good fortune. She died just as he was starting."

Harry shook his head. "Then we can definitely expect more."

"I'd say so. And it depends."

"On what, Dan? On what?"

"On whether it's local. Someone developing his ritual. Or if it's something international that's been relocated here."

"International?"

"Ask Sheehan to check with Interpol or whoever you guys work with now. Find case similarities. Forced dental extractions. Post- and *ante*-mortem."

"Can you come down to Sydney?"

"Phone me Monday and I'll let you know. I need to speak with someone first. You could stay around. Visit some wineries, come over for dinner tonight. Annie would love to see you."

They both knew it wouldn't go that way. Not this time. Not yet. "Sorry, Dan. I need to get going with this. Take a rain check?"

"Roger that," Dan said.

At 2:00 P.M. that afternoon, Dan met with Peter Rait and Phillip Crow at a picnic table sheltered by the largest Moreton Bay Fig in the hospital grounds. Peter, thin, black-haired, pale-skinned, on any ordinary day looked a decade younger than his forty-two years, but his recent nightmares had given him an intense, peaked quality that Dan found unsettling. He sat with a manila folder in front of him.

To his left on the same bench was Phil, four years older, fair-headed, stocky, with the sort of weathered but pleasant face that Carla liked to call "old-school Australian." He looked up and smiled as Dan arrived. "Just like old times, Doctor Dan."

"It is, Phil," Dan said as he sat across from them. He had to work not to smile. Peter and Phil were his "psychosleuths," their talent pretty well dormant these last three years. Officially, both men had been rehabilitated back into society; both had elected to stay, their choice, taking accommodation and rations in return for doing odd jobs. And called it Blackwater Psychiatric Hospital, of course.

Given Peter's present state, Dan couldn't enjoy the reunion as much as he would have liked. He went straight to the heart of it.

"Peter, tell me about the voices."

Peter took two typed pages from the folder in front of him. "Here are the transcripts," he said, sounding every bit as tired as he looked.

Dan was surprised by the odd choice of words. "Transcripts? How did you manage that?"

"They keep playing over. Two different conversations now. Two different victims."

"But how—?"

"I just can, Doctor Dan, okay? It's pretty distressing. You can't know how awful it is."

Dan saw that Peter wasn't just tired; he was exhausted. "You can't stop it?"

"Giving you these might do it. Getting them out."

"Nothing else?"

"Not yet. Please, just read them."

Dan looked at the first page.

TRANSCRIPT 1

[miscellaneous sounds]
[male voice / mature, controlled]
"As they say, there is the good news and the bad news."
[terrified female voice, quite young]
"What do you mean?"
"You have a choice here. The good news is that you'll wake up. All your teeth will be gone, but we'll have a relatively easy time with the extractions and you *will* wake up. You'll be alive. The alternative—you make my job difficult and you won't wake up. That's the deal."
"Why are you doing this?"
"What's it to be?"
"Why?"
"It's necessary. What's it to be?"
"There has to be a reason!"
"I'll count to three."
"Just tell me why! Please!"
"One."
"For God's sake! Why are you doing this? Why?"
"Two. Choose or I will."
"You can't expect me—"

"Three. Too late."

"No! No! I want to wake up! Please! I want to wake up!"

"All right. Just this once."

"One question."

"Go ahead."

"You could drug me and do it. Do whatever you want. Why do I even have to choose?"

"Now that's the thing. And, really, you already know why. I need you conscious for it. I may drug you at the end. Oh, dear, look. You're pissing yourself."

[sobbing]

"Why? Why? Why?"

"You're not listening. It's my thing. I need to see your eyes while I'm doing it."

"Another question."

"There always is. What is it?"

"What will you do with—with *them*? Afterward?"

"Make a nice set of dentures. Maybe I could sell them back to you. That would be a rather nice irony, wouldn't it? Irony is quite our thing."

"What about me? Afterward?"

"You'll wake up. Hate us forever. Go on with the rest of your life."

"But I'll wake up? I *will* wake up?"

"Make it easy for us now and, yes. You have my word."

"You're saying 'us' and 'our.'"

"Oh, dear. So I am."

"What's that over there?"

"I think that's enough questions."

"What *is* that?"

[sundry sounds]

[victim screaming]

[audio ends]

Dan looked up. "Peter—"

"The next one, Doctor Dan. Read the next one, please. Same male voice. Different female victim."

Dan turned to it at once.

TRANSCRIPT 2

[miscellaneous sounds]

"You're crazy!"

"I hope not, for your sake. Major dental work needs a degree of control."

"But why? Why me?"

"The usual reason. Chance. Purest hazard. You were on hand."

"Then pick someone else!"

"From someone else's viewpoint I did. But enough talk. We have a lot to do."

"Listen. Listen to me. My name is Pamela Deering. I'm a mother. I have two little girls. Emma and Grace. Aged seven and five. My husband's name—"

[muffled sounds]

"Ssh now, Pamela. No more bonding. We have a lot to do."

"What? What do we have to do?"

"Let's just say that your girls and hubby will have to call you Gummy instead of Mummy." [pause] "That's our little joke, Pamela."

[sobbing]

"Please. Please don't do this."

"We have to, Mu—er—Gummy. It's our thing. It won't take long."

"You're saying 'we,' 'us.' You're not alone. There's someone else."

"Tsk. How rude of me. You want to meet my associate. Over here. Try to turn your head a little more."

[sundry sounds]

"But that's not—"

[victim screaming]

[audio ends]

Dan lowered the pages. "There are two of them. He's not a loner."

"Seems that way," Peter said.

"Do you get accents at all?"

"Educated male. Educated enough. Enunciates s carefully so it's hard to know. The first woman sounds English. The Deering woman sounds Australian."

"But not recent. Over time, you said."

Peter nodded. "Sixties, seventies." He gestured to include Phil, as if he were equally part of this, both of them hearing the voices. "You have to protect us, Doctor Dan."

"I always do. That comes first."

"How will you?"

"Our old method. You aren't mentioned. Any locations you give, I'll have Harry say a phone call came in, anonymous. Someone overheard a disturbance, cries, screaming. Wouldn't give their name."

"They'll buy it?"

"Why not? It happens more and more these days. Remember, we *all* need to stay out of this."

Phil leaned forward. "What happens now?"

"We have a name," Dan said. "Pamela Deering. Harry can check that out. Meanwhile, Peter—"

"I'll keep dreaming."

"You don't have to. We can give you a sedative."

"No," Peter said. "I'm doing it for them."

Dan saw the haunted look in the tired dark eyes. "We need this, Peter."

"I know."

Thirty-two cases were listed in the international database, Harry told Dan on the phone that Monday morning, different countries, different cities, different decades, though it was the sort of statistic that convinced them both that many others existed.

"They say two thousand people a year in New Guinea are killed by coconuts falling on their heads," Harry said. "How do you get a statistic like that? It can only ever be the ones you *hear* about. It's like that here. These are just the ones that came to the attention of different national authorities and have anything approximating a similar MO."

"What about the time frame, Harry?"

"Dan, we've got cases going back to the thirties and forties, even earlier. Prague.

Krakow. Trieste. Bangkok, for heaven's sake! They can't be the same person. It can't be a generational thing. It doesn't work like that."

"I'd normally agree," Dan said. "But you say the MOs are similar for these thirty-two?"

"Victims bitten to death, post- or ante-mortem; the various odontologists' findings give both. Their own teeth removed before, during, or after; again there's a range. Older fragments in the wounds in some instances, say, nineteen, twenty percent."

"Harry—"

"You're not going to say a secret society. An international brotherhood of toothers."

Dan gave a grim smile. "No, but look how it presents. It's as if a very old, well-traveled sociopath has been able to find agents across a lifetime and still has at least one accomplice now, doing his dirty work. The Reid disinterment was done manually, not using a backhoe. That took a lot of effort."

"You believe this? Sheehan may not buy it."

"At this point I'm just trying to understand it, Harry. Rookwood and Darlinghurst suggest he may be local, at least for now."

"Can you come down to Sydney?"

"On Thursday. I'll be bringing Peter Rait."

Harry knew enough about Peter's gifts not to question it. "He has something?"

"For your eyes only."

"What, Dan?"

"Check if you have a missing person, a possible victim named Pamela Deering." He spelled out the name. "It could be from the sixties or seventies."

"How on earth did—?"

"Harry, you know how this has to be done. Yes or no?"

"Yes. Yes. Pamela Deering. Bring Peter with you. You got somewhere to stay?"

"I've arranged for unofficial digs at the old Gladesville Hospital on Victoria Road. There's a coffee shop on the grounds called Cornucopia. Meet us there around midday Thursday, okay?"

"Cornucopia. Got it."

"And bring a map of Rookwood Cemetery will you? The adjacent streets."

"You think he lives in the area?"

"Peter needs it."

"Done."

At a convenience store roadstop in Branxton on their drive down that Thursday morning, Peter presented Dan with a third transcript.

"You need to factor this in," was all Peter said as he handed it over. He looked more drawn than ever, as if he had barely slept the night before.

"Last night?"

"Last two nights."

"You kept it to yourself."

Peter ran a hand through his dark hair. "Look, I have to be sure, okay? I have to know that it's not—just coming from me. That I can trust it."

"And you do?"

"I'm satisfied now, Doctor Dan. I couldn't make this up."

Dan leaned against the car door and read the carefully typed words.

TRANSCRIPT 3

[miscellaneous sounds]

"You're the one who took the Kellar woman. Those poor women in Zurich. You're going to take out all my teeth!"

[sounds]

"Take them out? Oh, no. Not this time. Toother was very specific."

[sounds, like things being shaken in a metal box]

"Toother?"

"Yes. Your name please?"

"What difference does it make?"

"But isn't that what the experts advise? Always try to use names? Don't let them dehumanize you. My name is Paul."

"Your real name? Not Toother?"

"It'll do for today."

"Then I'll be Janice. For today. Who is Toother?"

"Why, your host, Janice-for-today. The one who taught me all I know. Mostly he takes, but sometimes he gives."

"Gives?"

"Sometimes. I have my little hammer and my little punch, see? And you have such a full, generous mouth. Today we are going to put teeth back in. Lots and lots, see?"

[more rattling sounds]

"Big teeth. Men's teeth. We're going to call you Smiler."

[more rattling sounds]

[victim sobbing]

[victim screaming]

Dan left Peter to drowse for much of the journey south, but as they were on the bridge crossing the Hawkesbury River, he glanced aside and saw the dark eyes watching him.

"You okay?" he asked.

"Sorry for losing it back there," Peter said, as if resuming a conversation from moments before. "Things are escalating for me too. With this latest—exchange—I get something about his trophies."

Dan wished he weren't driving right then. He pulled into the low-speed lane. "You see them?"

"Just lots of—grimaces. You know, teeth without lips. It's the most terrifying thing. Bared teeth. No skin covering. Like eyes without lids. Horrible."

"Are they on shelves, in drawers, boxes, what?"

"Displayed. Arranged somehow, secretly. Nothing like smiles or grins. I just see them as bared teeth, Doctor Dan. In a private space. Sorry. It isn't much."

"Try, Peter. Whatever you get. These voices—"

"It's more than just voices. It's reciprocal now."

"Reciprocal? What does that mean?"

"It isn't just going one way. He knows I've been listening. Accessing his files. He was very angry at first, but now he's enjoying it. He's fighting back."

"How, Peter? How does he fight back?"

"Sending things, thoughts, images. They're not mine. It's more than delusions, Doctor Dan, I'm sure of it. More than my usual hypersensitivity. I just had to be sure."

"Understood. Go on."

"It's Rookwood. All those graves. I keep seeing the bodies, vulnerable, helpless, keep seeing the teeth. They're mostly all teeth, lots of dentures too. But there's such anguish. Such rage."

"Female burials?"

"Female *and* male. They're all murmuring, chattering. Some desperately wanting to be picked, calling 'Pick me! Pick me!' Others hiding. Desperately hiding. As if alive. They're not, but it's like they are for him."

"Is there a voice talking to you now?"

"*Like* a voice, Doctor Dan. *Not* a voice, but like one. I have certainties, just know things. He wants it like that."

"He's found someone he can share with. He hears the bodies calling to him you say?"

"How he sees them. Calling, begging. 'Pick me! Pick me!' Or hiding, resisting. Furious. Either way he sees it as liberation, sees them as all waiting to be chosen. The living victims too."

"He's *saving* them?"

"Liberating them is his word, yes. Living or dead, it doesn't matter. It just means a different method of retrieval."

"Retrieval!" Dan gave a laugh, completely without humor. "But he's in the area?"

Peter shrugged. "It's a huge cemetery, Doctor Dan. It's not called the Sleeping City for nothing. He's committed so many desecrations there. You can't begin to know. Secretly. Passionately. This is his place for now."

"Peter, I trust you completely. Just let me know what you get. Anything."

It was strange to walk the grounds of the decommissioned, largely deserted mental hospital at Gladesville later that morning. The former wards and outbuildings had been turned into offices for various governmental health services, so by day it was like a stately, manicured museum estate. There were still vehicles in the car parks, people walking the paths, roadways, and lawns, giving the place a semblance of its former life.

Dan walked those daylight roads now, glad that he wasn't doing it at night. After dark the offices and car parks were deserted, but had a strange new half-life, quarter-life, life-in-death. Instead of being left to stand as part of a vast col of blackness overlooking the Parramatta River, the old sandstone buildings and empty roads were lit, as if beckoning, urging, waiting for those willing to surrender bits of their sanity to make the place live again.

When Dan reached Cornucopia, he found Harry waiting at a table outside the café door.

"I've driven past this place a thousand times," Harry said, "and never knew how big it was. Where's Peter?"

"He sends his apologies. Said he wants to keep his mind off this for now."

"Doesn't want me asking questions," Harry said. "I can understand that."

"Harry—"

"Dan, I know how it can be for him. How it *was*. Just say hi for me."

They went in and placed their orders, then sat watching the clear autumn sky above the sandstone walls. Harry took out his notebook.

"The Deering woman went missing from a holiday house at Cottesloe Beach in 1967."

"That's Western Australia, isn't it?"

"Right. There was blood, definite signs of a struggle, but no body. And before you ask, there were no teeth fragments."

"You've been thorough."

"Now that there's international scrutiny, we have different resources available."

"What did you tell Sheehan?"

"That it came up in a missing persons keyword sweep. In the last three decades alone there are thirty-six names of missing persons nationally where blood mixed with saliva was found at locations where each of them was last seen."

"Oral blood?"

"Right. So tell me what Peter has found."

Dan passed him the transcript folder. "Harry, you might want to finish eating first."

Dan found it hard to sleep that night. They were in separate rooms in an otherwise empty, former staff residence at the southern end of the hospital grounds, a converted single-story brick house. It was a cool, late autumn night, pleasant for sleeping, but with all that had happened, Dan felt restless, too keenly aware of the empty roads outside and the lit, abandoned buildings, so normal, yet—the only word for it—so abnormal, waiting in the night.

The lights are on but nobody's home.

The old euphemism for madness kept coming back to him. No doubt there were security personnel doing the rounds, one, possibly more, but just the same, there was the distinct sense that Peter and he were the only living souls in the place.

Dan kept thinking of what Peter had told him that morning, of the bodies as repositories for teeth, grimaces, smiles, lying there waiting, hiding, some calling, chattering in darkness, wanting any kind of life, others dreading such attention.

It was absurd, foolish, but Rookwood Necropolis was barely ten kilometers away, 285 hectares of one of the largest dedicated cemeteries in the world, site of nearly a million interments.

In his half-drowsing state, Dan kept thinking, too, of the old 1963 movie *Jason and the Argonauts*, of King Aeëtes collecting and sowing the teeth from the skull of the slain Hydra, raising up an army of skeletons to combat Jason and his crew. Dan imagined human teeth being first plucked and then sown in Rookwood's older, less tended fields. If the Hydra's teeth raised up *human* skeletons, what sort of creature would human teeth raise up?

He must have fallen asleep at last, for the next thing he knew Peter was rousing him.

"Doctor Dan?" Peter said, switching on Dan's bedside light.

"Peter? What is it?"

Peter was fully dressed, his hair and eyes wild. "He's got someone! Right now. He has someone!"

Dan grabbed his watch, saw that it was 12:16 A.M. "He told you this?"

"No. But I saw anyway. He's furious that I saw."

Dan climbed out of bed, began dressing. "The reciprocal thing?"

"It backfired, yes. Showed me more than he wanted. He's so angry, but he's enjoying it too! He's still enjoying it."

"The drama. The added excitement."

"Yes. We have to hurry!"

Dan reached for his mobile. "Where, Peter? I need to call Harry."

"Good. Yes. An old factory site in Somersby Road. A few streets back from the cemetery. But I need to be there. I have to be closer, Doctor Dan. Her life depends on it."

"Those women in the transcripts . . . ?"

"Never woke up. None of them."

"Understood."

Harry answered his mobile before Dan's call went to voice mail. He sounded leaden from sleep until Dan explained what they had. "You'll be there before I will, Dan, but I'll have two units there. Four officers. Best I can do for now. Where are you?"

"Still at the hospital. Heading out to the car. We'll need an ambulance too, Harry. The Somersby Road corner closest to the cemetery. Tell them to wait for us. No sirens."

"Right. You're sure about this, Dan?"

"Peter is."

"I'm on my way!"

"Harry, Peter stays out of it. How do we cover ourselves?"

"Anonymous tip. A neighbor heard screaming. I'll have a word with whoever turns up. Go!"

Two patrol cars and an ambulance were waiting at the corner of Somersby Road, lights off, ready. There was no sign of Harry's car yet.

"You Dr. Truswell?" an officer asked, appearing at Dan's driver-side window when he pulled up.

"Yes. Look—"

"Harry explained. I'm Senior Constable Banners. Warwick Banners. Just tell us where to go."

"It's there!" Peter said, pointing. "That building there!"

"Right. Follow us in but stay well back, hear?"

"We hear you," Dan said, and turned to Peter. "You have to stay in the car, okay?"

"I know," Peter said. "And keep the doors locked."

Dan joined the police officers and paramedics waiting at the curb. It took them seconds to reach the building two doors down, a large brick factory-front with closed and locked roller-doors and smaller street door. The premises looked so quiet and innocent in the night, and not for the first time Dan wondered if Peter could be mistaken.

There was a single crash as the street door was forced. In moments they were in off the street, standing in utter quiet, in darkness lit by the beams of five torches.

Again it was all so ordinary, so commonplace. But Dan knew only too well how such places could be terrifying in their simplicity. He had seen the Piggyback Killer's rooms in Newtown, such a mundane blend of walls, hallways, and furniture until you opened that one door, found the two coffins. He had seen Corinne Kester's balcony view and the shed with its treacherous windows, had seen Peter Rait's own room come alive in a wholly unexpected way right there at Blackwater. Such simple, terrifying places.

This, too, was such an ordinary, extraordinary space. Who knew what it had been originally: a warehouse, a meatpacking plant, some other kind of factory, but taking up the entire ground floor, large and low-ceilinged, with painted-out windows and a large, windowless inner section that took up most of the back half of the premises. Given the absence of screams being reported in the neighborhood, it was very likely double brick or soundproofed in some other way.

Dan followed the police and paramedics as they pushed through the double doors into that inner precinct. At first, it seemed totally dark. Then Dan saw that intervening pillars concealed an area off to the left lit by a dim yellow bulb. The police deployed immediately, guns ready, and crossed to it. There was no one there, just signs of where the occupant had been: a table and chair, a cupboard, a modest camp bed with tangled bedclothes, a hot plate and bar fridge to one side where it all stretched off into darkness again.

Deliberate darkness. Darkness as controlled theatrical flourish, prelude to shocking revelations, precisely calculated anguish and despair.

The police led the way around more pillars. The stark white light of their torches soon found the old dentistry chair near the back wall, securely bolted to the floor, revealed the victim strapped down, alive but barely conscious, gurgling through a ruined mouth filled with her own blood.

The paramedics rushed to her aid, began working by torchlight as best they could.

Dan made himself look away, forced himself to look at what else there was in the shifting torchlight that *wasn't* this poor woman, gurgling, groaning, and sobbing. He noted the straps for securing the chair's occupant, the elaborate padded clamp for holding the head, the metal tables and dental tools, other tools that had no place in dental work, the stains on the floor, dark and rusty-looking. The air smelled of disinfectant, urine, and blood and something else, something sour.

An officer finally located a light switch. A single spot came on overhead, illuminating the chair and the woman, showing her ruined face and more: an array of mirrors on adjustable stands, video and audio equipment, shelves with old-style video and audio tapes, newer-style DVDs.

Souvenirs. An archive.

Dan scanned the row of audio tapes; the first were dated from the sixties.

Peter Rait's voices.

But all so mundane in a worrying sense. Though terrible to say, these were the workaday trappings of sociopaths and psychopaths the world over, how they, too, made mundane lives for themselves out of their horrific acts.

But there was a large heavy door beyond the woman in the chair, like a rusted walk-in freezer door with a sturdy latch. Dan focused his attention on it as soon as the torch beams revealed the pitted metal surface. An exit? A hideaway? Another inner sanctum in this hellish place?

An officer approached the door, weapon ready, and pulled it back.

It was a storeroom, a small square room empty but for a large chalk-white post nearly two meters tall. The post was as round as three dinner plates, set in concrete or freestanding, it was hard to tell, but standing like a bollard, one of those removable traffic posts used to stop illegal parking, though larger, much larger, and set all over with encrustations.

Not just any encrustations, Dan knew. Sets of teeth in false mouths, fitted at different heights, randomly but carefully, lovingly, set into the white plaster, fiberglass, concrete, whatever it was. Dentures made from real teeth, corpse teeth, teeth taken post- and ante-mortem, some of them, all of them spring-loaded and deadly!

A trophy post.

This was where Toother kept his terrible collection, displayed it for his pleasure—and, yes, for the calculated and utter terror of others.

A door slammed somewhere in the building.

The police reacted at once. The officer holding the storeroom door let it go. It was on a counterweight and closed with a resounding boom. Another shouted orders. One hurried back to secure the main entrance. The rest rushed to search the outer premises, to find other exits and locate their quarry. Footsteps echoed in the empty space.

It all happened so quickly. Dan stood listening, hoping, trusting that Peter was still out in the car, safe.

Movement close by caught his attention, brought him back. The paramedics had the woman on their gurney at last. The awful gurgling had stopped and they were now wheeling her away.

For a terrible moment, Dan was left alone with the chair under its single spot, with the tables and instruments, the archive shelves and heavy metal door, now mercifully closed.

Then there were cries off in the darkness, sounds of running, more shouting. Two gunshots echoed in the night.

Then, in seconds, minutes, however long it was, Harry was there, two officers with him.

"We got him, Dan."

"Harry. What? What's that?"

"We got him. Toother. He's dead."

"Dead?" Peter was there too, appearing out of the darkness. "You did? You really got him?"

"We did, Peter," Harry said. "He was running out when we arrived. Officer Burns and me. He was armed and wouldn't stop. Colin here had to shoot."

Dan placed a hand on Peter's arm. "No more voices?"

"No," Peter said. "No voices at all now."

"We got him, Peter," Harry said.

But Peter frowned, gave an odd, puzzled look as if hearing something, then crossed to the heavy door and pulled it back. "Harry, I don't think we did. Not this time. Not yet."

The storeroom was empty, of course.

LISA TUTTLE

Closet Dreams

Lisa Tuttle is the author of seven novels—most recently The Silver Bough—
and five short story collections, two of which, My Pathology *and* Ghosts and
Other Lovers, *are available as e-books. She has also written nonfiction, including* Encyclopedia of Feminism *and* Writing Fantasy and Science Fiction, *and more than a dozen books for younger readers. Born and raised in
Houston, Texas, she now lives on the west coast of Scotland with her family.*

"Closet Dreams" was first published in Postscripts #10, *Spring issue,
edited by Peter Crowther.*

—E. D.

Something terrible happened to me when I was a little girl.

I don't want to go into details. I had to do that far too often in the year after it happened, first telling the police everything I could remember in the
(vain) hope it would help them catch the monster, then talking for hours and
hours to all sorts of therapists, doctors, shrinks, and specialists brought in to help me.
Talking about it was supposed to help me understand what had happened, achieve
closure, and move on.

I just wanted to forget—I thought that's what "putting it behind me" meant—but
they said to do that, first I had to *remember*. I thought I did remember—in fact, I was
sure I did—but they wouldn't believe what I told them. They said it was a fantasy,
created to cover something I couldn't bear to admit. For my own good (and also to
help the police catch that monster) I had to remember the truth.

So I racked my brain and forced myself to relive my darkest memories, giving
them more and more specifics, suffering through every horrible moment a second,
third, and fourth time before belatedly realizing it wasn't the stuff the monster had
done to me that they could not believe. There was nothing at all impossible about a
single detail of my abduction, imprisonment, and abuse, not even the sick particu-
lars of what he called "playing." I had been an innocent; it was all new to me, but
they were adults, professionals who had dealt with too many victims. It came as no
surprise to them that there were monsters living among us, looking just like ordinary
men, but really the worst kind of sexual predator.

The only thing they did not believe in was my escape. It could not have happened the way I said. Surely I must see that?

But it had. When I understood what they were questioning, it made me first tear-
ful and then mad. I was not a liar. Impossible or not, it had happened, and my presence there, telling them about it, ought to be proof enough.

One of them—her name escapes me, but she was an older lady who always wore turtleneck sweaters or big scarves, and who reminded me a little of my granny with her high cheekbones, narrow blue eyes, and gentle voice—told me that she knew I wasn't lying. What I had described was my own experience of the escape, and true on those terms—but all the same, I was a big girl now and I could surely understand that it could not have happened that way in actuality. She said I could think of it like a dream. The dream was my experience, what happened inside my brain while I was asleep, but something else was happening at the same time. Maybe, if we worked with the details of my dream, we might get some clues as to what that was.

She asked me to tell her something about my dreams. I told her there was only one. Ever since I'd escaped I'd had a recurring nightmare, night after night, unlike any dream I'd ever had before, twice as real and ten times more horrible.

It went like this: I'd come awake, in darkness too intense for seeing, my body aching, wooden floor hard beneath my naked body, the smell of dust and ancient varnish in my nose, and my legs would jerk, a spasm of shock, before I returned to lying motionless again, eyes tightly shut, trying desperately, against all hope, to fall back into the safe oblivion of sleep. Sometimes it was only a matter of seconds before I woke again in my own bedroom, where the light was always left on for just such moments, but sometimes I would seemingly remain in that prison for hours before I could wake. Nothing ever happened; I never saw him; there was just the closet, and that was bad enough. The true horror of the dream was that it didn't seem like a dream, and so turned reality inside-out, stripping my illusory freedom from me.

When I was much younger I'd made the discovery that I guess most kids make, that if you can only manage to scream out loud when you're dreaming—especially when you've started to realize that it *is* just a dream—you'll wake yourself up.

But I never tried that in the closet dream; I didn't dare. The monster had taught me not to scream. If I made any noise in the closet, any noise loud enough for him to hear from another room, he would tape my mouth shut and tie my hands together behind my back.

I knew I was his prisoner. Before he did that, it wouldn't have occurred to me that I still had *some* freedom.

So I didn't scream.

I guess the closet dream didn't offer much scope for analysis. She tried to get me to recall other dreams, but when I insisted I didn't have any, she didn't press. Instead, she told me that it wouldn't always be that way, and taught me some relaxation techniques that would make it easier to slip into an undisturbed sleep.

It wasn't only for my peace of mind that I kept having these sessions with psychiatrists. Anything I remembered might help the police.

Nobody but me knew what my abductor looked like. I'd done my best to describe him, but my descriptions, while detailed, were probably too personal, intimate, and distorted by fear. I had no idea how an outsider would see him; I rarely even saw him dressed. I didn't know what he did for a living or where he lived.

I was his prisoner for nearly four months, but I'd been unconscious when he took me into his house, and all I knew of it, all I was ever allowed to see, was one bedroom, bathroom, and closet. Under careful questioning from the police, with help from an architect, a very vague and general picture emerged: it was a single-story house on a quiet residential street, in a neighborhood that probably dated back to the 1940s or even earlier. (Nobody had used bathroom tiles like that since the 1950s; the small size of the closet dated it, and so did the thickness of the internal doors.)

There were no houses like that in my parents' neighborhood, and all the newer sub-divisions in the city could be ruled out, but that still left a lot of ground. It was even possible, since I had no idea how long I'd been unconscious in the back of his van after he grabbed me, that the monster lived and worked in another town entirely.

I wanted to help them catch him, of course. So although I hated thinking about it, and wanted only to absorb myself back into my own life with my parents, friends, and school, I made myself return, in memory, to my prison and concentrated on de-tails, but what was most vivid to me—the smell of dusty varnish or the pictures I thought I could make out in the grain of the wood floor; a crack in the ceiling, or the low roaring surf sound made by the central air-conditioning at night—did not supply any useful clues to the police.

Five mornings a week the monster left the house and stayed away all day. He would let me out to use the bathroom before he left, and then lock me into the closet. He'd fixed a sliding bolt on the outside of the big, heavy closet door, and once the door was shut and he slid the bolt home, I was trapped. But that was not enough for him: he added a padlock, to which he carried the only key. As he told me, if he didn't come home to let me out, I would *die* inside that closet, of hunger and thirst, so I had better pray nothing happened to him, because if it did, no one would ever find me.

That padlock wasn't his last word in security, either. He also locked the bedroom door, and before he left the house I always heard an electronic bleeping sound I rec-ognized as being part of a security system. He had a burglar alarm, as well as locks on everything that could be secured shut.

All he left me with in the closet was a plastic bottle full of water, a blanket and a child's plastic potty that I couldn't bear to use. There was a light fixture in the ceiling, but he'd removed the lightbulb, and the switch was on the other side of the locked door. At first I thought his decision to deprive me of light was just more of his meaning-less cruelty, but later it occurred to me that it was just another example—like the pad-lock and the burglar alarm—of his overly cautious nature. He'd even removed the wooden hanging rod from the closet, presumably afraid that I might have been able to wrench it loose and use it as a weapon against him. I might have scratched him with a broken lightbulb; big deal. It wouldn't have incapacitated him, but it might have hurt, and he wouldn't risk even the tiniest of hurts. He wanted total control.

So, all those daylight hours when I was locked in the closet, I was in the dark ex-cept for the light that seeped in around the edges of the door; mainly from the ap-proximately three-quarters of an inch that was left between the bottom of the door and the floor. That was my window on the world. I thought it was larger than the gap beneath our doors at home; the police architect said it might have been because the carpet it had been cut to accommodate had been removed; alternatively, my captor might have replaced the original door because he didn't find it sturdy enough for the prison he had planned.

Whatever the reason, I was grateful that the gap was wide enough for me to look through. I would spend hours sometimes lying with my cheek flat against the floor peering sideways into the bedroom, not because it was interesting, but simply for the light and space that it offered in comparison to the tiny closet.

When I was in the closet, I could use my fingernails to scrape the dirt and varnish from the floorboards, or make pictures out of the shadows all around me; there was nothing else to look at except the dirty cream walls, and the most interesting thing there—the only thing that caught my eye and made me think—was a square outlined in silvery duct tape.

I knew what it was, because there was something very similar on one wall of my closet at home, and my parents had explained to me that it was only an access hatch, so a plumber could get at the bathroom plumbing, in case it ever needed to be fixed.

Once that had been explained, and I knew it wasn't the entrance to a secret passage or a hidden room, it became uninteresting to me. In the monster's closet, though, a plumbing access hatch took on a whole new glamour.

I thought it might be my way out. Even though I knew there was no window in the bathroom, and the only door connected it to the bedroom—it was at least an escape from the closet. I wasn't sure an adult could crawl through what looked like a square-foot opening, but I knew I could manage; I didn't care if I left a little skin behind.

I peeled off the strips of tape, got my fingers into the gap, and, with a little bit of effort, managed to pry out the square of painted Sheetrock. But I didn't uncover a way out. There were pipes revealed in a space between the walls, but that was all. There was no opening into the bathroom, no space for a creature larger than a mouse to squeeze into. And I probably don't need to say that I didn't find anything useful left behind by a forgetful plumber; no tools or playthings or stale snacks.

I wept with disappointment, and then I sealed it up again—carefully enough, I hoped, that the monster would never notice what I'd done. After that, for the next thirteen weeks or so, I never touched it.

But I looked at it often, that small square that so resembled a secret hatchway, a closed-off window, a hidden opening to somewhere else. There was so little else to look at in the closet, and my longing, my need, for escape was so strong that of course I was drawn back to it. For the first few days I kept my back to it, and flinched away even from the thought of it, because it had been such a letdown, but after a week or so I chose to forget what I knew about it, and pretended that it really *was* a way out of the closet, a secret that the monster didn't know.

My favorite thing to think about, and the only thing that could comfort me enough to let me fall asleep, was home. Going home again. Being safely back at home with my parents and my little brother and Puzzle the cat, surrounded by all my own familiar things in my bedroom. It wasn't like the relaxation techniques the psychiatrist suggested, thinking myself into a place I loved. That didn't work. Just thinking about my home could make me cry, and bring me more rigidly awake on the hard floor in the dark narrow closet, too aware of all that I had lost, and how impossibly far away it was now. I had to do something else, I had to create a little routine, almost like a magic spell, a mental exercise that let me relax enough to sleep.

What I did was, I pretended I had never before stripped away the tape and lifted out that square of Sheetrock in the wall. I was doing it for the first time. And this time, instead of pipes in a shallow cavity between two walls, I saw only darkness, a much deeper darkness than that which surrounded me in the closet, and which I knew was the opening to a tunnel.

It was kind of scary. I felt excited by the possibility of escape, but that dark entry into the unknown also frightened me. I didn't know where it went. Maybe it didn't go anywhere at all; maybe it would take me into even greater danger. But there was no real question about it; it looked like a way out, so of course I was going to take it.

I squeezed through the opening and crawled through darkness along a tunnel that ended abruptly in a blank wall. Only the wall was not entirely blank; when I ran my hands over it I could feel the faint outline of a square had been cut away—just like in the closet I'd escaped from, only at this end the tape was on the other side.

I gave it a good, hard punch and knocked out the piece of Sheetrock, and then I crawled through and found myself in another closet. Only this one was ordinary, familiar and friendly, with carpet comfy underfoot, clothes hanging down overhead, and when I grasped the smooth metal of the doorknob it turned easily in my hand and let me out into my own beloved bedroom.

After that, the fantasy could take different courses. Sometimes I rushed to find my parents. I might find them downstairs, awake and drinking coffee in the kitchen, or they might be asleep in their bed, and I'd crawl in beside them to be cuddled and comforted as they assured me there was nothing to fear, it was only a bad dream. At other times I just wandered around the house, rediscovering the ordinary domestic landscape, reclaiming it for my own, until finally I fell asleep.

My captivity continued, with little to distinguish one day from another until the time that I got sick. Then, the monster was so disgusted by me, or so fearful of contagion, that he hardly touched me for a couple of days; his abstinence was no sign of compassion. It didn't matter to him if I was vomiting, or shaking with feverish chills, I was locked in the closet and left to suffer alone as usual.

I tried to lose myself in my comfort-dream, but the fever made it difficult to concentrate on anything. Even in the well-rehearsed routine, I kept mentally losing my place, having to go back and start over again, continuously peeling the tape off the wall and prying out that square of Sheetrock, again and again, until finding it unexpectedly awkward to hold, I lost my grip and the thing came crashing down painfully on my foot.

It was only then, as I blinked away the reflexive tears and rubbed the soreness out of my foot, that I realized it had really happened: I wasn't just imagining it; in my feverish stupor I'd actually stood up, pulled off the tape, and opened a hole in the wall.

And it really *was* a hole this time.

I stared, dumbfounded, not at pipes in a shallow cavity, but into blackness.

My heart began to pound. Fearful that I was just seeing things, I bent over and stuck my head into it, flinching a little, expecting to meet resistance. But my head went in, and my chest and arms . . . I stretched forward and wriggled into the tunnel.

It was much lower than in my fantasy, not big enough to allow me to crawl. If I'd been a couple of years older or five pounds heavier I don't think I would have made it. Only because I was such a flat-chested, narrow-hipped, skinny little kid did I fit, and I had to wriggle and worm my way along like some legless creature.

I didn't care. I didn't think about getting stuck, and I didn't worry about the absolute, suffocating blackness stretching ahead. This was freedom. I kept my eyes shut and hauled myself forward on hands and elbows, pushing myself ahead with my toes. Somehow, I kept going, although the energy it took was immense, almost more than I possessed. I was drenched in sweat and gasping—the sound of my own breathing was like that of a monster in pursuit—but I didn't give up. I could not.

And then I came to the end, a blank wall. But that didn't worry me, because I'd already dreamed of this moment, and I knew what to do. I just had to knock out the bit of plasterboard. Nothing but tape held it in. One good punch would do it.

Only I was so weak from illness, from captivity, from the long, slow journey through the dark, that I doubted I had a good punch in me. But I couldn't give up now. I braced my legs on either side of the tunnel and pushed with all my might, pushed so hard I thought my lungs would burst. I battered it with my fists, and heard the feeble sound of my useless blows like hollow laughter. Finally, trembling with exhaustion, sweating rivers, I hauled back, gathered all the power I had left, and launched myself forward, using my head as a battering ram.

And that did it. On the other side of the wall the tape tore away, and as the square of Sheetrock fell out and into my bedroom closet, so did I.

I was home. I was really and truly home at last.

I wanted to go running and calling for my mother, but first I stopped to repair the wall, carefully fitting the square of Sheetrock back into place, and restoring the pieces of tape that had held it in, smoothing over the torn bits as best I could. It seemed important to do this, as if I might be drawn back along through the tunnel, back to that prison house, if I didn't seal up the exit.

By the time I finished that, I was exhausted. I walked out of the closet, tottered across the room to my bed, pulled back the sheet and lay down, naked as I was.

It was there, like that, my little brother found me a few hours later.

Even I knew my escape was impossible. At least, it could not have happened in the way I remembered. Just to be sure, my parents opened the plumbing access hatch in my closet, to prove that's all it was. There was no tunnel; no way in or out.

Yet I had come home.

My parents—and I guess the police, too—thought the monster had been frightened by my illness into believing I might die, and had brought me home. Maybe he'd picked the locks (we didn't have a burglar alarm), or maybe—because a small window in one of the upstairs bathrooms turned out to have been left unfastened— he'd carried me up a ladder and pushed me through. My "memory" was only a fevered, feverish dream.

Did it matter that I couldn't remember what really happened? My parents decided it did not, and that the excruciating regime of having to talk about my ordeal was only delaying my recovery, and they brought it to an end.

The years passed. I went to a new junior high, and then on to high school. I learned to drive. I started thinking about college. I didn't have a boyfriend, but it began to seem like a possibility. I'm not saying I forgot what had happened to me, but it was no longer fresh, it wasn't present, it belonged to the past, which became more and more blurred and distant as I struck out for adulthood and independence. The only thing that really bothered me, the real, continuing legacy of those few months when I'd been the monster's prisoner and plaything, were the dreams. Or, I should say, dream, because there was just the one, the closet dream.

Even after so many years, I did not have ordinary dreams. Night after night—and it was a rare night it did not happen—I fell asleep only to wake, suddenly, and find myself in that closet again. It was awful, but I kind of got used to it. You can get used to almost anything. So when it happened, I didn't panic, but tried practicing the relaxation techniques I'd been taught when I was younger, and eventually—sometimes it took just a few minutes, while other nights it seemed to take hours—I escaped back into sleep.

One Saturday, a few weeks before my seventeenth birthday, I happened to be in a part of town that was strange to me. I was looking for a summer job, and was on my way to a shopping mall I knew only by name, and somehow or other, because I wanted to avoid the freeways, I got a little lost. I saw a sign for a U-Tote-'Em and pulled into the parking lot to figure it out. Although I had an indexed map book, I must have been looking on the wrong page; after a few hot, sweaty minutes of frustration I threw it down and got out of the car, deciding to go into the store to ask directions and buy myself a drink to cool me down.

I had just taken a Dr Pepper out of the refrigerator cabinet when something made me look around. It was him. The monster was standing in the very next aisle, a loaf of white bread in one hand as he browsed a display of chips and dips.

My hands were colder than the bottle. My feet felt very far away from my head. I couldn't move, and I couldn't stop looking at him.

My attention made him look up. For a moment he just looked blank and kind of stupid, his lower lip thrust out and shining with saliva. Then his mouth snapped shut as he tensed up, and his eyes kind of bulged, and I knew that he'd recognized me, too.

I dropped the plastic bottle and ran. Somebody said something—I think it was the guy behind the counter—but I didn't stop. I didn't even pause, just hurled myself at the door and got out. I couldn't think about anything but escape; it never occurred to me that *he* might have had more to fear than I did, that I could have asked the guy behind the counter to call the police, or just dialed 911 myself on my cell. All that was too rational, and I was way too frightened to reason. The old animal brain, instinct, had taken over, and all I could think of was running away and hiding.

I was so out of my mind with fear that instead of going back to my car I turned in the other direction, ran around to the back of the store, then past the dry cleaner's next door, and hid myself, gasping for breath in the torrid afternoon heat, behind a Dumpster.

Still panting with terror, shaking so much I could barely control my movements, I fumbled inside my purse, searching for my phone. My hands were so cold I couldn't feel a thing; impatient, I sank into a squat and dumped the contents on the gritty cement surface, found the little silver gadget and snatched it up.

Then I hesitated. Maybe I shouldn't call 911; that was supposed to be for emergencies only, wasn't it? Years ago the police had given me a phone number to call if I ever remembered something more or learned something that might give them a handle on the monster's identity. That number was pinned to the bulletin board in the kitchen where I saw it every single day. It was engraved on my memory still, although I'd never used it, I knew exactly what numbers to press. But when I tried, my fingers were still so stiff and clumsy with fear that I kept messing up.

I stopped and concentrated on calming myself. Looking around the side of the Dumpster I could see a quiet, tree-lined residential street. It was an old neighborhood—you could tell that by the age of the trees, and the fact that it had sidewalks. I was gazing at this peaceful view, feeling my breath and pulse rate going back to normal, when I caught another glimpse of the monster.

Immediately I shrank back and held my breath, but he never looked up as he walked, hunched a little forward as he clutched a brown paper bag to his chest, eyes on the sidewalk in front of him. He never suspected my eyes were on him, and as I watched his jerky, shuffling progress—as if he wanted to run but didn't dare—I realized how much our encounter had rattled him. All at once I was calmer. He must know I would call the police, and he was trying to get away, to hide. That he was on foot told me he must live nearby; probably the clerk in the convenience store would recognize him as a local, and the police would not have far to look for him.

But that was only if he stayed put. What if he was planning to leave? He might hurry home, grab a few things, jump in the car, and lose himself in another city where he'd never be found.

I was filled with a righteous fury. I was not going to let him escape. He'd just passed out of sight when I decided to follow him.

I kept well back and off the sidewalk, darting in and out of the trees, keeping to the shade, not because I was afraid, but because I didn't want to alert him. I was determined to find out where he lived, to get his address and the license number of his car, and then I'd hand him over to the police.

After two blocks, he turned onto another street. I hung back, looking for the name of it, but the street sign was on the opposite corner where the lacy fronds of a mimosa tree hung down, obscuring it.

That didn't really matter. All I had to do was tell the police his house was two blocks off Montrose—was that the name? All at once I was uncertain of where I'd just been, the name of the thoroughfare the U-Tote-'Em was on, where I'd left my car. But I could find my way back and meet the police there, just as soon as I saw which house the monster went in to.

So I hurried after, suddenly fearful that he might give me the slip, and I was just in time to see him going up the front walk of a single-story, pink-brick house, digging into his pocket for the key to the shiny black front door.

I made no effort to hide now, stopping directly across the street in the open, beneath the burning sun. I looked across at the raised curbstone where the house number had been painted. But the paint had been laid down a long time ago and not renewed; black and white had together faded into the gray of the concrete, and I couldn't be sure after the first number—definitely a two—if the next three were sixes, or eights, or some combination.

As he slipped the key into the lock the monster suddenly turned his head and stared across the street. He was facing me, looking right at me, and yet I had the impression he didn't see me watching him, because he didn't look scared or worried anymore. In fact, he was smiling; a horrible, familiar smile that I knew all too well.

I raised the phone to summon the police, but my hand was empty. I grabbed for my purse, but it had gone, too. There was no canvas strap slung across my shoulder. As I groped for it, my fingers felt only skin: my own naked flesh. Where were my clothes? How could I have come out without getting dressed?

The smells of dust and ancient varnish and my own sour sweat filled my nose and I began to tremble as I heard the sound of his key in the lock and woke from the dream that was my only freedom, and remembered.

Something terrible happened to me when I was a little girl.

It's still happening.

KIJ JOHNSON

The Evolution of Trickster Stories Among the Dogs of North Park After the Change

Kij Johnson, whose story "At the Mouth of the River of Bees" (SCI FIC-TION) was reprinted in the seventeenth volume of this series, gives us another kind of dog story in "The Evolution of Trickster Stories Among the Dogs of North Park After the Change," originally published in Ellen Datlow and Terri Windling's anthology The Coyote Road. *Johnson is an author, editor, and publishing production manager. Her stories have appeared in* Analog, Asimov's, Duelist Magazine, The Magazine of Fantasy & Science Fiction, *and* Realms of Fantasy, *and have won the Sturgeon and Crawford Awards. Since 1994, she has assisted at the Writer's Workshop for Science Fiction, hosted by the Center for the Study of Science Fiction at the University of Kansas. She divides her time between the Midwest and the West Coast.*

—K. L. & G. G.

North Park is a backwater tucked into a loop of the Kaw River: pale dirt and baked grass, aging playground equipment, silver-leafed cottonwoods, underbrush: mosquitoes and gnats blackening the air at dusk. To the south is a busy street. Engine noise and the hissing of tires on pavement mean it's no retreat. By late afternoon the air smells of hot tar and summertime river bottoms. There are two entrances to North Park: the formal one, of silvered railroad ties framing an arch of sorts; and an accidental little gap in the fence, back where Second Street dead ends into the park's west side, just by the river.

A few stray dogs have always lived here, too clever or shy or easily hidden to be caught and taken to the shelter. On nice days (and this is a nice day, a smell like boiling sweet corn easing in on the south wind to blunt the sharper scents), Linna sits at one of the faded picnic tables with a reading assignment from her summer class and a paper bag full of old fast food, the remains of her lunch. She waits to see who visits her.

The squirrels come first, and she ignores them. At last she sees the little dust-colored dog, the one she calls Gold.

"What'd you bring?" he says. His voice, like all dogs' voices, is hoarse and rasping.

He has trouble making certain sounds. Linna understands him the way one understands a bad lisp or someone speaking with a harelip.

(It's a universal fantasy, isn't it?—that the animals learn to speak, and at last we learn what they're thinking, our cats and dogs and horses: a new era in cross-species understanding. But nothing ever works out quite as we imagine. When the Change happened, it affected all the mammals we have shaped to meet our own needs. They all could talk a little, and they all could frame their thoughts well enough to talk. Cattle, horses, goats, llamas; rats, too. Pigs. Minks. And dogs and cats. And we found that, really, we prefer our slaves mute.

(The cats mostly leave, even ones who love their owners. Their pragmatic sociopathy makes us uncomfortable, and we bore them; and they leave. They slip out between our legs and lope into summer dusks. We hear them at night, fighting as they sort out ranges, mates, boundaries. The savage sounds frighten us, a fear that does not ease when our cat Klio returns home for a single night, asking to be fed and to sleep on the bed. A lot of cats die in fights or under car wheels, but they seem to prefer that to living under our roofs; and as I said, we fear them.

(Some dogs run away. Others are thrown out by the owners who loved them. Some were always free.)

"Chicken and French fries," Linna tells the dog, Gold. Linna has a summer cold that ruins her appetite, and in any case it's too hot to eat. She brought her lunch leftovers, hours-old but still lukewarm: half of a Chik-fil-A and some French fries. He never takes anything from her hand, so she tosses the food onto the ground just beyond kicking range. Gold likes French fries, so he eats them first.

Linna tips her head toward the two dogs she sees peeking from the bushes. (She knows better than to lift her hand suddenly, even to point or wave.) "Who are these two?"

"Hope and Maggie."

"Hi, Hope," Linna says. "Hi, Maggie." The dogs dip their heads nervously as if bowing. They don't meet her eyes. She recognizes their expressions, the hurt wariness: she's seen it a few times, on the recent strays of North Park, the ones whose owners threw them out after the Change. There are five North Park dogs she's seen so far: these two are new.

"Story," says the collie, Hope.

2. One Dog Loses Her Collar.

This is the same dog. She lives in a little room with her master. She has a collar that itches, so she claws at it. When her master comes home, he ties a leash to the collar and takes her outside to the sidewalk. There's a busy street outside. The dog wants to play on the street with the cars, which smell strong and move very fast. When her master tries to take her back inside, she sits down and won't move. He pulls on the leash and her collar slips over her ears and falls to the ground. When she sees this, she runs into the street. She gets hit by a car and dies.

This is not the first story Linna has heard the dogs tell. The first one was about a dog who's been inside all day and rushes outside with his master to urinate against a tree. When he's done, his master hits him, because his master was standing too close and his shoe is covered with urine. *One Dog Pisses on a Person.* The dog in the story has no name, but the dogs all call him (or her: she changes sex with each telling) One Dog. Each story starts: "This is the same dog."

The little dust-colored dog, Gold, is the storyteller. As the sky dims and the mosquitoes swarm, the strays of North Park ease from the underbrush and sit or lie belly-down in the dirt to listen to Gold. Linna listens, as well.

(Perhaps the dogs always told these stories and we could not understand them. Now they tell their stories here in North Park, as does the pack in Cruz Park a little to the south, and so across the world. The tales are not all the same, though there are similarities. There is no possibility of gathering them all. The dogs do not welcome eager anthropologists with their tape recorders and their agendas.

(The cats after the Change tell stories as well, but no one will ever know what they are.)

When the story is done, and the last of the French fries eaten, Linna asks Hope, "Why are you here?" The collie turns her face away, and it is Maggie, the little Jack Russell, who answers: "Our mother made us leave. She has a baby." Maggie's tone is matter-of-fact: it is Hope who mourns for the woman and child she loved, who compulsively licks her paw as if she were dirty and cannot be cleaned.

Linna knows this story. She's heard it from the other new strays of North Park: all but Gold, who has been feral all his life.

(Sometimes we think we want to know what our dogs think. We don't, not really. Someone who watches us with unclouded eyes and sees who we really are is more frightening than a man with a gun. We can fight or flee or avoid the man, but the truth sticks like pine sap. After the Change, some dog owners feel a cold place in the pit of their stomachs when they meet their pets' eyes. Sooner or later, they ask their dogs to find new homes, or they forget to latch the gate, or they force the dogs out with the ends of brooms and curses. Or the dogs leave, unable to bear the look in their masters' eyes.

(The dogs gather in parks and gardens, anywhere close to food and water where they can stay out of people's way. Cruz Park ten blocks away is big, fifteen acres in the middle of town, and sixty or more dogs already have gathered there. They raid trash or beg from their former owners or strangers. They sleep under the bushes and bandstand and the inexpensive civic sculptures. No one goes to Cruz Park on their lunch breaks anymore.

(In contrast North Park is a little dead end. No one ever did go there, and so no one really worries much about the dogs there. Not yet.)

3. One Dog Tries to Mate.

This is the same dog. There is a female he very much wants to mate with. All the other dogs want to mate with her, too, but her master keeps her in a yard surrounded by a chain-link fence. She whines and rubs against the fence. All the dogs try to dig under the fence, but its base is buried too deep to find. They try to jump over, but it is too tall for even the biggest or most agile dogs.

One Dog has an idea. He finds a cigarette butt on the street and tucks it in his mouth. He finds a shirt in a Dumpster and pulls it on. He walks right up to the master's front door and presses the bell-button. When the master answers the door, One Dog says, "I'm from the men with white trucks. I have to check your electrical statico-pressure. Can you let me into your yard?"

The man nods and lets him go in back. One Dog takes off his shirt and drops the cigarette and mates with the female. It feels very nice, but when he is done and they are still linked together, he starts to whine.

The man hears and comes out. He's very angry. He shoots One Dog and kills him.

The female tells One Dog, "You would have been better off if you had found another female."

The next day after classes (hot again, and heavy with the smell of cut grass), Linna finds a dog. She hears crying and crouches to peek under a hydrangea, its blue-gray flowers as fragile as paper. It's a Maltese with filthy fur matted with twigs and burrs. There are stains under her eyes and she is moaning, the terrible sound of an injured animal.

The Maltese comes nervous to Linna's outstretched fingers and the murmur of her voice. "I won't hurt you," Linna says. "It's okay."

Linna picks the dog up carefully, feeling the dog flinch under her hand as she checks for injuries. Linna knows already that the pain is not physical; she knows the dog's story before she hears it.

The house nearby is massive, a graceful collection of Edwardian gingerbread and oriel windows and dark green roof tiles. The garden is large, with a low fence just tall enough to keep a Maltese in. Or out. A woman answers the doorbell: Linna can feel the Maltese vibrate in her arms at the sight of the woman: excitement, not fear.

"Is this your dog?" Linna asks with a smile. "I found her outside, scared."

The woman's eyes flicker to the dog and away, back to Linna's face. "We don't have a dog," she says.

(We like our slaves mute. We like to imagine they love us, and they do. But they are also with us because freedom and security war in each of us, and sometimes security wins out. They do love us. But.)

In those words Linna has already seen how this conversation will go, the denials and the tangled fear and anguish and self-loathing of the woman. Linna turns away in the middle of the woman's words and walks down the stairs, the brick walkway, through the gate and north, toward North Park.

The dog's name is Sophie. The other dogs are kind to her.

(When George Washington died, his will promised freedom for his slaves, but only after his wife had also passed on. A terrified Martha freed them within hours of his death. Though the dogs love us, thoughtful owners can't help but wonder what they think when they sit on the floor beside our beds as we sleep, teeth slightly bared as they pant in the heat. Do the dogs realize that their freedom hangs by the thread of our lives? The curse of speech, the things they could say and yet choose not to say, makes that thread seem very thin.

(Some people keep their dogs, even after the Change. Some people have the strength to love, no matter what. But many of us only learn the limits of our love when they have been breached. Some people keep their dogs; many do not.

(The dogs who stay seem to tell no stories.)

4. One Dog Catches Possums.

This is the same dog. She is very hungry because her master forgot to feed her, and there's no good trash because the possums have eaten it all. "If I catch the possums," she says, "I can eat them now and then the trash later, because then they won't be getting it all."

She knows that possums are very hard to catch, so she lies down next to a trash bin and starts moaning. Sure enough, when the possums come to eat trash, they hear her and waddle over.

"Oh, oh oh," moans the dog. "I told the rats a great secret and now they won't let me rest."

·The possums look around but they don't see any rats. "Where are they?" the oldest possum asks.

One Dog says, "Everything I eat ends up in a place inside me like a giant garbage heap. I told the rats and they snuck in, and they've been there ever since." And she let out a great howl. "Their cold feet are horrible!"

The possums think for a time and then the oldest says, "This garbage heap, is it large?"

"Huge," One Dog says.

"Are the rats fierce?" says the youngest.

"Not at all," One Dog tells the possums. "If they weren't inside me, they wouldn't be any trouble, even for a possum. Ow! I can feel one dragging bits of bacon around."

After whispering among themselves for a time, the possums say, "We can go in and chase out the rats, but you must promise not to hunt us ever again."

"If you catch any rats, I'll never eat another possum," she promises.

One by one the possums crawl into her mouth. She eats all but the oldest, because she's too full to eat any more.

"This is much better than dog food or trash," she says.

(Dogs love us. We have bred them to do this for ten thousand, a hundred thousand, a million years. It's hard to make a dog hate people, though we have at times tried, with our junkyard guards and our attack dogs.

(It's hard to make dogs hate people, but it is possible.)

Another day, just at dusk, the sky an indescribable violet. Linna has a hard time telling how many dogs there are now: ten or twelve, perhaps. The dogs around her snuffle, yip, bark. One moans, the sound of a sled dog trying to howl. Words float up: *dry, bite, food, piss.*

The sled dog continues its moaning howl, and one by one the others join in with drawn-out barks and moans. They are trying to howl as a pack, but none of them know how to do this, nor what it is supposed to sound like. It's a wolf secret, and they do not know any of those.

Sitting on a picnic table, Linna closes her eyes to listen. The dogs outyell the trees' restless whispers, the river's wet sliding, even the hissing roaring street. Ten dogs, or fifteen. Or more: Linna can't tell, because they are all around her now, in the brush, down by the Kaw's muddy bank, behind the cottonwoods, beside the tall fence that separates the park from the street.

The misformed howl, the hint of killing animals gathered to work efficiently together—it awakens a monkey-place somewhere in her corpus callosum, or even deeper, stained into her genes. Adrenaline hits hot as panic. Her heart beats so hard that it feels as though she's torn it. Her monkey-self opens her eyes to watch the dogs through pupils constricted enough to dim the twilight; it clasps her arms tight over her soft belly to protect the intestines and liver that are the first parts eaten; it tucks her head between her shoulders to protect her neck and throat. She pants through bared teeth, fighting a keening noise.

Several of the dogs don't even try to howl. Gold is one of them. (The howling would have defined them before the poisoned gift of speech; but the dogs have words now. They will never be free of stories, though their stories may free them. Gold may understand this.

(They were wolves once, ten thousand, twenty thousand, a hundred thousand years ago. Or more. And before we were men and women, we were monkeys and fair game for them. After a time we grew taller and stronger and smarter: human, eventually. We learned about fire and weapons. If you can tame it, a wolf is an effective weapon, a useful tool. If you can keep it. We learned how to keep wolves close.

(But we were monkeys first, and they were wolves. Blood doesn't forget.)

After a thousand heartbeats fast as birds', long after the howl has decayed into snuffling and play-barks and speech, Linna eases back into her forebrain. Alive and safe. But not untouched. Gold tells a tale.

5. One Dog Tries to Become Like Men.

This is the same dog. There is a party, and people are eating and drinking and using their clever fingers to do things. The dog wants to do everything they do, so he says, "Look, I'm human," and he starts barking and dancing about.

The people say, "You're not human. You're just a dog pretending. If you wanted to be human, you have to be bare, with just a little hair here and there."

One Dog goes off and bites his hairs out and rubs the places he can't reach against the sidewalk until there are bloody patches where he scraped off his skin, as well.

He returns to the people and says, "Now I am human," and he shows his bare skin.

"That's not human," the people say. "We stand on our hind legs and sleep on our backs. First you must do these things."

One Dog goes off and practices standing on his hind legs until he no longer cries out loud when he does it. He leans against a wall to sleep on his back, but it hurts and he does not sleep much. He returns and says, "Now I am human," and he walks on his hind legs from place to place.

"That's not human," the people say. "Look at these, we have fingers. First you must have fingers."

One Dog goes off and he bites at his front paws until his toes are separated. They bleed and hurt and do not work well, but he returns and says, "Now I am human," and he tries to take food from a plate.

"That's not human," say the people. "First you must dream, as we do."

"What do you dream of?" the dog asks.

"Work and failure and shame and fear," the people say.

"I will try," the dog says. He rolls onto his back and sleeps. Soon he is crying out loud and his bloody paws beat at the air. He is dreaming of all they told him.

"That dog is making too much noise," the people say and they kill him.

Linna calls the Humane Society the next day, though she feels like a traitor to the dogs for doing this. The sky is sullen with the promise of rainstorms, and even though she knows that rain is not such a big problem in the life of a dog, she worries a little, remembering her own dog when she was a little girl, who had been terrified of thunder.

So she calls. The phone rings fourteen times before someone picks it up. Linna tells the woman about the dogs of North Park. "Is there anything we can do?"

The woman barks a single unamused laugh. "I wish. People keep bringing them— been doing that since right after the Change. We're packed to the rafters—and they *keep* bringing them in, or just dumping them in the parking lot, too chickenshit to come in and tell anyone."

"So—" Linna begins, but she has no idea what to ask. She can see the scene in her mind, a hundred or more terrified angry confused grieving hungry thirsty dogs. At least the dogs of North Park have some food and water, and the shelter of the underbrush at night.

The woman has continued! "—they can't take care of themselves—"

"Do you know that?" Linna asks, but the woman talks on.

"—and we don't have the resources—"

"So what do you do?" Linna interrupts. "Put them to sleep?"

"If we have to," the woman says, and her voice is so weary that Linna wants suddenly to comfort her. "They're in the runs, four and five in each one because we don't have anywhere to put them, and we can't get them outside because the paddocks are full; it smells like you wouldn't believe. And they tell these stories—"

"What's going to happen to them?" Linna means all the dogs, now that they have speech, now that they are equals.

"Oh, hon, I don't know." The woman's voice trembles. "But I know we can't save them all."

(Why do we fear them when they learn speech? They are still dogs, still subordinate. It doesn't change who they are or their loyalty.

(It is not always fear we run from. Sometimes it is shame.)

6. One Dog Invents Death.

This is the same dog. She lives in a nice house with people. They do not let her run outside a fence and they did things to her so that she can't have puppies, but they feed her well and are kind, and they rub places on her back that she can't reach.

At this time, there is no death for dogs, they live forever. After a while, One Dog becomes bored with her fence and her food and even the people's pats. But she can't convince the people to allow her outside the fence.

"There should be death," she decides. "Then there will be no need for boredom."

(How do the dogs know things? How do they frame an abstract like *thank you* or a collective concept like *chicken*? Since the Change, everyone has been asking that question. If awareness is dependent on linguistics, an answer is that the dogs have learned to use words, so the words themselves are the frame they use. But it is still *our* frame, *our* language. They are still not free.

(Any more than we are.)

It is a moonless night, and the hot wet air blurs the streetlights so that they illuminate nothing except their own glass globes. Linna is there, though it is very late. She no longer attends her classes and has switched to the dogs' schedule, sleeping the afternoons away in the safety of her apartment. She cannot bring herself to sleep in the dogs' presence. In the park, she is taut as a strung wire, a single monkey among wolves; but she returns each dusk, and listens, and sometimes speaks. There are maybe fifteen dogs now, though she's sure more hide in the bushes, or doze, or prowl for food.

"I remember," a voice says hesitantly. (*Remember* is a frame; they did not "remember" before the word, only lived in a series of nows longer or shorter in duration. Memory breeds resentment. Or so we fear.) "I had a home, food, a warm place, something I chewed—a, a blanket. A woman and a man and she gave me all these things, patted me." Voices in assent: pats remembered. "But she wasn't always nice. She yelled sometimes. She took the blanket away. And she'd drag at my collar until it hurt sometimes. But when she made food she'd put a piece on the floor for me to eat. Beef, it was. That was nice again."

Another voice in the darkness: "Beef. That is a hamburger." The dogs are trying out the concept of *beef* and the concept of *hamburger* and they are connecting them.

"*Nice* is not being hurt," a dog says.

"Not nice is collars and leashes."

"And rules."

"Being inside and only coming out to shit and piss."

"People are nice and not nice," says the first voice. Linna finally sees that it belongs to a small dusty black dog sitting near the roots of an immense oak. Its enormous fringed ears look like radar dishes. "I learned to think and the woman brought me here. She was sad, but she hit me with stones until I ran away, and then she left. A person is nice and not nice."

The dogs are silent, digesting this. "Linna?" Hope says. "How can people be nice and then not nice?"

"I don't know," she says, because she knows the real question is, *How can they stop loving us?*

(The answer even Linna has trouble seeing is that *nice* and *not nice* have nothing to do with love. And even loving someone doesn't always mean you can share your house and the fine thread of your life, or sleep safely in the same place.)

7. One Dog Tricks the White-Truck Man.

This is the same dog. He is very hungry and looking through the alleys for something to eat. He sees a man with a white truck coming toward him. One Dog knows that the white-truck men catch dogs sometimes, so he's afraid. He drags some old bones out of the trash and heaps them up and settles on top of them. He pretends not to see the white-truck man but says loudly, "Boy, that was a delicious man I just killed, but I'm still starved. I hope I can catch another one."

Well, that white-truck man runs right away. But someone was watching all this from her kitchen window and she runs out to the man and tells him, "One Dog never killed a man! That's just a pile of bones from my barbecue last week, and he's making a mess out of my backyard. Come catch him."

The white-truck man and the person run back to where One Dog is still gnawing on one of the bones in his pile. He sees them and guesses what has happened, so he's afraid. But he pretends not to see them and says loudly, "I'm still starved! I hope that human comes back soon with that white-truck man I asked her to get for me."

The white-truck man and the woman both run away, and he does not see them again that day.

"Why is she here?"

It's one of the new dogs, a lean Lab-cross with a limp. He doesn't talk to her but to Gold, but Linna sees his anger in his liquid-brown eyes, feels it like a hot scent rising from his back. He's one of the half strays, an outdoor dog who lived on a chain. It was no effort at all for his owner to unhook the chain and let him go; no effort for the Lab-cross to leave his owner's yard and drift across town killing cats and raiding trash cans, and end up in North Park.

There are thirty dogs now and maybe more. The newcomers are warier around her than the earlier dogs. Some, the ones who have taken several days to end up here, dodging police cruisers and pedestrians' Mace, are actively hostile.

"She's no threat," Gold says.

The Lab-cross says nothing but approaches with head lowered and hackles raised. Linna sits on the picnic table's bench and tries not to screech, to bare her teeth and scratch and run. The situation is as charged as the air before a thunderstorm. Gold is no longer the pack's leader—there's a German shepherd dog who holds his tail higher—but he still has status as the one who tells the stories. The German shepherd doesn't care whether Linna's there or not; he won't stop another dog from attacking if it wishes. Linna spends much of her time with her hands flexed to bare claws she doesn't have.

"She listens, that's all," says Hope: frightened Hope standing up for her. "And brings food sometimes." Others speak up: *she got rid of my collar when it got burrs under it. She took the tick off me. She stroked my head.*

The Lab-cross's breath on her ankles is hot, his nose wet and surprisingly warm. Dogs were once wolves; right now this burns in her mind. She tries not to shiver. "You're sick," the dog says at last.

"I'm well enough," Linna says.

Just like that the dog loses interest and turns back to the others.

(Why does Linna come here at all? Her parents had a dog when she was a little girl. Ruthie was so obviously grateful for Linna's love and the home she was offered, the old quilt on the floor, the dog food that fell from the sky twice a day like manna. Linna wondered even then whether Ruthie dreamed of a Holy Land, and what that place would have looked like. Linna's parents were kind and generous, denied Ruthie's needs only when they couldn't help it; paid for her medical bills without too much complaining; didn't put her to sleep until she became incontinent and messed on the living-room floor.

(Even we dog-lovers wrestle with our consciences. We promised to keep our pets forever until they died; but that was from a comfortable height, when we were the masters and they the slaves. Some Inuit tribes believe all animals have souls—except for dogs. This is a convenient stance. They could not use their dogs as they do—beat them, work them, starve them, eat them, feed them one to the other—if dogs were men's equals.

(Or perhaps they could. Our record with our own species is not so exemplary.)

8. One Dog and the Eating Man.

This is the same dog. She lives with the Eating Man, who eats only good things while One Dog has only dry kibble. The Eating Man is always hungry. He orders a pizza but he is still hungry, so he eats all the meat and vegetables he finds in the refrigerator. But he's still hungry, so he opens all the cupboards and eats the cereal and noodles and flour and sugar in there. And he's still hungry. There is nothing left, so he eats all One Dog's dry kibble, leaving nothing for One Dog.

So One Dog kills the Eating Man. "It was him or me," One Dog says. The Eating Man is the best thing One Dog has ever eaten.

Linna has been sleeping the days away so that she can be with the dogs at night, when they feel safest out on the streets looking for food. So now it's hot dusk, a day later, and she's just awakened in tangled sheets in a bedroom with flaking walls: the sky a hard haze, air warm and wet as laundry. Linna is walking past Cruz Park, on her way to North Park. She has a bag with a loaf of day-old bread, some cheap sandwich meat, and an extra order of French fries. The fatty smell of the fries sticks in her nostrils. Gold never gets them anymore, unless she saves them from the other dogs and gives them to him specially.

She thinks nothing of the blue and red and strobing white lights ahead of her on Mass street until she gets close enough to see that this is no traffic stop. There's no wrecked car, no distraught student who turned left across traffic because she was late for her job and was T-boned. Half a dozen police cars perch on the sidewalks around the park, and she can see reflected lights from others otherwise hidden by the park's shrubs. Fifteen or twenty policemen stand around in clumps, like dead leaves caught for a moment in an eddy and released according to some unseen current.

Everyone knows Cruz Park is full of dogs—sixty or seventy according to today's editorial in the local paper, each one a health and safety risk—but very few dogs are visible at the moment, and none look familiar to her, either as neighbors' ex-pets or wanderers from the North Park pack.

Linna approaches an eddy of policemen; its elements drift apart, rejoin other groups.

"Cruz Park is closed," the remaining officer says to Linna. He's a tall man with a military cut that makes him look older than he is.

It's no surprise that the flashing lights, the cars, the yellow CAUTION tape, and the policemen are about the dogs. There've been complaints from the people neighboring the park—overturned trash cans, feces on the sidewalks, even one attack when a man tried to grab a stray's collar and the stray fought to get away. Today's editorial merely crystallized what everyone already felt.

Linna thinks of Gold, Sophie, Hope. "They're just dogs."

The officer looks a little uncomfortable. "The park is closed until we can address current health and safety concerns." Linna can practically hear the quote marks from the official statement.

"What are you going to do?" she asks.

He relaxes a little. "Right now we're waiting for Animal Control. Any dogs they capture will go to Douglas County Humane Society, they'll try to track down the owners—"

"The ones who kicked the dogs out in the first place?" Linna asks. "No one's gonna want these dogs back, you know that."

"That's the procedure," he says, his back stiff again, tone harsh. "If the Humane—"

"Do you have a dog?" Linna interrupts him. "I mean, did you? Before this started?"

He turns and walks away without a word.

Linna runs the rest of the way to North Park, slowing to a lumbering trot when she gets a cramp in her side. There are no police cars up here, but yellow plastic police tape stretches across the entry: CAUTION. She walks around to the side entrance, the break in the fence off Second Street. The police don't seem to know about this place.

9. One Dog Meets Tame Dogs.

This is the same dog. He lives in a park, and eats at the restaurants across the street. On his way to the restaurants one day, he walks past a yard with two dogs. They laugh at her and say, "We get dog food every day and our master lets us sleep in the kitchen, which is cool in the summer and warm in the winter. And you have to cross Sixth Street to get food where you might get run over, and you have to sleep in the heat and the cold."

The dog walks past them to get to the restaurants, and he eats the fallen tacos and French fries and burgers around the Dumpster. When he sits by the restaurant doors, many people give him bits of food; one person gives him chicken in a paper dish. He walks back to the yard and lets the two dogs smell the chicken and grease on his breath through the fence. "Ha on you," he says, and then goes back to his park and sleeps on a pile of dry rubbish under the bridge, where the breeze is cool. When night comes, he goes looking for a mate and no one stops him.

(Whatever else it is, the Change of the animals—mute to speaking, dumb to dreaming—is a test for us. We pass the test when we accept that their dreams and desires and goals may not be ours. Many people fail this test. But we don't have to, and even failing we can try again. And again. And pass at last.

(A slave is trapped, choiceless and voiceless; but so is her owner. Those we have injured may forgive us, but how can we know? Can we trust them with our homes, our lives, our hearts? Animals did not forgive before the Change; mostly they forgot. But the Change brought memory, and memory requires forgiveness, and how can we trust them to forgive us?

(And how do we forgive ourselves? Mostly we don't. Mostly we pretend to forget, and hope it becomes true.)

At noon the next day, Linna jerks awake, monkey-self already dragging her to her feet. Even before she's fully awake, she knows that what woke her wasn't a car's backfire. It was a shotgun blast, and it was only a couple of blocks away, and she already knows why.

She drags on clothes and runs to Cruz Park, no stitch in her side this time. The flashing police cars and CAUTION tape and men are all still there, but now she sees dogs everywhere, twenty or more laid flat near the sidewalk, the way dogs sleep on hot summer days. Too many of the rib cages are still; too many of the eyes open, dust and pollen already gathering.

Linna has no words, can only watch speechless; but the men say enough. First thing in the morning, the Animal Control people went to Dillon's grocery store and bought fifty one-pound packages of cheap hamburger on sale, and they poisoned them all, and then scattered them around the park. Linna can see little blue styrene squares from the packaging scattered here and there, among the dogs.

The dying dogs don't say much. Most have fallen back on the ancient language of pain, wordless yelps and keening. Men walk among them, shooting the suffering dogs, jabbing poles into the underbrush looking for any who might have slipped away.

People come in cars and trucks and on bicycles and scooters and on their feet. The police officers around Cruz Park keep sending them away—"a health risk" says one officer: "safety," says another, but the people keep coming back, or new people.

Linna's eyes are blind with tears; she blinks and they slide down her face, oddly cool and thick.

"Killing them is the answer?" says a woman beside her. Her face is wet as well, but her voice is even, as if they are debating this in a class, she and Linna. The woman holds her baby in her arms, a white cloth thrown over its face so that it can't see. "I have three dogs at home, and they've never hurt anything. Words don't change that."

"What if they change?" Linna asks. "What if they ask for real food and a bed soft as yours, the chance to dream their own dreams?"

"I'll try to give it to them," the woman says, but her attention is focused on the park, the dogs. "They can't do this!"

"Try and stop them." Linna turns away tasting her tears. She should feel comforted by the woman's words, the fact that not everyone has forgotten how to love animals when they are no longer slaves, but she feels nothing. And she walks north, carved hollow.

10. One Dog Goes to the Place of Pieces.

This is the same dog. She is hit by a car and part of her flies off and runs into a dark culvert. She does not know what the piece is, so she chases it. The culvert is long and it gets so cold that her breath puffs out in front of her. When she gets to the end, there's no light and the world smells like cold metal. She walks along a road. Cold cars rush past but they don't slow down. None of them hit her.

One Dog comes to a parking lot that has nothing in it but the legs of dogs. The legs walk from place to place, but they cannot see or smell or eat. None of them are her legs, so she walks on. After this she finds a parking lot filled with the ears of dogs, and then one filled with the assholes of dogs, and the eyes of dogs and the bodies of dogs; but none of the ears and assholes and eyes and bodies are hers, so she walks on.

The last parking lot she comes to has nothing at all in it except for little smells, like puppies. She can tell one of the little smells is hers, so she calls to it and it comes to her. She doesn't know where the little smell belongs on her body, so she carries it in her mouth and walks back past the parking lots and through the culvert.

One Dog cannot leave the culvert because a man stands in the way. She puts the little smell down carefully and says, "I want to go back."

The man says, "You can't unless all your parts are where they belong."

One Dog can't think of where the little smell belongs. She picks up the little smell and tries to sneak past the man, but the man catches her and hits her. One Dog tries to hide it under a hamburger wrapper and pretend it's not there, but the man catches that, too.

One Dog thinks some more and finally says, "Where does the little smell belong?"

The man says, "Inside you."

So One Dog swallows the little smell. She realizes that the man has been trying to keep her from returning home but that the man cannot lie about the little smell. One Dog growls and runs past him, and returns to our world.

There are two police cars pulled onto the sidewalk before North Park's main entrance. Linna takes in the sight of them in three stages: first, she has seen police everywhere today, so they are no shock; second, they are *here*, at *her* park, threatening *her* dogs, and this is like being kicked in the stomach; and third, she thinks: *I have to get past them.*

North Park has two entrances, but one isn't used much. Linna walks down a side street and enters the park by the little narrow dirt path from Second Avenue. The police haven't remembered this one yet.

The park is never quiet. There's busy Sixth Street just south, and the river and its noises to the north and east and west; trees and bushes hissing with the hot wind; the hum of insects.

But the dogs are quiet. She's never seen them all in the daylight, but they're gathered now, silent and loll-tongued in the bright daylight. There are forty or more. Everyone is dirty, now. Any long fur is matted; anything white is dust-colored. Most of them are thinner than they were when they arrived. The dogs face one of the tables, as orderly as the audience at a string quartet; but the tension in the air is so obvious that Linna stops short.

Gold stands on the table. There are a couple of dogs she doesn't recognize in the dust nearby: flopped flat with their sides heaving, tongues long and flecked with white foam. One is hunched over; he drools onto the ground and retches helplessly.

The other dog has a scratch along her flank. The blood is the brightest thing Linna can see in the sunlight, a red so strong it hurts her eyes.

The Cruz Park cordon was permeable, of course. These two managed to slip past the police cars. The vomiting one is dying.

She realizes suddenly that every dog's muzzle is swiveled toward her. The air snaps with something that makes her back-brain bare its teeth and scream, her hackles rise. The monkey-self looks for escape, but the trees are not close enough to climb (and she is no climber), the road and river too far away. She is a spy in a gulag; the prisoners have little to lose by killing her.

"You shouldn't have come back," Gold says.

"I came to tell you—warn you." Even through her monkey-self's defiance, Linna weeps helplessly.

"We already know." The pack's leader, the German shepherd dog, says, "They're killing us all. We're leaving the park."

She shakes her head, fighting for breath. "They'll kill you. There are police cars on Sixth—they'll shoot you however you get out. They're *waiting.*"

"Will it be better here?" Gold asks. "They'll kill us anyway, with their poisoned meat. We *know.* You're afraid, all of you—"

"I'm not—" Linna starts, but he breaks in.

"We smell it on everyone, even the people who take care of us or feed us. We have to get out of here."

"They'll *kill* you," Linna says again.

"Some of us might make it."

"Wait! Maybe there's a way," Linna says, and then: "I have stories."

In the stifling air, Linna can hear the dogs pant, even over the street noises. "People have their own stories," Gold says at last. "Why should we listen to yours?"

"We made you into what we wanted; we *owned* you. Now you are becoming what *you* want. You belong to yourselves. But we have stories, too, and we learned from them. Will you listen?"

The air shifts, but whether it is the first movement of the still air or the shifting of the dogs, she can't tell.

"Tell your story," says the German shepherd.

Linna struggles to remember half-read textbooks from a sophomore course on folklore, framing her thoughts as she speaks them. "We used to tell a lot of stories about Coyote. The animals were here before humans were, and Coyote was one of them. He did a lot of stuff, got in a lot of trouble. Fooled everyone."

"I know about coyotes," a dog says. "There were some by where I used to live. They eat puppies sometimes."

"I bet they do," Linna says. "Coyotes eat everything. But this wasn't *a* coyote, it's *Coyote.* The one and only."

The dogs murmur. She hears them work it out: *coyote* is the same as *this is the same dog.*

"So. Coyote disguised himself as a female so that he could hang out with a bunch of females, just so he could mate with them. He pretended to be dead, and then when the crows came down to eat him, he snatched them up and ate every one! When a greedy man was keeping all the animals for himself, Coyote pretended to be a very rich person and then freed them all, so that everyone could eat. He—" She pauses to think, looks down at the dogs all around her. The monkey-fear is gone: she is the storyteller, the maker of thoughts. They will not kill her, she knows. "Coyote did all these things, and a lot more things. I bet you'll think of some, too.

"I have an idea of how to save you," she says. "Some of you might die, but some chance is better than no chance."

"Why would we trust you?" says the Lab-cross who has never liked her, but the other dogs are with her. She feels it, and answers.

"Because this trick, maybe it's even good enough for Coyote. Will you let me show you?"

We people are so proud of our intelligence, but that makes it easier to trick us. We see the white-truck men and we believe they're whatever we're expecting to see. Linna goes to U-Haul and rents a pickup truck for the afternoon. She digs out a white shirt she used to wear when she ushered at the concert hall. She knows *clipboard with printout* means *official responsibilities*, so she throws one on the dashboard of the truck.

She backs the pickup to the little entrance on Second Street. The dogs slip through the gap in the fence and scramble into the pickup's bed. She lifts the ones that are too small to jump so high. And then they arrange themselves carefully, flat on their sides. There's a certain amount of snapping and snarling as later dogs step on the ears and rib cages on the earlier dogs, but eventually everyone is settled, everyone able to breathe a little, every eye tight shut.

She pulls onto Sixth Street with a truck heaped with dogs. When the police stop her, she tells them a little story. Animal Control has too many calls these days: cattle loose on the highways, horses leaping fences that are too high and breaking their legs; and the dogs, the scores and scores of dogs at Cruz Park. Animal Control is renting trucks now, whatever they can find. The dogs of North Park were slated for poisoning this morning.

"I didn't hear about this in briefing," one of the policemen says. He pokes at the heap of dogs with a black club; they shift like dead meat. They reek; an inexperienced man might not recognize the stench as mingled dog-breath and shit.

Linna smiles, baring her teeth. "I'm on my way back to the shelter," she says. "They have an incinerator." She waves an open cell phone at him, and hopes he does not ask to talk to whoever's on the line, because there is no one.

But people believe stories, and then they make them real: the officer pokes at the dogs one more time and then wrinkles his nose and waves her on.

Clinton Lake is a vast place, trees and bushes and impenetrable brambles ringing a big lake, open country in every direction. When Linna unlatches the pickup's bed, the dogs drop stiffly to the ground, and stretch. Three died of overheating, stifled beneath the weight of so many others. Gold is one of them, but Linna does not cry. She knew she couldn't save them all, but she has saved some of them. That has to be enough. And the stories will continue: stories do not easily die.

The dogs can go wherever they wish from here, and they will. They and all the other dogs who have tricked or slipped or stumbled to safety will spread across the Midwest, the world. Some will find homes with men and women who treat them not as slaves but as friends, freeing themselves, as well. Linna herself returns home with little shivering Sophie and sad Hope.

Some will die, killed by men and cougars and cars and even other dogs. Others will raise litters. The fathers of some of those litters will be coyotes. Eventually the Changed dogs will find their place in the changed world.

(When we first fashioned animals to suit our needs, we treated them as if they were stories and we the authors, and we clung desperately to an imagined copyright that would permit us to change them, sell them, even delete them. But some stories cannot be controlled. Perhaps we started them, but they change and they are no longer ours—if they ever were. A wise author or dog owner listens, and learns, and says at last, "I never knew that.")

11. One Dog Creates the World.

This is the same dog. There wasn't any world when this happens, just a man and a dog. They lived in a house that didn't have any windows to look out of. Nothing had any smells. The dog shit and pissed on a paper in the bathroom, but not even this had a smell. Her food had no taste, either. The man suppressed all these things. This was because the man didn't want One Dog to create the universe and he knew it would be done by smell.

One night One Dog was sleeping and she felt the strangest thing that any dog has ever felt. It was the smells of the world pouring from her nose. When the smell of grass came out, there was grass outside. When the smell of shit came out, there was shit outside. She made the whole world that way. And when the smell of other dogs came out, there were dogs everywhere, big ones and little ones all over the world.

"I think I'm done," she said, and she left.

Honorable Mentions: 2007

Addison, Linda D., "Living Between the Blows" (poem), *Being Full of Light, Insubstantial*.
Adrian, Chris, "Promise Breaker," *Esquire*, December.
Akers, Tim, "Toke," *Interzone* 210.
Albrecht, Aaron, "Medicine Business," *All Hallows* 42.
Allen, Mike, "The Button Bin," *Helix*, Fall.
——, "The Hiker's Tale," *Cabinet des Fées* 2.
——, "The Hollow Sphere" (poem), *Lone Star Stories* 19.
Alten, Steve, "Lost in Time," *Out of the Gutter* 2.
Amundsen, Erik, "Summer of Smoke" (poem), *Jabberwocky* 3.
Anderson, Barth, "Clockmaker's Requiem," *Clarkesworld*, March.
Anderson, Sue, "The Ice Game," *Dark Horizons* 50.
Andrew, Jason, "The Dead Man's Hand," *Frontier Cthulhu*.
Armstrong, Kelley, "Twilight," *Many Bloody Returns*.
Arnett, Melinda, "Sometimes They Call Us the Werewolf," *Outer Darkness* 34.
Arnold, Joel, "October Blizzard," *Doorways* 4.
——, "The Starlite," *Dark Recesses Press* 7.
Arruin, A. M., "The Lullaby Stream" (poem), *On Spec*, Fall.
Asher, Neal, "Bioship," *The Solaris Book of New Science Fiction*.
Ashford, Jenny, "The Anatomy Lesson," *History Is Dead*.
Astruc, R. J., "The Perfume Eater," *Strange Horizons*, July 16.
Atkins, Peter, "Last of the Invisible Kings," *The Twilight Limited*.
——, "Stacy and Her Idiot," *Dark Delicacies II: Fear*.
Atkinson, Astrid, "Things with Sharp Teeth," *Ideomancer* Vol. 6, Issue 2.
Aton-Osias, Kate, "The River Stone Heart of Maria Dela Rosa," *Serendipity* 3.
Attanasio, A. A., "Fractal Freaks," *Horrors Beyond* 2.
Atwater-Rhodes, Amelia, "Empire of Dirt," *666: The Number of the Beast*.
Averbuch, Hagy, "Let's Come Together," *Zombies*.
Avery, Simon, "Bury the Carnival," *Black Static* 1.
Ayres, Neil, "The Listening," *Gratia Placenti*.
Bacigalupi, Paolo, "Softer," *Logorrhea*.
Baker, Linda P., "A Better Place," *Time Twisters*.
Barford, Duncan, "The Sofa," *Supernatural Tales* 12.
Barker, R. J., "The Dry Heat, the Dust, the Martinis, and the Insects," *In Bad Dreams*.
——, "Portrait of the Artist as a Good Host," *Whispers of Wickedness* 5.
Barras, Jamie, "Pale Saints and Dark Madonnas," *Black Static* 1.

Barron, Laird, "Procession of the Black Sloth" (novella), *The Imago Sequence*.

Barzak, Christopher, "Little Miss Apocalypse," *Realms of Fantasy*, August.

——, "Realer Than You," *The Coyote Road*.

——, "What We Know About the Lost Families of — House," *Interfictions*.

Bates, Paul L., "No Second Chance," *New Writings in the Fantastic*.

Battersby, Lee, "Father Muertes & the Joy of Warfare," *Aurealis* 37.

Batykefer, Erinn, "Egyptology" (poem), *Mid-American Review* Vol. XXVII, No. 2.

Baugh, Matthew, "Clown Fish," *High Seas Cthulhu*.

——, "Snake Oil," *Frontier Cthulhu*.

Baumer, Jennifer Rachel, "The Forgotten Tastes of Chocolate and Joy," *Jabberwocky* 3.

——, "Old People and Dogs: A Death in the Desert," *On Spec*, Spring.

Beagle, Peter S., "Barrens Dance," *Wizards*.

——, "We Never Talk About My Brother," *Orson Scott Card's Intergalactic Medicine Show*.

Beal, Anthony, "And Death Rode with Him," *Whispers in the Night*.

Bear, Elizabeth, "Cryptic Coloration," *Baen's Universe*, June.

——, "Inelastic Collisions," *Inferno*.

——, "Limerent," *Subterranean* 6.

——, "Orm the Beautiful," *Clarkesworld*, January.

Beazley, J. J., "The Charlie Club," *At Ease with the Dead*.

Bell, Chris, "The Locum, Yellow Rose," *Not One of Us* 37.

Bell, Peter, "The Light of the World," *At Ease with the Dead*.

Benedict, Laura, "The Erstwhile Groom," *Ellery Queen's Mystery Magazine*, Sept./Oct.

Benson, John &Taaffe, Sonya, "The Waters Where Once We Lay" (poem), *Jabberwocky* 3.

Berman, Judith, "Awakening," *Black Gate* 10.

Berry, Jedediah, "The Other Labyrinth," *The Coyote Road*.

Bestwick, Simon, "Hushabye," *Inferno*.

——, "A Small Cold Hand," *At Ease with the Dead*.

Bey, Matthew, "Deadtown Taxi," *Flesh Feast*.

Bishop, Michael, "The Pile," *Subterranean Online*, Winter.

Bisson, Terry, "Pirates of the Somali Coast," *Subterranean* 7.

Black, Holly, "The Poison Eaters," *The Restless Dead*.

Blackmore, Leigh, "The Return of Zoth-Ommog," *Daikaiju! 3: Giant Monsters vs the World*.

Bobet, Leah, "Bears," *Strange Horizons*, November 5.

——, "Fitcher's Third Wife" (poem), *Mythic Delirium* 17.

——, "The Girl from Another World," *Strange Horizons*, August 13.

——, "Three Deaths" (poem), *Lone Star Stories* 21.

Boon, Kevin, "As the Day Would Quake," *Flesh Feast*.

Borski, Robert, "Mrs. McGregor" (poem), *The Magazine of Speculative Poetry*, Vol. 8, No. 2.

Bounds, Sydney J., "Downmarket," *The Mammoth Book of Monsters*.

Bowes, Richard, "The King of the Big Night Hours," *Subterranean* 7.

Boyce, Frank Cottrell, "The Part of Me that Died," *Phobic*.

Boyle, William, "Neighborhood Girl," *Out of the Gutter* 2.

Bradley, Lisa M., "Mourning Cricket" (poem), *Star*Line*, July/August.

Braunbeck, Gary A., "Afterward, There Will Be a Hallway" (novella), *Five Strokes to Midnight*.

——, "Onlookers," *Midnight Premiere*.

——, "The Queen of Talley's Corner," *Five Strokes to Midnight*.

Brenchley, Chaz, "The Deadly Space Between," *Phantoms at the Phil II*.

——, "Summer's Lease," *Phantoms at the Phil III, Postscripts* 10.

Brennan, Marie, "Nine Sketches, in Charcoal and Blood," *On Spec*, Fall.

Brown, Elizabeth, "Llanfihangel," *Strange Tales Volume II*.

Brown, Mike, "Zombie Girl," *Zombies*.

Browne, Adam, "An Account of an Experiment Conducted by Fra Salimbene . . ." *Orb* 7.

Budnitz, Judy, "Abroad," *Tin House* 33.

Bull, Scott Emerson, "Killing Mr. Softly," *New Writings in the Fantastic*.

Burgis, Stephanie, "Locked Doors," *Strange Horizons*, January 1.

Burke, Kealan Patrick, "Cobwebs," *Postscripts* 11.

——, "How the Night Receives Them," *Legends of the Mountain State*.

——, "Visiting Hours," *At Ease with the Dead*.

——, "You In?" (chapbook) *Bad Moon Books*.

Bursztynski, Sue, "Of Loaves, Fishes, and Mars Bars," *Andromeda Spaceways Inflight Magazine* 29.

Busk, Michael Reid, "The Demon Butterflies: A Visitor's Guide," *Night Train*, Oct. 28.

Butcher, Jim, "It's My Birthday, Too," *Many Bloody Returns*.

Cacek, P. D., "Autumn Coming Home," *Doorways* 3.

——, "Black and White and Shades of Gray," *Horror World*.

——, "The Keeper," *Inferno*.

——, "Smoke and Mirrors," *The Secret History of Vampires*.

Cadigan, Pat, "Stilled Life," *Inferno*.

Cailas, Joanna Paula L., "Hamog," *Philippine Speculative Fiction* III.

Caines, Nicola, "Time's Winged Chariot," *Albedo One* 32.

Campanile, Carri M., "In Wolves' Clothing" (poem), *Mag. of Spec. Poetry*, Vol. 8, No. 1.

Campbell, Ramsey, "Digging Deep," *Phobic*.

——, "Peep," *Postscripts* 10.

Campbell-Such, Julia, "The Baby Blues," *On Spec*, Summer.

Campbell-Wise, Alison, "Little Red," *Jabberwocky* 3.

Campisi, Stephanie, "The Ringing Sounds of Death on the Water Tank," *In Bad Dreams*.

Car, Von, "The White Isle," *Realms of Fantasy*, December.

Carroll, David, "Two Zombies," *All Tomorrow's Zombies*.

Carter, Scott William, "Directions to Mourning's Deep," *Weird Tales* 344.

——, "The World in Primary Colors," *EQMM*, Sept./Oct.

Casey, Rosalind L., "Reflected" (poem), *Goblin Fruit*, Summer.

Casson, Tim, "Lady of the Crows," *Black Static* 1.

Catton, John Paul, "The Flowers of Edo," *Midnight Street* 9.

Cave, Hugh B., "House of Shadows," *Astounding Hero Tales*.

Chadbourne, Kate, "How does he know?" (poem) *Goblin Fruit*, Summer.

Chambers, Christopher, "Mr. Bones," *Whispers in the Night*.

Chambers, Stephen, "Pennsylvania Dragon," *Realms of Fantasy*, June.

Chappell, Fred, "Dance of Shadows," *The Magazine of Fantasy & Science Fiction*, March.

Charlton, David, "Moon Over Yodok," *Clarkesworld*, June.

Châteaureynaud, Georges-Olivier, "The Denham Inheritance," *Trois Contes*.

Chenier, Nancy, "Night Transit," *On Spec*, Winter 2006.

Chrulew, Matthew, "Between the Memories," *Aurealis* 38/39.

——, "How I Learned to Keep Tidy," *Andromeda Spaceways* 31.

Church, Suzanne, "Hell's Deadline," *Book of Dead Things*.

Cisco, Michael, "Dr. Bondi's Methods," *Secret Hours*.

——, "Ice Age of Dreams," ibid.

——, "What He Chanced to Mould in Play," ibid.

Cleeves, Ann, "The Midwife's Assistant," *Phantoms at the Phil II*.

Cockle, Kevin, "Eight Precious Spiced Jewels," *On Spec*, Winter 2006.

Comeau, Joey, "Tradition," *Strange Horizons*, February 5.

Conyers, David, "From the Sick Trees" (chapbook), *Cthulhu Australis*.

——, "Weapon Grade," *The Spiraling Worm*.

——, and Sunseri, John, "The Spiraling Worm" (novella), ibid.

Cook, Rob, "Weathermen" (poem), *Mythic Delirium* 16.

Cooley, Holly, "After Appomattox" (poem), *Mythic Delirium* 17.

Cooper, James, "The Constant Eye," *You Are the Fly*.

——, "In Each Dark Body There Lies," *The First Humdrumming Book of Horror*.

——, "Shortly Comes the Harvest," *You Are the Fly*.

Corbacho, Jaime, "Honeymoon," *New Genre* 5.

Cornell, Paul, "Horror Story," *Phobic*.

Cox, F. Brett, "The Serpent and the Hatchet Gang," *Black Static* 2.

Crawford, Gary William, "Love Letters" (poem), *Star*Line*, July/August.

Creasey, Ian, "Memories of the Knacker's Yard," *Apex* 10.

Crook, Jeff, "Man for a Moment," *Hub* 12.

Crow, Jennifer, "Her Last Murder" (poem), *Goblin Fruit*, Autumn.

——, "Stains," *Space and Time* 100.

——, ". . . And the Other" (poem), *Lone Star Stories* 24.

Crowther, Peter, "Dark Times," *Travellers in Darkness*.

Cunningham, P. E., "Car 17," *F & SF*, July.

Curran, Tim, "Cemetery, Nevada," *Frontier Cthulhu*.

——, "Wormwood" (novella), *Horrors Beyond* 2.

——, "The Wreck of the Ghost," *High Seas Cthulhu*.

Currier, Jameson, "The Woman in the Window," *All Hallows* 42.

Czyzniejewski, Michael, "The Death of Purple," *American Short Fiction* 37.

Dansky, Richard, "Missing Pages," *Astounding Hero Tales*.

Davies, Liam, "When the Shark Bites," *Raw Meat*.

Davis, Joel James, "She Kept Them in Jars," *Redivider*, Vol. 5, No. 1.

Day, R. W., "Stranger at the Wedding," *Cabinet des Fées* 2.

de Beer, David, "The Man Who Eats Angels," *ChiZine* 32.

de Bodard, Aliette, "Autumn's Country," *Andromeda Spaceways* 30.

de Lint, Charles, "Yellow Dog," chapbook.

De Luca, Michael J., "The Utter Proximity of God," *Interfictions*.

De Winter, Corrine, "You Dreamed" (poem), *Tango in the Ninth Circle*.

Depestre, Yohamna, "Abikú" (trans. Achy Obejas), *Havana Noir*.

Dianne, Marlo, "The Monkey's Eye" (poem), *Goblin Fruit*, Autumn.

Dines, Steven J., "Unzipped," *GUD*, Spring.

Doig, James, "Threads," *At Ease with the Dead*.

Dowling, Terry, "Jarkman at the Othergates," *Exotic Gothic*.

——, "The Suits at Auderlene," *Inferno*.

Downum, Amanda, "Catch," *Weird Tales* 347.

——, "Ebb," *Not One of Us* 37.

——, "The Salvation Game," *Fantasy*.

Doyle, Noreen, "The Rope," *Realms of Fantasy*, April.

Doyle, Tom, "The Wizard of Macatawa," *Paradox* 11.

Duane, Diane, "Theobroma," *Wizards, Inc.*

Dudman, Clare, "Eczema," *Logorrhea*.

Due, Tananarive, "Amusement," *Dark Delicacies II: Fear*.

——, "Summer," *Whispers in the Night*.

Duffy, Steve, "Lie Still, Sleep Becalmed," *At Ease with the Dead*.

Dumitru, David, "Oak," *All Hallows* 42.

Dunbar, Robert, "Red Soil," *Bare Bone* 10.

Duncan, Hal, "Island of the Pirate Gods," *Postscripts* 13.

Durbin, Fredric S., "The Bone Man," *F & SF*, December.

Dyson, Jeremy, "The Coué," *Phobic*.

Edelman, Scott, "The Man He Had Been Before," *The Mammoth Book of Monsters*.

Edwards, Graham, "Still Point," *Realms of Fantasy*, December.

Elliott, Julia, "The Wilds," *Tin House* 33.

Elrod, P. N., "Grave-Robbed," *Many Bloody Returns*.

Elvidge, Suzanne, "The Door," *Read by Dawn: Volume II*.

Emshwiller, Carol, "At Sixes and Sevens," *Asimov's Science Fiction*, Oct./Nov.

Enge, James, "The Lawless Hours," *Black Gate* 11.

English, Tom, "Lightning Rod," *All Hallows* 43.

Etchemendy, Nancy, "Honey in the Wound," *The Restless Dead*.

Evenson, Brian, "Alfons Kuylers," *Columbia* 45.

Everson, John, "Something Inside," *Needles & Sins*.

——, "You Never Got Used to the Needle," ibid.

Every, Gary, "Hohokam Eclipse," *Dreams and Nightmares* 76.

Ewing, Murray, "The Bookshop," *Dark Horizons* 50.

Ezzo, Joseph A., "The Strange Summer of Duke Bogardis," *New Genre* 5.

Faber, Michael, "Fortress/Deer Park," *Perverted by Language*.

Fabian, Karina L., "Amateurs," *The Sword Review*, October.

Fagan, Robert, "Inhuman Remedies," *Stand* 183.

Falgui, Raymond G., "The Datu's Daughter," *Philippine Spec. Fic.* III.

Fallon, Jennifer, "Demons of Fear," *Andromeda Spaceways* 27.

Farris, John, "First Born," *Dark Delicacies II: Fear*.

Fazi, "Mélanie, "In the Shape of a Dragon," *Black Static* 2.

Fetzer, Bret, "The Devil Factory" *Cabinet des Feés* 2.

Fiesler, Casey, "I Met a Mermaid on the Metro" (poem), *Goblin Fruit*, Spring.

Files, Gemma, "Pen Umbra" (novella), *Thrillers* 2.

——, "Villa Locusta," *The Harrow*, Volume 10, No. 1.

——, "Words Written Backwards," chapbook.

Finch, Paul, "Bethany's Wood," *Inferno*.

——, "The Gatehouse" (novella), *Stains*.

——, "Questionnaire," *Bare Bone* 10.

——, "The Stain" (novella), ibid.

——, "The Tank," *At Ease with the Dead*.

——, "When . . ." *New Writings in the Fantastic*.

Flynn, Nick, "Fire" (poem), *Tin House* 31.

Forbes, Amy Beth, "The Gardener of Hell," *Flytrap* 7.

Ford, Jeffrey, "The Manticore Spell," *Wizards*.

Ford, John B., "The Transition in the Jester's House," *The Mechanics of False Hilarity* (chapbook).

——, "A Treatment for Coulrophobia," ibid.

Forsyth, Kate, "Moths" (poem), *Andromeda Spaceways* 27.

Foster, Eugie, "The Music Company," *Hub* 26.

——, "Year of the Fox," *So Fey*.

Fowler, Christopher, "All Packed," *Old Devil Moon*.

——, "Cupped Hands," ibid.

——, "Invulnerable," ibid.

——, "The Night Museum," ibid.

——, "The Threads," *Summer Chills*.

——, "The Twilight Express," *Old Devil Moon*.

——, "The Uninvited," *Inferno*.

Freeman, Kyri, "Winner," *Ideomancer*, Vol. 6, Issue 3.

Frost, Gregory, "Ill-Met in Ilium," *The Secret History of Vampires*.

Frost, M., "The Witch's Daughter" (poem), *Mythic Delirium* 17.

Fry, Gary, "Figure of Fun," *Supernatural Tales* 12.

——, "In the Absence of . . ." *Humdrumming*.

——, "It Can Also End at Home," *Sanity and Other Delusions*.

——, "No Oil Painting," ibid.

——, "Out of Body, Out of Mind," *World Wide Web*.

Fulda, Nancy, "Monument," *Apex* 10.

Gage, Joshua, "Tales for Children" (poem), *Goblin Fruit*, Summer.

Gaiman, Neil, "Feminine Endings," *Four Letter Word: New Love Letters*.

——, "The Witch's Headstone," *Wizards*.

Gallagher, Stephen, "Eels," *Postscripts* 10.

——, "Misadventure," *Inferno*.

Garrett, Kay Weathersby, "Sagebrush Inn," *On Spec*, Winter 2006.

Garris, Mick, "Ocular," *Midnight Premiere*.

Garton, Ray, "Everything Must Go," ibid.

Gates, Patrick R., "Midnight Popeye," *Thrillers* 2.

Gavin, Richard, "& On the Eve of Yule . . ." *Omens*.

Gee, Joshua, "Incident Report," *666: The Number of the Beast*.

Glover, Elizabeth M., "Metaphysics," *Realms of Fantasy*, August.

Glover, J. T., "Alabama Ghost Pool" (poem), *Goblin Fruit*, Autumn.

Goble, Steve, "The Gods-Forsaken World," *Grendelsong* 2.

Goet, Lise, "Thantos," *Farrago's Wainscot*, Fall.

Golaski, Adam, "What Water Reveals," *Strange Tales Volume II*.

——, "Woods (Marion)," *Essays and Fictions*, Volume 1.

Golden, Christopher, "Breathe My Name," *Five Strokes to Midnight*.

——, "Under Cover of Night," ibid.

Goldman, Ken, "Rite of Passage," *Read by Dawn: Volume II*.

——, "There's Something in Autumn Parks Lake," *Midnight Street* 9.

Goldstein, Lisa, "Dark Rooms," *Asimov's*, October/November.

Gordon, Justin C., "The Dream Machine," *Southern Gothic* online.

Goss, Theodora, "Catherine and the Satyr," *Strange Horizons*, October 1.

Goulart, Ron, "The Devil Bats Will Be a Little Late This Year," *F & SF*, March.

Grant, Helen, "The Calvary at Banská Bystrica," *At Ease with the Dead*.

——, "The Sea Change," *Supernatural Tales* 11.

——, "Self Catering," *All Hallows* 43.

Grant, John, "Lives," *Inferno*.

Grassly, M. C., "Within a Mile of an Oak," *All Hallows* 42.

Graves, Doug, "Alecsander's Empire," *Loving the Undead*.

Gregory, Daryl, "Unpossible," *F & SF*, October/November.

Grey, John, "Explanation to a Child" (poem), *Tales of the Talisman*, Vol. 2, No. 4.

Grimsley, Jim," The Sanguine," *Asimov's*, March.

Grove, Richard & Morton, Lisa, "Forces of Evil, Starring Robert Fields," *Midnight Premiere*.

Hand, Elizabeth, "Illyria" (novella), chapbook.

——, "Vignette," *Logorrhea*.

Hansen, Jon, "Under the Garden in Dreams" (poem), *Electric Velocipede* 13.

Harding, Ian, "The Moonshot Goodnight," *All Hallows* 42.

Hardinge, Frances, "Black Grass," *All Hallows* 43.

Harland, Richard, "Special Perceptions," *At Ease with the Dead.*

Harman, Christopher, "Dinckley Green" (novella), *Strange Tales Volume II.*

Harris, Jeff, "Working Stiffs," *Zombies.*

Harrison, John, "The Accompanist," *Dark Delicacies II: Fear.*

Harrison, M. John, "The Good Detective," *Interzone* 209.

Harvey, Euan, "The Tao of Crocodiles," *Realms of Fantasy*, April.

Harvey-Fitzhenry, Alyxandra, "Little Red" (poem), *Tesseracts Eleven.*

Hawkins, Christopher, "Carpenter's Thumb," *The Harrow*, Volume 10, No. 3.

Hellisen, Catherine L., "This Reflection of Me," *Jabberwocky* 3.

Henderson, C. J., "Folly," *Dark Wisdom* 11.

Henderson, Samantha, "The Black Hole in Auntie Sutra's Handbag," *Lone Star Stories* 20.

——, "Bottles," *Realms of Fantasy*, April.

——, "King's Man" (poem), *Mythic Delirium* 16.

——, "Nemesis" (poem), *Lone Star Stories* 22.

——, "The Tithing Hunt" (poem), *Sporty Spec.*

Hergenrader, Trent, "Black Jack Davy," *Realms of Fantasy*, April.

Heuler, Karen, "Down on the Farm," *Bandersnatch.*

Hill, Joe, "Thumbprint," *Postscripts* 10.

Hirshberg, Glen, "I Am Coming to Live in Your Mouth," *Dark Delicacies II: Fear.*

——, "The Janus Tree," *Inferno.*

——, "Miss Ill-Kept Runt," *The Twilight Limited.*

Hobson, M.K., "The Hotel Astarte," *Realms of Fantasy*, June.

Hodge, Brian, "And They Will Come in the Hour of Our Greatest Need," *A Dark and Deadly Valley.*

——, "The Passion of the Beast," *Midnight Premiere.*

Hodson, Brad, "Picked Last," *Midnight Lullabies.*

Hollander, Barry, "Hatchie Bottom," *ChiZine* 34.

Holm, Janis Butler, "Red," *Falling from the Sky.*

Holman, Stephen, "Mr. Poppy," *Strange Tales Volume II.*

Holness, Matthew, "Sounds Between," *Phobic.*

Hood, Robert, "Monstrous Bright Tomorrows," *In Bad Dreams.*

Hopkinson, Nalo, "Soul Case," *Foundation* 100.

Hosek, Paul, "Made," *On Spec*, Spring.

Houarner, Gerard, "Between the Storms," *Midnight Premiere.*

——, "Like Smoke Rising from the Burning Ghats," *Road from Hell.*

——, "Night Service," *Horror Literature Quarterly* 2.

Hughes, Rhys, "The Upper Reaches," *All Hallows* 43.

Hults, Matt, "The Show Must Live On," *Horror Library, Volume II.*

Humphrey, Andrew, "Holding Pattern," *Black Static* 2.

Hunter, Ian, "The Woman with the Hair," *Dark Horizons* 50.

Hutcheson, Douglas, "The Travellin' Show," *History Is Dead.*

Ings, Simon, "The Wedding Party," *The Solaris Book of New Science Fiction.*

Ireland, Davin, "The Kingdom of Grey," *Zahir* 13.

Irvine, Alex, "Semaphore," *Logorrhea.*

——, "Wizard's Six," *F & SF*, June.

Isle, Sue, "Stranger and Sojourner," *Orb* 7.

Jackson, Nick, "Paper Wraps the Stone," *Midnight Street* 8.

Jacob, Charlee, "Heresy," *Heresy.*

——, "My Eye" (poem), ibid.

——, "My Eye's Sequel: Where Blindness Fails" (poem), ibid.

——, "The Sticks," *Cemetery Dance* 57.

Jeffrey, Shaun, "Envy," *Voyeurs of Death*.

Jemisin, N. K., "The You Train," *Strange Horizons*, December 10.

Jessup, Paul, "Ghost Technology from the Sun," *Postscripts* 12.

Jeter, K. W., "Riding Bitch," *Inferno*.

Jones, Stephen Graham, "Father, Son, Holy Rabbit," *Cemetery Dance* 57.

——, "The Sons of Billy Clay," *Doorways* 4.

Jordan, Andrew, "The General Election" (poem), *Stand* 184.

Joyce, Graham, "The Last Testament of Seamus Todd—Soldier of the Queen," *Postscripts* 10.

Justice, Mark, "Martin's Walk," *New Writings in the Fantastic*.

Kalamaras, George, "Just to Become Human" (poem), *Mag. of Spec. Poetry*, Vol. 8, No. 1.

Kaufmann, Nicholas, "General Slocum's Gold," chapbook.

Keene, Brian, "The Black Wave," *A Dark and Deadly Valley*.

Kelly, James Patrick, "Don't Stop," *Asimov's*, June.

Kelly, Michael, "Winter Birds," *City Slab* 10.

——, "Wolves and Angels," *Scratching the Surface*.

——, "Worse Things," ibid.

——, and Thomas, Scott, "Boulevard of Broken Dreams," ibid.

Kemble, Gary, "Dead Air," *Zombies*.

Kemp, Paul S., "The Signal," *Horrors Beyond 2*.

Kennett, Rick, "The Dark and What It Said," *Andromeda Spaceways* 28.

Keohane, Daniel G., "Ray Gun," *Apex* 11.

Ketchum, Jack, "Elusive," *Midnight Premiere*.

Khanna, Rajan, "The Furies," *Shimmer*, The Pirate Issue.

Kiernan, Caitlin R., "The Ammonite Violin (Murder Ballad No.4)," *Dark Delicacies II: Fear*.

——, "The Ape's Wife," *Clarkesworld*, September.

——, "The Daughter of the Four of Pentacles," *Thrillers 2*.

——, "Houses Under the Sea," ibid.

——, "Night Games in the Crimson Court," *Sirenia Digest* 17.

——, "A Season of Broken Dolls," *Sirenia Digest* 15.

Kiesbye, Sanaz and Stefan, "Rico's Journey Through Hell," *Hobart* 7.

Kilpatrick, Nancy, "The Vechi Barbat," *Travellers in Darkness*.

Kilpatrick, Stephen, "The Night Bride," *New Writings in the Fantastic*.

Kilworth, Garry, "The Sacrificial Anode," *Humdrumming*.

King, Stephen, "Ayana," *The Paris Review* 182.

——, "The Gingerbread Girl," *Esquire*, July.

——, "Graduation Afternoon," *Postscripts* 10.

Kivett, Henry S., "Making Bread," *Pindeldyboz*, February 7.

Klause, Annette Curtis, "Kissing Dead Boys," *The Restless Dead*.

Klein, T. E. D., "Imagining Things," *666: The Number of the Beast*.

Knight, Joel, "Calico Black, Calico Blue," *Strange Tales Volume II*.

Kohler, Sheila, "Limpopo," *EQMM*, Sept./Oct.

Komunyakaa, Yusef, "From Love in the Time of War" (poem), *McSweeney's* 22.

Kosmatka, Ted, "The Prophet of Flores," *Asimov's*, September.

Kowal, Mary Robinette, "Tomorrow and Tomorrow," *Gratia Placenti*.

Kress, Nancy, "By Fools Like Me," *Asimov's*, September.

Kte'pi, Bill, "The Vine That Ate the South," *ChiZine* 33.

Laben, Carrie, "Something in the Mermaid Way," *Clarkesworld*, March.

Lake, Jay, "Fat Man," *The Mammoth Book of Monsters*.

——, "The God-Clown Is Near," *Dark Discoveries* 10.

——, "Number of the Bus," *Realms of Fantasy*, February.

——, "Trinity" (poem), *Lone Star Stories* 19.

Lalumière, Claude, "The Beginning of Time," *Reflection's Edge*, August.

——, "The Object of Worship," *Tesseracts Eleven*.

Lanagan, Margo, "She-Creatures," *Eclipse One*.

Lane, Joel, "Blue Train," *At Ease with the Dead*.

——, "My Stone Desire," *Black Static* 1.

——, "Still Water," *Supernatural Tales* 11.

——, and Pelan, John, "City of Night," *Subterranean* 7.

Langan, John, "Episode Seven: Last Stand Against the Pack . . ." *F & SF*, Sept.

Lanham, Carole, "The Forgotten Orphan," *Midnight Lullabies*.

——, "The Moribund Room," *History Is Dead*.

Lannes, Roberta, "The Anguish of Departure," *Summer Chills*.

Lansdale, Joe R., "Dog," *Dark Delicacies II: Fear*.

——, "The Gentleman's Hotel," *The Shadows, Kith and Kin*.

——, "The Lone Dead Day," *Subterranean* 6.

Lecard, Marc, "The Admiral's House," *At Ease with the Dead*.

Leckie, Ann, "The Snake's Wife," *Helix*, October.

Lee, Tanith, "Cold Fire," *Asimov's*, February.

——, "Green Wallpaper," *The Secret History of Vampires*.

Lee, Yoon Ha, "Notes on the Necromantic Symphony," *Farrago's Wainscot*, Fall.

Lejano-Massebieau, Apol, "Pedro Diyego's Homecoming," *Philippine Spec. Fic.* III.

Lewis, E. Michael, "Rubber Soul," *All Hallows* 43.

Lewis, Joshua, "Ever So Much More than Twenty," *So Fey*.

Lilley, Sharyn, "Winter Solstice," *In Bad Dreams*.

Lingen, Marissa, "Scribing a Line," *Fictitious Force* 4.

Link, Kelly, "Light" *Tin House* 33.

——, "The Wrong Grave," *The Restless Dead*.

Lippman, Laura, "Pony Girl," *New Orleans Noir*.

Littlewood, Alison J., "To Sleep a Dreamless Sleep," *Midnight Lullabies*.

Litton, Claire, "Djeme el-Fina" (poem), *On Spec*, Summer.

——, "Thanksgiving" (poem), *On Spec*, Spring.

Livings, Martin, "There Was Darkness," *Fantastic Wonder Stories*.

Livingston, Michael, "The Angel of Marye's Heights," *Paradox* 11.

Llewellyn, Livia, "Take Your Daughters to Work," *Subterranean* 6.

Lock, Norman, "The Monster in Winter," *New England Review* Vol. 28, No. 3.

Lockley, Steve & Lewis, Paul, "Death Knock," *At Ease with the Dead*.

Lodi, Edward, "The Greyness of Ghosts," *All Hallows* 42.

Long, Beth Adele, "Fish Girl," *Fantasy* 6.

Lovell, Tony, "Figures," *All Hallows* 42.

Lupoff, Richard A., "Wyshes.com," *Horrors Beyond* 2.

Lynch, Mark Patrick, "Lies We Tell the Trojans," *Supernatural Tales* 12.

——, "The Music Box," *At Ease with the Dead*.

MacArthur, Maxine, "Breaking the Ice," *Daikaiju! 2: Revenge of the Giant Monsters*.

MacFarlane, Alex Dally, "Old House" (poem), *Goblin Fruit*, Autumn.

MacLeod, Catherine, "The Laws of Motion," *On Spec*, Summer.

MacLeod, Ian R., "The Master Miller's Tale," *F & SF*, May.

Magrs, Paul, "The Foster Parents," *Phobic*.

Maguire, Gregory, Excerpts from the initial stanzas of "The Oziad" (poem), *Prairie Schooner*, Fall.

Mah, Emily, "Coyote Discovers Mars," *Coyote Wild*, Summer.

Mamatas, Nick, "A Sudden Absence of Bees," *Nature*, Vol 450, #7166.

——, "Summon Bind Banish," *Bandersnatch*.

Manning, Dan, "On Foot," *Aoife's Kiss*, March.

Mantchev, Lisa, "Six Scents," *Weird Tales* 344.

Marvin, Cate, "All My Wives" (poem), *Tin House* 31.

Massie, Elizabeth, "Brazen Bull," chapbook.

Masterton, Graham, "Son of Beast," *Dark Passions: Hot Blood XIII*.

Mathews, Michael, "A Trail of Stars Swirling," *Albedo One* 33.

Maynard, L. H. and Sims, M. P. N., "North and South," *Midnight Street* 8.

McAllister, Bruce, "Poison," *Asimov's*, January.

McCormick, Darren, "The Negotiators," *Whispers of Wickedness*, March 19.

McHugh, Ian, "Grace," *Andromeda Spaceways* 28.

——, "The Greatest Adventure of All," *Coyote Wild*, Autumn.

McHugh, Maura, "Bone Mother," *Fantasy*.

McKenna, Andrew, "Barrelhouse," *Albedo One* 33.

McKinney, Joe, "Starvation Army," *History Is Dead*.

McLaughlin, Mark, "Cthulhu Royale," *Lovecraft's Disciples* 7.

McMahon, Gary, "Family Fishing," *The Black Book of Horror*.

——, "All Your Gods Are Dead" (novella), chapbook.

——, "Borrowed Times," *Dirty Prayers*.

——, "The Bungalow People," ibid.

——, "Comeback," ibid.

——, "Face the Strange" (novella), ibid.

——, "The In-Between," ibid.

——, "Meg 'o Green Weeds," *Beyond the Borderland 2*, December 2006.

——, "Pray Dirty," *Dirty Prayers*.

——, "Raise Your Hands," *New Writings in the Fantastic*.

——, "The Sand King," *All Hallows* 42.

——, "The Wrong Town," *Supernatural Tales* 12.

McNeil, Dan, "The View from Mrs. Mote," *Whispers of Wickedness* 15.

McNew, Pam, "Ursine Conversation" (poem), *Lone Star Stories* 20.

Meadows, Kriscinda, "Wall-Eyed," *Flesh Feast*.

Mellick, Carlton, III., "City Hobgoblins," *Perverted by Language*.

Melniczek, Paul, "Predicting Perdition," *Horrors Beyond 2*.

Meloy, Paul, "Islington Crocodiles," *Interzone* 208.

Merriam, Michael, "And a Song in Her Hair," *Andromeda Spaceways* 26.

Messner-Loebs, William, "Wolf Train West," *Astounding Hero Tales*.

Miller, Christopher K., "A Hawk Circling the Wind," *Nossa Morte*, Nov.

Miller, Scott Stainton, "The Night Animals," *Read by Dawn: Volume II*.

Mills, Katharine, "Golem Branle" (poem), *Goblin Fruit*, Autumn.

——, "Seducing the Crone" (poem), *Goblin Fruit*, Summer.

Mills, Steven, "If Giants Are Thunder," *Tesseracts Eleven*.

Mingin, William, "Which Leads to What Comes Next," *Tales of the Unanticipated* 28.

Mitchell, David, "Dénouement," *Guardian Review*, May 26.

Monette, Sarah, "The Bone Key," *Say . . . What's the Combination?/The Bone Key*.

——, "Listening to Bone," *The Bone Key*.

——, "Somewhere Beneath Those Waves Was Her Home," *Fantasy*.

——, "Under the Beansidhe's Pillow," *Lone Star Stories* 22.

Monk, Devon, "When the Train Calls Lonely," *Realms of Fantasy*, October.

Monteleone, Thomas F., "End of Story," *Midnight Premiere*.

Moody, Christian, "In the Middle of the Woods," *The Cincinnati Review*, Summer.

Moody, David, "Grandma Kelly," *666: The Number of the Beast*.

Moore, Jarrah, "The Keepsake Purse," *Ticonderoga Online*, Autumn.

Moorer, M. Brock, "The Third Kind of Darkness," *Lady Churchill's Rosebud Wristlet* 20.

Morden, Simon, "Seeing Things," *Phantoms at the Phil II*.

Morgan, Christine, "The Barrow Maid," *History Is Dead*.

Morlan, A. R., "Holes," *Cemetery Dance* 57.

——, "Milan, March, 1972," *Smothered Dolls*.

——, "Smothered Dolls," ibid.

Morris, Keith Lee, "Mighty Blue Sea," *The Cincinnati Review*, Summer.

Morris, Mark, "Nothing Prepares You," *Postscripts* 10.

Morrison, Trevor J., "A Coil of Thread," *On Spec*, Fall.

Motil, Rebecca, "When Earth Collides with Space," *Kiss the Sky: Fiction and Poetry Starring Jimi Hendrix*.

Moyer, Jaime Lee, "Longing" (poem), *Goblin Fruit*, Autumn.

Muir, Charles A., "Ding-Dong-Ditch," *Whispers of Wickedness* 15.

Myers, E. C., "In the Closet," *Loving the Undead*.

Myers, Ryan Neal, "The Underthing," *Aeon* 11.

Nellen, Stefani, "Spinnetje," *Apex* 11.

Newman, Kim, "Cold Snap" (novella), *Secret Files of the Diogenes Club*.

Nicholas, Frank, "Crows" (novella), *The Black Book of Horror*.

Nicholls, Mark, "Ramoth-Gilead," *Supernatural Tales* 11.

Niles, Steve, "Nocturnal Invasions," *Dark Passions: Hot Blood XIII*.

——, "The Y Incision," *Dark Delicacies II: Fear*.

Noyes, Deborah, "No Visible Power," *The Restless Dead*.

Nix, Garth, "Holly and Iron," *Wizards*.

Nutting, Alissa, "My Trip to Space," *Swink* 3.

Ó Guilín, Peadar, "The Drain," *Weird Tales, The 21st Century*, volume 1.

O'Brien, Sean, "The Cricket Match at Green Lock," *Phantoms at the Phil III*.

——, "In the Silence Room," ibid.

O'Driscoll, Mike, "Thirteen O'Clock," *Inferno*.

Oates, Joyce Carol, "Hi, Howya Doin," *Ploughshares*, Spring.

Oldknow, Antony, "Dr. Upex and the Great God Ing," *At Ease with the Dead*.

Oliver, Reggie, "Blind Man's Box," *Masques of Satan*.

——, "The Children of Monte Rosa," ibid.

——, "The Man in the Grey Bedroom," ibid.

——, "Mmm-Delicious," *Nemonymous 7: Zencore! Scriptus Innominatus*.

——, "The Old Silence," *Masques of Satan*.

——, "Puss-Cat," ibid.

——, "The Road from Damascus," ibid.

——, "Shades of the Prison House," ibid.

Osundu, E. C., "Waiting for the Gods to Die," *Pindeldyboz*, January 24.

Overton, Mary, "Mother's Milk," *Zahir* 13.

Pagliassotti, Dru, "Nookmarked," *Reflection's Edge*, October.

Palwick, Susan, "Sorrell's Heart," *The Fate of Mice*.

——, "Stormdusk," ibid.

Paoletti, Marc, "Apple," *Horror Library, Volume II*.

Parks, Richard, "Diva," *Worshipping Small Gods*.

——, "Touch of Hell," *Realms of Fantasy*, April.

Pearlberg, Gerry Gomez, "Jimi Comes to Me in the Visage of a Tree-God" (poem), *Kiss the Sky . . .*

Peek, Ben, "Black Betty," *Lone Star Stories* 23.

Pendarvis, Jack, "My Derby," *American Short Fiction* 37.

Pendergrass, Tom, "Immortal Remains," *Horror Library, Volume II.*

Percy, Benjamin, "The Long Black Coat," *Hobart* 8.

Petersen, Kristi, "Wailing Station," *Toasted Cheese* contest.

Peterson, Jim, "Original Face" (poem), *Cave Wall* 1.

Phi, Bao, "The Godzilla Sestina" (poem), *Illumen*, Spring.

Philips, Holly, "The Oracle Spoke," *Clarkesworld*, June.

——, "The Past Never Dies," *Weird Tales* 346.

Piccirilli, Tom, "Bereavement," *Five Strokes to Midnight.*

——, "Loss," ibid.

——, "Shadder," *Midnight Premiere.*

Pignatella, Michael, "Remember the Face of Your Son," *Withersin: Birth* 1.

Pinborough, Sarah, "The Bohemian of the Arbat," *Summer Chills.*

——, "The Fear," *Waiting for October.*

Pinn, Paul, "Borderline Charm," *New Writings in the Fantastic.*

Pirie, Steven, "Mary's Gift, the Stars, and Frank's Pisser," *Zencore!.*

Poulson, Christine, "Safe as Houses," *Phobic.*

Powell, James, "A Cozy for the Jack O'Lanterns," *EQMM*, Sept./Oct.

Prater, Lon, "Something to Hold the Door Closed," *Frontier Cthulhu.*

Pratt, Tim, "From Around Here," *Logorrhea.*

Priest, Cherie, "Bad Sushi," *Apex* 10.

——, "Following Piper," *Subterranean* 6.

Prill, David, "Show of Hands," *Subterranean* online, Fall.

——, "Vivisepulture," *Logorrhea.*

——, "White Pumpkins," *Cemetery Dance* 57.

Probert, John Llewellyn, "Between the Pipes," *All Hallows* 42.

Pulker, Donald, "The Willow Path," ibid.

Rambo, Cat, "Foam on the Water," *Strange Horizons*, February 19.

——, "I'll Gnaw Your Bones, the Manticore Said," *Clarkesworld*, July.

——, "Sugar," *Fantasy.*

Randall, Marta, "The Dark Boy," *F & SF*, January.

Rawlings, Wendy, "Again," *Cincinnati Review*, Winter.

Redekop, Fred, "Paging Daryl and Java Man," *New England Rev.*, Vol. 28, No. 1.

Redwood, Steve, "Hot Cross Son," *New Writings in the Fantastic.*

Reed, Kit, "What Wolves Know," *Asimov's*, September.

Reed, Robert, "Magic with Thirteen-Year-Old Boys," *F & SF*, March.

Reich, Claudius, "Fragments of a Barbary Coast," *The Paranormal Appreciation Society.*

Reynolds, Joshua, "Sharp Things," *Read by Dawn: Volume II.*

Richards, Tony, "Man, You Gotta See This!" *Going Back.*

——, "The Moon Also Rises," *Dark Discoveries* 9.

Richmond, Michelle, "Logorrhea," *Logorrhea.*

Rickert, M., "Don't Ask," *F & SF*, December.

——, "Memoir of a Deer Woman," *F & SF*, March.

Riedel, Kate, "Phoebus Gins Arise," *Tesseracts Eleven.*

——, "Song Cycle," *New Writings in the Fantastic.*

Rigney, Mark, "His Master's Voice," *Talebones* 34.

Rix, David, "The Magpies" (novella), *Strange Tales Volume II*.

Roberts, Maria, "By the River," *Phobic*.

Roden, Barbara, "The Palace," *At Ease with the Dead*.

——, "The Wide Wide Sea," *Exotic Gothic*.

Rogers, Ian, "Relaxed Best," *Not One of Us* 38.

Romanko, Karen, "They Threw Their Daughters into the Sea" (poem), *Goblin Fruit*, Spring.

Roque, Mariela Varona, "The Orchid" (trans. Achy Obejas), *Havana Noir*.

Rosenbaum, Ben and Ackert, David, "Stray" *F & SF*, December.

Rountree, Josh, "In the Thicket with Wolves," *Realms of Fantasy*, February.

——, "When the Rain Comes," *Lone Star Stories* 20.

Royle, Nicholas, "Lancashire," *Phobic*.

Rucker, Lynda E., "Ash-Mouth," *Black Static* 2.

Runolfson, J. C., "Windborne" (poem), *Goblin Fruit*, Winter.

Rusch, Kristine Kathryn, "Craters," *Future Weapons of War*.

——, "Substitutions," *Places to Be, People to Kill*.

Russell, Benjamin, "Bird Brain" (poem), *Mid-American Review*, Vol. XXVIII, No. 1.

Russo, Patricia, "Fugly," *Zencore!*.

——, "In Comes I," *Tales of the Unanticipated* 28.

——, "Sally," *Read by Dawn: Volume 2*.

Ruwe, Donelle, "On Playing the Hoedown 'Sally Goodin'" (poem), *Another Message You Miss the Point Of*.

Ryan, Michael, "A Cartoon of Hurt" (poem), *The New Yorker*, May 23.

Sadanand, Sunil, "Trapped Light Medium," *Horror Library, Volume II*.

Sakmyster, David, "Ladders," *ChiZine* 33.

Sallis, James, "Season Premiere," *Dark Delicacies II: Fear*.

Sampson, Susan, "Fishing Off Mount Olympus" (poem), *Alimentum* 3.

Samuels, Mark, "Ghorla," *Inferno*.

Santoro, Lawrence, "At Angels Sixteen," *A Dark and Deadly Valley*.

Santos, Rodello M., "In Earthen Vessels," *Philippine Spec. Fic.* III.

Sarath, Patrice E., "Bagged Lunch," *Weird Tales* 345.

——, "Pigs and Feaches," *Apex* 10.

Sargeant, J. Kenneth, "Fort Bliss," *Paradox* 11.

Savile, Steve, "A Madness of Ravens," *Daikaiju!* 3.

Savory, Brett Alexander, "Marching the Hate Machines into the Sun," *No Further Messages*.

——, "Scenario B," ibid.

Sazynski, Shirl, "The King of Hell's Daughter" (poem), *Jabberwocky* 3.

Schmitt, Margit Elland, "Under Janey's Garden," *Orson Scott Card's Intergalactic Medicine Show*, July.

Schoffstall, John, "Bullet Dance," *Asimov's*, July.

Schow, David J., "What Scares You," *Dark Passions: Hot Blood XIII*.

Schwader, Ann K., "Paradigm Wash," *Dark Wisdom*, 10 & 11.

Schwartz, David J., "Oma Dortchen and the Pillar of Story," *Farrago's Wainscot*, Summer.

Schwartz, Jason, "A Map of Her Town," Web *Conjunctions*, 3/14.

Schweitzer, Darrell, "The Copyist" (poem), *Dreams and Nightmares* 77.

Scott, Matthew David, "Industrial Estate," *Perverted by Language*.

Sedia, E., "The Clockmaker's Daughter," *Horrors Beyond* 2.

——, "Torsion," *Zencore!*.

Sedia, Ekaterina, "Seas of the World," *Sybil's Garage* 4.

——, "Zombie Lenin," *Fantasy*.

Selke, Lori, "Dead. Nude. Girls." *Strange Horizons*, February 12.

Shapter, Lisa, "Gilvaethwy," *Aoife's Kiss*, March.

Shea, Michael, "The Pool," *Weird Tales* 343.

Shearman, Robert, "Mortal Coil," *Phobic*.

Shell, J. Michael, "Tucker's Girl," *Southern Fried Weirdness*.

Shepard, Jim, "Pleasure Boating in Lituya Bay," *Ploughshares*, Spring.

Shepard, Lucius, "Dead Money" (novella), *Asimov's*, April/May.

——, "Dinner at Baldassaro's," *Postscripts* 10.

——, "The Ease with Which We Freed the Beast," *Inferno*.

——, "Soft Spoken" (novella), chapbook.

——, "Stars Seen Through Stone" (novella), *F & SF*, July.

——, "Vacancy" (novella), *Subterranean* 7.

Sherez, Stav, "God-Box," *Perverted by Language*.

Shipp, Jeremy C., "Those Below," *Love and Sacrifice*.

——, "Watching," *Bare Bone* 10.

Shire, John, "The Tip of the Iceberg," *High Seas Cthulhu*.

Shirley, John, "Seven Knives," *Living Shadows*.

Shumante, David, "The Supernatural," *Mid-American Review*, Vol. XXVIII, No. 1.

Siddall, D., "Going Back," *Supernatural Tales* 11.

Siemienowicz, Miranda, "Lion's Breath," *Island* 108.

Silcox, Mark, "Only One Game," *All Hallows* 42.

Silverthorne, Lisa, "Permanent Ink," *New Writings in the Fantastic*.

Simmons, Adrian, "Hot Pursuit," *Allegory* 3.

Simms, Chris, "Mother's Milk," *EQMM*, May.

Simon, Marge, "When Again I Feel My Hands" (poem), *ChiZine* 32.

Sims, M. P. N. and Maynard, L. H., "Fractured Souls," *Doorways* 4.

Singleton, Sarah and Butler, Chris, "Songs of the Dead," *GUD*, Spring.

Sinisalo, Johanna, "Baby Doll," *The SFWA European Hall of Fame*.

Sisson, Amy, "Fella Down a Hole: Unlikely Patron Saints No. 2," *Strange Horizons*, April 30.

Skillingstead, Jack, "Strangers on a Bus," *Asimov's*, December.

Slatter, A. G., "Sourdough," *Strange Tales Volume II*.

Smale, Alan, "Wearing the Dead," *Book of Dead Things*.

Smith, D. Lynn, "The Charnel House," *Summer Chills*.

Smith, Douglas, "Out of the Light," *Dark Wisdom* 11.

Smith, Michael Marshall, "Old Flame," *Postscripts* 10.

——, "One Two Three," ibid.

——, "The Things He Said," *Travellers in Darkness*.

Smith, Rodney J., "Giggles," *Midnight Lullabies*.

Snyder, Lucy A., "Wake Up Naked Monkey You're Going to Die," *Horror World*.

Soderstrom, Martin R., "Spark," *Zombies*.

Somers, Garrison, "Oracle," *The Blotter*, May.

Souban, Lucien, "Serenade," *Horrors Beyond* 2.

Sparks, Cat, "Champagne and Ice," *Aurealis* 38/39.

——, "Hollywood Roadkill," *On Spec*, Summer.

——, "A Lady of Adestan," *Orb* 7.

——, "A Million Shades of Nightmare," *Dark Animus*, 10/11.

Spencer, William Browning, "Stone and the Librarian," *F & SF*, February.

Steel, Jim, "The Fog Catcher," *Whispers of Wickedness* 14.

Sternberg, Stewart, "The Others," *High Seas Cthulhu*.

Stewart, Michael, "The Devil, a Digression," *Web Conjunctions*, 4/25.

Strahan, Mike, "In the Beginning, Nothing Lasts," *Orson Scott Card's Intergalactic Medicine Show*.

Strantzas, Simon, "Something New," *All Hallows* 42.

——, "You Are Here," *Supernatural Tales* 12.

Strikha, Yaroslava, "Mountain-Hunting for Beginners," *Behind the Wainscot* 6.

Stueart, Jerome, "Why the Poets Were Banned from the City," *On Spec*, Spring.

Sunseri, John, "The Innsmouth Affair," chapbook.

——, "Resurgence," *The Spiraling Worm*.

Sutton, David A., "The Fisherman," chapbook.

Swain, Tiki, "Birder," *Borderlands* 9.

Swanwick, Michael, "Urdumheim," *F & SF*, October/November.

Taaffe, Sonya, "Kameraden Obscure: A Retrospective" (poem), *Not One of Us* 27.

——, "Notes Toward the Classification of the Lesser Moly," *Zahir* 12.

——, "Perdidit Spolia" (poem), *Midrash*.

——, "Plague-Bearer" (poem), *Lone Star Stories* 24.

——, "Postscripts from the Red Sea" (poem), *Goblin Fruit*, Summer.

——, "The Wedding in Hell," *Jabberwocky* 3.

Tan, Yvette Natalie U., "Sidhi," *Philippine Spec. Fic. III*.

——, "Stella for Star," *Expeditions*.

Tate, James, "The Native Americans" (poem), *Columbia* 45.

Taylor, John Alfred, "Where Your Treasure Is," *All Hallows* 43.

Taylor, Terence, "Wet Pain," *Whispers in the Night*.

Tem, Melanie, "Dhost," *At Ease with the Dead*.

Tem, Steve Rasnic, "Strangeness," *Sybil's Garage* 4.

Tennant, Peter, "13, on the Ghost Train," *Midnight Street* 8.

Tensei, Kono, "Hikari," trans. Dana Lewis, *Speculative Japan*.

Tentchoff, Marcie Lynn, "The Catch" (poem), *Sometimes While Dreaming*.

——, "Crow Counting" (poem), ibid.

——, "The Rope Trick" (poem), ibid.

Thao Worra, Bryan, "The Watermelon" (poem), *On the Other Side of the Eye*.

Thomas, Jeffrey, "In His Sights," *The Solaris Book of New Science Fiction*.

Thomas, Lee, "An Apiary of White Bees," *Inferno*.

——, "Sweet Fields," *Space and Time* 100.

——, "They Would Say She Danced," *Horrorworld*, April.

——, "Turtle," *Doorways* 4.

Thomas, M., and Tremblay, Paul G., "Figure 5," *Weird Tales* 347.

Thomas, Scott, "Cabin 13," *Over the Darkening Fields*.

——, "The Cinnamon Mask," ibid.

——, "The Franklin Stove," *Midnight in New England*.

——, "The House of Murals," *Over the Darkening Fields*.

——, "A Million Dying Leaves," *Midnight in New England*.

——, "The Second Parsonage," ibid.

——, "Wrought Iron Skeleton," ibid.

Thornburg, Mary, "Guile," *Cicada*, March/April.

Tidhar, Lavie, "The Burial of the Dead," *ChiZine* 31.

——, "The Prisoner in the Forest," *Electric Velocipede* 12.

Tijam, Mia, "The Ascension of Our Lady Boy," *Philippine Spec. Fic. III*.

Tisbert, Andrew, "A Little Animal Throb," *Talebones* 35.

Tolbert, Jeremiah, "Captain Blood's B00ty," *Shimmer*, Vol. 2, No. 3.

Totton, Sarah, "Bluecoat Jack," *Text: Ur, the New Book of Masks*.

Travis, John, "Dissertation on a Mouthful of Seaweed," *Humdrumming*.

Travis, John, "We, the Remedials," *At Ease with the Dead*.

Tremblay, Paul G., "There's No Light Between Floors," *Clarkesworld*, May.

——, "The Teacher," *ChiZine* 31.

Trenholm, Hayden, "Iron Ties," *Talebones* 35.

Tullis, S. D., "The Reflection," *All Hallows* 43.

——, "Terminus," *Zencore!*.

Tumasonis, Don, "Sejanus' Daughter," *Strange Tales Volume II*.

Turnbull, David, "Father's Day," *Dark Horizons* 51.

Turowski, Eric, "Ile Faim," *Flesh Feast*.

Turtledove, Harry, "Under St. Peter's," *The Secret History of Vampires*.

Turzillo, Mary, "Consolations of Bast" (poem), *Your Cat and Other Space Aliens*.

——, "Gacy" (poem), ibid.

——, "Hibiscus Island, 2304 AD" (poem), ibid.

——, "She Who Was the Beautiful Helmet Maker's Wife" (poem), ibid.

Turzillo, Mary, "Surrogate" (poem), *Star*Line*, May/June.

Tuttle, Lisa and Utley, Steven, "In the Hole," *Black Static* 2.

Tyndall, Richard, "The Gallows Grave," *All Hallows* 43.

Unsworth, Emma, "Saturday Mary," *Phobic*.

Urbancik, John, "The Thousandth Dream," *Space and Time* 100.

Valente, Catherynne M., "The Ballad of the Sinister Mr. Mouth," *Lone Star Stories* 22.

——, "Crow" (poem), *Jabberwocky* 3.

——, "A Dirge for Prester John," *Interfictions*.

——, "Flax" (poem), *Goblin Fruit*, Winter.

Valentine, Mark, "Undergrowth," *Zencore!*.

——, "The White Sea Company," *At Ease with the Dead*.

Van Pelt, James, "How Music Begins," *Asimov's*, September.

Vance, Michael, "Quiet Empire," *On Spec*, Summer.

Vanderhooft, JoSelle, "Beauty, Between the Bones" (poem), *Ossuary*.

——, "Elise" (poem), *Goblin Fruit*, Winter.

——, "Flesh into Sand" (poem), *Sybil's Garage* 4.

——, "Gleipnir Diaries" (poem), *Mythic Delirium* 17.

——, "Handless Came the Maiden" (poem), *Goblin Fruit*, Winter.

——, "The Tale of the Sands" (poem), *Star*Line*, May/June.

——, "When Beauty Dreams" (poem), *Ossuary*.

——, "When Kraken Wakes" (poem), *The Minotaur's Last Letter to His Mother*.

——, "Wizened-Wise" (poem), *Ossuary*.

VanderMeer, Jeff, "Appoggiatura," *Logorrhea*.

——, "A New Face in Hell," *Perverted by Language*.

——, "The Third Bear," *Clarkesworld*, April.

——, and Rambo, Cat, "The Surgeon's Tale," *Subterranean* online, Winter.

Vaughn, Carrie, "Kitty's Zombie New Year," *Weird Tales* 345.

——, "A Princess of Spain," *The Secret History of Vampires*.

Vedeler, Torger, "Ilium," *Midrash*.

Vernon, Steve, "In the Dark and the Deep," *A Dark and Deadly Valley*.

——, "Trolling Lures" (novella), *Hard Roads*.

Volk, Stephen, "Who Dies Best," *Postscripts* 10.

Waggoner, Tim, "The Faces That We Meet," *Thrillers* 2.

Walker, Leslie Claire, "Max Velocity," *GUD*, Spring.

Wallace, Matt, "The End of Flesh," *Tattered Souls*.

Walther, Paul, "We Fall on Each Other," *Horror Library*, Volume II.

Warren, Kaaron, "Coalescence," *Aurealis* 37.

——, "Cooling the Crows," *In Bad Dreams*.

——, "His Lipstick Minx," *The Workers' Paradise*.

——, "Polish," *Andromeda Spaceways* 28.

Waters, Dan, "Perfect Rings of Calamari," *Book of Dead Things*.

Watkins, William John, "The Polka Man," *Orson Scott Card's Intergalactic Medicine Show*.

Weagly, John, "Love in the House of Nowhere," *Book of Dead Things*.

Webb, Don, "The Great White Bed," *F & SF*, May.

Weinberg, Robert, "The Margins," *Horrors Beyond 2*.

Wells, Martha, "Holy Places," *Black Gate* 11.

Wentworth, K. D., "Kaleidoscope," *F & SF*, May.

Weston, Robert, "Stop Plate Tectonics," *On Spec*, Spring.

Whitbourn, John, "A Pillar of the Church," *At Ease with the Dead*.

White, Wrath James, "Scab," *Whispers in the Night*.

Wick, Jessica Paige, "After the Voice Was Taken" (poem), *Mythic Delirium* 16.

——, "The Cat-Skin Coat," *Cabinet des Fées* 2.

Wilce, Ysabeau S., "Quartermaster Returns," *Eclipse One*.

Williams, Liz, "Debatable Lands," *Asimov's*, October/November.

Williams, Conrad, "Perhaps the Last," *Inferno*.

——, "The Scalding Rooms" (novella), chapbook.

——, "Tight Wrappers," *Phobic*.

Williamson, Chet, "Blanket Man," *Kaikon*.

Winter, Laurel, "Emily Dickinson, as far as we know" (poem), *Tales of the Unanticipated* 28.

Worley, Brian, "Smother," *Not One of Us* 37.

Worra, Bryan Thao, "Heresies of Thread, Flint, and Stone" (poem), *Tales of the Unanticipated* 28.

Wright, T. M., "After Dunkirk," *A Dark and Deadly Valley*.

——, "Murder Victim," *Midnight Premiere*.

Yellin, Tamar, "Strangers on a Train," *Text: Ur, the New Book of Masks*.

Yolen, Jane, "The Bull" (poem), *Helix*.

Youmans, Marly, "Drunk Bay," *Postscripts* 13.

——, "Seven Crooked Tinies," *Fantasy* 6.

Young, Marty, "The Wildflowers," *Fantastic Wonder Stories*.

Zaglanis, Charles P., "The Isle of Dreams," *High Seas Cthulhu*.

Zeidler, Catherine, "Julian the Hospitaler," *Hobart in America* 8.

Zerbe, Bradley, "Fishing with the Devil," *Himmelskabet* 15.

Ziemska, Elizabeth, "A Murder of Crows," *Tin House* 31.

Zimring, Kim, "My Heart as Dry as Dust," *Asimov's*, September.

Zumpe, Lee Clark, "Passage to Oblivion," *High Seas Cthulhu*.

The People Behind the Book .

Ellen Datlow was editor of *SCI FICTION*, the multi-award-winning fiction section of SCIFI.COM, for six years, editor of Event Horizon: Science Fiction and Fantasy for one and a half years, and fiction editor of *OMNI* and *OMNI* Online. She continues to edit anthologies for adults, young adults, and children.

Her most recent anthologies are *Inferno*, *The Dark*, *The Del Rey Book of Science Fiction and Fantasy*, *Salon Fantastique*, and *The Coyote Road* (the latter two with Terri Windling). She's been coediting *The Year's Best Fantasy and Horror* for over twenty years. Datlow has won eight World Fantasy Awards, two Bram Stoker Awards, three Hugo Awards, five Locus Awards, the British Fantasy Award, and the International Horror Guild Award for her editing. She lives in New York City. For more information and lots of photos see: www.datlow.com.

Kelly Link and Gavin J. Grant started Small Beer Press in 2000. They have published the zine *Lady Churchill's Rosebud Wristlet* ("Tiny, but celebrated"—*Washington Post*) for eleven years. An anthology, *The Best of Lady Churchill's Rosebud Wristlet*, was published last autumn. With Ellen Datlow they have won the Bram Stoker Award and the Locus Award for editing *The Year's Best Fantasy and Horror*. Link and Grant live in Northampton, Massachusetts.

Kelly Link is the author of three collections, *Stranger Things Happen*, *Magic for Beginners* (one of *Time* magazine's Best Books of the Year), and most recently a young adult collection, *Pretty Monsters*. She edited the anthology *Trampoline*. Stories from her collections have won the Nebula, Hugo, World Fantasy, Tiptree, and Locus Awards, and her work has recently appeared in *Tin House*, *The Starry Rift*, and *The Coyote Road*.

Originally from Scotland, Gavin J. Grant regularly reviews fantasy and science fiction. Publications where his work has appeared include the *Los Angeles Times*, *BookPage*, SCI FICTION, *Strange Horizons*, and *Salon Fantastique*.

Media critic Edward Bryant is an award-winning author of science fiction, fantasy, and horror, having published short fiction in countless anthologies and magazines. He's won the Nebula Award for his science fiction, and other works of his short fiction have been nominated for many other awards. He's also written for television. He lives in Denver, Colorado.

Jeff VanderMeer is a two-time winner of the World Fantasy Award, and has made the year's best lists of *Publishers Weekly*, *The San Francisco Chronicle*, *The Los Angeles Weekly*, *Publishers' News*, and Amazon.com. His fiction has been shortlisted for *Best American Short Stories* and appeared in several year's best anthologies. His most recent novels are *City of Saints and Madmen, Shriek: An Afterword,* and *Strange Tales of Secret Lives.* Read more at www.jeffvandermeer.com.

Music critic **Charles de Lint** is a full-time writer and musician who presently makes his home in Ottawa, Canada, with his wife, MaryAnn Harris, an artist and musician. His most recent books are *Dingo, What the Mouse Found,* and *Promises to Keep.* Other recent publications include the chapbook *Yellow Dog* and collections *Triskell Tales 2* and *The Hour Before Dawn.* For more information about his work, visit his Web site at www.charlesdelint.com.

Series jacket artist **Thomas Canty** has won the World Fantasy Award for Best Artist. He has painted and/or designed covers for many books, and has art-directed many other covers, in a career that spans more than twenty-five years. He lives outside Boston, Massachusetts.

Packager **James Frenkel**, a book editor since 1971, has been an editor for Tor Books since 1983, and is currently a senior editor. He has also edited various anthologies, including *True Names and the Opening of the Cyberspace Frontier, Technohorror,* and *Bangs and Whimpers.* He lives in Madison, Wisconsin.

NOV   2008